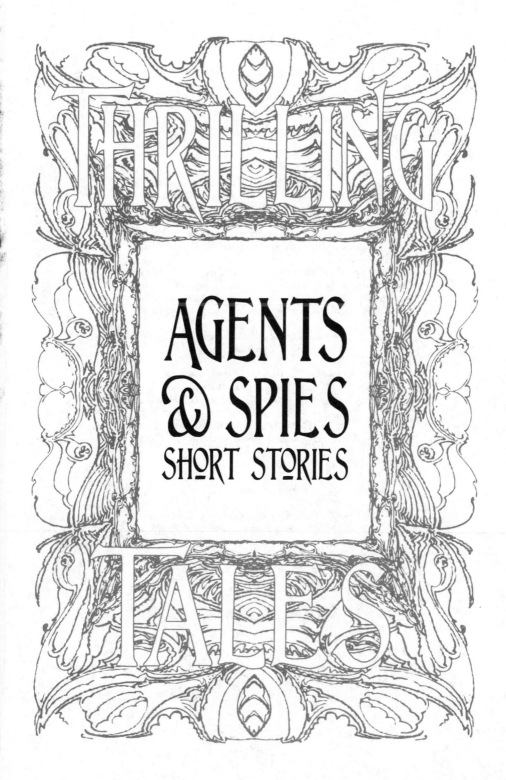

THRILLING

AGENTS
& SPIES
SHORT STORIES

TALES

Publisher & Creative Director: Nick Wells
Project Editor: Laura Bulbeck
Editorial Board: Gillian Whitaker, Josie Mitchell, Catherine Taylor

FLAME TREE PUBLISHING
6 Melbray Mews, Fulham,
London SW6 3NS,
United Kingdom

First published 2017

The cover image is created by Flame Tree Studio
based on artwork by Slava Gerj and Gabor Ruszkai.

ISBN: 978-1-78664-557-9
Special ISBN: 978-1-78664-665-1

13 5 7 9 10 8 6 4 2

Manufactured in China

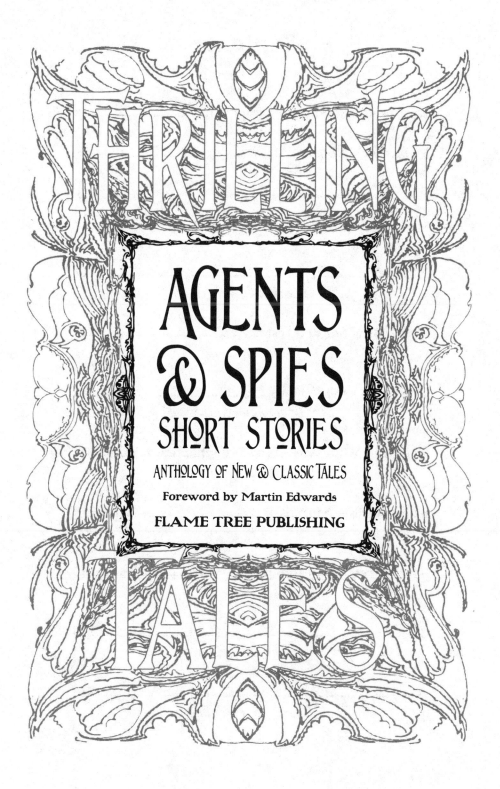

THRILLING

AGENTS
& SPIES
SHORT STORIES

ANTHOLOGY OF NEW & CLASSIC TALES

Foreword by Martin Edwards

FLAME TREE PUBLISHING

TALES

Contents

Foreword by Martin Edwards.......................................8

Publisher's Note 9

The Youngest Brother 12
   Sara Dobie Bauer

Murder!.. 17
   Arnold Bennett

The Tilling Shaw Mystery 28
   Ernest Bramah

The Thirty-Nine Steps............................... 43
   John Buchan

The Man Who Was Thursday (chapters I–VIII).. 105
   G.K. Chesterton

The Invisible Man.................................. 149
   G.K. Chesterton

The Secret Agent (chapters I–V)............................. 160
   Joseph Conrad

The Vigil.. 209
   Joseph Cusumano

Afriti..218
   David R. Downing

The Adventure of the Second Stain **224**
Arthur Conan Doyle

The Moabite Cipher................................**241**
R. Austin Freeman

Spooks **256**
Shane Halbach

Kim (chapters I–IV).................................**267**
Rudyard Kipling

Under the Shield **314**
Stephen Kotowych

Induction **331**
Colt Leasure

The Mysterious Railway Passenger **335**
Maurice Leblanc

To Catch A Mole **345**
Jonathan MacGregor

The Empathy Bomb **353**
Jo Miles

The Defenestration of Prague........................**364**
Josh Pachter

We Who Steal Faces................................ **371**
Tony Pi

The Black Hand....................................**382**
Arthur B. Reeve

The Creaking Door **395**
Sapper

Spies and Taboos **408**
S.L. Scott

The Hula-Hoop Heart **415**
Dan Stout

No Regrets on Fourth Street **421**
Lauren C. Teffeau

The Ebony Box **435**
Ellen Wood

Biographies & Sources **472**

GOTHIC FANTASY

Foreword: Agents & Spies Short Stories

STORIES ABOUT detective agents and spies have an eternal appeal. This meaty anthology follows the same pattern as earlier volumes published by Flame Tree, combining the work of classic authors with that of newer names which may – at present – be much less familiar. The result is an eclectic and entertaining mix.

The spy story is often regarded as an off-shoot of the crime novel, and it's sometimes said that the genre was inaugurated in 1903 by Erskine Childers' classic *The Riddle of the Sands*. But its roots are deeper than that. James Fenimore Cooper published *The Spy* as long ago as 1821 – long before Edgar Allan Poe wrote what is commonly regarded as the first detective short story, 'The Murders in the Rue Morgue' in 1841. The first detective novel is widely reckoned to be *The Notting Hill Mystery* by Charles Warren Adams, writing as Charles Felix, which began life as a magazine serial 41 years after *The Spy* appeared.

So spy stories have a notable pedigree, and the authors featured in this collection include some legendary figures. Rudyard Kipling was the first English-language writer to receive the Nobel Prize for Literature. *Kim*, an extract from which is included here, is a fine story notable not only for its account of 'the Great Game' of espionage, but also as the source of the nickname of one of real life's most infamous double agents, Harold 'Kim' Philby.

Agents & Spies Short Stories also samples superb novels by three more authors of distinction: G.K. Chesterton, Joseph Conrad, and John Buchan. Those who have not yet had the pleasure of reading their books will, I hope, be duly encouraged to seek out the complete texts. Other contributors include Ellen Wood, often known as Mrs Henry Wood, who wrote that classic novel of sensation *East Lynne* (1861). Here she is represented by 'The Ebony Box', a story about her series character Johnny Ludlow, important enough to be chosen by Dorothy L. Sayers for her landmark anthology *The Omnibus of Crime* (1928).

A collection of this kind would not be complete without a story by Sir Arthur Conan Doyle. In 1927, Doyle included 'The Second Stain' among his dozen favourite Holmes adventures for its treatment of 'high diplomacy and intrigue'. One of Doyle's disciples on continental Europe was Maurice Leblanc, creator of Arsene Lupin, and one of Lupin's finest cases appears in this book.

The mix also includes Arnold Bennett, a bestseller whose work fell out of fashion but is enjoying a deserved revival of interest, and H.C. McNeile, whose thrillers written under the pen-name Sapper once enjoyed huge popularity. Ernest Bramah and R. Austin Freeman had a particular flair for the short detective story, and Max Carrados and Dr. Thorndyke remain two of the most notable British detectives from the 'Golden Age of Murder' between the wars. Reading this book, you have the chance to compare and contrast the best of the past with the work of writers of the twenty-first century. Enjoy!

Martin Edwards
www.martinedwardsbooks.com

Publisher's Note

These stories featuring agents and spies take us into worlds of dark alleys, midnight vigils and anarchist plots. Spy and detective fiction comes in all sorts of forms, and within this volume you'll find characters that encompass it all: from the well-known Dr. Thorndyke with his expert medical knowledge, to Max Carrados the blind detective, Franklin P. Scudder the freelance spy and Kim, an orphan living on the streets of Lahore. Due to the recent publication of our *Edgar Allan Poe Short Stories* anthology we have chosen not to include any stories by Poe, despite his undisputable contribution to detective fiction. His story 'The Murders in the Rue Morgue' paved the way for many detective stories that have followed and influenced a number of writers in this anthology, most notably Arthur Conan Doyle.

Every year the response to our call for submissions seems to grow and grow, giving us a rich universe of stories to choose from, but making our job all the more difficult in narrowing down the final selection. We've loved delving into such secret worlds, and ultimately chose a selection of stories we hope sit alongside each other and with the classic selection, to provide a fantastic *Agents & Spies* book for all to enjoy.

THRILLING

AGENTS & SPIES
SHORT STORIES

ANTHOLOGY OF NEW & CLASSIC TALES

Foreword by Martin Edwards

FLAME TREE PUBLISHING

TALES

The Youngest Brother

Sara Dobie Bauer

IN THE CROWDED BAR, it was easy to spot the man who'd just lost his father and come straight from the funeral to forget as much. He looked gentle, quiet. The youngest of four brothers, he was a senior at Harvard, where he attended as a history major, of all the wasteful things. He had not been admitted to the prestigious university thanks to his father's abundant funds but on the basis of his own intellect. Of the four brothers, she considered him the second most handsome, shadowed only by the eldest – the man who'd hired her.

Yes, she easily recognized the youngest brother amidst a crowd of posh academics, near as they were to the university where he studied. Not that he looked very different; on the contrary, he was clean-shaven and in an expensive, black suit. Expensive? She recognized those sorts of things, considered *those sorts of things* part of her job. Knowing the cut of a man's suit said a lot about him, and she was all about knowing.

For instance, take the mournful man at the bar. Simple black meant he wasn't showy, didn't have a big ego, not like the guys who wore suits with silver pinstripes or slick, red ties. Thin lapels meant modern, not retro, so he didn't look to the past for respite. Finally, the suit was slimly cut, snugly tailored, which meant someone who was used to movement – someone in good shape, athletic.

Of course, she cheated on all accounts. She knew these things about the young man; his brother had told her. She knew he was intelligent and subdued. She knew he swam laps every night at six p.m., and his name was Duncan Sadler.

She had arranged to be surrounded by people that night so as not to arouse suspicion. Being an attractive woman, playing pool alone in a bar, only attracted attention from men, and there was only one man she planned on talking to at The Sphinx – Duncan Sadler's bar of choice. She knew that about him, too.

Her so-called friends, more like acquaintances, were in on it, in her same profession. They understood the need to blend in, so they all played pool together until someone won. Then, she took a sip of beer. With her eyes, she told them she was going in and didn't need their backup anymore. It had all been arranged. Once she struck up the youngest Sadler in conversation, her friends would leave, say they were going somewhere else. She could play the lonely damsel card, if only long enough to get Duncan to the alley.

She approached the bar. In her sky-high heels, it was easy to feign a fall, right against the man in the smart black suit. She made a show of spilling the end of her beer on his arm. Then, she sputtered, acted embarrassed. "Oh, shit, I am so sorry."

He barely moved, only to lean back on his barstool. He didn't seem to notice his wet arm, which she pawed at as if his suit was a table she could merely dust until clean. "It's all right." He didn't look at her.

"I could get you a napkin or something." She giggled.

"No, I'm –" He saw her for the first time. "I'm fine."

She stood on her tiptoes and did a little hip dance. "I could buy you a drink."

"No. Please, just go back to your pool game."

"How'd you know I was playing pool?" She leaned closer and put her hand on his shoulder. "You keeping an eye on me?"

He leaned away from her but moved like a man in mud. His hands touched the bar, slow and clumsy, and even in dim light, she saw his eyes were red.

He said, "There are a couple dozen men in this bar who probably enjoy giggling and flirting and your fucking tight jeans. Why don't you talk to one of them?"

Time to change direction, she thought. She used her real voice and dropped the flirty girl routine. "You looked like an easy mark."

He folded his arms. "I suppose I do."

She slid onto the barstool at his side. "You're not even going to ask for what?"

"Dunno, money, drinks?"

"Either. Both." She reached her hand out to him. "I'm Jossa."

He didn't take her hand, perhaps didn't notice it. "Duncan."

"What's the matter with you, Duncan?"

"Right now, just you."

She leaned forward so she could see his face and smiled, which had the desired effect: a little twitch on the outside of his lips.

He glanced over his shoulder. "So are your friends waiting outside in the alley to beat me up?"

She looked at the now empty pool table. "Not that I know of. They're going to a rave." She gestured to the bartender. "I'm not big on raves."

Jossa ordered another crappy light beer from the girl with curly blonde hair who stood in front of them. She usually drank tequila, but she needed to stay alert while fitting into the bar atmosphere.

Then, the blonde looked at Duncan. "You want another, sweetie?"

"Thanks, Cleo."

"How you holding up?" she asked.

Jossa watched his response. He didn't speak, just looked up at the bartender and squinted his eyes.

The girl reached across the bar and touched his hand. "I'll keep 'em coming."

"Have a bad day?"

He finished the last of his rocks glass. "Jesus, are you still here?"

"You bet. Now you got me intrigued."

"I have never seen you here before. Did you show up tonight just to bother me?"

"It's possible." She leaned her elbow on the bar closer to him. He didn't back away at her advancement, but she suspected that was because he didn't want to move and perhaps even feared falling from his seat. She could smell the whiskey on his breath, along with something else, something sweet, like white lilies – perfume from a funeral.

She may have been wrong about him, maybe. Duncan Sadler may have been the best looking brother. All of them, all four, had the same deep, black hair, of varying lengths and thickness. Duncan and his eldest brother had their mother's eyes, large and dark brown, but only Duncan had his father's face. Whereas the other brothers looked like their mother with round, soft, full features, Duncan looked like Daddy Sadler – thin nose, sharp angles, and carved out cheeks.

The bartender returned with their drinks.

"So tell me about your day."

"I don't want to be your mark."

"You're not my mark anymore. Now, you're just interesting."

She did it, made him smile, even if it was small.

Jossa put her hand on his knee. "Come on. Be interesting."

"I had a funeral today."

"Oh." She pulled her hand away. "Well, that blows. Someone you knew well?"

"That's a matter of opinion."

"Who then?"

"My dad."

She stayed quiet for a reasonable amount of time, as though taking in the unfortunate news for the first time. "I'm sorry, Duncan."

"You don't even know me." He took a sip of whiskey. "You don't have to be sorry."

"What was your dad like?"

"A criminal."

She smiled, acted like she thought he was joking. Then, she kept acting. She went through the motions of amused, thoughtful, and then, light bulb. "Holy shit, you're not Doug Sadler's son."

He didn't look at her. "So she reads the news."

"Wow. Okay. Well, you look really clean cut for being part of a crime syndicate."

"I'm not part of a crime syndicate."

Jossa knew that wasn't true – Duncan was known on the street for some dark dealings – but then, his expression changed. He looked scared, but he chased his fear with whiskey and the fear soon disappeared.

"This would be a good time for you to stop talking to me. Make up some excuse about checking on your cat."

"I don't want to stop talking to you," she said.

He turned to look at her. His brow crinkled into rows of wrinkles, and his right eye twitched on the outside. The resemblance to his father was uncanny. It could have been Duncan, aged forty years, in the casket a couple blocks away.

"Why are you interested in me?"

"Because you're the hottest guy in this bar."

"That can't be true, and if it is, I'm sorry."

Jossa mirrored his wrinkled look. "Do you know how to talk to girls?"

He chuckled. "On occasion, I've been told I'm quite good at it."

"So when a girl is hitting on you, you usually reciprocate?"

He poked at a cocktail napkin. "It's been known to happen."

"So hit on me." She scooted closer until she felt the warmth of his skin.

He had his elbow on the bar, his forehead resting in the open palm of his hand. "You have a nice mouth."

She laughed, which made him laugh, too, if only for a second. In that second, she remembered he was only twenty-three. The suit made him seem older, as did the grief. If his father hadn't died, he'd be thinking about graduation. He would be playing pool, hitting on girls, getting laid, because she knew that about Duncan, too. Those were the things he did, but not on the day of his father's funeral.

"I'm going to have a smoke outside. Will you come with me?"

He sighed. "Friends in the alley."

She stood up. "No one's gonna beat you up in the alley, okay? Just come with me."

It took some doing for him to escape the edge of the bar and his barstool. He finished his newest glass of whiskey before waving at Cleo. He pantomimed a cigarette, and the blonde bartender gave him a thumbs-up. Then, Jossa moved. She walked out the front of the bar and didn't look back to see if he followed; she knew he would because he was drunk and not thinking properly.

She stepped around the corner of The Sphinx, into an alley that felt wet and smelled of stale beer. She ignored the lacking ambience, and as soon as he turned the corner, grabbed the lapels of his suit. Jossa wanted to stretch things out. She wanted to taste his mouth and know how his lips felt – soft, warm, forceful. He didn't feel surprised or hesitant; she suspected the alcohol was to thank.

She considered a quick screw, and why not? Give a man his last rites, but then, his hands traveled where they weren't supposed to, never expected, and he pulled her revolver from the hidden holster between her shoulder blades. She pulled back enough to head butt him in the face, but he didn't seem to register the pain. He just shoved her away, into the center of the alley. He leaned his back against the brick wall of the bar's exterior and pointed her pistol.

"Who sent you?"

She put her hands in her pockets and watched his lip bleed. He used the back of his hand to wipe his chin. "Your brother," she said.

"Which one?"

"Does it matter?"

His expression said no. "Why?"

"Because they found out your father left you everything in the will and that he wants you to run the family business."

"Fuck, how did they find out?"

"Tortured the family lawyer."

His chest rose and fell much too fast, and she watched his alcohol-soaked gaze jump back and forth over pavement. "I never wanted this. God, I never did." His voice cracked, but he kept the gun pointed at her chest. "What did they hire you to do? Kill me?"

"No. It's supposed to look like you picked up some girl in a bar. You took me home, we had sex, and then…" She moved her hand in a circle mid-air. "In reality, I'm supposed to knock you out and take you to them. They're going to suicide you."

His hand shook.

"There are worse ways to go."

"Are there?"

She shrugged. "I can't let you run."

She watched his grip tighten on her revolver. "You talk as if there's a gun in your hand."

"It doesn't matter, Duncan." She took a step forward, certain he wouldn't shoot. "I already drugged your drink."

She could tell he knew that, could see the way his body leaned against the building and the way his dark eyes shined with unwelcome tears. "I didn't want this."

"I know." She stepped closer, and the gun dropped to his side.

He melted in front of her until he was nothing more than a dark shape in the angle where building met floor. She knelt down and used her fingers to brush the hair off his forehead.

"You really are the best looking brother."

"Will you do something for me?"

She nodded but realized he wasn't seeing her anymore.

"Will you kill me here?" he asked.

"I can't do that."

"Don't you think I deserve it?"

There would be a massive investigation if she did – federal, of course. The son of a recently offed crime boss found shot to death in an alley was front-page news. His oldest brother said Duncan was smart, and he was. He knew an investigation would lead back to his family, especially when the news broke about his father's will.

Jossa smiled. She leaned down and kissed his broken bottom lip and decided, *What the hell?* She could say he took off running, and she had no choice but to bump him off. She really hated when she had to suicide people, and Duncan Sadler seemed like an okay guy, but as she reached for her gun, held limply in his hand, her head went fuzzy. His face took on a soft glow, and her tongue felt like a soaked sponge. Jossa leaned back on her heels.

"Duncan." Her head spun. She used his knee for ballast, but then, he moved, and her palms met the cold, wet ground.

She closed her eyes and tried to focus – on the sound of him moving, the scent of him like dying flowers, and the feel of his hands on her face. "I'm sorry," he said.

"Is she dead yet?"

Jossa recognized the blonde bartender's voice from the back of the alley – probably a delivery entrance.

"Did you give her enough to kill her?" he asked.

"I thought that was what you wanted."

"Go back inside, Cleo." Jossa felt his hands still on her face and his warm breath against her lips. "You didn't drug my drink. Cleo replaced mine and drugged yours."

"You're not even drunk, are you?" she asked.

He didn't speak, but she knew the answer.

Jossa forced her eyes open long enough to look at him, see him *really*. True, he had his father's face, but not his countenance. Duncan was gentle, sweet maybe, a history major at Harvard. Or he had been, until someone killed his father, and that was where he'd beat her: the woman good at knowing things. She knew the Duncan Sadler his brothers knew, the one they grew up with, and that was the man they'd told her about. They didn't know this person in the alley with the black eyes and calm composure – this Oscar-worthy actor, no, they didn't know Duncan Sadler anymore.

"What will you do now?" She had trouble putting words together.

"What my father expected: run the family business."

She took in the young face, the playful smirk.

He leaned forward and kissed her forehead before letting her lie limp on the ground. She heard the sound of his suit above her, the sound of tight material moving over skin. "And you're right," he said, "I am the best looking brother, now that the rest of them are dead."

Jossa smelled stale beer. The asphalt felt cool beneath her cheek, and the earth seemed to shake with the sound of his dress shoes, footsteps returning him to the bar. She assumed they wouldn't just leave her corpse out there. That would leave too many questions. He probably had a car ready to take her away, once she was dead, because she now knew Duncan Sadler was the kind of man who arranged things, even better than she did.

Murder!

Arnold Bennett

Chapter I

MANY GREAT ONES of the earth have justified murder as a social act, defensible, and even laudable in certain instances. There is something to be said for murder, though perhaps not much. All of us, or nearly all of us, have at one time or another had the desire and the impulse to commit murder. At any rate, murder is not an uncommon affair. On an average, two people are murdered every week in England, and probably about two hundred every week in the United States. And forty per cent of the murderers are not brought to justice. These figures take no account of the undoubtedly numerous cases where murder has been done but never suspected. Murders and murderesses walk safely abroad among us, and it may happen to us to shake hands with them. A disturbing thought! But such is life, and such is homicide.

Chapter II

Two men, named respectively Lomax Harder and John Franting, were walking side by side one autumn afternoon, on the Marine Parade of the seaside resort and port of Quangate (English Channel). Both were well-dressed and had the air of moderate wealth, and both were about thirty-five years of age. At this point the resemblances between them ceased. Lomax Harder had refined features, an enormous forehead, fair hair, and a delicate, almost apologetic manner. John Franting was low-browed, heavy chinned, scowling, defiant, indeed what is called a tough customer. Lomax Harder corresponded in appearance with the popular notion of a poet – save that he was carefully barbered. He was in fact a poet, and not unknown in the tiny, trifling, mad world where poetry is a matter of first-rate interest. John Franting corresponded in appearance with the popular notion of a gambler, an amateur boxer, and, in spare time, a deluder of women. Popular notions sometimes fit the truth.

Lomax Harder, somewhat nervously buttoning his overcoat, said in a quiet but firm and insistent tone:

"Haven't you got anything to say?"

John Franting stopped suddenly in front of a shop whose façade bore the sign: 'Gontle. Gunsmith.'

"Not in words," answered Franting. "I'm going in here."

And he brusquely entered the small, shabby shop.

Lomax Harder hesitated half a second, and then followed his companion.

The shopman was a middle-aged gentleman wearing a black velvet coat.

"Good afternoon," he greeted Franting, with an expression and in a tone of urbane condescension which seemed to indicate that Franting was a wise as well as a fortunate man in that he knew of the excellence of Gontle's and had the wit to come into Gontle's.

For the name of Gontle was favourably and respectfully known wherever triggers are pressed. Not only along the whole length of the Channel coast, but throughout England, was Gontle's renowned. Sportsmen would travel to Quangate from the far north, and even from London, to buy guns. To say: 'I bought it at Gontle's,' or 'Old Gontle recommended it,' was sufficient to silence any dispute concerning the merits of a fire-arm. Experts bowed the head before the unique reputation of Gontle. As for old Gontle, he was extremely and pardonably conceited. His conviction that no other gunsmith in the wide world could compare with him was absolute. He sold guns and rifles with the gesture of a monarch conferring an honour. He never argued; he stated; and the customer who contradicted him was as likely as not to be courteously and icily informed by Gontle of the geographical situation of the shop-door. Such shops exist in the English provinces, and nobody knows how they have achieved their renown. They could exist nowhere else.

"'d afternoon," said Franting gruffly, and paused.

"What can I do for you?" asked Mr. Gontle, as if saying: 'Now don't be afraid. This shop is tremendous, and I am tremendous; but I shall not eat you.'

"I want a revolver," Franting snapped.

"Ah! A revolver!" commented Mr. Gontle, as if saying: 'A gun or a rifle, yes! But a revolver – an arm without individuality, manufactured wholesale! ... However, I suppose I must deign to accommodate you.'

"I presume you know something about revolvers?" asked Mr. Gontle, as he began to produce the weapons.

"A little."

"Do you know the Webley Mark III?"

"Can't say that I do."

"Ah! It is the best for all common purposes." And Mr. Gontle's glance said: 'Have the goodness not to tell me it isn't.'

Franting examined the Webley Mark III.

"You see," said Mr. Gontle. "The point about it is that until the breach is properly closed it cannot be fired. So that it can't blow open and maim or kill the would-be murderer." Mr. Gontle smiled archly at one of his oldest jokes.

"What about suicides?" Franting grimly demanded.

"Ah!"

"You might show me just how to load it," said Franting.

Mr. Gontle, having found ammunition, complied with this reasonable request.

"The barrel's a bit scratched," said Franting.

Mr. Gontle inspected the scratch with pain. He would have denied the scratch, but could not.

"Here's another one," said he, "since you're so particular." He simply had to put customers in their place.

"You might load it," said Franting.

Mr. Gontle loaded the second revolver.

"I'd like to try it," said Franting.

"Certainly," said Mr. Gontle, and led Franting out of the shop by the back, and down to a cellar where revolvers could be experimented with.

Lomax Harder was now alone in the shop. He hesitated a long time and then picked up the revolver rejected by Franting, fingered it, put it down, and picked it up again. The back-door of the shop opened suddenly, and, startled, Harder dropped the revolver into his overcoat pocket: a thoughtless, quite unpremeditated act. He dared not remove the revolver. The revolver was as fast in his pocket as though the pocket had been sewn up.

"And cartridges?" asked Mr. Gontle of Franting.

"Oh," said Franting, "I've only had one shot. Five'll be more than enough for the present. What does it weigh?"

"Let me see. Four inch barrel? Yes. One pound four ounces."

Franting paid for the revolver, receiving thirteen shillings in change from a five-pound note, and strode out of the shop, weapon in hand. He was gone before Lomax Harder decided upon a course of action.

"And for you, sir?" said Mr. Gontle, addressing the poet.

Harder suddenly comprehended that Mr. Gontle had mistaken him for a separate customer, who had happened to enter the shop a moment after the first one. Harder and Franting had said not a word to one another during the purchase, and Harder well knew that in the most exclusive shops it is the custom utterly to ignore a second customer until the first one has been dealt with.

"I want to see some foils." Harder spoke stammeringly the only words that came into his head.

"Foils!" exclaimed Mr. Gontle, shocked, as if to say: 'Is it conceivable that you should imagine that I, Gontle, gunsmith, sell such things as foils?'

After a little talk Harder apologized and departed – a thief.

"I'll call later and pay the fellow," said Harder to his restive conscience. "No. I can't do that. I'll send him some anonymous postal orders."

He crossed the Parade and saw Franting, a small left-handed figure all alone far below on the deserted sands, pointing the revolver. He thought that his ear caught the sound of a discharge, but the distance was too great for him to be sure. He continued to watch, and at length Franting walked westward diagonally across the beach.

"He's going back to the Bellevue," thought Harder, the Bellevue being the hotel from which he had met Franting coming out half an hour earlier. He strolled slowly towards the white hotel. But Franting, who had evidently come up the face of the cliff in the penny lift, was before him. Harder, standing outside, saw Franting seated in the lounge. Then Franting rose and vanished down a long passage at the rear of the lounge. Harder entered the hotel rather guiltily. There was no hall-porter at the door, and not a soul in the lounge or in sight of the lounge. Harder went down the long passage.

Chapter III

AT THE END of the passage Lomax Harder found himself in a billiard-room – an apartment built partly of brick and partly of wood on a sort of courtyard behind the main structure of the hotel. The roof, of iron and grimy glass, rose to a point in the middle. On two sides the high walls of the hotel obscured the light. Dusk was already closing in. A small fire burned feebly in the grate. A large radiator under the window was steel-cold, for though summer was finished, winter had not officially begun in the small economically-run hotel: so that the room was chilly; nevertheless, in deference to the English passion for fresh air and discomfort, the window was wide open.

Franting, in his overcoat, and an unlit cigarette between his lips, stood lowering with his back to the bit of fire. At sight of Harder he lifted his chin in a dangerous challenge.

"So you're still following me about," he said resentfully to Harder.

"Yes," said the latter, with his curious gentle primness of manner. "I came down here specially to talk to you. I should have said all I had to say earlier, only you happened to be going out of the hotel just as I was coming in. You didn't seem to want to talk in the street; but there's some talking has to be done. I've a few things I must tell you." Harder appeared to be perfectly calm, and he felt perfectly calm. He advanced from the door towards the billiard-table.

Franting raised his hand, displaying his square-ended, brutal fingers in the twilight.

"Now listen to me," he said with cold, measured ferocity. "You can't tell me anything I don't know. If there's some talking to be done I'll do it myself, and when I've finished you can get out. I know that my wife has taken a ticket for Copenhagen by the steamer from Harwich, and that she's been seeing to her passport, and packing. And of course I know that you have interests in Copenhagen and spend about half your precious time there. I'm not worrying to connect the two things. All that's got nothing to do with me. Emily has always seen a great deal of you, and I know that the last week or two she's been seeing you more than ever. Not that I mind that. I know that she objects to my treatment of her and my conduct generally. That's all right, but it's a matter that only concerns her and me. I mean that it's no concern of yours, for instance, or anybody else's. If she objects enough she can try and divorce me. I doubt if she'd succeed, but you can never be sure – with these new laws. Anyhow she's my wife till she does divorce me, and so she has the usual duties and responsibilities towards me – even though I was the worst husband in the world. That's how I look at it, in my old-fashioned way. I've just had a letter from her – she knew I was here, and I expect that explains how you knew I was here."

"It does," said Lomax Harder quietly.

Franting pulled a letter out of his inner pocket and unfolded it.

"Yes," he said, glancing at it, and read some sentences aloud: "'I have absolutely decided to leave you, and I won't hide from you that I know you know who is doing what he can to help me. I can't live with you any longer. You may be very fond of me, as you say, but I find your way of showing your fondness too humiliating and painful. I've said this to you before, and now I'm saying it for the last time.' And so on and so on."

Franting tore the letter in two, dropped one half on the floor, twisted the other half into a spill, turned to the fire, and lit his cigarette.

"That's what I think of her letter," he proceeded, the cigarette between his teeth. "You're helping her, are you? Very well. I don't say you're in love with her, or she with you. I'll make no wild statements. But if you aren't in love with her I wonder why you're taking all this trouble over her. Do you go about the world helping ladies who say they're unhappy just for the pure sake of helping? Never mind. Emily isn't going to leave me. Get that into your head. I shan't let her leave me. She has money, and I haven't. I've been living on her, and it would be infernally awkward for me if she left me for good. That's a reason for keeping her, isn't it? But you may believe me or not – it isn't my reason. She's right enough when she says I'm very fond of her. That's a reason for keeping her too. But it isn't my reason. My reason is that a wife's a wife, and she can't break her word just because everything isn't lovely in the garden. I've heard it said I'm unmoral. I'm not all unmoral. And I feel particularly strongly about what's called the marriage tie." He drew the revolver from his overcoat pocket, and held it up to view. "You see this thing. You saw me buy it. Now you needn't be afraid. I'm not threatening you; and it's no part of my game to shoot you. I've nothing to do with your goings-on. What I have to do with is the goings-on of my wife. If she deserts me – for you or for anybody or for nobody – I shall follow her, whether it's to Copenhagen or Bangkok or the North Pole, and I shall kill her – with just this very revolver that you saw me buy. And now you can get out."

Franting replaced the revolver, and began to consume the cigarette with fierce and larger puffs.

Lomax Harder looked at the grim, set, brutal, scowling bitter face, and knew that Franting meant what he had said. Nothing would stop him from carrying out his threat. The fellow was not an arguifier; he could not reason; but he had unmistakable grit and would never recoil from the fear of consequences. If Emily left him, Emily was a dead woman; nothing in the end could protect her from the execution of her husband's menace. On the other hand, nothing would persuade her to remain with her husband. She had decided to go, and she would go. And indeed the mere thought of this lady to whom he, Harder, was utterly devoted, staying with her husband and continuing to suffer the tortures and humiliations which she had been suffering for years – this thought revolted him. He could not think it.

He stepped forward along the side of the billiard-table, and simultaneously Franting stepped forward to meet him. Lomax Harder snatched the revolver which was in his pocket, aimed, and pulled the trigger.

Franting collapsed, with the upper half of his body somehow balanced on the edge of the billiard-table. He was dead. The sound of the report echoed in Harder's ear like the sound of a violin string loudly twanged by a finger. He saw a little reddish hole in Franting's bronzed right temple.

"Well," he thought, "somebody had to die. And it's better him than Emily." He felt that he had performed a righteous act. Also he felt a little sorry for Franting.

Then he was afraid. He was afraid for himself, because he wanted not to die, especially on the scaffold; but also for Emily Franting who would be friendless and helpless without him; he could not bear to think of her alone in the world – the central point of a terrific scandal. He must get away instantly....

Not down the corridor back into the hotel-lounge! No! That would be fatal! The window. He glanced at the corpse. It was more odd, curious, than affrighting. He had made the corpse. Strange! He could not unmake it. He had accomplished the irrevocable. Impressive! He saw Franting's cigarette glowing on the linoleum in the deepening dusk, and picked it up and threw it into the fender.

Lace curtains hung across the whole width of the window. He drew one aside, and looked forth. The light was much stronger in the courtyard than within the room. He put his gloves on. He gave a last look at the corpse, straddled the window-sill, and was on the brick pavement of the courtyard. He saw that the curtain had fallen back into the perpendicular.

He gazed around. Nobody! Not a light in any window! He saw a green wooden gate, pushed it; it yielded; then a sort of entry-passage.... In a moment, after two half-turns, he was on the Marine Parade again. He was a fugitive. Should he fly to the right, to the left? Then he had an inspiration. An idea of genius for baffling pursuers. He would go into the hotel by the main-entrance. He went slowly and deliberately into the portico, where a middle-aged hall-porter was standing in the gloom.

"Good evening, sir."

"Good evening. Have you got any rooms?"

"I think so, sir. The housekeeper is out, but she'll be back in a moment – if you'd like a seat. The manager's away in London."

The hall-porter suddenly illuminated the lounge, and Lomax Harder, blinking, entered and sat down.

"I might have a cocktail while I'm waiting," the murderer suggested with a bright and friendly smile. "A Bronx."

"Certainly, sir. The page is off duty. He sees to orders in the lounge, but I'll attend to you myself."

"What a hotel!" thought the murderer, solitary in the chilly lounge, and gave a glance down the long passage. "Is the whole place run by the hall-porter? But of course it's the dead season."

Was it conceivable that nobody had heard the sound of the shot?

Harder had a strong impulse to run away. But no! To do so would be highly dangerous. He restrained himself.

"How much?" he asked of the hall-porter, who had arrived with surprising quickness, tray in hand and glass on tray.

"A shilling, sir."

The murderer gave him eighteenpence, and drank off the cocktail.

"Thank you very much, sir." The hall-porter took the glass.

"See here!" said the murderer. "I'll look in again. I've got one or two little errands to do."

And he went, slowly, into the obscurity of the Marine Parade.

Chapter IV

LOMAX HARDER leant over the left arm of the sea-wall of the man-made port of Quangate. Not another soul was there. Night had fallen. The lighthouse at the extremity of the right arm was occulting. The lights – some red, some green, many white – of ships at sea passed in both directions in endless processions. Waves plashed gently against the vast masonry of the wall. The wind, blowing steadily from the north-west, was not cold. Harder, looking about – thought he knew he was absolutely alone, took his revolver from his overcoat pocket and stealthily dropped it into the sea. Then he turned round and gazed across the small harbour at the mysterious amphitheatre of the lighted town, and heard public clocks and religious clocks striking the hour.

He was a murderer, but why should he not successfully escape detection? Other murderers had done so. He had all his wits. He was not excited. He was not morbid. His perspective of things was not askew. The hall-porter had not seen his first entrance into the hotel, nor his exit after the crime. Nobody had seen them. He had left nothing behind in the billiard-room. No finger marks on the window-sill. (The putting-on of his gloves was in itself a clear demonstration that he had fully kept his presence of mind.) No footmarks on the hard, dry pavement of the courtyard.

Of course there was the possibility that some person unseen had seen him getting out of the window. Slight: but still a possibility! And there was also the possibility that someone who knew Franting by sight had noted him walking by Franting's side in the streets. If such a person informed the police and gave a description of him, inquiries might be made.... No! Nothing in it. His appearance offered nothing remarkable to the eye of a casual observer – except his forehead, of which he was rather proud, but which was hidden by his hat.

It was generally believed that criminals always did something silly. But so far he had done nothing silly, and he was convinced that, in regard to the crime, he never would do anything silly. He had none of the desire, supposed to be common among murderers, to revisit the scene of the crime or to look upon the corpse once more. Although he regretted the necessity for his act, he felt no slightest twinge of conscience. Somebody had to die, and surely it was better that a brute should die than the heavenly, enchanting, martyrized creature whom his act had rescued for ever from the brute! He was aware within himself of an ecstasy of devotion to Emily Franting – now a widow and free. She was a unique woman. Strange that a woman of such gifts should have come under the sway of so obvious a scoundrel as Franting. But she was very young at the time, and such freaks of sex had happened before and would happen again; they were a widespread phenomenon in the history of the relations of men and women. He would have killed a hundred men if a hundred men had threatened her felicity. His heart was pure; he wanted nothing from Emily in exchange for what he had done in her defence. He was passionate in her defence. When he reflected upon the coarseness and cruelty of the gesture by which Franting had used Emily's letter to light his cigarette, Harder's cheeks grew hot with burning resentment.

A clock struck the quarter. Harder walked quickly to the harbour front, where was a taxi-rank, and drove to the station.… A sudden apprehension! The crime might have been discovered! Police might already be watching for suspicious-looking travellers! Absurd! Still, the apprehension remained despite its absurdity. The taxi-driver looked at him queerly. No! Imagination! He hesitated on the threshold of the station, then walked boldly in, and showed his return ticket to the ticket-inspector. No sign of a policeman. He got into the Pullman car, where five other passengers were sitting. The train started.

Chapter V

HE NEARLY MISSED the boat-train at Liverpool Street because according to its custom the Quangate flyer arrived twenty minutes late at Victoria. And at Victoria the foolish part of him, as distinguished from the common-sense part, suffered another spasm of fear. Would detectives, instructed by telegraph, be waiting for the train? No! An absurd idea! The boat-train from Liverpool Street was crowded with travellers, and the platform crowded with senders-off. He gathered from scraps of talk overheard that an international conference was about to take place at Copenhagen. And he had known nothing of it – not seen a word of it in the papers! Excusable perhaps; graver matters had held his attention.

Useless to look for Emily in the vast bustle of the compartments! She had her through ticket (which she had taken herself, in order to avoid possible complications), and she happened to be the only woman in the world who was never late and never in a hurry. She was certain to be in the train. But was she in the train? Something sinister might have come to pass. For instance, a telephone message to the flat that her husband had been found dead with a bullet in his brain.

The swift two-hour journey to Harwich was terrible for Lomax Harder. He remembered that he had left the unburnt part of the letter lying under the billiard-table. Forgetful!

Silly! One of the silly things that criminals did! And on Parkeston Quay the confusion was enormous. He did not walk, he was swept, on to the great shaking steamer whose dark funnels rose amid wisps of steam into the starry sky. One advantage: detectives would have no chance in that multitudinous scene, unless indeed they held up the ship.

The ship roared a warning, and slid away from the quay, groped down the tortuous channel to the harbour mouth, and was in the North Sea; and England dwindled to naught but a string of lights. He searched every deck from stem to stern, and could not find Emily. She had not caught the train, or, if she had caught the train, she had not boarded the steamer because he had failed to appear. His misery was intense. Everything was going wrong. And on the arrival at Esbjerg would not detectives be lying in wait for the Copenhagen train?

Then he descried her, and she him. She too had been searching. Only chance had kept them apart. Her joy at finding him was ecstatic; tears came into his eyes at sight of it. He was everything to her, absolutely everything. He clasped her right hand in both his hands and gazed at her in the dim, diffused light blended of stars, moon and electricity. No woman was ever like her: mature, innocent, wise, trustful, honest. And the touching beauty of her appealing, sad, happy face, and the pride of her carriage! A unique jewel – snatched from the brutal grasp of that fellow – who had ripped her solemn letter in two and used it as a spill for his cigarette! She related her movements; and he his. Then she said:

"Well?"

"I didn't go," he answered. "Thought it best not to. I'm convinced it wouldn't have been any use."

He had not intended to tell her this lie. Yet when it came to the point, what else could he say? He told one lie instead of twenty. He was deceiving her, but for her sake. Even if the worst occurred, she was for ever safe from that brutal grasp. And he had saved her. As for the conceivable complications of the future, he refused to front them; he could live in the marvellous present. He felt suddenly the amazing beauty of the night at sea, and beneath all his other sensations was the obscure sensation of a weight at his heart.

"I expect you were right," she angelically acquiesced.

Chapter VI

THE SUPERINTENDENT of Police (Quangate was the county town of the western half of the county), and a detective-sergeant were in the billiard-room of the Bellevue. Both wore mufti. The powerful green-shaded lamps usual in billiard-rooms shone down ruthlessly on the green table, and on the reclining body of John Franting, which had not moved and had not been moved.

A charwoman was just leaving these officers when a stout gentleman, who had successfully beguiled a policeman guarding the other end of the long corridor, squeezed past her, greeted the two officers, and shut the door.

The Superintendent, a thin man, with lips to match, and a moustache, stared hard at the arrival.

"I am staying with my friend Dr. Furnival," said the arrival cheerfully. "You telephoned for him, and as he had to go out to one of those cases in which nature will not wait, I offered to come in his place. I've met you before, Superintendent, at Scotland Yard."

"Dr. Austin Bond!" exclaimed the Superintendent.

"He," said the other.

They shook hands, Dr. Bond genially, the Superintendent half-consequential, half-deferential, as one who had his dignity to think about; also as one who resented an intrusion, but dared not show resentment.

The detective-sergeant recoiled at the dazzling name of the great amateur detective, a genius who had solved the famous mysteries of 'The Yellow Hat,' 'The Three Towns,' 'The Three Feathers,' 'The Gold Spoon,' etc., etc., etc., whose devilish perspicacity had again and again made professional detectives both look and feel foolish, and whose notorious friendship with the loftiest heads of Scotland Yard compelled all police forces to treat him very politely indeed.

"Yes," said Dr. Austin Bond, after detailed examination. "Been shot about ninety minutes, poor fellow! Who found him?"

"That woman who's just gone out. Some servant here. Came in to look after the fire."

"How long since?"

"Oh! About an hour ago."

"Found the bullet? I see it hit the brass on that cue-rack there."

The detective-sergeant glanced at the Superintendent, who, however, resolutely remained unastonished.

"Here's the bullet," said the Superintendent.

"Ah!" commented Dr. Austin Bond, glinting through his spectacles at the bullet as it lay in the Superintendent's hand. "Decimal 38, I see. Flattened. It would be."

"Sergeant," said the Superintendent. "You can get help and have the body moved, now Dr. Bond has made his examination. Eh, doctor?"

"Certainly," answered Dr. Bond, at the fireplace. "He was smoking a cigarette, I see."

"Either he or his murderer."

"You've got a clue?"

"Oh yes," the Superintendent answered, not without pride. "Look here. Your torch, sergeant."

The detective-sergeant produced a pocket electric-lamp, and the Superintendent turned to the window-sill.

"I've got a stronger one than that," said Dr. Austin Bond, producing another torch.

The Superintendent displayed finger-prints on the window-frame, footmarks on the sill, and a few strands of inferior blue cloth. Dr. Austin Bond next produced a magnifying glass, and inspected the evidence at very short range.

"The murderer must have been a tall man – you can judge that from the angle of fire; he wore a blue suit, which he tore slightly on this splintered wood of the window-frame; one of his boots had a hole in the middle of the sole, and he'd only three fingers on his left hand. He must have come in by the window and gone out by the window, because the hall-porter is sure that nobody except the dead man entered the lounge by any door within an hour of the time when the murder must have been committed." The Superintendent proudly gave many more details, and ended by saying that he had already given instructions to circulate a description.

"Curious," said Dr. Austin Bond, "that a man like John Franting should let anyone enter the room by the window! Especially a shabby-looking man!"

"You knew the deceased personally then?"

"No! But I know he was John Franting."

"How, Doctor?"

"Luck."

"Sergeant," said the Superintendent, piqued. "Tell the constable to fetch the hall-porter."

Dr. Austin Bond walked to and fro, peering everywhere, and picked up a piece of paper that had lodged against the step of the platform which ran round two sides of the room for the raising of the spectators' benches. He glanced at the paper casually, and dropped it again.

"My man," the Superintendent addressed the hall-porter. "How can you be sure that nobody came in here this afternoon?"

"Because I was in my cubicle all the time, sir."

The hall-porter was lying. But he had to think of his own welfare. On the previous day he had been reprimanded for quitting his post against the rule. Taking advantage of the absence of the manager, he had sinned once again, and he lived in fear of dismissal if found out.

"With a full view of the lounge?"

"Yes, sir."

"Might have been in there beforehand," Dr. Austin Bond suggested.

"No," said the Superintendent. "The charwoman came in twice. Once just before Franting came in. She saw the fire wanted making up and she went for some coal, and then returned later with some coal. But the look of Franting frightened her, and she went back with her coal."

"Yes," said the hall-porter. "I saw that."

Another lie.

At a sign from the Superintendent he withdrew.

"I should like to have a word with that charwoman," said Dr. Austin Bond.

The Superintendent hesitated. Why should the great amateur meddle with what did not concern him? Nobody had asked his help. But the Superintendent thought of the amateur's relations with Scotland Yard, and sent for the charwoman.

"Did you clean the window here today?" Dr. Austin Bond interrogated her.

"Yes, please, sir."

"Show me your left hand." The slattern obeyed. "How did you lose your little finger?"

"In a mangle accident, sir."

"Just come to the window, will you, and put your hands on it. But take off your left boot first."

The slattern began to weep.

"It's quite all right, my good creature." Dr. Austin Bond reassured her. "Your skirt is torn at the hem, isn't it?"

When the slattern was released from her ordeal and had gone, carrying one boot in her grimy hand, Dr. Austin Bond said genially to the Superintendent:

"Just a fluke. I happened to notice she'd only three fingers on her left hand when she passed me in the corridor. Sorry I've destroyed your evidence. But I felt sure almost from the first that the murderer hadn't either entered or decamped by the window."

"How?"

"Because I think he's still here in the room."

The two police officers gazed about them as if exploring the room for the murderer.

"I think he's there."

Dr. Austin Bond pointed to the corpse.

"And where did he hide the revolver after he'd killed himself?" demanded the thin-lipped Superintendent icily, when he had somewhat recovered his aplomb.

"I'd thought of that, too," said Dr. Austin Bond, beaming. "It is always a very wise course to leave a dead body absolutely untouched until a professional man has seen it. But *looking* at the body can do no harm. You see the left-hand pocket of the overcoat. Notice how it bulges. Something unusual in it. Something that has the shape of a —. Just feel inside it, will you?"

The Superintendent, obeying, drew a revolver from the overcoat pocket of the dead man.

"Ah! Yes!" said Dr. Austin Bond. "A Webley Mark III. Quite new. You might take out the ammunition." The Superintendent dismantled the weapon. "Yes, yes! Three chambers empty. Wonder how he used the other two! Now, where's that bullet? You see? He fired. His arm dropped, and the revolver happened to fall into the pocket."

"Fired with his left hand, did he?" asked the Superintendent, foolishly ironic.

"Certainly. A dozen years ago Franting was perhaps the finest amateur light-weight boxer in England. And one reason for it was that he bewildered his opponents by being left-handed. His lefts were much more fatal than his rights. I saw him box several times."

Whereupon Dr. Austin Bond strolled to the step of the platform near the door and picked up the fragment of very thin paper that was lying there.

"This," said he, "must have blown from the hearth to here by the draught from the window when the door was opened. It's part of a letter. You can see the burnt remains of the other part in the corner of the fender. He probably lighted the cigarette with it. Out of bravado! His last bravado! Read this."

The Superintendent read:

"… repeat that I realize how fond you are of me, but you have killed my affection for you, and I shall leave our home tomorrow. This is absolutely final. E."

Dr. Austin Bond, having for the nth time satisfactorily demonstrated in his own unique, rapid way, that police-officers were a set of numskulls, bade the Superintendent a most courteous good evening, nodded amicably to the detective-sergeant, and left in triumph.

Chapter VII

I MUST get some mourning and go back to the flat," said Emily Franting.

She was sitting one morning in the lobby of the Palads Hotel, Copenhagen. Lomax Harder had just called on her with an English newspaper containing an account of the inquest at which the jury had returned a verdict of suicide upon the body of her late husband. Her eyes filled with tears.

"Time will put her right," thought Lomax Harder, tenderly watching her. "I was bound to do what I did. And I can keep a secret for ever."

The Tilling Shaw Mystery

Ernest Bramah

"I WILL SEE Miss George now," assented Carrados. Parkinson retired and Greatorex looked round from his chair. The morning 'clearing-up' was still in progress.

"Shall I go?" he inquired.

"Not unless the lady desires it. I don't know her at all."

The secretary was not unobservant and he had profited from his association with Mr. Carrados. Without more ado, he began to get his papers quietly together.

The door opened and a girl of about twenty came eagerly yet half timorously into the room. Her eyes for a moment swept Carrados with an anxious scrutiny. Then, with a slight shade of disappointment, she noticed that they were not alone.

"I have come direct from Oakshire to see you, Mr. Carrados," she announced, in a quick, nervous voice that was evidently the outcome of a desperate resolution to be brave and explicit. "The matter is a dreadfully important one to me and I should very much prefer to tell it to you alone."

There was no need for Carrados to turn towards his secretary; that discriminating young gentleman was already on his way. Miss George flashed him a shy look of thanks and filled in the moment with a timid survey of the room.

"Is it something that you think I can help you with?"

"I had hoped so. I had heard in a roundabout way of your wonderful power – ought I to tell you how – does it matter?"

"Not in the least if it has nothing to do with the case," replied Carrados.

"When this dreadful thing happened I instinctively thought of you. I felt sure that I ought to come and get you to help me at once. But I – I have very little money, Mr. Carrados, only a few pounds, and I am not so childish as not to know that very clever men require large fees. Then when I got here my heart sank, for I saw at once from your house and position that what seemed little even to me would be ridiculous to you – that if you did help me it would be purely out of kindness of heart and generosity."

"Suppose you tell me what the circumstances are," suggested Carrados cautiously. Then, to afford an opening, he added: "You have recently gone into mourning, I see."

"See!" exclaimed the girl almost sharply. "Then you are not blind?"

"Oh yes," he replied; "only I use the familiar expression, partly from custom, partly because it sounds unnecessarily pedantic to say, 'I deduce from certain observations.'"

"I beg your pardon. I suppose I was startled not so much by the expression as by your knowledge. I ought to have been prepared. But I am already wasting your time and I came so determined to be business-like. I got a copy of the local paper on the way, because I thought that the account in it would be clearer to you than I could tell it. Shall I read it?"

"Please; if that was your intention."

"It is *The Stinbridge Herald*," explained the girl, taking a closely folded newspaper from the handbag which she carried. "Stinbridge is our nearest town – about six miles from Tilling Shaw, where we live. This is the account:

"'MYSTERIOUS TRAGEDY AT TILLING

"'Well-known Agriculturalist Attempts Murder and Commits Suicide

"'The districts of Great Tilling, Tilling Shaw and the immediate neighbourhood were thrown into a state of unusual excitement on Thursday last by the report of a tragedy in their midst such as has rarely marked the annals of our law-abiding countryside.

"'A *Herald* representative was early on the scene, and his inquiries elucidated the fact that it was only too true that in this case rumour had not exaggerated the circumstances, rather the reverse indeed.

"'On the afternoon of the day in question, Mr. Frank Whitmarsh, of High Barn, presented himself at Barony, the residence of his uncle, Mr. William Whitmarsh, with the intention of seeing him in reference to a dispute that was pending between them. This is understood to be connected with an alleged trespass in pursuit of game, each relative claiming exclusive sporting rights over a piece of water known as Hunstan Mere.

"'On this occasion the elder gentleman was not at home and Mr. Frank Whitmarsh, after waiting for some time, departed, leaving a message to the effect that he would return, and, according to one report, "have it out with Uncle William," later in the evening.

"'This resolution he unfortunately kept. Returning about eight-forty-five p.m. he found his uncle in and for some time the two men remained together in the dining-room. What actually passed between them has not yet transpired, but it is said that for half-an-hour there had been nothing to indicate to the other occupants of the house that anything unusual was in progress when suddenly two shots rang out in rapid succession. Mrs. Lawrence, the housekeeper at Barony, and a servant were the soonest on the spot, and, conquering the natural terror that for a moment held them outside the now silent room, they summoned up courage to throw open the door and to enter. The first thing that met their eyes was the body of Mr. Frank Whitmarsh lying on the floor almost at their feet. In their distressed state it was immediately assumed by the horrified women that he was dead, or at least seriously wounded, but a closer examination revealed the fact that the gentleman had experienced an almost miraculous escape. At the time of the tragedy he was wearing a large old-fashioned silver watch; and in this the bullet intended for his heart was found, literally embedded deep in the works. The second shot had, however, effected its purpose, for at the other side of the room, still seated at the table, was Mr. William Whitmarsh, already quite dead, with a terrible wound in his head and the weapon, a large-bore revolver of obsolete pattern, lying at his feet.

"'Mr. Frank Whitmarsh subsequently explained that the shock of the attack, and the dreadful appearance presented by his uncle when, immediately afterwards, he turned his hand against himself, must have caused him to faint.

"'Readers of *The Herald* will join in our expression of sympathy for all members of the Whitmarsh family, and in our congratulations to Mr. Frank Whitmarsh on his providential escape.

"'The inquest is fixed for Monday and it is anticipated that the funeral will take place on the following day.'"

"That is all," concluded Miss George.

"All that is in the paper," amended Carrados.

"It is the same everywhere – 'attempted murder and suicide' – that is what everyone accepts as a matter of course," went on the girl quickly. "How do they know that my father tried to kill Frank, or that he killed himself? How can they know, Mr. Carrados?"

"Your father, Miss George?"

"Yes. My name is Madeline Whitmarsh. At home everyone looks at me as if I was an object of mingled pity and reproach. I thought that they might know the name here, so I gave the first that came into my head. I think it is a street I was directed along. Besides, I don't want it to be known that I came to see you in any case."

"Why?"

Much of the girl's conscious nervousness had stiffened into an attitude of unconscious hardness. Grief takes many forms, and whatever she had been before, the tragic episode had left Miss Whitmarsh a little hurt and cynical.

"You are a man living in a town and can do as you like. I am a girl living in the country and have therefore to do largely as my neighbours like. For me to set up my opinion against popular feeling would constitute no small offence; to question its justice would be held to be adding outrageous insult to enormous injury."

"So far I am unable to go beyond the newspaper account. On the face of it, your father – with what provocation of course I do not know – did attempt this Mr. Frank Whitmarsh's life and then take his own. You imply another version. What reason have you?"

"That is the terrible part of it," exclaimed the girl, with rising distress. "It was that which made me so afraid of coming to you, although I felt that I must, for I dreaded that when you asked me for proofs and I could give you none you would refuse to help me. We were not even in time to hear him speak, and yet I know, *know* with absolute conviction, that my father would not have done this. There are things that you cannot explain, Mr. Carrados, and – well, there is an end of it."

Her voice sank to an absent-minded whisper.

"Everyone will condemn him now that he cannot defend himself, and yet he could not even have had the revolver that was found at his feet."

"What is that?" demanded Carrados sharply. "Do you mean that?"

"Mean what?" she asked, with the blankness of one who has lost the thread of her own thoughts.

"What you said about the revolver – that your father could not have had it?"

"The revolver?" she repeated half wearily; "oh yes. It was a heavy, old-fashioned affair. It had been lying in a drawer of his desk for more than ten years because once a dog came into the orchard in broad daylight light and worried half-a-dozen lambs before anyone could do anything."

"Yes, but why could he not have it on Thursday?"

"I noticed that it was gone. After Frank had left in the afternoon I went into the room where he had been waiting, to finish dusting. The paper says the dining-room, but it was really papa's business-room and no one else used it. Then when I was dusting the desk I saw that the revolver was no longer there."

"You had occasion to open the drawer?"

"It is really a very old bureau and none of the drawers fit closely. Dust lies on the ledges and you always have to open them a little to dust properly. They were never kept locked."

"Possibly your father had taken the revolver with him."

"No. I had seen it there after he had gone. He rode to Stinbridge immediately after lunch and did not return until nearly eight. After he left I went to dust his room. It was then that I saw it. I was doing the desk when Frank knocked and interrupted me. That is how I came to be there twice."

"But you said that you had no proof, Miss Whitmarsh," Carrados reminded her, with deep seriousness. "Do you not recognize the importance – the deadly importance – that this one shred of evidence may assume?"

"Does it?" she replied simply. "I am afraid that I am rather dull just now. All yesterday I was absolutely dazed; I could not do the most ordinary things. I found myself looking at the clock for minutes together, yet absolutely incapable of grasping what time it was. In the same way I know that it struck me as being funny about the revolver but I always had to give it up. It was as though everything was there but things would not fit in."

"You are sure, absolutely sure, that you saw the revolver there after your father had left, and missed it before he returned?"

"Oh yes," said the girl quickly; "I remember realizing how curious it was at the time. Besides there is something else. I so often had things to ask papa about when he was out of the house that I got into the way of making little notes to remind me later. This morning I found on my dressing-table one that I had written on Thursday afternoon."

"About this weapon?"

"Yes; to ask him what could have become of it."

Carrados made a further inquiry, and this was Madeline Whitmarsh's account of affairs existing between the two branches of the family:

Until the time of William Whitmarsh, father of the William Whitmarsh just deceased, the properties of Barony and High Barn had formed one estate, descending from a William senior to a William junior down a moderately long line of yeomen Whitmarshes. Through the influence of his second wife this William senior divided the property, leaving Barony with its four hundred acres of good land to William junior, and High Barn, with which went three hundred acres of poor land, to his other son, father of the Frank implicated in the recent tragedy. But though divided, the two farms still had one common link. Beneath their growing corn and varied pasturage lay, it was generally admitted, a seam of coal at a depth and of a thickness that would render its working a paying venture. Even in William the Divider's time, when the idea was new, money in plenty would have been forthcoming, but he would have none of it, and when he died his will contained a provision restraining either son from mining or exploiting his land for mineral without the consent and co-operation of the other.

This restriction became a legacy of hate. The brothers were only half-brothers and William having suffered unforgettably at the hands of his step-mother had old scores to pay off. Quite comfortably prosperous on his own rich farm, and quite satisfied with the excellent shooting and the congenial life, he had not the slightest desire to increase his wealth. He had the old dour, peasant-like instinct to cling to the house and the land of his forefathers. From this position no argument moved him.

In the meanwhile, on the other side of the new boundary fence, Frank senior was growing poorer year by year. To his periodical entreaties that William would agree to shafts being sunk on High Barn he received an emphatic "Never in my time!" The poor man argued, besought, threatened and swore; the prosperous one shook his head and grinned. Carrados did not need to hear the local saying: "Half brothers: whole haters; like the Whitmarshes," to read the situation.

"Of course I do not really understand the business part of it," said Madeline, "and many people blamed poor papa, especially when Uncle Frank drank himself to death. But I know that it was not mere obstinacy. He loved the undisturbed, peaceful land just as it was, and his father had wished it to remain the same. Collieries would bring swarms of strange men into the neighbourhood, poachers and trespassers, he said. The smoke and dust would ruin the land for miles round and drive away the game, and in the end, if the work did not turn out profitable, we should all be much worse off than before."

"Does the restriction lapse now; will Mr. Frank junior be able to mine?"

"It will now lie with Frank and my brother William, just as it did before with their fathers. I should expect Willie to be quite favourable. He is more – modern."

"You have not spoken of your brother."

"I have two. Bob, the younger, is in Mexico," she explained; "and Willie in Canada with an engineering firm. They did not get on very well with papa and they went away."

It did not require preternatural observation to deduce that the late William Whitmarsh had been 'a little difficult.'

"When Uncle Frank died, less than six months ago, Frank came back to High Barn from South Africa. He had been away about two years."

"Possibly he did not get on well with his father?"

Madeline smiled sadly.

"I am afraid that no two Whitmarsh men ever did get on well together," she admitted.

"Your father and young Frank, for instance?"

"Their lands adjoin; there were always quarrels and disputes," she replied. "Then Frank had his father's grievance over again."

"He wished to mine?"

"Yes. He told me that he had had experience of coal in Natal."

"There was no absolute ostracism between you then? You were to some extent friends?"

"Scarcely." She appeared to reflect. "Acquaintances…. We met occasionally, of course, at people's houses."

"You did not visit High Barn?"

"Oh no."

"But there was no particular reason why you should not?"

"Why do you ask me that?" she demanded quickly, and in a tone that was quite incompatible with the simple inquiry. Then, recognizing the fact, she added, with shamefaced penitence: "I beg your pardon, Mr. Carrados. I am afraid that my nerves have gone to pieces since Thursday. The most ordinary things affect me inexplicably."

"That is a common experience in such circumstances," said Carrados reassuringly. "Where were you at the time of the tragedy?"

"I was in my bedroom, which is rather high up, changing. I had driven down to the village, to give an order, and had just returned. Mrs. Lawrence told me that she had been afraid there might be quarrelling, but no one would ever have dreamed of this, and then came a loud shot and then, after a few seconds, another not so loud, and we rushed to the door – she and Mary first – and everything was absolutely still."

"A loud shot *and then another not so loud*?"

"Yes; I noticed that even at the time. I happened to speak to Mrs. Lawrence of it afterwards and then she also remembered that it had been like that."

Afterwards Carrados often recalled with grim pleasantry that the two absolutely vital points in the fabric of circumstantial evidence that was to exonerate her father and fasten the guilt upon another had dropped from the girl's lips utterly by chance. But at the moment the facts themselves monopolized his attention.

"You are not disappointed that I can tell you so little?" she asked timidly.

"Scarcely," he replied. "A suicide who could not have had the weapon he dies by, a victim who is miraculously preserved by an opportune watch, and two shots from the same pistol that differ materially in volume, all taken together do not admit of disappointment."

"I am very stupid," she said. "I do not seem able to follow things. But you will come and clear my father's name?"

"I will come," he replied. "Beyond that who shall prophesy?"

It had been arranged between them that the girl should return at once, while Carrados would travel down to Great Tilling late that same afternoon and put up at the local fishing inn. In the evening he would call at Barony, where Madeline would accept him as a distant connexion of the family. The arrangement was only for the benefit of the domestics and any casual visitor who might be present, for there was no possibility of a near relation being in attendance. Nor was there any appreciable danger of either his name or person being recognized in those parts, a consideration that seemed to have some weight with the girl, for, more than once, she entreated him not to disclose to anyone his real business there until he had arrived at a definite conclusion.

It was nine o'clock, but still just light enough to distinguish the prominent features of the landscape, when Carrados, accompanied by Parkinson, reached Barony. The house, as described by the man-servant, was a substantial grey stone building, very plain, very square, very exposed to the four winds. It had not even a porch to break the flat surface, and here and there in the line of its three solid storeys a window had been built up by some frugal, tax-evading Whitmarsh of a hundred years ago.

"Sombre enough," commented Carrados, "but the connexion between environment and crime is not yet capable of analysis. We get murders in brand-new suburban villas and the virtues, light-heartedness and good-fellowship, in moated granges. What should you say about it, eh, Parkinson?"

"I should say it was damp, sir," observed Parkinson, with his wisest air.

Madeline Whitmarsh herself opened the door. She took them down the long flagged hall to the dining-room, a cheerful enough apartment whatever its exterior might forebode.

"I am glad you have come now, Mr. Carrados," she said hurriedly, when the door was closed. "Sergeant Brewster is here from Stinbridge police station to make some arrangements for the inquest. It is to be held at the schools here on Monday. He says that he must take the revolver with him to produce. Do you want to see it before he goes?"

"I should like to," replied Carrados.

"Will you come into papa's room then? He is there."

The sergeant was at the table, making notes in his pocket-book, when they entered. An old-fashioned revolver lay before him.

"This gentleman has come a long way on hearing about poor papa," said the girl. "He would like to see the revolver before you take it, Mr. Brewster."

"Good evening, sir," said Brewster. "It's a bad business that brings us here."

Carrados 'looked' round the room and returned the policeman's greeting. Madeline hesitated for a moment, and then, picking up the weapon, put it into the blind man's hand.

"A bit out of date, sir," remarked Brewster, with a nod. "But in good order yet, I find."

"An early French make, I should say; one of Lefaucheux's probably," said Carrados. "You have removed the cartridges?"

"Why, yes," admitted the sergeant, producing a matchbox from his pocket. "They're pin-fire, you see, and I'm not too fond of carrying a thing like that loaded in my pocket as I'm riding a young horse."

"Quite so," agreed Carrados, fingering the cartridges. "I wonder if you happened to mark the order of these in the chambers?"

"That was scarcely necessary, sir. Two, together, had been fired; the other four had not."

"I once knew a case – possibly I read of it – where a pack of cards lay on the floor. It was a murder case and the guilt or innocence of an accused man depended on the relative positions of the fifty-first and fifty-second cards."

"I think you must have read of that, sir," replied Brewster, endeavouring to implicate first Miss Whitmarsh and then Parkinson in his meaning smile. "However, this is straightforward enough."

"Then, of course, you have not thought it worth while to look for anything else?"

"I have noted all the facts that have any bearing on the case. Were you referring to any particular point, sir?"

"I was only wondering," suggested Carrados, with apologetic mildness, "whether you, or anyone, had happened to find a wad lying about anywhere."

The sergeant stroked his well-kept moustache to hide the smile that insisted, however, on escaping through his eyes.

"Scarcely, sir," he replied, with fine irony. "Bulleted revolver cartridges contain no wad. You are thinking of a shot-gun, sir."

"Oh," said Carrados, bending over the spent cartridge he was examining, "that settles it, of course."

"I think so, sir," assented the sergeant, courteously but with a quiet enjoyment of the situation. "Well, miss, I'll be getting back now. I think I have everything I want."

"You will excuse me a few minutes?" said Miss Whitmarsh, and the two callers were left alone.

"Parkinson," said Carrados softly, as the door closed, "look round on the floor. There is no wad lying within sight?"

"No, sir."

"Then take the lamp and look behind things. But if you find one don't disturb it."

For a minute strange and gigantic shadows chased one another across the ceiling as Parkinson moved the table-lamp to and fro behind the furniture. The man to whom blazing sunlight and the deepest shade were as one sat with his eyes fixed tranquilly on the unseen wall before him.

"There is a little pellet of paper here behind the couch, sir," announced Parkinson.

"Then put the lamp back."

Together they drew the cumbrous old piece of furniture from the wall and Carrados went behind. On hands and knees, with his face almost to the floor, he appeared to be studying even the dust that lay there. Then with a light, unerring touch he carefully picked up the thing that Parkinson had found. Very gently he unrolled it, using his long, delicate fingers so skilfully that even at the end the particles of dust still clung here and there to the surface of the paper.

"What do you make of it, Parkinson?"

Parkinson submitted it to the judgment of a single sense.

"A cigarette-paper to all appearance, sir. I can't say it's a kind that I've had experience of. It doesn't seem to have any distinct watermark but there is a half-inch of glossy paper along one edge."

"Amber-tipped. Yes?"

"Another edge is a little uneven; it appears to have been cut."

"This edge opposite the mouthpiece. Yes, yes."

"Patches are blackened, and little holes – like pinpricks – burned through. In places it is scorched brown."

"Anything else?"

"I hope there is nothing I have failed to observe, sir," said Parkinson, after a pause.

Carrados's reply was a strangely irrelevant question.

"What is the ceiling made of?" he demanded.

"Oak boards, sir, with a heavy cross-beam."

"Are there any plaster figures about the room?"

"No, sir."

"Or anything at all that is whitewashed?"

"Nothing, sir."

Carrados raised the scrap of tissue paper to his nose again, and for the second time he touched it with his tongue.

"Very interesting, Parkinson," he remarked, and Parkinson's responsive "Yes, sir" was a model of discreet acquiescence.

"I am sorry that I had to leave you," said Miss Whitmarsh, returning, "but Mrs. Lawrence is out and my father made a practice of offering everyone refreshment."

"Don't mention it," said Carrados. "We have not been idle. I came from London to pick up a scrap of paper, lying on the floor of this room. Well, here it is." He rolled the tissue into a pellet again and held it before her eyes.

"The wad!" she exclaimed eagerly. "Oh, that proves that I was right?"

"Scarcely 'proves,' Miss Whitmarsh."

"But it shows that one of the shots was a blank charge, as you suggested this morning might have been the case."

"Hardly even that."

"What then?" she demanded, with her large dark eyes fixed in a curious fascination on his inscrutable face.

"That behind the couch we have found this scrap of powder-singed paper."

There was a moment's silence. The girl turned away her head.

"I am afraid that I am a little disappointed," she murmured.

"Perhaps better now than later. I wished to warn you that we must prove every inch of ground. Does your cousin Frank smoke cigarettes?"

"I cannot say, Mr. Carrados. You see... I knew so little of him."

"Quite so; there was just the chance. And your father?"

"He never did. He despised them."

"That is all I need ask you now. What time tomorrow shall I find you in, Miss Whitmarsh? It is Sunday, you remember."

"At any time. The curiosity I inspire doesn't tempt me to encounter my friends, I can assure you," she replied, her face hardening at the recollection. "But... Mr. Carrados –"

"Yes?"

"The inquest is on Monday afternoon.... I had a sort of desperate faith that you would be able to vindicate papa."

"By the time of the inquest, you mean?"

"Yes. Otherwise –"

"The verdict of a coroner's jury means nothing, Miss Whitmarsh. It is the merest formality."

"It means a very great deal to me. It haunts and oppresses me. If they say – if it goes out that papa is guilty of the attempt of murder, and of suicide, I shall never raise my head again."

Carrados had no desire to prolong a futile discussion.

"Goodnight," he said, holding out his hand.

"Goodnight, Mr. Carrados." She detained him a moment, her voice vibrant with quiet feeling. "I already owe you more than I can ever hope to express. Your wonderful kindness –"

"A strange case," moralized Carrados, as they walked out of the quadrangular yard into the silent lane. "Instructive, but I more than half wish I'd never heard of it."

"The young lady seems grateful, sir," Parkinson ventured to suggest.

"The young lady is the case, Parkinson," replied his master rather grimly.

A few score yards farther on a swing gate gave access to a field-path, cutting off the corner that the high road made with the narrow lane. This was their way, but instead of following the brown line of trodden earth Carrados turned to the left and indicated the line of buildings that formed the back of one side of the quadrangle they had passed through.

"We will investigate here," he said. "Can you see a way in?"

Most of the buildings opened on to the yard, but at one end of the range Parkinson discovered a door, secured only by a wooden latch. The place beyond was impenetrably dark, but the sweet, dusty smell of hay, and, from beyond, the occasional click of a horse's shoe on stone and the rattle of a head-stall chain through the manger ring told them that they were in the chaff-pen at the back of the stable.

Carrados stretched out his hand and touched the wall with a single finger.

"We need go no farther," he remarked, and as they resumed their way across the field he took out a handkerchief to wipe the taste of whitewash off his tongue.

Madeline had spoken of the gradual decay of High Barn, but Carrados was hardly prepared for the poverty-stricken desolation which Parkinson described as they approached the homestead on the following afternoon. He had purposely selected a way that took them across many of young Whitmarsh's ill-stocked fields, fields in which sedge and charlock wrote an indictment of neglected drains and half-hearted tillage. On the land, the gates and hedges had been broken and unkempt; the buildings, as they passed through the farmyard, were empty and showed here and there a skeletonry of bare rafters to the sky.

"Starved," commented the blind man, as he read the signs. "The thirsty owner and the hungry land: they couldn't both be fed."

Although it was afternoon the bolts and locks of the front door had to be unfastened in answer to their knock. When at last the door was opened a shrivelled little old woman, rather wicked-looking in a comic way, and rather begrimed, stood there.

"Mr. Frank Whitmarsh?" she replied to Carrados's polite inquiry; "oh yes, he lives here. Frank," she called down the passage, "you're wanted."

"What is it, mother?" responded a man's full, strong voice rather lazily.

"Come and see!" and the old creature ogled Carrados with her beady eyes as though the situation constituted an excellent joke between them.

There was the sound of a chair being moved and at the end of the passage a tall man appeared in his shirt sleeves.

"I am a stranger to you," explained Carrados, "but I am staying at the Bridge Inn and I heard of your wonderful escape on Thursday. I was so interested that I have taken the liberty of coming across to congratulate you on it."

"Oh, come in, come in," said Whitmarsh. "Yes... it was a sort of miracle, wasn't it?"

He led the way back into the room he had come from, half kitchen, half parlour. It at least had the virtue of an air of rude comfort, and some of the pewter and china that ornamented its mantelpiece and dresser would have rejoiced a collector's heart.

"You find us a bit rough," apologized the young man, with something of contempt towards his surroundings. "We weren't expecting visitors."

"And I was hesitating to come because I thought that you would be surrounded by your friends."

This very ordinary remark seemed to afford Mrs. Whitmarsh unbounded entertainment and for quite a number of seconds she was convulsed with silent amusement at the idea.

"Shut up, mother," said her dutiful son. "Don't take any notice of her," he remarked to his visitors, "she often goes on like that. The fact is," he added, "we Whitmarshes aren't popular in these parts. Of course that doesn't trouble me; I've seen too much of things. And, taken as a boiling, the Whitmarshes deserve it."

"Ah, wait till you touch the coal, my boy, then you'll see," put in the old lady, with malicious triumph.

"I reckon we'll show them then, eh, mother?" he responded bumptiously. "Perhaps you've heard of that, Mr. –?"

"Carrados – Wynn Carrados. This is my man, Parkinson. I have to be attended because my sight has failed me. Yes, I had heard something about coal. Providence seems to be on your side just now, Mr. Whitmarsh. May I offer you a cigarette?"

"Thanks, I don't mind for once in a way."

"They're Turkish; quite innocuous, I believe."

"Oh, it isn't that. I can smoke cutty with any man, I reckon, but the paper affects my lips. I make my own and use a sort of paper with an end that doesn't stick."

"The paper is certainly a drawback sometimes," agreed Carrados. "I've found that. Might I try one of yours?"

They exchanged cigarettes and Whitmarsh returned to the subject of the tragedy.

"This has made a bit of a stir, I can tell you," he remarked, with complacency.

"I am sure it would. Well, it was the chief topic of conversation when I was in London."

"Is that a fact?" Avowedly indifferent to the opinion of his neighbours, even Whitmarsh was not proof against the pronouncement of the metropolis. "What do they say about it up there?"

"I should be inclined to think that the interest centres round the explanation you will give at the inquest of the cause of the quarrel."

"There! What did I tell you?" exclaimed Mrs. Whitmarsh.

"Be quiet, mother. That's easily answered, Mr. Carrados. There was a bit of duck shooting that lay between our two places. But perhaps you saw that in the papers?"

"Yes," admitted Carrados, "I saw that. Frankly, the reason seemed inadequate to so deadly a climax."

"What did I say?" demanded the irrepressible dame. "They won't believe it."

The young man cast a wrathful look in his mother's direction and turned again to the visitor.

"That's because you don't know Uncle William. *Any* reason was good enough for him to quarrel over. Here, let me give you an instance. When I went in on Thursday he was smoking a pipe. Well, after a bit I took out a cigarette and lit it. I'm damned if he didn't turn round and start on me for that. How does that strike you for one of your own family, Mr. Carrados?"

"Unreasonable, I am bound to admit. I am afraid that I should have been inclined to argue the point. What did you do, Mr. Whitmarsh?"

"I hadn't gone there to quarrel," replied the young man, half sulky at the recollection. "It was his house. I threw it into the fireplace."

"Very obliging," said Carrados. "But, if I may say so, it isn't so much a matter of speculation why he should shoot you as why he should shoot himself."

"The gentleman seems friendly. Better ask his advice, Frank," put in the old woman in a penetrating whisper.

"Stow it, mother!" said Whitmarsh sharply. "Are you crazy? Her idea of a coroner's inquest," he explained to Carrados, with easy contempt, "is that I am being tried for murder. As a matter of fact, Uncle William was a very passionate man, and, like many of that kind, he frequently went beyond himself. I don't doubt that he was sure he'd killed me, for he was a good shot and the force of the blow sent me backwards. He was a very proud man too, in a way – wouldn't stand correction or any kind of authority, and when he realized what he'd done and saw in a flash that he would be tried and hanged for it, suicide seemed the easiest way out of his difficulties, I suppose."

"Yes; that sounds reasonable enough," admitted Carrados.

"Then you don't think there will be any trouble, sir?" insinuated Mrs. Whitmarsh anxiously.

Frank had already professed his indifference to local opinion, but Carrados was conscious that both of them hung rather breathlessly on to his reply.

"Why, no," he declared weightily. "I should see no reason for anticipating any. Unless," he added thoughtfully, "some clever lawyer was instructed to insist that there must be more in the dispute than appears on the surface."

"Oh, them lawyers, them lawyers!" moaned the old lady in a panic. "They can make you say anything."

"They can't make me say anything." A cunning look came into his complacent face. "And, besides, who's going to engage a lawyer?"

"The family of the deceased gentleman might wish to do so."

"Both of the sons are abroad and could not be back in time."

"But is there not a daughter here? I understood so."

Whitmarsh gave a short, unpleasant laugh and turned to look at his mother.

"Madeline won't. You may bet your bottom tikkie it's the last thing she would want."

The little old creature gazed admiringly at her big showy son and responded with an appreciative grimace that made her look more humorously rat-like than ever.

"He! He! Missie won't," she tittered. "That would never do. He! He!" Wink succeeded nod and meaning smile until she relapsed into a state of quietness; and Parkinson, who had been fascinated by her contortions, was unable to decide whether she was still laughing or had gone to sleep.

Carrados stayed a few more minutes and before they left he asked to see the watch.

"A unique memento, Mr. Whitmarsh," he remarked, examining it. "I should think this would become a family heirloom."

"It's no good for anything else," said Whitmarsh practically. "A famous time-keeper it was, too."

"The fingers are both gone."

"Yes; the glass was broken, of course, and they must have caught in the cloth of my pocket and ripped off."

"They naturally would; it was ten minutes past nine when the shot was fired."

The young man thought and then nodded.

"About that," he agreed.

"Nearer than 'about,' if your watch was correct. Very interesting, Mr. Whitmarsh. I am glad to have seen the watch that saved your life."

Instead of returning to the inn Carrados directed Parkinson to take the road to Barony. Madeline was at home, and from the sound of voices it appeared that she had other visitors, but she came out to Carrados at once, and at his request took him into the empty dining-room while Parkinson stayed in the hall.

"Yes?" she said eagerly.

"I have come to tell you that I must throw up my brief," he said. "There is nothing more to be done and I return to town tonight."

"Oh!" she stammered helplessly. "I thought – I thought –"

"Your cousin did not abstract the revolver when he was here on Thursday, Miss Whitmarsh. He did not at his leisure fire a bullet into his own watch to make it appear, later in the day, as if he had been attacked. He did not reload the cartridge with a blank charge. He did not deliberately shoot your father and then fire off the blank cartridge. He *was* attacked and the newspaper version is substantially correct. The whole fabric so delicately suggested by inference and innuendo falls to pieces."

"Then you desert me, Mr. Carrados?" she said, in a low, bitter voice.

"I have seen the watch – the watch that saved Whitmarsh's life," he continued, unmoved. "It would save it again if necessary. It indicates ten minutes past nine – the time to a minute at which it is agreed the shot was fired. By what prescience was he to know at what exact minute his opportunity would occur?"

"When I saw the watch on Thursday night the fingers were not there."

"They are not, but the shaft remains. It is of an old-fashioned pattern and it will only take the fingers in one position. That position indicates ten minutes past nine."

"Surely it would have been an easy matter to have altered that afterwards?"

"In this case fate has been curiously systematic, Miss Whitmarsh. The bullet that shattered the works has so locked the action that it will not move a fraction this way or that."

"There is something more than this – something that I do not understand," she persisted. "I think I have a right to know."

"Since you insist, there is. There is the wad of the blank cartridge that you fired in the outbuilding."

"Oh!" she exclaimed, in the moment of startled undefence, "how do you – how can you –"

"You must leave the conjurer his few tricks for effect. Of course you naturally would fire it where the precious pellet could not get lost – the paper you steamed off the cigarette that Whitmarsh threw into the empty fire-grate; and of course the place must be some distance from the house or even that slight report might occasion remark."

"Yes," she confessed, in a sudden abandonment to weary indifference, "it has been useless. I was a fool to set my cleverness against yours. Now, I suppose, Mr. Carrados, you will have to hand me over to justice?

"Well; why don't you say something?" she demanded impatiently, as he offered no comment.

"People frequently put me in this embarrassing position," he explained diffidently, "and throw the responsibility on me. Now a number of years ago a large and stately building was set up in London and it was beautifully called 'The Royal Palace of Justice.' That was its official name and that was what it was to be; but very soon people got into the way of calling it the Law Courts, and today, if you asked a Londoner to direct you to the Palace of Justice he would undoubtedly set you down as a religious maniac. You see my difficulty?"

"It is very strange," she said, intent upon her own reflections, "but I do not feel a bit ashamed to you of what I have done. I do not even feel afraid to tell you all about it, although of some of that I must certainly be ashamed. Why is it?"

"Because I am blind?"

"Oh no," she replied very positively.

Carrados smiled at her decision but he did not seek to explain that when he could no longer see the faces of men the power was gradually given to him of looking into their hearts, to which some in their turn – strong, free spirits – instinctively responded.

"There is such a thing as friendship at first sight," he suggested.

"Why, yes; like quite old friends," she agreed. "It is a pity that I had no very trusty friend, since my mother died when I was quite little. Even my father has been – it is queer to think of it now – well, almost a stranger to me really."

She looked at Carrados's serene and kindly face and smiled.

"It is a great relief to be able to talk like this, without the necessity for lying," she remarked. "Did you know that I was engaged?"

"No; you had not told me that."

"Oh no, but you might have heard of it. He is a clergyman whom I met last summer. But, of course, that is all over now."

"You have broken it off?"

"Circumstances have broken it off. The daughter of a man who had the misfortune to be murdered might just possibly be tolerated as a vicar's wife, but the daughter of a murderer and suicide – it is unthinkable! You see, the requirements for the office are largely social, Mr. Carrados."

"Possibly your vicar may have other views."

"Oh, he isn't a vicar yet, but he is rather well-connected, so it is quite assured. And he would be dreadfully torn if the choice lay with him. As it is, he will perhaps rather soon get over my absence. But, you see, if we married he could never get over my presence; it would always stand in the way of his preferment. I worked very hard to make it possible, but it could not be."

"You were even prepared to send an innocent man to the gallows?"

"I think so, at one time," she admitted frankly. "But I scarcely thought it would come to that. There are so many well-meaning people who always get up petitions.... No, as I stand here looking at myself over there, I feel that I couldn't quite have hanged Frank, no matter how much he deserved it.... You are very shocked, Mr. Carrados?"

"Well," admitted Carrados, with pleasant impartiality, "I have seen the young man, but the penalty, even with a reprieve, still seems to me a little severe."

"Yet how do you know, even now, that he is, as you say, an innocent man?"

"I don't," was the prompt admission. "I only know, in this astonishing case, that so far as my investigation goes, he did not murder your father by the act of his hand."

"Not according to your Law Courts?" she suggested. "But in the great Palace of Justice? ... Well, you shall judge."

She left his side, crossed the room, and stood by the square, ugly window, looking out, but as blind as Carrados to the details of the somnolent landscape.

"I met Frank for the first time after I was at all grown-up about three years ago, when I returned from boarding-school. I had not seen him since I was a child, and I thought him very tall and manly. It seemed a frightfully romantic thing in the circumstances to meet him secretly – of course my thoughts flew to Romeo and Juliet. We put impassioned letters for one another in a hollow tree that stood on the boundary hedge. But presently I found out – gradually and incredulously at first and then one night with a sudden terrible certainty – that my ideas of romance were not his.... I had what is called, I believe, a narrow escape. I was glad when he went abroad, for it was only my self-conceit that had suffered. I was never in love with him: only in love with the idea of being in love with him.

"A few months ago Frank came back to High Barn. I tried never to meet him anywhere, but one day he overtook me in the lanes. He said that he had thought a lot about me while he was away, and would I marry him. I told him that it was impossible in any case, and, besides, I was engaged. He coolly replied that he knew. I was dumbfounded and asked him what he meant.

"Then he took out a packet of my letters that he had kept somewhere all the time. He insisted on reading parts of them up and telling me what this and that meant and what everyone would say it proved. I was horrified at the construction that seemed capable of being put on my foolish but innocent gush. I called him a coward and a blackguard and a mean cur and a sneaking cad and everything I could think of in one long breath, until I found myself faint and sick with excitement and the nameless growing terror of it.

"He only laughed and told me to think it over, and then walked on, throwing the letters up into the air and catching them.

"It isn't worth while going into all the times he met and threatened me. I was to marry him or he would expose me. He would never allow me to marry anyone else. And then finally he turned round and said that he didn't really want to marry me at all; he only wanted to force father's consent to start mining and this had seemed the easiest way."

"That is what is called blackmail, Miss Whitmarsh; a word you don't seem to have applied to him. The punishment ranges up to penal servitude for life in extreme cases."

"Yes, that is what it really was. He came on Thursday with the letters in his pocket. That was his last threat when he could not move me. I can guess what happened. He read the letters and proposed a bargain. And my father, who was a very passionate man, and very proud in certain ways, shot him as he thought, and then, in shame and in the madness of despair, took his own life…. Now, Mr. Carrados, you were to be my judge."

"I think," said the blind man, with a great pity in his voice, "that it will be sufficient for you to come up for Judgment when called upon."

* * *

Three weeks later a registered letter bearing the Liverpool postmark was delivered at The Turrets. After he had read it Carrados put it away in a special drawer of his desk, and once or twice in after years, when his work seemed rather barren, he took it out and read it. This is what it contained:

"Dear Mr. Carrados, – Some time after you had left me that Sunday afternoon, a man came in the dark to the door and asked for me. I did not see his face for he kept in the shade, but his figure was not very unlike that of your servant Parkinson. A packet was put into my hands and he was gone without a word. From this I imagine that perhaps you did not leave quite as soon as you had intended.

"Thank you very much indeed for the letters. I was glad to have the miserable things, to drop them into the fire, and to see them pass utterly out of my own and everybody else's life. I wonder who else in the world would have done so much for a forlorn creature who just flashed across a few days of his busy life? And then I wonder who else could.

"But there is something else for which I thank you now far, far more, and that is for saving me from the blindness of my own passionate folly. When I look back on the abyss of meanness, treachery and guilt into which I would have wilfully cast myself, and been condemned to live in all my life, I can scarcely trust myself to write.

"I will not say that I do not suffer now. I think I shall for many years to come, but all the bitterness and I think all the hardness have been drawn out.

"You will see that I am writing from Liverpool. I have taken a second-class passage to Canada and we sail tonight. Willie, who returned to Barony last week, has lent me all the money I shall need until I find work. Do not be apprehensive. It is not with the vague uncertainty of an indifferent typist or a downtrodden governess that I go, but as an efficient domestic servant – a capable cook, housemaid or 'general,' as need be. It sounds rather incredible at first, does it not, but such things happen, and I shall get on very well.

"Goodbye, Mr. Carrados; I shall remember you very often and very gratefully.

"Madeline Whitmarsh.

"*P.S.* – Yes, there is friendship at first sight."

The Thirty-Nine Steps

John Buchan

Chapter I
The Man Who Died

I RETURNED from the City about three o'clock on that May afternoon pretty well disgusted with life. I had been three months in the Old Country, and was fed up with it. If anyone had told me a year ago that I would have been feeling like that I should have laughed at him; but there was the fact. The weather made me liverish, the talk of the ordinary Englishman made me sick. I couldn't get enough exercise, and the amusements of London seemed as flat as soda-water that has been standing in the sun. "Richard Hannay," I kept telling myself, "you have got into the wrong ditch, my friend, and you had better climb out."

It made me bite my lips to think of the plans I had been building up those last years in Bulawayo. I had got my pile – not one of the big ones, but good enough for me; and I had figured out all kinds of ways of enjoying myself. My father had brought me out from Scotland at the age of six, and I had never been home since; so England was a sort of Arabian Nights to me, and I counted on stopping there for the rest of my days.

But from the first I was disappointed with it. In about a week I was tired of seeing sights, and in less than a month I had had enough of restaurants and theatres and race-meetings. I had no real pal to go about with, which probably explains things. Plenty of people invited me to their houses, but they didn't seem much interested in me. They would fling me a question or two about South Africa, and then get on their own affairs. A lot of Imperialist ladies asked me to tea to meet schoolmasters from New Zealand and editors from Vancouver, and that was the dismalest business of all. Here was I, thirty-seven years old, sound in wind and limb, with enough money to have a good time, yawning my head off all day. I had just about settled to clear out and get back to the veld, for I was the best bored man in the United Kingdom.

That afternoon I had been worrying my brokers about investments to give my mind something to work on, and on my way home I turned into my club – rather a pot-house, which took in Colonial members. I had a long drink, and read the evening papers. They were full of the row in the Near East, and there was an article about Karolides, the Greek Premier. I rather fancied the chap. From all accounts he seemed the one big man in the show; and he played a straight game too, which was more than could be said for most of them. I gathered that they hated him pretty blackly in Berlin and Vienna, but that we were going to stick by him, and one paper said that he was the only barrier between Europe and Armageddon. I remember wondering if I could get a job in those parts. It struck me that Albania was the sort of place that might keep a man from yawning.

About six o'clock I went home, dressed, dined at the Cafe Royal, and turned into a music-hall. It was a silly show, all capering women and monkey-faced men, and I did not stay long. The night was fine and clear as I walked back to the flat I had hired near Portland Place. The crowd surged past me on the pavements, busy and chattering, and I envied the people for having something to do. These shop-girls and clerks and dandies and policemen had some interest in life that kept them going. I gave half-a-crown to a beggar because I saw him yawn; he was a fellow-sufferer. At Oxford Circus I looked up into the spring sky and I made a vow. I would give the Old Country another day to fit me into something; if nothing happened, I would take the next boat for the Cape.

My flat was the first floor in a new block behind Langham Place. There was a common staircase, with a porter and a liftman at the entrance, but there was no restaurant or anything of that sort, and each flat was quite shut off from the others. I hate servants on the premises, so I had a fellow to look after me who came in by the day. He arrived before eight o'clock every morning and used to depart at seven, for I never dined at home.

I was just fitting my key into the door when I noticed a man at my elbow. I had not seen him approach, and the sudden appearance made me start. He was a slim man, with a short brown beard and small, gimlety blue eyes. I recognized him as the occupant of a flat on the top floor, with whom I had passed the time of day on the stairs.

"Can I speak to you?" he said. "May I come in for a minute?" He was steadying his voice with an effort, and his hand was pawing my arm.

I got my door open and motioned him in. No sooner was he over the threshold than he made a dash for my back room, where I used to smoke and write my letters. Then he bolted back.

"Is the door locked?" he asked feverishly, and he fastened the chain with his own hand.

"I'm very sorry," he said humbly. "It's a mighty liberty, but you looked the kind of man who would understand. I've had you in my mind all this week when things got troublesome. Say, will you do me a good turn?"

"I'll listen to you," I said. "That's all I'll promise." I was getting worried by the antics of this nervous little chap.

There was a tray of drinks on a table beside him, from which he filled himself a stiff whisky-and-soda. He drank it off in three gulps, and cracked the glass as he set it down.

"Pardon," he said, "I'm a bit rattled tonight. You see, I happen at this moment to be dead."

I sat down in an armchair and lit my pipe.

"What does it feel like?" I asked. I was pretty certain that I had to deal with a madman.

A smile flickered over his drawn face. "I'm not mad – yet. Say, Sir, I've been watching you, and I reckon you're a cool customer. I reckon, too, you're an honest man, and not afraid of playing a bold hand. I'm going to confide in you. I need help worse than any man ever needed it, and I want to know if I can count you in."

"Get on with your yarn," I said, "and I'll tell you."

He seemed to brace himself for a great effort, and then started on the queerest rigmarole. I didn't get hold of it at first, and I had to stop and ask him questions. But here is the gist of it:

He was an American, from Kentucky, and after college, being pretty well off, he had started out to see the world. He wrote a bit, and acted as war correspondent for a Chicago paper, and spent a year or two in South-Eastern Europe. I gathered that he was a fine linguist, and had got to know pretty well the society in those parts. He spoke familiarly of many names that I remembered to have seen in the newspapers.

He had played about with politics, he told me, at first for the interest of them, and then because he couldn't help himself. I read him as a sharp, restless fellow, who always wanted to get down to the roots of things. He got a little further down than he wanted.

I am giving you what he told me as well as I could make it out. Away behind all the Governments and the armies there was a big subterranean movement going on, engineered by very dangerous people. He had come on it by accident; it fascinated him; he went further, and then he got caught. I gathered that most of the people in it were the sort of educated anarchists that make revolutions, but that beside them there were financiers who were playing for money. A clever man can make big profits on a falling market, and it suited the book of both classes to set Europe by the ears.

He told me some queer things that explained a lot that had puzzled me – things that happened in the Balkan War, how one state suddenly came out on top, why alliances were made and broken, why certain men disappeared, and where the sinews of war came from. The aim of the whole conspiracy was to get Russia and Germany at loggerheads.

When I asked why, he said that the anarchist lot thought it would give them their chance. Everything would be in the melting-pot, and they looked to see a new world emerge. The capitalists would rake in the shekels, and make fortunes by buying up wreckage. Capital, he said, had no conscience and no fatherland. Besides, the Jew was behind it, and the Jew hated Russia worse than hell.

"Do you wonder?" he cried. "For three hundred years they have been persecuted, and this is the return match for the pogroms. The Jew is everywhere, but you have to go far down the backstairs to find him. Take any big Teutonic business concern. If you have dealings with it the first man you meet is Prince von und Zu Something, an elegant young man who talks Eton-and-Harrow English. But he cuts no ice. If your business is big, you get behind him and find a prognathous Westphalian with a retreating brow and the manners of a hog. He is the German business man that gives your English papers the shakes. But if you're on the biggest kind of job and are bound to get to the real boss, ten to one you are brought up against a little white-faced Jew in a bath-chair with an eye like a rattlesnake. Yes, Sir, he is the man who is ruling the world just now, and he has his knife in the Empire of the Tzar, because his aunt was outraged and his father flogged in some one-horse location on the Volga."

I could not help saying that his Jew-anarchists seemed to have got left behind a little.

"Yes and no," he said. "They won up to a point, but they struck a bigger thing than money, a thing that couldn't be bought, the old elemental fighting instincts of man. If you're going to be killed you invent some kind of flag and country to fight for, and if you survive you get to love the thing. Those foolish devils of soldiers have found something they care for, and that has upset the pretty plan laid in Berlin and Vienna. But my friends haven't played their last card by a long sight. They've gotten the ace up their sleeves, and unless I can keep alive for a month they are going to play it and win."

"But I thought you were dead," I put in.

"*Mors janua vitae*," he smiled. (I recognized the quotation: it was about all the Latin I knew.) "I'm coming to that, but I've got to put you wise about a lot of things first. If you read your newspaper, I guess you know the name of Constantine Karolides?"

I sat up at that, for I had been reading about him that very afternoon.

"He is the man that has wrecked all their games. He is the one big brain in the whole show, and he happens also to be an honest man. Therefore he has been marked down these twelve months past. I found that out – not that it was difficult, for any fool could guess as much. But I found out the way they were going to get him, and that knowledge was deadly. That's why I have had to decease."

He had another drink, and I mixed it for him myself, for I was getting interested in the beggar.

"They can't get him in his own land, for he has a bodyguard of Epirotes that would skin their grandmothers. But on the 15th day of June he is coming to this city. The British Foreign Office has taken to having International tea-parties, and the biggest of them is due on that date. Now Karolides is reckoned the principal guest, and if my friends have their way he will never return to his admiring countrymen."

"That's simple enough, anyhow," I said. "You can warn him and keep him at home."

"And play their game?" he asked sharply. "If he does not come they win, for he's the only man that can straighten out the tangle. And if his Government are warned he won't come, for he does not know how big the stakes will be on June the 15th."

"What about the British Government?" I said. "They're not going to let their guests be murdered. Tip them the wink, and they'll take extra precautions."

"No good. They might stuff your city with plain-clothes detectives and double the police and Constantine would still be a doomed man. My friends are not playing this game for candy. They want a big occasion for the taking off, with the eyes of all Europe on it. He'll be murdered by an Austrian, and there'll be plenty of evidence to show the connivance of the big folk in Vienna and Berlin. It will all be an infernal lie, of course, but the case will look black enough to the world. I'm not talking hot air, my friend. I happen to know every detail of the hellish contrivance, and I can tell you it will be the most finished piece of blackguardism since the Borgias. But it's not going to come off if there's a certain man who knows the wheels of the business alive right here in London on the 15th day of June. And that man is going to be your servant, Franklin P. Scudder."

I was getting to like the little chap. His jaw had shut like a rat-trap, and there was the fire of battle in his gimlety eyes. If he was spinning me a yarn he could act up to it.

"Where did you find out this story?" I asked.

"I got the first hint in an inn on the Achensee in Tyrol. That set me inquiring, and I collected my other clues in a fur-shop in the Galician quarter of Buda, in a Strangers' Club in Vienna, and in a little bookshop off the Racknitzstrasse in Leipsic. I completed my evidence ten days ago in Paris. I can't tell you the details now, for it's something of a history. When I was quite sure in my own mind I judged it my business to disappear, and I reached this city by a mighty queer circuit. I left Paris a dandified young French-American, and I sailed from Hamburg a Jew diamond merchant. In Norway I was an English student of Ibsen collecting materials for lectures, but when I left Bergen I was a cinema-man with special ski films. And I came here from Leith with a lot of pulp-wood propositions in my pocket to put before the London newspapers. Till yesterday I thought I had muddied my trail some, and was feeling pretty happy. Then..."

The recollection seemed to upset him, and he gulped down some more whisky.

"Then I saw a man standing in the street outside this block. I used to stay close in my room all day, and only slip out after dark for an hour or two. I watched him for a bit from my window, and I thought I recognized him.... He came in and spoke to the porter.... When I came back from my walk last night I found a card in my letter-box. It bore the name of the man I want least to meet on God's earth."

I think that the look in my companion's eyes, the sheer naked scare on his face, completed my conviction of his honesty. My own voice sharpened a bit as I asked him what he did next.

"I realized that I was bottled as sure as a pickled herring, and that there was only one way out. I had to die. If my pursuers knew I was dead they would go to sleep again."

"How did you manage it?"

"I told the man that valets me that I was feeling pretty bad, and I got myself up to look like death. That wasn't difficult, for I'm no slouch at disguises. Then I got a corpse – you can always get a body in London if you know where to go for it. I fetched it back in a trunk on the top of a four-wheeler, and I had to be assisted upstairs to my room. You see I had to pile up some evidence for the inquest. I went to bed and got my man to mix me a sleeping-draught, and then told him to clear out. He wanted to fetch a doctor, but I swore some and said I couldn't abide leeches. When I was left alone I started in to fake up that corpse. He was my size, and I judged had perished from too much alcohol, so I put some spirits handy about the place. The jaw was the weak point in the likeness, so I blew it away with a revolver. I daresay there will be somebody tomorrow to swear to having heard a shot, but there are no neighbours on my floor, and I guessed I could risk it. So I left the body in bed dressed up in my pyjamas, with a revolver lying on the bed-clothes and a considerable mess around. Then I got into a suit of clothes I had kept waiting for emergencies. I didn't dare to shave for fear of leaving tracks, and besides, it wasn't any kind of use my trying to get into the streets. I had had you in my mind all day, and there seemed nothing to do but to make an appeal to you. I watched from my window till I saw you come home, and then slipped down the stair to meet you ... There, Sir, I guess you know about as much as me of this business."

He sat blinking like an owl, fluttering with nerves and yet desperately determined. By this time I was pretty well convinced that he was going straight with me. It was the wildest sort of narrative, but I had heard in my time many steep tales which had turned out to be true, and I had made a practice of judging the man rather than the story. If he had wanted to get a location in my flat, and then cut my throat, he would have pitched a milder yarn.

"Hand me your key," I said, "and I'll take a look at the corpse. Excuse my caution, but I'm bound to verify a bit if I can."

He shook his head mournfully. "I reckoned you'd ask for that, but I haven't got it. It's on my chain on the dressing-table. I had to leave it behind, for I couldn't leave any clues to breed suspicions. The gentry who are after me are pretty bright-eyed citizens. You'll have to take me on trust for the night, and tomorrow you'll get proof of the corpse business right enough."

I thought for an instant or two. "Right. I'll trust you for the night. I'll lock you into this room and keep the key. Just one word, Mr. Scudder. I believe you're straight, but if so be you are not I should warn you that I'm a handy man with a gun."

"Sure," he said, jumping up with some briskness. "I haven't the privilege of your name, Sir, but let me tell you that you're a white man. I'll thank you to lend me a razor."

I took him into my bedroom and turned him loose. In half an hour's time a figure came out that I scarcely recognized. Only his gimlety, hungry eyes were the same. He was shaved clean, his hair was parted in the middle, and he had cut his eyebrows.

Further, he carried himself as if he had been drilled, and was the very model, even to the brown complexion, of some British officer who had had a long spell in India. He had a monocle, too, which he stuck in his eye, and every trace of the American had gone out of his speech.

"My hat! Mr. Scudder –" I stammered.

"Not Mr. Scudder," he corrected; "Captain Theophilus Digby, of the 40th Gurkhas, presently home on leave. I'll thank you to remember that, Sir."

I made him up a bed in my smoking-room and sought my own couch, more cheerful than I had been for the past month. Things did happen occasionally, even in this God-forgotten metropolis.

I woke next morning to hear my man, Paddock, making the deuce of a row at the smoking-room door. Paddock was a fellow I had done a good turn to out on the Selakwe, and I had inspanned him as my servant as soon as I got to England. He had about as much gift of the gab as a hippopotamus, and was not a great hand at valeting, but I knew I could count on his loyalty.

"Stop that row, Paddock," I said. "There's a friend of mine, Captain – Captain" (I couldn't remember the name) "dossing down in there. Get breakfast for two and then come and speak to me."

I told Paddock a fine story about how my friend was a great swell, with his nerves pretty bad from overwork, who wanted absolute rest and stillness. Nobody had got to know he was here, or he would be besieged by communications from the India Office and the Prime Minister and his cure would be ruined. I am bound to say Scudder played up splendidly when he came to breakfast. He fixed Paddock with his eyeglass, just like a British officer, asked him about the Boer War, and slung out at me a lot of stuff about imaginary pals. Paddock couldn't learn to call me 'Sir', but he 'sirred' Scudder as if his life depended on it.

I left him with the newspaper and a box of cigars, and went down to the City till luncheon. When I got back the lift-man had an important face.

"Nawsty business 'ere this morning, Sir. Gent in No. 15 been and shot 'isself. They've just took 'im to the mortiary. The police are up there now."

I ascended to No. 15, and found a couple of bobbies and an inspector busy making an examination. I asked a few idiotic questions, and they soon kicked me out. Then I found the man that had valeted Scudder, and pumped him, but I could see he suspected nothing. He was a whining fellow with a churchyard face, and half-a-crown went far to console him.

I attended the inquest next day. A partner of some publishing firm gave evidence that the deceased had brought him wood-pulp propositions, and had been, he believed, an agent of an American business. The jury found it a case of suicide while of unsound mind, and the few effects were handed over to the American Consul to deal with. I gave Scudder a full account of the affair, and it interested him greatly. He said he wished he could have attended the inquest, for he reckoned it would be about as spicy as to read one's own obituary notice.

The first two days he stayed with me in that back room he was very peaceful. He read and smoked a bit, and made a heap of jottings in a note-book, and every night we had a game of chess, at which he beat me hollow. I think he was nursing his nerves back to health, for he had had a pretty trying time. But on the third day I could see he was beginning to get restless. He fixed up a list of the days till June 15th, and ticked each off with a red pencil, making remarks in shorthand against them. I would find him sunk in a brown study, with his sharp eyes abstracted, and after those spells of meditation he was apt to be very despondent.

Then I could see that he began to get edgy again. He listened for little noises, and was always asking me if Paddock could be trusted. Once or twice he got very peevish, and apologized for it. I didn't blame him. I made every allowance, for he had taken on a fairly stiff job.

It was not the safety of his own skin that troubled him, but the success of the scheme he had planned. That little man was clean grit all through, without a soft spot in him. One night he was very solemn.

"Say, Hannay," he said, "I judge I should let you a bit deeper into this business. I should hate to go out without leaving somebody else to put up a fight." And he began to tell me in detail what I had only heard from him vaguely.

I did not give him very close attention. The fact is, I was more interested in his own adventures than in his high politics. I reckoned that Karolides and his affairs were not my business, leaving all that to him. So a lot that he said slipped clean out of my memory. I remember that he was very clear that the danger to Karolides would not begin till he had got to London, and would come from the very highest quarters, where there would be no thought of suspicion. He mentioned the name of a woman – Julia Czechenyi – as having something to do with the danger. She would be the decoy, I gathered, to get Karolides out of the care of his guards. He talked, too, about a Black Stone and a man that lisped in his speech, and he described very particularly somebody that he never referred to without a shudder – an old man with a young voice who could hood his eyes like a hawk.

He spoke a good deal about death, too. He was mortally anxious about winning through with his job, but he didn't care a rush for his life.

"I reckon it's like going to sleep when you are pretty well tired out, and waking to find a summer day with the scent of hay coming in at the window. I used to thank God for such mornings way back in the Blue-Grass country, and I guess I'll thank Him when I wake up on the other side of Jordan."

Next day he was much more cheerful, and read the life of Stonewall Jackson much of the time. I went out to dinner with a mining engineer I had got to see on business, and came back about half-past ten in time for our game of chess before turning in.

I had a cigar in my mouth, I remember, as I pushed open the smoking-room door. The lights were not lit, which struck me as odd. I wondered if Scudder had turned in already.

I snapped the switch, but there was nobody there. Then I saw something in the far corner which made me drop my cigar and fall into a cold sweat.

My guest was lying sprawled on his back. There was a long knife through his heart which skewered him to the floor.

Chapter II
The Milkman Sets Out on his Travels

I SAT DOWN in an armchair and felt very sick. That lasted for maybe five minutes, and was succeeded by a fit of the horrors. The poor staring white face on the floor was more than I could bear, and I managed to get a table-cloth and cover it. Then I staggered to a cupboard, found the brandy and swallowed several mouthfuls. I had seen men die violently before; indeed I had killed a few myself in the Matabele War; but this cold-blooded indoor business was different. Still I managed to pull myself together. I looked at my watch, and saw that it was half-past ten.

An idea seized me, and I went over the flat with a small-tooth comb. There was nobody there, nor any trace of anybody, but I shuttered and bolted all the windows and put the chain on the door. By this time my wits were coming back to me, and I could think again. It took me about an hour to figure the thing out, and I did not hurry, for, unless the murderer came back, I had till about six o'clock in the morning for my cogitations.

I was in the soup – that was pretty clear. Any shadow of a doubt I might have had about the truth of Scudder's tale was now gone. The proof of it was lying under the table-cloth. The men who knew that he knew what he knew had found him, and had taken the best way to make certain of his silence. Yes; but he had been in my rooms four days, and his enemies must have reckoned that he had confided in me. So I would be the next to go. It might be that very night, or next day, or the day after, but my number was up all right.

Then suddenly I thought of another probability. Supposing I went out now and called in the police, or went to bed and let Paddock find the body and call them in the morning. What kind of a story was I to tell about Scudder? I had lied to Paddock about him, and the whole thing looked desperately fishy. If I made a clean breast of it and told the police everything he had told me, they would simply laugh at me. The odds were a thousand to one that I would be charged with the murder, and the circumstantial evidence was strong enough to hang me. Few people knew me in England; I had no real pal who could come forward and swear to my character. Perhaps that was what those secret enemies were playing for. They were clever enough for anything, and an English prison was as good a way of getting rid of me till after June 15th as a knife in my chest.

Besides, if I told the whole story, and by any miracle was believed, I would be playing their game. Karolides would stay at home, which was what they wanted. Somehow or other the sight of Scudder's dead face had made me a passionate believer in his scheme. He was gone, but he had taken me into his confidence, and I was pretty well bound to carry on his work.

You may think this ridiculous for a man in danger of his life, but that was the way I looked at it. I am an ordinary sort of fellow, not braver than other people, but I hate to see a good man downed, and that long knife would not be the end of Scudder if I could play the game in his place.

It took me an hour or two to think this out, and by that time I had come to a decision. I must vanish somehow, and keep vanished till the end of the second week in June. Then I must somehow find a way to get in touch with the Government people and tell them what Scudder had told me. I wished to Heaven he had told me more, and that I had listened more carefully to the little he had told me. I knew nothing but the barest facts. There was a big risk that, even if I weathered the other dangers, I would not be believed in the end. I must take my chance of that, and hope that something might happen which would confirm my tale in the eyes of the Government.

My first job was to keep going for the next three weeks. It was now the 24th day of May, and that meant twenty days of hiding before I could venture to approach the powers that be. I reckoned that two sets of people would be looking for me – Scudder's enemies to put me out of existence, and the police, who would want me for Scudder's murder. It was going to be a giddy hunt, and it was queer how the prospect comforted me. I had been slack so long that almost any chance of activity was welcome. When I had to sit alone with that corpse and wait on Fortune I was no better than a crushed worm, but if my neck's safety was to hang on my own wits I was prepared to be cheerful about it.

My next thought was whether Scudder had any papers about him to give me a better clue to the business. I drew back the table-cloth and searched his pockets, for I had no longer any shrinking from the body. The face was wonderfully calm for a man who had been struck down in a moment. There was nothing in the breast-pocket, and only a few loose coins and a cigar-holder in the waistcoat. The trousers held a little penknife and some silver, and the side pocket of his jacket contained an old crocodile-skin cigar-case. There was no sign of the little black book in which I had seen him making notes. That had no doubt been taken by his murderer.

But as I looked up from my task I saw that some drawers had been pulled out in the writing-table. Scudder would never have left them in that state, for he was the tidiest of mortals. Someone must have been searching for something – perhaps for the pocket-book.

I went round the flat and found that everything had been ransacked – the inside of books, drawers, cupboards, boxes, even the pockets of the clothes in my wardrobe, and the sideboard in the dining-room. There was no trace of the book. Most likely the enemy had found it, but they had not found it on Scudder's body.

Then I got out an atlas and looked at a big map of the British Isles. My notion was to get off to some wild district, where my veldcraft would be of some use to me, for I would be like a trapped rat in a city. I considered that Scotland would be best, for my people were Scotch and I could pass anywhere as an ordinary Scotsman. I had half an idea at first to be a German tourist, for my father had had German partners, and I had been brought up to speak the tongue pretty fluently, not to mention having put in three years prospecting for copper in German Damaraland. But I calculated that it would be less conspicuous to be a Scot, and less in a line with what the police might know of my past. I fixed on Galloway as the best place to go. It was the nearest wild part of Scotland, so far as I could figure it out, and from the look of the map was not over thick with population.

A search in Bradshaw informed me that a train left St Pancras at 7.10, which would land me at any Galloway station in the late afternoon. That was well enough, but a more important matter was how I was to make my way to St Pancras, for I was pretty certain that Scudder's friends would be watching outside. This puzzled me for a bit; then I had an inspiration, on which I went to bed and slept for two troubled hours.

I got up at four and opened my bedroom shutters. The faint light of a fine summer morning was flooding the skies, and the sparrows had begun to chatter. I had a great revulsion of feeling, and felt a God-forgotten fool. My inclination was to let things slide, and trust to the British police taking a reasonable view of my case. But as I reviewed the situation I could find no arguments to bring against my decision of the previous night, so with a wry mouth I resolved to go on with my plan. I was not feeling in any particular funk; only disinclined to go looking for trouble, if you understand me.

I hunted out a well-used tweed suit, a pair of strong nailed boots, and a flannel shirt with a collar. Into my pockets I stuffed a spare shirt, a cloth cap, some handkerchiefs, and a tooth-brush. I had drawn a good sum in gold from the bank two days before, in case Scudder should want money, and I took fifty pounds of it in sovereigns in a belt which I had brought back from Rhodesia. That was about all I wanted. Then I had a bath, and cut my moustache, which was long and drooping, into a short stubbly fringe.

Now came the next step. Paddock used to arrive punctually at 7.30 and let himself in with a latch-key. But about twenty minutes to seven, as I knew from bitter experience, the milkman turned up with a great clatter of cans, and deposited my share outside my door. I had seen that milkman sometimes when I had gone out for an early ride. He was a young man about my own height, with an ill-nourished moustache, and he wore a white overall. On him I staked all my chances.

I went into the darkened smoking-room where the rays of morning light were beginning to creep through the shutters. There I breakfasted off a whisky-and-soda and some biscuits from the cupboard. By this time it was getting on for six o'clock. I put a pipe in my pocket and filled my pouch from the tobacco jar on the table by the fireplace.

As I poked into the tobacco my fingers touched something hard, and I drew out Scudder's little black pocket-book…

That seemed to me a good omen. I lifted the cloth from the body and was amazed at the peace and dignity of the dead face. "Goodbye, old chap," I said; "I am going to do my best for you. Wish me well, wherever you are."

Then I hung about in the hall waiting for the milkman. That was the worst part of the business, for I was fairly choking to get out of doors. Six-thirty passed, then six-forty, but still he did not come. The fool had chosen this day of all days to be late.

At one minute after the quarter to seven I heard the rattle of the cans outside. I opened the front door, and there was my man, singling out my cans from a bunch he carried and whistling through his teeth. He jumped a bit at the sight of me.

"Come in here a moment," I said. "I want a word with you." And I led him into the dining-room.

"I reckon you're a bit of a sportsman," I said, "and I want you to do me a service. Lend me your cap and overall for ten minutes, and here's a sovereign for you."

His eyes opened at the sight of the gold, and he grinned broadly. "Wot's the gyme?" he asked.

"A bet," I said. "I haven't time to explain, but to win it I've got to be a milkman for the next ten minutes. All you've got to do is to stay here till I come back. You'll be a bit late, but nobody will complain, and you'll have that quid for yourself."

"Right-o!" he said cheerily. "I ain't the man to spoil a bit of sport. 'Ere's the rig, guv'nor."

I stuck on his flat blue hat and his white overall, picked up the cans, banged my door, and went whistling downstairs. The porter at the foot told me to shut my jaw, which sounded as if my make-up was adequate.

At first I thought there was nobody in the street. Then I caught sight of a policeman a hundred yards down, and a loafer shuffling past on the other side. Some impulse made me raise my eyes to the house opposite, and there at a first-floor window was a face. As the loafer passed he looked up, and I fancied a signal was exchanged.

I crossed the street, whistling gaily and imitating the jaunty swing of the milkman. Then I took the first side street, and went up a left-hand turning which led past a bit of vacant ground. There was no one in the little street, so I dropped the milk-cans inside the hoarding and sent the cap and overall after them. I had only just put on my cloth cap when a postman came round the corner. I gave him good morning and he answered me unsuspiciously. At the moment the clock of a neighbouring church struck the hour of seven.

There was not a second to spare. As soon as I got to Euston Road I took to my heels and ran. The clock at Euston Station showed five minutes past the hour. At St Pancras I had no time to take a ticket, let alone that I had not settled upon my destination. A porter told me the platform, and as I entered it I saw the train already in motion. Two station officials blocked the way, but I dodged them and clambered into the last carriage.

Three minutes later, as we were roaring through the northern tunnels, an irate guard interviewed me. He wrote out for me a ticket to Newton-Stewart, a name which had suddenly come back to my memory, and he conducted me from the first-class compartment where I had ensconced myself to a third-class smoker, occupied by a sailor and a stout woman with a child. He went off grumbling, and as I mopped my brow I observed to my companions in my broadest Scots that it was a sore job catching trains. I had already entered upon my part.

"The impidence o' that gyaird!" said the lady bitterly. "He needit a Scotch tongue to pit him in his place. He was complainin' o' this wean no haein' a ticket and her no fower till August twalmonth, and he was objectin' to this gentleman spittin'."

The sailor morosely agreed, and I started my new life in an atmosphere of protest against authority. I reminded myself that a week ago I had been finding the world dull.

Chapter III
The Adventure of the Literary Innkeeper

I HAD A solemn time travelling north that day. It was fine May weather, with the hawthorn flowering on every hedge, and I asked myself why, when I was still a free man, I had stayed on in London and not got the good of this heavenly country. I didn't dare face the restaurant car, but I got a luncheon-basket at Leeds and shared it with the fat woman. Also I got the morning's papers, with news about starters for the Derby and the beginning of the cricket season, and some paragraphs about how Balkan affairs were settling down and a British squadron was going to Kiel.

When I had done with them I got out Scudder's little black pocket-book and studied it. It was pretty well filled with jottings, chiefly figures, though now and then a name was printed in. For example, I found the words 'Hofgaard', 'Luneville', and 'Avocado' pretty often, and especially the word 'Pavia'.

Now I was certain that Scudder never did anything without a reason, and I was pretty sure that there was a cypher in all this. That is a subject which has always interested me, and I did a bit at it myself once as intelligence officer at Delagoa Bay during the Boer War. I have a head for things like chess and puzzles, and I used to reckon myself pretty good at finding out cyphers. This one looked like the numerical kind where sets of figures correspond to the letters of the alphabet, but any fairly shrewd man can find the clue to that sort after an hour or two's work, and I didn't think Scudder would have been content with anything so easy. So I fastened on the printed words, for you can make a pretty good numerical cypher if you have a key word which gives you the sequence of the letters.

I tried for hours, but none of the words answered. Then I fell asleep and woke at Dumfries just in time to bundle out and get into the slow Galloway train. There was a man on the platform whose looks I didn't like, but he never glanced at me, and when I caught sight of myself in the mirror of an automatic machine I didn't wonder. With my brown face, my old tweeds, and my slouch, I was the very model of one of the hill farmers who were crowding into the third-class carriages.

I travelled with half a dozen in an atmosphere of shag and clay pipes. They had come from the weekly market, and their mouths were full of prices. I heard accounts of how the lambing had gone up the Cairn and the Deuch and a dozen other mysterious waters. Above half the men had lunched heavily and were highly flavoured with whisky, but they took no notice of me. We rumbled slowly into a land of little wooded glens and then to a great wide moorland place, gleaming with lochs, with high blue hills showing northwards.

About five o'clock the carriage had emptied, and I was left alone as I had hoped. I got out at the next station, a little place whose name I scarcely noted, set right in the heart of a bog. It reminded me of one of those forgotten little stations in the Karroo. An old station-master was digging in his garden, and with his spade over his shoulder sauntered to the train, took charge of a parcel, and went back to his potatoes. A child of ten received my ticket, and I emerged on a white road that straggled over the brown moor.

It was a gorgeous spring evening, with every hill showing as clear as a cut amethyst. The air had the queer, rooty smell of bogs, but it was as fresh as mid-ocean, and it had the strangest effect on my spirits. I actually felt light-hearted. I might have been a boy out for a spring holiday tramp, instead of a man of thirty-seven very much wanted by the police. I felt just as I used to feel when I was starting for a big trek on a frosty morning on the high veld. If you believe me, I swung along that road whistling. There was no plan of campaign in my head, only just to go on and on in this blessed, honest-smelling hill country, for every mile put me in better humour with myself.

In a roadside planting I cut a walking-stick of hazel, and presently struck off the highway up a bypath which followed the glen of a brawling stream. I reckoned that I was still far ahead of any pursuit, and for that night might please myself. It was some hours since I had tasted food, and I was getting very hungry when I came to a herd's cottage set in a nook beside a waterfall. A brown-faced woman was standing by the door, and greeted me with the kindly shyness of moorland places. When I asked for a night's lodging she said I was welcome to the 'bed in the loft', and very soon she set before me a hearty meal of ham and eggs, scones, and thick sweet milk.

At the darkening her man came in from the hills, a lean giant, who in one step covered as much ground as three paces of ordinary mortals. They asked me no questions, for they had the perfect breeding of all dwellers in the wilds, but I could see they set me down as a kind of dealer, and I took some trouble to confirm their view. I spoke a lot about cattle, of which my host knew little, and I picked up from him a good deal about the local Galloway markets, which I tucked away in my memory for future use. At ten I was nodding in my chair, and the 'bed in the loft' received a weary man who never opened his eyes till five o'clock set the little homestead a-going once more.

They refused any payment, and by six I had breakfasted and was striding southwards again. My notion was to return to the railway line a station or two farther on than the place where I had alighted yesterday and to double back. I reckoned that that was the safest way, for the police would naturally assume that I was always making farther from London in the direction of some western port. I thought I had still a good bit of a start, for, as I reasoned, it would take some hours to fix the blame on me, and several more to identify the fellow who got on board the train at St Pancras.

It was the same jolly, clear spring weather, and I simply could not contrive to feel careworn. Indeed I was in better spirits than I had been for months. Over a long ridge of moorland I took my road, skirting the side of a high hill which the herd had called Cairnsmore of Fleet. Nesting curlews and plovers were crying everywhere, and the links of green pasture by the streams were dotted with young lambs. All the slackness of the past months was slipping from my bones, and I stepped out like a four-year-old. By-and-by I came to a swell of moorland which dipped to the vale of a little river, and a mile away in the heather I saw the smoke of a train.

The station, when I reached it, proved to be ideal for my purpose. The moor surged up around it and left room only for the single line, the slender siding, a waiting-room, an office, the station-master's cottage, and a tiny yard of gooseberries and sweet-william. There seemed no road to it from anywhere, and to increase the desolation the waves of a tarn lapped on their grey granite beach half a mile away. I waited in the deep heather till I saw the smoke of an east-going train on the horizon. Then I approached the tiny booking-office and took a ticket for Dumfries.

The only occupants of the carriage were an old shepherd and his dog – a wall-eyed brute that I mistrusted. The man was asleep, and on the cushions beside him was that morning's *Scotsman*. Eagerly I seized on it, for I fancied it would tell me something.

There were two columns about the Portland Place Murder, as it was called. My man Paddock had given the alarm and had the milkman arrested. Poor devil, it looked as if the latter had earned his sovereign hardly; but for me he had been cheap at the price, for he seemed to have occupied the police for the better part of the day. In the latest news I found a further instalment of the story. The milkman had been released, I read, and the true criminal, about whose identity the police were reticent, was believed to have got away from London by one of the northern lines. There was a short note about me as the owner of the flat. I guessed the police had stuck that in, as a clumsy contrivance to persuade me that I was unsuspected.

There was nothing else in the paper, nothing about foreign politics or Karolides, or the things that had interested Scudder. I laid it down, and found that we were approaching the station at which I had got out yesterday. The potato-digging station-master had been gingered up into some activity, for the west-going train was waiting to let us pass, and from it had descended three men who were asking him questions. I supposed that they were the local police, who had been stirred up by Scotland Yard, and had traced me as far as this one-horse siding. Sitting well back in the shadow I watched them carefully. One of them had a book, and took down notes. The old potato-digger seemed to have turned peevish, but the child who had collected my ticket was talking volubly. All the party looked out across the moor where the white road departed. I hoped they were going to take up my tracks there.

As we moved away from that station my companion woke up. He fixed me with a wandering glance, kicked his dog viciously, and inquired where he was. Clearly he was very drunk.

"That's what comes o' bein' a teetotaller," he observed in bitter regret.

I expressed my surprise that in him I should have met a blue-ribbon stalwart.

"Ay, but I'm a strong teetotaller," he said pugnaciously. "I took the pledge last Martinmas, and I havena touched a drop o' whisky sinsyne. Not even at Hogmanay, though I was sair temptit."

He swung his heels up on the seat, and burrowed a frowsy head into the cushions.

"And that's a' I get," he moaned. "A heid better than hell fire, and twae een lookin' different ways for the Sabbath."

"What did it?" I asked.

"A drink they ca' brandy. Bein' a teetotaller I keepit off the whisky, but I was nip-nippin' a' day at this brandy, and I doubt I'll no be weel for a fortnicht." His voice died away into a splutter, and sleep once more laid its heavy hand on him.

My plan had been to get out at some station down the line, but the train suddenly gave me a better chance, for it came to a standstill at the end of a culvert which spanned a brawling porter-coloured river. I looked out and saw that every carriage window was closed and no human figure appeared in the landscape. So I opened the door, and dropped quickly into the tangle of hazels which edged the line.

It would have been all right but for that infernal dog. Under the impression that I was decamping with its master's belongings, it started to bark, and all but got me by the trousers. This woke up the herd, who stood bawling at the carriage door in the belief that I had committed suicide. I crawled through the thicket, reached the edge of the stream, and in cover of the bushes put a hundred yards or so behind me. Then from my shelter I peered back, and saw the guard and several passengers gathered round the open carriage door and staring in my direction. I could not have made a more public departure if I had left with a bugler and a brass band.

Happily the drunken herd provided a diversion. He and his dog, which was attached by a rope to his waist, suddenly cascaded out of the carriage, landed on their heads on the track, and rolled some way down the bank towards the water. In the rescue which followed the dog bit somebody, for I could hear the sound of hard swearing. Presently they had forgotten me, and when after a quarter of a mile's crawl I ventured to look back, the train had started again and was vanishing in the cutting.

I was in a wide semicircle of moorland, with the brown river as radius, and the high hills forming the northern circumference. There was not a sign or sound of a human being, only the plashing water and the interminable crying of curlews. Yet, oddly enough, for the first time I felt the terror of the hunted on me. It was not the police that I thought of, but the other folk, who knew that I knew Scudder's secret and dared not let me live. I was certain that they would pursue me with a keenness and vigilance unknown to the British law, and that once their grip closed on me I should find no mercy.

I looked back, but there was nothing in the landscape. The sun glinted on the metals of the line and the wet stones in the stream, and you could not have found a more peaceful sight in the world. Nevertheless I started to run. Crouching low in the runnels of the bog, I ran till the sweat blinded my eyes. The mood did not leave me till I had reached the rim of mountain and flung myself panting on a ridge high above the young waters of the brown river.

From my vantage-ground I could scan the whole moor right away to the railway line and to the south of it where green fields took the place of heather. I have eyes like a hawk, but I could see nothing moving in the whole countryside. Then I looked east beyond the ridge and saw a new kind of landscape – shallow green valleys with plentiful fir plantations and the faint lines of dust which spoke of highroads. Last of all I looked into the blue May sky, and there I saw that which set my pulses racing...

Low down in the south a monoplane was climbing into the heavens. I was as certain as if I had been told that that aeroplane was looking for me, and that it did not belong to the police. For an hour or two I watched it from a pit of heather. It flew low along the hill-tops, and then in narrow circles over the valley up which I had come. Then it seemed to change its mind, rose to a great height, and flew away back to the south.

I did not like this espionage from the air, and I began to think less well of the countryside I had chosen for a refuge. These heather hills were no sort of cover if my enemies were in the sky, and I must find a different kind of sanctuary. I looked with more satisfaction to the green country beyond the ridge, for there I should find woods and stone houses.

About six in the evening I came out of the moorland to a white ribbon of road which wound up the narrow vale of a lowland stream. As I followed it, fields gave place to bent, the glen became a plateau, and presently I had reached a kind of pass where a solitary house smoked in the twilight. The road swung over a bridge, and leaning on the parapet was a young man.

He was smoking a long clay pipe and studying the water with spectacled eyes. In his left hand was a small book with a finger marking the place. Slowly he repeated –

As when a Gryphon through the wilderness
With winged step, o'er hill and moory dale
Pursues the Arimaspian.

He jumped round as my step rung on the keystone, and I saw a pleasant sunburnt boyish face.

"Good evening to you," he said gravely. "It's a fine night for the road."

The smell of peat smoke and of some savoury roast floated to me from the house.

"Is that place an inn?" I asked.

"At your service," he said politely. "I am the landlord, Sir, and I hope you will stay the night, for to tell you the truth I have had no company for a week."

I pulled myself up on the parapet of the bridge and filled my pipe. I began to detect an ally.

"You're young to be an innkeeper," I said.

"My father died a year ago and left me the business. I live there with my grandmother. It's a slow job for a young man, and it wasn't my choice of profession."

"Which was?"

He actually blushed. "I want to write books," he said.

"And what better chance could you ask?" I cried. "Man, I've often thought that an innkeeper would make the best story-teller in the world."

"Not now," he said eagerly. "Maybe in the old days when you had pilgrims and ballad-makers and highwaymen and mail-coaches on the road. But not now. Nothing comes here but motor-cars full of fat women, who stop for lunch, and a fisherman or two in the spring, and the shooting tenants in August. There is not much material to be got out of that. I want to see life, to travel the world, and write things like Kipling and Conrad. But the most I've done yet is to get some verses printed in *Chambers's Journal*." I looked at the inn standing golden in the sunset against the brown hills.

"I've knocked a bit about the world, and I wouldn't despise such a hermitage. D'you think that adventure is found only in the tropics or among gentry in red shirts? Maybe you're rubbing shoulders with it at this moment."

"That's what Kipling says," he said, his eyes brightening, and he quoted some verse about "Romance bringing up the 9.15".

"Here's a true tale for you then," I cried, "and a month from now you can make a novel out of it."

Sitting on the bridge in the soft May gloaming I pitched him a lovely yarn. It was true in essentials, too, though I altered the minor details. I made out that I was a mining magnate from Kimberley, who had had a lot of trouble with I.D.B. and had shown up a gang. They had pursued me across the ocean, and had killed my best friend, and were now on my tracks.

I told the story well, though I say it who shouldn't. I pictured a flight across the Kalahari to German Africa, the crackling, parching days, the wonderful blue-velvet nights. I described an attack on my life on the voyage home, and I made a really horrid affair of the Portland Place murder. "You're looking for adventure," I cried; "well, you've found it here. The devils are after me, and the police are after them. It's a race that I mean to win."

"By God!" he whispered, drawing his breath in sharply, "it is all pure Rider Haggard and Conan Doyle."

"You believe me," I said gratefully.

"Of course I do," and he held out his hand. "I believe everything out of the common. The only thing to distrust is the normal."

He was very young, but he was the man for my money.

"I think they're off my track for the moment, but I must lie close for a couple of days. Can you take me in?"

He caught my elbow in his eagerness and drew me towards the house. "You can lie as snug here as if you were in a moss-hole. I'll see that nobody blabs, either. And you'll give me some more material about your adventures?"

As I entered the inn porch I heard from far off the beat of an engine. There silhouetted against the dusky West was my friend, the monoplane.

He gave me a room at the back of the house, with a fine outlook over the plateau, and he made me free of his own study, which was stacked with cheap editions of his favourite authors. I never saw the grandmother, so I guessed she was bedridden. An old woman called Margit brought me my meals, and the innkeeper was around me at all hours. I wanted some time to myself, so I invented a job for him. He had a motor-bicycle, and I sent him off next morning for the daily paper, which usually arrived with the post in the late afternoon. I told him to keep his eyes skinned, and make note of any strange figures he saw, keeping a special sharp look-out for motors and aeroplanes. Then I sat down in real earnest to Scudder's note-book.

He came back at midday with the *Scotsman*. There was nothing in it, except some further evidence of Paddock and the milkman, and a repetition of yesterday's statement that the murderer had gone North. But there was a long article, reprinted from *The Times*, about Karolides and the state of affairs in the Balkans, though there was no mention of any visit to England. I got rid of the innkeeper for the afternoon, for I was getting very warm in my search for the cypher.

As I told you, it was a numerical cypher, and by an elaborate system of experiments I had pretty well discovered what were the nulls and stops. The trouble was the key word, and when I thought of the odd million words he might have used I felt pretty hopeless. But about three o'clock I had a sudden inspiration.

The name Julia Czechenyi flashed across my memory. Scudder had said it was the key to the Karolides business, and it occurred to me to try it on his cypher.

It worked. The five letters of 'Julia' gave me the position of the vowels. A was J, the tenth letter of the alphabet, and so represented by X in the cypher. E was XXI, and so on. 'Czechenyi' gave me the numerals for the principal consonants. I scribbled that scheme on a bit of paper and sat down to read Scudder's pages.

In half an hour I was reading with a whitish face and fingers that drummed on the table.

I glanced out of the window and saw a big touring-car coming up the glen towards the inn. It drew up at the door, and there was the sound of people alighting. There seemed to be two of them, men in aquascutums and tweed caps.

Ten minutes later the innkeeper slipped into the room, his eyes bright with excitement.

"There's two chaps below looking for you," he whispered. "They're in the dining-room having whiskies-and-sodas. They asked about you and said they had hoped to meet you here. Oh! And they described you jolly well, down to your boots and shirt. I told them you had been here last night and had gone off on a motor bicycle this morning, and one of the chaps swore like a navvy."

I made him tell me what they looked like. One was a dark-eyed thin fellow with bushy eyebrows, the other was always smiling and lisped in his talk. Neither was any kind of foreigner; on this my young friend was positive.

I took a bit of paper and wrote these words in German as if they were part of a letter –

> ... *Black Stone. Scudder had got on to this, but he could not act for a fortnight. I doubt if I can do any good now, especially as Karolides is uncertain about his plans. But if Mr. T. advises I will do the best I...*

I manufactured it rather neatly, so that it looked like a loose page of a private letter.

"Take this down and say it was found in my bedroom, and ask them to return it to me if they overtake me."

Three minutes later I heard the car begin to move, and peeping from behind the curtain caught sight of the two figures. One was slim, the other was sleek; that was the most I could make of my reconnaissance.

The innkeeper appeared in great excitement. "Your paper woke them up," he said gleefully. "The dark fellow went as white as death and cursed like blazes, and the fat one whistled and looked ugly. They paid for their drinks with half-a-sovereign and wouldn't wait for change."

"Now I'll tell you what I want you to do," I said. "Get on your bicycle and go off to Newton-Stewart to the Chief Constable. Describe the two men, and say you suspect them of having had something to do with the London murder. You can invent reasons. The two will come back, never fear. Not tonight, for they'll follow me forty miles along the road, but first thing tomorrow morning. Tell the police to be here bright and early."

He set off like a docile child, while I worked at Scudder's notes. When he came back we dined together, and in common decency I had to let him pump me. I gave him a lot of stuff about lion hunts and the Matabele War, thinking all the while what tame businesses these were compared to this I was now engaged in! When he went to bed I sat up and finished Scudder. I smoked in a chair till daylight, for I could not sleep.

About eight next morning I witnessed the arrival of two constables and a sergeant. They put their car in a coach-house under the innkeeper's instructions, and entered the house. Twenty minutes later I saw from my window a second car come across the plateau from the opposite direction. It did not come up to the inn, but stopped two hundred yards off in the shelter of a patch of wood. I noticed that its occupants carefully reversed it before leaving it. A minute or two later I heard their steps on the gravel outside the window.

My plan had been to lie hid in my bedroom, and see what happened. I had a notion that, if I could bring the police and my other more dangerous pursuers together, something might work out of it to my advantage. But now I had a better idea. I scribbled a line of thanks to my host, opened the window, and dropped quietly into a gooseberry bush. Unobserved I crossed the dyke, crawled down the side of a tributary burn, and won the highroad on the far side of the patch of trees. There stood the car, very spick and span in the morning sunlight, but with the dust on her which told of a long journey. I started her, jumped into the chauffeur's seat, and stole gently out on to the plateau.

Almost at once the road dipped so that I lost sight of the inn, but the wind seemed to bring me the sound of angry voices.

Chapter IV
The Adventure of the Radical Candidate

YOU MAY picture me driving that 40 h.p. car for all she was worth over the crisp moor roads on that shining May morning; glancing back at first over my shoulder, and looking anxiously to the next turning; then driving with a vague eye, just wide enough awake to keep on the highway. For I was thinking desperately of what I had found in Scudder's pocket-book.

The little man had told me a pack of lies. All his yarns about the Balkans and the Jew-Anarchists and the Foreign Office Conference were eyewash, and so was Karolides. And yet not quite, as you shall hear. I had staked everything on my belief in his story, and had been let down; here was his book telling me a different tale, and instead of being once-bitten-twice-shy, I believed it absolutely.

Why, I don't know. It rang desperately true, and the first yarn, if you understand me, had been in a queer way true also in spirit. The fifteenth day of June was going to be a day of destiny, a bigger destiny than the killing of a Dago. It was so big that I didn't blame Scudder for keeping me out of the game and wanting to play a lone hand. That, I was pretty clear, was his intention. He had told me something which sounded big enough, but the real thing was so immortally big that he, the man who had found it out, wanted it all for himself. I didn't blame him. It was risks after all that he was chiefly greedy about.

The whole story was in the notes – with gaps, you understand, which he would have filled up from his memory. He stuck down his authorities, too, and had an odd trick of giving them all a numerical value and then striking a balance, which stood for the reliability of each stage in the yarn. The four names he had printed were authorities, and there was a man, Ducrosne, who got five out of a possible five; and another fellow, Ammersfoort, who got three. The bare bones of the tale were all that was in the book – these, and one queer phrase which occurred half a dozen times inside brackets. '(Thirty-nine steps)' was the phrase; and at its last time of use it ran – '(Thirty-nine steps, I counted them – high tide 10.17 p.m.)'. I could make nothing of that.

The first thing I learned was that it was no question of preventing a war. That was coming, as sure as Christmas: had been arranged, said Scudder, ever since February 1912. Karolides was going to be the occasion. He was booked all right, and was to hand in his checks on June 14th, two weeks and four days from that May morning. I gathered from Scudder's notes that nothing on earth could prevent that. His talk of Epirote guards that would skin their own grandmothers was all billy-o.

The second thing was that this war was going to come as a mighty surprise to Britain. Karolides' death would set the Balkans by the ears, and then Vienna would chip in with an ultimatum. Russia wouldn't like that, and there would be high words. But Berlin would play the peacemaker, and pour oil on the waters, till suddenly she would find a good cause for a quarrel, pick it up, and in five hours let fly at us. That was the idea, and a pretty good one too. Honey and fair speeches, and then a stroke in the dark. While we were talking about the goodwill and good intentions of Germany our coast would be silently ringed with mines, and submarines would be waiting for every battleship.

But all this depended upon the third thing, which was due to happen on June 15th. I would never have grasped this if I hadn't once happened to meet a French staff officer, coming back from West Africa, who had told me a lot of things. One was that, in spite of all the nonsense talked in Parliament, there was a real working alliance between France and Britain, and that the two General Staffs met every now and then, and made plans for joint action in case of war. Well, in June a very great swell was coming over from Paris, and he was going to get nothing less than a statement of the disposition of the British Home Fleet on mobilization. At least I gathered it was something like that; anyhow, it was something uncommonly important.

But on the 15th day of June there were to be others in London – others, at whom I could only guess. Scudder was content to call them collectively the 'Black Stone'. They represented not our Allies, but our deadly foes; and the information, destined for France, was to be diverted to their pockets. And it was to be used, remember – used a week or two later, with great guns and swift torpedoes, suddenly in the darkness of a summer night.

This was the story I had been deciphering in a back room of a country inn, overlooking a cabbage garden. This was the story that hummed in my brain as I swung in the big touring-car from glen to glen.

My first impulse had been to write a letter to the Prime Minister, but a little reflection convinced me that that would be useless. Who would believe my tale? I must show a sign, some token in proof, and Heaven knew what that could be. Above all, I must keep going myself, ready to act when things got riper, and that was going to be no light job with the police of the British Isles in full cry after me and the watchers of the Black Stone running silently and swiftly on my trail.

I had no very clear purpose in my journey, but I steered east by the sun, for I remembered from the map that if I went north I would come into a region of coalpits and industrial towns. Presently I was down from the moorlands and traversing the broad haugh of a river. For miles I ran alongside a park wall, and in a break of the trees I saw a great castle. I swung through little old thatched villages, and over peaceful lowland streams, and past gardens blazing with hawthorn and yellow laburnum. The land was so deep in peace that I could scarcely believe that somewhere behind me were those who sought my life; ay, and that in a month's time, unless I had the almightiest of luck, these round country faces would be pinched and staring, and men would be lying dead in English fields.

About mid-day I entered a long straggling village, and had a mind to stop and eat. Half-way down was the Post Office, and on the steps of it stood the postmistress and a policeman hard at work conning a telegram. When they saw me they wakened up, and the policeman advanced with raised hand, and cried on me to stop.

I nearly was fool enough to obey. Then it flashed upon me that the wire had to do with me; that my friends at the inn had come to an understanding, and were united in desiring to see more of me, and that it had been easy enough for them to wire the description of me and the car to thirty villages through which I might pass. I released the brakes just in time. As it was, the policeman made a claw at the hood, and only dropped off when he got my left in his eye.

I saw that main roads were no place for me, and turned into the byways. It wasn't an easy job without a map, for there was the risk of getting on to a farm road and ending in a duck-pond or a stable-yard, and I couldn't afford that kind of delay. I began to see what an ass I had been to steal the car. The big green brute would be the safest kind of clue to me over the breadth of Scotland. If I left it and took to my feet, it would be discovered in an hour or two and I would get no start in the race.

The immediate thing to do was to get to the loneliest roads. These I soon found when I struck up a tributary of the big river, and got into a glen with steep hills all about me, and a corkscrew road at the end which climbed over a pass. Here I met nobody, but it was taking me too far north, so I slewed east along a bad track and finally struck a big double-line railway. Away below me I saw another broadish valley, and it occurred to me that if I crossed it I might find some remote inn to pass the night. The evening was now drawing in, and I was furiously hungry, for I had eaten nothing since breakfast except a couple of buns I had bought from a baker's cart. Just then I heard a noise in the sky, and lo and behold there was that infernal aeroplane, flying low, about a dozen miles to the south and rapidly coming towards me.

I had the sense to remember that on a bare moor I was at the aeroplane's mercy, and that my only chance was to get to the leafy cover of the valley. Down the hill I went like blue lightning, screwing my head round, whenever I dared, to watch that damned flying machine. Soon I was on a road between hedges, and dipping to the deep-cut glen of a stream. Then came a bit of thick wood where I slackened speed.

Suddenly on my left I heard the hoot of another car, and realized to my horror that I was almost up on a couple of gate-posts through which a private road debouched on the highway. My horn gave an agonized roar, but it was too late. I clapped on my brakes, but my impetus was too great, and there before me a car was sliding athwart my course. In a second there would have been the deuce of a wreck. I did the only thing possible, and ran slap into the hedge on the right, trusting to find something soft beyond.

But there I was mistaken. My car slithered through the hedge like butter, and then gave a sickening plunge forward. I saw what was coming, leapt on the seat and would have jumped out. But a branch of hawthorn got me in the chest, lifted me up and held me, while a ton or two of expensive metal slipped below me, bucked and pitched, and then dropped with an almighty smash fifty feet to the bed of the stream.

Slowly that thorn let me go. I subsided first on the hedge, and then very gently on a bower of nettles. As I scrambled to my feet a hand took me by the arm, and a sympathetic and badly scared voice asked me if I were hurt.

I found myself looking at a tall young man in goggles and a leather ulster, who kept on blessing his soul and whinnying apologies. For myself, once I got my wind back, I was rather glad than otherwise. This was one way of getting rid of the car.

"My blame, Sir," I answered him. "It's lucky that I did not add homicide to my follies. That's the end of my Scotch motor tour, but it might have been the end of my life."

He plucked out a watch and studied it. "You're the right sort of fellow," he said. "I can spare a quarter of an hour, and my house is two minutes off. I'll see you clothed and fed and snug in bed. Where's your kit, by the way? Is it in the burn along with the car?"

"It's in my pocket," I said, brandishing a toothbrush. "I'm a Colonial and travel light."

"A Colonial," he cried. "By Gad, you're the very man I've been praying for. Are you by any blessed chance a Free Trader?"

"I am," said I, without the foggiest notion of what he meant.

He patted my shoulder and hurried me into his car. Three minutes later we drew up before a comfortable-looking shooting box set among pine-trees, and he ushered me indoors. He took me first to a bedroom and flung half a dozen of his suits before me, for my own had been pretty well reduced to rags. I selected a loose blue serge, which differed most conspicuously from my former garments, and borrowed a linen collar. Then he haled me to the dining-room, where the remnants of a meal stood on the table, and announced that I had just five minutes to feed. "You can take a snack in your pocket, and we'll have supper when we get back. I've got to be at the Masonic Hall at eight o'clock, or my agent will comb my hair."

I had a cup of coffee and some cold ham, while he yarned away on the hearth-rug.

"You find me in the deuce of a mess, Mr. – by-the-by, you haven't told me your name. Twisdon? Any relation of old Tommy Twisdon of the Sixtieth? No? Well, you see I'm Liberal Candidate for this part of the world, and I had a meeting on tonight at Brattleburn – that's my chief town, and an infernal Tory stronghold. I had got the Colonial ex-Premier fellow, Crumpleton, coming to speak for me tonight, and had the thing tremendously billed and the whole place ground-baited. This afternoon I had a wire from the ruffian saying he had got influenza at Blackpool, and here am I left to do the whole thing myself. I had meant to speak for ten minutes and must now go on for forty, and, though I've been racking my brains for three hours to think of something, I simply cannot last the course. Now you've got to be a good chap and help me. You're a Free Trader and can tell our people what a wash-out Protection is in the Colonies. All you fellows have the gift of the gab – I wish to Heaven I had it. I'll be for evermore in your debt."

I had very few notions about Free Trade one way or the other, but I saw no other chance to get what I wanted. My young gentleman was far too absorbed in his own difficulties to think how odd it was to ask a stranger who had just missed death by an ace and had lost a 1,000-guinea car to address a meeting for him on the spur of the moment. But my necessities did not allow me to contemplate oddnesses or to pick and choose my supports.

"All right," I said. "I'm not much good as a speaker, but I'll tell them a bit about Australia."

At my words the cares of the ages slipped from his shoulders, and he was rapturous in his thanks. He lent me a big driving coat – and never troubled to ask why I had started on a motor tour without possessing an ulster – and, as we slipped down the dusty roads, poured into my ears the simple facts of his history. He was an orphan, and his uncle had brought him up – I've forgotten the uncle's name, but he was in the Cabinet, and you can read his speeches in the papers. He had gone round the world after leaving Cambridge, and then, being short of a job, his uncle had advised politics. I gathered that he had no preference in parties. "Good chaps in both," he said cheerfully, "and plenty of blighters, too. I'm Liberal, because my family have always been Whigs." But if he was lukewarm politically he had strong views on other things. He found out I knew a bit about horses, and jawed away about the Derby entries; and he was full of plans for improving his shooting. Altogether, a very clean, decent, callow young man.

As we passed through a little town two policemen signalled us to stop, and flashed their lanterns on us.

"Beg pardon, Sir Harry," said one. "We've got instructions to look out for a car, and the description's no unlike yours."

"Right-o," said my host, while I thanked Providence for the devious ways I had been brought to safety. After that he spoke no more, for his mind began to labour heavily with his coming speech. His lips kept muttering, his eye wandered, and I began to prepare myself for a second catastrophe. I tried to think of something to say myself, but my mind was dry as a stone. The next thing I knew we had drawn up outside a door in a street, and were being welcomed by some noisy gentlemen with rosettes. The hall had about five hundred in it, women mostly, a lot of bald heads, and a dozen or two young men. The chairman, a weaselly minister with a reddish nose, lamented Crumpleton's absence, soliloquized on his influenza, and gave me a certificate as a 'trusted leader of Australian thought'. There were two policemen at the door, and I hoped they took note of that testimonial. Then Sir Harry started.

I never heard anything like it. He didn't begin to know how to talk. He had about a bushel of notes from which he read, and when he let go of them he fell into one prolonged stutter. Every now and then he remembered a phrase he had learned by heart, straightened his back, and gave it off like Henry Irving, and the next moment he was bent double and crooning over his papers. It was the most appalling rot, too. He talked about the 'German menace', and said it was all a Tory invention to cheat the poor of their rights and keep back the great flood of social reform, but that 'organized labour' realized this and laughed the Tories to scorn. He was all for reducing our Navy as a proof of our good faith, and then sending Germany an ultimatum telling her to do the same or we would knock her into a cocked hat. He said that, but for the Tories,

Germany and Britain would be fellow-workers in peace and reform. I thought of the little black book in my pocket! A giddy lot Scudder's friends cared for peace and reform.

Yet in a queer way I liked the speech. You could see the niceness of the chap shining out behind the muck with which he had been spoon-fed. Also it took a load off my mind. I mightn't be much of an orator, but I was a thousand per cent better than Sir Harry.

I didn't get on so badly when it came to my turn. I simply told them all I could remember about Australia, praying there should be no Australian there – all about its labour party and emigration and universal service. I doubt if I remembered to mention Free Trade, but I said there were no Tories in Australia, only Labour and Liberals. That fetched a cheer, and I woke them up a bit when I started in to tell them the kind of glorious business I thought could be made out of the Empire if we really put our backs into it.

Altogether I fancy I was rather a success. The minister didn't like me, though, and when he proposed a vote of thanks, spoke of Sir Harry's speech as 'statesmanlike' and mine as having 'the eloquence of an emigration agent'.

When we were in the car again my host was in wild spirits at having got his job over. "A ripping speech, Twisdon," he said. "Now, you're coming home with me. I'm all alone, and if you'll stop a day or two I'll show you some very decent fishing."

We had a hot supper – and I wanted it pretty badly – and then drank grog in a big cheery smoking-room with a crackling wood fire. I thought the time had come for me to put my cards on the table. I saw by this man's eye that he was the kind you can trust.

"Listen, Sir Harry," I said. "I've something pretty important to say to you. You're a good fellow, and I'm going to be frank. Where on earth did you get that poisonous rubbish you talked tonight?"

His face fell. "Was it as bad as that?" he asked ruefully. "It did sound rather thin. I got most of it out of the *Progressive* magazine and pamphlets that agent chap of mine keeps sending me. But you surely don't think Germany would ever go to war with us?"

"Ask that question in six weeks and it won't need an answer," I said. "If you'll give me your attention for half an hour I am going to tell you a story."

I can see yet that bright room with the deers' heads and the old prints on the walls, Sir Harry standing restlessly on the stone curb of the hearth, and myself lying back in an armchair, speaking. I seemed to be another person, standing aside and listening to my own voice, and judging carefully the reliability of my tale. It was the first time I had ever told anyone the exact truth, so far as I understood it, and it did me no end of good, for it straightened out the thing in my own mind. I blinked no detail. He heard all about Scudder, and the milkman, and the note-book, and my doings in Galloway. Presently he got very excited and walked up and down the hearth-rug.

"So you see," I concluded, "you have got here in your house the man that is wanted for the Portland Place murder. Your duty is to send your car for the police and give me up. I don't think I'll get very far. There'll be an accident, and I'll have a knife in my ribs an hour or so after arrest. Nevertheless, it's your duty, as a law-abiding citizen. Perhaps in a month's time you'll be sorry, but you have no cause to think of that."

He was looking at me with bright steady eyes. "What was your job in Rhodesia, Mr. Hannay?" he asked.

"Mining engineer," I said. "I've made my pile cleanly and I've had a good time in the making of it."

"Not a profession that weakens the nerves, is it?"

I laughed. "Oh, as to that, my nerves are good enough." I took down a hunting-knife from a stand on the wall, and did the old Mashona trick of tossing it and catching it in my lips. That wants a pretty steady heart.

He watched me with a smile. "I don't want proof. I may be an ass on the platform, but I can size up a man. You're no murderer and you're no fool, and I believe you are speaking the truth. I'm going to back you up. Now, what can I do?"

"First, I want you to write a letter to your uncle. I've got to get in touch with the Government people sometime before the 15th of June."

He pulled his moustache. "That won't help you. This is Foreign Office business, and my uncle would have nothing to do with it. Besides, you'd never convince him. No, I'll go one better. I'll write to the Permanent Secretary at the Foreign Office. He's my godfather, and one of the best going. What do you want?"

He sat down at a table and wrote to my dictation. The gist of it was that if a man called Twisdon (I thought I had better stick to that name) turned up before June 15th he was to entreat him kindly. He said Twisdon would prove his bona fides by passing the word 'Black Stone' and whistling 'Annie Laurie'.

"Good," said Sir Harry. "That's the proper style. By the way, you'll find my godfather – his name's Sir Walter Bullivant – down at his country cottage for Whitsuntide. It's close to Artinswell on the Kenner. That's done. Now, what's the next thing?"

"You're about my height. Lend me the oldest tweed suit you've got. Anything will do, so long as the colour is the opposite of the clothes I destroyed this afternoon. Then show me a map of the neighbourhood and explain to me the lie of the land. Lastly, if the police come seeking me, just show them the car in the glen. If the other lot turn up, tell them I caught the south express after your meeting."

He did, or promised to do, all these things. I shaved off the remnants of my moustache, and got inside an ancient suit of what I believe is called heather mixture. The map gave me some notion of my whereabouts, and told me the two things I wanted to know – where the main railway to the south could be joined and what were the wildest districts near at hand. At two o'clock he wakened me from my slumbers in the smoking-room armchair, and led me blinking into the dark starry night. An old bicycle was found in a tool-shed and handed over to me.

"First turn to the right up by the long fir-wood," he enjoined. "By daybreak you'll be well into the hills. Then I should pitch the machine into a bog and take to the moors on foot. You can put in a week among the shepherds, and be as safe as if you were in New Guinea."

I pedalled diligently up steep roads of hill gravel till the skies grew pale with morning. As the mists cleared before the sun, I found myself in a wide green world with glens falling on every side and a far-away blue horizon. Here, at any rate, I could get early news of my enemies.

Chapter V
The Adventure of the Spectacled Roadman

I SAT DOWN on the very crest of the pass and took stock of my position.

Behind me was the road climbing through a long cleft in the hills, which was the upper glen of some notable river. In front was a flat space of maybe a mile, all pitted with bog-holes and rough with tussocks, and then beyond it the road fell steeply down another glen to a plain whose blue dimness melted into the distance. To left and right were round-shouldered green hills as smooth as pancakes, but to the south – that is, the left hand – there was a glimpse of high heathery mountains, which I remembered from the map as the big knot of hill which I had chosen for my sanctuary. I was on the central boss of a huge upland country, and could see everything moving for miles. In the meadows below the road half a mile back a cottage smoked, but it was the only sign of human life. Otherwise there was only the calling of plovers and the tinkling of little streams.

It was now about seven o'clock, and as I waited I heard once again that ominous beat in the air. Then I realized that my vantage-ground might be in reality a trap. There was no cover for a tomtit in those bald green places.

I sat quite still and hopeless while the beat grew louder. Then I saw an aeroplane coming up from the east. It was flying high, but as I looked it dropped several hundred feet and began to circle round the knot of hill in narrowing circles, just as a hawk wheels before it pounces. Now it was flying very low, and now the observer on board caught sight of me. I could see one of the two occupants examining me through glasses.

Suddenly it began to rise in swift whorls, and the next I knew it was speeding eastward again till it became a speck in the blue morning.

That made me do some savage thinking. My enemies had located me, and the next thing would be a cordon round me. I didn't know what force they could command, but I was certain it would be sufficient. The aeroplane had seen my bicycle, and would conclude that I would try to escape by the road. In that case there might be a chance on the moors to the right or left. I wheeled the machine a hundred yards from the highway, and plunged it into a moss-hole, where it sank among pond-weed and water-buttercups. Then I climbed to a knoll which gave me a view of the two valleys. Nothing was stirring on the long white ribbon that threaded them.

I have said there was not cover in the whole place to hide a rat. As the day advanced it was flooded with soft fresh light till it had the fragrant sunniness of the South African veld. At other times I would have liked the place, but now it seemed to suffocate me. The free moorlands were prison walls, and the keen hill air was the breath of a dungeon.

I tossed a coin – heads right, tails left – and it fell heads, so I turned to the north. In a little I came to the brow of the ridge which was the containing wall of the pass. I saw the highroad for maybe ten miles, and far down it something that was moving, and that I took to be a motor-car. Beyond the ridge I looked on a rolling green moor, which fell away into wooded glens.

Now my life on the veld has given me the eyes of a kite, and I can see things for which most men need a telescope... Away down the slope, a couple of miles away, several men were advancing, like a row of beaters at a shoot...

I dropped out of sight behind the sky-line. That way was shut to me, and I must try the bigger hills to the south beyond the highway. The car I had noticed was getting nearer, but it was still a long way off with some very steep gradients before it. I ran hard, crouching low except in the hollows, and as I ran I kept scanning the brow of the hill before me. Was it imagination, or did I see figures – one, two, perhaps more – moving in a glen beyond the stream?

If you are hemmed in on all sides in a patch of land there is only one chance of escape. You must stay in the patch, and let your enemies search it and not find you.

That was good sense, but how on earth was I to escape notice in that table-cloth of a place? I would have buried myself to the neck in mud or lain below water or climbed the tallest tree. But there was not a stick of wood, the bog-holes were little puddles, the stream was a slender trickle. There was nothing but short heather, and bare hill bent, and the white highway.

Then in a tiny bight of road, beside a heap of stones, I found the roadman.

He had just arrived, and was wearily flinging down his hammer. He looked at me with a fishy eye and yawned.

"Confoond the day I ever left the herdin'!" he said, as if to the world at large. "There I was my ain maister. Now I'm a slave to the Goavernment, tethered to the roadside, wi' sair een, and a back like a suckle."

He took up the hammer, struck a stone, dropped the implement with an oath, and put both hands to his ears. "Mercy on me! My heid's burstin'!" he cried.

He was a wild figure, about my own size but much bent, with a week's beard on his chin, and a pair of big horn spectacles.

"I canna dae't," he cried again. "The Surveyor maun just report me. I'm for my bed."

I asked him what was the trouble, though indeed that was clear enough.

"The trouble is that I'm no sober. Last nicht my dochter Merran was waddit, and they danced till fower in the byre. Me and some ither chiels sat down to the drinkin', and here I am. Peety that I ever lookit on the wine when it was red!"

I agreed with him about bed. "It's easy speakin'," he moaned. "But I got a postcard yestreen sayin' that the new Road Surveyor would be round the day. He'll come and he'll no find me, or else he'll find me fou, and either way I'm a done man. I'll awa' back to my bed and say I'm no weel, but I doot that'll no help me, for they ken my kind o' no-weel-ness."

Then I had an inspiration. "Does the new Surveyor know you?" I asked.

"No him. He's just been a week at the job. He rins about in a wee motor-cawr, and wad speir the inside oot o' a whelk."

"Where's your house?" I asked, and was directed by a wavering finger to the cottage by the stream.

"Well, back to your bed," I said, "and sleep in peace. I'll take on your job for a bit and see the Surveyor."

He stared at me blankly; then, as the notion dawned on his fuddled brain, his face broke into the vacant drunkard's smile.

"You're the billy," he cried. "It'll be easy eneuch managed. I've finished that bing o' stanes, so you needna chap ony mair this forenoon. Just take the barry, and wheel eneuch metal frae yon quarry doon the road to mak anither bing the morn. My name's Alexander Turnbull, and I've been seeven year at the trade, and twenty afore that herdin' on Leithen Water. My freens ca' me Ecky, and whiles Specky, for I wear glesses, being waik i' the sicht. Just you speak the Surveyor fair, and ca' him Sir, and he'll be fell pleased. I'll be back or mid-day."

I borrowed his spectacles and filthy old hat; stripped off coat, waistcoat, and collar, and gave him them to carry home; borrowed, too, the foul stump of a clay pipe as an extra property. He indicated my simple tasks, and without more ado set off at an amble bedwards. Bed may have been his chief object, but I think there was also something left in the foot of a bottle. I prayed that he might be safe under cover before my friends arrived on the scene.

Then I set to work to dress for the part. I opened the collar of my shirt – it was a vulgar blue-and-white check such as ploughmen wear – and revealed a neck as brown as any tinker's. I rolled up my sleeves, and there was a forearm which might have been a blacksmith's, sunburnt and rough with old scars. I got my boots and trouser-legs all white from the dust of the road, and hitched up my trousers, tying them with string below the knee. Then I set to work on my face. With a handful of dust I made a water-mark round my neck, the place where Mr. Turnbull's Sunday ablutions might be expected to stop. I rubbed a good deal of dirt also into the sunburn of my cheeks. A roadman's eyes would no doubt be a little inflamed, so I contrived to get some dust in both of mine, and by dint of vigorous rubbing produced a bleary effect.

The sandwiches Sir Harry had given me had gone off with my coat, but the roadman's lunch, tied up in a red handkerchief, was at my disposal. I ate with great relish several of the thick slabs of scone and cheese and drank a little of the cold tea. In the handkerchief was a local paper tied with string and addressed to Mr. Turnbull – obviously meant to solace his mid-day leisure. I did up the bundle again, and put the paper conspicuously beside it.

My boots did not satisfy me, but by dint of kicking among the stones I reduced them to the granite-like surface which marks a roadman's foot-gear. Then I bit and scraped my finger-nails till the edges were all cracked and uneven. The men I was matched against would miss no detail. I broke one of the bootlaces and retied it in a clumsy knot, and loosed the other so that my thick grey socks bulged over the uppers. Still no sign of anything on the road. The motor I had observed half an hour ago must have gone home.

My toilet complete, I took up the barrow and began my journeys to and from the quarry a hundred yards off.

I remember an old scout in Rhodesia, who had done many queer things in his day, once telling me that the secret of playing a part was to think yourself into it. You could never keep it up, he said, unless you could manage to convince yourself that you were it. So I shut off all other thoughts and switched them on to the road-mending. I thought of the little white cottage as my home, I recalled the years I had spent herding on Leithen Water, I made my mind dwell lovingly on sleep in a box-bed and a bottle of cheap whisky. Still nothing appeared on that long white road.

Now and then a sheep wandered off the heather to stare at me. A heron flopped down to a pool in the stream and started to fish, taking no more notice of me than if I had been a milestone. On I went, trundling my loads of stone, with the heavy step of the professional. Soon I grew warm, and the dust on my face changed into solid and abiding grit. I was already counting the hours till evening should put a limit to Mr. Turnbull's monotonous toil. Suddenly a crisp voice spoke from the road, and looking up I saw a little Ford two-seater, and a round-faced young man in a bowler hat.

"Are you Alexander Turnbull?" he asked. "I am the new County Road Surveyor. You live at Blackhopefoot, and have charge of the section from Laidlawbyres to the Riggs? Good! A fair bit of road, Turnbull, and not badly engineered. A little soft about a mile off, and the edges want cleaning. See you look after that. Good morning. You'll know me the next time you see me."

Clearly my get-up was good enough for the dreaded Surveyor. I went on with my work, and as the morning grew towards noon I was cheered by a little traffic. A baker's van breasted the hill, and sold me a bag of ginger biscuits which I stowed in my trouser-pockets against emergencies. Then a herd passed with sheep, and disturbed me somewhat by asking loudly, "What had become o' Specky?"

"In bed wi' the colic," I replied, and the herd passed on ... just about mid-day a big car stole down the hill, glided past and drew up a hundred yards beyond. Its three occupants descended as if to stretch their legs, and sauntered towards me.

Two of the men I had seen before from the window of the Galloway inn – one lean, sharp, and dark, the other comfortable and smiling. The third had the look of a countryman – a vet, perhaps, or a small farmer. He was dressed in ill-cut knickerbockers, and the eye in his head was as bright and wary as a hen's.

"Morning," said the last. "That's a fine easy job o' yours."

I had not looked up on their approach, and now, when accosted, I slowly and painfully straightened my back, after the manner of roadmen; spat vigorously, after the manner of the low Scot; and regarded them steadily before replying. I confronted three pairs of eyes that missed nothing.

"There's waur jobs and there's better," I said sententiously. "I wad rather hae yours, sittin' a' day on your hinderlands on thae cushions. It's you and your muckle cawrs that wreck my roads! If we a' had oor richts, ye sud be made to mend what ye break."

The bright-eyed man was looking at the newspaper lying beside Turnbull's bundle.

"I see you get your papers in good time," he said.

I glanced at it casually. "Aye, in gude time. Seein' that that paper cam' out last Setterday I'm just Sax days late."

He picked it up, glanced at the superscription, and laid it down again. One of the others had been looking at my boots, and a word in German called the speaker's attention to them.

"You've a fine taste in boots," he said. "These were never made by a country shoemaker."

"They were not," I said readily. "They were made in London. I got them frae the gentleman that was here last year for the shootin'. What was his name now?" And I scratched a forgetful head. Again the sleek one spoke in German. "Let us get on," he said. "This fellow is all right."

They asked one last question.

"Did you see anyone pass early this morning? He might be on a bicycle or he might be on foot."

I very nearly fell into the trap and told a story of a bicyclist hurrying past in the grey dawn. But I had the sense to see my danger. I pretended to consider very deeply.

"I wasna up very early," I said. "Ye see, my dochter was merrit last nicht, and we keepit it up late. I opened the house door about seeven and there was naebody on the road then. Since I cam' up here there has just been the baker and the Ruchill herd, besides you gentlemen."

One of them gave me a cigar, which I smelt gingerly and stuck in Turnbull's bundle. They got into their car and were out of sight in three minutes.

My heart leaped with an enormous relief, but I went on wheeling my stones. It was as well, for ten minutes later the car returned, one of the occupants waving a hand to me. Those gentry left nothing to chance.

I finished Turnbull's bread and cheese, and pretty soon I had finished the stones. The next step was what puzzled me. I could not keep up this roadmaking business for long. A merciful Providence had kept Mr. Turnbull indoors, but if he appeared on the scene there would be trouble. I had a notion that the cordon was still tight round the glen, and that if I walked in any direction I should meet with questioners. But get out I must. No man's nerve could stand more than a day of being spied on.

I stayed at my post till five o'clock. By that time I had resolved to go down to Turnbull's cottage at nightfall and take my chance of getting over the hills in the darkness. But suddenly a new car came up the road, and slowed down a yard or two from me. A fresh wind had risen, and the occupant wanted to light a cigarette. It was a touring car, with the tonneau full of an assortment of baggage. One man sat in it, and by an amazing chance I knew him. His name was Marmaduke Jopley, and he was an offence to creation. He was a sort of blood stockbroker, who did his business by toadying eldest sons and rich young peers and foolish old ladies. 'Marmie' was a familiar figure, I understood, at balls and polo-weeks and country houses. He was an adroit scandal-monger, and would crawl a mile on his belly to anything that had a title or a million. I had a business introduction to his firm when I came to London, and he was good enough to ask me to dinner at his club. There he showed off at a great rate, and pattered about his duchesses till the snobbery of the creature turned me sick. I asked a man afterwards why nobody kicked him, and was told that Englishmen reverenced the weaker sex.

Anyhow there he was now, nattily dressed, in a fine new car, obviously on his way to visit some of his smart friends. A sudden daftness took me, and in a second I had jumped into the tonneau and had him by the shoulder.

"Hullo, Jopley," I sang out. "Well met, my lad!" He got a horrid fright. His chin dropped as he stared at me. "Who the devil are YOU?" he gasped.

"My name's Hannay," I said. "From Rhodesia, you remember."

"Good God, the murderer!" he choked.

"Just so. And there'll be a second murder, my dear, if you don't do as I tell you. Give me that coat of yours. That cap, too."

He did as bid, for he was blind with terror. Over my dirty trousers and vulgar shirt I put on his smart driving-coat, which buttoned high at the top and thereby hid the deficiencies of my collar. I stuck the cap on my head, and added his gloves to my get-up. The dusty roadman in a minute was transformed into one of the neatest motorists in Scotland. On Mr. Jopley's head I clapped Turnbull's unspeakable hat, and told him to keep it there.

Then with some difficulty I turned the car. My plan was to go back the road he had come, for the watchers, having seen it before, would probably let it pass unremarked, and Marmie's figure was in no way like mine.

"Now, my child," I said, "sit quite still and be a good boy. I mean you no harm. I'm only borrowing your car for an hour or two. But if you play me any tricks, and above all if you open your mouth, as sure as there's a God above me I'll wring your neck. SAVEZ?"

I enjoyed that evening's ride. We ran eight miles down the valley, through a village or two, and I could not help noticing several strange-looking folk lounging by the roadside. These were the watchers who would have had much to say to me if I had come in other garb or company. As it was, they looked incuriously on. One touched his cap in salute, and I responded graciously.

As the dark fell I turned up a side glen which, as I remember from the map, led into an unfrequented corner of the hills. Soon the villages were left behind, then the farms, and then even the wayside cottage. Presently we came to a lonely moor where the night was blackening the sunset gleam in the bog pools. Here we stopped, and I obligingly reversed the car and restored to Mr. Jopley his belongings.

"A thousand thanks," I said. "There's more use in you than I thought. Now be off and find the police."

As I sat on the hillside, watching the tail-light dwindle, I reflected on the various kinds of crime I had now sampled. Contrary to general belief, I was not a murderer, but I had become an unholy liar, a shameless impostor, and a highwayman with a marked taste for expensive motor-cars.

Chapter VI
The Adventure of the Bald Archaeologist

I SPENT the night on a shelf of the hillside, in the lee of a boulder where the heather grew long and soft. It was a cold business, for I had neither coat nor waistcoat. These were in Mr. Turnbull's keeping, as was Scudder's little book, my watch and – worst of all – my pipe and tobacco pouch. Only my money accompanied me in my belt, and about half a pound of ginger biscuits in my trousers pocket.

I supped off half those biscuits, and by worming myself deep into the heather got some kind of warmth. My spirits had risen, and I was beginning to enjoy this crazy game of hide-and-seek. So far I had been miraculously lucky. The milkman, the literary innkeeper, Sir Harry, the roadman, and the idiotic Marmie, were all pieces of undeserved good fortune. Somehow the first success gave me a feeling that I was going to pull the thing through.

My chief trouble was that I was desperately hungry. When a Jew shoots himself in the City and there is an inquest, the newspapers usually report that the deceased was 'well-nourished'. I remember thinking that they would not call me well-nourished if I broke my neck in a bog-hole. I lay and tortured myself – for the ginger biscuits merely emphasized the aching void – with the memory of all the good food I had thought so little of in London. There were Paddock's crisp sausages and fragrant shavings of bacon, and shapely poached eggs – how often I had turned up my nose at them! There were the cutlets they did at the club, and a particular ham that stood on the cold table, for which my soul lusted. My thoughts hovered over all varieties of mortal edible, and finally settled on a porterhouse steak and a quart of bitter with a welsh rabbit to follow. In longing hopelessly for these dainties I fell asleep.

I woke very cold and stiff about an hour after dawn. It took me a little while to remember where I was, for I had been very weary and had slept heavily. I saw first the pale blue sky through a net of heather, then a big shoulder of hill, and then my own boots placed neatly in a blaeberry bush. I raised myself on my arms and looked down into the valley, and that one look set me lacing up my boots in mad haste.

For there were men below, not more than a quarter of a mile off, spaced out on the hillside like a fan, and beating the heather. Marmie had not been slow in looking for his revenge.

I crawled out of my shelf into the cover of a boulder, and from it gained a shallow trench which slanted up the mountain face. This led me presently into the narrow gully of a burn, by way of which I scrambled to the top of the ridge. From there

I looked back, and saw that I was still undiscovered. My pursuers were patiently quartering the hillside and moving upwards.

Keeping behind the skyline I ran for maybe half a mile, till I judged I was above the uppermost end of the glen. Then I showed myself, and was instantly noted by one of the flankers, who passed the word to the others. I heard cries coming up from below, and saw that the line of search had changed its direction. I pretended to retreat over the skyline, but instead went back the way I had come, and in twenty minutes was behind the ridge overlooking my sleeping place. From that viewpoint I had the satisfaction of seeing the pursuit streaming up the hill at the top of the glen on a hopelessly false scent.

I had before me a choice of routes, and I chose a ridge which made an angle with the one I was on, and so would soon put a deep glen between me and my enemies. The exercise had warmed my blood, and I was beginning to enjoy myself amazingly. As I went I breakfasted on the dusty remnants of the ginger biscuits.

I knew very little about the country, and I hadn't a notion what I was going to do. I trusted to the strength of my legs, but I was well aware that those behind me would be familiar with the lie of the land, and that my ignorance would be a heavy handicap. I saw in front of me a sea of hills, rising very high towards the south, but northwards breaking down into broad ridges which separated wide and shallow dales. The ridge I had chosen seemed to sink after a mile or two to a moor which lay like a pocket in the uplands. That seemed as good a direction to take as any other.

My stratagem had given me a fair start – call it twenty minutes – and I had the width of a glen behind me before I saw the first heads of the pursuers. The police had evidently called in local talent to their aid, and the men I could see had the appearance of herds or gamekeepers. They hallooed at the sight of me, and I waved my hand. Two dived into the glen and began to climb my ridge, while the others kept their own side of the hill. I felt as if I were taking part in a schoolboy game of hare and hounds.

But very soon it began to seem less of a game. Those fellows behind were hefty men on their native heath. Looking back I saw that only three were following direct, and I guessed that the others had fetched a circuit to cut me off. My lack of local knowledge might very well be my undoing, and I resolved to get out of this tangle of glens to the pocket of moor I had seen from the tops. I must so increase my distance as to get clear away from them, and I believed I could do this if I could find the right ground for it. If there had been cover I would have tried a bit of stalking, but on these bare slopes you could see a fly a mile off. My hope must be in the length of my legs and the soundness of my wind, but I needed easier ground for that, for I was not bred a mountaineer. How I longed for a good Afrikander pony!

I put on a great spurt and got off my ridge and down into the moor before any figures appeared on the skyline behind me. I crossed a burn, and came out on a highroad which made a pass between two glens. All in front of me was a big field of heather sloping up to a crest which was crowned with an odd feather of trees. In the dyke by the roadside was a gate, from which a grass-grown track led over the first wave of the moor.

I jumped the dyke and followed it, and after a few hundred yards – as soon as it was out of sight of the highway – the grass stopped and it became a very respectable road, which was evidently kept with some care. Clearly it ran to a house, and I began to think of doing the same. Hitherto my luck had held, and it might be that my best chance would be found in this remote dwelling. Anyhow there were trees there, and that meant cover.

I did not follow the road, but the burnside which flanked it on the right, where the bracken grew deep and the high banks made a tolerable screen. It was well I did so, for no sooner had I gained the hollow than, looking back, I saw the pursuit topping the ridge from which I had descended.

After that I did not look back; I had no time. I ran up the burnside, crawling over the open places, and for a large part wading in the shallow stream. I found a deserted cottage with a row of phantom peat-stacks and an overgrown garden. Then I was among young hay, and very soon had come to the edge of a plantation of wind-blown firs. From there I saw the chimneys of the house smoking a few hundred yards to my left. I forsook the burnside, crossed another dyke, and almost before I knew was on a rough lawn. A glance back told me that I was well out of sight of the pursuit, which had not yet passed the first lift of the moor.

The lawn was a very rough place, cut with a scythe instead of a mower, and planted with beds of scrubby rhododendrons. A brace of black-game, which are not usually garden birds, rose at my approach. The house before me was the ordinary moorland farm, with a more pretentious whitewashed wing added. Attached to this wing was a glass veranda, and through the glass I saw the face of an elderly gentleman meekly watching me.

I stalked over the border of coarse hill gravel and entered the open veranda door. Within was a pleasant room, glass on one side, and on the other a mass of books. More books showed in an inner room. On the floor, instead of tables, stood cases such as you see in a museum, filled with coins and queer stone implements.

There was a knee-hole desk in the middle, and seated at it, with some papers and open volumes before him, was the benevolent old gentleman. His face was round and shiny, like Mr. Pickwick's, big glasses were stuck on the end of his nose, and the top of his head was as bright and bare as a glass bottle. He never moved when I entered, but raised his placid eyebrows and waited on me to speak.

It was not an easy job, with about five minutes to spare, to tell a stranger who I was and what I wanted, and to win his aid. I did not attempt it. There was something about the eye of the man before me, something so keen and knowledgeable, that I could not find a word. I simply stared at him and stuttered.

"You seem in a hurry, my friend," he said slowly.

I nodded towards the window. It gave a prospect across the moor through a gap in the plantation, and revealed certain figures half a mile off straggling through the heather.

"Ah, I see," he said, and took up a pair of field-glasses through which he patiently scrutinized the figures.

"A fugitive from justice, eh? Well, we'll go into the matter at our leisure. Meantime I object to my privacy being broken in upon by the clumsy rural policeman. Go into my study, and you will see two doors facing you. Take the one on the left and close it behind you. You will be perfectly safe."

And this extraordinary man took up his pen again.

I did as I was bid, and found myself in a little dark chamber which smelt of chemicals, and was lit only by a tiny window high up in the wall. The door had swung behind me with a click like the door of a safe. Once again I had found an unexpected sanctuary.

All the same I was not comfortable. There was something about the old gentleman which puzzled and rather terrified me. He had been too easy and ready, almost as if he had expected me. And his eyes had been horribly intelligent.

No sound came to me in that dark place. For all I knew the police might be searching the house, and if they did they would want to know what was behind this door. I tried to possess my soul in patience, and to forget how hungry I was.

Then I took a more cheerful view. The old gentleman could scarcely refuse me a meal, and I fell to reconstructing my breakfast. Bacon and eggs would content me, but I wanted the better part of a flitch of bacon and half a hundred eggs. And then, while my mouth was watering in anticipation, there was a click and the door stood open.

I emerged into the sunlight to find the master of the house sitting in a deep armchair in the room he called his study, and regarding me with curious eyes.

"Have they gone?" I asked.

"They have gone. I convinced them that you had crossed the hill. I do not choose that the police should come between me and one whom I am delighted to honour. This is a lucky morning for you, Mr. Richard Hannay."

As he spoke his eyelids seemed to tremble and to fall a little over his keen grey eyes. In a flash the phrase of Scudder's came back to me, when he had described the man he most dreaded in the world. He had said that he 'could hood his eyes like a hawk'. Then I saw that I had walked straight into the enemy's headquarters.

My first impulse was to throttle the old ruffian and make for the open air. He seemed to anticipate my intention, for he smiled gently, and nodded to the door behind me.

I turned, and saw two men-servants who had me covered with pistols.

He knew my name, but he had never seen me before. And as the reflection darted across my mind I saw a slender chance.

"I don't know what you mean," I said roughly. "And who are you calling Richard Hannay? My name's Ainslie."

"So?" he said, still smiling. "But of course you have others. We won't quarrel about a name."

I was pulling myself together now, and I reflected that my garb, lacking coat and waistcoat and collar, would at any rate not betray me. I put on my surliest face and shrugged my shoulders.

"I suppose you're going to give me up after all, and I call it a damned dirty trick. My God, I wish I had never seen that cursed motor-car! Here's the money and be damned to you," and I flung four sovereigns on the table.

He opened his eyes a little. "Oh no, I shall not give you up. My friends and I will have a little private settlement with you, that is all. You know a little too much, Mr. Hannay. You are a clever actor, but not quite clever enough."

He spoke with assurance, but I could see the dawning of a doubt in his mind.

"Oh, for God's sake stop jawing," I cried. "Everything's against me. I haven't had a bit of luck since I came on shore at Leith. What's the harm in a poor devil with an empty stomach picking up some money he finds in a bust-up motor-car? That's all I done, and for that I've been chivvied for two days by those blasted bobbies over those blasted hills. I tell you I'm fair sick of it. You can do what you like, old boy! Ned Ainslie's got no fight left in him."

I could see that the doubt was gaining.

"Will you oblige me with the story of your recent doings?" he asked.

"I can't, guv'nor," I said in a real beggar's whine. "I've not had a bite to eat for two days. Give me a mouthful of food, and then you'll hear God's truth."

I must have showed my hunger in my face, for he signalled to one of the men in the doorway. A bit of cold pie was brought and a glass of beer, and I wolfed them down like a pig – or rather, like Ned Ainslie, for I was keeping up my character. In the middle of my meal he spoke suddenly to me in German, but I turned on him a face as blank as a stone wall.

Then I told him my story – how I had come off an Archangel ship at Leith a week ago, and was making my way overland to my brother at Wigtown. I had run short of cash – I hinted vaguely at a spree – and I was pretty well on my uppers when I had come on a hole in a hedge, and, looking through, had seen a big motor-car lying in the burn. I had poked about to see what had happened, and had found three sovereigns lying on the seat and one on the floor. There was nobody there or any sign of an owner, so I had pocketed the cash. But somehow the law had got after me. When I had tried to change a sovereign in a baker's shop, the woman had cried on the police, and a little later, when I was washing my face in a burn, I had been nearly gripped, and had only got away by leaving my coat and waistcoat behind me.

"They can have the money back," I cried, "for a fat lot of good it's done me. Those perishers are all down on a poor man. Now, if it had been you, guv'nor, that had found the quids, nobody would have troubled you."

"You're a good liar, Hannay," he said.

I flew into a rage. "Stop fooling, damn you! I tell you my name's Ainslie, and I never heard of anyone called Hannay in my born days. I'd sooner have the police than you with your Hannays and your monkey-faced pistol tricks…. No, guv'nor, I beg pardon, I don't mean that. I'm much obliged to you for the grub, and I'll thank you to let me go now the coast's clear."

It was obvious that he was badly puzzled. You see he had never seen me, and my appearance must have altered considerably from my photographs, if he had got one of them. I was pretty smart and well dressed in London, and now I was a regular tramp.

"I do not propose to let you go. If you are what you say you are, you will soon have a chance of clearing yourself. If you are what I believe you are, I do not think you will see the light much longer."

He rang a bell, and a third servant appeared from the veranda.

"I want the Lanchester in five minutes," he said. "There will be three to luncheon."

Then he looked steadily at me, and that was the hardest ordeal of all.

There was something weird and devilish in those eyes, cold, malignant, unearthly, and most hellishly clever. They fascinated me like the bright eyes of a snake. I had a strong impulse to throw myself on his mercy and offer to join his side, and if you consider the way I felt about the whole thing you will see that that impulse must have been purely physical, the weakness of a brain mesmerized and mastered by a stronger spirit. But I managed to stick it out and even to grin.

"You'll know me next time, guv'nor," I said.

"Karl," he spoke in German to one of the men in the doorway, "you will put this fellow in the storeroom till I return, and you will be answerable to me for his keeping."

I was marched out of the room with a pistol at each ear.

The storeroom was a damp chamber in what had been the old farmhouse. There was no carpet on the uneven floor, and nothing to sit down on but a school form. It was black as pitch, for the windows were heavily shuttered. I made out by groping that the walls were lined with boxes and barrels and sacks of some heavy stuff. The whole place smelt of mould and disuse. My gaolers turned the key in the door, and I could hear them shifting their feet as they stood on guard outside.

I sat down in that chilly darkness in a very miserable frame of mind. The old boy had gone off in a motor to collect the two ruffians who had interviewed me yesterday. Now, they had seen me as the roadman, and they would remember me, for I was in the same rig. What was a roadman doing twenty miles from his beat, pursued by the police? A question or two would put them on the track. Probably they had seen Mr. Turnbull, probably Marmie too; most likely they could link me up with Sir Harry, and then the whole thing would be crystal clear. What chance had I in this moorland house with three desperadoes and their armed servants?

I began to think wistfully of the police, now plodding over the hills after my wraith. They at any rate were fellow-countrymen and honest men, and their tender mercies would be kinder than these ghoulish aliens. But they wouldn't have listened to me. That old devil with the eyelids had not taken long to get rid of them. I thought he probably had some kind of graft with the constabulary. Most likely he had letters from Cabinet Ministers saying he was to be given every facility for plotting against Britain. That's the sort of owlish way we run our politics in the Old Country.

The three would be back for lunch, so I hadn't more than a couple of hours to wait. It was simply waiting on destruction, for I could see no way out of this mess. I wished that I had Scudder's courage, for I am free to confess I didn't feel any great fortitude. The only thing that kept me going was that I was pretty furious. It made me boil with rage to think of those three spies getting the pull on me like this. I hoped that at any rate I might be able to twist one of their necks before they downed me.

The more I thought of it the angrier I grew, and I had to get up and move about the room. I tried the shutters, but they were the kind that lock with a key, and I couldn't move them. From the outside came the faint clucking of hens in the warm sun. Then I groped among the sacks and boxes. I couldn't open the latter, and the sacks seemed to be full of things like dog-biscuits that smelt of cinnamon. But, as I circumnavigated the room, I found a handle in the wall which seemed worth investigating.

It was the door of a wall cupboard – what they call a 'press' in Scotland – and it was locked. I shook it, and it seemed rather flimsy. For want of something better to do I put out my strength on that door, getting some purchase on the handle by looping my braces round it. Presently the thing gave with a crash which I thought would bring in my warders to inquire. I waited for a bit, and then started to explore the cupboard shelves.

There was a multitude of queer things there. I found an odd vesta or two in my trouser pockets and struck a light. It was out in a second, but it showed me one thing. There was a little stock of electric torches on one shelf. I picked up one, and found it was in working order.

With the torch to help me I investigated further. There were bottles and cases of queer-smelling stuffs, chemicals no doubt for experiments, and there were coils of fine copper wire and yanks and yanks of thin oiled silk. There was a box of detonators, and a lot of cord for fuses. Then away at the back of the shelf I found a stout brown cardboard box, and inside it a wooden case. I managed to wrench it open, and within lay half a dozen little grey bricks, each a couple of inches square.

I took up one, and found that it crumbled easily in my hand. Then I smelt it and put my tongue to it. After that I sat down to think. I hadn't been a mining engineer for nothing, and I knew lentonite when I saw it.

With one of these bricks I could blow the house to smithereens. I had used the stuff in Rhodesia and knew its power. But the trouble was that my knowledge wasn't exact. I had forgotten the proper charge and the right way of preparing it, and I wasn't sure about the timing. I had only a vague notion, too, as to its power, for though I had used it I had not handled it with my own fingers.

But it was a chance, the only possible chance. It was a mighty risk, but against it was an absolute black certainty. If I used it the odds were, as I reckoned, about five to one in favour of my blowing myself into the tree-tops; but if I didn't I should very likely be occupying a six-foot hole in the garden by the evening. That was the way I had to look at it. The prospect was pretty dark either way, but anyhow there was a chance, both for myself and for my country.

The remembrance of little Scudder decided me. It was about the beastliest moment of my life, for I'm no good at these cold-blooded resolutions. Still I managed to rake up the pluck to set my teeth and choke back the horrid doubts that flooded in on me. I simply shut off my mind and pretended I was doing an experiment as simple as Guy Fawkes fireworks.

I got a detonator, and fixed it to a couple of feet of fuse. Then I took a quarter of a lentonite brick, and buried it near the door below one of the sacks in a crack of the floor, fixing the detonator in it. For all I knew half those boxes might be dynamite. If the cupboard held such deadly explosives, why not the boxes? In that case there would be a glorious skyward journey for me and the German servants and about an acre of surrounding country. There was also the risk that the detonation might set off the other bricks in the cupboard, for I had forgotten most that I knew about lentonite. But it didn't do to begin thinking about the possibilities. The odds were horrible, but I had to take them.

I ensconced myself just below the sill of the window, and lit the fuse. Then I waited for a moment or two. There was dead silence – only a shuffle of heavy boots in the passage, and the peaceful cluck of hens from the warm out-of-doors. I commended my soul to my Maker, and wondered where I would be in five seconds...]

A great wave of heat seemed to surge upwards from the floor, and hang for a blistering instant in the air. Then the wall opposite me flashed into a golden yellow and dissolved with a rending thunder that hammered my brain into a pulp. Something dropped on me, catching the point of my left shoulder.

And then I think I became unconscious.

My stupor can scarcely have lasted beyond a few seconds. I felt myself being choked by thick yellow fumes, and struggled out of the debris to my feet. Somewhere behind me I felt fresh air. The jambs of the window had fallen, and through the ragged rent the smoke was pouring out to the summer noon. I stepped over the broken lintel, and found myself standing in a yard in a dense and acrid fog. I felt very sick and ill, but I could move my limbs, and I staggered blindly forward away from the house.

A small mill-lade ran in a wooden aqueduct at the other side of the yard, and into this I fell. The cool water revived me, and I had just enough wits left to think of escape. I squirmed up the lade among the slippery green slime till I reached the mill-wheel. Then I wriggled through the axle hole into the old mill and tumbled on to a bed of chaff. A nail caught the seat of my trousers, and I left a wisp of heather-mixture behind me.

The mill had been long out of use. The ladders were rotten with age, and in the loft the rats had gnawed great holes in the floor. Nausea shook me, and a wheel in my head kept turning, while my left shoulder and arm seemed to be stricken with the palsy. I looked out of the window and saw a fog still hanging over the house and smoke escaping from an upper window. Please God I had set the place on fire, for I could hear confused cries coming from the other side.

But I had no time to linger, since this mill was obviously a bad hiding-place. Anyone looking for me would naturally follow the lade, and I made certain the search would begin as soon as they found that my body was not in the storeroom. From another window I saw that on the far side of the mill stood an old stone dovecot. If I could get there without leaving tracks I might find a hiding-place, for I argued that my enemies, if they thought I could move, would conclude I had made for open country, and would go seeking me on the moor.

I crawled down the broken ladder, scattering chaff behind me to cover my footsteps. I did the same on the mill floor, and on the threshold where the door hung on broken hinges. Peeping out, I saw that between me and the dovecot was a piece of bare cobbled ground, where no footmarks would show. Also it was mercifully hid by the mill buildings from any view from the house. I slipped across the space, got to the back of the dovecot and prospected a way of ascent.

That was one of the hardest jobs I ever took on. My shoulder and arm ached like hell, and I was so sick and giddy that I was always on the verge of falling. But I managed it somehow. By the use of out-jutting stones and gaps in the masonry and a tough ivy root I got to the top in the end. There was a little parapet behind which I found space to lie down. Then I proceeded to go off into an old-fashioned swoon.

I woke with a burning head and the sun glaring in my face. For a long time I lay motionless, for those horrible fumes seemed to have loosened my joints and dulled my brain. Sounds came to me from the house – men speaking throatily and the throbbing of a stationary car. There was a little gap in the parapet to which I wriggled, and from which I had some sort of prospect of the yard. I saw figures come out – a servant with his head bound up, and then a younger man in knickerbockers. They were looking for something, and moved towards the mill. Then one of them caught sight of the wisp of cloth on the nail, and cried out to the other. They both went back to the house, and brought two more to look at it. I saw the rotund figure of my late captor, and I thought I made out the man with the lisp. I noticed that all had pistols.

For half an hour they ransacked the mill. I could hear them kicking over the barrels and pulling up the rotten planking. Then they came outside, and stood just below the dovecot arguing fiercely. The servant with the bandage was being soundly rated. I heard them fiddling with the door of the dovecote and for one horrid moment I fancied they were coming up. Then they thought better of it, and went back to the house.

All that long blistering afternoon I lay baking on the rooftop. Thirst was my chief torment. My tongue was like a stick, and to make it worse I could hear the cool drip of water from the mill-lade. I watched the course of the little stream as it came in from the moor, and my fancy followed it to the top of the glen, where it must issue from an icy fountain fringed with cool ferns and mosses. I would have given a thousand pounds to plunge my face into that.

I had a fine prospect of the whole ring of moorland. I saw the car speed away with two occupants, and a man on a hill pony riding east. I judged they were looking for me, and I wished them joy of their quest.

But I saw something else more interesting. The house stood almost on the summit of a swell of moorland which crowned a sort of plateau, and there was no higher point nearer than the big hills six miles off. The actual summit, as I have mentioned, was a biggish clump of trees – firs mostly, with a few ashes and beeches. On the dovecot I was almost on a level with the tree-tops, and could see what lay beyond. The wood was not solid, but only a ring, and inside was an oval of green turf, for all the world like a big cricket-field.

I didn't take long to guess what it was. It was an aerodrome, and a secret one. The place had been most cunningly chosen. For suppose anyone were watching an aeroplane descending here, he would think it had gone over the hill beyond the trees. As the place was on the top of a rise in the midst of a big amphitheatre, any observer from any direction would conclude it had passed out of view behind the hill. Only a man very close at hand would realize that the aeroplane had not gone over but had descended in the midst of the wood. An observer with a telescope on one of the higher hills might have discovered the truth, but only herds went there, and herds do not carry spy-glasses. When I looked from the dovecot I could see far away a blue line which I knew was the sea, and I grew furious to think that our enemies had this secret conning-tower to rake our waterways.

Then I reflected that if that aeroplane came back the chances were ten to one that I would be discovered. So through the afternoon I lay and prayed for the coming of darkness, and glad I was when the sun went down over the big western hills and the twilight haze crept over the moor. The aeroplane was late. The gloaming was far advanced when I heard the beat of wings and saw it volplaning downward to its home in the wood. Lights twinkled for a bit and there was much coming and going from the house. Then the dark fell, and silence.

Thank God it was a black night. The moon was well on its last quarter and would not rise till late. My thirst was too great to allow me to tarry, so about nine o'clock, so far as I could judge, I started to descend. It wasn't easy, and half-way down I heard the back door of the house open, and saw the gleam of a lantern against the mill wall. For some agonizing minutes I hung by the ivy and prayed that whoever it was would not come round by the dovecot. Then the light disappeared, and I dropped as softly as I could on to the hard soil of the yard.

I crawled on my belly in the lee of a stone dyke till I reached the fringe of trees which surrounded the house. If I had known how to do it I would have tried to put that aeroplane out of action, but I realized that any attempt would probably be futile. I was pretty certain that there would be some kind of defence round the house, so I went through the wood on hands and knees, feeling carefully every inch before me. It was as well, for presently I came on a wire about two feet from the ground. If I had tripped over that, it would doubtless have rung some bell in the house and I would have been captured.

A hundred yards farther on I found another wire cunningly placed on the edge of a small stream. Beyond that lay the moor, and in five minutes I was deep in bracken and heather. Soon I was round the shoulder of the rise, in the little glen from which the mill-lade flowed. Ten minutes later my face was in the spring, and I was soaking down pints of the blessed water.

But I did not stop till I had put half a dozen miles between me and that accursed dwelling.

Chapter VII
The Dry-Fly Fisherman

I SAT DOWN on a hill-top and took stock of my position. I wasn't feeling very happy, for my natural thankfulness at my escape was clouded by my severe bodily discomfort. Those lentonite fumes had fairly poisoned me, and the baking hours on the dovecot hadn't helped matters. I had a crushing headache, and felt as sick as a cat. Also my shoulder was in a bad way. At first I thought it was only a bruise, but it seemed to be swelling, and I had no use of my left arm.

My plan was to seek Mr. Turnbull's cottage, recover my garments, and especially Scudder's note-book, and then make for the main line and get back to the south. It seemed to me that the sooner I got in touch with the Foreign Office man, Sir Walter Bullivant, the better. I didn't see how I could get more proof than I had got already. He must just take or leave my story, and anyway, with him I would be in better hands than those devilish Germans. I had begun to feel quite kindly towards the British police.

It was a wonderful starry night, and I had not much difficulty about the road. Sir Harry's map had given me the lie of the land, and all I had to do was to steer a point or two west of south-west to come to the stream where I had met the roadman. In all these travels I never knew the names of the places, but I believe this stream was no less than the upper waters of the river Tweed. I calculated I must be about eighteen miles distant, and that meant I could not get there before morning. So I must lie up a day somewhere, for I was too outrageous a figure to be seen in the sunlight. I had neither coat, waistcoat, collar, nor hat, my trousers were badly torn, and my face and hands were black with the explosion. I daresay I had other beauties, for my eyes felt as if they were furiously bloodshot. Altogether I was no spectacle for God-fearing citizens to see on a highroad.

Very soon after daybreak I made an attempt to clean myself in a hill burn, and then approached a herd's cottage, for I was feeling the need of food. The herd was away from home, and his wife was alone, with no neighbour for five miles. She was a decent old body, and a plucky one, for though she got a fright when she saw me, she had an axe handy, and would have used it on any evil-doer. I told her that I had had a fall – I didn't say how – and she saw by my looks that I was pretty sick. Like a true Samaritan she asked no questions, but gave me a bowl of milk with a dash of whisky in it, and let me sit for a little by her kitchen fire. She would have bathed my shoulder, but it ached so badly that I would not let her touch it.

I don't know what she took me for – a repentant burglar, perhaps; for when I wanted to pay her for the milk and tendered a sovereign which was the smallest coin I had, she shook her head and said something about 'giving it to them that had a right to it'. At this I protested so strongly that I think she believed me honest, for she took the money and gave me a warm new plaid for it, and an old hat of her man's. She showed me how to wrap the plaid around my shoulders, and when I left that cottage I was the living image of the kind of Scotsman you see in the illustrations to Burns's poems. But at any rate I was more or less clad.

It was as well, for the weather changed before midday to a thick drizzle of rain. I found shelter below an overhanging rock in the crook of a burn, where a drift of dead brackens made a tolerable bed. There I managed to sleep till nightfall, waking very cramped and wretched, with my shoulder gnawing like a toothache. I ate the oatcake and cheese the old wife had given me and set out again just before the darkening.

I pass over the miseries of that night among the wet hills. There were no stars to steer by, and I had to do the best I could from my memory of the map. Twice I lost my way, and I had some nasty falls into peat-bogs. I had only about ten miles to go as the crow flies, but my mistakes made it nearer twenty. The last bit was completed with set teeth and a very light and dizzy head. But I managed it, and in the early dawn I was knocking at Mr. Turnbull's door. The mist lay close and thick, and from the cottage I could not see the highroad.

Mr. Turnbull himself opened to me – sober and something more than sober. He was primly dressed in an ancient but well-tended suit of black; he had been shaved not later than the night before; he wore a linen collar; and in his left hand he carried a pocket Bible. At first he did not recognize me.

"Whae are ye that comes stravaigin' here on the Sabbath mornin'?" he asked.

I had lost all count of the days. So the Sabbath was the reason for this strange decorum.

My head was swimming so wildly that I could not frame a coherent answer. But he recognized me, and he saw that I was ill.

"Hae ye got my specs?" he asked.

I fetched them out of my trouser pocket and gave him them.

"Ye'll hae come for your jaicket and westcoat," he said. "Come in-bye. Losh, man, ye're terrible dune i' the legs. Haud up till I get ye to a chair."

I perceived I was in for a bout of malaria. I had a good deal of fever in my bones, and the wet night had brought it out, while my shoulder and the effects of the fumes combined to make me feel pretty bad. Before I knew, Mr. Turnbull was helping me off with my clothes, and putting me to bed in one of the two cupboards that lined the kitchen walls.

He was a true friend in need, that old roadman. His wife was dead years ago, and since his daughter's marriage he lived alone.

For the better part of ten days he did all the rough nursing I needed. I simply wanted to be left in peace while the fever took its course, and when my skin was cool again I found that the bout had more or less cured my shoulder. But it was a baddish go, and though I was out of bed in five days, it took me some time to get my legs again.

He went out each morning, leaving me milk for the day, and locking the door behind him; and came in in the evening to sit silent in the chimney corner. Not a soul came near the place. When I was getting better, he never bothered me with a question. Several times he fetched me a two days' old *Scotsman*, and I noticed that the interest in the Portland Place murder seemed to have died down. There was no mention of it, and I could find very little about anything except a thing called the General Assembly – some ecclesiastical spree, I gathered.

One day he produced my belt from a lockfast drawer. "There's a terrible heap o' siller in't," he said. "Ye'd better coont it to see it's a' there."

He never even sought my name. I asked him if anybody had been around making inquiries subsequent to my spell at the road-making.

"Ay, there was a man in a motor-cawr. He speired whae had ta'en my place that day, and I let on I thocht him daft. But he keepit on at me, and syne I said he maun be thinkin' o' my gude-brither frae the Cleuch that whiles lent me a haun'. He was a wersh-lookin' sowl, and I couldna understand the half o' his English tongue."

I was getting restless those last days, and as soon as I felt myself fit I decided to be off. That was not till the twelfth day of June, and as luck would have it a drover went past that morning taking some cattle to Moffat. He was a man named Hislop, a friend of Turnbull's, and he came in to his breakfast with us and offered to take me with him.

I made Turnbull accept five pounds for my lodging, and a hard job I had of it. There never was a more independent being. He grew positively rude when I pressed him, and shy and red, and took the money at last without a thank you. When I told him how much I owed him, he grunted something about 'ae guid turn deservin' anither'. You would have thought from our leave-taking that we had parted in disgust.

Hislop was a cheery soul, who chattered all the way over the pass and down the sunny vale of Annan. I talked of Galloway markets and sheep prices, and he made up his mind I was a 'pack-shepherd' from those parts – whatever that may be. My plaid and my old hat, as I have said, gave me a fine theatrical Scots look. But driving cattle is a mortally slow job, and we took the better part of the day to cover a dozen miles.

If I had not had such an anxious heart I would have enjoyed that time. It was shining blue weather, with a constantly changing prospect of brown hills and far green meadows, and a continual sound of larks and curlews and falling streams. But I had no mind for the summer, and little for Hislop's conversation, for as the fateful fifteenth of June drew near I was overweighed with the hopeless difficulties of my enterprise.

I got some dinner in a humble Moffat public-house, and walked the two miles to the junction on the main line. The night express for the south was not due till near midnight, and to fill up the time I went up on the hillside and fell asleep, for the walk had tired me. I all but slept too long, and had to run to the station and catch the train with two minutes to spare. The feel of the hard third-class cushions and the smell of stale tobacco cheered me up wonderfully. At any rate, I felt now that I was getting to grips with my job.

I was decanted at Crewe in the small hours and had to wait till six to get a train for Birmingham. In the afternoon I got to Reading, and changed into a local train which journeyed into the deeps of Berkshire. Presently I was in a land of lush water-meadows and slow reedy streams. About eight o'clock in the evening, a weary and travel-stained being – a cross between a farm-labourer and a vet – with a checked black-and-white plaid over his arm (for I did not dare to wear it south of the Border), descended at the little station of Artinswell. There were several people on the platform, and I thought I had better wait to ask my way till I was clear of the place.

The road led through a wood of great beeches and then into a shallow valley, with the green backs of downs peeping over the distant trees. After Scotland the air smelt heavy and flat, but infinitely sweet, for the limes and chestnuts and lilac bushes were domes of blossom. Presently I came to a bridge, below which a clear slow stream flowed between snowy beds of water-buttercups. A little above it was a mill; and the lasher made a pleasant cool sound in the scented dusk. Somehow the place soothed me and put me at my ease. I fell to whistling as I looked into the green depths, and the tune which came to my lips was 'Annie Laurie'.

A fisherman came up from the waterside, and as he neared me he too began to whistle. The tune was infectious, for he followed my suit. He was a huge man in untidy old flannels and a wide-brimmed hat, with a canvas bag slung on his shoulder. He nodded to me, and I thought I had never seen a shrewder or better-tempered face. He leaned his delicate ten-foot split-cane rod against the bridge, and looked with me at the water.

"Clear, isn't it?" he said pleasantly. "I back our Kenner any day against the Test. Look at that big fellow. Four pounds if he's an ounce. But the evening rise is over and you can't tempt 'em."

"I don't see him," said I.

"Look! There! A yard from the reeds just above that stickle."

"I've got him now. You might swear he was a black stone."

"So," he said, and whistled another bar of 'Annie Laurie'.

"Twisdon's the name, isn't it?" he said over his shoulder, his eyes still fixed on the stream.

"No," I said. "I mean to say, Yes." I had forgotten all about my alias.

"It's a wise conspirator that knows his own name," he observed, grinning broadly at a moor-hen that emerged from the bridge's shadow.

I stood up and looked at him, at the square, cleft jaw and broad, lined brow and the firm folds of cheek, and began to think that here at last was an ally worth having. His whimsical blue eyes seemed to go very deep.

Suddenly he frowned. "I call it disgraceful," he said, raising his voice. "Disgraceful that an able-bodied man like you should dare to beg. You can get a meal from my kitchen, but you'll get no money from me."

A dog-cart was passing, driven by a young man who raised his whip to salute the fisherman. When he had gone, he picked up his rod.

"That's my house," he said, pointing to a white gate a hundred yards on. "Wait five minutes and then go round to the back door." And with that he left me.

I did as I was bidden. I found a pretty cottage with a lawn running down to the stream, and a perfect jungle of guelder-rose and lilac flanking the path. The back door stood open, and a grave butler was awaiting me.

"Come this way, Sir," he said, and he led me along a passage and up a back staircase to a pleasant bedroom looking towards the river. There I found a complete outfit laid out for me – dress clothes with all the fixings, a brown flannel suit, shirts, collars, ties, shaving things and hair-brushes, even a pair of patent shoes. "Sir Walter thought as how Mr. Reggie's things would fit you, Sir," said the butler. "He keeps some clothes 'ere, for he comes regular on the week-ends. There's a bathroom next door, and I've prepared a 'ot bath. Dinner in 'alf an hour, Sir. You'll 'ear the gong."

The grave being withdrew, and I sat down in a chintz-covered easy-chair and gaped. It was like a pantomime, to come suddenly out of beggardom into this orderly comfort. Obviously Sir Walter believed in me, though why he did I could not guess. I looked at myself in the mirror and saw a wild, haggard brown fellow, with a fortnight's ragged beard, and dust in ears and eyes, collarless, vulgarly shirted, with shapeless old tweed clothes and boots that had not been cleaned for the better part of a month. I made a fine tramp and a fair drover; and here I was ushered by a prim butler into this temple of gracious ease. And the best of it was that they did not even know my name.

I resolved not to puzzle my head but to take the gifts the gods had provided. I shaved and bathed luxuriously, and got into the dress clothes and clean crackling shirt, which fitted me not so badly. By the time I had finished the looking-glass showed a not unpersonable young man.

Sir Walter awaited me in a dusky dining-room where a little round table was lit with silver candles. The sight of him – so respectable and established and secure, the embodiment of law and government and all the conventions – took me aback and made me feel an interloper. He couldn't know the truth about me, or he wouldn't treat me like this. I simply could not accept his hospitality on false pretences.

"I'm more obliged to you than I can say, but I'm bound to make things clear," I said. "I'm an innocent man, but I'm wanted by the police. I've got to tell you this, and I won't be surprised if you kick me out."

He smiled. "That's all right. Don't let that interfere with your appetite. We can talk about these things after dinner." I never ate a meal with greater relish, for I had had nothing all day but railway sandwiches. Sir Walter did me proud, for we drank a good champagne and had some uncommon fine port afterwards. It made me almost hysterical to be sitting there, waited on by a footman and a sleek butler, and remember that I had been living for three weeks like a brigand, with every man's hand against me. I told Sir Walter about tiger-fish in the Zambesi that bite off your fingers if you give them a chance, and we discussed sport up and down the globe, for he had hunted a bit in his day.

We went to his study for coffee, a jolly room full of books and trophies and untidiness and comfort. I made up my mind that if ever I got rid of this business and had a house of my own, I would create just such a room. Then when the coffee-cups were cleared away, and we had got our cigars alight, my host swung his long legs over the side of his chair and bade me get started with my yarn.

"I've obeyed Harry's instructions," he said, "and the bribe he offered me was that you would tell me something to wake me up. I'm ready, Mr. Hannay."

I noticed with a start that he called me by my proper name.

I began at the very beginning. I told of my boredom in London, and the night I had come back to find Scudder gibbering on my doorstep. I told him all Scudder had told me about Karolides and the Foreign Office conference, and that made him purse his lips and grin.

Then I got to the murder, and he grew solemn again. He heard all about the milkman and my time in Galloway, and my deciphering Scudder's notes at the inn.

"You've got them here?" he asked sharply, and drew a long breath when I whipped the little book from my pocket.

I said nothing of the contents. Then I described my meeting with Sir Harry, and the speeches at the hall. At that he laughed uproariously.

"Harry talked dashed nonsense, did he? I quite believe it. He's as good a chap as ever breathed, but his idiot of an uncle has stuffed his head with maggots. Go on, Mr. Hannay."

My day as roadman excited him a bit. He made me describe the two fellows in the car very closely, and seemed to be raking back in his memory. He grew merry again when he heard of the fate of that ass Jopley.

But the old man in the moorland house solemnized him. Again I had to describe every detail of his appearance.

"Bland and bald-headed and hooded his eyes like a bird.... He sounds a sinister wild-fowl! And you dynamited his hermitage, after he had saved you from the police. Spirited piece of work, that!" Presently I reached the end of my wanderings. He got up slowly, and looked down at me from the hearth-rug.

"You may dismiss the police from your mind," he said. "You're in no danger from the law of this land."

"Great Scot!" I cried. "Have they got the murderer?"

"No. But for the last fortnight they have dropped you from the list of possibles."

"Why?" I asked in amazement.

"Principally because I received a letter from Scudder. I knew something of the man, and he did several jobs for me. He was half crank, half genius, but he was wholly honest. The trouble about him was his partiality for playing a lone hand. That made him pretty well useless in any Secret Service – a pity, for he had uncommon gifts. I think he was the bravest man in the world, for he was always shivering with fright, and yet nothing would choke him off. I had a letter from him on the 31st of May."

"But he had been dead a week by then."

"The letter was written and posted on the 23rd. He evidently did not anticipate an immediate decease. His communications usually took a week to reach me, for they were sent under cover to Spain and then to Newcastle. He had a mania, you know, for concealing his tracks."

"What did he say?" I stammered.

"Nothing. Merely that he was in danger, but had found shelter with a good friend, and that I would hear from him before the 15th of June. He gave me no address, but said he was living near Portland Place. I think his object was to clear you if anything happened. When I got it I went to Scotland Yard, went over the details of the inquest, and concluded that you were the friend. We made inquiries about you, Mr. Hannay, and found you were respectable. I thought I knew the motives for your disappearance – not only the police, the other one too – and when I got Harry's scrawl I guessed at the rest. I have been expecting you any time this past week." You can imagine what a load this took off my mind. I felt a free man once more, for I was now up against my country's enemies only, and not my country's law.

"Now let us have the little note-book," said Sir Walter.

It took us a good hour to work through it. I explained the cypher, and he was jolly quick at picking it up. He emended my reading of it on several points, but I had been fairly correct, on the whole. His face was very grave before he had finished, and he sat silent for a while.

"I don't know what to make of it," he said at last. "He is right about one thing – what is going to happen the day after tomorrow. How the devil can it have got known? That is ugly enough in itself. But all this about war and the Black Stone – it reads like some wild melodrama. If only I had more confidence in Scudder's judgement. The trouble about him was that he was too romantic. He had the artistic temperament, and wanted a story to be better than God meant it to be. He had a lot of odd biases, too. Jews, for example, made him see red. Jews and the high finance.

"The Black Stone," he repeated. "*Der Schwarze Stein*. It's like a penny novelette. And all this stuff about Karolides. That is the weak part of the tale, for I happen to know that the virtuous Karolides is likely to outlast us both. There is no State in Europe that wants him gone. Besides, he has just been playing up to Berlin and Vienna and giving my Chief some uneasy moments. No! Scudder has gone off the track there. Frankly, Hannay, I don't believe that part of his story. There's some nasty business afoot, and he found out too much and lost his life over it. But I am ready to take my oath that it is ordinary spy work. A certain great European Power makes a hobby of her spy system, and her methods are not too particular. Since she pays by piecework her blackguards are not likely to stick at a murder or two. They want our naval dispositions for their collection at the Marineamt; but they will be pigeon-holed – nothing more."

Just then the butler entered the room.

"There's a trunk-call from London, Sir Walter. It's Mr. 'Eath, and he wants to speak to you personally."

My host went off to the telephone.

He returned in five minutes with a whitish face. "I apologize to the shade of Scudder," he said. "Karolides was shot dead this evening at a few minutes after seven."

Chapter VIII
The Coming of the Black Stone

I CAME DOWN to breakfast next morning, after eight hours of blessed dreamless sleep, to find Sir Walter decoding a telegram in the midst of muffins and marmalade. His fresh rosiness of yesterday seemed a thought tarnished.

"I had a busy hour on the telephone after you went to bed," he said. "I got my Chief to speak to the First Lord and the Secretary for War, and they are bringing Royer over a day sooner. This wire clinches it. He will be in London at five. Odd that the code word for a *Sous-chef d'état Major-General* should be 'Porker'."

He directed me to the hot dishes and went on.

"Not that I think it will do much good. If your friends were clever enough to find out the first arrangement they are clever enough to discover the change. I would give my head to know where the leak is. We believed there were only five men in England who knew about Royer's visit, and you may be certain there were fewer in France, for they manage these things better there."

While I ate he continued to talk, making me to my surprise a present of his full confidence.

"Can the dispositions not be changed?" I asked.

"They could," he said. "But we want to avoid that if possible. They are the result of immense thought, and no alteration would be as good. Besides, on one or two points change is simply impossible. Still, something could be done, I suppose, if it were absolutely necessary. But you see the difficulty, Hannay. Our enemies are not going to be such fools as to pick Royer's pocket or any childish game like that. They know that would mean a row and put us on our guard. Their aim is to get the details without any one of us knowing, so that Royer will go back to Paris in the belief that the whole business is still deadly secret. If they can't do that they fail, for, once we suspect, they know that the whole thing must be altered."

"Then we must stick by the Frenchman's side till he is home again," I said. "If they thought they could get the information in Paris they would try there. It means that they have some deep scheme on foot in London which they reckon is going to win out."

"Royer dines with my Chief, and then comes to my house where four people will see him – Whittaker from the Admiralty, myself, Sir Arthur Drew, and General Winstanley. The First Lord is ill, and has gone to Sheringham. At my house he will get a certain document from Whittaker, and after that he will be motored to Portsmouth where a destroyer will take him to Havre. His journey is too important for the ordinary boat-train. He will never be left unattended for a moment till he is safe on French soil. The same with Whittaker till he meets Royer. That is the best we can do, and it's hard to see how there can be any miscarriage. But I don't mind admitting that I'm horribly nervous. This murder of Karolides will play the deuce in the chancelleries of Europe."

After breakfast he asked me if I could drive a car. "Well, you'll be my chauffeur today and wear Hudson's rig. You're about his size. You have a hand in this business and we are taking no risks. There are desperate men against us, who will not respect the country retreat of an overworked official."

When I first came to London I had bought a car and amused myself with running about the south of England, so I knew something of the geography. I took Sir Walter to town by the Bath Road and made good going. It was a soft breathless June morning, with a promise of sultriness later, but it was delicious enough swinging through the little towns with their freshly watered streets, and past the summer gardens of the Thames valley. I landed Sir Walter at his house in Queen Anne's Gate punctually by half-past eleven. The butler was coming up by train with the luggage.

The first thing he did was to take me round to Scotland Yard. There we saw a prim gentleman, with a clean-shaven, lawyer's face.

"I've brought you the Portland Place murderer," was Sir Walter's introduction.

The reply was a wry smile. "It would have been a welcome present, Bullivant. This, I presume, is Mr. Richard Hannay, who for some days greatly interested my department."

"Mr. Hannay will interest it again. He has much to tell you, but not today. For certain grave reasons his tale must wait for four hours. Then, I can promise you, you will be entertained and possibly edified. I want you to assure Mr. Hannay that he will suffer no further inconvenience."

This assurance was promptly given. "You can take up your life where you left off," I was told. "Your flat, which probably you no longer wish to occupy, is waiting for you, and your man is still there. As you were never publicly accused, we considered that there was no need of a public exculpation. But on that, of course, you must please yourself."

"We may want your assistance later on, MacGillivray," Sir Walter said as we left.

Then he turned me loose.

"Come and see me tomorrow, Hannay. I needn't tell you to keep deadly quiet. If I were you I would go to bed, for you must have considerable arrears of sleep to overtake. You had better lie low, for if one of your Black Stone friends saw you there might be trouble."

I felt curiously at a loose end. At first it was very pleasant to be a free man, able to go where I wanted without fearing anything. I had only been a month under the ban of the law, and it was quite enough for me. I went to the Savoy and ordered very carefully a very good luncheon, and then smoked the best cigar the house could provide. But I was still feeling nervous. When I saw anybody look at me in the lounge, I grew shy, and wondered if they were thinking about the murder.

After that I took a taxi and drove miles away up into North London. I walked back through fields and lines of villas and terraces and then slums and mean streets, and it took me pretty nearly two hours. All the while my restlessness was growing worse. I felt that great things, tremendous things, were happening or about to happen, and I, who was the cog-wheel of the whole business, was out of it. Royer would be landing at Dover, Sir Walter would be making plans with the few people in England who were in the secret, and somewhere in the darkness the Black Stone would be working. I felt the sense of danger and impending calamity, and I had the curious feeling, too, that I alone could avert it, alone could grapple with it. But I was out of the game now. How could it be otherwise? It was not likely that Cabinet Ministers and Admiralty Lords and Generals would admit me to their councils.

I actually began to wish that I could run up against one of my three enemies. That would lead to developments. I felt that I wanted enormously to have a vulgar scrap with those gentry, where I could hit out and flatten something. I was rapidly getting into a very bad temper.

I didn't feel like going back to my flat. That had to be faced some time, but as I still had sufficient money I thought I would put it off till next morning, and go to a hotel for the night.

My irritation lasted through dinner, which I had at a restaurant in Jermyn Street. I was no longer hungry, and let several courses pass untasted. I drank the best part of a bottle of Burgundy, but it did nothing to cheer me. An abominable restlessness had taken possession of me. Here was I, a very ordinary fellow, with no particular brains, and yet I was convinced that somehow I was needed to help this business through – that without me it would all go to blazes. I told myself it was sheer silly conceit, that four or five of the cleverest people living, with all the might of the British Empire at their back, had the job in hand. Yet I couldn't be convinced. It seemed as if a voice kept speaking in my ear, telling me to be up and doing, or I would never sleep again.

The upshot was that about half-past nine I made up my mind to go to Queen Anne's Gate. Very likely I would not be admitted, but it would ease my conscience to try.

I walked down Jermyn Street, and at the corner of Duke Street passed a group of young men. They were in evening dress, had been dining somewhere, and were going on to a music-hall. One of them was Mr. Marmaduke Jopley.

He saw me and stopped short.

"By God, the murderer!" he cried. "Here, you fellows, hold him! That's Hannay, the man who did the Portland Place murder!" He gripped me by the arm, and the others crowded round. I wasn't looking for any trouble, but my ill-temper made me play the fool. A policeman came up, and I should have told him the truth, and, if he didn't believe it, demanded to be taken to Scotland Yard, or for that matter to the nearest police station. But a delay at that moment seemed to me unendurable, and the sight of Marmie's imbecile face was more than I could bear. I let out with my left, and had the satisfaction of seeing him measure his length in the gutter.

Then began an unholy row. They were all on me at once, and the policeman took me in the rear. I got in one or two good blows, for I think, with fair play, I could have licked the lot of them, but the policeman pinned me behind, and one of them got his fingers on my throat.

Through a black cloud of rage I heard the officer of the law asking what was the matter, and Marmie, between his broken teeth, declaring that I was Hannay the murderer.

"Oh, damn it all," I cried, "make the fellow shut up. I advise you to leave me alone, constable. Scotland Yard knows all about me, and you'll get a proper wigging if you interfere with me."

"You've got to come along of me, young man," said the policeman. "I saw you strike that gentleman crool 'ard. You began it too, for he wasn't doing nothing. I seen you. Best go quietly or I'll have to fix you up."

Exasperation and an overwhelming sense that at no cost must I delay gave me the strength of a bull elephant. I fairly wrenched the constable off his feet, floored the man who was gripping my collar, and set off at my best pace down Duke Street. I heard a whistle being blown, and the rush of men behind me.

I have a very fair turn of speed, and that night I had wings. In a jiffy I was in Pall Mall and had turned down towards St James's Park. I dodged the policeman at the Palace gates, dived through a press of carriages at the entrance to the Mall, and was making for the bridge before my pursuers had crossed the roadway. In the open ways of the Park I put on a spurt. Happily there were few people about and no one tried to stop me. I was staking all on getting to Queen Anne's Gate.

When I entered that quiet thoroughfare it seemed deserted. Sir Walter's house was in the narrow part, and outside it three or four motor-cars were drawn up. I slackened speed some yards off and walked briskly up to the door. If the butler refused me admission, or if he even delayed to open the door, I was done.

He didn't delay. I had scarcely rung before the door opened.

"I must see Sir Walter," I panted. "My business is desperately important."

That butler was a great man. Without moving a muscle he held the door open, and then shut it behind me. "Sir Walter is engaged, Sir, and I have orders to admit no one. Perhaps you will wait."

The house was of the old-fashioned kind, with a wide hall and rooms on both sides of it. At the far end was an alcove with a telephone and a couple of chairs, and there the butler offered me a seat.

"See here," I whispered. "There's trouble about and I'm in it. But Sir Walter knows, and I'm working for him. If anyone comes and asks if I am here, tell him a lie."

He nodded, and presently there was a noise of voices in the street, and a furious ringing at the bell. I never admired a man more than that butler. He opened the door, and with a face like a graven image waited to be questioned. Then he gave them it. He told them whose house it was, and what his orders were, and simply froze them off the doorstep. I could see it all from my alcove, and it was better than any play.

I hadn't waited long till there came another ring at the bell. The butler made no bones about admitting this new visitor.

While he was taking off his coat I saw who it was. You couldn't open a newspaper or a magazine without seeing that face – the grey beard cut like a spade, the firm fighting mouth, the blunt square nose, and the keen blue eyes. I recognized the First Sea Lord, the man, they say, that made the new British Navy.

He passed my alcove and was ushered into a room at the back of the hall. As the door opened I could hear the sound of low voices. It shut, and I was left alone again.

For twenty minutes I sat there, wondering what I was to do next. I was still perfectly convinced that I was wanted, but when or how I had no notion. I kept looking at my watch, and as the time crept on to half-past ten I began to think that the conference must soon end. In a quarter of an hour Royer should be speeding along the road to Portsmouth...

Then I heard a bell ring, and the butler appeared. The door of the back room opened, and the First Sea Lord came out. He walked past me, and in passing he glanced in my direction, and for a second we looked each other in the face.

Only for a second, but it was enough to make my heart jump. I had never seen the great man before, and he had never seen me. But in that fraction of time something sprang into his eyes, and that something was recognition. You can't mistake it. It is a flicker, a spark of light, a minute shade of difference which means one thing and one thing only. It came involuntarily, for in a moment it died, and he passed on. In a maze of wild fancies I heard the street door close behind him.

I picked up the telephone book and looked up the number of his house. We were connected at once, and I heard a servant's voice.

"Is his Lordship at home?" I asked.

"His Lordship returned half an hour ago," said the voice, "and has gone to bed. He is not very well tonight. Will you leave a message, Sir?"

I rang off and almost tumbled into a chair. My part in this business was not yet ended. It had been a close shave, but I had been in time.

Not a moment could be lost, so I marched boldly to the door of that back room and entered without knocking.

Five surprised faces looked up from a round table. There was Sir Walter, and Drew the War Minister, whom I knew from his photographs. There was a slim elderly man, who was probably Whittaker, the Admiralty official, and there was General Winstanley, conspicuous from the long scar on his forehead. Lastly, there was a short stout man with an iron-grey moustache and bushy eyebrows, who had been arrested in the middle of a sentence.

Sir Walter's face showed surprise and annoyance.

"This is Mr. Hannay, of whom I have spoken to you," he said apologetically to the company. "I'm afraid, Hannay, this visit is ill-timed."

I was getting back my coolness. "That remains to be seen, Sir," I said; "but I think it may be in the nick of time. For God's sake, gentlemen, tell me who went out a minute ago?"

"Lord Alloa," Sir Walter said, reddening with anger.

"It was not," I cried; "it was his living image, but it was not Lord Alloa. It was someone who recognized me, someone I have seen in the last month. He had scarcely left the doorstep when I rang up Lord Alloa's house and was told he had come in half an hour before and had gone to bed."

"Who – who –" someone stammered.

"The Black Stone," I cried, and I sat down in the chair so recently vacated and looked round at five badly scared gentlemen.

Chapter IX
The Thirty-Nine Steps

"NONSENSE!" said the official from the Admiralty.

Sir Walter got up and left the room while we looked blankly at the table. He came back in ten minutes with a long face. "I have spoken to Alloa," he said. "Had him out of bed – very grumpy. He went straight home after Mulross's dinner."

"But it's madness," broke in General Winstanley. "Do you mean to tell me that that man came here and sat beside me for the best part of half an hour and that I didn't detect the imposture? Alloa must be out of his mind."

"Don't you see the cleverness of it?" I said. "You were too interested in other things to have any eyes. You took Lord Alloa for granted. If it had been anybody else you might have looked more closely, but it was natural for him to be here, and that put you all to sleep."

Then the Frenchman spoke, very slowly and in good English.

"The young man is right. His psychology is good. Our enemies have not been foolish!"

He bent his wise brows on the assembly.

"I will tell you a tale," he said. "It happened many years ago in Senegal. I was quartered in a remote station, and to pass the time used to go fishing for big barbel in the river. A little Arab mare used to carry my luncheon basket – one of the salted dun breed you got at Timbuctoo in the old days. Well, one morning I had good sport, and the mare was unaccountably restless. I could hear her whinnying and squealing and stamping her feet, and I kept soothing her with my voice while my mind was intent on fish. I could see her all the time, as I thought, out of a corner of my eye, tethered to a tree twenty yards away. After a couple of hours I began to think of food. I collected my fish in a tarpaulin bag, and moved down the stream towards the mare, trolling my line. When I got up to her I flung the tarpaulin on her back –"

He paused and looked round.

"It was the smell that gave me warning. I turned my head and found myself looking at a lion three feet off.... An old man-eater, that was the terror of the village.... What was left of the mare, a mass of blood and bones and hide, was behind him."

"What happened?" I asked. I was enough of a hunter to know a true yarn when I heard it.

"I stuffed my fishing-rod into his jaws, and I had a pistol. Also my servants came presently with rifles. But he left his mark on me." He held up a hand which lacked three fingers.

"Consider," he said. "The mare had been dead more than an hour, and the brute had been patiently watching me ever since. I never saw the kill, for I was accustomed to the mare's fretting, and I never marked her absence, for my consciousness of her was only of something tawny, and the lion filled that part. If I could blunder thus, gentlemen, in a land where men's senses are keen, why should we busy preoccupied urban folk not err also?"

Sir Walter nodded. No one was ready to gainsay him.

"But I don't see," went on Winstanley. "Their object was to get these dispositions without our knowing it. Now it only required one of us to mention to Alloa our meeting tonight for the whole fraud to be exposed."

Sir Walter laughed dryly. "The selection of Alloa shows their acumen. Which of us was likely to speak to him about tonight? Or was he likely to open the subject?"

I remembered the First Sea Lord's reputation for taciturnity and shortness of temper.

"The one thing that puzzles me," said the General, "is what good his visit here would do that spy fellow? He could not carry away several pages of figures and strange names in his head."

"That is not difficult," the Frenchman replied. "A good spy is trained to have a photographic memory. Like your own Macaulay. You noticed he said nothing, but went through these papers again and again. I think we may assume that he has every detail stamped on his mind. When I was younger I could do the same trick."

"Well, I suppose there is nothing for it but to change the plans," said Sir Walter ruefully.

Whittaker was looking very glum. "Did you tell Lord Alloa what has happened?" he asked. "No? Well, I can't speak with absolute assurance, but I'm nearly certain we can't make any serious change unless we alter the geography of England."

"Another thing must be said," it was Royer who spoke. "I talked freely when that man was here. I told something of the military plans of my Government. I was permitted to say so much. But that information would be worth many millions to our enemies. No, my friends, I see no other way. The man who came here and his confederates must be taken, and taken at once."

"Good God," I cried, "and we have not a rag of a clue."

"Besides," said Whittaker, "there is the post. By this time the news will be on its way."

"No," said the Frenchman. "You do not understand the habits of the spy. He receives personally his reward, and he delivers personally his intelligence. We in France know something of the breed. There is still a chance, *mes amis*. These men must cross the sea, and there are ships to be searched and ports to be watched. Believe me, the need is desperate for both France and Britain."

Royer's grave good sense seemed to pull us together. He was the man of action among fumblers. But I saw no hope in any face, and I felt none. Where among the fifty millions of these islands and within a dozen hours were we to lay hands on the three cleverest rogues in Europe?

Then suddenly I had an inspiration.

"Where is Scudder's book?" I cried to Sir Walter. "Quick, man, I remember something in it."

He unlocked the door of a bureau and gave it to me.

I found the place. *Thirty-nine steps*, I read, and again, *Thirty-nine steps – I counted them – high tide 10.17 P.M.*

The Admiralty man was looking at me as if he thought I had gone mad.

"Don't you see it's a clue," I shouted. "Scudder knew where these fellows laired – he knew where they were going to leave the country, though he kept the name to himself. Tomorrow was the day, and it was some place where high tide was at 10.17."

"They may have gone tonight," someone said.

"Not they. They have their own snug secret way, and they won't be hurried. I know Germans, and they are mad about working to a plan. Where the devil can I get a book of Tide Tables?"

Whittaker brightened up. "It's a chance," he said. "Let's go over to the Admiralty."

We got into two of the waiting motor-cars – all but Sir Walter, who went off to Scotland Yard – to 'mobilize MacGillivray', so he said. We marched through empty corridors and big bare chambers where the charwomen were busy, till we reached a little room lined with books and maps. A resident clerk was unearthed, who presently fetched from the library the Admiralty Tide Tables. I sat at the desk and the others stood round, for somehow or other I had got charge of this expedition.

It was no good. There were hundreds of entries, and so far as I could see 10.17 might cover fifty places. We had to find some way of narrowing the possibilities.

I took my head in my hands and thought. There must be some way of reading this riddle. What did Scudder mean by steps? I thought of dock steps, but if he had meant that I didn't think he would have mentioned the number. It must be some place where there were several staircases, and one marked out from the others by having thirty-nine steps.

Then I had a sudden thought, and hunted up all the steamer sailings. There was no boat which left for the Continent at 10.17 p.m.

Why was high tide so important? If it was a harbour it must be some little place where the tide mattered, or else it was a heavy-draught boat. But there was no regular steamer sailing at that hour, and somehow I didn't think they would travel by a big boat from a regular harbour. So it must be some little harbour where the tide was important, or perhaps no harbour at all.

But if it was a little port I couldn't see what the steps signified. There were no sets of staircases on any harbour that I had ever seen. It must be some place which a particular staircase identified, and where the tide was full at 10.17. On the whole it seemed to me that the place must be a bit of open coast. But the staircases kept puzzling me.

Then I went back to wider considerations. Whereabouts would a man be likely to leave for Germany, a man in a hurry, who wanted a speedy and a secret passage? Not from any of the big harbours. And not from the Channel or the West Coast or Scotland, for, remember, he was starting from London. I measured the distance on the map, and tried to put myself in the enemy's shoes. I should try for Ostend or Antwerp or Rotterdam, and I should sail from somewhere on the East Coast between Cromer and Dover.

All this was very loose guessing, and I don't pretend it was ingenious or scientific. I wasn't any kind of Sherlock Holmes. But I have always fancied I had a kind of instinct about questions like this. I don't know if I can explain myself, but I used to use my brains as far as they went, and after they came to a blank wall I guessed, and I usually found my guesses pretty right.

So I set out all my conclusions on a bit of Admiralty paper. They ran like this:

FAIRLY CERTAIN

(1) Place where there are several sets of stairs; one that matters distinguished by having thirty-nine steps.

(2) Full tide at 10.17 p.m. Leaving shore only possible at full tide.

(3) Steps not dock steps, and so place probably not harbour.

(4) No regular night steamer at 10.17. Means of transport must be tramp (unlikely), yacht, or fishing-boat.

There my reasoning stopped. I made another list, which I headed 'Guessed', but I was just as sure of the one as the other.

GUESSED
(1) Place not harbour but open coast.
(2) Boat small – trawler, yacht, or launch.
(3) Place somewhere on East Coast between Cromer and Dover.

It struck me as odd that I should be sitting at that desk with a Cabinet Minister, a Field-Marshal, two high Government officials, and a French General watching me, while from the scribble of a dead man I was trying to drag a secret which meant life or death for us.

Sir Walter had joined us, and presently MacGillivray arrived. He had sent out instructions to watch the ports and railway stations for the three men whom I had described to Sir Walter. Not that he or anybody else thought that that would do much good.

"Here's the most I can make of it," I said. "We have got to find a place where there are several staircases down to the beach, one of which has thirty-nine steps. I think it's a piece of open coast with biggish cliffs, somewhere between the Wash and the Channel. Also it's a place where full tide is at 10.17 tomorrow night."

Then an idea struck me. "Is there no Inspector of Coastguards or some fellow like that who knows the East Coast?"

Whittaker said there was, and that he lived in Clapham. He went off in a car to fetch him, and the rest of us sat about the little room and talked of anything that came into our heads. I lit a pipe and went over the whole thing again till my brain grew weary.

About one in the morning the coastguard man arrived. He was a fine old fellow, with the look of a naval officer, and was desperately respectful to the company. I left the War Minister to cross-examine him, for I felt he would think it cheek in me to talk.

"We want you to tell us the places you know on the East Coast where there are cliffs, and where several sets of steps run down to the beach."

He thought for a bit. "What kind of steps do you mean, Sir? There are plenty of places with roads cut down through the cliffs, and most roads have a step or two in them. Or do you mean regular staircases – all steps, so to speak?"

Sir Arthur looked towards me. "We mean regular staircases," I said.

He reflected a minute or two. "I don't know that I can think of any. Wait a second. There's a place in Norfolk – Brattlesham – beside a golf-course, where there are a couple of staircases, to let the gentlemen get a lost ball."

"That's not it," I said.

"Then there are plenty of Marine Parades, if that's what you mean. Every seaside resort has them."

I shook my head. "It's got to be more retired than that," I said.

"Well, gentlemen, I can't think of anywhere else. Of course, there's the Ruff –"

"What's that?" I asked.

"The big chalk headland in Kent, close to Bradgate. It's got a lot of villas on the top, and some of the houses have staircases down to a private beach. It's a very high-toned sort of place, and the residents there like to keep by themselves."

I tore open the Tide Tables and found Bradgate. High tide there was at 10.27 P.M. on the 15th of June.

"We're on the scent at last," I cried excitedly. "How can I find out what is the tide at the Ruff?"

"I can tell you that, Sir," said the coastguard man. "I once was lent a house there in this very month, and I used to go out at night to the deep-sea fishing. The tide's ten minutes before Bradgate."

I closed the book and looked round at the company.

"If one of those staircases has thirty-nine steps we have solved the mystery, gentlemen," I said. "I want the loan of your car, Sir Walter, and a map of the roads. If Mr. MacGillivray will spare me ten minutes, I think we can prepare something for tomorrow."

It was ridiculous in me to take charge of the business like this, but they didn't seem to mind, and after all I had been in the show from the start. Besides, I was used to rough jobs, and these eminent gentlemen were too clever not to see it. It was General Royer who gave me my commission. "I for one," he said, "am content to leave the matter in Mr. Hannay's hands."

By half-past three I was tearing past the moonlit hedgerows of Kent, with MacGillivray's best man on the seat beside me.

Chapter X
Various Parties Converging on the Sea

A PINK AND BLUE June morning found me at Bradgate looking from the Griffin Hotel over a smooth sea to the lightship on the Cock sands which seemed the size of a bell-buoy. A couple of miles farther south and much nearer the shore a small destroyer was anchored. Scaife, MacGillivray's man, who had been in the Navy, knew the boat, and told me her name and her commander's, so I sent off a wire to Sir Walter.

After breakfast Scaife got from a house-agent a key for the gates of the staircases on the Ruff. I walked with him along the sands, and sat down in a nook of the cliffs while he investigated the half-dozen of them. I didn't want to be seen, but the place at this hour was quite deserted, and all the time I was on that beach I saw nothing but the sea-gulls.

It took him more than an hour to do the job, and when I saw him coming towards me, conning a bit of paper, I can tell you my heart was in my mouth. Everything depended, you see, on my guess proving right.

He read aloud the number of steps in the different stairs. 'Thirty-four, thirty-five, thirty-nine, forty-two, forty-seven,' and 'twenty-one' where the cliffs grew lower. I almost got up and shouted.

We hurried back to the town and sent a wire to MacGillivray. I wanted half a dozen men, and I directed them to divide themselves among different specified hotels. Then Scaife set out to prospect the house at the head of the thirty-nine steps.

He came back with news that both puzzled and reassured me. The house was called Trafalgar Lodge, and belonged to an old gentleman called Appleton – a retired stockbroker, the house-agent said. Mr. Appleton was there a good deal in the summer time, and was in residence now – had been for the better part of a week. Scaife could pick up very little information about him, except that he was a decent old fellow, who paid his bills regularly, and was always good for a fiver for a local charity. Then Scaife seemed to have penetrated to the back door of the house, pretending he was an agent for sewing-machines. Only three servants were kept, a cook, a parlour-maid, and a housemaid, and they were just the sort that you would find in a respectable middle-class household. The cook was not the gossiping kind, and had pretty soon shut the door in his face, but Scaife said he was positive she knew nothing. Next door there was a new house building which would give good cover for observation, and the villa on the other side was to let, and its garden was rough and shrubby.

I borrowed Scaife's telescope, and before lunch went for a walk along the Ruff. I kept well behind the rows of villas, and found a good observation point on the edge of the golf-course. There I had a view of the line of turf along the cliff top, with seats placed at intervals, and the little square plots, railed in and planted with bushes, whence the staircases descended to the beach. I saw Trafalgar Lodge very plainly, a red-brick villa with a veranda, a tennis lawn behind, and in front the ordinary seaside flower-garden full of marguerites and scraggy geraniums. There was a flagstaff from which an enormous Union Jack hung limply in the still air.

Presently I observed someone leave the house and saunter along the cliff. When I got my glasses on him I saw it was an old man, wearing white flannel trousers, a blue serge jacket, and a straw hat. He carried field-glasses and a newspaper, and sat down on one of the iron seats and began to read. Sometimes he would lay down the paper and turn his glasses on the sea. He looked for a long time at the destroyer. I watched him for half an hour, till he got up and went back to the house for his luncheon, when I returned to the hotel for mine.

I wasn't feeling very confident. This decent common-place dwelling was not what I had expected. The man might be the bald archaeologist of that horrible moorland farm, or he might not. He was exactly the kind of satisfied old bird you will find in every suburb and every holiday place. If you wanted a type of the perfectly harmless person you would probably pitch on that.

But after lunch, as I sat in the hotel porch, I perked up, for I saw the thing I had hoped for and had dreaded to miss. A yacht came up from the south and dropped anchor pretty well opposite the Ruff. She seemed about a hundred and fifty tons, and I saw she belonged to the Squadron from the white ensign. So Scaife and I went down to the harbour and hired a boatman for an afternoon's fishing.

I spent a warm and peaceful afternoon. We caught between us about twenty pounds of cod and lythe, and out in that dancing blue sea I took a cheerier view of things. Above the white cliffs of the Ruff I saw the green and red of the villas, and especially the great flagstaff of Trafalgar Lodge. About four o'clock, when we had fished enough, I made the boatman row us round the yacht, which lay like a delicate white bird, ready at a moment to flee. Scaife said she must be a fast boat for her build, and that she was pretty heavily engined.

Her name was the *Ariadne*, as I discovered from the cap of one of the men who was polishing brasswork. I spoke to him, and got an answer in the soft dialect of Essex. Another hand that came along passed me the time of day in an unmistakable English tongue. Our boatman had an argument with one of them about the weather, and for a few minutes we lay on our oars close to the starboard bow.

Then the men suddenly disregarded us and bent their heads to their work as an officer came along the deck. He was a pleasant, clean-looking young fellow, and he put a question to us about our fishing in very good English. But there could be no doubt about him. His close-cropped head and the cut of his collar and tie never came out of England.

That did something to reassure me, but as we rowed back to Bradgate my obstinate doubts would not be dismissed. The thing that worried me was the reflection that my enemies knew that I had got my knowledge from Scudder, and it was Scudder who had given me the clue to this place. If they knew that Scudder had this clue, would they not be certain to change their plans? Too much depended on their success for them to take any risks. The whole question was how much they understood about Scudder's knowledge. I had talked confidently last night about Germans always sticking to a scheme, but if they had any suspicions that I was on their track they would be fools not to cover it. I wondered if the man last night had seen that I recognized him. Somehow I did not think he had, and to that I had clung. But the whole business had never seemed so difficult as that afternoon when by all calculations I should have been rejoicing in assured success.

In the hotel I met the commander of the destroyer, to whom Scaife introduced me, and with whom I had a few words. Then I thought I would put in an hour or two watching Trafalgar Lodge.

I found a place farther up the hill, in the garden of an empty house. From there I had a full view of the court, on which two figures were having a game of tennis. One was the old man, whom I had already seen; the other was a younger fellow, wearing some club colours in the scarf round his middle. They played with tremendous zest, like two city gents who wanted hard exercise to open their pores. You couldn't conceive a more innocent spectacle. They shouted and laughed and stopped for drinks, when a maid brought out two tankards on a salver. I rubbed my eyes and asked myself if I was not the most immortal fool on earth. Mystery and darkness had hung about the men who hunted me over the Scotch moor in aeroplane and motor-car, and notably about that infernal antiquarian. It was easy enough to connect those folk with the knife that pinned Scudder to the floor, and with fell designs on the world's peace. But here were two guileless citizens taking their innocuous exercise, and soon about to go indoors to a humdrum dinner, where they would talk of market prices and the last cricket scores and the gossip of their native Surbiton. I had been making a net to catch vultures and falcons, and lo and behold! two plump thrushes had blundered into it.

Presently a third figure arrived, a young man on a bicycle, with a bag of golf-clubs slung on his back. He strolled round to the tennis lawn and was welcomed riotously by the players. Evidently they were chaffing him, and their chaff sounded horribly English. Then the plump man, mopping his brow with a silk handkerchief, announced that he must have a tub. I heard his very words – "I've got into a proper lather," he said. "This will bring down my weight and my handicap, Bob. I'll take you on tomorrow and give you a stroke a hole." You couldn't find anything much more English than that.

They all went into the house, and left me feeling a precious idiot. I had been barking up the wrong tree this time. These men might be acting; but if they were, where was their audience? They didn't know I was sitting thirty yards off in a rhododendron. It was simply impossible to believe that these three hearty fellows were anything but what they seemed – three ordinary, game-playing, suburban Englishmen, wearisome, if you like, but sordidly innocent.

And yet there were three of them; and one was old, and one was plump, and one was lean and dark; and their house chimed in with Scudder's notes; and half a mile off was lying a steam yacht with at least one German officer. I thought of Karolides lying dead and all Europe trembling on the edge of earthquake, and the men I had left behind me in London who were waiting anxiously for the events of the next hours. There was no doubt that hell was afoot somewhere. The Black Stone had won, and if it survived this June night would bank its winnings.

There seemed only one thing to do – go forward as if I had no doubts, and if I was going to make a fool of myself to do it handsomely. Never in my life have I faced a job with greater disinclination. I would rather in my then mind have walked into a den of anarchists, each with his Browning handy, or faced a charging lion with a popgun, than enter that happy home of three cheerful Englishmen and tell them that their game was up. How they would laugh at me!

But suddenly I remembered a thing I once heard in Rhodesia from old Peter Pienaar. I have quoted Peter already in this narrative. He was the best scout I ever knew, and before he had turned respectable he had been pretty often on the windy side of the law, when he had been wanted badly by the authorities. Peter once discussed with me the question of disguises, and he had a theory which struck me at the time. He said, barring absolute certainties like fingerprints, mere physical traits were very little use for identification if the fugitive really knew his business. He laughed at things like dyed hair and false beards and such childish follies. The only thing that mattered was what Peter called 'atmosphere'.

If a man could get into perfectly different surroundings from those in which he had been first observed, and – this is the important part – really play up to these surroundings and behave as if he had never been out of them, he would puzzle the cleverest detectives on earth. And he used to tell a story of how he once borrowed a black coat and went to church and shared the same hymn-book with the man that was looking for him. If that man had seen him in decent company before he would have recognized him; but he had only seen him snuffing the lights in a public-house with a revolver.

The recollection of Peter's talk gave me the first real comfort that I had had that day. Peter had been a wise old bird, and these fellows I was after were about the pick of the aviary. What if they were playing Peter's game? A fool tries to look different: a clever man looks the same and is different.

Again, there was that other maxim of Peter's which had helped me when I had been a roadman. 'If you are playing a part, you will never keep it up unless you convince yourself that you are it.' That would explain the game of tennis. Those chaps didn't need to act, they just turned a handle and passed into another life, which came as naturally to them as the first. It sounds a platitude, but Peter used to say that it was the big secret of all the famous criminals.

It was now getting on for eight o'clock, and I went back and saw Scaife to give him his instructions. I arranged with him how to place his men, and then I went for a walk, for I didn't feel up to any dinner. I went round the deserted golf-course, and then to a point on the cliffs farther north beyond the line of the villas.

On the little trim newly-made roads I met people in flannels coming back from tennis and the beach, and a coastguard from the wireless station, and donkeys and pierrots padding homewards. Out at sea in the blue dusk I saw lights appear on the *Ariadne* and on the destroyer away to the south, and beyond the Cock sands the bigger lights of steamers making for the Thames. The whole scene was so peaceful and ordinary that I got more dashed in spirits every second. It took all my resolution to stroll towards Trafalgar Lodge about half-past nine.

On the way I got a piece of solid comfort from the sight of a greyhound that was swinging along at a nursemaid's heels. He reminded me of a dog I used to have in Rhodesia, and of the time when I took him hunting with me in the Pali hills. We were after rhebok, the dun kind, and I recollected how we had followed one beast, and both he and I had clean lost it. A greyhound works by sight, and my eyes are good enough, but that buck simply leaked out of the landscape. Afterwards I found out how it managed it. Against the grey rock of the kopjes it showed no more than a crow against a thundercloud. It didn't need to run away; all it had to do was to stand still and melt into the background.

Suddenly as these memories chased across my brain I thought of my present case and applied the moral. The Black Stone didn't need to bolt. They were quietly absorbed into the landscape. I was on the right track, and I jammed that down in my mind and vowed never to forget it. The last word was with Peter Pienaar.

Scaife's men would be posted now, but there was no sign of a soul. The house stood as open as a market-place for anybody to observe. A three-foot railing separated it from the cliff road; the windows on the ground-floor were all open, and shaded lights and the low sound of voices revealed where the occupants were finishing dinner. Everything was as public and above-board as a charity bazaar. Feeling the greatest fool on earth, I opened the gate and rang the bell.

A man of my sort, who has travelled about the world in rough places, gets on perfectly well with two classes, what you may call the upper and the lower. He understands them and they understand him. I was at home with herds and tramps and roadmen, and I was sufficiently at my ease with people like Sir Walter and the men I had met the night before. I can't explain why, but it is a fact. But what fellows like me don't understand is the great comfortable, satisfied middle-class world, the folk that live in villas and suburbs. He doesn't know how they look at things, he doesn't understand their conventions, and he is as shy of them as of a black mamba. When a trim parlour-maid opened the door, I could hardly find my voice.

I asked for Mr. Appleton, and was ushered in. My plan had been to walk straight into the dining-room, and by a sudden appearance wake in the men that start of recognition which would confirm my theory. But when I found myself in that neat hall the place mastered me. There were the golf-clubs and tennis-rackets, the straw hats and caps, the rows of gloves, the sheaf of walking-sticks, which you will find in ten thousand British homes. A stack of neatly folded coats and waterproofs covered the top of an old oak chest; there was a grandfather clock ticking; and some polished brass warming-pans on the walls, and a barometer, and a print of Chiltern winning the St Leger. The place was as orthodox as an Anglican church. When the maid asked me for my name I gave it automatically, and was shown into the smoking-room, on the right side of the hall.

That room was even worse. I hadn't time to examine it, but I could see some framed group photographs above the mantelpiece, and I could have sworn they were English public school or college. I had only one glance, for I managed to pull myself together and go after the maid. But I was too late. She had already entered the dining-room and given my name to her master, and I had missed the chance of seeing how the three took it.

When I walked into the room the old man at the head of the table had risen and turned round to meet me. He was in evening dress – a short coat and black tie, as was the other, whom I called in my own mind the plump one. The third, the dark fellow, wore a blue serge suit and a soft white collar, and the colours of some club or school.

The old man's manner was perfect. "Mr. Hannay?" he said hesitatingly. "Did you wish to see me? One moment, you fellows, and I'll rejoin you. We had better go to the smoking-room."

Though I hadn't an ounce of confidence in me, I forced myself to play the game. I pulled up a chair and sat down on it.

"I think we have met before," I said, "and I guess you know my business."

The light in the room was dim, but so far as I could see their faces, they played the part of mystification very well.

"Maybe, maybe," said the old man. "I haven't a very good memory, but I'm afraid you must tell me your errand, Sir, for I really don't know it."

"Well, then," I said, and all the time I seemed to myself to be talking pure foolishness – "I have come to tell you that the game's up. I have a warrant for the arrest of you three gentlemen."

"Arrest," said the old man, and he looked really shocked. "Arrest! Good God, what for?"

"For the murder of Franklin Scudder in London on the 23rd day of last month."

"I never heard the name before," said the old man in a dazed voice.

One of the others spoke up. "That was the Portland Place murder. I read about it. Good heavens, you must be mad, Sir! Where do you come from?"

"Scotland Yard," I said.

After that for a minute there was utter silence. The old man was staring at his plate and fumbling with a nut, the very model of innocent bewilderment.

Then the plump one spoke up. He stammered a little, like a man picking his words.

"Don't get flustered, uncle," he said. "It is all a ridiculous mistake; but these things happen sometimes, and we can easily set it right. It won't be hard to prove our innocence. I can show that I was out of the country on the 23rd of May, and Bob was in a nursing home. You were in London, but you can explain what you were doing."

"Right, Percy! Of course that's easy enough. The 23rd! That was the day after Agatha's wedding. Let me see. What was I doing? I came up in the morning from Woking, and lunched at the club with Charlie Symons. Then – oh yes, I dined with the Fishmongers. I remember, for the punch didn't agree with me, and I was seedy next morning. Hang it all, there's the cigar-box I brought back from the dinner." He pointed to an object on the table, and laughed nervously.

"I think, Sir," said the young man, addressing me respectfully, "you will see you are mistaken. We want to assist the law like all Englishmen, and we don't want Scotland Yard to be making fools of themselves. That's so, uncle?"

"Certainly, Bob." The old fellow seemed to be recovering his voice. "Certainly, we'll do anything in our power to assist the authorities. But – but this is a bit too much. I can't get over it."

"How Nellie will chuckle," said the plump man. "She always said that you would die of boredom because nothing ever happened to you. And now you've got it thick and strong," and he began to laugh very pleasantly.

"By Jove, yes. Just think of it! What a story to tell at the club. Really, Mr. Hannay, I suppose I should be angry, to show my innocence, but it's too funny! I almost forgive you the fright you gave me! You looked so glum, I thought I might have been walking in my sleep and killing people."

It couldn't be acting, it was too confoundedly genuine. My heart went into my boots, and my first impulse was to apologize and clear out. But I told myself I must see it through, even though I was to be the laughing-stock of Britain. The light from the dinner-table candlesticks was not very good, and to cover my confusion I got up, walked to the door and switched on the electric light. The sudden glare made them blink, and I stood scanning the three faces.

Well, I made nothing of it. One was old and bald, one was stout, one was dark and thin. There was nothing in their appearance to prevent them being the three who had hunted me in Scotland, but there was nothing to identify them. I simply can't explain why I who, as a roadman, had looked into two pairs of eyes, and as Ned Ainslie into another pair, why I, who have a good memory and reasonable powers of observation, could find no satisfaction. They seemed exactly what they professed to be, and I could not have sworn to one of them.

There in that pleasant dining-room, with etchings on the walls, and a picture of an old lady in a bib above the mantelpiece, I could see nothing to connect them with the moorland desperadoes. There was a silver cigarette-box beside me, and I saw that it had been won by Percival Appleton, Esq., of the St Bede's Club, in a golf tournament. I had to keep a firm hold of Peter Pienaar to prevent myself bolting out of that house.

"Well," said the old man politely, "are you reassured by your scrutiny, Sir?"

I couldn't find a word.

"I hope you'll find it consistent with your duty to drop this ridiculous business. I make no complaint, but you'll see how annoying it must be to respectable people."

I shook my head.

"O Lord," said the young man. "This is a bit too thick!"

"Do you propose to march us off to the police station?" asked the plump one. "That might be the best way out of it, but I suppose you won't be content with the local branch. I have the right to ask to see your warrant, but I don't wish to cast any aspersions upon you. You are only doing your duty. But you'll admit it's horribly awkward. What do you propose to do?"

There was nothing to do except to call in my men and have them arrested, or to confess my blunder and clear out. I felt mesmerized by the whole place, by the air of obvious innocence – not innocence merely, but frank honest bewilderment and concern in the three faces.

"Oh, Peter Pienaar," I groaned inwardly, and for a moment I was very near damning myself for a fool and asking their pardon.

"Meantime I vote we have a game of bridge," said the plump one. "It will give Mr. Hannay time to think over things, and you know we have been wanting a fourth player. Do you play, Sir?"

I accepted as if it had been an ordinary invitation at the club. The whole business had mesmerized me. We went into the smoking-room where a card-table was set out, and I was offered things to smoke and drink. I took my place at the table in a kind of dream. The window was open and the moon was flooding the cliffs and sea with a great tide of yellow light. There was moonshine, too, in my head. The three had recovered their composure, and were talking easily – just the kind of slangy talk you will hear in any golf club-house. I must have cut a rum figure, sitting there knitting my brows with my eyes wandering.

My partner was the young dark one. I play a fair hand at bridge, but I must have been rank bad that night. They saw that they had got me puzzled, and that put them more than ever at their ease. I kept looking at their faces, but they conveyed nothing to me. It was not that they looked different; they were different. I clung desperately to the words of Peter Pienaar.

Then something awoke me.

The old man laid down his hand to light a cigar. He didn't pick it up at once, but sat back for a moment in his chair, with his fingers tapping on his knees.

It was the movement I remembered when I had stood before him in the moorland farm, with the pistols of his servants behind me.

A little thing, lasting only a second, and the odds were a thousand to one that I might have had my eyes on my cards at the time and missed it. But I didn't, and, in a flash, the air seemed to clear. Some shadow lifted from my brain, and I was looking at the three men with full and absolute recognition.

The clock on the mantelpiece struck ten o'clock.

The three faces seemed to change before my eyes and reveal their secrets. The young one was the murderer. Now I saw cruelty and ruthlessness, where before I had only seen good-humour. His knife, I made certain, had skewered Scudder to the floor. His kind had put the bullet in Karolides.

The plump man's features seemed to dislimn, and form again, as I looked at them. He hadn't a face, only a hundred masks that he could assume when he pleased. That chap must have been a superb actor. Perhaps he had been Lord Alloa of the night before; perhaps not; it didn't matter. I wondered if he was the fellow who had first tracked Scudder, and left his card on him. Scudder had said he lisped, and I could imagine how the adoption of a lisp might add terror.

But the old man was the pick of the lot. He was sheer brain, icy, cool, calculating, as ruthless as a steam hammer. Now that my eyes were opened I wondered where I had seen the benevolence. His jaw was like chilled steel, and his eyes had the inhuman luminosity of a bird's. I went on playing, and every second a greater hate welled up in my heart. It almost choked me, and I couldn't answer when my partner spoke. Only a little longer could I endure their company.

"Whew! Bob! Look at the time," said the old man. "You'd better think about catching your train. Bob's got to go to town tonight," he added, turning to me. The voice rang now as false as hell. I looked at the clock, and it was nearly half-past ten.

"I am afraid he must put off his journey," I said.

"Oh, damn," said the young man. "I thought you had dropped that rot. I've simply got to go. You can have my address, and I'll give any security you like."

"No," I said, "you must stay."

At that I think they must have realized that the game was desperate. Their only chance had been to convince me that I was playing the fool, and that had failed. But the old man spoke again.

"I'll go bail for my nephew. That ought to content you, Mr. Hannay." Was it fancy, or did I detect some halt in the smoothness of that voice?

There must have been, for as I glanced at him, his eyelids fell in that hawk-like hood which fear had stamped on my memory.

I blew my whistle.

In an instant the lights were out. A pair of strong arms gripped me round the waist, covering the pockets in which a man might be expected to carry a pistol.

"*Schnell, Franz,*" cried a voice, "*Das Boot, das Boot!*" As it spoke I saw two of my fellows emerge on the moonlit lawn.

The young dark man leapt for the window, was through it, and over the low fence before a hand could touch him. I grappled the old chap, and the room seemed to fill with figures. I saw the plump one collared, but my eyes were all for the out-of-doors, where Franz sped on over the road towards the railed entrance to the beach stairs. One man followed him, but he had no chance. The gate of the stairs locked behind the fugitive, and I stood staring, with my hands on the old boy's throat, for such a time as a man might take to descend those steps to the sea.

Suddenly my prisoner broke from me and flung himself on the wall. There was a click as if a lever had been pulled. Then came a low rumbling far, far below the ground, and through the window I saw a cloud of chalky dust pouring out of the shaft of the stairway.

Someone switched on the light.

The old man was looking at me with blazing eyes.

"He is safe," he cried. "You cannot follow in time.... He is gone.... He has triumphed ... *Der Schwarze Stein ist in der Siegeskrone.*"

There was more in those eyes than any common triumph. They had been hooded like a bird of prey, and now they flamed with a hawk's pride. A white fanatic heat burned in them, and I realized for the first time the terrible thing I had been up against. This man was more than a spy; in his foul way he had been a patriot.

As the handcuffs clinked on his wrists I said my last word to him.

"I hope Franz will bear his triumph well. I ought to tell you that the *Ariadne* for the last hour has been in our hands."

Three weeks later, as all the world knows, we went to war. I joined the New Army the first week, and owing to my Matabele experience got a captain's commission straight off. But I had done my best service, I think, before I put on khaki.

The Man Who Was Thursday
Chapters I–VIII
G.K. Chesterton

Chapter I
The Two Poets of Saffron Park

THE SUBURB of Saffron Park lay on the sunset side of London, as red and ragged as a cloud of sunset. It was built of a bright brick throughout; its skyline was fantastic, and even its ground plan was wild. It had been the outburst of a speculative builder, faintly tinged with art, who called its architecture sometimes Elizabethan and sometimes Queen Anne, apparently under the impression that the two sovereigns were identical. It was described with some justice as an artistic colony, though it never in any definable way produced any art. But although its pretensions to be an intellectual centre were a little vague, its pretensions to be a pleasant place were quite indisputable. The stranger who looked for the first time at the quaint red houses could only think how very oddly shaped the people must be who could fit in to them. Nor when he met the people was he disappointed in this respect. The place was not only pleasant, but perfect, if once he could regard it not as a deception but rather as a dream. Even if the people were not 'artists,' the whole was nevertheless artistic. That young man with the long, auburn hair and the impudent face – that young man was not really a poet; but surely he was a poem. That old gentleman with the wild, white beard and the wild, white hat – that venerable humbug was not really a philosopher; but at least he was the cause of philosophy in others. That scientific gentleman with the bald, egg-like head and the bare, bird-like neck had no real right to the airs of science that he assumed. He had not discovered anything new in biology; but what biological creature could he have discovered more singular than himself? Thus, and thus only, the whole place had properly to be regarded; it had to be considered not so much as a workshop for artists, but as a frail but finished work of art. A man who stepped into its social atmosphere felt as if he had stepped into a written comedy.

More especially this attractive unreality fell upon it about nightfall, when the extravagant roofs were dark against the afterglow and the whole insane village seemed as separate as a drifting cloud. This again was more strongly true of the many nights of local festivity, when the little gardens were often illuminated, and the big Chinese lanterns glowed in the dwarfish trees like some fierce and monstrous fruit. And this was strongest of all on one particular evening, still vaguely remembered in the locality, of which the auburn-haired poet was the hero. It was not by any means the only evening of which he was the hero. On many nights those passing by his little back garden might hear his high, didactic voice laying down the law to men and particularly to women. The attitude of women in such cases was indeed one of the paradoxes of the place. Most of the women were of the kind vaguely called emancipated, and professed some protest against male supremacy. Yet these new women would always pay to a man the extravagant compliment which no ordinary woman ever pays to him, that of listening while he is talking. And Mr. Lucian Gregory, the red-haired poet, was really (in some sense) a man worth listening to, even if one only laughed at the end of it. He put the old cant of the lawlessness of art and the art of lawlessness with a certain impudent freshness which gave at least a momentary pleasure. He was helped in some degree by the arresting oddity of his appearance, which he worked, as the phrase goes, for all it was worth. His dark red hair parted in the middle was literally like a woman's, and curved into the slow curls of a virgin in a pre-Raphaelite picture. From within this almost saintly oval, however, his face projected suddenly broad and brutal, the chin carried forward with a look of cockney contempt. This combination at once tickled and terrified the nerves of a neurotic population. He seemed like a walking blasphemy, a blend of the angel and the ape.

This particular evening, if it is remembered for nothing else, will be remembered in that place for its strange sunset. It looked like the end of the world. All the heaven seemed covered with a quite vivid and palpable plumage; you could only say that the sky was full of feathers, and of feathers that almost brushed the face. Across the great part of the dome they were grey, with the strangest tints of violet and mauve and an unnatural pink or pale green; but towards the west the whole grew past description, transparent and passionate, and the last red-hot plumes of it covered up the sun like something too good to be seen. The whole was so close about the earth, as to express nothing but a violent secrecy. The very empyrean seemed to be a secret. It expressed that splendid smallness which is the soul of local patriotism. The very sky seemed small.

I say that there are some inhabitants who may remember the evening if only by that oppressive sky. There are others who may remember it because it marked the first appearance in the place of the second poet of Saffron Park. For a long time the red-haired revolutionary had reigned without a rival; it was upon the night of the sunset that his solitude suddenly ended. The new poet, who introduced himself by the name of Gabriel Syme was a very mild-looking mortal, with a fair, pointed beard and faint, yellow hair. But an impression grew that he was less meek than he looked. He signalised his entrance by differing with the established poet, Gregory, upon the whole nature of poetry. He said that he (Syme) was poet of law, a poet of order; nay, he said he was a poet of respectability. So all the Saffron Parkers looked at him as if he had that moment fallen out of that impossible sky.

In fact, Mr. Lucian Gregory, the anarchic poet, connected the two events.

"It may well be," he said, in his sudden lyrical manner, "it may well be on such a night of clouds and cruel colours that there is brought forth upon the earth such a portent as a respectable poet. You say you are a poet of law; I say you are a contradiction in terms. I only wonder there were not comets and earthquakes on the night you appeared in this garden."

The man with the meek blue eyes and the pale, pointed beard endured these thunders with a certain submissive solemnity. The third party of the group, Gregory's sister Rosamond, who had her brother's braids of red hair, but a kindlier face underneath them, laughed with such mixture of admiration and disapproval as she gave commonly to the family oracle.

Gregory resumed in high oratorical good humour.

"An artist is identical with an anarchist," he cried. "You might transpose the words anywhere. An anarchist is an artist. The man who throws a bomb is an artist, because he prefers a great moment to everything. He sees how much more valuable is one burst of blazing light, one peal of perfect thunder, than the mere common bodies of a few shapeless policemen. An artist disregards all governments, abolishes all conventions. The poet delights in disorder only. If it were not so, the most poetical thing in the world would be the Underground Railway."

"So it is," said Mr. Syme.

"Nonsense!" said Gregory, who was very rational when anyone else attempted paradox. "Why do all the clerks and navvies in the railway trains look so sad and tired, so very sad and tired? I will tell you. It is because they know that the train is going right. It is because they know that whatever place they have taken a ticket for that place they will reach. It is because after they have passed Sloane Square they know that the next station must be Victoria, and nothing but Victoria. Oh, their wild rapture! Oh, their eyes like stars and their souls again in Eden, if the next station were unaccountably Baker Street!"

"It is you who are unpoetical," replied the poet Syme. "If what you say of clerks is true, they can only be as prosaic as your poetry. The rare, strange thing is to hit the mark; the gross, obvious thing is to miss it. We feel it is epical when man with one wild arrow strikes a distant bird. Is it not also epical when man with one wild engine strikes a distant station? Chaos is dull; because in chaos the train might indeed go anywhere, to Baker Street or to Bagdad. But man is a magician, and his whole magic is in this, that he does say Victoria, and lo! it is Victoria. No, take your books of mere poetry and prose; let me read a time table, with tears of pride. Take your Byron, who commemorates the defeats of man; give me Bradshaw, who commemorates his victories. Give me Bradshaw, I say!"

"Must you go?" inquired Gregory sarcastically.

"I tell you," went on Syme with passion, "that every time a train comes in I feel that it has broken past batteries of besiegers, and that man has won a battle against chaos. You say contemptuously that when one has left Sloane Square one must come to Victoria. I say that one might do a thousand things instead, and that whenever I really come there I have the sense of hairbreadth escape. And when I hear the guard shout out the word 'Victoria,' it is not an unmeaning word. It is to me the cry of a herald announcing conquest. It is to me indeed 'Victoria'; it is the victory of Adam."

Gregory wagged his heavy, red head with a slow and sad smile.

"And even then," he said, "we poets always ask the question, 'And what is Victoria now that you have got there?' You think Victoria is like the New Jerusalem. We know that the New Jerusalem will only be like Victoria. Yes, the poet will be discontented even in the streets of heaven. The poet is always in revolt."

"There again," said Syme irritably, "what is there poetical about being in revolt? You might as well say that it is poetical to be sea-sick. Being sick is a revolt. Both being sick and being rebellious may be the wholesome thing on certain desperate occasions; but I'm hanged if I can see why they are poetical. Revolt in the abstract is – revolting. It's mere vomiting."

The girl winced for a flash at the unpleasant word, but Syme was too hot to heed her.

"It is things going right," he cried, "that is poetical! Our digestions, for instance, going sacredly and silently right, that is the foundation of all poetry. Yes, the most poetical thing, more poetical than the flowers, more poetical than the stars – the most poetical thing in the world is not being sick."

"Really," said Gregory superciliously, "the examples you choose –".

"I beg your pardon," said Syme grimly, "I forgot we had abolished all conventions."

For the first time a red patch appeared on Gregory's forehead.

"You don't expect me," he said, "to revolutionise society on this lawn?"

Syme looked straight into his eyes and smiled sweetly.

"No, I don't," he said; "but I suppose that if you were serious about your anarchism, that is exactly what you would do."

Gregory's big bull's eyes blinked suddenly like those of an angry lion, and one could almost fancy that his red mane rose.

"Don't you think, then," he said in a dangerous voice, "that I am serious about my anarchism?"

"I beg your pardon?" said Syme.

"Am I not serious about my anarchism?" cried Gregory, with knotted fists.

"My dear fellow!" said Syme, and strolled away.

With surprise, but with a curious pleasure, he found Rosamond Gregory still in his company.

"Mr. Syme," she said, "do the people who talk like you and my brother often mean what they say? Do you mean what you say now?"

Syme smiled.

"Do you?" he asked.

"What do you mean?" asked the girl, with grave eyes.

"My dear Miss Gregory," said Syme gently, "there are many kinds of sincerity and insincerity. When you say 'thank you' for the salt, do you mean what you say? No. When you say 'the world is round,' do you mean what you say? No. It is true, but you don't mean it. Now, sometimes a man like your brother really finds a thing he does mean. It may be only a half-truth, quarter-truth, tenth-truth; but then he says more than he means – from sheer force of meaning it."

She was looking at him from under level brows; her face was grave and open, and there had fallen upon it the shadow of that unreasoning responsibility which is at the bottom of the most frivolous woman, the maternal watch which is as old as the world.

"Is he really an anarchist, then?" she asked.

"Only in that sense I speak of," replied Syme; "or if you prefer it, in that nonsense."

She drew her broad brows together and said abruptly –

"He wouldn't really use – bombs or that sort of thing?"

Syme broke into a great laugh, that seemed too large for his slight and somewhat dandified figure.

"Good Lord, no!" he said, "that has to be done anonymously."

And at that the corners of her own mouth broke into a smile, and she thought with a simultaneous pleasure of Gregory's absurdity and of his safety.

Syme strolled with her to a seat in the corner of the garden, and continued to pour out his opinions. For he was a sincere man, and in spite of his superficial airs and graces, at root a humble one. And it is always the humble man who talks too much; the proud man watches himself too closely. He defended respectability with violence and exaggeration. He grew passionate in his praise of tidiness and propriety. All the time there was a smell of lilac all round him. Once he heard very faintly in some distant street a barrel-organ begin to play, and it seemed to him that his heroic words were moving to a tiny tune from under or beyond the world.

He stared and talked at the girl's red hair and amused face for what seemed to be a few minutes; and then, feeling that the groups in such a place should mix, rose to his feet. To his astonishment, he discovered the whole garden empty. Everyone had gone long ago, and he went himself with a rather hurried apology. He left with a sense of champagne in his head, which he could not afterwards explain. In the wild events which were to follow this girl had no part at all; he never saw her again until all his tale was over. And yet, in some indescribable way, she kept recurring like a motive in music through all his mad adventures afterwards, and the glory of her strange hair ran like a red thread through those dark and ill-drawn tapestries of the night. For what followed was so improbable, that it might well have been a dream.

When Syme went out into the starlit street, he found it for the moment empty. Then he realised (in some odd way) that the silence was rather a living silence than a dead one. Directly outside the door stood a street lamp, whose gleam gilded the leaves of the tree that bent out over the fence behind him. About a foot from the lamp-post stood a figure almost as rigid and motionless as the lamp-post itself. The tall hat and long frock coat were black; the face, in an abrupt shadow, was almost as dark. Only a fringe of fiery hair against the light, and also something aggressive in the attitude, proclaimed that it was the poet Gregory. He had something of the look of a masked bravo waiting sword in hand for his foe.

He made a sort of doubtful salute, which Syme somewhat more formally returned.

"I was waiting for you," said Gregory. "Might I have a moment's conversation?"

"Certainly. About what?" asked Syme in a sort of weak wonder.

Gregory struck out with his stick at the lamp-post, and then at the tree. "About this and this," he cried; "about order and anarchy. There is your precious order, that lean, iron lamp, ugly and barren; and there is anarchy, rich, living, reproducing itself – there is anarchy, splendid in green and gold."

"All the same," replied Syme patiently, "just at present you only see the tree by the light of the lamp. I wonder when you would ever see the lamp by the light of the tree." Then after a pause he said, "But may I ask if you have been standing out here in the dark only to resume our little argument?"

"No," cried out Gregory, in a voice that rang down the street, "I did not stand here to resume our argument, but to end it for ever."

The silence fell again, and Syme, though he understood nothing, listened instinctively for something serious. Gregory began in a smooth voice and with a rather bewildering smile.

"Mr. Syme," he said, "this evening you succeeded in doing something rather remarkable. You did something to me that no man born of woman has ever succeeded in doing before."

"Indeed!"

"Now I remember," resumed Gregory reflectively, "one other person succeeded in doing it. The captain of a penny steamer (if I remember correctly) at Southend. You have irritated me."

"I am very sorry," replied Syme with gravity.

"I am afraid my fury and your insult are too shocking to be wiped out even with an apology," said Gregory very calmly. "No duel could wipe it out. If I struck you dead I could not wipe it out. There is only one way by which that insult can be erased, and that way I choose. I am going, at the possible sacrifice of my life and honour, to prove to you that you were wrong in what you said."

"In what I said?"

"You said I was not serious about being an anarchist."

"There are degrees of seriousness," replied Syme. "I have never doubted that you were perfectly sincere in this sense, that you thought what you said well worth saying, that you thought a paradox might wake men up to a neglected truth."

Gregory stared at him steadily and painfully.

"And in no other sense," he asked, "you think me serious? You think me a flaneur who lets fall occasional truths. You do not think that in a deeper, a more deadly sense, I am serious."

Syme struck his stick violently on the stones of the road.

"Serious!" he cried. "Good Lord! Is this street serious? Are these damned Chinese lanterns serious? Is the whole caboodle serious? One comes here and talks a pack of bosh, and perhaps some sense as well, but I should think very little of a man who didn't keep something in the background of his life that was more serious than all this talking – something more serious, whether it was religion or only drink."

"Very well," said Gregory, his face darkening, "you shall see something more serious than either drink or religion."

Syme stood waiting with his usual air of mildness until Gregory again opened his lips.

"You spoke just now of having a religion. Is it really true that you have one?"

"Oh," said Syme with a beaming smile, "we are all Catholics now."

"Then may I ask you to swear by whatever gods or saints your religion involves that you will not reveal what I am now going to tell you to any son of Adam, and especially not to the police? Will you swear that! If you will take upon yourself this awful abnegation if you will consent to burden your soul with a vow that you should never make and a knowledge you should never dream about, I will promise you in return –"

"You will promise me in return?" inquired Syme, as the other paused.

"I will promise you a very entertaining evening." Syme suddenly took off his hat.

"Your offer," he said, "is far too idiotic to be declined. You say that a poet is always an anarchist. I disagree; but I hope at least that he is always a sportsman. Permit me, here and now, to swear as a Christian, and promise as a good comrade and a fellow-artist, that I will not report anything of this, whatever it is, to the police. And now, in the name of Colney Hatch, what is it?"

"I think," said Gregory, with placid irrelevancy, "that we will call a cab."

He gave two long whistles, and a hansom came rattling down the road. The two got into it in silence. Gregory gave through the trap the address of an obscure public-house on the Chiswick bank of the river. The cab whisked itself away again, and in it these two fantastics quitted their fantastic town.

Chapter II
The Secret of Gabriel Syme

THE CAB pulled up before a particularly dreary and greasy beershop, into which Gregory rapidly conducted his companion. They seated themselves in a close and dim sort of bar-parlour, at a stained wooden table with one wooden leg. The room was so small and dark, that very little could be seen of the attendant who was summoned, beyond a vague and dark impression of something bulky and bearded.

"Will you take a little supper?" asked Gregory politely. "The pâté de foie gras is not good here, but I can recommend the game."

Syme received the remark with stolidity, imagining it to be a joke. Accepting the vein of humour, he said, with a well-bred indifference –

"Oh, bring me some lobster mayonnaise."

To his indescribable astonishment, the man only said "Certainly, sir!" and went away apparently to get it.

"What will you drink?" resumed Gregory, with the same careless yet apologetic air. "I shall only have a creme de menthe myself; I have dined. But the champagne can really be trusted. Do let me start you with a half-bottle of Pommery at least?"

"Thank you!" said the motionless Syme. "You are very good."

His further attempts at conversation, somewhat disorganised in themselves, were cut short finally as by a thunderbolt by the actual appearance of the lobster. Syme tasted it, and found it particularly good. Then he suddenly began to eat with great rapidity and appetite.

"Excuse me if I enjoy myself rather obviously!" he said to Gregory, smiling. "I don't often have the luck to have a dream like this. It is new to me for a nightmare to lead to a lobster. It is commonly the other way."

"You are not asleep, I assure you," said Gregory. "You are, on the contrary, close to the most actual and rousing moment of your existence. Ah, here comes your champagne! I admit that there may be a slight disproportion, let us say, between the inner arrangements of this excellent hotel and its simple and unpretentious exterior. But that is all our modesty. We are the most modest men that ever lived on earth."

"And who are we?" asked Syme, emptying his champagne glass.

"It is quite simple," replied Gregory. "We are the serious anarchists, in whom you do not believe."

"Oh!" said Syme shortly. "You do yourselves well in drinks."

"Yes, we are serious about everything," answered Gregory.

Then after a pause he added –

"If in a few moments this table begins to turn round a little, don't put it down to your inroads into the champagne. I don't wish you to do yourself an injustice."

"Well, if I am not drunk, I am mad," replied Syme with perfect calm; "but I trust I can behave like a gentleman in either condition. May I smoke?"

"Certainly!" said Gregory, producing a cigar-case. "Try one of mine."

Syme took the cigar, clipped the end off with a cigar-cutter out of his waistcoat pocket, put it in his mouth, lit it slowly, and let out a long cloud of smoke. It is not a little to his credit that he performed these rites with so much composure, for almost before he had begun them the table at which he sat had begun to revolve, first slowly, and then rapidly, as if at an insane seance.

"You must not mind it," said Gregory; "it's a kind of screw."

"Quite so," said Syme placidly, "a kind of screw. How simple that is!"

The next moment the smoke of his cigar, which had been wavering across the room in snaky twists, went straight up as if from a factory chimney, and the two, with their chairs and table, shot down through the floor as if the earth had swallowed them. They went rattling down a kind of roaring chimney as rapidly as a lift cut loose, and they came with an abrupt bump to the bottom. But when Gregory threw open a pair of doors and let in a red subterranean light, Syme was still smoking with one leg thrown over the other, and had not turned a yellow hair.

Gregory led him down a low, vaulted passage, at the end of which was the red light. It was an enormous crimson lantern, nearly as big as a fireplace, fixed over a small but heavy iron door. In the door there was a sort of hatchway or grating, and on this Gregory struck five times. A heavy voice with a foreign accent asked him who he was. To this he gave the more or less unexpected reply, "Mr. Joseph Chamberlain." The heavy hinges began to move; it was obviously some kind of password.

Inside the doorway the passage gleamed as if it were lined with a network of steel. On a second glance, Syme saw that the glittering pattern was really made up of ranks and ranks of rifles and revolvers, closely packed or interlocked.

"I must ask you to forgive me all these formalities," said Gregory; "we have to be very strict here."

"Oh, don't apologise," said Syme. "I know your passion for law and order," and he stepped into the passage lined with the steel weapons. With his long, fair hair and rather foppish frock-coat, he looked a singularly frail and fanciful figure as he walked down that shining avenue of death.

They passed through several such passages, and came out at last into a queer steel chamber with curved walls, almost spherical in shape, but presenting, with its tiers of benches, something of the appearance of a scientific lecture-theatre. There were no rifles or pistols in this apartment, but round the walls of it were hung more dubious and dreadful shapes, things that looked like the bulbs of iron plants, or the eggs of iron birds. They were bombs, and the very room itself seemed like the inside of a bomb. Syme knocked his cigar ash off against the wall, and went in.

"And now, my dear Mr. Syme," said Gregory, throwing himself in an expansive manner on the bench under the largest bomb, "now we are quite cosy, so let us talk properly. Now no human words can give you any notion of why I brought you here. It was one of those quite arbitrary emotions, like jumping off a cliff or falling in love. Suffice it to say that you were an inexpressibly irritating fellow, and, to do you justice, you are still. I would break twenty oaths of secrecy for the pleasure of taking you down a peg. That way you have of lighting a cigar would make a priest break the seal of confession. Well, you said that you were quite certain I was not a serious anarchist. Does this place strike you as being serious?"

"It does seem to have a moral under all its gaiety," assented Syme; "but may I ask you two questions? You need not fear to give me information, because, as you remember, you very wisely extorted from me a promise not to tell the police, a promise I shall certainly keep. So it is in mere curiosity that I make my queries. First of all, what is it really all about? What is it you object to? You want to abolish Government?"

"To abolish God!" said Gregory, opening the eyes of a fanatic. "We do not only want to upset a few despotisms and police regulations; that sort of anarchism does exist, but it is a mere branch of the Nonconformists. We dig deeper and we blow you higher. We wish to deny all those arbitrary distinctions of vice and virtue, honour and treachery, upon which mere rebels base themselves. The silly sentimentalists of the French Revolution talked of the Rights of Man! We hate Rights as we hate Wrongs. We have abolished Right and Wrong."

"And Right and Left," said Syme with a simple eagerness, "I hope you will abolish them too. They are much more troublesome to me."

"You spoke of a second question," snapped Gregory.

"With pleasure," resumed Syme. "In all your present acts and surroundings there is a scientific attempt at secrecy. I have an aunt who lived over a shop, but this is the first time I have found people living from preference under a public-house. You have a heavy iron door. You cannot pass it without submitting to the humiliation of calling yourself Mr. Chamberlain. You surround yourself with steel instruments which make the place, if I may say so, more impressive than homelike. May I ask why, after taking all this trouble to barricade yourselves in the bowels of the earth, you then parade your whole secret by talking about anarchism to every silly woman in Saffron Park?"

Gregory smiled.

"The answer is simple," he said. "I told you I was a serious anarchist, and you did not believe me. Nor do they believe me. Unless I took them into this infernal room they would not believe me."

Syme smoked thoughtfully, and looked at him with interest. Gregory went on.

"The history of the thing might amuse you," he said. "When first I became one of the New Anarchists I tried all kinds of respectable disguises. I dressed up as a bishop. I read up all about bishops in our anarchist pamphlets, in Superstition the Vampire and Priests of Prey. I certainly understood from them that bishops are strange and terrible old men keeping a cruel secret from mankind. I was misinformed. When on my first appearing in episcopal gaiters in a drawing-room I cried out in a voice of thunder, 'Down! Down! Presumptuous human reason!' they found out in some way that I was not a bishop at all. I was nabbed at once. Then I made up as a millionaire; but I defended Capital with so much intelligence that a fool could see that I was quite poor. Then I tried being a major. Now I am a humanitarian myself, but I have, I hope, enough intellectual breadth to understand the position of those who, like Nietzsche, admire violence – the proud, mad war of Nature and all that, you know. I threw myself into the major. I drew my sword and waved it constantly. I called out 'Blood!' abstractedly, like a man calling for wine. I often said, 'Let the weak perish; it is the Law.' Well, well, it seems majors don't do this. I was nabbed again. At last I went in despair to the President of the Central Anarchist Council, who is the greatest man in Europe."

"What is his name?" asked Syme.

"You would not know it," answered Gregory. "That is his greatness. Caesar and Napoleon put all their genius into being heard of, and they were heard of. He puts all his genius into not being heard of, and he is not heard of. But you cannot be for five minutes in the room with him without feeling that Caesar and Napoleon would have been children in his hands."

He was silent and even pale for a moment, and then resumed –

"But whenever he gives advice it is always something as startling as an epigram, and yet as practical as the Bank of England. I said to him, 'What disguise will hide me from the world? What can I find more respectable than bishops and majors?' He looked at me with his large but indecipherable face. 'You want a safe disguise, do you? You want a dress which will guarantee you harmless; a dress in which no one would ever look for a bomb?' I nodded. He suddenly lifted his lion's voice. 'Why, then, dress up as an anarchist, you fool!' he roared so that the room shook. 'Nobody will ever expect you to do anything dangerous then.' And he turned his broad back on me without another word. I took his advice, and have never regretted it. I preached blood and murder to those women day and night, and – by God! – they would let me wheel their perambulators."

Syme sat watching him with some respect in his large, blue eyes.

"You took me in," he said. "It is really a smart dodge."

Then after a pause he added –

"What do you call this tremendous President of yours?"

"We generally call him Sunday," replied Gregory with simplicity. "You see, there are seven members of the Central Anarchist Council, and they are named after days of the week. He is called Sunday, by some of his admirers Bloody Sunday. It is curious you should mention the matter, because the very night you have dropped in (if I may so express it) is the night on which our London branch, which assembles in this room, has to elect its own deputy to fill a vacancy in the Council. The gentleman who has for some time past played, with propriety and general applause, the difficult part of Thursday, has died quite suddenly. Consequently, we have called a meeting this very evening to elect a successor."

He got to his feet and strolled across the room with a sort of smiling embarrassment.

"I feel somehow as if you were my mother, Syme," he continued casually. "I feel that I can confide anything to you, as you have promised to tell nobody. In fact, I will confide to you something that I would not say in so many words to the anarchists who will be coming to the room in about ten minutes. We shall, of course, go through a form of election; but I don't mind telling you that it is practically certain what the result will be." He looked down for a moment modestly. "It is almost a settled thing that I am to be Thursday."

"My dear fellow," said Syme heartily, "I congratulate you. A great career!"

Gregory smiled in deprecation, and walked across the room, talking rapidly.

"As a matter of fact, everything is ready for me on this table," he said, "and the ceremony will probably be the shortest possible."

Syme also strolled across to the table, and found lying across it a walking-stick, which turned out on examination to be a sword-stick, a large Colt's revolver, a sandwich case, and a formidable flask of brandy. Over the chair, beside the table, was thrown a heavy-looking cape or cloak.

"I have only to get the form of election finished," continued Gregory with animation, "then I snatch up this cloak and stick, stuff these other things into my pocket, step out of a door in this cavern, which opens on the river, where there is a steam-tug already waiting for me, and then – then – oh, the wild joy of being Thursday!" And he clasped his hands.

Syme, who had sat down once more with his usual insolent languor, got to his feet with an unusual air of hesitation.

"Why is it," he asked vaguely, "that I think you are quite a decent fellow? Why do I positively like you, Gregory?" He paused a moment, and then added with a sort of fresh curiosity, "Is it because you are such an ass?"

There was a thoughtful silence again, and then he cried out –

"Well, damn it all! This is the funniest situation I have ever been in in my life, and I am going to act accordingly. Gregory, I gave you a promise before I came into this place. That promise I would keep under red-hot pincers. Would you give me, for my own safety, a little promise of the same kind?"

"A promise?" asked Gregory, wondering.

"Yes," said Syme very seriously, "a promise. I swore before God that I would not tell your secret to the police. Will you swear by Humanity, or whatever beastly thing you believe in, that you will not tell my secret to the anarchists?"

"Your secret?" asked the staring Gregory. "Have you got a secret?"

"Yes," said Syme, "I have a secret." Then after a pause, "Will you swear?"

Gregory glared at him gravely for a few moments, and then said abruptly –

"You must have bewitched me, but I feel a furious curiosity about you. Yes, I will swear not to tell the anarchists anything you tell me. But look sharp, for they will be here in a couple of minutes."

Syme rose slowly to his feet and thrust his long, white hands into his long, grey trousers' pockets. Almost as he did so there came five knocks on the outer grating, proclaiming the arrival of the first of the conspirators.

"Well," said Syme slowly, "I don't know how to tell you the truth more shortly than by saying that your expedient of dressing up as an aimless poet is not confined to you or your President. We have known the dodge for some time at Scotland Yard."

Gregory tried to spring up straight, but he swayed thrice.

"What do you say?" he asked in an inhuman voice.

"Yes," said Syme simply, "I am a police detective. But I think I hear your friends coming."

From the doorway there came a murmur of "Mr. Joseph Chamberlain." It was repeated twice and thrice, and then thirty times, and the crowd of Joseph Chamberlains (a solemn thought) could be heard trampling down the corridor.

Chapter III
The Man Who Was Thursday

BEFORE ONE of the fresh faces could appear at the doorway, Gregory's stunned surprise had fallen from him. He was beside the table with a bound, and a noise in his throat like a wild beast. He caught up the Colt's revolver and took aim at Syme. Syme did not flinch, but he put up a pale and polite hand.

"Don't be such a silly man," he said, with the effeminate dignity of a curate. "Don't you see it's not necessary? Don't you see that we're both in the same boat? Yes, and jolly sea-sick."

Gregory could not speak, but he could not fire either, and he looked his question.

"Don't you see we've checkmated each other?" cried Syme. "I can't tell the police you are an anarchist. You can't tell the anarchists I'm a policeman. I can only watch you, knowing what you are; you can only watch me, knowing what I am. In short, it's a lonely, intellectual duel, my head against yours. I'm a policeman deprived of the help of the police. You, my poor fellow, are an anarchist deprived of the help of that law and organisation which is so essential to anarchy. The one solitary difference is in your favour. You are not surrounded by inquisitive policemen; I am surrounded by inquisitive anarchists. I cannot betray you, but I might betray myself. Come, come! Wait and see me betray myself. I shall do it so nicely."

Gregory put the pistol slowly down, still staring at Syme as if he were a sea-monster.

"I don't believe in immortality," he said at last, "but if, after all this, you were to break your word, God would make a hell only for you, to howl in for ever."

"I shall not break my word," said Syme sternly, "nor will you break yours. Here are your friends."

The mass of the anarchists entered the room heavily, with a slouching and somewhat weary gait; but one little man, with a black beard and glasses – a man somewhat of the type of Mr. Tim Healy – detached himself, and bustled forward with some papers in his hand.

"Comrade Gregory," he said, "I suppose this man is a delegate?"

Gregory, taken by surprise, looked down and muttered the name of Syme; but Syme replied almost pertly –

"I am glad to see that your gate is well enough guarded to make it hard for anyone to be here who was not a delegate."

The brow of the little man with the black beard was, however, still contracted with something like suspicion.

"What branch do you represent?" he asked sharply.

"I should hardly call it a branch," said Syme, laughing; "I should call it at the very least a root."

"What do you mean?"

"The fact is," said Syme serenely, "the truth is I am a Sabbatarian. I have been specially sent here to see that you show a due observance of Sunday."

The little man dropped one of his papers, and a flicker of fear went over all the faces of the group. Evidently the awful President, whose name was Sunday, did sometimes send down such irregular ambassadors to such branch meetings.

"Well, comrade," said the man with the papers after a pause, "I suppose we'd better give you a seat in the meeting?"

"If you ask my advice as a friend," said Syme with severe benevolence, "I think you'd better."

When Gregory heard the dangerous dialogue end, with a sudden safety for his rival, he rose abruptly and paced the floor in painful thought. He was, indeed, in an agony of diplomacy. It was clear that Syme's inspired impudence was likely to bring him out of all merely accidental dilemmas. Little was to be hoped from them. He could not himself betray Syme, partly from honour, but partly also because, if he betrayed him and for some reason failed to destroy him, the Syme who escaped would be a Syme freed from all obligation of secrecy, a Syme who would simply walk to the nearest police station. After all, it was only one night's discussion, and only one detective who would know of it. He would let out as little as possible of their plans that night, and then let Syme go, and chance it.

He strode across to the group of anarchists, which was already distributing itself along the benches.

"I think it is time we began," he said; "the steam-tug is waiting on the river already. I move that Comrade Buttons takes the chair."

This being approved by a show of hands, the little man with the papers slipped into the presidential seat.

"Comrades," he began, as sharp as a pistol-shot, "our meeting tonight is important, though it need not be long. This branch has always had the honour of electing Thursdays for the Central European Council. We have elected many and splendid Thursdays. We all lament the sad decease of the heroic worker who occupied the post until last week. As you know, his services to the cause were considerable. He organised the great dynamite coup of Brighton which, under happier circumstances, ought to have killed everybody on the pier. As you also know, his death was as self-denying as his life, for he died through his faith in a hygienic mixture of chalk and water as a substitute for milk, which beverage he regarded as barbaric, and as involving cruelty to the cow. Cruelty, or anything approaching to cruelty, revolted him always. But it is not to acclaim his virtues that we are met, but for a harder task. It is difficult properly to praise his qualities, but it is more difficult to replace them. Upon you, comrades, it devolves this evening to choose out of the company present the man who shall be Thursday. If any comrade suggests a name I will put it to the vote. If no comrade suggests a name, I can only tell myself that that dear dynamiter, who is gone from us, has carried into the unknowable abysses the last secret of his virtue and his innocence."

There was a stir of almost inaudible applause, such as is sometimes heard in church. Then a large old man, with a long and venerable white beard, perhaps the only real working-man present, rose lumberingly and said –

"I move that Comrade Gregory be elected Thursday," and sat lumberingly down again.

"Does anyone second?" asked the chairman.

A little man with a velvet coat and pointed beard seconded.

"Before I put the matter to the vote," said the chairman, "I will call on Comrade Gregory to make a statement."

Gregory rose amid a great rumble of applause. His face was deadly pale, so that by contrast his queer red hair looked almost scarlet. But he was smiling and altogether at ease. He had made up his mind, and he saw his best policy quite plain in front of him like a white road. His best chance was to make a softened and ambiguous speech, such as would leave on the detective's mind the impression that the anarchist brotherhood was a very mild affair after all. He believed in his own literary power, his capacity for suggesting fine shades and picking perfect words. He thought that with care he could succeed, in spite of all the people around him, in conveying an impression of the institution, subtly and delicately false. Syme had once thought that anarchists, under all their bravado, were only playing the fool. Could he not now, in the hour of peril, make Syme think so again?

"Comrades," began Gregory, in a low but penetrating voice, "it is not necessary for me to tell you what is my policy, for it is your policy also. Our belief has been slandered, it has been disfigured, it has been utterly confused and concealed, but it has never been altered. Those who talk about anarchism and its dangers go everywhere and anywhere to get their information, except to us, except to the fountain head. They learn about anarchists from sixpenny novels; they learn about anarchists from tradesmen's newspapers; they learn about anarchists from Ally Sloper's Half-Holiday and the Sporting Times. They never learn about anarchists from anarchists. We have no chance of denying the mountainous slanders which are heaped upon our heads from one end of Europe to another. The man who has always heard that we are walking plagues has never heard our reply. I know that he will not hear it tonight, though my passion were to rend the roof. For it is deep, deep under the earth that the persecuted are permitted to assemble, as the Christians assembled in the Catacombs. But if, by some incredible accident, there were here tonight a man who all his life had thus immensely misunderstood us, I would put this question to him: 'When those Christians met in those Catacombs, what sort of moral reputation had they in the streets above? What tales were told of their atrocities by one educated Roman to another? Suppose' (I would say to him), 'suppose that we are only repeating that still mysterious paradox of history. Suppose we seem as shocking as the Christians because we are really as harmless as the Christians. Suppose we seem as mad as the Christians because we are really as meek.'"

The applause that had greeted the opening sentences had been gradually growing fainter, and at the last word it stopped suddenly. In the abrupt silence, the man with the velvet jacket said, in a high, squeaky voice –

"I'm not meek!"

"Comrade Witherspoon tells us," resumed Gregory, "that he is not meek. Ah, how little he knows himself! His words are, indeed, extravagant; his appearance is ferocious, and even (to an ordinary taste) unattractive. But only the eye of a friendship as deep and delicate as mine can perceive the deep foundation of solid meekness which lies at the base of him, too deep even for himself to see. I repeat, we are the true early Christians, only that we come too late. We are simple, as they revere simple – look at Comrade Witherspoon. We are modest, as they were modest – look at me. We are merciful –"

"No, no!" called out Mr. Witherspoon with the velvet jacket.

"I say we are merciful," repeated Gregory furiously, "as the early Christians were merciful. Yet this did not prevent their being accused of eating human flesh. We do not eat human flesh –"

"Shame!" cried Witherspoon. "Why not?"

"Comrade Witherspoon," said Gregory, with a feverish gaiety, "is anxious to know why nobody eats him (laughter). In our society, at any rate, which loves him sincerely, which is founded upon love –"

"No, no!" said Witherspoon, "down with love."

"Which is founded upon love," repeated Gregory, grinding his teeth, "there will be no difficulty about the aims which we shall pursue as a body, or which I should pursue were I chosen as the representative of that body. Superbly careless of the slanders that represent us as assassins and enemies of human society, we shall pursue with moral courage and quiet intellectual pressure, the permanent ideals of brotherhood and simplicity."

Gregory resumed his seat and passed his hand across his forehead. The silence was sudden and awkward, but the chairman rose like an automaton, and said in a colourless voice –

"Does anyone oppose the election of Comrade Gregory?"

The assembly seemed vague and sub-consciously disappointed, and Comrade Witherspoon moved restlessly on his seat and muttered in his thick beard. By the sheer rush of routine, however, the motion would have been put and carried. But as the chairman was opening his mouth to put it, Syme sprang to his feet and said in a small and quiet voice –

"Yes, Mr. Chairman, I oppose."

The most effective fact in oratory is an unexpected change in the voice. Mr. Gabriel Syme evidently understood oratory. Having said these first formal words in a moderated tone and with a brief simplicity, he made his next word ring and volley in the vault as if one of the guns had gone off.

"Comrades!" he cried, in a voice that made every man jump out of his boots, "have we come here for this? Do we live underground like rats in order to listen to talk like this? This is talk we might listen to while eating buns at a Sunday School treat. Do we line these walls with weapons and bar that door with death lest anyone should come and hear Comrade Gregory saying to us, 'Be good, and you will be happy,' 'Honesty is the best policy,' and 'Virtue is its own reward'? There was not a word in Comrade Gregory's address to which a curate could not have listened with pleasure (hear, hear). But I am not a curate (loud cheers), and I did not listen to it with pleasure (renewed cheers). The man who is fitted to make a good curate is not fitted to make a resolute, forcible, and efficient Thursday (hear, hear)."

"Comrade Gregory has told us, in only too apologetic a tone, that we are not the enemies of society. But I say that we are the enemies of society, and so much the worse for society. We are the enemies of society, for society is the enemy of humanity, its oldest and its most pitiless enemy (hear, hear). Comrade Gregory has told us (apologetically again) that we are not murderers. There I agree. We are not murderers, we are executioners (cheers)."

Ever since Syme had risen Gregory had sat staring at him, his face idiotic with astonishment. Now in the pause his lips of clay parted, and he said, with an automatic and lifeless distinctness –

"You damnable hypocrite!"

Syme looked straight into those frightful eyes with his own pale blue ones, and said with dignity –

"Comrade Gregory accuses me of hypocrisy. He knows as well as I do that I am keeping all my engagements and doing nothing but my duty. I do not mince words. I do not pretend to. I say that Comrade Gregory is unfit to be Thursday for all his amiable qualities. He is unfit to be Thursday because of his amiable qualities. We do not want the Supreme Council of Anarchy infected with a maudlin mercy (hear, hear). This is no time for ceremonial politeness, neither is it a time for ceremonial modesty. I set myself against Comrade Gregory as I would set myself against all the Governments of Europe, because the anarchist who has given himself to anarchy has forgotten modesty as much as he has forgotten pride (cheers). I am not a man at all. I am a cause (renewed cheers). I set myself against Comrade Gregory as impersonally and as calmly as I should choose one pistol rather than another out of that rack upon the wall; and I say that rather than have Gregory and his milk-and-water methods on the Supreme Council, I would offer myself for election –"

His sentence was drowned in a deafening cataract of applause. The faces, that had grown fiercer and fiercer with approval as his tirade grew more and more uncompromising, were now distorted with grins of anticipation or cloven with delighted cries. At the moment when he announced himself as ready to stand for the post of Thursday, a roar of excitement and assent broke forth, and became uncontrollable, and at the same moment Gregory sprang to his feet, with foam upon his mouth, and shouted against the shouting.

"Stop, you blasted madmen!" he cried, at the top of a voice that tore his throat. "Stop, you –"

But louder than Gregory's shouting and louder than the roar of the room came the voice of Syme, still speaking in a peal of pitiless thunder –

"I do not go to the Council to rebut that slander that calls us murderers; I go to earn it (loud and prolonged cheering). To the priest who says these men are the enemies of religion, to the judge who says these men are the enemies of law, to the fat parliamentarian who says these men are the enemies of order and public decency, to all these I will reply, 'You are false kings, but you are true prophets. I am come to destroy you, and to fulfil your prophecies.'"

The heavy clamour gradually died away, but before it had ceased Witherspoon had jumped to his feet, his hair and beard all on end, and had said –

"I move, as an amendment, that Comrade Syme be appointed to the post."

"Stop all this, I tell you!" cried Gregory, with frantic face and hands. "Stop it, it is all –"

The voice of the chairman clove his speech with a cold accent.

"Does anyone second this amendment?" he said. A tall, tired man, with melancholy eyes and an American chin beard, was observed on the back bench to be slowly rising to his feet. Gregory had been screaming for some time past; now there was a change in his accent, more shocking than any scream. "I end all this!" he said, in a voice as heavy as stone.

"This man cannot be elected. He is a –"

"Yes," said Syme, quite motionless, "what is he?" Gregory's mouth worked twice without sound; then slowly the blood began to crawl back into his dead face. "He is a man quite inexperienced in our work," he said, and sat down abruptly.

Before he had done so, the long, lean man with the American beard was again upon his feet, and was repeating in a high American monotone –

"I beg to second the election of Comrade Syme."

"The amendment will, as usual, be put first," said Mr. Buttons, the chairman, with mechanical rapidity.

"The question is that Comrade Syme –"

Gregory had again sprung to his feet, panting and passionate.

"Comrades," he cried out, "I am not a madman."

"Oh, oh!" said Mr. Witherspoon.

"I am not a madman," reiterated Gregory, with a frightful sincerity which for a moment staggered the room, "but I give you a counsel which you can call mad if you like. No, I will not call it a counsel, for I can give you no reason for it. I will call it a command. Call it a mad command, but act upon it. Strike, but hear me! Kill me, but obey me! Do not elect this man." Truth is so terrible, even in fetters, that for a moment Syme's slender and insane victory swayed like a reed. But you could not have guessed it from Syme's bleak blue eyes. He merely began –

"Comrade Gregory commands –"

Then the spell was snapped, and one anarchist called out to Gregory –

"Who are you? You are not Sunday;" and another anarchist added in a heavier voice, "And you are not Thursday."

"Comrades," cried Gregory, in a voice like that of a martyr who in an ecstacy of pain has passed beyond pain, "it is nothing to me whether you detest me as a tyrant or detest me as a slave. If you will not take my command, accept my degradation. I kneel to you. I throw myself at your feet. I implore you. Do not elect this man."

"Comrade Gregory," said the chairman after a painful pause, "this is really not quite dignified."

For the first time in the proceedings there was for a few seconds a real silence. Then Gregory fell back in his seat, a pale wreck of a man, and the chairman repeated, like a piece of clock-work suddenly started again –

"The question is that Comrade Syme be elected to the post of Thursday on the General Council."

The roar rose like the sea, the hands rose like a forest, and three minutes afterwards Mr. Gabriel Syme, of the Secret Police Service, was elected to the post of Thursday on the General Council of the Anarchists of Europe.

Everyone in the room seemed to feel the tug waiting on the river, the sword-stick and the revolver, waiting on the table. The instant the election was ended and irrevocable, and Syme had received the paper proving his election, they all sprang to their feet, and the fiery groups moved and mixed in the room. Syme found himself, somehow or other, face to face with Gregory, who still regarded him with a stare of stunned hatred. They were silent for many minutes.

"You are a devil!" said Gregory at last.

"And you are a gentleman," said Syme with gravity.

"It was you that entrapped me," began Gregory, shaking from head to foot, "entrapped me into –"

"Talk sense," said Syme shortly. "Into what sort of devils' parliament have you entrapped me, if it comes to that? You made me swear before I made you. Perhaps we are both doing what we think right. But what we think right is so damned different that there can be nothing between us in the way of concession. There is nothing possible between us but honour and death," and he pulled the great cloak about his shoulders and picked up the flask from the table.

"The boat is quite ready," said Mr. Buttons, bustling up. "Be good enough to step this way."

With a gesture that revealed the shop-walker, he led Syme down a short, iron-bound passage, the still agonised Gregory following feverishly at their heels. At the end of the passage was a door, which Buttons opened sharply, showing a sudden blue and silver picture of the moonlit river, that looked like a scene in a theatre. Close to the opening lay a dark, dwarfish steam-launch, like a baby dragon with one red eye.

Almost in the act of stepping on board, Gabriel Syme turned to the gaping Gregory.

"You have kept your word," he said gently, with his face in shadow. "You are a man of honour, and I thank you. You have kept it even down to a small particular. There was one special thing you promised me at the beginning of the affair, and which you have certainly given me by the end of it."

"What do you mean?" cried the chaotic Gregory. "What did I promise you?"

"A very entertaining evening," said Syme, and he made a military salute with the sword-stick as the steamboat slid away.

Chapter IV
The Tale of a Detective

GABRIEL SYME was not merely a detective who pretended to be a poet; he was really a poet who had become a detective. Nor was his hatred of anarchy hypocritical. He was one of those who are driven early in life into too conservative an attitude by the bewildering folly of most revolutionists. He had not attained it by any tame tradition.

His respectability was spontaneous and sudden, a rebellion against rebellion. He came of a family of cranks, in which all the oldest people had all the newest notions. One of his uncles always walked about without a hat, and another had made an unsuccessful attempt to walk about with a hat and nothing else. His father cultivated art and self-realisation; his mother went in for simplicity and hygiene. Hence the child, during his tenderer years, was wholly unacquainted with any drink between the extremes of absinth and cocoa, of both of which he had a healthy dislike. The more his mother preached a more than Puritan abstinence the more did his father expand into a more than pagan latitude; and by the time the former had come to enforcing vegetarianism, the latter had pretty well reached the point of defending cannibalism.

Being surrounded with every conceivable kind of revolt from infancy, Gabriel had to revolt into something, so he revolted into the only thing left – sanity. But there was just enough in him of the blood of these fanatics to make even his protest for common sense a little too fierce to be sensible. His hatred of modern lawlessness had been crowned also by an accident. It happened that he was walking in a side street at the instant of a dynamite outrage. He had been blind and deaf for a moment, and then seen, the smoke clearing, the broken windows and the bleeding faces. After that he went about as usual – quiet, courteous, rather gentle; but there was a spot on his mind that was not sane. He did not regard anarchists, as most of us do, as a handful of morbid men, combining ignorance with intellectualism. He regarded them as a huge and pitiless peril, like a Chinese invasion.

He poured perpetually into newspapers and their waste-paper baskets a torrent of tales, verses and violent articles, warning men of this deluge of barbaric denial. But he seemed to be getting no nearer his enemy, and, what was worse, no nearer a living. As he paced the Thames embankment, bitterly biting a cheap cigar and brooding on the advance of Anarchy, there was no anarchist with a bomb in his pocket so savage or so solitary as he. Indeed, he always felt that Government stood alone and desperate, with its back to the wall. He was too quixotic to have cared for it otherwise.

He walked on the Embankment once under a dark red sunset. The red river reflected the red sky, and they both reflected his anger. The sky, indeed, was so swarthy, and the light on the river relatively so lurid, that the water almost seemed of fiercer flame than the sunset it mirrored. It looked like a stream of literal fire winding under the vast caverns of a subterranean country.

Syme was shabby in those days. He wore an old-fashioned black chimney-pot hat; he was wrapped in a yet more old-fashioned cloak, black and ragged; and the combination gave him the look of the early villains in Dickens and Bulwer Lytton. Also his yellow beard and hair were more unkempt and leonine than when they appeared long afterwards, cut and pointed, on the lawns of Saffron Park. A long, lean, black cigar, bought in Soho for twopence, stood out from between his tightened teeth, and altogether he looked a very satisfactory specimen of the anarchists upon whom he had vowed a holy war. Perhaps this was why a policeman on the Embankment spoke to him, and said "Good evening."

Syme, at a crisis of his morbid fears for humanity, seemed stung by the mere stolidity of the automatic official, a mere bulk of blue in the twilight.

"A good evening is it?" he said sharply. "You fellows would call the end of the world a good evening. Look at that bloody red sun and that bloody river! I tell you that if that were literally human blood, spilt and shining, you would still be standing here as solid as ever, looking out for some poor harmless tramp whom you could move on. You policemen are cruel to the poor, but I could forgive you even your cruelty if it were not for your calm."

"If we are calm," replied the policeman, "it is the calm of organised resistance."

"Eh?" said Syme, staring.

"The soldier must be calm in the thick of the battle," pursued the policeman. "The composure of an army is the anger of a nation."

"Good God, the Board Schools!" said Syme. "Is this undenominational education?"

"No," said the policeman sadly, "I never had any of those advantages. The Board Schools came after my time. What education I had was very rough and old-fashioned, I am afraid."

"Where did you have it?" asked Syme, wondering.

"Oh, at Harrow," said the policeman

The class sympathies which, false as they are, are the truest things in so many men, broke out of Syme before he could control them.

"But, good Lord, man," he said, "you oughtn't to be a policeman!"

The policeman sighed and shook his head.

"I know," he said solemnly, "I know I am not worthy."

"But why did you join the police?" asked Syme with rude curiosity.

"For much the same reason that you abused the police," replied the other. "I found that there was a special opening in the service for those whose fears for humanity were concerned rather with the aberrations of the scientific intellect than with the normal and excusable, though excessive, outbreaks of the human will. I trust I make myself clear."

"If you mean that you make your opinion clear," said Syme, "I suppose you do. But as for making yourself clear, it is the last thing you do. How comes a man like you to be talking philosophy in a blue helmet on the Thames embankment?"

"You have evidently not heard of the latest development in our police system," replied the other. "I am not surprised at it. We are keeping it rather dark from the educated class, because that class contains most of our enemies. But you seem to be exactly in the right frame of mind. I think you might almost join us."

"Join you in what?" asked Syme.

"I will tell you," said the policeman slowly. "This is the situation: the head of one of our departments, one of the most celebrated detectives in Europe, has long been of opinion that a purely intellectual conspiracy would soon threaten the very existence of civilisation. He is certain that the scientific and artistic worlds are silently bound in a crusade against the Family and the State. He has, therefore, formed a special corps of policemen, policemen who are also philosophers. It is their business to watch the beginnings of this conspiracy, not merely in a criminal but in a controversial sense. I am a democrat myself, and I am fully aware of the value of the ordinary man in matters of ordinary valour or virtue. But it would obviously be undesirable to employ the common policeman in an investigation which is also a heresy hunt."

Syme's eyes were bright with a sympathetic curiosity.

"What do you do, then?" he said.

"The work of the philosophical policeman," replied the man in blue, "is at once bolder and more subtle than that of the ordinary detective. The ordinary detective goes to pot-houses to arrest thieves; we go to artistic tea-parties to detect pessimists.

The ordinary detective discovers from a ledger or a diary that a crime has been committed. We discover from a book of sonnets that a crime will be committed. We have to trace the origin of those dreadful thoughts that drive men on at last to intellectual fanaticism and intellectual crime. We were only just in time to prevent the assassination at Hartlepool, and that was entirely due to the fact that our Mr. Wilks (a smart young fellow) thoroughly understood a triolet."

"Do you mean," asked Syme, "that there is really as much connection between crime and the modern intellect as all that?"

"You are not sufficiently democratic," answered the policeman, "but you were right when you said just now that our ordinary treatment of the poor criminal was a pretty brutal business. I tell you I am sometimes sick of my trade when I see how perpetually it means merely a war upon the ignorant and the desperate. But this new movement of ours is a very different affair. We deny the snobbish English assumption that the uneducated are the dangerous criminals. We remember the Roman Emperors. We remember the great poisoning princes of the Renaissance. We say that the dangerous criminal is the educated criminal. We say that the most dangerous criminal now is the entirely lawless modern philosopher. Compared to him, burglars and bigamists are essentially moral men; my heart goes out to them. They accept the essential ideal of man; they merely seek it wrongly. Thieves respect property. They merely wish the property to become their property that they may more perfectly respect it. But philosophers dislike property as property; they wish to destroy the very idea of personal possession. Bigamists respect marriage, or they would not go through the highly ceremonial and even ritualistic formality of bigamy. But philosophers despise marriage as marriage. Murderers respect human life; they merely wish to attain a greater fulness of human life in themselves by the sacrifice of what seems to them to be lesser lives. But philosophers hate life itself, their own as much as other people's."

Syme struck his hands together.

"How true that is," he cried. "I have felt it from my boyhood, but never could state the verbal antithesis. The common criminal is a bad man, but at least he is, as it were, a conditional good man. He says that if only a certain obstacle be removed – say a wealthy uncle – he is then prepared to accept the universe and to praise God. He is a reformer, but not an anarchist. He wishes to cleanse the edifice, but not to destroy it. But the evil philosopher is not trying to alter things, but to annihilate them. Yes, the modern world has retained all those parts of police work which are really oppressive and ignominious, the harrying of the poor, the spying upon the unfortunate. It has given up its more dignified work, the punishment of powerful traitors in the State and powerful heresiarchs in the Church. The moderns say we must not punish heretics. My only doubt is whether we have a right to punish anybody else."

"But this is absurd!" cried the policeman, clasping his hands with an excitement uncommon in persons of his figure and costume, "but it is intolerable! I don't know what you're doing, but you're wasting your life. You must, you shall, join our special army against anarchy. Their armies are on our frontiers. Their bolt is ready to fall. A moment more, and you may lose the glory of working with us, perhaps the glory of dying with the last heroes of the world."

"It is a chance not to be missed, certainly," assented Syme, "but still I do not quite understand. I know as well as anybody that the modern world is full of lawless little men and mad little movements. But, beastly as they are, they generally have the one merit of disagreeing with each other. How can you talk of their leading one army or hurling one bolt. What is this anarchy?"

"Do not confuse it," replied the constable, "with those chance dynamite outbreaks from Russia or from Ireland, which are really the outbreaks of oppressed, if mistaken, men. This is a vast philosophic movement, consisting of an outer and an inner ring. You might even call the outer ring the laity and the inner ring the priesthood. I prefer to call the outer ring the innocent section, the inner ring the supremely guilty section. The outer ring – the main mass of their supporters – are merely anarchists; that is, men who believe that rules and formulas have destroyed human happiness. They believe that all the evil results of human crime are the results of the system that has called it crime. They do not believe that the crime creates the punishment. They believe that the punishment has created the crime. They believe that if a man seduced seven women he would naturally walk away as blameless as the flowers of spring. They believe that if a man picked a pocket he would naturally feel exquisitely good. These I call the innocent section."

"Oh!" said Syme.

"Naturally, therefore, these people talk about 'a happy time coming'; 'the paradise of the future'; 'mankind freed from the bondage of vice and the bondage of virtue,' and so on. And so also the men of the inner circle speak – the sacred priesthood. They also speak to applauding crowds of the happiness of the future, and of mankind freed at last. But in their mouths" – and the policeman lowered his voice – "in their mouths these happy phrases have a horrible meaning. They are under no illusions; they are too intellectual to think that man upon this earth can ever be quite free of original sin and the struggle. And they mean death. When they say that mankind shall be free at last, they mean that mankind shall commit suicide. When they talk of a paradise without right or wrong, they mean the grave.

"They have but two objects, to destroy first humanity and then themselves. That is why they throw bombs instead of firing pistols. The innocent rank and file are disappointed because the bomb has not killed the king; but the high-priesthood are happy because it has killed somebody."

"How can I join you?" asked Syme, with a sort of passion.

"I know for a fact that there is a vacancy at the moment," said the policeman, "as I have the honour to be somewhat in the confidence of the chief of whom I have spoken. You should really come and see him. Or rather, I should not say see him, nobody ever sees him; but you can talk to him if you like."

"Telephone?" inquired Syme, with interest.

"No," said the policeman placidly, "he has a fancy for always sitting in a pitch-dark room. He says it makes his thoughts brighter. Do come along."

Somewhat dazed and considerably excited, Syme allowed himself to be led to a side-door in the long row of buildings of Scotland Yard. Almost before he knew what he was doing, he had been passed through the hands of about four intermediate officials, and was suddenly shown into a room, the abrupt blackness of which startled him like a blaze of light. It was not the ordinary darkness, in which forms can be faintly traced; it was like going suddenly stone-blind.

"Are you the new recruit?" asked a heavy voice.

And in some strange way, though there was not the shadow of a shape in the gloom, Syme knew two things: first, that it came from a man of massive stature; and second, that the man had his back to him.

"Are you the new recruit?" said the invisible chief, who seemed to have heard all about it. "All right. You are engaged."

Syme, quite swept off his feet, made a feeble fight against this irrevocable phrase.

"I really have no experience," he began.

"No one has any experience," said the other, "of the Battle of Armageddon."

"But I am really unfit –"

"You are willing, that is enough," said the unknown.

"Well, really," said Syme, "I don't know any profession of which mere willingness is the final test."

"I do," said the other – "martyrs. I am condemning you to death. Good day."

Thus it was that when Gabriel Syme came out again into the crimson light of evening, in his shabby black hat and shabby, lawless cloak, he came out a member of the New Detective Corps for the frustration of the great conspiracy. Acting under the advice of his friend the policeman (who was professionally inclined to neatness), he trimmed his hair and beard, bought a good hat, clad himself in an exquisite summer suit of light blue-grey, with a pale yellow flower in the button-hole, and, in short, became that elegant and rather insupportable person whom Gregory had first encountered in the little garden of Saffron Park. Before he finally left the police premises his friend provided him with a small blue card, on which was written, 'The Last Crusade,' and a number, the sign of his official authority. He put this carefully in his upper waistcoat pocket, lit a cigarette, and went forth to track and fight the enemy in all the drawing-rooms of London. Where his adventure ultimately led him we have already seen. At about half-past one on a February night he found himself steaming in a small tug up the silent Thames, armed with swordstick and revolver, the duly elected Thursday of the Central Council of Anarchists.

When Syme stepped out on to the steam-tug he had a singular sensation of stepping out into something entirely new; not merely into the landscape of a new land, but even into the landscape of a new planet. This was mainly due to the insane yet solid decision of that evening, though partly also to an entire change in the weather and the sky since he entered the little tavern some two hours before. Every trace of the passionate plumage of the cloudy sunset had been swept away, and a naked moon stood in a naked sky. The moon was so strong and full that (by a paradox often to be noticed) it seemed like a weaker sun. It gave, not the sense of bright moonshine, but rather of a dead daylight.

Over the whole landscape lay a luminous and unnatural discoloration, as of that disastrous twilight which Milton spoke of as shed by the sun in eclipse; so that Syme fell easily into his first thought, that he was actually on some other and emptier planet, which circled round some sadder star. But the more he felt this glittering desolation in the moonlit land, the more his own chivalric folly glowed in the night like a great fire. Even the common things he carried with him – the food and the brandy and the loaded pistol – took on exactly that concrete and material poetry which a child feels when he takes a gun upon a journey or a bun with him to bed. The sword-stick and the brandy-flask, though in themselves only the tools of morbid conspirators, became the expressions of his own more healthy romance. The sword-stick became almost the sword of chivalry, and the brandy the wine of the stirrup-cup. For even the most dehumanised modern fantasies depend on some older and simpler figure; the adventures may be mad, but the adventurer must be sane. The dragon without St. George would not even be grotesque. So this inhuman landscape was only imaginative by the presence of a man really human. To Syme's exaggerative mind the bright, bleak houses and terraces by the Thames looked as empty as the mountains of the moon. But even the moon is only poetical because there is a man in the moon.

The tug was worked by two men, and with much toil went comparatively slowly. The clear moon that had lit up Chiswick had gone down by the time that they passed Battersea, and when they came under the enormous bulk of Westminster day had already begun to break. It broke like the splitting of great bars of lead, showing bars of silver; and these had brightened like white fire when the tug, changing its onward course, turned inward to a large landing stage rather beyond Charing Cross.

The great stones of the Embankment seemed equally dark and gigantic as Syme looked up at them. They were big and black against the huge white dawn. They made him feel that he was landing on the colossal steps of some Egyptian palace; and, indeed, the thing suited his mood, for he was, in his own mind, mounting to attack the solid thrones of horrible and heathen kings. He leapt out of the boat on to one slimy step, and stood, a dark and slender figure, amid the enormous masonry. The two men in the tug put her off again and turned up stream. They had never spoken a word.

Chapter V
The Feast of Fear

AT FIRST the large stone stair seemed to Syme as deserted as a pyramid; but before he reached the top he had realised that there was a man leaning over the parapet of the Embankment and looking out across the river. As a figure he was quite conventional, clad in a silk hat and frock-coat of the more formal type of fashion; he had a red flower in his buttonhole. As Syme drew nearer to him step by step, he did not even move a hair; and Syme could come close enough to notice even in the dim, pale morning light that his face was long, pale and intellectual, and ended in a small triangular tuft of dark beard at the very point of the chin, all else being clean-shaven. This scrap of hair almost seemed a mere oversight; the rest of the face was of the type that is best shaven – clear-cut, ascetic, and in its way noble. Syme drew closer and closer, noting all this, and still the figure did not stir.

At first an instinct had told Syme that this was the man whom he was meant to meet. Then, seeing that the man made no sign, he had concluded that he was not. And now again he had come back to a certainty that the man had something to do with his mad adventure. For the man remained more still than would have been natural if a stranger had come so close. He was as motionless as a wax-work, and got on the nerves somewhat in the same way. Syme looked again and again at the pale, dignified and delicate face, and the face still looked blankly across the river. Then he took out of his pocket the note from Buttons proving his election, and put it before that sad and beautiful face. Then the man smiled, and his smile was a shock, for it was all on one side, going up in the right cheek and down in the left.

There was nothing, rationally speaking, to scare anyone about this. Many people have this nervous trick of a crooked smile, and in many it is even attractive. But in all

Syme's circumstances, with the dark dawn and the deadly errand and the loneliness on the great dripping stones, there was something unnerving in it.

There was the silent river and the silent man, a man of even classic face. And there was the last nightmare touch that his smile suddenly went wrong.

The spasm of smile was instantaneous, and the man's face dropped at once into its harmonious melancholy. He spoke without further explanation or inquiry, like a man speaking to an old colleague.

"If we walk up towards Leicester Square," he said, "we shall just be in time for breakfast. Sunday always insists on an early breakfast. Have you had any sleep?"

"No," said Syme.

"Nor have I," answered the man in an ordinary tone. "I shall try to get to bed after breakfast."

He spoke with casual civility, but in an utterly dead voice that contradicted the fanaticism of his face. It seemed almost as if all friendly words were to him lifeless conveniences, and that his only life was hate. After a pause the man spoke again.

"Of course, the Secretary of the branch told you everything that can be told. But the one thing that can never be told is the last notion of the President, for his notions grow like a tropical forest. So in case you don't know, I'd better tell you that he is carrying out his notion of concealing ourselves by not concealing ourselves to the most extraordinary lengths just now. Originally, of course, we met in a cell underground, just as your branch does. Then Sunday made us take a private room at an ordinary restaurant. He said that if you didn't seem to be hiding nobody hunted you out. Well, he is the only man on earth, I know; but sometimes I really think that his huge brain is going a little mad in its old age. For now we flaunt ourselves before the public. We have our breakfast on a balcony – on a balcony, if you please – overlooking Leicester Square."

"And what do the people say?" asked Syme.

"It's quite simple what they say," answered his guide.

"They say we are a lot of jolly gentlemen who pretend they are anarchists."

"It seems to me a very clever idea," said Syme.

"Clever! God blast your impudence! Clever!" cried out the other in a sudden, shrill voice which was as startling and discordant as his crooked smile. "When you've seen Sunday for a split second you'll leave off calling him clever."

With this they emerged out of a narrow street, and saw the early sunlight filling Leicester Square. It will never be known, I suppose, why this square itself should look so alien and in some ways so continental. It will never be known whether it was the foreign look that attracted the foreigners or the foreigners who gave it the foreign look. But on this particular morning the effect seemed singularly bright and clear. Between the open square and the sunlit leaves and the statue and the Saracenic outlines of the Alhambra, it looked the replica of some French or even Spanish public place. And this effect increased in Syme the sensation, which in many shapes he had had through the whole adventure, the eerie sensation of having strayed into a new world. As a fact, he had bought bad cigars round Leicester Square ever since he was a boy. But as he turned that corner, and saw the trees and the Moorish cupolas, he could have sworn that he was turning into an unknown Place de something or other in some foreign town.

At one corner of the square there projected a kind of angle of a prosperous but quiet hotel, the bulk of which belonged to a street behind. In the wall there was one large French window, probably the window of a large coffee-room; and outside this window, almost literally overhanging the square, was a formidably buttressed balcony, big enough to contain a dining-table. In fact, it did contain a dining-table, or more strictly a breakfast-table; and round the breakfast-table, glowing in the sunlight and evident to the street, were a group of noisy and talkative men, all dressed in the insolence of fashion, with white waistcoats and expensive button-holes. Some of their jokes could almost be heard across the square. Then the grave Secretary gave his unnatural smile, and Syme knew that this boisterous breakfast party was the secret conclave of the European Dynamiters.

Then, as Syme continued to stare at them, he saw something that he had not seen before. He had not seen it literally because it was too large to see. At the nearest end of the balcony, blocking up a great part of the perspective, was the back of a great mountain of a man. When Syme had seen him, his first thought was that the weight of him must break down the balcony of stone. His vastness did not lie only in the fact that he was abnormally tall and quite incredibly fat. This man was planned enormously in his original proportions, like a statue carved deliberately as colossal. His head, crowned with white hair, as seen from behind looked bigger than a head ought to be. The ears that stood out from it looked larger than human ears. He was enlarged terribly to scale; and this sense of size was so staggering, that when Syme saw him all the other figures seemed quite suddenly to dwindle and become dwarfish. They were still sitting there as before with their flowers and frock-coats, but now it looked as if the big man was entertaining five children to tea.

As Syme and the guide approached the side door of the hotel, a waiter came out smiling with every tooth in his head.

"The gentlemen are up there, sare," he said. "They do talk and they do laugh at what they talk. They do say they will throw bombs at ze king."

And the waiter hurried away with a napkin over his arm, much pleased with the singular frivolity of the gentlemen upstairs.

The two men mounted the stairs in silence.

Syme had never thought of asking whether the monstrous man who almost filled and broke the balcony was the great President of whom the others stood in awe. He knew it was so, with an unaccountable but instantaneous certainty. Syme, indeed, was one of those men who are open to all the more nameless psychological influences in a degree a little dangerous to mental health. Utterly devoid of fear in physical dangers, he was a great deal too sensitive to the smell of spiritual evil. Twice already that night little unmeaning things had peeped out at him almost pruriently, and given him a sense of drawing nearer and nearer to the head-quarters of hell. And this sense became overpowering as he drew nearer to the great President.

The form it took was a childish and yet hateful fancy. As he walked across the inner room towards the balcony, the large face of Sunday grew larger and larger; and Syme was gripped with a fear that when he was quite close the face would be too big to be possible, and that he would scream aloud. He remembered that as a child he would not look at the mask of Memnon in the British Museum, because it was a face, and so large.

By an effort, braver than that of leaping over a cliff, he went to an empty seat at the breakfast-table and sat down. The men greeted him with good-humoured raillery as if they had always known him. He sobered himself a little by looking at their conventional coats and solid, shining coffee-pot; then he looked again at Sunday. His face was very large, but it was still possible to humanity.

In the presence of the President the whole company looked sufficiently commonplace; nothing about them caught the eye at first, except that by the President's caprice they had been dressed up with a festive respectability, which gave the meal the look of a wedding breakfast. One man indeed stood out at even a superficial glance. He at least was the common or garden Dynamiter. He wore, indeed, the high white collar and satin tie that were the uniform of the occasion; but out of this collar there sprang a head quite unmanageable and quite unmistakable, a bewildering bush of brown hair and beard that almost obscured the eyes like those of a Skye terrier. But the eyes did look out of the tangle, and they were the sad eyes of some Russian serf. The effect of this figure was not terrible like that of the President, but it had every diablerie that can come from the utterly grotesque. If out of that stiff tie and collar there had come abruptly the head of a cat or a dog, it could not have been a more idiotic contrast.

The man's name, it seemed, was Gogol; he was a Pole, and in this circle of days he was called Tuesday. His soul and speech were incurably tragic; he could not force himself to play the prosperous and frivolous part demanded of him by President Sunday. And, indeed, when Syme came in the President, with that daring disregard of public suspicion which was his policy, was actually chaffing Gogol upon his inability to assume conventional graces.

"Our friend Tuesday," said the President in a deep voice at once of quietude and volume, "our friend Tuesday doesn't seem to grasp the idea. He dresses up like a gentleman, but he seems to be too great a soul to behave like one. He insists on the ways of the stage conspirator. Now if a gentleman goes about London in a top hat and a frock-coat, no one need know that he is an anarchist. But if a gentleman puts on a top hat and a frock-coat, and then goes about on his hands and knees – well, he may attract attention. That's what Brother Gogol does. He goes about on his hands and knees with such inexhaustible diplomacy, that by this time he finds it quite difficult to walk upright."

"I am not good at goncealment," said Gogol sulkily, with a thick foreign accent; "I am not ashamed of the cause."

"Yes you are, my boy, and so is the cause of you," said the President good-naturedly. "You hide as much as anybody; but you can't do it, you see, you're such an ass! You try to combine two inconsistent methods. When a householder finds a man under his bed, he will probably pause to note the circumstance. But if he finds a man under his bed in a top hat, you will agree with me, my dear Tuesday, that he is not likely even to forget it. Now when you were found under Admiral Biffin's bed –"

"I am not good at deception," said Tuesday gloomily, flushing.

"Right, my boy, right," said the President with a ponderous heartiness, "you aren't good at anything."

While this stream of conversation continued, Syme was looking more steadily at the men around him. As he did so, he gradually felt all his sense of something spiritually queer return.

He had thought at first that they were all of common stature and costume, with the evident exception of the hairy Gogol. But as he looked at the others, he began to see in each of them exactly what he had seen in the man by the river, a demoniac detail somewhere. That lop-sided laugh, which would suddenly disfigure the fine face of his original guide, was typical of all these types. Each man had something about him, perceived perhaps at the tenth or twentieth glance, which was not normal, and which seemed hardly human. The only metaphor he could think of was this, that they all looked as men of fashion and presence would look, with the additional twist given in a false and curved mirror.

Only the individual examples will express this half-concealed eccentricity. Syme's original cicerone bore the title of Monday; he was the Secretary of the Council, and his twisted smile was regarded with more terror than anything, except the President's horrible, happy laughter. But now that Syme had more space and light to observe him, there were other touches. His fine face was so emaciated, that Syme thought it must be wasted with some disease; yet somehow the very distress of his dark eyes denied this. It was no physical ill that troubled him. His eyes were alive with intellectual torture, as if pure thought was pain.

He was typical of each of the tribe; each man was subtly and differently wrong. Next to him sat Tuesday, the tousle-headed Gogol, a man more obviously mad. Next was Wednesday, a certain Marquis de St. Eustache, a sufficiently characteristic figure. The first few glances found nothing unusual about him, except that he was the only man at table who wore the fashionable clothes as if they were really his own. He had a black French beard cut square and a black English frock-coat cut even squarer. But Syme, sensitive to such things, felt somehow that the man carried a rich atmosphere with him, a rich atmosphere that suffocated. It reminded one irrationally of drowsy odours and of dying lamps in the darker poems of Byron and Poe. With this went a sense of his being clad, not in lighter colours, but in softer materials; his black seemed richer and warmer than the black shades about him, as if it were compounded of profound colour. His black coat looked as if it were only black by being too dense a purple. His black beard looked as if it were only black by being too deep a blue. And in the gloom and thickness of the beard his dark red mouth showed sensual and scornful. Whatever he was he was not a Frenchman; he might be a Jew; he might be something deeper yet in the dark heart of the East. In the bright coloured Persian tiles and pictures showing tyrants hunting, you may see just those almond eyes, those blue-black beards, those cruel, crimson lips.

Then came Syme, and next a very old man, Professor de Worms, who still kept the chair of Friday, though every day it was expected that his death would leave it empty. Save for his intellect, he was in the last dissolution of senile decay. His face was as grey as his long grey beard, his forehead was lifted and fixed finally in a furrow of mild despair. In no other case, not even that of Gogol, did the bridegroom brilliancy of the morning dress express a more painful contrast. For the red flower in his button-hole showed up against a face that was literally discoloured like lead; the whole hideous effect was as if some drunken dandies had put their clothes upon a corpse. When he rose or sat down, which was with long labour and peril, something worse was expressed than mere weakness, something indefinably connected with the horror of the whole scene. It did not express decrepitude merely, but corruption. Another hateful fancy crossed Syme's quivering mind. He could not help thinking that whenever the man moved a leg or arm might fall off.

Right at the end sat the man called Saturday, the simplest and the most baffling of all. He was a short, square man with a dark, square face clean-shaven, a medical practitioner going by the name of Bull. He had that combination of savoir-faire with a sort of well-groomed coarseness which is not uncommon in young doctors. He carried his fine clothes with confidence rather than ease, and he mostly wore a set smile.

There was nothing whatever odd about him, except that he wore a pair of dark, almost opaque spectacles. It may have been merely a crescendo of nervous fancy that had gone before, but those black discs were dreadful to Syme; they reminded him of half-remembered ugly tales, of some story about pennies being put on the eyes of the dead. Syme's eye always caught the black glasses and the blind grin. Had the dying Professor worn them, or even the pale Secretary, they would have been appropriate. But on the younger and grosser man they seemed only an enigma. They took away the key of the face. You could not tell what his smile or his gravity meant. Partly from this, and partly because he had a vulgar virility wanting in most of the others it seemed to Syme that he might be the wickedest of all those wicked men. Syme even had the thought that his eyes might be covered up because they were too frightful to see.

Chapter VI
The Exposure

SUCH WERE THE six men who had sworn to destroy the world. Again and again Syme strove to pull together his common sense in their presence. Sometimes he saw for an instant that these notions were subjective, that he was only looking at ordinary men, one of whom was old, another nervous, another short-sighted. The sense of an unnatural symbolism always settled back on him again. Each figure seemed to be, somehow, on the borderland of things, just as their theory was on the borderland of thought. He knew that each one of these men stood at the extreme end, so to speak, of some wild road of reasoning. He could only fancy, as in some old-world fable, that if a man went westward to the end of the world he would find something – say a tree – that was more or less than a tree, a tree possessed by a spirit; and that if he went east to the end of the world he would find something else that was not wholly itself – a tower, perhaps, of which the very shape was wicked. So these figures seemed to stand up, violent and unaccountable, against an ultimate horizon, visions from the verge. The ends of the earth were closing in.

Talk had been going on steadily as he took in the scene; and not the least of the contrasts of that bewildering breakfast-table was the contrast between the easy and unobtrusive tone of talk and its terrible purport. They were deep in the discussion of an actual and immediate plot. The waiter downstairs had spoken quite correctly when he said that they were talking about bombs and kings. Only three days afterwards the Czar was to meet the President of the French Republic in Paris, and over their bacon and eggs upon their sunny balcony these beaming gentlemen had decided how both should die. Even the instrument was chosen; the black-bearded Marquis, it appeared, was to carry the bomb.

Ordinarily speaking, the proximity of this positive and objective crime would have sobered Syme, and cured him of all his merely mystical tremors. He would have thought of nothing but the need of saving at least two human bodies from being ripped in pieces with iron and roaring gas. But the truth was that by this time he had begun to feel a third kind of fear, more piercing and practical than either his moral revulsion or his social responsibility. Very simply, he had no fear to spare for the French President or the Czar; he had begun to fear for himself. Most of the talkers took little heed of him, debating now with their faces closer together, and almost uniformly grave, save when for an instant the smile of the Secretary ran aslant across his face as the jagged lightning runs aslant across the sky. But there was one persistent thing which first troubled Syme and at last terrified him. The President was always looking at him, steadily, and with a great and baffling interest. The enormous man was quite quiet, but his blue eyes stood out of his head. And they were always fixed on Syme.

Syme felt moved to spring up and leap over the balcony. When the President's eyes were on him he felt as if he were made of glass. He had hardly the shred of a doubt that in some silent and extraordinary way Sunday had found out that he was a spy. He looked over the edge of the balcony, and saw a policeman, standing abstractedly just beneath, staring at the bright railings and the sunlit trees.

Then there fell upon him the great temptation that was to torment him for many days. In the presence of these powerful and repulsive men, who were the princes of anarchy, he had almost forgotten the frail and fanciful figure of the poet Gregory, the mere aesthete of anarchism. He even thought of him now with an old kindness, as if they had played together when children. But he remembered that he was still tied to Gregory by a great promise. He had promised never to do the very thing that he now felt himself almost in the act of doing. He had promised not to jump over that balcony and speak to that policeman. He took his cold hand off the cold stone balustrade. His soul swayed in a vertigo of moral indecision. He had only to snap the thread of a rash vow made to a villainous society, and all his life could be as open and sunny as the square beneath him. He had, on the other hand, only to keep his antiquated honour, and be delivered inch by inch into the power of this great enemy of mankind, whose very intellect was a torture-chamber. Whenever he looked down into the square he saw the comfortable policeman, a pillar of common sense and common order. Whenever he looked back at the breakfast-table he saw the President still quietly studying him with big, unbearable eyes.

In all the torrent of his thought there were two thoughts that never crossed his mind. First, it never occurred to him to doubt that the President and his Council could crush him if he continued to stand alone. The place might be public, the project might seem impossible. But Sunday was not the man who would carry himself thus easily without having, somehow or somewhere, set open his iron trap. Either by anonymous poison or sudden street accident, by hypnotism or by fire from hell, Sunday could certainly strike him. If he defied the man he was probably dead, either struck stiff there in his chair or long afterwards as by an innocent ailment. If he called in the police promptly, arrested everyone, told all, and set against them the whole energy of England, he would probably escape; certainly not otherwise. They were a balconyful of gentlemen overlooking a bright and busy square; but he felt no more safe with them than if they had been a boatful of armed pirates overlooking an empty sea.

There was a second thought that never came to him. It never occurred to him to be spiritually won over to the enemy. Many moderns, inured to a weak worship of intellect and force, might have wavered in their allegiance under this oppression of a great personality. They might have called Sunday the super-man. If any such creature be conceivable, he looked, indeed, somewhat like it, with his earth-shaking abstraction, as of a stone statue walking. He might have been called something above man, with his large plans, which were too obvious to be detected, with his large face, which was too frank to be understood. But this was a kind of modern meanness to which Syme could not sink even in his extreme morbidity. Like any man, he was coward enough to fear great force; but he was not quite coward enough to admire it.

The men were eating as they talked, and even in this they were typical. Dr. Bull and the Marquis ate casually and conventionally of the best things on the table – cold pheasant or Strasbourg pie. But the Secretary was a vegetarian, and he spoke earnestly of the projected murder over half a raw tomato and three quarters of a glass of tepid water. The old Professor had such slops as suggested a sickening second childhood. And even in this President Sunday preserved his curious predominance of mere mass. For he ate like twenty men; he ate incredibly, with a frightful freshness of appetite, so that it was like watching a sausage factory. Yet continually, when he had swallowed a dozen crumpets or drunk a quart of coffee, he would be found with his great head on one side staring at Syme.

"I have often wondered," said the Marquis, taking a great bite out of a slice of bread and jam, "whether it wouldn't be better for me to do it with a knife. Most of the best things have been brought off with a knife. And it would be a new emotion to get a knife into a French President and wriggle it round."

"You are wrong," said the Secretary, drawing his black brows together. "The knife was merely the expression of the old personal quarrel with a personal tyrant. Dynamite is not only our best tool, but our best symbol. It is as perfect a symbol of us as is incense of the prayers of the Christians. It expands; it only destroys because it broadens; even so, thought only destroys because it broadens. A man's brain is a bomb," he cried out, loosening suddenly his strange passion and striking his own skull with violence. "My brain feels like a bomb, night and day. It must expand! It must expand! A man's brain must expand, if it breaks up the universe."

"I don't want the universe broken up just yet," drawled the Marquis. "I want to do a lot of beastly things before I die. I thought of one yesterday in bed."

"No, if the only end of the thing is nothing," said Dr. Bull with his sphinx-like smile, "it hardly seems worth doing."

The old Professor was staring at the ceiling with dull eyes.

"Every man knows in his heart," he said, "that nothing is worth doing."

There was a singular silence, and then the Secretary said –

"We are wandering, however, from the point. The only question is how Wednesday is to strike the blow. I take it we should all agree with the original notion of a bomb. As to the actual arrangements, I should suggest that tomorrow morning he should go first of all to –"

The speech was broken off short under a vast shadow. President Sunday had risen to his feet, seeming to fill the sky above them.

"Before we discuss that," he said in a small, quiet voice, "let us go into a private room. I have something very particular to say."

Syme stood up before any of the others. The instant of choice had come at last, the pistol was at his head. On the pavement before he could hear the policeman idly stir and stamp, for the morning, though bright, was cold.

A barrel-organ in the street suddenly sprang with a jerk into a jovial tune. Syme stood up taut, as if it had been a bugle before the battle. He found himself filled with a supernatural courage that came from nowhere. That jingling music seemed full of the vivacity, the vulgarity, and the irrational valour of the poor, who in all those unclean streets were all clinging to the decencies and the charities of Christendom. His youthful prank of being a policeman had faded from his mind; he did not think of himself as the representative of the corps of gentlemen turned into fancy constables, or of the old eccentric who lived in the dark room. But he did feel himself as the ambassador of all these common and kindly people in the street, who every day marched into battle to the music of the barrel-organ. And this high pride in being human had lifted him unaccountably to an infinite height above the monstrous men around him. For an instant, at least, he looked down upon all their sprawling eccentricities from the starry pinnacle of the commonplace. He felt towards them all that unconscious and elementary superiority that a brave man feels over powerful beasts or a wise man over powerful errors. He knew that he had neither the intellectual nor the physical strength of President Sunday; but in that moment he minded it no more than the fact that he had not the muscles of a tiger or a horn on his nose like a rhinoceros. All was swallowed up in an ultimate certainty that the President was wrong and that the barrel-organ was right. There clanged in his mind that unanswerable and terrible truism in the song of Roland –

'Pagens ont tort et Chretiens ont droit'

which in the old nasal French has the clang and groan of great iron. This liberation of his spirit from the load of his weakness went with a quite clear decision to embrace death. If the people of the barrel-organ could keep their old-world obligations, so could he. This very pride in keeping his word was that he was keeping it to miscreants. It was his last triumph over these lunatics to go down into their dark room and die for something that they could not even understand. The barrel-organ seemed to give the marching tune with the energy and the mingled noises of a whole orchestra; and he could hear deep and rolling, under all the trumpets of the pride of life, the drums of the pride of death.

The conspirators were already filing through the open window and into the rooms behind. Syme went last, outwardly calm, but with all his brain and body throbbing with romantic rhythm. The President led them down an irregular side stair, such as might be used by servants, and into a dim, cold, empty room, with a table and benches, like an abandoned boardroom. When they were all in, he closed and locked the door.

The first to speak was Gogol, the irreconcilable, who seemed bursting with inarticulate grievance.

"Zso! Zso!" he cried, with an obscure excitement, his heavy Polish accent becoming almost impenetrable. "You zay you nod 'ide. You zay you show himselves. It is all nuzzinks. Ven you vant talk importance you run yourselves in a dark box!"

The President seemed to take the foreigner's incoherent satire with entire good humour.

"You can't get hold of it yet, Gogol," he said in a fatherly way. "When once they have heard us talking nonsense on that balcony they will not care where we go afterwards. If we had come here first, we should have had the whole staff at the keyhole. You don't seem to know anything about mankind."

"I die for zem," cried the Pole in thick excitement, "and I slay zare oppressors. I care not for these games of gonzealment. I would zmite ze tyrant in ze open square."

"I see, I see," said the President, nodding kindly as he seated himself at the top of a long table. "You die for mankind first, and then you get up and smite their oppressors. So that's all right. And now may I ask you to control your beautiful sentiments, and sit down with the other gentlemen at this table. For the first time this morning something intelligent is going to be said."

Syme, with the perturbed promptitude he had shown since the original summons, sat down first. Gogol sat down last, grumbling in his brown beard about gombromise. No one except Syme seemed to have any notion of the blow that was about to fall. As for him, he had merely the feeling of a man mounting the scaffold with the intention, at any rate, of making a good speech.

"Comrades," said the President, suddenly rising, "we have spun out this farce long enough. I have called you down here to tell you something so simple and shocking that even the waiters upstairs (long inured to our levities) might hear some new seriousness in my voice. Comrades, we were discussing plans and naming places. I propose, before saying anything else, that those plans and places should not be voted by this meeting, but should be left wholly in the control of some one reliable member. I suggest Comrade Saturday, Dr. Bull."

They all stared at him; then they all started in their seats, for the next words, though not loud, had a living and sensational emphasis. Sunday struck the table.

"Not one word more about the plans and places must be said at this meeting. Not one tiny detail more about what we mean to do must be mentioned in this company."

Sunday had spent his life in astonishing his followers; but it seemed as if he had never really astonished them until now. They all moved feverishly in their seats, except Syme. He sat stiff in his, with his hand in his pocket, and on the handle of his loaded revolver. When the attack on him came he would sell his life dear. He would find out at least if the President was mortal.

Sunday went on smoothly –

"You will probably understand that there is only one possible motive for forbidding free speech at this festival of freedom. Strangers overhearing us matters nothing. They assume that we are joking. But what would matter, even unto death, is this, that there should be one actually among us who is not of us, who knows our grave purpose, but does not share it, who –"

The Secretary screamed out suddenly like a woman.

"It can't be!" he cried, leaping. "There can't –"

The President flapped his large flat hand on the table like the fin of some huge fish.

"Yes," he said slowly, "there is a spy in this room. There is a traitor at this table. I will waste no more words. His name –"

Syme half rose from his seat, his finger firm on the trigger.

"His name is Gogol," said the President. "He is that hairy humbug over there who pretends to be a Pole."

Gogol sprang to his feet, a pistol in each hand. With the same flash three men sprang at his throat. Even the Professor made an effort to rise. But Syme saw little of the scene, for he was blinded with a beneficent darkness; he had sunk down into his seat shuddering, in a palsy of passionate relief.

Chapter VII
The Unaccountable Conduct of Professor de Worms

"SIT DOWN!" said Sunday in a voice that he used once or twice in his life, a voice that made men drop drawn swords.

The three who had risen fell away from Gogol, and that equivocal person himself resumed his seat.

"Well, my man," said the President briskly, addressing him as one addresses a total stranger, "will you oblige me by putting your hand in your upper waistcoat pocket and showing me what you have there?"

The alleged Pole was a little pale under his tangle of dark hair, but he put two fingers into the pocket with apparent coolness and pulled out a blue strip of card. When Syme saw it lying on the table, he woke up again to the world outside him. For although the card lay at the other extreme of the table, and he could read nothing of the inscription on it, it bore a startling resemblance to the blue card in his own pocket, the card which had been given to him when he joined the anti-anarchist constabulary.

"Pathetic Slav," said the President, "tragic child of Poland, are you prepared in the presence of that card to deny that you are in this company – shall we say de trop?"

"Right oh!" said the late Gogol. It made everyone jump to hear a clear, commercial and somewhat cockney voice coming out of that forest of foreign hair. It was irrational, as if a Chinaman had suddenly spoken with a Scotch accent.

"I gather that you fully understand your position," said Sunday.

"You bet," answered the Pole. "I see it's a fair cop. All I say is, I don't believe any Pole could have imitated my accent like I did his."

"I concede the point," said Sunday. "I believe your own accent to be inimitable, though I shall practise it in my bath. Do you mind leaving your beard with your card?"

"Not a bit," answered Gogol; and with one finger he ripped off the whole of his shaggy head-covering, emerging with thin red hair and a pale, pert face. "It was hot," he added.

"I will do you the justice to say," said Sunday, not without a sort of brutal admiration, "that you seem to have kept pretty cool under it. Now listen to me. I like you. The consequence is that it would annoy me for just about two and a half minutes if I heard that you had died in torments. Well, if you ever tell the police or any human soul about us, I shall have that two and a half minutes of discomfort. On your discomfort I will not dwell. Good day. Mind the step."

The red-haired detective who had masqueraded as Gogol rose to his feet without a word, and walked out of the room with an air of perfect nonchalance. Yet the astonished Syme was able to realise that this ease was suddenly assumed; for there was a slight stumble outside the door, which showed that the departing detective had not minded the step.

"Time is flying," said the President in his gayest manner, after glancing at his watch, which like everything about him seemed bigger than it ought to be. "I must go off at once; I have to take the chair at a Humanitarian meeting."

The Secretary turned to him with working eyebrows.

"Would it not be better," he said a little sharply, "to discuss further the details of our project, now that the spy has left us?"

"No, I think not," said the President with a yawn like an unobtrusive earthquake. "Leave it as it is. Let Saturday settle it. I must be off. Breakfast here next Sunday."

But the late loud scenes had whipped up the almost naked nerves of the Secretary. He was one of those men who are conscientious even in crime.

"I must protest, President, that the thing is irregular," he said. "It is a fundamental rule of our society that all plans shall be debated in full council. Of course, I fully appreciate your forethought when in the actual presence of a traitor –"

"Secretary," said the President seriously, "if you'd take your head home and boil it for a turnip it might be useful. I can't say. But it might."

The Secretary reared back in a kind of equine anger.

"I really fail to understand –" he began in high offense.

"That's it, that's it," said the President, nodding a great many times. "That's where you fail right enough. You fail to understand. Why, you dancing donkey," he roared, rising, "you didn't want to be overheard by a spy, didn't you? How do you know you aren't overheard now?"

And with these words he shouldered his way out of the room, shaking with incomprehensible scorn.

Four of the men left behind gaped after him without any apparent glimmering of his meaning. Syme alone had even a glimmering, and such as it was it froze him to the bone. If the last words of the President meant anything, they meant that he had not after all passed unsuspected. They meant that while Sunday could not denounce him like Gogol, he still could not trust him like the others.

The other four got to their feet grumbling more or less, and betook themselves elsewhere to find lunch, for it was already well past midday. The Professor went last, very slowly and painfully. Syme sat long after the rest had gone, revolving his strange position. He had escaped a thunderbolt, but he was still under a cloud. At last he rose and made his way out of the hotel into Leicester Square. The bright, cold day had grown increasingly colder, and when he came out into the street he was surprised by a few flakes of snow. While he still carried the sword-stick and the rest of Gregory's portable luggage, he had thrown the cloak down and left it somewhere, perhaps on the steam-tug, perhaps on the balcony. Hoping, therefore, that the snow-shower might be slight, he stepped back out of the street for a moment and stood up under the doorway of a small and greasy hair-dresser's shop, the front window of which was empty, except for a sickly wax lady in evening dress.

Snow, however, began to thicken and fall fast; and Syme, having found one glance at the wax lady quite sufficient to depress his spirits, stared out instead into the white and empty street. He was considerably astonished to see, standing quite still outside the shop and staring into the window, a man. His top hat was loaded with snow like the hat of Father Christmas, the white drift was rising round his boots and ankles; but it seemed as if nothing could tear him away from the contemplation of the colourless wax doll in dirty evening dress. That any human being should stand in such weather looking into such a shop was a matter of sufficient wonder to Syme; but his idle wonder turned suddenly into a personal shock; for he realised that the man standing there was the paralytic old Professor de Worms. It scarcely seemed the place for a person of his years and infirmities.

Syme was ready to believe anything about the perversions of this dehumanized brotherhood; but even he could not believe that the Professor had fallen in love with that particular wax lady. He could only suppose that the man's malady (whatever it was) involved some momentary fits of rigidity or trance. He was not inclined, however, to feel in this case any very compassionate concern. On the contrary, he rather congratulated himself that the Professor's stroke and his elaborate and limping walk would make it easy to escape from him and leave him miles behind. For Syme thirsted first and last to get clear of the whole poisonous atmosphere, if only for an hour. Then he could collect his thoughts, formulate his policy, and decide finally whether he should or should not keep faith with Gregory.

He strolled away through the dancing snow, turned up two or three streets, down through two or three others, and entered a small Soho restaurant for lunch. He partook reflectively of four small and quaint courses, drank half a bottle of red wine, and ended up over black coffee and a black cigar, still thinking. He had taken his seat in the upper room of the restaurant, which was full of the chink of knives and the chatter of foreigners. He remembered that in old days he had imagined that all these harmless and kindly aliens were anarchists. He shuddered, remembering the real thing. But even the shudder had the delightful shame of escape. The wine, the common food, the familiar place, the faces of natural and talkative men, made him almost feel as if the Council of the Seven Days had been a bad dream; and although he knew it was nevertheless an objective reality, it was at least a distant one. Tall houses and populous streets lay between him and his last sight of the shameful seven; he was free in free London, and drinking wine among the free. With a somewhat easier action, he took his hat and stick and strolled down the stair into the shop below.

When he entered that lower room he stood stricken and rooted to the spot. At a small table, close up to the blank window and the white street of snow, sat the old anarchist Professor over a glass of milk, with his lifted livid face and pendent eyelids. For an instant Syme stood as rigid as the stick he leant upon. Then with a gesture as of blind hurry, he brushed past the Professor, dashing open the door and slamming it behind him, and stood outside in the snow.

"Can that old corpse be following me?" he asked himself, biting his yellow moustache. "I stopped too long up in that room, so that even such leaden feet could catch me up. One comfort is, with a little brisk walking I can put a man like that as far away as Timbuctoo. Or am I too fanciful? Was he really following me? Surely Sunday would not be such a fool as to send a lame man?"

He set off at a smart pace, twisting and whirling his stick, in the direction of Covent Garden. As he crossed the great market the snow increased, growing blinding and bewildering as the afternoon began to darken. The snow-flakes tormented him like a swarm of silver bees. Getting into his eyes and beard, they added their unremitting futility to his already irritated nerves; and by the time that he had come at a swinging pace to the beginning of Fleet Street, he lost patience, and finding a Sunday teashop, turned into it to take shelter. He ordered another cup of black coffee as an excuse. Scarcely had he done so, when Professor de Worms hobbled heavily into the shop, sat down with difficulty and ordered a glass of milk.

Syme's walking-stick had fallen from his hand with a great clang, which confessed the concealed steel. But the Professor did not look round. Syme, who was commonly a cool character, was literally gaping as a rustic gapes at a conjuring trick. He had seen no cab following; he had heard no wheels outside the shop; to all mortal appearances the man had come on foot. But the old man could only walk like a snail, and Syme had walked like the wind. He started up and snatched his stick, half crazy with the contradiction in mere arithmetic, and swung out of the swinging doors, leaving his coffee untasted. An omnibus going to the Bank went rattling by with an unusual rapidity. He had a violent run of a hundred yards to reach it; but he managed to spring, swaying upon the splash-board and, pausing for an instant to pant, he climbed on to the top. When he had been seated for about half a minute, he heard behind him a sort of heavy and asthmatic breathing.

Turning sharply, he saw rising gradually higher and higher up the omnibus steps a top hat soiled and dripping with snow, and under the shadow of its brim the short-sighted face and shaky shoulders of Professor de Worms. He let himself into a seat with characteristic care, and wrapped himself up to the chin in the mackintosh rug.

Every movement of the old man's tottering figure and vague hands, every uncertain gesture and panic-stricken pause, seemed to put it beyond question that he was helpless, that he was in the last imbecility of the body. He moved by inches, he let himself down with little gasps of caution. And yet, unless the philosophical entities called time and space have no vestige even of a practical existence, it appeared quite unquestionable that he had run after the omnibus.

Syme sprang erect upon the rocking car, and after staring wildly at the wintry sky, that grew gloomier every moment, he ran down the steps. He had repressed an elemental impulse to leap over the side.

Too bewildered to look back or to reason, he rushed into one of the little courts at the side of Fleet Street as a rabbit rushes into a hole. He had a vague idea, if this incomprehensible old Jack-in-the-box was really pursuing him, that in that labyrinth of little streets he could soon throw him off the scent. He dived in and out of those crooked lanes, which were more like cracks than thoroughfares; and by the time that he had completed about twenty alternate angles and described an unthinkable polygon, he paused to listen for any sound of pursuit. There was none; there could not in any case have been much, for the little streets were thick with the soundless snow. Somewhere behind Red Lion Court, however, he noticed a place where some energetic citizen had cleared away the snow for a space of about twenty yards, leaving the wet, glistening cobble-stones. He thought little of this as he passed it, only plunging into yet another arm of the maze. But when a few hundred yards farther on he stood still again to listen, his heart stood still also, for he heard from that space of rugged stones the clinking crutch and labouring feet of the infernal cripple.

The sky above was loaded with the clouds of snow, leaving London in a darkness and oppression premature for that hour of the evening. On each side of Syme the walls of the alley were blind and featureless; there was no little window or any kind of eve. He felt a new impulse to break out of this hive of houses, and to get once more into the open and lamp-lit street. Yet he rambled and dodged for a long time before he struck the main thoroughfare. When he did so, he struck it much farther up than he had fancied. He came out into what seemed the vast and void of Ludgate Circus, and saw St. Paul's Cathedral sitting in the sky.

At first he was startled to find these great roads so empty, as if a pestilence had swept through the city. Then he told himself that some degree of emptiness was natural; first because the snow-storm was even dangerously deep, and secondly because it was Sunday. And at the very word Sunday he bit his lip; the word was henceforth for hire like some indecent pun. Under the white fog of snow high up in the heaven the whole atmosphere of the city was turned to a very queer kind of green twilight, as of men under the sea. The sealed and sullen sunset behind the dark dome of St. Paul's had in it smoky and sinister colours – colours of sickly green, dead red or decaying bronze, that were just bright enough to emphasise the solid whiteness of the snow. But right up against these dreary colours rose the black bulk of the cathedral; and upon the top of the cathedral was a random splash and great stain of snow, still clinging as to an Alpine peak. It had fallen accidentally, but just so fallen as to half drape the dome from its very topmost point, and to pick out in perfect silver the great orb and the cross. When Syme saw it he suddenly straightened himself, and made with his sword-stick an involuntary salute.

He knew that that evil figure, his shadow, was creeping quickly or slowly behind him, and he did not care.

It seemed a symbol of human faith and valour that while the skies were darkening that high place of the earth was bright. The devils might have captured heaven, but they had not yet captured the cross. He had a new impulse to tear out the secret of this dancing, jumping and pursuing paralytic; and at the entrance of the court as it opened upon the Circus he turned, stick in hand, to face his pursuer.

Professor de Worms came slowly round the corner of the irregular alley behind him, his unnatural form outlined against a lonely gas-lamp, irresistibly recalling that very imaginative figure in the nursery rhymes, "the crooked man who went a crooked mile." He really looked as if he had been twisted out of shape by the tortuous streets he had been threading. He came nearer and nearer, the lamplight shining on his lifted spectacles, his lifted, patient face. Syme waited for him as St. George waited for the dragon, as a man waits for a final explanation or for death. And the old Professor came right up to him and passed him like a total stranger, without even a blink of his mournful eyelids.

There was something in this silent and unexpected innocence that left Syme in a final fury. The man's colourless face and manner seemed to assert that the whole following had been an accident. Syme was galvanised with an energy that was something between bitterness and a burst of boyish derision. He made a wild gesture as if to knock the old man's hat off, called out something like "Catch me if you can," and went racing away across the white, open Circus. Concealment was impossible now; and looking back over his shoulder, he could see the black figure of the old gentleman coming after him with long, swinging strides like a man winning a mile race. But the head upon that bounding body was still pale, grave and professional, like the head of a lecturer upon the body of a harlequin.

This outrageous chase sped across Ludgate Circus, up Ludgate Hill, round St. Paul's Cathedral, along Cheapside, Syme remembering all the nightmares he had ever known. Then Syme broke away towards the river, and ended almost down by the docks. He saw the yellow panes of a low, lighted public-house, flung himself into it and ordered beer. It was a foul tavern, sprinkled with foreign sailors, a place where opium might be smoked or knives drawn.

A moment later Professor de Worms entered the place, sat down carefully, and asked for a glass of milk.

Chapter VIII
The Professor Explains

WHEN GABRIEL SYME found himself finally established in a chair, and opposite to him, fixed and final also, the lifted eyebrows and leaden eyelids of the Professor, his fears fully returned. This incomprehensible man from the fierce council, after all, had certainly pursued him. If the man had one character as a paralytic and another character as a pursuer, the antithesis might make him more interesting, but scarcely more soothing. It would be a very small comfort that he could not find the Professor out, if by some serious accident the Professor should find him out. He emptied a whole pewter pot of ale before the professor had touched his milk.

One possibility, however, kept him hopeful and yet helpless. It was just possible that this escapade signified something other than even a slight suspicion of him.

Perhaps it was some regular form or sign. Perhaps the foolish scamper was some sort of friendly signal that he ought to have understood. Perhaps it was a ritual. Perhaps the new Thursday was always chased along Cheapside, as the new Lord Mayor is always escorted along it. He was just selecting a tentative inquiry, when the old Professor opposite suddenly and simply cut him short. Before Syme could ask the first diplomatic question, the old anarchist had asked suddenly, without any sort of preparation –

"Are you a policeman?"

Whatever else Syme had expected, he had never expected anything so brutal and actual as this. Even his great presence of mind could only manage a reply with an air of rather blundering jocularity.

"A policeman?" he said, laughing vaguely. "Whatever made you think of a policeman in connection with me?"

"The process was simple enough," answered the Professor patiently. "I thought you looked like a policeman. I think so now."

"Did I take a policeman's hat by mistake out of the restaurant?" asked Syme, smiling wildly. "Have I by any chance got a number stuck on to me somewhere? Have my boots got that watchful look? Why must I be a policeman? Do, do let me be a postman."

The old Professor shook his head with a gravity that gave no hope, but Syme ran on with a feverish irony.

"But perhaps I misunderstood the delicacies of your German philosophy. Perhaps policeman is a relative term. In an evolutionary sense, sir, the ape fades so gradually into the policeman, that I myself can never detect the shade. The monkey is only the policeman that may be. Perhaps a maiden lady on Clapham Common is only the policeman that might have been. I don't mind being the policeman that might have been. I don't mind being anything in German thought."

"Are you in the police service?" said the old man, ignoring all Syme's improvised and desperate raillery. "Are you a detective?"

Syme's heart turned to stone, but his face never changed.

"Your suggestion is ridiculous," he began. "Why on earth –"

The old man struck his palsied hand passionately on the rickety table, nearly breaking it.

"Did you hear me ask a plain question, you pattering spy?" he shrieked in a high, crazy voice. "Are you, or are you not, a police detective?"

"No!" answered Syme, like a man standing on the hangman's drop.

"You swear it," said the old man, leaning across to him, his dead face becoming as it were loathsomely alive. "You swear it! You swear it! If you swear falsely, will you be damned? Will you be sure that the devil dances at your funeral? Will you see that the nightmare sits on your grave? Will there really be no mistake? You are an anarchist, you are a dynamiter! Above all, you are not in any sense a detective? You are not in the British police?"

He leant his angular elbow far across the table, and put up his large loose hand like a flap to his ear.

"I am not in the British police," said Syme with insane calm.

Professor de Worms fell back in his chair with a curious air of kindly collapse.

"That's a pity," he said, "because I am."

Syme sprang up straight, sending back the bench behind him with a crash.

"Because you are what?" he said thickly. "You are what?"

"I am a policeman," said the Professor with his first broad smile, and beaming through his spectacles. "But as you think policeman only a relative term, of course I have nothing to do with you. I am in the British police force; but as you tell me you are not in the British police force, I can only say that I met you in a dynamiters' club. I suppose I ought to arrest you." And with these words he laid on the table before Syme an exact facsimile of the blue card which Syme had in his own waistcoat pocket, the symbol of his power from the police.

Syme had for a flash the sensation that the cosmos had turned exactly upside down, that all trees were growing downwards and that all stars were under his feet. Then came slowly the opposite conviction. For the last twenty-four hours the cosmos had really been upside down, but now the capsized universe had come right side up again. This devil from whom he had been fleeing all day was only an elder brother of his own house, who on the other side of the table lay back and laughed at him. He did not for the moment ask any questions of detail; he only knew the happy and silly fact that this shadow, which had pursued him with an intolerable oppression of peril, was only the shadow of a friend trying to catch him up. He knew simultaneously that he was a fool and a free man. For with any recovery from morbidity there must go a certain healthy humiliation. There comes a certain point in such conditions when only three things are possible: first a perpetuation of Satanic pride, secondly tears, and third laughter. Syme's egotism held hard to the first course for a few seconds, and then suddenly adopted the third. Taking his own blue police ticket from his own waist coat pocket, he tossed it on to the table; then he flung his head back until his spike of yellow beard almost pointed at the ceiling, and shouted with a barbaric laughter.

Even in that close den, perpetually filled with the din of knives, plates, cans, clamorous voices, sudden struggles and stampedes, there was something Homeric in Syme's mirth which made many half-drunken men look round.

"What yer laughing at, guv'nor?" asked one wondering labourer from the docks.

"At myself," answered Syme, and went off again into the agony of his ecstatic reaction.

"Pull yourself together," said the Professor, "or you'll get hysterical. Have some more beer. I'll join you."

"You haven't drunk your milk," said Syme.

"My milk!" said the other, in tones of withering and unfathomable contempt, "my milk! Do you think I'd look at the beastly stuff when I'm out of sight of the bloody anarchists? We're all Christians in this room, though perhaps," he added, glancing around at the reeling crowd, "not strict ones. Finish my milk? Great blazes! Yes, I'll finish it right enough!" and he knocked the tumbler off the table, making a crash of glass and a splash of silver fluid.

Syme was staring at him with a happy curiosity.

"I understand now," he cried; "of course, you're not an old man at all."

"I can't take my face off here," replied Professor de Worms. "It's rather an elaborate make-up. As to whether I'm an old man, that's not for me to say. I was thirty-eight last birthday."

"Yes, but I mean," said Syme impatiently, "there's nothing the matter with you."

"Yes," answered the other dispassionately. "I am subject to colds."

Syme's laughter at all this had about it a wild weakness of relief. He laughed at the idea of the paralytic Professor being really a young actor dressed up as if for the footlights. But he felt that he would have laughed as loudly if a pepperpot had fallen over.

The false Professor drank and wiped his false beard.

"Did you know," he asked, "that that man Gogol was one of us?"

"I? No, I didn't know it," answered Syme in some surprise. "But didn't you?"

"I knew no more than the dead," replied the man who called himself de Worms. "I thought the President was talking about me, and I rattled in my boots."

"And I thought he was talking about me," said Syme, with his rather reckless laughter. "I had my hand on my revolver all the time."

"So had I," said the Professor grimly; "so had Gogol evidently."

Syme struck the table with an exclamation.

"Why, there were three of us there!" he cried. "Three out of seven is a fighting number. If we had only known that we were three!"

The face of Professor de Worms darkened, and he did not look up.

"We were three," he said. "If we had been three hundred we could still have done nothing."

"Not if we were three hundred against four?" asked Syme, jeering rather boisterously.

"No," said the Professor with sobriety, "not if we were three hundred against Sunday."

And the mere name struck Syme cold and serious; his laughter had died in his heart before it could die on his lips. The face of the unforgettable President sprang into his mind as startling as a coloured photograph, and he remarked this difference between Sunday and all his satellites, that their faces, however fierce or sinister, became gradually blurred by memory like other human faces, whereas Sunday's seemed almost to grow more actual during absence, as if a man's painted portrait should slowly come alive.

They were both silent for a measure of moments, and then Syme's speech came with a rush, like the sudden foaming of champagne.

"Professor," he cried, "it is intolerable. Are you afraid of this man?"

The Professor lifted his heavy lids, and gazed at Syme with large, wide-open, blue eyes of an almost ethereal honesty.

"Yes, I am," he said mildly. "So are you."

Syme was dumb for an instant. Then he rose to his feet erect, like an insulted man, and thrust the chair away from him.

"Yes," he said in a voice indescribable, "you are right. I am afraid of him. Therefore I swear by God that I will seek out this man whom I fear until I find him, and strike him on the mouth. If heaven were his throne and the earth his footstool, I swear that I would pull him down."

"How?" asked the staring Professor. "Why?"

"Because I am afraid of him," said Syme; "and no man should leave in the universe anything of which he is afraid."

De Worms blinked at him with a sort of blind wonder. He made an effort to speak, but Syme went on in a low voice, but with an undercurrent of inhuman exaltation –

"Who would condescend to strike down the mere things that he does not fear? Who would debase himself to be merely brave, like any common prizefighter? Who would stoop to be fearless – like a tree? Fight the thing that you fear. You remember the old tale of the English clergyman who gave the last rites to the brigand of Sicily, and how on his death-bed the great robber said, 'I can give you no money, but I can give you advice for a lifetime: your thumb on the blade, and strike upwards.' So I say to you, strike upwards, if you strike at the stars."

The other looked at the ceiling, one of the tricks of his pose.

"Sunday is a fixed star," he said.

"You shall see him a falling star," said Syme, and put on his hat.

The decision of his gesture drew the Professor vaguely to his feet.

"Have you any idea," he asked, with a sort of benevolent bewilderment, "exactly where you are going?"

"Yes," replied Syme shortly, "I am going to prevent this bomb being thrown in Paris."

"Have you any conception how?" inquired the other.

"No," said Syme with equal decision.

"You remember, of course," resumed the soi-disant de Worms, pulling his beard and looking out of the window, "that when we broke up rather hurriedly the whole arrangements for the atrocity were left in the private hands of the Marquis and Dr. Bull. The Marquis is by this time probably crossing the Channel. But where he will go and what he will do it is doubtful whether even the President knows; certainly we don't know. The only man who does know is Dr. Bull."

"Confound it!" cried Syme. "And we don't know where he is."

"Yes," said the other in his curious, absent-minded way, "I know where he is myself."

"Will you tell me?" asked Syme with eager eyes.

"I will take you there," said the Professor, and took down his own hat from a peg.

Syme stood looking at him with a sort of rigid excitement.

"What do you mean?" he asked sharply. "Will you join me? Will you take the risk?"

"Young man," said the Professor pleasantly, "I am amused to observe that you think I am a coward. As to that I will say only one word, and that shall be entirely in the manner of your own philosophical rhetoric. You think that it is possible to pull down the President. I know that it is impossible, and I am going to try it," and opening the tavern door, which let in a blast of bitter air, they went out together into the dark streets by the docks.

Most of the snow was melted or trampled to mud, but here and there a clot of it still showed grey rather than white in the gloom. The small streets were sloppy and full of pools, which reflected the flaming lamps irregularly, and by accident, like fragments of some other and fallen world. Syme felt almost dazed as he stepped through this growing confusion of lights and shadows; but his companion walked on with a certain briskness, towards where, at the end of the street, an inch or two of the lamplit river looked like a bar of flame.

"Where are you going?" Syme inquired.

"Just now," answered the Professor, "I am going just round the corner to see whether Dr. Bull has gone to bed. He is hygienic, and retires early."

"Dr. Bull!" exclaimed Syme. "Does he live round the corner?"

"No," answered his friend. "As a matter of fact he lives some way off, on the other side of the river, but we can tell from here whether he has gone to bed."

Turning the corner as he spoke, and facing the dim river, flecked with flame, he pointed with his stick to the other bank. On the Surrey side at this point there ran out into the Thames, seeming almost to overhang it, a bulk and cluster of those tall tenements, dotted with lighted windows, and rising like factory chimneys to an almost insane height. Their special poise and position made one block of buildings especially look like a Tower of Babel with a hundred eyes. Syme had never seen any of the skyscraping buildings in America, so he could only think of the buildings in a dream.

Even as he stared, the highest light in this innumerably lighted turret abruptly went out, as if this black Argus had winked at him with one of his innumerable eyes.

Professor de Worms swung round on his heel, and struck his stick against his boot.

"We are too late," he said, "the hygienic Doctor has gone to bed."

"What do you mean?" asked Syme. "Does he live over there, then?"

"Yes," said de Worms, "behind that particular window which you can't see. Come along and get some dinner. We must call on him tomorrow morning."

Without further parley, he led the way through several by-ways until they came out into the flare and clamour of the East India Dock Road. The Professor, who seemed to know his way about the neighbourhood, proceeded to a place where the line of lighted shops fell back into a sort of abrupt twilight and quiet, in which an old white inn, all out of repair, stood back some twenty feet from the road.

"You can find good English inns left by accident everywhere, like fossils," explained the Professor. "I once found a decent place in the West End."

"I suppose," said Syme, smiling, "that this is the corresponding decent place in the East End?"

"It is," said the Professor reverently, and went in.

In that place they dined and slept, both very thoroughly. The beans and bacon, which these unaccountable people cooked well, the astonishing emergence of Burgundy from their cellars, crowned Syme's sense of a new comradeship and comfort. Through all this ordeal his root horror had been isolation, and there are no words to express the abyss between isolation and having one ally. It may be conceded to the mathematicians that four is twice two. But two is not twice one; two is two thousand times one. That is why, in spite of a hundred disadvantages, the world will always return to monogamy.

Syme was able to pour out for the first time the whole of his outrageous tale, from the time when Gregory had taken him to the little tavern by the river. He did it idly and amply, in a luxuriant monologue, as a man speaks with very old friends. On his side, also, the man who had impersonated Professor de Worms was not less communicative. His own story was almost as silly as Syme's.

"That's a good get-up of yours," said Syme, draining a glass of Macon; "a lot better than old Gogol's. Even at the start I thought he was a bit too hairy."

"A difference of artistic theory," replied the Professor pensively. "Gogol was an idealist. He made up as the abstract or platonic ideal of an anarchist. But I am a realist. I am a portrait painter. But, indeed, to say that I am a portrait painter is an inadequate expression. I am a portrait."

"I don't understand you," said Syme.

"I am a portrait," repeated the Professor. "I am a portrait of the celebrated Professor de Worms, who is, I believe, in Naples."

"You mean you are made up like him," said Syme. "But doesn't he know that you are taking his nose in vain?"

"He knows it right enough," replied his friend cheerfully.

"Then why doesn't he denounce you?"

"I have denounced him," answered the Professor.

"Do explain yourself," said Syme.

"With pleasure, if you don't mind hearing my story," replied the eminent foreign philosopher. "I am by profession an actor, and my name is Wilks. When I was on the stage I mixed with all sorts of Bohemian and blackguard company. Sometimes I touched the edge of the turf, sometimes the riff-raff of the arts, and occasionally the political refugee. In some den of exiled dreamers I was introduced to the great German

Nihilist philosopher, Professor de Worms. I did not gather much about him beyond his appearance, which was very disgusting, and which I studied carefully. I understood that he had proved that the destructive principle in the universe was God; hence he insisted on the need for a furious and incessant energy, rending all things in pieces. Energy, he said, was the All. He was lame, shortsighted, and partially paralytic. When I met him I was in a frivolous mood, and I disliked him so much that I resolved to imitate him. If I had been a draughtsman I would have drawn a caricature. I was only an actor, I could only act a caricature. I made myself up into what was meant for a wild exaggeration of the old Professor's dirty old self. When I went into the room full of his supporters I expected to be received with a roar of laughter, or (if they were too far gone) with a roar of indignation at the insult. I cannot describe the surprise I felt when my entrance was received with a respectful silence, followed (when I had first opened my lips) with a murmur of admiration. The curse of the perfect artist had fallen upon me. I had been too subtle, I had been too true. They thought I really was the great Nihilist Professor. I was a healthy-minded young man at the time, and I confess that it was a blow. Before I could fully recover, however, two or three of these admirers ran up to me radiating indignation, and told me that a public insult had been put upon me in the next room. I inquired its nature. It seemed that an impertinent fellow had dressed himself up as a preposterous parody of myself. I had drunk more champagne than was good for me, and in a flash of folly I decided to see the situation through. Consequently it was to meet the glare of the company and my own lifted eyebrows and freezing eyes that the real Professor came into the room.

"I need hardly say there was a collision. The pessimists all round me looked anxiously from one Professor to the other Professor to see which was really the more feeble. But I won. An old man in poor health, like my rival, could not be expected to be so impressively feeble as a young actor in the prime of life. You see, he really had paralysis, and working within this definite limitation, he couldn't be so jolly paralytic as I was. Then he tried to blast my claims intellectually. I countered that by a very simple dodge. Whenever he said something that nobody but he could understand, I replied with something which I could not even understand myself. 'I don't fancy,' he said, 'that you could have worked out the principle that evolution is only negation, since there inheres in it the introduction of lacuna, which are an essential of differentiation.' I replied quite scornfully, 'You read all that up in Pinckwerts; the notion that involution functioned eugenically was exposed long ago by Glumpe.' It is unnecessary for me to say that there never were such people as Pinckwerts and Glumpe. But the people all round (rather to my surprise) seemed to remember them quite well, and the Professor, finding that the learned and mysterious method left him rather at the mercy of an enemy slightly deficient in scruples, fell back upon a more popular form of wit. 'I see,' he sneered, 'you prevail like the false pig in Aesop.' 'And you fail,' I answered, smiling, 'like the hedgehog in Montaigne.' Need I say that there is no hedgehog in Montaigne? 'Your claptrap comes off,' he said; 'so would your beard.' I had no intelligent answer to this, which was quite true and rather witty. But I laughed heartily, answered, 'Like the Pantheist's boots,' at random, and turned on my heel with all the honours of victory. The real Professor was thrown out, but not with violence, though one man tried very patiently to pull off his nose. He is now, I believe, received everywhere in Europe as a delightful impostor. His apparent earnestness and anger, you see, make him all the more entertaining."

"Well," said Syme, "I can understand your putting on his dirty old beard for a night's practical joke, but I don't understand your never taking it off again."

"That is the rest of the story," said the impersonator. "When I myself left the company, followed by reverent applause, I went limping down the dark street, hoping that I should soon be far enough away to be able to walk like a human being. To my astonishment, as I was turning the corner, I felt a touch on the shoulder, and turning, found myself under the shadow of an enormous policeman. He told me I was wanted. I struck a sort of paralytic attitude, and cried in a high German accent, 'Yes, I am wanted – by the oppressed of the world. You are arresting me on the charge of being the great anarchist, Professor de Worms.' The policeman impassively consulted a paper in his hand, 'No, sir,' he said civilly, 'at least, not exactly, sir. I am arresting you on the charge of not being the celebrated anarchist, Professor de Worms.' This charge, if it was criminal at all, was certainly the lighter of the two, and I went along with the man, doubtful, but not greatly dismayed. I was shown into a number of rooms, and eventually into the presence of a police officer, who explained that a serious campaign had been opened against the centres of anarchy, and that this, my successful masquerade, might be of considerable value to the public safety. He offered me a good salary and this little blue card. Though our conversation was short, he struck me as a man of very massive common sense and humour; but I cannot tell you much about him personally, because –"

Syme laid down his knife and fork.

"I know," he said, "because you talked to him in a dark room."

Professor de Worms nodded and drained his glass.

The complete and unabridged text is available online, from *flametreepublishing.com/extras*

The Invisible Man

G.K. Chesterton

IN THE COOL blue twilight of two steep streets in Camden Town, the shop at the corner, a confectioner's, glowed like the butt of a cigar. One should rather say, perhaps, like the butt of a firework, for the light was of many colours and some complexity, broken up by many mirrors and dancing on many gilt and gaily-coloured cakes and sweetmeats. Against this one fiery glass were glued the noses of many gutter-snipes, for the chocolates were all wrapped in those red and gold and green metallic colours which are almost better than chocolate itself; and the huge white wedding-cake in the window was somehow at once remote and satisfying, just as if the whole North Pole were good to eat. Such rainbow provocations could naturally collect the youth of the neighbourhood up to the ages of ten or twelve. But this corner was also attractive to youth at a later stage; and a young man, not less than twenty-four, was staring into the same shop window. To him, also, the shop was of fiery charm, but this attraction was not wholly to be explained by chocolates; which, however, he was far from despising.

He was a tall, burly, red-haired young man, with a resolute face but a listless manner. He carried under his arm a flat, grey portfolio of black-and-white sketches, which he had sold with more or less success to publishers ever since his uncle (who was an admiral) had disinherited him for Socialism, because of a lecture which he had delivered against that economic theory. His name was John Turnbull Angus.

Entering at last, he walked through the confectioner's shop to the back room, which was a sort of pastry-cook restaurant, merely raising his hat to the young lady who was serving there. She was a dark, elegant, alert girl in black, with a high colour and very quick, dark eyes; and after the ordinary interval she followed him into the inner room to take his order.

His order was evidently a usual one. "I want, please," he said with precision, "one halfpenny bun and a small cup of black coffee." An instant before the girl could turn away he added, "Also, I want you to marry me."

The young lady of the shop stiffened suddenly and said, "Those are jokes I don't allow."

The red-haired young man lifted grey eyes of an unexpected gravity.

"Really and truly," he said, "it's as serious – as serious as the halfpenny bun. It is expensive, like the bun; one pays for it. It is indigestible, like the bun. It hurts."

The dark young lady had never taken her dark eyes off him, but seemed to be studying him with almost tragic exactitude. At the end of her scrutiny she had something like the shadow of a smile, and she sat down in a chair.

"Don't you think," observed Angus, absently, "that it's rather cruel to eat these halfpenny buns? They might grow up into penny buns. I shall give up these brutal sports when we are married."

The dark young lady rose from her chair and walked to the window, evidently in a state of strong but not unsympathetic cogitation. When at last she swung round again with an air of resolution she was bewildered to observe that the young man was carefully laying out on the table various objects from the shop-window. They included a pyramid of highly coloured sweets, several plates of sandwiches, and the two decanters containing that mysterious port and sherry which are peculiar to pastry-cooks. In the middle of this neat arrangement he had carefully let down the enormous load of white sugared cake which had been the huge ornament of the window.

"What on earth are you doing?" she asked.

"Duty, my dear Laura," he began.

"Oh, for the Lord's sake, stop a minute," she cried, "and don't talk to me in that way. I mean, what is all that?"

"A ceremonial meal, Miss Hope."

"And what is that?" she asked impatiently, pointing to the mountain of sugar.

"The wedding-cake, Mrs. Angus," he said.

The girl marched to that article, removed it with some clatter, and put it back in the shop window; she then returned, and, putting her elegant elbows on the table, regarded the young man not unfavourably but with considerable exasperation.

"You don't give me any time to think," she said.

"I'm not such a fool," he answered; "that's my Christian humility."

She was still looking at him; but she had grown considerably graver behind the smile.

"Mr. Angus," she said steadily, "before there is a minute more of this nonsense I must tell you something about myself as shortly as I can.'"

"Delighted," replied Angus gravely. "You might tell me something about myself, too, while you are about it."

"Oh, do hold your tongue and listen," she said. "It's nothing that I'm ashamed of, and it isn't even anything that I'm specially sorry about. But what would you say if there were something that is no business of mine and yet is my nightmare?"

"In that case," said the man seriously, "I should suggest that you bring back the cake."

"Well, you must listen to the story first," said Laura, persistently. "To begin with, I must tell you that my father owned the inn called the 'Red Fish' at Ludbury, and I used to serve people in the bar."

"I have often wondered," he said, "why there was a kind of a Christian air about this one confectioner's shop."

"Ludbury is a sleepy, grassy little hole in the Eastern Counties, and the only kind of people who ever came to the 'Red Fish' were occasional commercial travellers, and for the rest, the most awful people you can see, only you've never seen them. I mean little, loungy men, who had just enough to live on and had nothing to do but lean about in bar-rooms and bet on horses, in bad clothes that were just too good for them. Even these wretched young rotters were not very common at our house; but there were two of them that were a lot too common – common in every sort of way. They both lived on money of their own, and were wearisomely idle and over-dressed. But yet I was a bit sorry for them, because I half believe they slunk into our little empty bar because each of them had a slight deformity; the sort of thing that some yokels laugh at. It wasn't exactly a deformity either; it was more an oddity. One of them was a surprisingly small man, something like a dwarf, or at least like a jockey. He was not at all jockeyish to look at, though; he had a round black head and a well-trimmed black beard, bright eyes like a bird's; he jingled money in his pockets; he jangled a great gold watch chain; and he never turned up except dressed just too much like a gentleman to be one. He was no fool though, though a futile idler; he was curiously clever at all kinds of things that couldn't be the slightest use; a sort of impromptu conjuring; making fifteen matches set fire to each other like a regular firework; or cutting a banana or some such thing into a dancing doll. His name was Isidore Smythe; and I can see him still, with his little dark face, just coming up to the counter, making a jumping kangaroo out of five cigars.

"The other fellow was more silent and more ordinary; but somehow he alarmed me much more than poor little Smythe. He was very tall and slight, and light-haired; his nose had a high bridge, and he might almost have been handsome in a spectral sort of way; but he had one of the most appalling squints I have ever seen or heard of. When he looked straight at you, you didn't know where you were yourself, let alone what he was looking at. I fancy this sort of disfigurement embittered the poor chap a little; for while Smythe was ready to show off his monkey tricks anywhere, James Welkin (that was the squinting man's name) never did anything except soak in our bar parlour, and go for great walks by himself in the flat, grey country all round. All the same, I think Smythe, too, was a little sensitive about being so small, though he carried it off more smartly. And so it was that I was really puzzled, as well as startled, and very sorry, when they both offered to marry me in the same week.

"Well, I did what I've since thought was perhaps a silly thing. But, after all, these freaks were my friends in a way; and I had a horror of their thinking I refused them for the real reason, which was that they were so impossibly ugly. So I made up some gas of another sort, about never meaning to marry anyone who hadn't carved his way in the world. I said it was a point of principle with me not to live on money that was just inherited like theirs. Two days after I had talked in this well-meaning sort of way, the whole trouble began. The first thing I heard was that both of them had gone off to seek their fortunes, as if they were in some silly fairy tale.

"Well, I've never seen either of them from that day to this. But I've had two letters from the little man called Smythe, and really they were rather exciting."

"Ever heard of the other man?" asked Angus.

"No, he never wrote," said the girl, after an instant's hesitation. "Smythe's first letter was simply to say that he had started out walking with Welkin to London; but Welkin was such a good walker that the little man dropped out of it, and took a rest by the roadside. He happened to be picked up by some travelling show, and, partly because he was nearly a dwarf, and partly because he was really a clever little wretch, he got on quite well in the show business, and was soon sent up to the Aquarium, to do some tricks that I forget. That was his first letter. His second was much more of a startler, and I only got it last week."

The man called Angus emptied his coffee-cup and regarded her with mild and patient eyes. Her own mouth took a slight twist of laughter as she resumed, "I suppose you've seen on the hoardings all about this 'Smythe's Silent Service'? Or you must be the only person that hasn't. Oh, I don't know much about it, it's some clockwork invention for doing all the housework by machinery. You know the sort of thing: 'Press a Button – A Butler who Never Drinks.' 'Turn a Handle – Ten Housemaids who Never Flirt.' You must have seen the advertisements. Well, whatever these machines are, they are making pots of money; and they are making it all for that little imp whom I knew down in Ludbury. I can't help feeling pleased the poor little chap has fallen on his feet; but the plain fact is, I'm in terror of his turning up any minute and telling me he's carved his way in the world – as he certainly has."

"And the other man?" repeated Angus with a sort of obstinate quietude.

Laura Hope got to her feet suddenly. "My friend," she said, "I think you are a witch. Yes, you are quite right. I have not seen a line of the other man's writing; and I have no more notion than the dead of what or where he is. But it is of him that I am frightened. It is he who is all about my path. It is he who has half driven me mad. Indeed, I think he has driven me mad; for I have felt him where he could not have been, and I have heard his voice when he could not have spoken."

"Well, my dear," said the young man, cheerfully, "if he were Satan himself, he is done for now you have told somebody. One goes mad all alone, old girl. But when was it you fancied you felt and heard our squinting friend?"

"I heard James Welkin laugh as plainly as I hear you speak," said the girl, steadily. "There was nobody there, for I stood just outside the shop at the corner, and could see down both streets at once. I had forgotten how he laughed, though his laugh was as odd as his squint. I had not thought of him for nearly a year. But it's a solemn truth that a few seconds later the first letter came from his rival."

"Did you ever make the spectre speak or squeak, or anything?" asked Angus, with some interest.

Laura suddenly shuddered, and then said, with an unshaken voice, "Yes. Just when I had finished reading the second letter from Isidore Smythe announcing his success. Just then, I heard Welkin say, 'He shan't have you, though.' It was quite plain, as if he were in the room. It is awful, I think I must be mad."

"If you really were mad," said the young man, "you would think you must be sane. But certainly there seems to me to be something a little rum about this unseen gentleman. Two heads are better than one – I spare you allusions to any other organs and really, if you would allow me, as a sturdy, practical man, to bring back the wedding-cake out of the window –"

Even as he spoke, there was a sort of steely shriek in the street outside, and a small motor, driven at devilish speed, shot up to the door of the shop and stuck there. In the same flash of time a small man in a shiny top hat stood stamping in the outer room.

Angus, who had hitherto maintained hilarious ease from motives of mental hygiene, revealed the strain of his soul by striding abruptly out of the inner room and confronting the new-comer. A glance at him was quite sufficient to confirm the savage guesswork of a man in love. This very dapper but dwarfish figure, with the spike of black beard carried insolently forward, the clever unrestful eyes, the neat but very nervous fingers, could be none other than the man just described to him: Isidore Smythe, who made dolls out of banana skins and match-boxes; Isidore Smythe, who made millions out of undrinking butlers and unflirting housemaids of metal. For a moment the two men, instinctively understanding each other's air of possession, looked at each other with that curious cold generosity which is the soul of rivalry.

Mr. Smythe, however, made no allusion to the ultimate ground of their antagonism, but said simply and explosively, "Has Miss Hope seen that thing on the window?"

"On the window?" repeated the staring Angus.

"There's no time to explain other things," said the small millionaire shortly. "There's some tomfoolery going on here that has to be investigated."

He pointed his polished walking-stick at the window, recently depleted by the bridal preparations of Mr. Angus; and that gentleman was astonished to see along the front of the glass a long strip of paper pasted, which had certainly not been on the window when he looked through it some time before. Following the energetic Smythe outside into the street, he found that some yard and a half of stamp paper had been carefully gummed along the glass outside, and on this was written in straggly characters, "If you marry Smythe, he will die."

"Laura," said Angus, putting his big red head into the shop, "you're not mad."

"It's the writing of that fellow Welkin," said Smythe gruffly. "I haven't seen him for years, but he's always bothering me. Five times in the last fortnight he's had threatening letters left at my flat, and I can't even find out who leaves them, let alone if it is Welkin himself. The porter of the flats swears that no suspicious characters have been seen, and here he has pasted up a sort of dado on a public shop window, while the people in the shop –"

"Quite so," said Angus modestly, "while the people in the shop were having tea. Well, sir, I can assure you I appreciate your common sense in dealing so directly with the matter. We can talk about other things afterwards. The fellow cannot be very far off yet, for I swear there was no paper there when I went last to the window, ten or fifteen minutes ago. On the other hand, he's too far off to be chased, as we don't even know the direction. If you'll take my advice, Mr. Smythe, you'll put this at once in the hands of some energetic inquiry man, private rather than public. I know an extremely clever fellow, who has set up in business five minutes from here in your car. His name's Flambeau, and though his youth was a bit stormy, he's a strictly honest man now, and his brains are worth money. He lives in Lucknow Mansions, Hampstead."

"That is odd," said the little man, arching his black eyebrows. "I live, myself, in Himylaya Mansions, round the corner. Perhaps you might care to come with me; I can go to my rooms and sort out these queer Welkin documents, while you run round and get your friend the detective."

"You are very good," said Angus politely. "Well, the sooner we act the better."

Both men, with a queer kind of impromptu fairness, took the same sort of formal farewell of the lady, and both jumped into the brisk little car. As Smythe took the handles and they turned the great corner of the street, Angus was amused to see a gigantesque poster of 'Smythe's Silent Service,' with a picture of a huge headless iron doll, carrying a saucepan with the legend, 'A Cook Who is Never Cross.'

"I use them in my own flat," said the little black-bearded man, laughing, "partly for advertisements, and partly for real convenience. Honestly, and all above board, those big clockwork dolls of mine do bring your coals or claret or a timetable quicker than any live servants I've ever known, if you know which knob to press. But I'll never deny, between ourselves, that such servants have their disadvantages, too."

"Indeed?" said Angus; "is there something they can't do?"

"Yes," replied Smythe coolly; "they can't tell me who left those threatening letters at my flat."

The man's motor was small and swift like himself; in fact, like his domestic service, it was of his own invention. If he was an advertising quack, he was one who believed in his own wares. The sense of something tiny and flying was accentuated as they swept up long white curves of road in the dead but open daylight of evening. Soon the white curves came sharper and dizzier; they were upon ascending spirals, as they say in the modern religions. For, indeed, they were cresting a corner of London which is almost as precipitous as Edinburgh, if not quite so picturesque. Terrace rose above terrace, and the special tower of flats they sought, rose above them all to almost Egyptian height, gilt by the level sunset. The change, as they turned the corner and entered the crescent known as Himylaya Mansions, was as abrupt as the opening of a window; for they found that pile of flats sitting above London as above a green sea of slate. Opposite to the mansions, on the other side of the gravel crescent, was a bushy enclosure more like a steep hedge or dyke than a garden, and some way below that ran a strip of artificial water, a sort of canal, like the moat of that embowered fortress. As the car swept round the crescent it passed, at one corner, the stray stall of a man selling chestnuts; and right away at the other end of the curve, Angus could see a dim blue policeman walking slowly. These were the only human shapes in that high suburban solitude; but he had an irrational sense that they expressed the speechless poetry of London. He felt as if they were figures in a story.

The little car shot up to the right house like a bullet, and shot out its owner like a bomb shell. He was immediately inquiring of a tall commissionaire in shining braid, and a short porter in shirt sleeves, whether anybody or anything had been seeking his apartments. He was assured that nobody and nothing had passed these officials since his last inquiries; whereupon he and the slightly bewildered Angus were shot up in the lift like a rocket, till they reached the top floor.

"Just come in for a minute," said the breathless Smythe. "I want to show you those Welkin letters. Then you might run round the corner and fetch your friend." He pressed a button concealed in the wall, and the door opened of itself.

It opened on a long, commodious ante-room, of which the only arresting features, ordinarily speaking, were the rows of tall half-human mechanical figures that stood up on both sides like tailors' dummies. Like tailors' dummies they were headless; and like tailors' dummies they had a handsome unnecessary humpiness in the shoulders, and a pigeon-breasted protuberance of chest; but barring this, they were not much more like a human figure than any automatic machine at a station that is about the human height. They had two great hooks like arms, for carrying trays; and they were painted pea-green, or vermilion, or black for convenience of distinction; in every other way they were only automatic machines and nobody would have looked twice at them. On this occasion, at least, nobody did. For between the two rows of these domestic dummies lay something more interesting than most of the mechanics of the world. It was a white, tattered scrap of paper scrawled with red ink; and the agile inventor had snatched it up almost as soon as the door flew open. He handed it to Angus without a word. The red ink on it actually was not dry, and the message ran, "If you have been to see her today, I shall kill you."

There was a short silence, and then Isidore Smythe said quietly, "Would you like a little whiskey? I rather feel as if I should."

"Thank you; I should like a little Flambeau," said Angus, gloomily. "This business seems to me to be getting rather grave. I'm going round at once to fetch him."

"Right you are," said the other, with admirable cheerfulness. "Bring him round here as quick as you can."

But as Angus closed the front door behind him he saw Smythe push back a button, and one of the clockwork images glided from its place and slid along a groove in the floor carrying a tray with syphon and decanter. There did seem something a trifle weird about leaving the little man alone among those dead servants, who were coming to life as the door closed.

Six steps down from Smythe's landing the man in shirt sleeves was doing something with a pail. Angus stopped to extract a promise, fortified with a prospective bribe, that he would remain in that place until the return with the detective, and would keep count of any kind of stranger coming up those stairs. Dashing down to the front hall he then laid similar charges of vigilance on the commissionaire at the front door, from whom he learned the simplifying circumstances that there was no back door. Not content with this, he captured the floating policeman and induced him to stand opposite the entrance and watch it; and finally paused an instant for a pennyworth of chestnuts, and an inquiry as to the probable length of the merchant's stay in the neighbourhood.

The chestnut seller, turning up the collar of his coat, told him he should probably be moving shortly, as he thought it was going to snow. Indeed, the evening was growing grey and bitter, but Angus, with all his eloquence, proceeded to nail the chestnut man to his post.

"Keep yourself warm on your own chestnuts," he said earnestly. "Eat up your whole stock; I'll make it worth your while. I'll give you a sovereign if you'll wait here till I come back, and then tell me whether any man, woman, or child has gone into that house where the commissionaire is standing."

He then walked away smartly, with a last look at the besieged tower.

"I've made a ring round that room, anyhow," he said. "They can't all four of them be Mr. Welkin's accomplices."

Lucknow Mansions were, so to speak, on a lower platform of that hill of houses, of which Himylaya Mansions might be called the peak. Mr. Flambeau's semi-official flat was on the ground floor, and presented in every way a marked contrast to the American machinery and cold hotel-like luxury of the flat of the Silent Service. Flambeau, who was a friend of Angus, received him in a rococo artistic den behind his office, of which the ornaments were sabres, harquebuses, Eastern curiosities, flasks of Italian wine, savage cooking-pots, a plumy Persian cat, and a small dusty-looking Roman Catholic priest, who looked particularly out of place.

"This is my friend Father Brown," said Flambeau. "I've often wanted you to meet him. Splendid weather, this; a little cold for Southerners like me."

"Yes, I think it will keep clear," said Angus, sitting down on a violet-striped Eastern ottoman.

"No," said the priest quietly, "it has begun to snow."

And, indeed, as he spoke, the first few flakes, foreseen by the man of chestnuts, began to drift across the darkening windowpane.

"Well," said Angus heavily. "I'm afraid I've come on business, and rather jumpy business at that. The fact is, Flambeau, within a stone's throw of your house is a fellow who badly wants your help; he's perpetually being haunted and threatened by an invisible enemy – a scoundrel whom nobody has even seen." As Angus proceeded to tell the whole tale of Smythe and Welkin, beginning with Laura's story, and going on with his own, the supernatural laugh at the corner of two empty streets, the strange distinct words spoken in an empty room, Flambeau grew more and more vividly concerned, and the little priest seemed to be left out of it, like a piece of furniture. When it came to the scribbled stamp-paper pasted on the window, Flambeau rose, seeming to fill the room with his huge shoulders.

"If you don't mind," he said, "I think you had better tell me the rest on the nearest road to this man's house. It strikes me, somehow, that there is no time to be lost."

"Delighted," said Angus, rising also, "though he's safe enough for the present, for I've set four men to watch the only hole to his burrow."

They turned out into the street, the small priest trundling after them with the docility of a small dog. He merely said, in a cheerful way, like one making conversation, "How quick the snow gets thick on the ground."

As they threaded the steep side streets already powdered with silver, Angus finished his story; and by the time they reached the crescent with the towering flats, he had leisure to turn his attention to the four sentinels. The chestnut seller, both before and after receiving a sovereign, swore stubbornly that he had watched the door and seen no visitor enter. The policeman was even more emphatic. He said he had had experience of crooks of all kinds, in top hats and in rags; he wasn't so green as to expect suspicious characters to look suspicious; he looked out for anybody, and, so help him, there had been nobody. And when all three men gathered round the gilded commissionaire, who still stood smiling astride of the porch, the verdict was more final still.

"I've got a right to ask any man, duke or dustman, what he wants in these flats," said the genial and gold-laced giant, "and I'll swear there's been nobody to ask since this gentleman went away."

The unimportant Father Brown, who stood back, looking modestly at the pavement, here ventured to say meekly, "Has nobody been up and down stairs, then, since the snow began to fall? It began while we were all round at Flambeau's."

"Nobody's been in here, sir, you can take it from me," said the official, with beaming authority.

"Then I wonder what that is?" said the priest, and stared at the ground blankly like a fish.

The others all looked down also; and Flambeau used a fierce exclamation and a French gesture. For it was unquestionably true that down the middle of the entrance guarded by the man in gold lace, actually between the arrogant, stretched legs of that colossus, ran a stringy pattern of grey footprints stamped upon the white snow.

"God!" cried Angus involuntarily, "the Invisible Man!"

Without another word he turned and dashed up the stairs, with Flambeau following; but Father Brown still stood looking about him in the snow-clad street as if he had lost interest in his query.

Flambeau was plainly in a mood to break down the door with his big shoulders; but the Scotchman, with more reason, if less intuition, fumbled about on the frame of the door till he found the invisible button; and the door swung slowly open.

It showed substantially the same serried interior; the hall had grown darker, though it was still struck here and there with the last crimson shafts of sunset, and one or two of the headless machines had been moved from their places for this or that purpose, and stood here and there about the twilit place. The green and red of their coats were all darkened in the dusk; and their likeness to human shapes slightly increased by their very shapelessness. But in the middle of them all, exactly where the paper with the red ink had lain, there lay something that looked like red ink spilt out of its bottle. But it was not red ink.

With a French combination of reason and violence Flambeau simply said "Murder!" and, plunging into the flat, had explored, every corner and cupboard of it in five minutes.

But if he expected to find a corpse he found none. Isidore Smythe was not in the place, either dead or alive. After the most tearing search the two men met each other in the outer hall, with streaming faces and staring eyes. "My friend," said Flambeau, talking French in his excitement, "not only is your murderer invisible, but he makes invisible also the murdered man."

Angus looked round at the dim room full of dummies, and in some Celtic corner of his Scotch soul a shudder started. One of the life-size dolls stood immediately overshadowing the blood stain, summoned, perhaps, by the slain man an instant before he fell. One of the high-shouldered hooks that served the thing for arms, was a little lifted, and Angus had suddenly the horrid fancy that poor Smythe's own iron child had struck him down. Matter had rebelled, and these machines had killed their master. But even so, what had they done with him?

"Eaten him?" said the nightmare at his ear; and he sickened for an instant at the idea of rent, human remains absorbed and crushed into all that acephalous clockwork.

He recovered his mental health by an emphatic effort, and said to Flambeau, "Well, there it is. The poor fellow has evaporated like a cloud and left a red streak on the floor. The tale does not belong to this world."

"There is only one thing to be done," said Flambeau, "whether it belongs to this world or the other. I must go down and talk to my friend."

They descended, passing the man with the pail, who again asseverated that he had let no intruder pass, down to the commissionaire and the hovering chestnut man, who rigidly reasserted their own watchfulness. But when Angus looked round for his fourth confirmation he could not see it, and called out with some nervousness, "Where is the policeman?"

"I beg your pardon," said Father Brown; "that is my fault. I just sent him down the road to investigate something – that I just thought worth investigating."

"Well, we want him back pretty soon," said Angus abruptly, "for the wretched man upstairs has not only been murdered, but wiped out."

"How?" asked the priest.

"Father," said Flambeau, after a pause, "upon my soul I believe it is more in your department than mine. No friend or foe has entered the house, but Smythe is gone, as if stolen by the fairies. If that is not supernatural, I –"

As he spoke they were all checked by an unusual sight; the big blue policeman came round the corner of the crescent, running. He came straight up to Brown.

"You're right, sir," he panted, "they've just found poor Mr. Smythe's body in the canal down below."

Angus put his hand wildly to his head. "Did he run down and drown himself?" he asked.

"He never came down, I'll swear," said the constable, "and he wasn't drowned either, for he died of a great stab over the heart."

"And yet you saw no one enter?" said Flambeau in a grave voice.

"Let us walk down the road a little," said the priest.

As they reached the other end of the crescent he observed abruptly, "Stupid of me! I forgot to ask the policeman something. I wonder if they found a light brown sack."

"Why a light brown sack?" asked Angus, astonished.

"Because if it was any other coloured sack, the case must begin over again," said Father Brown; "but if it was a light brown sack, why, the case is finished."

"I am pleased to hear it," said Angus with hearty irony. "It hasn't begun, so far as I am concerned."

"You must tell us all about it," said Flambeau with a strange heavy simplicity, like a child.

Unconsciously they were walking with quickening steps down the long sweep of road on the other side of the high crescent, Father Brown leading briskly, though in silence. At last he said with an almost touching vagueness, "Well, I'm afraid you'll think it so prosy. We always begin at the abstract end of things, and you can't begin this story anywhere else.

"Have you ever noticed this – that people never answer what you say? They answer what you mean – or what they think you mean. Suppose one lady says to another in a country house, 'Is anybody staying with you?' the lady doesn't answer 'Yes; the butler, the three footmen, the parlourmaid, and so on,' though the parlourmaid may be in the room, or the butler behind her chair. She says 'There is nobody staying with us,' meaning nobody of the sort you mean. But suppose a doctor inquiring into an epidemic asks, 'Who is staying in the house?' then the lady will remember the butler, the parlourmaid, and the rest. All language is used like that; you never get a question answered literally, even when you get it answered truly. When those four quite honest men said that no man had gone into the Mansions, they did not really mean that no man had gone into them. They meant no man whom they could suspect of being your man. A man did go into the house, and did come out of it, but they never noticed him."

"An invisible man?" inquired Angus, raising his red eyebrows. "A mentally invisible man," said Father Brown.

A minute or two after he resumed in the same unassuming voice, like a man thinking his way. "Of course you can't think of such a man, until you do think of him. That's where his cleverness comes in. But I came to think of him through two or three little things in the tale Mr. Angus told us. First, there was the fact that this Welkin went for long walks. And then there was the vast lot of stamp paper on the window. And then, most of all, there were the two things the young lady said – things that couldn't be true. Don't get annoyed," he added hastily, noting a sudden movement of the Scotchman's head; "she thought they were true. A person can't be quite alone in a street a second before she receives a letter. She can't be quite alone in a street when she starts reading a letter just received. There must be somebody pretty near her; he must be mentally invisible."

"Why must there be somebody near her?" asked Angus.

"Because," said Father Brown, "barring carrier-pigeons, somebody must have brought her the letter."

"Do you really mean to say," asked Flambeau, with energy, "that Welkin carried his rival's letters to his lady?"

"Yes," said the priest. "Welkin carried his rival's letters to his lady. You see, he had to."

"Oh, I can't stand much more of this," exploded Flambeau. "Who is this fellow? What does he look like? What is the usual get-up of a mentally invisible man?"

"He is dressed rather handsomely in red, blue and gold," replied the priest promptly with precision, "and in this striking, and even showy, costume he entered Himylaya Mansions under eight human eyes; he killed Smythe in cold blood, and came down into the street again carrying the dead body in his arms –"

"Reverend sir," cried Angus, standing still, "are you raving mad, or am I?"

"You are not mad," said Brown, "only a little unobservant. You have not noticed such a man as this, for example."

He took three quick strides forward, and put his hand on the shoulder of an ordinary passing postman who had bustled by them unnoticed under the shade of the trees.

"Nobody ever notices postmen somehow," he said thoughtfully; "yet they have passions like other men, and even carry large bags where a small corpse can be stowed quite easily."

The postman, instead of turning naturally, had ducked and tumbled against the garden fence. He was a lean fair-bearded man of very ordinary appearance, but as he turned an alarmed face over his shoulder, all three men were fixed with an almost fiendish squint.

* * *

Flambeau went back to his sabres, purple rugs and Persian cat, having many things to attend to. John Turnbull Angus went back to the lady at the shop, with whom that imprudent young man contrives to be extremely comfortable. But Father Brown walked those snow-covered hills under the stars for many hours with a murderer, and what they said to each other will never be known.

The Secret Agent
Chapters I–V
Joseph Conrad

Chapter I

MR. VERLOC, going out in the morning, left his shop nominally in charge of his brother-in-law. It could be done, because there was very little business at any time, and practically none at all before the evening. Mr. Verloc cared but little about his ostensible business. And, moreover, his wife was in charge of his brother-in-law.

The shop was small, and so was the house. It was one of those grimy brick houses which existed in large quantities before the era of reconstruction dawned upon London. The shop was a square box of a place, with the front glazed in small panes. In the daytime the door remained closed; in the evening it stood discreetly but suspiciously ajar.

The window contained photographs of more or less undressed dancing girls; nondescript packages in wrappers like patent medicines; closed yellow paper envelopes, very flimsy, and marked two-and-six in heavy black figures; a few numbers of ancient French comic publications hung across a string as if to dry; a dingy blue china bowl, a casket of black wood, bottles of marking ink, and rubber stamps; a few books, with titles hinting at impropriety; a few apparently old copies of obscure newspapers, badly printed, with titles like *The Torch*, *The Gong* – rousing titles. And the two gas jets inside the panes were always turned low, either for economy's sake or for the sake of the customers.

These customers were either very young men, who hung about the window for a time before slipping in suddenly; or men of a more mature age, but looking generally as if they were not in funds. Some of that last kind had the collars of their overcoats turned right up to their moustaches, and traces of mud on the bottom of their nether garments, which had the appearance of being much worn and not very valuable. And the legs inside them did not, as a general rule, seem of much account either. With their hands plunged deep in the side pockets of their coats, they dodged in sideways, one shoulder first, as if afraid to start the bell going.

The bell, hung on the door by means of a curved ribbon of steel, was difficult to circumvent. It was hopelessly cracked; but of an evening, at the slightest provocation, it clattered behind the customer with impudent virulence.

It clattered; and at that signal, through the dusty glass door behind the painted deal counter, Mr. Verloc would issue hastily from the parlour at the back. His eyes were naturally heavy; he had an air of having wallowed, fully dressed, all day on an unmade bed. Another man would have felt such an appearance a distinct disadvantage. In a commercial transaction of the retail order much depends on the seller's engaging and amiable aspect. But Mr. Verloc knew his business, and remained undisturbed by any sort of aesthetic doubt about his appearance. With a firm, steady-eyed impudence, which seemed to hold back the threat of some abominable menace, he would proceed to sell over the counter some object looking obviously and scandalously not worth the money which passed in the transaction: a small cardboard box with apparently nothing inside, for instance, or one of those carefully closed yellow flimsy envelopes, or a soiled volume in paper covers with a promising title. Now and then it happened that one of the faded, yellow dancing girls would get sold to an amateur, as though she had been alive and young.

Sometimes it was Mrs. Verloc who would appear at the call of the cracked bell. Winnie Verloc was a young woman with a full bust, in a tight bodice, and with broad hips. Her hair was very tidy. Steady-eyed like her husband, she preserved an air of unfathomable indifference behind the rampart of the counter. Then the customer of comparatively tender years would get suddenly disconcerted at having to deal with a woman, and with rage in his heart would proffer a request for a bottle of marking ink, retail value sixpence (price in Verloc's shop one-and-sixpence), which, once outside, he would drop stealthily into the gutter.

The evening visitors – the men with collars turned up and soft hats rammed down – nodded familiarly to Mrs. Verloc, and with a muttered greeting, lifted up the flap at the end of the counter in order to pass into the back parlour, which gave access to a passage and to a steep flight of stairs. The door of the shop was the only means of entrance to the house in which Mr. Verloc carried on his business of a seller of shady wares, exercised his vocation of a protector of society, and cultivated his domestic virtues. These last were pronounced. He was thoroughly domesticated. Neither his spiritual, nor his mental, nor his physical needs were of the kind to take him much abroad. He found at home the ease of his body and the peace of his conscience, together with Mrs. Verloc's wifely attentions and Mrs. Verloc's mother's deferential regard.

Winnie's mother was a stout, wheezy woman, with a large brown face. She wore a black wig under a white cap. Her swollen legs rendered her inactive. She considered herself to be of French descent, which might have been true; and after a good many years of married life with a licensed victualler of the more common sort, she provided for the years of widowhood by letting furnished apartments for gentlemen near Vauxhall Bridge Road in a square once of some splendour and still included in the district of Belgravia. This topographical fact was of some advantage in advertising her rooms; but the patrons of the worthy widow were not exactly of the fashionable kind. Such as they were, her daughter Winnie helped to look after them. Traces of the French descent which the widow boasted of were apparent in Winnie too. They were apparent in the extremely neat and artistic arrangement of her glossy dark hair. Winnie had also other charms: her youth; her full, rounded form; her clear complexion; the provocation of her unfathomable reserve, which never went so far as to prevent conversation, carried on on the lodgers' part with animation, and on hers with an equable amiability. It must be that Mr. Verloc was susceptible to these fascinations. Mr. Verloc was an intermittent patron. He came and went without any very apparent reason. He generally arrived in London (like the influenza) from the Continent, only he arrived unheralded by the Press; and his visitations set in with great severity. He breakfasted in bed, and remained wallowing there with an air of quiet enjoyment till noon every day – and sometimes even to a later hour. But when he went out he seemed to experience a great difficulty in finding his way back to his temporary home in the Belgravian square. He left it late, and returned to it early – as early as three or four in the morning; and on waking up at ten addressed Winnie, bringing in the breakfast tray, with jocular, exhausted civility, in the hoarse, failing tones of a man who had been talking vehemently for many hours together. His prominent, heavy-lidded eyes rolled sideways amorously and languidly, the bedclothes were pulled up to his chin, and his dark smooth moustache covered his thick lips capable of much honeyed banter.

In Winnie's mother's opinion Mr. Verloc was a very nice gentleman. From her life's experience gathered in various 'business houses' the good woman had taken into her retirement an ideal of gentlemanliness as exhibited by the patrons of private-saloon bars. Mr. Verloc approached that ideal; he attained it, in fact.

"Of course, we'll take over your furniture, mother," Winnie had remarked.

The lodging-house was to be given up. It seems it would not answer to carry it on. It would have been too much trouble for Mr. Verloc. It would not have been convenient for his other business. What his business was he did not say; but after his engagement to Winnie he took the trouble to get up before noon, and descending the basement stairs, make himself pleasant to Winnie's mother in the breakfast-room downstairs where she had her motionless being. He stroked the cat, poked the fire, had his lunch served to him there. He left its slightly stuffy cosiness with evident reluctance, but, all the same, remained out till the night was far advanced. He never offered to take Winnie to theatres, as such a nice gentleman ought to have done. His evenings were occupied. His work was in a way political, he told Winnie once. She would have, he warned her, to be very nice to his political friends.

And with her straight, unfathomable glance she answered that she would be so, of course.

How much more he told her as to his occupation it was impossible for Winnie's mother to discover. The married couple took her over with the furniture. The mean aspect of the shop surprised her. The change from the Belgravian square to the narrow street in Soho affected her legs adversely. They became of an enormous size. On the other hand, she experienced a complete relief from material cares. Her son-in-law's heavy good nature inspired her with a sense of absolute safety. Her daughter's future was obviously assured, and even as to her son Stevie she need have no anxiety. She had not been able to conceal from herself that he was a terrible encumbrance, that poor Stevie. But in view of Winnie's fondness for her delicate brother, and of Mr. Verloc's kind and generous disposition, she felt that the poor boy was pretty safe in this rough world. And in her heart of hearts she was not perhaps displeased that the Verlocs had no children. As that circumstance seemed perfectly indifferent to Mr. Verloc, and as Winnie found an object of quasi-maternal affection in her brother, perhaps this was just as well for poor Stevie.

For he was difficult to dispose of, that boy. He was delicate and, in a frail way, good-looking too, except for the vacant droop of his lower lip. Under our excellent system of compulsory education he had learned to read and write, notwithstanding the unfavourable aspect of the lower lip. But as errand-boy he did not turn out a great success. He forgot his messages; he was easily diverted from the straight path of duty by the attractions of stray cats and dogs, which he followed down narrow alleys into unsavoury courts; by the comedies of the streets, which he contemplated open-mouthed, to the detriment of his employer's interests; or by the dramas of fallen horses, whose pathos and violence induced him sometimes to shriek pierceingly in a crowd, which disliked to be disturbed by sounds of distress in its quiet enjoyment of the national spectacle. When led away by a grave and protecting policeman, it would often become apparent that poor Stevie had forgotten his address – at least for a time. A brusque question caused him to stutter to the point of suffocation. When startled by anything perplexing he used to squint horribly. However, he never had any fits (which was encouraging); and before the natural outbursts of impatience on the part of his father he could always, in his childhood's days, run for protection behind the short skirts of his sister Winnie. On the other hand, he might have been suspected of hiding a fund of reckless naughtiness. When he had reached the age of fourteen a friend of his late father, an agent for a foreign preserved milk firm, having given him an opening as office-boy, he was discovered one foggy afternoon, in his chief's absence, busy letting off fireworks on the staircase. He touched off in quick succession a set of fierce rockets, angry catherine wheels, loudly exploding squibs – and the matter might have turned out very serious. An awful panic spread through the whole building. Wild-eyed, choking clerks stampeded through the passages full of smoke, silk hats and elderly business men could be seen rolling independently down the stairs. Stevie did not seem to derive any personal gratification from what he had done. His motives for this stroke of originality were difficult to discover. It was only later on that Winnie obtained from him a misty and confused confession. It seems that two other office-boys in the building had worked upon his feelings by tales of injustice and oppression till they had wrought his compassion to the pitch of that frenzy. But his father's friend, of course, dismissed him summarily as likely to ruin his business. After that altruistic exploit Stevie was put to help wash the dishes in the basement kitchen, and to black the boots of the gentlemen patronising the Belgravian mansion. There was obviously no future in such work. The gentlemen tipped him a shilling now and then. Mr. Verloc showed himself the most generous of lodgers. But altogether all that did not amount to much either in the way of gain or prospects; so that when Winnie announced her engagement to Mr. Verloc her mother could not help wondering, with a sigh and a glance towards the scullery, what would become of poor Stephen now.

It appeared that Mr. Verloc was ready to take him over together with his wife's mother and with the furniture, which was the whole visible fortune of the family. Mr. Verloc gathered everything as it came to his broad, good-natured breast. The furniture was disposed to the best advantage all over the house, but Mrs. Verloc's mother was confined to two back rooms on the first floor. The luckless Stevie slept in one of them. By this time a growth of thin fluffy hair had come to blur, like a golden mist, the sharp line of his small lower jaw. He helped his sister with blind love and docility in her household duties. Mr. Verloc thought that some occupation would be good for him. His spare time he occupied by drawing circles with compass and pencil on a piece of paper. He applied himself to that pastime with great industry, with his elbows spread out and bowed low over the kitchen table. Through the open door of the parlour at the back of the shop Winnie, his sister, glanced at him from time to time with maternal vigilance.

Chapter II

SUCH WAS the house, the household, and the business Mr. Verloc left behind him on his way westward at the hour of half-past ten in the morning. It was unusually early for him; his whole person exhaled the charm of almost dewy freshness; he wore his blue cloth overcoat unbuttoned; his boots were shiny; his cheeks, freshly shaven, had a sort of gloss; and even his heavy-lidded eyes, refreshed by a night of peaceful slumber, sent out glances of comparative alertness. Through the park railings these glances beheld men and women riding in the Row, couples cantering past harmoniously, others advancing sedately at a walk, loitering groups of three or four, solitary horsemen looking unsociable, and solitary women followed at a long distance by a groom with a cockade to his hat and a leather belt over his tight-fitting coat. Carriages went bowling by, mostly two-horse broughams, with here and there a victoria with the skin of some wild beast inside and a woman's face and hat emerging above the folded hood. And a peculiarly London sun – against which nothing could be said except that it looked bloodshot – glorified all this by its stare. It hung at a moderate elevation above Hyde Park Corner with an air of punctual and benign vigilance. The very pavement under Mr. Verloc's feet had an old-gold tinge in that diffused light, in which neither wall, nor tree, nor beast, nor man cast a shadow. Mr. Verloc was going westward through a town without shadows in an atmosphere of powdered old gold. There were red, coppery gleams on the roofs of houses, on the corners of walls, on the panels of carriages, on the very coats of the horses, and on the broad back of Mr. Verloc's overcoat, where they produced a dull effect of rustiness. But Mr. Verloc was not in the least conscious of having got rusty. He surveyed through the park railings the evidences of the town's opulence and luxury with an approving eye. All these people had to be protected. Protection is the first necessity of opulence and luxury. They had to be protected; and their horses, carriages, houses, servants had to be protected; and the source of their wealth had to be protected in the heart of the city and the heart of the country; the whole social order favourable to their hygienic idleness had to be protected against the shallow enviousness of unhygienic labour. It had to – and Mr. Verloc would have rubbed his hands with satisfaction had he not been constitutionally averse from every superfluous exertion. His idleness was not hygienic, but it suited him very well. He was in a manner devoted to it with a sort of inert fanaticism, or perhaps rather with a fanatical inertness. Born of industrious parents for a life of toil, he had embraced indolence from an impulse as profound as inexplicable and as imperious as the impulse which directs a man's preference for one particular woman in a given thousand. He was too lazy even for a mere demagogue, for a workman orator, for a leader of labour. It was too much trouble. He required a more perfect form of ease; or it might have been that he was the victim of a philosophical unbelief in the effectiveness of every human effort. Such a form of indolence requires, implies, a certain amount of intelligence. Mr. Verloc was not devoid of intelligence – and at the notion of a menaced social order he would perhaps have winked to himself if there had not been an effort to make in that sign of scepticism. His big, prominent eyes were not well adapted to winking. They were rather of the sort that closes solemnly in slumber with majestic effect.

Undemonstrative and burly in a fat-pig style, Mr. Verloc, without either rubbing his hands with satisfaction or winking sceptically at his thoughts, proceeded on his way. He trod the pavement heavily with his shiny boots, and his general get-up was that of a well-to-do mechanic in business for himself. He might have been anything from a picture-frame maker to a lock-smith; an employer of labour in a small way. But there was also about him an indescribable air which no mechanic could have acquired in the practice of his handicraft however dishonestly exercised: the air common to men who live on the vices, the follies, or the baser fears of mankind; the air of moral nihilism common to keepers of gambling hells and disorderly houses; to private detectives and inquiry agents; to drink sellers and, I should say, to the sellers of invigorating electric belts and to the inventors of patent medicines. But of that last I am not sure, not having carried my investigations so far into the depths. For all I know, the expression of these last may be perfectly diabolic. I shouldn't be surprised. What I want to affirm is that Mr. Verloc's expression was by no means diabolic.

Before reaching Knightsbridge, Mr. Verloc took a turn to the left out of the busy main thoroughfare, uproarious with the traffic of swaying omnibuses and trotting vans, in the almost silent, swift flow of hansoms. Under his hat, worn with a slight backward tilt, his hair had been carefully brushed into respectful sleekness; for his business was with an Embassy. And Mr. Verloc, steady like a rock – a soft kind of rock – marched now along a street which could with every propriety be described as private. In its breadth, emptiness, and extent it had the majesty of inorganic nature, of matter that never dies. The only reminder of mortality was a doctor's brougham arrested in august solitude close to the curbstone. The polished knockers of the doors gleamed as far as the eye could reach, the clean windows shone with a dark opaque lustre. And all was still. But a milk cart rattled noisily across the distant perspective; a butcher boy, driving with the noble recklessness of a charioteer at Olympic Games, dashed round the corner sitting high above a pair of red wheels. A guilty-looking cat issuing from under the stones ran for a while in front of Mr. Verloc, then dived into another basement; and a thick police constable, looking a stranger to every emotion, as if he too were part of inorganic nature, surging apparently out of a lamp-post, took not the slightest notice of Mr. Verloc. With a turn to the left Mr. Verloc pursued his way along a narrow street by the side of a yellow wall which, for some inscrutable reason, had No. 1 Chesham Square written on it in black letters. Chesham Square was at least sixty yards away, and Mr. Verloc, cosmopolitan enough not to be deceived by London's topographical mysteries, held on steadily, without a sign of surprise or indignation. At last, with business-like persistency, he reached the Square, and made diagonally for the number 10. This belonged to an imposing carriage gate in a high, clean wall between two houses, of which one rationally enough bore the number 9 and the other was numbered 37; but the fact that this last belonged to Porthill Street, a street well known in the neighbourhood, was proclaimed by an inscription placed above the ground-floor windows by whatever highly efficient authority is charged with the duty of keeping track of London's strayed houses. Why powers are not asked of Parliament (a short act would do) for compelling those edifices to return where they belong is one of the mysteries of municipal administration. Mr. Verloc did not trouble his head about it, his mission in life being the protection of the social mechanism, not its perfectionment or even its criticism.

It was so early that the porter of the Embassy issued hurriedly out of his lodge still struggling with the left sleeve of his livery coat. His waistcoat was red, and he wore knee-breeches, but his aspect was flustered. Mr. Verloc, aware of the rush on his flank, drove it off by simply holding out an envelope stamped with the arms of the Embassy, and passed on. He produced the same talisman also to the footman who opened the door, and stood back to let him enter the hall.

A clear fire burned in a tall fireplace, and an elderly man standing with his back to it, in evening dress and with a chain round his neck, glanced up from the newspaper he was holding spread out in both hands before his calm and severe face. He didn't move; but another lackey, in brown trousers and claw-hammer coat edged with thin yellow cord, approaching Mr. Verloc listened to the murmur of his name, and turning round on his heel in silence, began to walk, without looking back once. Mr. Verloc, thus led along a ground-floor passage to the left of the great carpeted staircase, was suddenly motioned to enter a quite small room furnished with a heavy writing-table and a few chairs. The servant shut the door, and Mr. Verloc remained alone. He did not take a seat. With his hat and stick held in one hand he glanced about, passing his other podgy hand over his uncovered sleek head.

Another door opened noiselessly, and Mr. Verloc immobilising his glance in that direction saw at first only black clothes, the bald top of a head, and a drooping dark grey whisker on each side of a pair of wrinkled hands. The person who had entered was holding a batch of papers before his eyes and walked up to the table with a rather mincing step, turning the papers over the while. Privy Councillor Wurmt, Chancelier d'Ambassade, was rather short-sighted. This meritorious official laying the papers on the table, disclosed a face of pasty complexion and of melancholy ugliness surrounded by a lot of fine, long dark grey hairs, barred heavily by thick and bushy eyebrows. He put on a black-framed pince-nez upon a blunt and shapeless nose, and seemed struck by Mr. Verloc's appearance. Under the enormous eyebrows his weak eyes blinked pathetically through the glasses.

He made no sign of greeting; neither did Mr. Verloc, who certainly knew his place; but a subtle change about the general outlines of his shoulders and back suggested a slight bending of Mr. Verloc's spine under the vast surface of his overcoat. The effect was of unobtrusive deference.

"I have here some of your reports," said the bureaucrat in an unexpectedly soft and weary voice, and pressing the tip of his forefinger on the papers with force. He paused; and Mr. Verloc, who had recognised his own handwriting very well, waited in an almost breathless silence. "We are not very satisfied with the attitude of the police here," the other continued, with every appearance of mental fatigue.

The shoulders of Mr. Verloc, without actually moving, suggested a shrug. And for the first time since he left his home that morning his lips opened.

"Every country has its police," he said philosophically. But as the official of the Embassy went on blinking at him steadily he felt constrained to add: "Allow me to observe that I have no means of action upon the police here."

"What is desired," said the man of papers, "is the occurrence of something definite which should stimulate their vigilance. That is within your province – is it not so?"

Mr. Verloc made no answer except by a sigh, which escaped him involuntarily, for instantly he tried to give his face a cheerful expression. The official blinked doubtfully, as if affected by the dim light of the room. He repeated vaguely.

"The vigilance of the police – and the severity of the magistrates. The general leniency of the judicial procedure here, and the utter absence of all repressive measures, are a scandal to Europe. What is wished for just now is the accentuation of the unrest – of the fermentation which undoubtedly exists –"

"Undoubtedly, undoubtedly," broke in Mr. Verloc in a deep deferential bass of an oratorical quality, so utterly different from the tone in which he had spoken before that his interlocutor remained profoundly surprised. "It exists to a dangerous degree. My reports for the last twelve months make it sufficiently clear."

"Your reports for the last twelve months," State Councillor Wurmt began in his gentle and dispassionate tone, "have been read by me. I failed to discover why you wrote them at all."

A sad silence reigned for a time. Mr. Verloc seemed to have swallowed his tongue, and the other gazed at the papers on the table fixedly. At last he gave them a slight push.

"The state of affairs you expose there is assumed to exist as the first condition of your employment. What is required at present is not writing, but the bringing to light of a distinct, significant fact – I would almost say of an alarming fact."

"I need not say that all my endeavours shall be directed to that end," Mr. Verloc said, with convinced modulations in his conversational husky tone. But the sense of being blinked at watchfully behind the blind glitter of these eye-glasses on the other side of the table disconcerted him. He stopped short with a gesture of absolute devotion. The useful, hard-working, if obscure member of the Embassy had an air of being impressed by some newly-born thought.

"You are very corpulent," he said.

This observation, really of a psychological nature, and advanced with the modest hesitation of an officeman more familiar with ink and paper than with the requirements of active life, stung Mr. Verloc in the manner of a rude personal remark. He stepped back a pace.

"Eh? What were you pleased to say?" he exclaimed, with husky resentment.

The Chancelier d'Ambassade entrusted with the conduct of this interview seemed to find it too much for him.

"I think," he said, "that you had better see Mr. Vladimir. Yes, decidedly I think you ought to see Mr. Vladimir. Be good enough to wait here," he added, and went out with mincing steps.

At once Mr. Verloc passed his hand over his hair. A slight perspiration had broken out on his forehead. He let the air escape from his pursed-up lips like a man blowing at a spoonful of hot soup. But when the servant in brown appeared at the door silently, Mr. Verloc had not moved an inch from the place he had occupied throughout the interview. He had remained motionless, as if feeling himself surrounded by pitfalls.

He walked along a passage lighted by a lonely gas-jet, then up a flight of winding stairs, and through a glazed and cheerful corridor on the first floor. The footman threw open a door, and stood aside. The feet of Mr. Verloc felt a thick carpet. The room was large, with three windows; and a young man with a shaven, big face, sitting in a roomy arm-chair before a vast mahogany writing-table, said in French to the Chancelier d'Ambassade, who was going out with the papers in his hand:

"You are quite right, mon cher. He's fat – the animal."

Mr. Vladimir, First Secretary, had a drawing-room reputation as an agreeable and entertaining man. He was something of a favourite in society. His wit consisted in discovering droll connections between incongruous ideas; and when talking in that strain he sat well forward of his seat, with his left hand raised, as if exhibiting his funny demonstrations between the thumb and forefinger, while his round and clean-shaven face wore an expression of merry perplexity.

But there was no trace of merriment or perplexity in the way he looked at Mr. Verloc. Lying far back in the deep arm-chair, with squarely spread elbows, and throwing one leg over a thick knee, he had with his smooth and rosy countenance the air of a preternaturally thriving baby that will not stand nonsense from anybody.

"You understand French, I suppose?" he said.

Mr. Verloc stated huskily that he did. His whole vast bulk had a forward inclination. He stood on the carpet in the middle of the room, clutching his hat and stick in one hand; the other hung lifelessly by his side. He muttered unobtrusively somewhere deep down in his throat something about having done his military service in the French artillery. At once, with contemptuous perversity, Mr. Vladimir changed the language, and began to speak idiomatic English without the slightest trace of a foreign accent.

"Ah! Yes. Of course. Let's see. How much did you get for obtaining the design of the improved breech-block of their new field-gun?"

"Five years' rigorous confinement in a fortress," Mr. Verloc answered unexpectedly, but without any sign of feeling.

"You got off easily," was Mr. Vladimir's comment. "And, anyhow, it served you right for letting yourself get caught. What made you go in for that sort of thing – eh?"

Mr. Verloc's husky conversational voice was heard speaking of youth, of a fatal infatuation for an unworthy –

"Aha! Cherchez la femme," Mr. Vladimir deigned to interrupt, unbending, but without affability; there was, on the contrary, a touch of grimness in his condescension. "How long have you been employed by the Embassy here?" he asked.

"Ever since the time of the late Baron Stott-Wartenheim," Mr. Verloc answered in subdued tones, and protruding his lips sadly, in sign of sorrow for the deceased diplomat. The First Secretary observed this play of physiognomy steadily.

"Ah! Ever since. Well! What have you got to say for yourself?" he asked sharply.

Mr. Verloc answered with some surprise that he was not aware of having anything special to say. He had been summoned by a letter – And he plunged his hand busily into the side pocket of his overcoat, but before the mocking, cynical watchfulness of Mr. Vladimir, concluded to leave it there.

"Bah!" said that latter. "What do you mean by getting out of condition like this? You haven't got even the physique of your profession. You – a member of a starving proletariat – never! You – a desperate socialist or anarchist – which is it?"

"Anarchist," stated Mr. Verloc in a deadened tone.

"Bosh!" went on Mr. Vladimir, without raising his voice. "You startled old Wurmt himself. You wouldn't deceive an idiot. They all are that by-the-by, but you seem to me simply impossible. So you began your connection with us by stealing the French gun designs. And you got yourself caught. That must have been very disagreeable to our Government. You don't seem to be very smart."

Mr. Verloc tried to exculpate himself huskily.

"As I've had occasion to observe before, a fatal infatuation for an unworthy –"

Mr. Vladimir raised a large white, plump hand. "Ah, yes. The unlucky attachment – of your youth. She got hold of the money, and then sold you to the police – eh?"

The doleful change in Mr. Verloc's physiognomy, the momentary drooping of his whole person, confessed that such was the regrettable case. Mr. Vladimir's hand clasped the ankle reposing on his knee. The sock was of dark blue silk.

"You see, that was not very clever of you. Perhaps you are too susceptible."

Mr. Verloc intimated in a throaty, veiled murmur that he was no longer young.

"Oh! That's a failing which age does not cure," Mr. Vladimir remarked, with sinister familiarity. "But no! You are too fat for that. You could not have come to look like this if you had been at all susceptible. I'll tell you what I think is the matter: you are a lazy fellow. How long have you been drawing pay from this Embassy?"

"Eleven years," was the answer, after a moment of sulky hesitation. "I've been charged with several missions to London while His Excellency Baron Stott-Wartenheim was still Ambassador in Paris. Then by his Excellency's instructions I settled down in London. I am English."

"You are! Are you? Eh?"

"A natural-born British subject," Mr. Verloc said stolidly. "But my father was French, and so –"

"Never mind explaining," interrupted the other. "I daresay you could have been legally a Marshal of France and a Member of Parliament in England – and then, indeed, you would have been of some use to our Embassy."

This flight of fancy provoked something like a faint smile on Mr. Verloc's face. Mr. Vladimir retained an imperturbable gravity.

"But, as I've said, you are a lazy fellow; you don't use your opportunities. In the time of Baron Stott-Wartenheim we had a lot of soft-headed people running this Embassy. They caused fellows of your sort to form a false conception of the nature of a secret service fund. It is my business to correct this misapprehension by telling you what the secret service is not. It is not a philanthropic institution. I've had you called here on purpose to tell you this."

Mr. Vladimir observed the forced expression of bewilderment on Verloc's face, and smiled sarcastically.

"I see that you understand me perfectly. I daresay you are intelligent enough for your work. What we want now is activity – activity."

On repeating this last word Mr. Vladimir laid a long white forefinger on the edge of the desk. Every trace of huskiness disappeared from Verloc's voice. The nape of his gross neck became crimson above the velvet collar of his overcoat. His lips quivered before they came widely open.

"If you'll only be good enough to look up my record," he boomed out in his great, clear oratorical bass, "you'll see I gave a warning only three months ago, on the occasion of the Grand Duke Romuald's visit to Paris, which was telegraphed from here to the French police, and –"

"Tut, tut!" broke out Mr. Vladimir, with a frowning grimace. "The French police had no use for your warning. Don't roar like this. What the devil do you mean?"

With a note of proud humility Mr. Verloc apologised for forgetting himself. His voice, – famous for years at open-air meetings and at workmen's assemblies in large halls, had contributed, he said, to his reputation of a good and trustworthy comrade. It was, therefore, a part of his usefulness. It had inspired confidence in his principles. "I was always put up to speak by the leaders at a critical moment," Mr. Verloc declared, with obvious satisfaction. There was no uproar above which he could not make himself heard, he added; and suddenly he made a demonstration.

"Allow me," he said. With lowered forehead, without looking up, swiftly and ponderously he crossed the room to one of the French windows. As if giving way to an uncontrollable impulse, he opened it a little. Mr. Vladimir, jumping up amazed from the depths of the arm-chair, looked over his shoulder; and below, across the courtyard of the Embassy, well beyond the open gate, could be seen the broad back of a policeman watching idly the gorgeous perambulator of a wealthy baby being wheeled in state across the Square.

"Constable!" said Mr. Verloc, with no more effort than if he were whispering; and Mr. Vladimir burst into a laugh on seeing the policeman spin round as if prodded by a sharp instrument. Mr. Verloc shut the window quietly, and returned to the middle of the room.

"With a voice like that," he said, putting on the husky conversational pedal, "I was naturally trusted. And I knew what to say, too."

Mr. Vladimir, arranging his cravat, observed him in the glass over the mantelpiece.

"I daresay you have the social revolutionary jargon by heart well enough," he said contemptuously. "Vox et... You haven't ever studied Latin – have you?"

"No," growled Mr. Verloc. "You did not expect me to know it. I belong to the million. Who knows Latin? Only a few hundred imbeciles who aren't fit to take care of themselves."

For some thirty seconds longer Mr. Vladimir studied in the mirror the fleshy profile, the gross bulk, of the man behind him. And at the same time he had the advantage of seeing his own face, clean-shaved and round, rosy about the gills, and with the thin sensitive lips formed exactly for the utterance of those delicate witticisms which had made him such a favourite in the very highest society. Then he turned, and advanced into the room with such determination that the very ends of his quaintly old-fashioned bow necktie seemed to bristle with unspeakable menaces. The movement was so swift and fierce that Mr. Verloc, casting an oblique glance, quailed inwardly.

"Aha! You dare be impudent," Mr. Vladimir began, with an amazingly guttural intonation not only utterly un-English, but absolutely un-European, and startling even to Mr. Verloc's experience of cosmopolitan slums. "You dare! Well, I am going to speak plain English to you. Voice won't do. We have no use for your voice. We don't want a voice. We want facts – startling facts – damn you," he added, with a sort of ferocious discretion, right into Mr. Verloc's face.

"Don't you try to come over me with your Hyperborean manners," Mr. Verloc defended himself huskily, looking at the carpet. At this his interlocutor, smiling mockingly above the bristling bow of his necktie, switched the conversation into French.

"You give yourself for an 'agent provocateur.' The proper business of an 'agent provocateur' is to provoke. As far as I can judge from your record kept here, you have done nothing to earn your money for the last three years."

"Nothing!" exclaimed Verloc, stirring not a limb, and not raising his eyes, but with the note of sincere feeling in his tone. "I have several times prevented what might have been –"

"There is a proverb in this country which says prevention is better than cure," interrupted Mr. Vladimir, throwing himself into the arm-chair. "It is stupid in a general way. There is no end to prevention. But it is characteristic. They dislike finality in this country. Don't you be too English. And in this particular instance, don't be absurd. The evil is already here. We don't want prevention – we want cure."

He paused, turned to the desk, and turning over some papers lying there, spoke in a changed business-like tone, without looking at Mr. Verloc.

"You know, of course, of the International Conference assembled in Milan?"

Mr. Verloc intimated hoarsely that he was in the habit of reading the daily papers. To a further question his answer was that, of course, he understood what he read.

At this Mr. Vladimir, smiling faintly at the documents he was still scanning one after another, murmured "As long as it is not written in Latin, I suppose."

"Or Chinese," added Mr. Verloc stolidly.

"H'm. Some of your revolutionary friends' effusions are written in a *charabia* every bit as incomprehensible as Chinese –" Mr. Vladimir let fall disdainfully a grey sheet of printed matter. "What are all these leaflets headed F.P., with a hammer, pen, and torch crossed? What does it mean, this F.P.?" Mr. Verloc approached the imposing writing-table.

"The Future of the Proletariat. It's a society," he explained, standing ponderously by the side of the arm-chair, "not anarchist in principle, but open to all shades of revolutionary opinion."

"Are you in it?"

"One of the Vice-Presidents," Mr. Verloc breathed out heavily; and the First Secretary of the Embassy raised his head to look at him.

"Then you ought to be ashamed of yourself," he said incisively. "Isn't your society capable of anything else but printing this prophetic bosh in blunt type on this filthy paper eh? Why don't you do something? Look here. I've this matter in hand now, and I tell you plainly that you will have to earn your money. The good old Stott-Wartenheim times are over. No work, no pay."

Mr. Verloc felt a queer sensation of faintness in his stout legs. He stepped back one pace, and blew his nose loudly.

He was, in truth, startled and alarmed. The rusty London sunshine struggling clear of the London mist shed a lukewarm brightness into the First Secretary's private room; and in the silence Mr. Verloc heard against a window-pane the faint buzzing of a fly – his first fly of the year – heralding better than any number of swallows the approach of spring. The useless fussing of that tiny energetic organism affected unpleasantly this big man threatened in his indolence.

In the pause Mr. Vladimir formulated in his mind a series of disparaging remarks concerning Mr. Verloc's face and figure. The fellow was unexpectedly vulgar, heavy, and impudently unintelligent. He looked uncommonly like a master plumber come to present his bill. The First Secretary of the Embassy, from his occasional excursions into the field of American humour, had formed a special notion of that class of mechanic as the embodiment of fraudulent laziness and incompetency.

This was then the famous and trusty secret agent, so secret that he was never designated otherwise but by the symbol Δ in the late Baron Stott-Wartenheim's official, semi-official, and confidential correspondence; the celebrated agent Δ whose warnings had the power to change the schemes and the dates of royal, imperial, grand ducal journeys, and sometimes caused them to be put off altogether! This fellow! And Mr. Vladimir indulged mentally in an enormous and derisive fit of merriment, partly at his own astonishment, which he judged naive, but mostly at the expense of the universally regretted Baron Stott-Wartenheim. His late Excellency, whom the august favour of his Imperial master had imposed as Ambassador upon several reluctant Ministers of Foreign Affairs, had enjoyed in his lifetime a fame for an owlish, pessimistic gullibility. His Excellency had the social revolution on the brain. He imagined himself to be a diplomatist set apart by a special dispensation to watch the end of diplomacy, and pretty nearly the end of the world, in a horrid democratic upheaval. His prophetic and doleful despatches had been for years the joke of Foreign Offices. He was said to have exclaimed on his deathbed (visited by his Imperial friend and master): "Unhappy Europe! Thou shalt perish by the moral insanity of thy children!" He was fated to be the victim of the first humbugging rascal that came along, thought Mr. Vladimir, smiling vaguely at Mr. Verloc.

"You ought to venerate the memory of Baron Stott-Wartenheim," he exclaimed suddenly.

The lowered physiognomy of Mr. Verloc expressed a sombre and weary annoyance.

"Permit me to observe to you," he said, "that I came here because I was summoned by a peremptory letter. I have been here only twice before in the last eleven years, and certainly never at eleven in the morning. It isn't very wise to call me up like this. There is just a chance of being seen. And that would be no joke for me."

Mr. Vladimir shrugged his shoulders.

"It would destroy my usefulness," continued the other hotly.

"That's your affair," murmured Mr. Vladimir, with soft brutality. "When you cease to be useful you shall cease to be employed. Yes. Right off. Cut short. You shall –" Mr. Vladimir, frowning, paused, at a loss for a sufficiently idiomatic expression, and instantly brightened up, with a grin of beautifully white teeth. "You shall be chucked," he brought out ferociously.

Once more Mr. Verloc had to react with all the force of his will against that sensation of faintness running down one's legs which once upon a time had inspired some poor devil with the felicitous expression: "My heart went down into my boots." Mr. Verloc, aware of the sensation, raised his head bravely.

Mr. Vladimir bore the look of heavy inquiry with perfect serenity.

"What we want is to administer a tonic to the Conference in Milan," he said airily. "Its deliberations upon international action for the suppression of political crime don't seem to get anywhere. England lags. This country is absurd with its sentimental regard for individual liberty. It's intolerable to think that all your friends have got only to come over to –"

"In that way I have them all under my eye," Mr. Verloc interrupted huskily.

"It would be much more to the point to have them all under lock and key. England must be brought into line. The imbecile bourgeoisie of this country make themselves the accomplices of the very people whose aim is to drive them out of their houses to starve in ditches. And they have the political power still, if they only had the sense to use it for their preservation. I suppose you agree that the middle classes are stupid?"

Mr. Verloc agreed hoarsely.

"They are."

"They have no imagination. They are blinded by an idiotic vanity. What they want just now is a jolly good scare. This is the psychological moment to set your friends to work. I have had you called here to develop to you my idea."

And Mr. Vladimir developed his idea from on high, with scorn and condescension, displaying at the same time an amount of ignorance as to the real aims, thoughts, and methods of the revolutionary world which filled the silent Mr. Verloc with inward consternation. He confounded causes with effects more than was excusable; the most distinguished propagandists with impulsive bomb throwers; assumed organisation where in the nature of things it could not exist; spoke of the social revolutionary party one moment as of a perfectly disciplined army, where the word of chiefs was supreme, and at another as if it had been the loosest association of desperate brigands that ever camped in a mountain gorge. Once Mr. Verloc had opened his mouth for a protest, but the raising of a shapely, large white hand arrested him. Very soon he became too appalled to even try to protest. He listened in a stillness of dread which resembled the immobility of profound attention.

"A series of outrages," Mr. Vladimir continued calmly, "executed here in this country; not only *planned* here – that would not do – they would not mind. Your friends could set half the Continent on fire without influencing the public opinion here in favour of a universal repressive legislation. They will not look outside their backyard here."

Mr. Verloc cleared his throat, but his heart failed him, and he said nothing.

"These outrages need not be especially sanguinary," Mr. Vladimir went on, as if delivering a scientific lecture, "but they must be sufficiently startling – effective. Let them be directed against buildings, for instance. What is the fetish of the hour that all the bourgeoisie recognise – eh, Mr. Verloc?"

Mr. Verloc opened his hands and shrugged his shoulders slightly.

"You are too lazy to think," was Mr. Vladimir's comment upon that gesture. "Pay attention to what I say. The fetish of today is neither royalty nor religion. Therefore the palace and the church should be left alone. You understand what I mean, Mr. Verloc?"

The dismay and the scorn of Mr. Verloc found vent in an attempt at levity.

"Perfectly. But what of the Embassies? A series of attacks on the various Embassies," he began; but he could not withstand the cold, watchful stare of the First Secretary.

"You can be facetious, I see," the latter observed carelessly. "That's all right. It may enliven your oratory at socialistic congresses. But this room is no place for it. It would be infinitely safer for you to follow carefully what I am saying. As you are being called upon to furnish facts instead of cock-and-bull stories, you had better try to make your profit off what I am taking the trouble to explain to you. The sacrosanct fetish of today is science. Why don't you get some of your friends to go for that wooden-faced panjandrum – eh? Is it not part of these institutions which must be swept away before the F.P. comes along?"

Mr. Verloc said nothing. He was afraid to open his lips lest a groan should escape him.

"This is what you should try for. An attempt upon a crowned head or on a president is sensational enough in a way, but not so much as it used to be. It has entered into the general conception of the existence of all chiefs of state. It's almost conventional – especially since so many presidents have been assassinated. Now let us take an outrage upon – say a church. Horrible enough at first sight, no doubt, and yet not so effective as a person of an ordinary mind might think. No matter how revolutionary and anarchist in inception, there would be fools enough to give such an outrage the character of a religious manifestation. And that would detract from the especial alarming significance we wish to give to the act. A murderous attempt on a restaurant or a theatre would suffer in the same way from the suggestion of non-political passion: the exasperation of a hungry man, an act of social revenge. All this is used up; it is no longer instructive as an object lesson in revolutionary anarchism. Every newspaper has ready-made phrases to explain such manifestations away. I am about to give you the philosophy of bomb throwing from my point of view; from the point of view you pretend to have been serving for the last eleven years. I will try not to talk above your head. The sensibilities of the class you are attacking are soon blunted. Property seems to them an indestructible thing. You can't count upon their emotions either of pity or fear for very long. A bomb outrage to have any influence on public opinion now must go beyond the intention of vengeance or terrorism. It must be purely destructive. It must be that, and only that, beyond the faintest suspicion of any other object. You anarchists should make it clear that you are perfectly determined to make a clean sweep of the whole social creation. But how to get that appallingly absurd notion into the heads of the middle classes so that there should be no mistake? That's the question. By directing your blows at something outside the ordinary passions of humanity is the answer. Of course, there is art. A bomb in the National Gallery would make some noise. But it would not be serious enough. Art has never been their fetish. It's like breaking a few back windows in a man's house; whereas, if you want to make him really sit up, you must try at least to raise the roof. There would be some screaming of course, but from whom? Artists – art critics and such like – people of no account. Nobody minds what they say. But there is learning – science. Any imbecile that has got an income believes in that. He does not know why, but he believes it matters somehow. It is the sacrosanct fetish. All the damned professors are radicals at heart. Let them know that their great panjandrum has got to go too, to make room for the Future of the Proletariat. A howl from all these intellectual idiots is bound to help forward the labours of the Milan Conference. They will be writing to the papers. Their indignation would be above suspicion, no material interests being openly at stake, and it will alarm every selfishness of the class which should be impressed. They believe that in some mysterious way science is at the source of their material prosperity. They do. And the absurd ferocity of such a demonstration will affect them more profoundly than the mangling of a whole street – or theatre – full of their own kind. To that last they can always say: 'Oh! It's mere class hate.' But what is one to say to an act of destructive ferocity so absurd as to be incomprehensible, inexplicable, almost unthinkable; in fact, mad? Madness alone is truly terrifying, inasmuch as you cannot placate it either by threats, persuasion, or bribes. Moreover, I am a civilised man. I would never dream of directing you to organise a mere butchery, even if I expected the best results from it. But I wouldn't expect from a butchery the result I want. Murder is always with us. It is almost an institution. The demonstration must be against learning – science. But not every science will do. The attack must have all the shocking senselessness of gratuitous blasphemy. Since bombs are your means of expression, it would be really telling if one could throw a bomb into pure mathematics. But that is impossible. I have been trying to educate you; I have expounded to you the higher philosophy of your usefulness, and suggested to you some serviceable arguments. The practical application of my teaching interests *you* mostly. But from the moment I have undertaken to interview you I have also given some attention to the practical aspect of the question. What do you think of having a go at astronomy?"

For sometime already Mr. Verloc's immobility by the side of the arm-chair resembled a state of collapsed coma – a sort of passive insensibility interrupted by slight convulsive starts, such as may be observed in the domestic dog having a nightmare on the hearthrug. And it was in an uneasy doglike growl that he repeated the word:

"Astronomy."

He had not recovered thoroughly as yet from that state of bewilderment brought about by the effort to follow Mr. Vladimir's rapid incisive utterance. It had overcome his power of assimilation. It had made him angry. This anger was complicated by incredulity. And suddenly it dawned upon him that all this was an elaborate joke. Mr. Vladimir exhibited his white teeth in a smile, with dimples on his round, full face posed with a complacent inclination above the bristling bow of his neck-tie. The favourite of intelligent society women had assumed his drawing-room attitude accompanying the delivery of delicate witticisms. Sitting well forward, his white hand upraised, he seemed to hold delicately between his thumb and forefinger the subtlety of his suggestion.

"There could be nothing better. Such an outrage combines the greatest possible regard for humanity with the most alarming display of ferocious imbecility. I defy the ingenuity of journalists to persuade their public that any given member of the proletariat can have a personal grievance against astronomy. Starvation itself could hardly be dragged in there – eh? And there are other advantages. The whole civilised world has heard of Greenwich. The very boot-blacks in the basement of Charing Cross Station know something of it. See?"

The features of Mr. Vladimir, so well known in the best society by their humorous urbanity, beamed with cynical self-satisfaction, which would have astonished the intelligent women his wit entertained so exquisitely. "Yes," he continued, with a contemptuous smile, "the blowing up of the first meridian is bound to raise a howl of execration."

"A difficult business," Mr. Verloc mumbled, feeling that this was the only safe thing to say.

"What is the matter? Haven't you the whole gang under your hand? The very pick of the basket? That old terrorist Yundt is here. I see him walking about Piccadilly in his green havelock almost every day. And Michaelis, the ticket-of-leave apostle – you don't mean to say you don't know where he is? Because if you don't, I can tell you," Mr. Vladimir went on menacingly. "If you imagine that you are the only one on the secret fund list, you are mistaken."

This perfectly gratuitous suggestion caused Mr. Verloc to shuffle his feet slightly.

"And the whole Lausanne lot – eh? Haven't they been flocking over here at the first hint of the Milan Conference? This is an absurd country."

"It will cost money," Mr. Verloc said, by a sort of instinct.

"That cock won't fight," Mr. Vladimir retorted, with an amazingly genuine English accent. "You'll get your screw every month, and no more till something happens. And if nothing happens very soon you won't get even that. What's your ostensible occupation? What are you supposed to live by?"

"I keep a shop," answered Mr. Verloc.

"A shop! What sort of shop?"

"Stationery, newspapers. My wife –"

"Your what?" interrupted Mr. Vladimir in his guttural Central Asian tones.

"My wife." Mr. Verloc raised his husky voice slightly. "I am married."

"That be damned for a yarn," exclaimed the other in unfeigned astonishment. "Married! And you a professed anarchist, too! What is this confounded nonsense? But I suppose it's merely a manner of speaking. Anarchists don't marry. It's well known. They can't. It would be apostasy."

"My wife isn't one," Mr. Verloc mumbled sulkily. "Moreover, it's no concern of yours."

"Oh yes, it is," snapped Mr. Vladimir. "I am beginning to be convinced that you are not at all the man for the work you've been employed on. Why, you must have discredited yourself completely in your own world by your marriage. Couldn't you have managed without? This is your virtuous attachment – eh? What with one sort of attachment and another you are doing away with your usefulness."

Mr. Verloc, puffing out his cheeks, let the air escape violently, and that was all. He had armed himself with patience. It was not to be tried much longer. The First Secretary became suddenly very curt, detached, final.

"You may go now," he said. "A dynamite outrage must be provoked. I give you a month. The sittings of the Conference are suspended. Before it reassembles again something must have happened here, or your connection with us ceases."

He changed the note once more with an unprincipled versatility.

"Think over my philosophy, Mr. – Mr. – Verloc," he said, with a sort of chaffing condescension, waving his hand towards the door. "Go for the first meridian. You don't know the middle classes as well as I do. Their sensibilities are jaded. The first meridian. Nothing better, and nothing easier, I should think."

He had got up, and with his thin sensitive lips twitching humorously, watched in the glass over the mantelpiece Mr. Verloc backing out of the room heavily, hat and stick in hand. The door closed.

The footman in trousers, appearing suddenly in the corridor, let Mr. Verloc another way out and through a small door in the corner of the courtyard. The porter standing at the gate ignored his exit completely; and Mr. Verloc retraced the path of his morning's pilgrimage as if in a dream – an angry dream. This detachment from the material world was so complete that, though the mortal envelope of Mr. Verloc had not hastened unduly along the streets, that part of him to which it would be unwarrantably rude to refuse immortality, found itself at the shop door all at once, as if borne from west to east on the wings of a great wind. He walked straight behind the counter, and sat down on a wooden chair that stood there. No one appeared to disturb his solitude. Stevie, put into a green baize apron, was now sweeping and dusting upstairs, intent and conscientious, as though he were playing at it; and Mrs. Verloc, warned in the kitchen by the clatter of the cracked bell, had merely come to the glazed door of the parlour, and putting the curtain aside a little, had peered into the dim shop. Seeing her husband sitting there shadowy and bulky, with his hat tilted far back on his head, she had at once returned to her stove. An hour or more later she took the green baize apron off her brother Stevie, and instructed him to wash his hands and face in the peremptory tone she had used in that connection for fifteen years or so – ever since she had, in fact, ceased to attend to the boy's hands and face herself. She spared presently a glance away from her dishing-up for the inspection of that face and those hands which Stevie, approaching the kitchen table, offered for her approval with an air of self-assurance hiding a perpetual residue of anxiety. Formerly the anger of the father was the supremely effective sanction of these rites, but Mr. Verloc's placidity in domestic life would have made all mention of anger incredible even to poor Stevie's nervousness. The theory was that Mr. Verloc would have been inexpressibly pained and shocked by any deficiency of cleanliness at meal times. Winnie after the death of her father found considerable consolation in the feeling that she need no longer tremble for poor Stevie. She could not bear to see the boy hurt. It maddened her. As a little girl she had often faced with blazing eyes the irascible licensed victualler in defence of her brother. Nothing now in Mrs. Verloc's appearance could lead one to suppose that she was capable of a passionate demonstration.

She finished her dishing-up. The table was laid in the parlour. Going to the foot of the stairs, she screamed out "Mother!" Then opening the glazed door leading to the shop, she said quietly "Adolf!" Mr. Verloc had not changed his position; he had not apparently stirred a limb for an hour and a half. He got up heavily, and came to his dinner in his overcoat and with his hat on, without uttering a word. His silence in itself had nothing startlingly unusual in this household, hidden in the shades of the sordid street seldom touched by the sun, behind the dim shop with its wares of disreputable rubbish. Only that day Mr. Verloc's taciturnity was so obviously thoughtful that the two women were impressed by it. They sat silent themselves, keeping a watchful eye on poor Stevie, lest he should break out into one of his fits of loquacity. He faced Mr. Verloc across the table, and remained very good and quiet, staring vacantly. The endeavour to keep him from making himself objectionable in any way to the master of the house put no inconsiderable anxiety into these two women's lives. "That boy," as they alluded to him softly between themselves, had been a source of that sort of anxiety almost from the very day of his birth. The late licensed victualler's humiliation at having such a very peculiar boy for a son manifested itself by a propensity to brutal treatment; for he was a person of fine sensibilities, and his sufferings as a man and a father were perfectly genuine. Afterwards Stevie had to be kept from making himself a nuisance to the single gentlemen lodgers, who are themselves a queer lot, and are easily aggrieved. And there was always the anxiety of his mere existence to face. Visions of a workhouse infirmary for her child had haunted the old woman in the basement breakfast-room of the decayed Belgravian house. "If you had not found such a good husband, my dear," she used to say to her daughter, "I don't know what would have become of that poor boy."

Mr. Verloc extended as much recognition to Stevie as a man not particularly fond of animals may give to his wife's beloved cat; and this recognition, benevolent and perfunctory, was essentially of the same quality. Both women admitted to themselves that not much more could be reasonably expected. It was enough to earn for Mr. Verloc the old woman's reverential gratitude. In the early days, made sceptical by the trials of friendless life, she used sometimes to ask anxiously: "You don't think, my dear, that Mr. Verloc is getting tired of seeing Stevie about?" To this Winnie replied habitually by a slight toss of her head. Once, however, she retorted, with a rather grim pertness: "He'll have to get tired of me first." A long silence ensued. The mother, with her feet propped up on a stool, seemed to be trying to get to the bottom of that answer, whose feminine profundity had struck her all of a heap. She had never really understood why Winnie had married Mr. Verloc. It was very sensible of her, and evidently had turned out for the best, but her girl might have naturally hoped to find somebody of a more suitable age. There had been a steady young fellow, only son of a butcher in the next street, helping his father in business, with whom Winnie had been walking out with obvious gusto. He was dependent on his father, it is true; but the business was good, and his prospects excellent. He took her girl to the theatre on several evenings. Then just as she began to dread to hear of their engagement (for what could she have done with that big house alone, with Stevie on her hands), that romance came to an abrupt end, and Winnie went about looking very dull. But Mr. Verloc, turning up providentially to occupy the first-floor front bedroom, there had been no more question of the young butcher. It was clearly providential.

Chapter III

"... **ALL IDEALISATION** makes life poorer. To beautify it is to take away its character of complexity – it is to destroy it. Leave that to the moralists, my boy. History is made by men, but they do not make it in their heads. The ideas that are born in their consciousness play an insignificant part in the march of events. History is dominated and determined by the tool and the production – by the force of economic conditions. Capitalism has made socialism, and the laws made by the capitalism for the protection of property are responsible for anarchism. No one can tell what form the social organisation may take in the future. Then why indulge in prophetic phantasies? At best they can only interpret the mind of the prophet, and can have no objective value. Leave that pastime to the moralists, my boy."

Michaelis, the ticket-of-leave apostle, was speaking in an even voice, a voice that wheezed as if deadened and oppressed by the layer of fat on his chest. He had come out of a highly hygienic prison round like a tub, with an enormous stomach and distended cheeks of a pale, semi-transparent complexion, as though for fifteen years the servants of an outraged society had made a point of stuffing him with fattening foods in a damp and lightless cellar. And ever since he had never managed to get his weight down as much as an ounce.

It was said that for three seasons running a very wealthy old lady had sent him for a cure to Marienbad – where he was about to share the public curiosity once with a crowned head – but the police on that occasion ordered him to leave within twelve hours. His martyrdom was continued by forbidding him all access to the healing waters. But he was resigned now.

With his elbow presenting no appearance of a joint, but more like a bend in a dummy's limb, thrown over the back of a chair, he leaned forward slightly over his short and enormous thighs to spit into the grate.

"Yes! I had the time to think things out a little," he added without emphasis. "Society has given me plenty of time for meditation."

On the other side of the fireplace, in the horse-hair arm-chair where Mrs. Verloc's mother was generally privileged to sit, Karl Yundt giggled grimly, with a faint black grimace of a toothless mouth. The terrorist, as he called himself, was old and bald, with a narrow, snow-white wisp of a goatee hanging limply from his chin. An extraordinary expression of underhand malevolence survived in his extinguished eyes. When he rose painfully the thrusting forward of a skinny groping hand deformed by gouty swellings suggested the effort of a moribund murderer summoning all his remaining strength for a last stab. He leaned on a thick stick, which trembled under his other hand.

"I have always dreamed," he mouthed fiercely, "of a band of men absolute in their resolve to discard all scruples in the choice of means, strong enough to give themselves frankly the name of destroyers, and free from the taint of that resigned pessimism which rots the world. No pity for anything on earth, including themselves, and death enlisted for good and all in the service of humanity – that's what I would have liked to see."

His little bald head quivered, imparting a comical vibration to the wisp of white goatee. His enunciation would have been almost totally unintelligible to a stranger. His worn-out passion, resembling in its impotent fierceness the excitement of a senile sensualist, was badly served by a dried throat and toothless gums which seemed to catch the tip of his tongue. Mr. Verloc, established in the corner of the sofa at the other end of the room, emitted two hearty grunts of assent.

The old terrorist turned slowly his head on his skinny neck from side to side.

"And I could never get as many as three such men together. So much for your rotten pessimism," he snarled at Michaelis, who uncrossed his thick legs, similar to bolsters, and slid his feet abruptly under his chair in sign of exasperation.

He a pessimist! Preposterous! He cried out that the charge was outrageous. He was so far from pessimism that he saw already the end of all private property coming along logically, unavoidably, by the mere development of its inherent viciousness. The possessors of property had not only to face the awakened proletariat, but they had also to fight amongst themselves. Yes. Struggle, warfare, was the condition of private ownership. It was fatal. Ah! He did not depend upon emotional excitement to keep up his belief, no declamations, no anger, no visions of blood-red flags waving, or metaphorical lurid suns of vengeance rising above the horizon of a doomed society. Not he! Cold reason, he boasted, was the basis of his optimism. Yes, optimism –

His laborious wheezing stopped, then, after a gasp or two, he added:

"Don't you think that, if I had not been the optimist I am, I could not have found in fifteen years some means to cut my throat? And, in the last instance, there were always the walls of my cell to dash my head against."

The shortness of breath took all fire, all animation out of his voice; his great, pale cheeks hung like filled pouches, motionless, without a quiver; but in his blue eyes, narrowed as if peering, there was the same look of confident shrewdness, a little crazy in its fixity, they must have had while the indomitable optimist sat thinking at night in his cell. Before him, Karl Yundt remained standing, one wing of his faded greenish havelock thrown back cavalierly over his shoulder. Seated in front of the fireplace, Comrade Ossipon, ex-medical student, the principal writer of the F.P. leaflets, stretched out his robust legs, keeping the soles of his boots turned up to the glow in the grate. A bush of crinkly yellow hair topped his red, freckled face, with a flattened nose and prominent mouth cast in the rough mould of the negro type. His almond-shaped eyes leered languidly over the high cheek-bones. He wore a grey flannel shirt, the loose ends of a black silk tie hung down the buttoned breast of his serge coat; and his head resting on the back of his chair, his throat largely exposed, he raised to his lips a cigarette in a long wooden tube, puffing jets of smoke straight up at the ceiling.

Michaelis pursued his idea – *the* idea of his solitary reclusion – the thought vouchsafed to his captivity and growing like a faith revealed in visions. He talked to himself, indifferent to the sympathy or hostility of his hearers, indifferent indeed to their presence, from the habit he had acquired of thinking aloud hopefully in the solitude of the four whitewashed walls of his cell, in the sepulchral silence of the great blind pile of bricks near a river, sinister and ugly like a colossal mortuary for the socially drowned.

He was no good in discussion, not because any amount of argument could shake his faith, but because the mere fact of hearing another voice disconcerted him painfully, confusing his thoughts at once – these thoughts that for so many years, in a mental solitude more barren than a waterless desert, no living voice had ever combatted, commented, or approved.

No one interrupted him now, and he made again the confession of his faith, mastering him irresistible and complete like an act of grace: the secret of fate discovered in the material side of life; the economic condition of the world responsible for the past and shaping the future; the source of all history, of all ideas, guiding the mental development of mankind and the very impulses of their passion –

A harsh laugh from Comrade Ossipon cut the tirade dead short in a sudden faltering of the tongue and a bewildered unsteadiness of the apostle's mildly exalted eyes. He closed them slowly for a moment, as if to collect his routed thoughts. A silence fell; but what with the two gas-jets over the table and the glowing grate the little parlour behind Mr. Verloc's shop had become frightfully hot. Mr. Verloc, getting off the sofa with ponderous reluctance, opened the door leading into the kitchen to get more air, and thus disclosed the innocent Stevie, seated very good and quiet at a deal table, drawing circles, circles, circles; innumerable circles, concentric, eccentric; a coruscating whirl of circles that by their tangled multitude of repeated curves, uniformity of form, and confusion of intersecting lines suggested a rendering of cosmic chaos, the symbolism of a mad art attempting the inconceivable. The artist never turned his head; and in all his soul's application to the task his back quivered, his thin neck, sunk into a deep hollow at the base of the skull, seemed ready to snap.

Mr. Verloc, after a grunt of disapproving surprise, returned to the sofa. Alexander Ossipon got up, tall in his threadbare blue serge suit under the low ceiling, shook off the stiffness of long immobility, and strolled away into the kitchen (down two steps) to look over Stevie's shoulder. He came back, pronouncing oracularly: "Very good. Very characteristic, perfectly typical."

"What's very good?" grunted inquiringly Mr. Verloc, settled again in the corner of the sofa. The other explained his meaning negligently, with a shade of condescension and a toss of his head towards the kitchen:

"Typical of this form of degeneracy – these drawings, I mean."

"You would call that lad a degenerate, would you?" mumbled Mr. Verloc.

Comrade Alexander Ossipon – nicknamed the Doctor, ex-medical student without a degree; afterwards wandering lecturer to working-men's associations upon the socialistic aspects of hygiene; author of a popular quasi-medical study (in the form of a cheap pamphlet seized promptly by the police) entitled "The Corroding Vices of the Middle Classes"; special delegate of the more or less mysterious Red Committee, together with Karl Yundt and Michaelis for the work of literary propaganda – turned upon the obscure familiar of at least two Embassies that glance of insufferable, hopelessly dense sufficiency which nothing but the frequentation of science can give to the dulness of common mortals.

"That's what he may be called scientifically. Very good type too, altogether, of that sort of degenerate. It's enough to glance at the lobes of his ears. If you read Lombroso –"

Mr. Verloc, moody and spread largely on the sofa, continued to look down the row of his waistcoat buttons; but his cheeks became tinged by a faint blush. Of late even the merest derivative of the word science (a term in itself inoffensive and of indefinite meaning) had the curious power of evoking a definitely offensive mental vision of Mr. Vladimir, in his body as he lived, with an almost supernatural clearness. And this phenomenon, deserving justly to be classed amongst the marvels of science, induced in Mr. Verloc an emotional state of dread and exasperation tending to express itself in violent swearing. But he said nothing. It was Karl Yundt who was heard, implacable to his last breath.

"Lombroso is an ass."

Comrade Ossipon met the shock of this blasphemy by an awful, vacant stare. And the other, his extinguished eyes without gleams blackening the deep shadows under the great, bony forehead, mumbled, catching the tip of his tongue between his lips at every second word as though he were chewing it angrily:

"Did you ever see such an idiot? For him the criminal is the prisoner. Simple, is it not? What about those who shut him up there – forced him in there? Exactly. Forced him in there. And what is crime? Does he know that, this imbecile who has made his way in this world of gorged fools by looking at the ears and teeth of a lot of poor, luckless devils? Teeth and ears mark the criminal? Do they? And what about the law that marks him still better – the pretty branding instrument invented by the overfed to protect themselves against the hungry? Red-hot applications on their vile skins – hey? Can't you smell and hear from here the thick hide of the people burn and sizzle? That's how criminals are made for your Lombrosos to write their silly stuff about."

The knob of his stick and his legs shook together with passion, whilst the trunk, draped in the wings of the havelock, preserved his historic attitude of defiance. He seemed to sniff the tainted air of social cruelty, to strain his ear for its atrocious sounds. There was an extraordinary force of suggestion in this posturing. The all but moribund veteran of dynamite wars had been a great actor in his time – actor on platforms, in secret assemblies, in private interviews. The famous terrorist had never in his life raised personally as much as his little finger against the social edifice. He was no man of action; he was not even an orator of torrential eloquence, sweeping the masses along in the rushing noise and foam of a great enthusiasm. With a more subtle intention, he took the part of an insolent and venomous evoker of sinister impulses which lurk in the blind envy and exasperated vanity of ignorance, in the suffering and misery of poverty, in all the hopeful and noble illusions of righteous anger, pity, and revolt. The shadow of his evil gift clung to him yet like the smell of a deadly drug in an old vial of poison, emptied now, useless, ready to be thrown away upon the rubbish-heap of things that had served their time.

Michaelis, the ticket-of-leave apostle, smiled vaguely with his glued lips; his pasty moon face drooped under the weight of melancholy assent. He had been a prisoner himself. His own skin had sizzled under the red-hot brand, he murmured softly. But Comrade Ossipon, nicknamed the Doctor, had got over the shock by that time.

"You don't understand," he began disdainfully, but stopped short, intimidated by the dead blackness of the cavernous eyes in the face turned slowly towards him with a blind stare, as if guided only by the sound. He gave the discussion up, with a slight shrug of the shoulders.

Stevie, accustomed to move about disregarded, had got up from the kitchen table, carrying off his drawing to bed with him. He had reached the parlour door in time to receive in full the shock of Karl Yundt's eloquent imagery. The sheet of paper covered with circles dropped out of his fingers, and he remained staring at the old terrorist, as if rooted suddenly to the spot by his morbid horror and dread of physical pain. Stevie knew very well that hot iron applied to one's skin hurt very much. His scared eyes blazed with indignation: it would hurt terribly. His mouth dropped open.

Michaelis by staring unwinkingly at the fire had regained that sentiment of isolation necessary for the continuity of his thought. His optimism had begun to flow from his lips. He saw Capitalism doomed in its cradle, born with the poison of the principle of competition in its system. The great capitalists devouring the little capitalists, concentrating the power and the tools of production in great masses, perfecting industrial processes, and in the madness of self-aggrandisement only preparing, organising, enriching, making ready the lawful inheritance of the suffering proletariat. Michaelis pronounced the great word 'Patience' – and his clear blue glance, raised to the low ceiling of Mr. Verloc's parlour, had a character of seraphic trustfulness. In the doorway Stevie, calmed, seemed sunk in hebetude.

Comrade Ossipon's face twitched with exasperation.

"Then it's no use doing anything – no use whatever."

"I don't say that," protested Michaelis gently. His vision of truth had grown so intense that the sound of a strange voice failed to rout it this time. He continued to look down at the red coals. Preparation for the future was necessary, and he was willing to admit that the great change would perhaps come in the upheaval of a revolution. But he argued that revolutionary propaganda was a delicate work of high conscience. It was the education of the masters of the world. It should be as careful as the education given to kings. He would have it advance its tenets cautiously, even timidly, in our ignorance of the effect that may be produced by any given economic change upon the happiness, the morals, the intellect, the history of mankind. For history is made with tools, not with ideas; and everything is changed by economic conditions – art, philosophy, love, virtue – truth itself!

The coals in the grate settled down with a slight crash; and Michaelis, the hermit of visions in the desert of a penitentiary, got up impetuously. Round like a distended balloon, he opened his short, thick arms, as if in a pathetically hopeless attempt to embrace and hug to his breast a self-regenerated universe. He gasped with ardour.

"The future is as certain as the past – slavery, feudalism, individualism, collectivism. This is the statement of a law, not an empty prophecy."

The disdainful pout of Comrade Ossipon's thick lips accentuated the negro type of his face.

"Nonsense," he said calmly enough. "There is no law and no certainty. The teaching propaganda be hanged. What the people knows does not matter, were its knowledge ever so accurate. The only thing that matters to us is the emotional state of the masses. Without emotion there is no action."

He paused, then added with modest firmness:

"I am speaking now to you scientifically – scientifically – Eh? What did you say, Verloc?"

"Nothing," growled from the sofa Mr. Verloc, who, provoked by the abhorrent sound, had merely muttered a "Damn."

The venomous spluttering of the old terrorist without teeth was heard.

"Do you know how I would call the nature of the present economic conditions? I would call it cannibalistic. That's what it is! They are nourishing their greed on the quivering flesh and the warm blood of the people – nothing else."

Stevie swallowed the terrifying statement with an audible gulp, and at once, as though it had been swift poison, sank limply in a sitting posture on the steps of the kitchen door.

Michaelis gave no sign of having heard anything. His lips seemed glued together for good; not a quiver passed over his heavy cheeks. With troubled eyes he looked for his round, hard hat, and put it on his round head. His round and obese body seemed to float low between the chairs under the sharp elbow of Karl Yundt. The old terrorist, raising an uncertain and clawlike hand, gave a swaggering tilt to a black felt sombrero shading the hollows and ridges of his wasted face. He got in motion slowly, striking the floor with his stick at every step. It was rather an affair to get him out of the house because, now and then, he would stop, as if to think, and did not offer to move again till impelled forward by Michaelis. The gentle apostle grasped his arm with brotherly care; and behind them, his hands in his pockets, the robust Ossipon yawned vaguely. A blue cap with a patent leather peak set well at the back of his yellow bush of hair gave him the aspect of a Norwegian sailor bored with the world after a thundering spree. Mr. Verloc saw his guests off the premises, attending them bareheaded, his heavy overcoat hanging open, his eyes on the ground.

He closed the door behind their backs with restrained violence, turned the key, shot the bolt. He was not satisfied with his friends. In the light of Mr. Vladimir's philosophy of bomb throwing they appeared hopelessly futile. The part of Mr. Verloc in revolutionary politics having been to observe, he could not all at once, either in his own home or in larger assemblies, take the initiative of action. He had to be cautious. Moved by the just indignation of a man well over forty, menaced in what is dearest to him – his repose and his security – he asked himself scornfully what else could have been expected from such a lot, this Karl Yundt, this Michaelis – this Ossipon.

Pausing in his intention to turn off the gas burning in the middle of the shop, Mr. Verloc descended into the abyss of moral reflections. With the insight of a kindred temperament he pronounced his verdict. A lazy lot – this Karl Yundt, nursed by a blear-eyed old woman, a woman he had years ago enticed away from a friend, and afterwards had tried more than once to shake off into the gutter. Jolly lucky for Yundt that she had persisted in coming up time after time, or else there would have been no one now to help him out of the bus by the Green Park railings, where that spectre took its constitutional crawl every fine morning. When that indomitable snarling old witch died the swaggering spectre would have to vanish too – there would be an end to fiery Karl Yundt. And Mr. Verloc's morality was offended also by the optimism of Michaelis, annexed by his wealthy old lady, who had taken lately to sending him to a cottage she had in the country. The ex-prisoner could moon about the shady lanes for days together in a delicious and humanitarian idleness. As to Ossipon, that beggar was sure to want for nothing as long as there were silly girls with savings-bank books in the world. And Mr. Verloc, temperamentally identical with his associates, drew fine distinctions in his mind on the strength of insignificant differences. He drew them with a certain complacency, because the instinct of conventional respectability was strong within him, being only overcome by his dislike of all kinds of recognised labour – a temperamental defect which he shared with a large proportion of revolutionary reformers of a given social state. For obviously one does not revolt against the advantages and opportunities of that state, but against the price which must be paid for the same in the coin of accepted morality, self-restraint, and toil. The majority of revolutionists are the enemies of discipline and fatigue mostly. There are natures too, to whose sense of justice the price exacted looms up monstrously enormous, odious, oppressive, worrying, humiliating, extortionate, intolerable. Those are the fanatics. The remaining portion of social rebels is accounted for by vanity, the mother of all noble and vile illusions, the companion of poets, reformers, charlatans, prophets, and incendiaries.

Lost for a whole minute in the abyss of meditation, Mr. Verloc did not reach the depth of these abstract considerations. Perhaps he was not able. In any case he had not the time. He was pulled up painfully by the sudden recollection of Mr. Vladimir, another of his associates, whom in virtue of subtle moral affinities he was capable of judging correctly. He considered him as dangerous. A shade of envy crept into his thoughts. Loafing was all very well for these fellows, who knew not Mr. Vladimir, and had women to fall back upon; whereas he had a woman to provide for –

At this point, by a simple association of ideas, Mr. Verloc was brought face to face with the necessity of going to bed some time or other that evening. Then why not go now – at once? He sighed. The necessity was not so normally pleasurable as it ought to have been for a man of his age and temperament. He dreaded the demon of sleeplessness, which he felt had marked him for its own. He raised his arm, and turned off the flaring gas-jet above his head.

A bright band of light fell through the parlour door into the part of the shop behind the counter. It enabled Mr. Verloc to ascertain at a glance the number of silver coins in the till. These were but few; and for the first time since he opened his shop he took a commercial survey of its value. This survey was unfavourable. He had gone into trade for no commercial reasons. He had been guided in the selection of this peculiar line of business by an instinctive leaning towards shady transactions, where money is picked up easily. Moreover, it did not take him out of his own sphere – the sphere which is watched by the police. On the contrary, it gave him a publicly confessed standing in that sphere, and as Mr. Verloc had unconfessed relations which made him familiar with yet careless of the police, there was a distinct advantage in such a situation. But as a means of livelihood it was by itself insufficient.

He took the cash-box out of the drawer, and turning to leave the shop, became aware that Stevie was still downstairs.

What on earth is he doing there? Mr. Verloc asked himself. What's the meaning of these antics? He looked dubiously at his brother-in-law, but he did not ask him for information. Mr. Verloc's intercourse with Stevie was limited to the casual mutter of a morning, after breakfast, "My boots," and even that was more a communication at large of a need than a direct order or request. Mr. Verloc perceived with some surprise that he did not know really what to say to Stevie. He stood still in the middle of the parlour, and looked into the kitchen in silence. Nor yet did he know what would happen if he did say anything. And this appeared very queer to Mr. Verloc in view of the fact, borne upon him suddenly, that he had to provide for this fellow too. He had never given a moment's thought till then to that aspect of Stevie's existence.

Positively he did not know how to speak to the lad. He watched him gesticulating and murmuring in the kitchen. Stevie prowled round the table like an excited animal in a cage. A tentative "Hadn't you better go to bed now?" produced no effect whatever; and Mr. Verloc, abandoning the stony contemplation of his brother-in-law's behaviour, crossed the parlour wearily, cash-box in hand. The cause of the general lassitude he felt while climbing the stairs being purely mental, he became alarmed by its inexplicable character. He hoped he was not sickening for anything. He stopped on the dark landing to examine his sensations. But a slight and continuous sound of snoring pervading the obscurity interfered with their clearness. The sound came from his mother-in-law's room. Another one to provide for, he thought – and on this thought walked into the bedroom.

Mrs. Verloc had fallen asleep with the lamp (no gas was laid upstairs) turned up full on the table by the side of the bed. The light thrown down by the shade fell dazzlingly on the white pillow sunk by the weight of her head reposing with closed eyes and dark hair done up in several plaits for the night. She woke up with the sound of her name in her ears, and saw her husband standing over her.

"Winnie! Winnie!"

At first she did not stir, lying very quiet and looking at the cash-box in Mr. Verloc's hand. But when she understood that her brother was "capering all over the place downstairs" she swung out in one sudden movement on to the edge of the bed. Her bare feet, as if poked through the bottom of an unadorned, sleeved calico sack buttoned tightly at neck and wrists, felt over the rug for the slippers while she looked upward into her husband's face.

"I don't know how to manage him," Mr. Verloc explained peevishly. "Won't do to leave him downstairs alone with the lights."

She said nothing, glided across the room swiftly, and the door closed upon her white form.

Mr. Verloc deposited the cash-box on the night table, and began the operation of undressing by flinging his overcoat on to a distant chair. His coat and waistcoat followed. He walked about the room in his stockinged feet, and his burly figure, with the hands worrying nervously at his throat, passed and repassed across the long strip of looking-glass in the door of his wife's wardrobe. Then after slipping his braces off his shoulders he pulled up violently the venetian blind, and leaned his forehead against the cold window-pane – a fragile film of glass stretched between him and the enormity of cold, black, wet, muddy, inhospitable accumulation of bricks, slates, and stones, things in themselves unlovely and unfriendly to man.

Mr. Verloc felt the latent unfriendliness of all out of doors with a force approaching to positive bodily anguish. There is no occupation that fails a man more completely than that of a secret agent of police. It's like your horse suddenly falling dead under you in the midst of an uninhabited and thirsty plain. The comparison occurred to Mr. Verloc because he had sat astride various army horses in his time, and had now the sensation of an incipient fall. The prospect was as black as the window-pane against which he was leaning his forehead. And suddenly the face of Mr. Vladimir, clean-shaved and witty, appeared enhaloed in the glow of its rosy complexion like a sort of pink seal, impressed on the fatal darkness.

This luminous and mutilated vision was so ghastly physically that Mr. Verloc started away from the window, letting down the venetian blind with a great rattle. Discomposed and speechless with the apprehension of more such visions, he beheld his wife re-enter the room and get into bed in a calm business-like manner which made him feel hopelessly lonely in the world. Mrs. Verloc expressed her surprise at seeing him up yet.

"I don't feel very well," he muttered, passing his hands over his moist brow.

"Giddiness?"

"Yes. Not at all well."

Mrs. Verloc, with all the placidity of an experienced wife, expressed a confident opinion as to the cause, and suggested the usual remedies; but her husband, rooted in the middle of the room, shook his lowered head sadly.

"You'll catch cold standing there," she observed.

Mr. Verloc made an effort, finished undressing, and got into bed. Down below in the quiet, narrow street measured footsteps approached the house, then died away unhurried and firm, as if the passer-by had started to pace out all eternity, from gas-lamp to gas-lamp in a night without end; and the drowsy ticking of the old clock on the landing became distinctly audible in the bedroom.

Mrs. Verloc, on her back, and staring at the ceiling, made a remark.

"Takings very small today."

Mr. Verloc, in the same position, cleared his throat as if for an important statement, but merely inquired:

"Did you turn off the gas downstairs?"

"Yes; I did," answered Mrs. Verloc conscientiously. "That poor boy is in a very excited state tonight," she murmured, after a pause which lasted for three ticks of the clock.

Mr. Verloc cared nothing for Stevie's excitement, but he felt horribly wakeful, and dreaded facing the darkness and silence that would follow the extinguishing of the lamp. This dread led him to make the remark that Stevie had disregarded his suggestion to go to bed. Mrs. Verloc, falling into the trap, started to demonstrate at length to her husband that this was not 'impudence' of any sort, but simply 'excitement.' There was no young man of his age in London more willing and docile than Stephen, she affirmed; none more affectionate and ready to please, and even useful, as long as people did not upset his poor head. Mrs. Verloc, turning towards her recumbent husband, raised herself on her elbow, and hung over him in her anxiety that he should believe Stevie to be a useful member of the family. That ardour of protecting compassion exalted morbidly in her childhood by the misery of another child tinged her sallow cheeks with a faint dusky blush, made her big eyes gleam under the dark lids. Mrs. Verloc then looked younger; she looked as young as Winnie used to look, and much more animated than the Winnie of the Belgravian mansion days had ever allowed herself to appear to gentlemen lodgers. Mr. Verloc's anxieties had prevented him from attaching any sense to what his wife was saying. It was as if her voice were talking on the other side of a very thick wall. It was her aspect that recalled him to himself.

He appreciated this woman, and the sentiment of this appreciation, stirred by a display of something resembling emotion, only added another pang to his mental anguish. When her voice ceased he moved uneasily, and said:

"I haven't been feeling well for the last few days."

He might have meant this as an opening to a complete confidence; but Mrs. Verloc laid her head on the pillow again, and staring upward, went on:

"That boy hears too much of what is talked about here. If I had known they were coming tonight I would have seen to it that he went to bed at the same time I did. He was out of his mind with something he overheard about eating people's flesh and drinking blood. What's the good of talking like that?"

There was a note of indignant scorn in her voice. Mr. Verloc was fully responsive now.

"Ask Karl Yundt," he growled savagely.

Mrs. Verloc, with great decision, pronounced Karl Yundt "a disgusting old man." She declared openly her affection for Michaelis. Of the robust Ossipon, in whose presence she always felt uneasy behind an attitude of stony reserve, she said nothing whatever. And continuing to talk of that brother, who had been for so many years an object of care and fears:

"He isn't fit to hear what's said here. He believes it's all true. He knows no better. He gets into his passions over it."

Mr. Verloc made no comment.

"He glared at me, as if he didn't know who I was, when I went downstairs. His heart was going like a hammer. He can't help being excitable. I woke mother up, and asked her to sit with him till he went to sleep. It isn't his fault. He's no trouble when he's left alone."

Mr. Verloc made no comment.

"I wish he had never been to school," Mrs. Verloc began again brusquely. "He's always taking away those newspapers from the window to read. He gets a red face poring over them. We don't get rid of a dozen numbers in a month. They only take up room in the front window. And Mr. Ossipon brings every week a pile of these F.P. tracts to sell at a halfpenny each. I wouldn't give a halfpenny for the whole lot. It's silly reading – that's what it is. There's no sale for it. The other day Stevie got hold of one, and there was a story in it of a German soldier officer tearing half-off the ear of a recruit, and nothing was done to him for it. The brute! I couldn't do anything with Stevie that afternoon. The story was enough, too, to make one's blood boil. But what's the use of printing things like that? We aren't German slaves here, thank God. It's not our business – is it?"

Mr. Verloc made no reply.

"I had to take the carving knife from the boy," Mrs. Verloc continued, a little sleepily now. "He was shouting and stamping and sobbing. He can't stand the notion of any cruelty. He would have stuck that officer like a pig if he had seen him then. It's true, too! Some people don't deserve much mercy." Mrs. Verloc's voice ceased, and the expression of her motionless eyes became more and more contemplative and veiled during the long pause. "Comfortable, dear?" she asked in a faint, far-away voice. "Shall I put out the light now?"

The dreary conviction that there was no sleep for him held Mr. Verloc mute and hopelessly inert in his fear of darkness. He made a great effort.

"Yes. Put it out," he said at last in a hollow tone.

Chapter IV

MOST OF THE THIRTY or so little tables covered by red cloths with a white design stood ranged at right angles to the deep brown wainscoting of the underground hall. Bronze chandeliers with many globes depended from the low, slightly vaulted ceiling, and the fresco paintings ran flat and dull all round the walls without windows, representing scenes of the chase and of outdoor revelry in mediaeval costumes. Varlets in green jerkins brandished hunting knives and raised on high tankards of foaming beer.

"Unless I am very much mistaken, you are the man who would know the inside of this confounded affair," said the robust Ossipon, leaning over, his elbows far out on the table and his feet tucked back completely under his chair. His eyes stared with wild eagerness.

An upright semi-grand piano near the door, flanked by two palms in pots, executed suddenly all by itself a valse tune with aggressive virtuosity. The din it raised was deafening. When it ceased, as abruptly as it had started, the be-spectacled, dingy little man who faced Ossipon behind a heavy glass mug full of beer emitted calmly what had the sound of a general proposition.

"In principle what one of us may or may not know as to any given fact can't be a matter for inquiry to the others."

"Certainly not," Comrade Ossipon agreed in a quiet undertone. "In principle."

With his big florid face held between his hands he continued to stare hard, while the dingy little man in spectacles coolly took a drink of beer and stood the glass mug back on the table. His flat, large ears departed widely from the sides of his skull, which looked frail enough for Ossipon to crush between thumb and forefinger; the dome of the forehead seemed to rest on the rim of the spectacles; the flat cheeks, of a greasy, unhealthy complexion, were merely smudged by the miserable poverty of a thin dark whisker. The lamentable inferiority of the whole physique was made ludicrous by the supremely self-confident bearing of the individual. His speech was curt, and he had a particularly impressive manner of keeping silent.

Ossipon spoke again from between his hands in a mutter.

"Have you been out much today?"

"No. I stayed in bed all the morning," answered the other. "Why?"

"Oh! Nothing," said Ossipon, gazing earnestly and quivering inwardly with the desire to find out something, but obviously intimidated by the little man's overwhelming air of unconcern. When talking with this comrade – which happened but rarely – the big Ossipon suffered from a sense of moral and even physical insignificance. However, he ventured another question. "Did you walk down here?"

"No; omnibus," the little man answered readily enough. He lived far away in Islington, in a small house down a shabby street, littered with straw and dirty paper, where out of school hours a troop of assorted children ran and squabbled with a shrill, joyless, rowdy clamour. His single back room, remarkable for having an extremely large cupboard, he rented furnished from two elderly spinsters, dressmakers in a humble way with a clientele of servant girls mostly. He had a heavy padlock put on the cupboard, but otherwise he was a model lodger, giving no trouble, and requiring practically no attendance. His oddities were that he insisted on being present when his room was being swept, and that when he went out he locked his door, and took the key away with him.

Ossipon had a vision of these round black-rimmed spectacles progressing along the streets on the top of an omnibus, their self-confident glitter falling here and there on the walls of houses or lowered upon the heads of the unconscious stream of people on the pavements. The ghost of a sickly smile altered the set of Ossipon's thick lips at the thought of the walls nodding, of people running for life at the sight of those spectacles. If they had only known! What a panic! He murmured interrogatively: "Been sitting long here?"

"An hour or more," answered the other negligently, and took a pull at the dark beer. All his movements – the way he grasped the mug, the act of drinking, the way he set the heavy glass down and folded his arms – had a firmness, an assured precision which made the big and muscular Ossipon, leaning forward with staring eyes and protruding lips, look the picture of eager indecision.

"An hour," he said. "Then it may be you haven't heard yet the news I've heard just now – in the street. Have you?"

The little man shook his head negatively the least bit. But as he gave no indication of curiosity Ossipon ventured to add that he had heard it just outside the place. A newspaper boy had yelled the thing under his very nose, and not being prepared for anything of that sort, he was very much startled and upset. He had to come in there with a dry mouth. "I never thought of finding you here," he added, murmuring steadily, with his elbows planted on the table.

"I come here sometimes," said the other, preserving his provoking coolness of demeanour.

"It's wonderful that you of all people should have heard nothing of it," the big Ossipon continued. His eyelids snapped nervously upon the shining eyes. "You of all people," he repeated tentatively. This obvious restraint argued an incredible and inexplicable timidity of the big fellow before the calm little man, who again lifted the glass mug, drank, and put it down with brusque and assured movements. And that was all.

Ossipon after waiting for something, word or sign, that did not come, made an effort to assume a sort of indifference.

"Do you," he said, deadening his voice still more, "give your stuff to anybody who's up to asking you for it?"

"My absolute rule is never to refuse anybody – as long as I have a pinch by me," answered the little man with decision.

"That's a principle?" commented Ossipon.

"It's a principle."

"And you think it's sound?"

The large round spectacles, which gave a look of staring self-confidence to the sallow face, confronted Ossipon like sleepless, unwinking orbs flashing a cold fire.

"Perfectly. Always. Under every circumstance. What could stop me? Why should I not? Why should I think twice about it?"

Ossipon gasped, as it were, discreetly.

"Do you mean to say you would hand it over to a 'teck' if one came to ask you for your wares?"

The other smiled faintly.

"Let them come and try it on, and you will see," he said. "They know me, but I know also every one of them. They won't come near me – not they."

His thin livid lips snapped together firmly. Ossipon began to argue.

"But they could send someone – rig a plant on you. Don't you see? Get the stuff from you in that way, and then arrest you with the proof in their hands."

"Proof of what? Dealing in explosives without a licence perhaps." This was meant for a contemptuous jeer, though the expression of the thin, sickly face remained unchanged, and the utterance was negligent. "I don't think there's one of them anxious to make that arrest. I don't think they could get one of them to apply for a warrant. I mean one of the best. Not one."

"Why?" Ossipon asked.

"Because they know very well I take care never to part with the last handful of my wares. I've it always by me." He touched the breast of his coat lightly. "In a thick glass flask," he added.

"So I have been told," said Ossipon, with a shade of wonder in his voice. "But I didn't know if –"

"They know," interrupted the little man crisply, leaning against the straight chair back, which rose higher than his fragile head. "I shall never be arrested. The game isn't good enough for any policeman of them all. To deal with a man like me you require sheer, naked, inglorious heroism." Again his lips closed with a self-confident snap. Ossipon repressed a movement of impatience.

"Or recklessness – or simply ignorance," he retorted. "They've only to get somebody for the job who does not know you carry enough stuff in your pocket to blow yourself and everything within sixty yards of you to pieces."

"I never affirmed I could not be eliminated," rejoined the other. "But that wouldn't be an arrest. Moreover, it's not so easy as it looks."

"Bah!" Ossipon contradicted. "Don't be too sure of that. What's to prevent half-a-dozen of them jumping upon you from behind in the street? With your arms pinned to your sides you could do nothing – could you?"

"Yes; I could. I am seldom out in the streets after dark," said the little man impassively, "and never very late. I walk always with my right hand closed round the india-rubber ball which I have in my trouser pocket. The pressing of this ball actuates a detonator inside the flask I carry in my pocket. It's the principle of the pneumatic instantaneous shutter for a camera lens. The tube leads up –"

With a swift disclosing gesture he gave Ossipon a glimpse of an india-rubber tube, resembling a slender brown worm, issuing from the armhole of his waistcoat and plunging into the inner breast pocket of his jacket. His clothes, of a nondescript brown mixture, were threadbare and marked with stains, dusty in the folds, with ragged button-holes. "The detonator is partly mechanical, partly chemical," he explained, with casual condescension.

"It is instantaneous, of course?" murmured Ossipon, with a slight shudder.

"Far from it," confessed the other, with a reluctance which seemed to twist his mouth dolorously. "A full twenty seconds must elapse from the moment I press the ball till the explosion takes place."

"Phew!" whistled Ossipon, completely appalled. "Twenty seconds! Horrors! You mean to say that you could face that? I should go crazy –"

"Wouldn't matter if you did. Of course, it's the weak point of this special system, which is only for my own use. The worst is that the manner of exploding is always the weak point with us. I am trying to invent a detonator that would adjust itself to all conditions of action, and even to unexpected changes of conditions. A variable and yet perfectly precise mechanism. A really intelligent detonator."

"Twenty seconds," muttered Ossipon again. "Ough! And then –"

With a slight turn of the head the glitter of the spectacles seemed to gauge the size of the beer saloon in the basement of the renowned Silenus Restaurant.

"Nobody in this room could hope to escape," was the verdict of that survey. "Nor yet this couple going up the stairs now."

The piano at the foot of the staircase clanged through a mazurka with brazen impetuosity, as though a vulgar and impudent ghost were showing off. The keys sank and rose mysteriously. Then all became still. For a moment Ossipon imagined the overlighted place changed into a dreadful black hole belching horrible fumes choked with ghastly rubbish of smashed brickwork and mutilated corpses. He had such a distinct perception of ruin and death that he shuddered again. The other observed, with an air of calm sufficiency:

"In the last instance it is character alone that makes for one's safety. There are very few people in the world whose character is as well established as mine."

"I wonder how you managed it," growled Ossipon.

"Force of personality," said the other, without raising his voice; and coming from the mouth of that obviously miserable organism the assertion caused the robust Ossipon to bite his lower lip. "Force of personality," he repeated, with ostentatious calm. "I have the means to make myself deadly, but that by itself, you understand, is absolutely nothing in the way of protection. What is effective is the belief those people have in my will to use the means. That's their impression. It is absolute. Therefore I am deadly."

"There are individuals of character amongst that lot too," muttered Ossipon ominously.

"Possibly. But it is a matter of degree obviously, since, for instance, I am not impressed by them. Therefore they are inferior. They cannot be otherwise. Their character is built upon conventional morality. It leans on the social order. Mine stands free from everything artificial. They are bound in all sorts of conventions. They depend on life, which, in this connection, is a historical fact surrounded by all sorts of restraints and considerations, a complex organised fact open to attack at every point; whereas I depend on death, which knows no restraint and cannot be attacked. My superiority is evident."

"This is a transcendental way of putting it," said Ossipon, watching the cold glitter of the round spectacles. "I've heard Karl Yundt say much the same thing not very long ago."

"Karl Yundt," mumbled the other contemptuously, "the delegate of the International Red Committee, has been a posturing shadow all his life. There are three of you delegates, aren't there? I won't define the other two, as you are one of them. But what you say means nothing. You are the worthy delegates for revolutionary propaganda, but the trouble is not only that you are as unable to think independently as any respectable grocer or journalist of them all, but that you have no character whatever."

Ossipon could not restrain a start of indignation.

"But what do you want from us?" he exclaimed in a deadened voice. "What is it you are after yourself?"

"A perfect detonator," was the peremptory answer. "What are you making that face for? You see, you can't even bear the mention of something conclusive."

"I am not making a face," growled the annoyed Ossipon bearishly.

"You revolutionists," the other continued, with leisurely self-confidence, "are the slaves of the social convention, which is afraid of you; slaves of it as much as the very police that stands up in the defence of that convention. Clearly you are, since you want to revolutionise it. It governs your thought, of course, and your action too, and thus neither your thought nor your action can ever be conclusive." He paused, tranquil, with that air of close, endless silence, then almost immediately went on. "You are not a bit better than the forces arrayed against you – than the police, for instance. The other day I came suddenly upon Chief Inspector Heat at the corner of Tottenham Court Road. He looked at me very steadily. But I did not look at him. Why should I give him more than a glance? He was thinking of many things – of his superiors, of his reputation, of the law courts, of his salary, of newspapers – of a hundred things. But I was thinking of my perfect detonator only. He meant nothing to me. He was as insignificant as – I can't call to mind anything insignificant enough to compare him with – except Karl Yundt perhaps. Like to like. The terrorist and the policeman both come from the same basket. Revolution, legality – counter moves in the same game; forms of idleness at bottom identical. He plays his little game – so do you propagandists. But I don't play; I work fourteen hours a day, and go hungry sometimes. My experiments cost money now and again, and then I must do without food for a day or two. You're looking at my beer. Yes. I have had two glasses already, and shall have another presently. This is a little holiday, and I celebrate it alone. Why not? I've the grit to work alone, quite alone, absolutely alone. I've worked alone for years."

Ossipon's face had turned dusky red.

"At the perfect detonator – eh?" he sneered, very low.

"Yes," retorted the other. "It is a good definition. You couldn't find anything half so precise to define the nature of your activity with all your committees and delegations. It is I who am the true propagandist."

"We won't discuss that point," said Ossipon, with an air of rising above personal considerations. "I am afraid I'll have to spoil your holiday for you, though. There's a man blown up in Greenwich Park this morning."

"How do you know?"

"They have been yelling the news in the streets since two o'clock. I bought the paper, and just ran in here. Then I saw you sitting at this table. I've got it in my pocket now."

He pulled the newspaper out. It was a good-sized rosy sheet, as if flushed by the warmth of its own convictions, which were optimistic. He scanned the pages rapidly.

"Ah! Here it is. Bomb in Greenwich Park. There isn't much so far. Half-past eleven. Foggy morning. Effects of explosion felt as far as Romney Road and Park Place. Enormous hole in the ground under a tree filled with smashed roots and broken branches. All round fragments of a man's body blown to pieces. That's all. The rest's mere newspaper gup. No doubt a wicked attempt to blow up the Observatory, they say. H'm. That's hardly credible."

He looked at the paper for a while longer in silence, then passed it to the other, who after gazing abstractedly at the print laid it down without comment.

It was Ossipon who spoke first – still resentful.

"The fragments of only *one* man, you note. Ergo: blew *himself* up. That spoils your day off for you – don't it? Were you expecting that sort of move? I hadn't the slightest idea – not the ghost of a notion of anything of the sort being planned to come off here – in this country. Under the present circumstances it's nothing short of criminal."

The little man lifted his thin black eyebrows with dispassionate scorn.

"Criminal! What is that? What *is* crime? What can be the meaning of such an assertion?"

"How am I to express myself? One must use the current words," said Ossipon impatiently. "The meaning of this assertion is that this business may affect our position very adversely in this country. Isn't that crime enough for you? I am convinced you have been giving away some of your stuff lately."

Ossipon stared hard. The other, without flinching, lowered and raised his head slowly.

"You have!" burst out the editor of the F.P. leaflets in an intense whisper. "No! And are you really handing it over at large like this, for the asking, to the first fool that comes along?"

"Just so! The condemned social order has not been built up on paper and ink, and I don't fancy that a combination of paper and ink will ever put an end to it, whatever you may think. Yes, I would give the stuff with both hands to every man, woman, or fool that likes to come along. I know what you are thinking about. But I am not taking my cue from the Red Committee. I would see you all hounded out of here, or arrested – or beheaded for that matter – without turning a hair. What happens to us as individuals is not of the least consequence."

He spoke carelessly, without heat, almost without feeling, and Ossipon, secretly much affected, tried to copy this detachment.

"If the police here knew their business they would shoot you full of holes with revolvers, or else try to sand-bag you from behind in broad daylight."

The little man seemed already to have considered that point of view in his dispassionate self-confident manner.

"Yes," he assented with the utmost readiness. "But for that they would have to face their own institutions. Do you see? That requires uncommon grit. Grit of a special kind."

Ossipon blinked.

"I fancy that's exactly what would happen to you if you were to set up your laboratory in the States. They don't stand on ceremony with their institutions there."

"I am not likely to go and see. Otherwise your remark is just," admitted the other. "They have more character over there, and their character is essentially anarchistic. Fertile ground for us, the States – very good ground. The great Republic has the root of the destructive matter in her. The collective temperament is lawless. Excellent. They may shoot us down, but –"

"You are too transcendental for me," growled Ossipon, with moody concern.

"Logical," protested the other. "There are several kinds of logic. This is the enlightened kind. America is all right. It is this country that is dangerous, with her idealistic conception of legality. The social spirit of this people is wrapped up in scrupulous prejudices, and that is fatal to our work. You talk of England being our only refuge! So much the worse. Capua! What do we want with refuges? Here you talk, print, plot, and do nothing. I daresay it's very convenient for such Karl Yundts."

He shrugged his shoulders slightly, then added with the same leisurely assurance: "To break up the superstition and worship of legality should be our aim. Nothing would please me more than to see Inspector Heat and his likes take to shooting us down in broad daylight with the approval of the public. Half our battle would be won then; the disintegration of the old morality would have set in in its very temple. That is what you ought to aim at. But you revolutionists will never understand that. You plan the future, you lose yourselves in reveries of economical systems derived from what is; whereas what's wanted is a clean sweep and a clear start for a new conception of life. That sort of future will take care of itself if you will only make room for it. Therefore I would shovel my stuff in heaps at the corners of the streets if I had enough for that; and as I haven't, I do my best by perfecting a really dependable detonator."

Ossipon, who had been mentally swimming in deep waters, seized upon the last word as if it were a saving plank.

"Yes. Your detonators. I shouldn't wonder if it weren't one of your detonators that made a clean sweep of the man in the park."

A shade of vexation darkened the determined sallow face confronting Ossipon.

"My difficulty consists precisely in experimenting practically with the various kinds. They must be tried after all. Besides –"

Ossipon interrupted.

"Who could that fellow be? I assure you that we in London had no knowledge. – Couldn't you describe the person you gave the stuff to?"

The other turned his spectacles upon Ossipon like a pair of searchlights.

"Describe him," he repeated slowly. "I don't think there can be the slightest objection now. I will describe him to you in one word – Verloc."

Ossipon, whom curiosity had lifted a few inches off his seat, dropped back, as if hit in the face.

"Verloc! Impossible."

The self-possessed little man nodded slightly once.

"Yes. He's the person. You can't say that in this case I was giving my stuff to the first fool that came along. He was a prominent member of the group as far as I understand."

"Yes," said Ossipon. "Prominent. No, not exactly. He was the centre for general intelligence, and usually received comrades coming over here. More useful than important. Man of no ideas. Years ago he used to speak at meetings – in France, I believe. Not very well, though. He was trusted by such men as Latorre, Moser and all that old lot. The only talent he showed really was his ability to elude the attentions of the police somehow. Here, for instance, he did not seem to be looked after very closely. He was regularly married, you know. I suppose it's with her money that he started that shop. Seemed to make it pay, too."

Ossipon paused abruptly, muttered to himself "I wonder what that woman will do now?" and fell into thought.

The other waited with ostentatious indifference. His parentage was obscure, and he was generally known only by his nickname of Professor. His title to that designation consisted in his having been once assistant demonstrator in chemistry at some technical institute. He quarrelled with the authorities upon a question of unfair treatment. Afterwards he obtained a post in the laboratory of a manufactory of dyes. There too he had been treated with revolting injustice. His struggles, his privations, his hard work to raise himself in the social scale, had filled him with such an exalted conviction of his merits that it was extremely difficult for the world to treat him with justice – the standard of that notion depending so much upon the patience of the individual. The Professor had genius, but lacked the great social virtue of resignation.

"Intellectually a nonentity," Ossipon pronounced aloud, abandoning suddenly the inward contemplation of Mrs. Verloc's bereaved person and business. "Quite an ordinary personality. You are wrong in not keeping more in touch with the comrades, Professor," he added in a reproving tone. "Did he say anything to you – give you some idea of his intentions? I hadn't seen him for a month. It seems impossible that he should be gone."

"He told me it was going to be a demonstration against a building," said the Professor. "I had to know that much to prepare the missile. I pointed out to him that I had hardly a sufficient quantity for a completely destructive result, but he pressed me very earnestly to do my best. As he wanted something that could be carried openly in the hand, I proposed to make use of an old one-gallon copal varnish can I happened to have by me. He was pleased at the idea. It gave me some trouble, because I had to cut out the bottom first and solder it on again afterwards. When prepared for use, the can enclosed a wide-mouthed, well-corked jar of thick glass packed around with some wet clay and containing sixteen ounces of X2 green powder. The detonator was connected with the screw top of the can. It was ingenious – a combination of time and shock. I explained the system to him. It was a thin tube of tin enclosing a –"

Ossipon's attention had wandered.

"What do you think has happened?" he interrupted.

"Can't tell. Screwed the top on tight, which would make the connection, and then forgot the time. It was set for twenty minutes. On the other hand, the time contact being made, a sharp shock would bring about the explosion at once. He either ran the time too close, or simply let the thing fall. The contact was made all right – that's clear to me at any rate. The system's worked perfectly. And yet you would think that a common fool in a hurry would be much more likely to forget to make the contact altogether. I was worrying myself about that sort of failure mostly. But there are more kinds of fools than one can guard against. You can't expect a detonator to be absolutely fool-proof."

He beckoned to a waiter. Ossipon sat rigid, with the abstracted gaze of mental travail. After the man had gone away with the money he roused himself, with an air of profound dissatisfaction.

"It's extremely unpleasant for me," he mused. "Karl has been in bed with bronchitis for a week. There's an even chance that he will never get up again. Michaelis's luxuriating in the country somewhere. A fashionable publisher has offered him five hundred pounds for a book. It will be a ghastly failure. He has lost the habit of consecutive thinking in prison, you know."

The Professor on his feet, now buttoning his coat, looked about him with perfect indifference.

"What are you going to do?" asked Ossipon wearily. He dreaded the blame of the Central Red Committee, a body which had no permanent place of abode, and of whose membership he was not exactly informed. If this affair eventuated in the stoppage of the modest subsidy allotted to the publication of the F.P. pamphlets, then indeed he would have to regret Verloc's inexplicable folly.

"Solidarity with the extremest form of action is one thing, and silly recklessness is another," he said, with a sort of moody brutality. "I don't know what came to Verloc. There's some mystery there. However, he's gone. You may take it as you like, but under the circumstances the only policy for the militant revolutionary group is to disclaim all connection with this damned freak of yours. How to make the disclaimer convincing enough is what bothers me."

The little man on his feet, buttoned up and ready to go, was no taller than the seated Ossipon. He levelled his spectacles at the latter's face point-blank.

"You might ask the police for a testimonial of good conduct. They know where every one of you slept last night. Perhaps if you asked them they would consent to publish some sort of official statement."

"No doubt they are aware well enough that we had nothing to do with this," mumbled Ossipon bitterly. "What they will say is another thing." He remained thoughtful, disregarding the short, owlish, shabby figure standing by his side. "I must lay hands on Michaelis at once, and get him to speak from his heart at one of our gatherings. The public has a sort of sentimental regard for that fellow. His name is known. And I am in touch with a few reporters on the big dailies. What he would say would be utter bosh, but he has a turn of talk that makes it go down all the same."

"Like treacle," interjected the Professor, rather low, keeping an impassive expression.

The perplexed Ossipon went on communing with himself half audibly, after the manner of a man reflecting in perfect solitude.

"Confounded ass! To leave such an imbecile business on my hands. And I don't even know if –"

He sat with compressed lips. The idea of going for news straight to the shop lacked charm. His notion was that Verloc's shop might have been turned already into a police trap. They will be bound to make some arrests, he thought, with something resembling virtuous indignation, for the even tenor of his revolutionary life was menaced by no fault of his. And yet unless he went there he ran the risk of remaining in ignorance of what perhaps it would be very material for him to know. Then he reflected that, if the man in the park had been so very much blown to pieces as the evening papers said, he could not have been identified. And if so, the police could have no special reason for watching Verloc's shop more closely than any other place known to be frequented by marked anarchists – no more reason, in fact, than for watching the doors of the Silenus. There would be a lot of watching all round, no matter where he went. Still –

"I wonder what I had better do now?" he muttered, taking counsel with himself.

A rasping voice at his elbow said, with sedate scorn:

"Fasten yourself upon the woman for all she's worth."

After uttering these words the Professor walked away from the table. Ossipon, whom that piece of insight had taken unawares, gave one ineffectual start, and remained still, with a helpless gaze, as though nailed fast to the seat of his chair. The lonely piano, without as much as a music stool to help it, struck a few chords courageously, and beginning a selection of national airs, played him out at last to the tune of 'Blue Bells of Scotland.' The painfully detached notes grew faint behind his back while he went slowly upstairs, across the hall, and into the street.

In front of the great doorway a dismal row of newspaper sellers standing clear of the pavement dealt out their wares from the gutter. It was a raw, gloomy day of the early spring; and the grimy sky, the mud of the streets, the rags of the dirty men, harmonised excellently with the eruption of the damp, rubbishy sheets of paper soiled with printers' ink. The posters, maculated with filth, garnished like tapestry the sweep of the curbstone. The trade in afternoon papers was brisk, yet, in comparison with the swift, constant march of foot traffic, the effect was of indifference, of a disregarded distribution. Ossipon looked hurriedly both ways before stepping out into the cross-currents, but the Professor was already out of sight.

Chapter V

The Professor had turned into a street to the left, and walked along, with his head carried rigidly erect, in a crowd whose every individual almost overtopped his stunted stature. It was vain to pretend to himself that he was not disappointed. But that was mere feeling; the stoicism of his thought could not be disturbed by this or any other failure. Next time, or the time after next, a telling stroke would be delivered – something really startling – a blow fit to open the first crack in the imposing front of the great edifice of legal conceptions sheltering the atrocious injustice of society. Of humble origin, and with an appearance really so mean as to stand in the way of his considerable natural abilities, his imagination had been fired early by the tales of men rising from the depths of poverty to positions of authority and affluence. The extreme, almost ascetic purity of his thought, combined with an astounding ignorance of worldly conditions, had set before him a goal of power and prestige to be attained without the medium of arts, graces, tact, wealth – by sheer weight of merit alone. On that view he considered himself entitled to undisputed success. His father, a delicate dark enthusiast with a sloping forehead, had been an itinerant and rousing preacher of some obscure but rigid Christian sect – a man supremely confident in the privileges of his righteousness. In the son, individualist by temperament, once the science of colleges had replaced thoroughly the faith of conventicles, this moral attitude translated itself into a frenzied puritanism of ambition. He nursed it as something secularly holy. To see it thwarted opened his eyes to the true nature of the world, whose morality was artificial, corrupt, and blasphemous. The way of even the most justifiable revolutions is prepared by personal impulses disguised into creeds. The Professor's indignation found in itself a final cause that absolved him from the sin of turning to destruction as the agent of his ambition. To destroy public faith in legality was the imperfect formula of his pedantic fanaticism; but the subconscious conviction that the framework of an established social order cannot be effectually shattered except by some form of collective or individual violence was precise and correct. He was a moral agent – that was settled in his mind. By exercising his agency with ruthless defiance he procured for himself the appearances of power and personal prestige. That was undeniable to his vengeful bitterness. It pacified its unrest; and in their own way the most ardent of revolutionaries are perhaps doing no more but seeking for peace in common with the rest of mankind – the peace of soothed vanity, of satisfied appetites, or perhaps of appeased conscience.

Lost in the crowd, miserable and undersized, he meditated confidently on his power, keeping his hand in the left pocket of his trousers, grasping lightly the india-rubber ball, the supreme guarantee of his sinister freedom; but after a while he became disagreeably affected by the sight of the roadway thronged with vehicles and of the pavement crowded with men and women. He was in a long, straight street, peopled by a mere fraction of an immense multitude; but all round him, on and on, even to the limits of the horizon hidden by the enormous piles of bricks, he felt the mass of mankind mighty in its numbers. They swarmed numerous like locusts, industrious like ants, thoughtless like a natural force, pushing on blind and orderly and absorbed, impervious to sentiment, to logic, to terror too perhaps.

That was the form of doubt he feared most. Impervious to fear! Often while walking abroad, when he happened also to come out of himself, he had such moments of dreadful and sane mistrust of mankind. What if nothing could move them? Such moments come to all men whose ambition aims at a direct grasp upon humanity – to artists, politicians, thinkers, reformers, or saints. A despicable emotional state this, against which solitude fortifies a superior character; and with severe exultation the Professor thought of the refuge of his room, with its padlocked cupboard, lost in a wilderness of poor houses, the hermitage of the perfect anarchist. In order to reach sooner the point where he could take his omnibus, he turned brusquely out of the populous street into a narrow and dusky alley paved with flagstones. On one side the low brick houses had in their dusty windows the sightless, moribund look of incurable decay – empty shells awaiting demolition. From the other side life had not departed wholly as yet. Facing the only gas-lamp yawned the cavern of a second-hand furniture dealer, where, deep in the gloom of a sort of narrow avenue winding through a bizarre forest of wardrobes, with an undergrowth tangle of table legs, a tall pier-glass glimmered like a pool of water in a wood. An unhappy, homeless couch, accompanied by two unrelated chairs, stood in the open. The only human being making use of the alley besides the Professor, coming stalwart and erect from the opposite direction, checked his swinging pace suddenly.

"Hallo!" he said, and stood a little on one side watchfully.

The Professor had already stopped, with a ready half turn which brought his shoulders very near the other wall. His right hand fell lightly on the back of the outcast couch, the left remained purposefully plunged deep in the trousers pocket, and the roundness of the heavy rimmed spectacles imparted an owlish character to his moody, unperturbed face.

It was like a meeting in a side corridor of a mansion full of life. The stalwart man was buttoned up in a dark overcoat, and carried an umbrella. His hat, tilted back, uncovered a good deal of forehead, which appeared very white in the dusk. In the dark patches of the orbits the eyeballs glimmered piercingly. Long, drooping moustaches, the colour of ripe corn, framed with their points the square block of his shaved chin.

"I am not looking for you," he said curtly.

The Professor did not stir an inch. The blended noises of the enormous town sank down to an inarticulate low murmur. Chief Inspector Heat of the Special Crimes Department changed his tone.

"Not in a hurry to get home?" he asked, with mocking simplicity.

The unwholesome-looking little moral agent of destruction exulted silently in the possession of personal prestige, keeping in check this man armed with the defensive mandate of a menaced society. More fortunate than Caligula, who wished that the Roman Senate had only one head for the better satisfaction of his cruel lust, he beheld in that one man all the forces he had set at defiance: the force of law, property, oppression, and injustice. He beheld all his enemies, and fearlessly confronted them all in a supreme satisfaction of his vanity. They stood perplexed before him as if before a dreadful portent. He gloated inwardly over the chance of this meeting affirming his superiority over all the multitude of mankind.

It was in reality a chance meeting. Chief Inspector Heat had had a disagreeably busy day since his department received the first telegram from Greenwich a little before eleven in the morning. First of all, the fact of the outrage being attempted less than a week after he had assured a high official that no outbreak of anarchist activity was to be apprehended was sufficiently annoying. If he ever thought himself safe in making a statement, it was then. He had made that statement with infinite satisfaction to himself, because it was clear that the high official desired greatly to hear that very thing. He had affirmed that nothing of the sort could even be thought of without the department being aware of it within twenty-four hours; and he had spoken thus in his consciousness of being the great expert of his department. He had gone even so far as to utter words which true wisdom would have kept back. But Chief Inspector Heat was not very wise – at least not truly so. True wisdom, which is not certain of anything in this world of contradictions, would have prevented him from attaining his present position. It would have alarmed his superiors, and done away with his chances of promotion. His promotion had been very rapid.

"There isn't one of them, sir, that we couldn't lay our hands on at any time of night and day. We know what each of them is doing hour by hour," he had declared. And the high official had deigned to smile. This was so obviously the right thing to say for an officer of Chief Inspector Heat's reputation that it was perfectly delightful. The high official believed the declaration, which chimed in with his idea of the fitness of things. His wisdom was of an official kind, or else he might have reflected upon a matter not of theory but of experience that in the close-woven stuff of relations between conspirator and police there occur unexpected solutions of continuity, sudden holes in space and time. A given anarchist may be watched inch by inch and minute by minute, but a moment always comes when somehow all sight and touch of him are lost for a few hours, during which something (generally an explosion) more or less deplorable does happen. But the high official, carried away by his sense of the fitness of things, had smiled, and now the recollection of that smile was very annoying to Chief Inspector Heat, principal expert in anarchist procedure.

This was not the only circumstance whose recollection depressed the usual serenity of the eminent specialist. There was another dating back only to that very morning. The thought that when called urgently to his Assistant Commissioner's private room he had been unable to conceal his astonishment was distinctly vexing. His instinct of a successful man had taught him long ago that, as a general rule, a reputation is built on manner as much as on achievement. And he felt that his manner when confronted with the telegram had not been impressive. He had opened his eyes widely, and had exclaimed "Impossible!" exposing himself thereby to the unanswerable retort of a finger-tip laid forcibly on the telegram which the Assistant Commissioner, after reading it aloud, had flung on the desk. To be crushed, as it were, under the tip of a forefinger was an unpleasant experience. Very damaging, too! Furthermore, Chief Inspector Heat was conscious of not having mended matters by allowing himself to express a conviction.

"One thing I can tell you at once: none of our lot had anything to do with this."

He was strong in his integrity of a good detective, but he saw now that an impenetrably attentive reserve towards this incident would have served his reputation better. On the other hand, he admitted to himself that it was difficult to preserve one's reputation if rank outsiders were going to take a hand in the business. Outsiders are the bane of the police as of other professions. The tone of the Assistant Commissioner's remarks had been sour enough to set one's teeth on edge.

And since breakfast Chief Inspector Heat had not managed to get anything to eat.

Starting immediately to begin his investigation on the spot, he had swallowed a good deal of raw, unwholesome fog in the park. Then he had walked over to the hospital; and when the investigation in Greenwich was concluded at last he had lost his inclination for food. Not accustomed, as the doctors are, to examine closely the mangled remains of human beings, he had been shocked by the sight disclosed to his view when a waterproof sheet had been lifted off a table in a certain apartment of the hospital.

Another waterproof sheet was spread over that table in the manner of a table-cloth, with the corners turned up over a sort of mound – a heap of rags, scorched and bloodstained, half concealing what might have been an accumulation of raw material for a cannibal feast. It required considerable firmness of mind not to recoil before that sight. Chief Inspector Heat, an efficient officer of his department, stood his ground, but for a whole minute he did not advance. A local constable in uniform cast a sidelong glance, and said, with stolid simplicity:

"He's all there. Every bit of him. It was a job."

He had been the first man on the spot after the explosion. He mentioned the fact again. He had seen something like a heavy flash of lightning in the fog. At that time he was standing at the door of the King William Street Lodge talking to the keeper. The concussion made him tingle all over. He ran between the trees towards the Observatory. "As fast as my legs would carry me," he repeated twice.

Chief Inspector Heat, bending forward over the table in a gingerly and horrified manner, let him run on. The hospital porter and another man turned down the corners of the cloth, and stepped aside. The Chief Inspector's eyes searched the gruesome detail of that heap of mixed things, which seemed to have been collected in shambles and rag shops.

"You used a shovel," he remarked, observing a sprinkling of small gravel, tiny brown bits of bark, and particles of splintered wood as fine as needles.

"Had to in one place," said the stolid constable. "I sent a keeper to fetch a spade. When he heard me scraping the ground with it he leaned his forehead against a tree, and was as sick as a dog."

The Chief Inspector, stooping guardedly over the table, fought down the unpleasant sensation in his throat. The shattering violence of destruction which had made of that body a heap of nameless fragments affected his feelings with a sense of ruthless cruelty, though his reason told him the effect must have been as swift as a flash of lightning. The man, whoever he was, had died instantaneously; and yet it seemed impossible to believe that a human body could have reached that state of disintegration without passing through the pangs of inconceivable agony. No physiologist, and still less of a metaphysician, Chief Inspector Heat rose by the force of sympathy, which is a form of fear, above the vulgar conception of time. Instantaneous! He remembered all he had ever read in popular publications of long and terrifying dreams dreamed in the instant of waking; of the whole past life lived with frightful intensity by a drowning man as his doomed head bobs up, streaming, for the last time. The inexplicable mysteries of conscious existence beset Chief Inspector Heat till he evolved a horrible notion that ages of atrocious pain and mental torture could be contained between two successive winks of an eye. And meantime the Chief Inspector went on, peering at the table with a calm face and the slightly anxious attention of an indigent customer bending over what may be called the by-products of a butcher's shop with a view to an inexpensive Sunday dinner. All the time his trained faculties of an excellent investigator, who scorns no chance of information, followed the self-satisfied, disjointed loquacity of the constable.

"A fair-haired fellow," the last observed in a placid tone, and paused. "The old woman who spoke to the sergeant noticed a fair-haired fellow coming out of Maze Hill Station." He paused. "And he was a fair-haired fellow. She noticed two men coming out of the station after the uptrain had gone on," he continued slowly. "She couldn't tell if they were together. She took no particular notice of the big one, but the other was a fair, slight chap, carrying a tin varnish can in one hand." The constable ceased.

"Know the woman?" muttered the Chief Inspector, with his eyes fixed on the table, and a vague notion in his mind of an inquest to be held presently upon a person likely to remain for ever unknown.

"Yes. She's housekeeper to a retired publican, and attends the chapel in Park Place sometimes," the constable uttered weightily, and paused, with another oblique glance at the table.

Then suddenly: "Well, here he is – all of him I could see. Fair. Slight – slight enough. Look at that foot there. I picked up the legs first, one after another. He was that scattered you didn't know where to begin."

The constable paused; the least flicker of an innocent self-laudatory smile invested his round face with an infantile expression.

"Stumbled," he announced positively. "I stumbled once myself, and pitched on my head too, while running up. Them roots do stick out all about the place. Stumbled against the root of a tree and fell, and that thing he was carrying must have gone off right under his chest, I expect."

The echo of the words 'Person unknown' repeating itself in his inner consciousness bothered the Chief Inspector considerably. He would have liked to trace this affair back to its mysterious origin for his own information. He was professionally curious. Before the public he would have liked to vindicate the efficiency of his department by establishing the identity of that man. He was a loyal servant. That, however, appeared impossible. The first term of the problem was unreadable – lacked all suggestion but that of atrocious cruelty.

Overcoming his physical repugnance, Chief Inspector Heat stretched out his hand without conviction for the salving of his conscience, and took up the least soiled of the rags. It was a narrow strip of velvet with a larger triangular piece of dark blue cloth hanging from it. He held it up to his eyes; and the police constable spoke.

"Velvet collar. Funny the old woman should have noticed the velvet collar. Dark blue overcoat with a velvet collar, she has told us. He was the chap she saw, and no mistake. And here he is all complete, velvet collar and all. I don't think I missed a single piece as big as a postage stamp."

At this point the trained faculties of the Chief Inspector ceased to hear the voice of the constable. He moved to one of the windows for better light. His face, averted from the room, expressed a startled intense interest while he examined closely the triangular piece of broad-cloth. By a sudden jerk he detached it, and *only* after stuffing it into his pocket turned round to the room, and flung the velvet collar back on the table –

"Cover up," he directed the attendants curtly, without another look, and, saluted by the constable, carried off his spoil hastily.

A convenient train whirled him up to town, alone and pondering deeply, in a third-class compartment. That singed piece of cloth was incredibly valuable, and he could not defend himself from astonishment at the casual manner it had come into his possession. It was as if Fate had thrust that clue into his hands. And after the manner of the average man, whose ambition is to command events, he began to mistrust such a gratuitous and accidental success – just because it seemed forced upon him. The practical value of success depends not a little on the way you look at it. But Fate looks at nothing. It has no discretion. He no longer considered it eminently desirable all round to establish publicly the identity of the man who had blown himself up that morning with such horrible completeness. But he was not certain of the view his department would take. A department is to those it employs a complex personality with ideas and even fads of its own. It depends on the loyal devotion of its servants, and the devoted loyalty of trusted servants is associated with a certain amount of affectionate contempt, which keeps it sweet, as it were. By a benevolent provision of Nature no man is a hero to his valet, or else the heroes would have to brush their own clothes. Likewise no department appears perfectly wise to the intimacy of its workers. A department does not know so much as some of its servants. Being a dispassionate organism, it can never be perfectly informed. It would not be good for its efficiency to know too much. Chief Inspector Heat got out of the train in a state of thoughtfulness entirely untainted with disloyalty, but not quite free of that jealous mistrust which so often springs on the ground of perfect devotion, whether to women or to institutions.

It was in this mental disposition, physically very empty, but still nauseated by what he had seen, that he had come upon the Professor. Under these conditions which make for irascibility in a sound, normal man, this meeting was specially unwelcome to Chief Inspector Heat. He had not been thinking of the Professor; he had not been thinking of any individual anarchist at all. The complexion of that case had somehow forced upon him the general idea of the absurdity of things human, which in the abstract is sufficiently annoying to an unphilosophical temperament, and in concrete instances becomes exasperating beyond endurance. At the beginning of his career Chief Inspector Heat had been concerned with the more energetic forms of thieving. He had gained his spurs in that sphere, and naturally enough had kept for it, after his promotion to another department, a feeling not very far removed from affection. Thieving was not a sheer absurdity. It was a form of human industry, perverse indeed, but still an industry exercised in an industrious world; it was work undertaken for the same reason as the work in potteries, in coal mines, in fields, in tool-grinding shops. It was labour, whose practical difference from the other forms of labour consisted in the nature of its risk, which did not lie in ankylosis, or lead poisoning, or fire-damp, or gritty dust, but in what may be briefly defined in its own special phraseology as 'Seven years hard.' Chief Inspector Heat was, of course, not insensible to the gravity of moral differences. But neither were the thieves he had been looking after. They submitted to the severe sanctions of a morality familiar to Chief Inspector Heat with a certain resignation.

They were his fellow-citizens gone wrong because of imperfect education, Chief Inspector Heat believed; but allowing for that difference, he could understand the mind of a burglar, because, as a matter of fact, the mind and the instincts of a burglar are of the same kind as the mind and the instincts of a police officer. Both recognise the same conventions, and have a working knowledge of each other's methods and of the routine of their respective trades. They understand each other, which is advantageous to both, and establishes a sort of amenity in their relations. Products of the same machine, one classed as useful and the other as noxious, they take the machine for granted in different ways, but with a seriousness essentially the same. The mind of Chief Inspector Heat was inaccessible to ideas of revolt. But his thieves were not rebels. His bodily vigour, his cool inflexible manner, his courage and his fairness, had secured for him much respect and some adulation in the sphere of his early successes. He had felt himself revered and admired. And

Chief Inspector Heat, arrested within six paces of the anarchist nick-named the Professor, gave a thought of regret to the world of thieves – sane, without morbid ideals, working by routine, respectful of constituted authorities, free from all taint of hate and despair.

After paying this tribute to what is normal in the constitution of society (for the idea of thieving appeared to his instinct as normal as the idea of property), Chief Inspector Heat felt very angry with himself for having stopped, for having spoken, for having taken that way at all on the ground of it being a short cut from the station to the headquarters. And he spoke again in his big authoritative voice, which, being moderated, had a threatening character.

"You are not wanted, I tell you," he repeated.

The anarchist did not stir. An inward laugh of derision uncovered not only his teeth but his gums as well, shook him all over, without the slightest sound. Chief Inspector Heat was led to add, against his better judgment:

"Not yet. When I want you I will know where to find you."

Those were perfectly proper words, within the tradition and suitable to his character of a police officer addressing one of his special flock. But the reception they got departed from tradition and propriety. It was outrageous. The stunted, weakly figure before him spoke at last.

"I've no doubt the papers would give you an obituary notice then. You know best what that would be worth to you. I should think you can imagine easily the sort of stuff that would be printed. But you may be exposed to the unpleasantness of being buried together with me, though I suppose your friends would make an effort to sort us out as much as possible."

With all his healthy contempt for the spirit dictating such speeches, the atrocious allusiveness of the words had its effect on Chief Inspector Heat. He had too much insight, and too much exact information as well, to dismiss them as rot. The dusk of this narrow lane took on a sinister tint from the dark, frail little figure, its back to the wall, and speaking with a weak, self-confident voice. To the vigorous, tenacious vitality of the Chief Inspector, the physical wretchedness of that being, so obviously not fit to live, was ominous; for it seemed to him that if he had the misfortune to be such a miserable object he would not have cared how soon he died. Life had such a strong hold upon him that a fresh wave of nausea broke out in slight perspiration upon his brow. The murmur of town life, the subdued rumble of wheels in the two invisible streets to the right and left, came through the curve of the sordid lane to his ears with a precious familiarity and an appealing sweetness. He was human. But Chief Inspector Heat was also a man, and he could not let such words pass.

"All this is good to frighten children with," he said. "I'll have you yet."

It was very well said, without scorn, with an almost austere quietness.

"Doubtless," was the answer; "but there's no time like the present, believe me. For a man of real convictions this is a fine opportunity of self-sacrifice. You may not find another so favourable, so humane. There isn't even a cat near us, and these condemned old houses would make a good heap of bricks where you stand. You'll never get me at so little cost to life and property, which you are paid to protect."

"You don't know who you're speaking to," said Chief Inspector Heat firmly. "If I were to lay my hands on you now I would be no better than yourself."

"Ah! The game!"

"You may be sure our side will win in the end. It may yet be necessary to make people believe that some of you ought to be shot at sight like mad dogs. Then that will be the game. But I'll be damned if I know what yours is. I don't believe you know yourselves. You'll never get anything by it."

"Meantime it's you who get something from it – so far. And you get it easily, too. I won't speak of your salary, but haven't you made your name simply by not understanding what we are after?"

"What are you after, then?" asked Chief Inspector Heat, with scornful haste, like a man in a hurry who perceives he is wasting his time.

The perfect anarchist answered by a smile which did not part his thin colourless lips; and the celebrated Chief Inspector felt a sense of superiority which induced him to raise a warning finger.

"Give it up – whatever it is," he said in an admonishing tone, but not so kindly as if he were condescending to give good advice to a cracksman of repute. "Give it up. You'll find we are too many for you."

The fixed smile on the Professor's lips wavered, as if the mocking spirit within had lost its assurance. Chief Inspector Heat went on:

"Don't you believe me eh? Well, you've only got to look about you. We are. And anyway, you're not doing it well. You're always making a mess of it. Why, if the thieves didn't know their work better they would starve."

The hint of an invincible multitude behind that man's back roused a sombre indignation in the breast of the Professor. He smiled no longer his enigmatic and mocking smile. The resisting power of numbers, the unattackable stolidity of a great multitude, was the haunting fear of his sinister loneliness. His lips trembled for some time before he managed to say in a strangled voice:

"I am doing my work better than you're doing yours."

"That'll do now," interrupted Chief Inspector Heat hurriedly; and the Professor laughed right out this time. While still laughing he moved on; but he did not laugh long. It was a sad-faced, miserable little man who emerged from the narrow passage into the bustle of the broad thoroughfare. He walked with the nerveless gait of a tramp going on, still going on, indifferent to rain or sun in a sinister detachment from the aspects of sky and earth. Chief Inspector Heat, on the other hand, after watching him for a while, stepped out with the purposeful briskness of a man disregarding indeed the inclemencies of the weather, but conscious of having an authorised mission on this earth and the moral support of his kind. All the inhabitants of the immense town, the population of the whole country, and even the teeming millions struggling upon the planet, were with him – down to the very thieves and mendicants. Yes, the thieves themselves were sure to be with him in his present work. The consciousness of universal support in his general activity heartened him to grapple with the particular problem.

The problem immediately before the Chief Inspector was that of managing the Assistant Commissioner of his department, his immediate superior. This is the perennial problem of trusty and loyal servants; anarchism gave it its particular complexion, but nothing more. Truth to say, Chief Inspector Heat thought but little of anarchism. He did not attach undue importance to it, and could never bring himself to consider it seriously. It had more the character of disorderly conduct; disorderly without the human excuse of drunkenness, which at any rate implies good feeling and an amiable leaning towards festivity. As criminals, anarchists were distinctly no class – no class at all. And recalling the Professor, Chief Inspector Heat, without checking his swinging pace, muttered through his teeth:

"Lunatic."

Catching thieves was another matter altogether. It had that quality of seriousness belonging to every form of open sport where the best man wins under perfectly comprehensible rules. There were no rules for dealing with anarchists. And that was distasteful to the Chief Inspector. It was all foolishness, but that foolishness excited the public mind, affected persons in high places, and touched upon international relations. A hard, merciless contempt settled rigidly on the Chief Inspector's face as he walked on. His mind ran over all the anarchists of his flock. Not one of them had half the spunk of this or that burglar he had known. Not half – not one-tenth.

At headquarters the Chief Inspector was admitted at once to the Assistant Commissioner's private room. He found him, pen in hand, bent over a great table bestrewn with papers, as if worshipping an enormous double inkstand of bronze and crystal. Speaking tubes resembling snakes were tied by the heads to the back of the Assistant Commissioner's wooden arm-chair, and their gaping mouths seemed ready to bite his elbows. And in this attitude he raised only his eyes, whose lids were darker than his face and very much creased. The reports had come in: every anarchist had been exactly accounted for.

After saying this he lowered his eyes, signed rapidly two single sheets of paper, and only then laid down his pen, and sat well back, directing an inquiring gaze at his renowned subordinate. The Chief Inspector stood it well, deferential but inscrutable.

"I daresay you were right," said the Assistant Commissioner, "in telling me at first that the London anarchists had nothing to do with this. I quite appreciate the excellent watch kept on them by your men. On the other hand, this, for the public, does not amount to more than a confession of ignorance."

The Assistant Commissioner's delivery was leisurely, as it were cautious. His thought seemed to rest poised on a word before passing to another, as though words had been the stepping-stones for his intellect picking its way across the waters of error. "Unless you have brought something useful from Greenwich," he added.

The Chief Inspector began at once the account of his investigation in a clear matter-of-fact manner. His superior turning his chair a little, and crossing his thin legs, leaned sideways on his elbow, with one hand shading his eyes. His listening attitude had a sort of angular and sorrowful grace. Gleams as of highly burnished silver played on the sides of his ebony black head when he inclined it slowly at the end.

Chief Inspector Heat waited with the appearance of turning over in his mind all he had just said, but, as a matter of fact, considering the advisability of saying something more. The Assistant Commissioner cut his hesitation short.

"You believe there were two men?" he asked, without uncovering his eyes.

The Chief Inspector thought it more than probable. In his opinion, the two men had parted from each other within a hundred yards from the Observatory walls. He explained also how the other man could have got out of the park speedily without being observed. The fog, though not very dense, was in his favour. He seemed to have escorted the other to the spot, and then to have left him there to do the job single-handed. Taking the time those two were seen coming out of Maze Hill Station by the old woman, and the time when the explosion was heard, the Chief Inspector thought that the other man might have been actually at the Greenwich Park Station, ready to catch the next train up, at the moment his comrade was destroying himself so thoroughly.

"Very thoroughly – eh?" murmured the Assistant Commissioner from under the shadow of his hand.

The Chief Inspector in a few vigorous words described the aspect of the remains. "The coroner's jury will have a treat," he added grimly.

The Assistant Commissioner uncovered his eyes.

"We shall have nothing to tell them," he remarked languidly.

He looked up, and for a time watched the markedly non-committal attitude of his Chief Inspector. His nature was one that is not easily accessible to illusions. He knew that a department is at the mercy of its subordinate officers, who have their own conceptions of loyalty. His career had begun in a tropical colony. He had liked his work there. It was police work. He had been very successful in tracking and breaking up certain nefarious secret societies amongst the natives. Then he took his long leave, and got married rather impulsively. It was a good match from a worldly point of view, but his wife formed an unfavourable opinion of the colonial climate on hearsay evidence. On the other hand, she had influential connections. It was an excellent match. But he did not like the work he had to do now. He felt himself dependent on too many subordinates and too many masters. The near presence of that strange emotional phenomenon called public opinion weighed upon his spirits, and alarmed him by its irrational nature. No doubt that from ignorance he exaggerated to himself its power for good and evil – especially for evil; and the rough east winds of the English spring (which agreed with his wife) augmented his general mistrust of men's motives and of the efficiency of their organisation. The futility of office work especially appalled him on those days so trying to his sensitive liver.

He got up, unfolding himself to his full height, and with a heaviness of step remarkable in so slender a man, moved across the room to the window. The panes streamed with rain, and the short street he looked down into lay wet and empty, as if swept clear suddenly by a great flood. It was a very trying day, choked in raw fog to begin with, and now drowned in cold rain. The flickering, blurred flames of gas-lamps seemed to be dissolving in a watery atmosphere. And the lofty pretensions of a mankind oppressed by the miserable indignities of the weather appeared as a colossal and hopeless vanity deserving of scorn, wonder, and compassion.

"Horrible, horrible!" thought the Assistant Commissioner to himself, with his face near the window-pane. "We have been having this sort of thing now for ten days; no, a fortnight – a fortnight." He ceased to think completely for a time. That utter stillness of his brain lasted about three seconds. Then he said perfunctorily: "You have set inquiries on foot for tracing that other man up and down the line?"

He had no doubt that everything needful had been done. Chief Inspector Heat knew, of course, thoroughly the business of man-hunting. And these were the routine steps, too, that would be taken as a matter of course by the merest beginner. A few inquiries amongst the ticket collectors and the porters of the two small railway stations would give additional details as to the appearance of the two men; the inspection of the collected tickets would show at once where they came from that morning. It was elementary, and could not have been neglected. Accordingly the Chief Inspector answered that all this had been done directly the old woman had come forward with her deposition. And he mentioned the name of a station. "That's where they came from, sir," he went on. "The porter who took the tickets at Maze Hill remembers two chaps answering to the description passing the barrier. They seemed to him two respectable working men of a superior sort – sign painters or house decorators. The big man got out of a third-class compartment backward, with a bright tin can in his hand. On the platform he gave it to carry to the fair young fellow who followed him. All this agrees exactly with what the old woman told the police sergeant in Greenwich."

The Assistant Commissioner, still with his face turned to the window, expressed his doubt as to these two men having had anything to do with the outrage. All this theory rested upon the utterances of an old charwoman who had been nearly knocked down by a man in a hurry. Not a very substantial authority indeed, unless on the ground of sudden inspiration, which was hardly tenable.

"Frankly now, could she have been really inspired?" he queried, with grave irony, keeping his back to the room, as if entranced by the contemplation of the town's colossal forms half lost in the night. He did not even look round when he heard the mutter of the word "Providential" from the principal subordinate of his department, whose name, printed sometimes in the papers, was familiar to the great public as that of one of its zealous and hard-working protectors. Chief Inspector Heat raised his voice a little.

"Strips and bits of bright tin were quite visible to me," he said. "That's a pretty good corroboration."

"And these men came from that little country station," the Assistant Commissioner mused aloud, wondering. He was told that such was the name on two tickets out of three given up out of that train at Maze Hill. The third person who got out was a hawker from Gravesend well known to the porters. The Chief Inspector imparted that information in a tone of finality with some ill humour, as loyal servants will do in the consciousness of their fidelity and with the sense of the value of their loyal exertions. And still the Assistant Commissioner did not turn away from the darkness outside, as vast as a sea.

"Two foreign anarchists coming from that place," he said, apparently to the window-pane. "It's rather unaccountable.'"

"Yes, sir. But it would be still more unaccountable if that Michaelis weren't staying in a cottage in the neighbourhood."

At the sound of that name, falling unexpectedly into this annoying affair, the Assistant Commissioner dismissed brusquely the vague remembrance of his daily whist party at his club. It was the most comforting habit of his life, in a mainly successful display of his skill without the assistance of any subordinate. He entered his club to play from five to seven, before going home to dinner, forgetting for those two hours whatever was distasteful in his life, as though the game were a beneficent drug for allaying the pangs of moral discontent. His partners were the gloomily humorous editor of a celebrated magazine; a silent, elderly barrister with malicious little eyes; and a highly martial, simple-minded old Colonel with nervous brown hands. They were his club acquaintances merely. He never met them elsewhere except at the card-table. But they all seemed to approach the game in the spirit of co-sufferers, as if it were indeed a drug against the secret ills of existence; and every day as the sun declined over the countless roofs of the town, a mellow, pleasurable impatience, resembling the impulse of a sure and profound friendship, lightened his professional labours. And now this pleasurable sensation went out of him with something resembling a physical shock, and was replaced by a special kind of interest in his work of social protection – an improper sort of interest, which may be defined best as a sudden and alert mistrust of the weapon in his hand.

The complete and unabridged text is available
online, from *flametreepublishing.com/extras*

The Vigil

Joseph Cusumano

March, 1941

MAX BAUER did his best to ignore the pain in his right leg as he walked to the meeting. The army surgeon had extracted as much shrapnel as possible, but more than two decades later he still walked with a limp. A taxi ride to his destination at an apartment building on New York City's West Side would have saved time and considerable discomfort, but Max was determined to stay fit. And for a stocky fifty-one year old German WWI veteran, he maintained a respectable pace.

When he arrived, most of the other members of the group, all European émigrés like himself, were seated and engrossed in several separate discussions. A dense cloud of cigarette smoke told Bauer that he must be a few minutes late; but Ira Koppel, the former editor of *Die Berliner* until Hitler had taken power, greeted him warmly. "Max! Glad you could make it. I've got some good news to share." Bauer took a seat next to Urzula Dabrowski, an attractive Polish chemist who made it difficult for Max to keep his mind on business.

"So what's this good news you've promised us, Herr Koppel?" Jean-Pierre Weiss, a former French industrialist, asked the group's moderator. Koppel stood at the end of the large table until the conversations quieted.

"I met with Senator Bullard last week in his office. It was very private, just he and I, and he gave me an update on the M3 tank. As you know, in October of last year the British government expressed interest in purchasing a new American tank, and in January of this year, the passage of the Lend-Lease Program put a deal within their reach. Senator Bullard let me know that Chrysler recently assembled the first M3 tanks in one of their Michigan factories, and the tanks are now on their way to the proving grounds at Aberdeen, Maryland." This elicited big smiles and a solid round of applause from all gathered, especially Horst Mullheim, who at Bullard's request had provided crucial testimony in closed-door sessions of the American Committee on Military Affairs.

That Mullheim was a member of a coterie of people who had fled Europe as German troops violated the borders established by the 1918 armistice was a source of amazement to Max Bauer. As recently as 8 months ago, Mullheim had been an adjutant to General Heinz Guderian, the originator of the blitzkrieg tactics used so successfully against Poland, Belgium and France in 1939 and 1940. But on learning that Hitler planned to invade the Soviet Union, Mullheim concluded that the Führer was about to make a colossal blunder. Hadn't Germany's experience from 1914 to 1918 proven the folly of fighting a two-front war, to say nothing of Napoleon's disastrous foray into Russia? So with his wife and two young children, Mullheim left Germany in the middle of the night. He would always love his fatherland, but was convinced that Hitler would lead Germany into another catastrophe.

"Now the information I've shared with you regarding the M3 tank is not classified," Koppel continued, "but the Senator has asked that we keep it to ourselves. He was willing to inform us only because we've been helpful to him and his committee."

"Bullard's coming up for election next year, and he's going to face a lot of opposition," Urzula Dabrowski said.

"Why?" Max Bauer asked.

"Because of the America First movement," she answered. "They're very strong in his state, close to 70,000 voters. Not only do they want to make sure that the U.S. stays out of the war in Europe, they're even opposed to shipping supplies to Britain."

"And they've got a powerful advocate and spokesman in Charles Lindbergh," Koppel added. Koppel turned to Weiss, the industrialist who had fled France when the Nazis encouraged the citizens of his occupied homeland to turn in their Jewish countrymen. "Jean-Pierre, can you help fund the Senator's reelection campaign?"

Without hesitating, Weiss answered. "How much does he need?"

"I'll find out," Koppel answered.

"Good. I'll need a little time to liquidate assets in order to raise cash, so let me know as soon as possible," Weiss said. Koppel thanked him and then began a report on the group's efforts to help recent émigrés find housing and employment.

Several hours later when the meeting ended, Max Bauer invited Urzula Dabrowski to come by his studio some time to see his latest works on canvas. "That would be lovely!" she replied, and Bauer couldn't agree more.

* * *

"Admiral, this arrived today and I thought you should see it," Leutnant Krebbs said.

Admiral Wilhelm Canaris, chief of the *Abwehr* – Germany's Intelligence Agency – looked up from the mess on his desk. He was irritated by the interruption, and his aide realized this wasn't the best time to be bringing alarming news.

"It was delivered from our embassy in New York City by diplomatic pouch. It's from Katapult. Several months ago, you instructed me to bring any message from Katapult to your immediate attention."

"Well, give me the gist of it," Canaris replied.

"Sir, last year Katapult infiltrated a group of approximately twenty European émigrés in New York City who are doing everything possible to convince the American government to step up aid to Britain. This group also wants the U.S. to become directly involved in the war by sending American soldiers and warships to Europe. Katapult says the Americans are currently testing a new tank which British troops will deploy in North Africa. In addition, one of the émigrés, Jean-Pierre Weiss, is about to make a major donation to support the reelection of Senator Nick Bullard, who has been convincing his fellow lawmakers that America needs to actively participate in the war."

Canaris perked up at the mention of Weiss, the Jewish industrialist who had fled France before he could be interrogated and sent to a camp. Weiss had also managed to take a considerable portion of his wealth with him, although his real estate holdings and manufacturing plants in France had all been confiscated. Ultimately, Canaris had had to take responsibility for Weiss's escape, and his standing among the governmental elite had been tarnished. As a result, the admiral's rivals in the Reich, sensing an opportunity, sought to have him replaced with one of their own men. This went on for several months until the Führer made it clear that Canaris would keep his position. But the admiral knew that if Weiss succeeded in getting Senator Bullard reelected, Hitler could lose the forbearance he had shown thus far and choose someone else to lead the *Abwehr*. In a private meeting with the Führer, the admiral was told that America's entry into the war must be delayed. German scientists were hard at work on new superweapons, including the Heisenberg device, but they needed time. Even a few extra months could be crucial to the eventual outcome of the war.

The aide, catching the expression of alarm on his chief's face, asked, "Admiral, what would you like me to do?"

The admiral knew he couldn't keep the new tank out of British hands, nor could Katapult try to obtain the specs for it without bringing suspicion on himself. But the situation with Weiss was another matter. Canaris said, "Refresh my memory. What did Katapult do during the Great War?"

"Infantry, sir. He served with distinction. In the trenches. But this is his first mission as an agent of the Abwehr."

"Who's his observer?"

"Raven, sir. But as you ordered, Katapult was not made aware of Raven."

Now Canaris remembered. He had selected Katapult for this intelligence-gathering mission because the Abwehr might have need of his special talent. Although unproven, Katapult had seemed to be the best available match at the time for what the mission might eventually demand. But Katapult had a quality that could be his undoing. His excess of initiative could make him difficult to rein in and function as part of an organization.

"Lieutenant, bring me Raven's file," Canaris ordered.

"Admiral, I don't have the clearance to access that file." That meant the file was in Canaris's office safe. After dismissing his aide, the admiral headed for the safe and entered the combination. Its contents were sufficiently well organized that he located Raven's dossier in moments. He returned to his desk, opened the file and reviewed the documents.

Raven was among the Abwehr's most valued agents, someone whom Canaris would be loathe to put at risk of exposure. A careful and restrained team member with an impressive compilation of successful missions, Raven was the polar opposite to Katapult. Nevertheless, Canaris had placed a bet that they could fulfill complementary roles and function as an effective duo.

As incautious as it might be to unleash Katapult, Canaris now felt that the information he had just received left him no choice. If Weiss's campaign contribution helped Bullard get reelected, the Abwehr would get a new chief. But Raven's identity had to be protected, even from Katapult, at any cost. If Germany's enemies ever uncovered Raven's identity, a number of vital operations established by Raven would be compromised.

Twenty minutes later, his aide aid left the Blenderblock office complex with two sets of orders to be delivered to the German embassy in NYC, one for Raven, the other for Katapult.

* * *

April, 1941

Jean-Pierre Weiss placed a recording of Gershwin's 'Rhapsody in Blue' on his phonograph and settled into an armchair in the parlor of his spacious Upper East Side home, and the moment he heard the opening clarinet riff, his mood began to lighten. His wife and daughter, out for an evening of ballet, had been gone only fifteen minutes when he had begun a descent into one of his moods. Sometimes feeling isolated even on the crowded sidewalks of his adopted city, Weiss missed the constant interaction and challenge he had enjoyed as an industrialist in France. He was not scientifically inclined but knew how to grow a business. The engineers, accountants, and other technical types could always be hired from the pool of young graduates of excellent French universities, and when necessary, lured from other corporations. Now, his wealth of unscheduled time was burdensome. At some point, he would have to start a new business if for no other reason than to protect his emotional wellbeing.

Jean-Pierre had been excited about living in America, especially in New York City, the birthplace of his favorite composer, and the famed metropolis had lived up to its reputation. Unlike Nantes, France where his corporate headquarters had been, Jean-Pierre's chosen sanctuary was a city of skyscrapers, the Chrysler Building his favorite. Never mind the greater height of the Empire State Building. And when Ira Koppel took him to Mama Leone's, he acquired a new appreciation for southern Italian cuisine.

But Jean-Pierre had not always been well fed. During the Great War, the French had struggled to provide for the men in the trenches just as the Germans had. Reduced rations during warm weather were bad enough. In cold weather, it meant pneumonia and death, and the soldiers weren't the only hungry ones in the trenches. Once he'd been awakened by a rat which had burrowed into his coat pocket in search of small piece of sausage. On another occasion, a dead horse seemed to be coming back to life, its undulating corpse full of scavenging rats. Weiss had swapped stories with Max Bauer, who convinced him that the terriers the German soldiers had were more effective in holding down the rat population than the cats used by the French. Unlike cats, terriers had no interest in tormenting their prey, and after killing a rat, took no time to eat it before grabbing the next victim by its neck.

Weiss rose from his armchair, lifted the tone arm of the phonograph before it reached the end of the recording, and headed for the wine cellar in the basement. He was halfway down the stairs when he heard the wind slam his front door shut into its frame. This occasionally happened when a new deliveryman arrived with an armload of groceries. Someone unfamiliar with the house had just gained entrance.

After descending the remaining steps to the basement, Weiss took hold of a thick walking stick he used when venturing out. He had a revolver in the bedroom he shared with his wife, but there was no way to retrieve it without risking an encounter. Better that he stay hidden. Most likely, this was a burglary that would end with nothing more than the loss of possessions easily replaced by his insurance.

But curious as to what the intruder was doing, Weiss allowed himself to partially ascend the basement stairs. He heard no conversation, and the pattern of creaking floorboards also suggested to him that there was only one man above him. This was fortunate, as an individual couldn't get away with his prized Zenith phonograph and radio. The wooden console was simply too bulky and heavy for one man to handle. Weiss listened for the opening and closing of drawers containing their fine silverware, but instead, the thief seemed to be making a quick inspection of the entire first floor.

Next there was a rapid and regular succession of muffled steps as the intruder climbed the carpeted front staircase. In order to keep track of him, Weiss further ascended the basement stairs.

When the intruder reached the second floor, he continued his quick survey of the rooms, apparently in search of a specific item. *But what is he looking for?* Weiss wondered. He could think of no particular possession that would motivate someone to break into his home.

Although it had been less than five minutes since the wind had suddenly slammed his front door shut, a growing sense of indignation at the intrusion began to supplant his fear, and when Weiss heard his unwelcomed visitor descend the back staircase, he maintained his position near the top of the basement steps. If the thief now intended to leave, he would pass the entrance to the basement where Weiss stood, so Weiss quickly shut off the light that illuminated the basement steps and gripped his walking stick a little tighter. Although he was becoming angrier by the moment, a part of him knew that the most sensible course of action was to take no action. *Just let him pass*, he ordered himself. At certain points in the Battle of the Somme when front lines had shifted in ways no strategist could have foreseen, a take-no-action tactic had been the only means of survival. *Stand down a little longer*, he ordered himself.

Then the intruder passed him and moments later was only several yards from the front door. The ordeal, whatever its purpose, was almost over, but then Weiss envisioned the man returning another day when his wife and daughter were alone in the house. And as if charging out of a trench, the former soldier leaped the last few steps up the staircase and hurled himself toward the enemy.

Hearing a creaking floorboard, the intruder turned and just managed to dodge a blow aimed at his head. But his assailant was quick to strike again, and a club smashed into his raised forearm. Cursing his crazed attacker, the intruder fought back with a ferocity born of instinct and honed with training.

* * *

"Jean-Pierre, what happened?" The other émigrés were equally shocked, but Ira Koppel managed to find his voice first. Dark splotchy bruises covered Weiss's neck, and his lower lip was split. His left eye was swollen shut, and when he began to turn his head to see all of them, a bolt of pain shot through his neck and down his left arm.

"I fought an intruder. In my house. Colette and Noelle were at the ballet. He got the front door open without a sound, but when the wind slammed it shut, I heard it from the basement," Weiss responded in a hoarse voice. He limped his way to the closest chair and carefully lowered himself into it.

"A robbery?" Urzula Dabrowski asked.

"That's what I thought, because he made a methodical search of the house. He was definitely searching for something. But as far as Colette and I can tell, nothing is missing."

"You got a look at him?" Koppel asked.

"No, he had a nylon stocking pulled over his head."

"But he attacked you! That's terrible," Urzula said, apparently even more upset than the others. Weiss privately welcomed her great concern for him, but didn't let on that he could have allowed the intruder to leave without a confrontation.

"Why did he have to attack you? Couldn't he just have run?" Horst Mullheim asked. Weiss shrugged. In truth, he was still trying to piece it all together, especially the man's intentions.

"Have the police come up with any clues that might help? Something he left behind?" Max Bauer spoke up for the first time.

"No," Weiss replied, shaking his head. "But when I smashed a walking stick into his forearm, he cursed me in German. He shouted *verdammt*!"

"Then he could be an émigré, like us," Koppel said. "Well, not exactly like us," he added. Taking a closer look at his friend's neck, Koppel said, "The bastard tried to choke you, Jean-Pierre... was he trying to kill you?" Weiss didn't answer right away. When he looked up from the table, all were staring at him.

"It felt like it at the time. He was *ungodly* strong," Weiss answered. "When he got his hands around my neck, I pretended to black out, and then kneed him hard in the groin. That's when he took off."

They sat silently around the table for some time, each wondering what to make of it all. The incident evoked a type of fear which they had consigned to the past. On crossing the Atlantic and reaching the New York City harbor, they had believed they were safe. No one dared voice any notion that the attack was related to what they had fled in Europe.

Eventually, the meeting resumed in subdued tones. The discussion of the conflicts in Europe continued, and most of the news was disheartening. The Greeks, who had fought with tremendous courage and managed to halt the invasion of their country by the Italian army, were crushed when Germany entered the fray. And in North Africa, General Erwin Rommel was living up to his reputation as the *Desert Fox*. The British forces were desperate for the first shipment of M3 tanks.

* * *

"Max, we have to convince Jean-Pierre," Urzula Dabrowski said. The two of them sat in a west side diner near Columbus Circle, their empty plates now pushed to the side. "He'll listen if we approach him together."

When Bauer had received a call from Urzula to meet for breakfast, he was delighted that she was showing more interest in him, but it turned out not to be a personal overture. Rather, Urzula wanted to talk tactics.

She told Max that their group must have been infiltrated by someone hostile to their objectives. "That's why Jean-Pierre was beaten in his home."

"You're saying it wasn't a robbery? That someone planned to attack or kill him?"

"Absolutely. The intruder and his associates wanted to stop him from making the donation to Bullard's reelection campaign. They want to delay or even prevent America's entry into the war. The attack came soon after our last meeting when Jean-Pierre promised to send money. Do you remember him telling Ira Koppel that it would take a little time to convert assets into cash? We have to convince Jean-Pierre not to send the money."

"But then these fanatics will have won. And it was you who pointed out that Bullard was facing a tough reelection battle because of the America First –"

"But I never thought we would be putting Jean-Pierre's life at risk," Urzula countered. "Are you willing to do that? And it might not be America First. Maybe the individual who has infiltrated our group is an agent of the German war machine."

"But Jean-Pierre's life would still be at risk. Even if he wrote the check today, they still might try to kill him," Max pointed out.

"We don't really know that. It's entirely possible the attack was a warning to him and the rest of us. If he withdraws from the group now and never sends the money to Bullard, they might leave him in peace. They know it would be far better to stop Jean-Pierre without resorting to murder. A murder would lead to a much bigger investigation, and it might be brought to the attention of the FBI. Right now, it's just a robbery being handled by the local police."

Bauer took a sip of his coffee, set the cup back on the table and leaned back in the wooden booth. Finally, he said, "Urzula, assuming we have been infiltrated, who among us do you suspect?"

"I don't know," she said quietly. She looked up at him. Do you have any thoughts?"

"If I *had* to pick someone, it would be Horst Mullheim."

"Why?"

"I had a conversation with him after one of our meetings. You're aware that until recently Mullheim was one of General Guderian's adjutants." Urzula nodded. "During the Great War he served in the infantry and was temporarily blinded by mustard gas. His vision eventually returned, but his lungs were permanently damaged. It's why he's so short of breath now. Mullheim told me that Germany was on the brink of winning in 1918 when it was betrayed by the 'November Criminals.' That's what Hitler called the German politicians who signed the armistice that was so punishing to Germany."

"Well, whoever is undermining us, there's one thing I'm certain of," Urzula replied. "We have to convince Jean-Pierre not to make the campaign contribution, and we have to do it at a meeting so that *everyone* in the group knows, including the mole."

After several moments of silence, Urzula said, "Max, I have an idea of how we can protect Jean-Pierre and possibly uncover the infiltrator. If we actually have one."

* * *

Nothing had happened during the first night of their vigil. With his wife and daughter still safely ensconced at the Waldorf Astoria, Jean-Pierre Weiss welcomed Max Bauer into his home where the two of them would spend a second night together. All the curtains were drawn to prevent observation from the outside.

As on the previous evening, each of them planned to pass the time reading and making sure the other stayed awake. The armchairs in the study were a bit too comfortable for watch duty, but the room was well illuminated. Although he could not offer Bauer a proper drink, Weiss had started a crackling blaze in the fireplace, and there were countless books in floor to ceiling shelves to keep the men occupied. Weiss asked Bauer if the two of them should stay in separate rooms to facilitate their plan, but Bauer said that it would increase the risk of one of them falling asleep. Weiss had to concur. They also agreed to keep their conversation to an absolute minimum. If the intruder returned, it was crucial that he believe that the owner of the house was alone.

After privately informing Weiss of Bauer's plan to protect him, Dabrowski had called for an emergency meeting of the group, and with everyone present, she and Bauer urged Weiss not to make the contribution to Senator Bullard's campaign. But Weiss – having been coached by Dabrowski and Bauer – proclaimed for all to hear that he had no intention of backing down. The sale of some of his assets almost complete, he would have the money in two days' time and planned on mailing the check promptly.

"We can't let the fascists intimidate us here also. There's nowhere else to run," he said. Almost everyone around the table nodded in agreement, but Weiss understood that if the group had been infiltrated, the informant would now have a very narrow window of opportunity to prevent the campaign contribution. None of the other émigrés were made aware that Max Bauer, properly armed, would be staying with Weiss. And by forcing the intruder to act so quickly, they could deny him much of the element of surprise. Dabrowski admired Bauer's clever plan to uncover the mole, but she worried that she and Max Bauer were now linked somehow in the minds of the other members of the émigré group.

The second night of their vigil passed without incident until 1 a.m. when Bauer and Weiss were startled by the sound of shattering glass. On entering the kitchen, they found Weiss's black tomcat standing on the breakfast table looking down at a broken bowl it had apparently shoved onto the tile floor. Weiss gave the cat some fresh food, and the two men returned to the study.

Even in the city that never sleeps, the sounds of cars passing in the street eventually subsided. Both men had been able to get some rest during the day, but fatigue inevitably crept up on them, and at one point, Weiss's head angled forward toward his chest. Before Bauer could rouse him, Weiss suddenly jerked his head upright. Awake and alarmed by his lapse, Jean-Pierre returned to the kitchen and made coffee for both of them. He also brought Max a confection from a neighborhood patisserie. Then they resumed their reading, and the evening passed uneventfully. For a while.

A little after 4 a.m., Jean-Pierre nodded off again. This time, his head was comfortably nestled in the space between the back of his overstuffed armchair and the chair's right wing. Bauer waited a few minutes, then rose and approached the back of his companion's chair. Bauer's 9 mm Glock rested untouched in a shoulder holster under the left side of his jacket, but he reached instead into the jacket's right inside pocket and withdrew another item.

Taking action before his own sense of fair play might assert itself, Bauer wrapped the strip of rawhide around Weiss's neck just below the larynx and pulled the ends of the cord with ungodly strength.

* * *

"Admiral, we've just received another message from Katapult," Leutnant Krebbs said.

"Report," Canaris ordered.

"Sir, Katapult has completed his mission."

A lifetime of stoic self-discipline reinforced by his training in the German Navy and the Abwehr had served Canaris well, but the admiral could barely suppress his elation on hearing this. Now, even if Bullard were reelected, it wouldn't be Weiss's doing. Besides, Canaris had put into play a scheme to funnel money to Bullard's opponents in the America First movement. He was achieving exactly what the Führer had instructed him to do; delay America's entrance into the war and provide the German scientists the time they needed to complete their superweapons. Hitler understood more than anyone a fundamental aspect of modern warfare – it was a race.

Recently, Canaris had been informed of Germany's plan to build what was being called the Amerika-Bomber. Piloted by brave volunteers, it would depart an airfield in occupied France and make a one-way flight over the Atlantic to drop a Heisenberg device on Washington D.C. Once this happened, the wars with Britain and the Soviet Union would end immediately. Canaris realized that the Führer's skeptics were wrong; Germany *could* fight a war on multiple fronts. And win it.

"Admiral, Katapult's message has a second part."

"What is it?"

"Katapult states that in order to safeguard his cover within the émigré group, he had to kill a second member of the group, Urzula Dabrowski." On seeing the horrified look on the admiral's face, the aide asked, "Sir, what's wrong?"

But the admiral stared at him in silence. Even dead, Raven's identity could not be revealed.

Afriti

David R. Downing

THE SPUTTERING campfire cast a dancing glimmer across the frozen desert, defying the night winds that hurried the cold breath of winter through the canyons. Beside the fire sat Kalat, though none in this frozen wasteland would know him by that name. He had the hood of his black cloak drawn up tight to ward against the growing cold, and sat close by the small fire. It was of small comfort. The flames flickered weakly, doing little to shield against the biting winds.

Kalat reached into a deep pocket and retrieved the last of the clues that had been provided for this assignment – a small trinket; a miniature oil lamp cast in pure copper. Kalat rubbed the lamp between chilled hands, frosting it with his breath as he brought the cold metal to his lips. "Afriti" he whispered into the icy night. It was a single word, yet in that was a name, a warning, and a summoning.

Across the frozen sands rose a distant whirlwind. The twister grew in intensity as it coursed into life, fed by the icy winds and nourished by the sage and sand that it sucked into its swirling might. The whirlwind staggered across the desert, laying a wayward path towards the one that had called it.

Kalat patiently awaited the storm's approach. He casually warmed his hands over the feeble flames and reflected on the information that the Messenger's pouch had provided for this assignment.

The first instruction had decoded simply as 'Desert Heart'. Kalat had resolved this clue with little difficulty. The heart of the vast and frozen Gobi was well known, though seldom entered, by the nomadic tribesmen that frequented these barren tracks. He had simply to accompany the local tribesmen on their nightly rounds of wine and women and allow their loose lips to reveal the location known to the tribesmen as the 'Fouad-Shamo', literally 'Heart of the Gobi'. This area, with its windswept plateaus and deeply carved canyons, lay near the center of the vast expanse of the wilderness. Indeed, the very heart of the immense and frozen desert.

The second instruction had also deciphered easily. The word, a secret and forbidden name in the guttural language of the nomads, immediately cast fear into those that heard it. The name was whispered around lonely campfires, drawn in cryptic runes along sand washed walls, and spoken loudly only by Majii in secret rituals that guarded the speaker. It was the name of power, of destruction, and of fear. It was the name of Djin whose name, 'Afriti', Kalat had dared utter into the night sky.

As usual there was a third instruction, and this Kalat found most difficult to resolve. The words had decoded as 'Fear is nothing'. Kalat, whose trail had led him through many such assignments, had little idea what to make of this instruction. He knew instinctively that this was no place for fear. This was to be an encounter, a challenging and a contest. Kalat's training had equipped him such assignments. He placed his faith in himself, his weapons, and his skill with the blades. He had trust in his abilities. Fear, he understood, was not part of his arsenal.

Along with the coded strips of parchment had come a handful of silver Denairi and the miniature lamp that he now returned to the pocket in his cloak. Kalat used the coins to purchase provisions before venturing out into the desert, but the lamp he had retained. It was of simple make, beaten with an economy of design. The small flame chamber, which could scarcely hold a palm-full of oil, was topped with a stopper attached with a delicate chain. The lamp was not much more than a child's toy, and of little use as a source of light in these endless wastelands. But Kalat hung onto it in any case; always mindful of the importance of any materials delivered on the silent wings of the Messenger.

The whirlwind swirled to a stop near the campfire, and from it emerged the one who had been summoned. Afriti was man-like, though much taller and stronger than any man that Kalat had ever seen. He was garbed in loose fitting silk garments that returned the light of the fire in a glittering reflection. In defiance of the cold, his bare arms protruded from a sleeveless vest. His head was turbaned, and his dark beard was braided nearly to his waist. His walk carried the swaggering arrogance of the desert gods. He was Djin, god among gods, not one to be lightly bothered with the concerns of men.

Afriti approached and casually sat across the small fire. Kalat acknowledged his presence, offering a cup of warm tea from the warming kettle. The Djin accepted Kalat's cup, yet he did not drink. Instead, he rolled the ceramic in the palms of his hands and sniffed at the steam rising from the brew. Afriti's size made the cup appear to be miniature, like a toy in the Djin's mighty hands. He raised his heavy eyebrows in question. "You know me?" Afriti's low voice resonated in the dark, rumbling in defiance of the howling winds.

Kalat shrugged. "I know of you. I know that you are feared."

Afriti chuckled. "Feared? Of course I am feared. Indeed, I am fear! I am not like you men. I am of the Djin. We have power beyond your comprehension." Afriti's words, spoken without malice, were laced with scorn. "Your kind can only fear that which it cannot grasp. You must cower before a power that you cannot contain or understand."

Kalat took a sip from the warm tea, letting the Djin's words echo across the canyons, but saying nothing in return.

Afriti looked up from the steaming cup to meet Kalat's eyes in a frozen gaze. "So tell me, who are you? Who is it that has dared to summon me from the pleasures of my harem? Who is it that has dared to call my name?"

This time Kalat did speak. "I have many names, but you may call me Executioner." Kalat met the Djin's icy stare. "I am also feared."

"Executioner, are you? I know of no man with such a name."

Again Kalat shrugged. "Perhaps I am nobody then." Kalat's eyes refused to retreat from the Djin's penetrating gaze. "Afriti, I ask you, does it really matter who I am?"

The Djin smiled, nodded slightly, and roared with a hearty laugh. "True, and well said! Executioner it is then, and Executioner it shall always be. You are correct, no one will care who you really are. And in truth, it matters little to me.

"I have been called to service many of your kind. In centuries forgotten, I have been summoned to provide strength and power to the leaders of men. I have served them all, providing muscle to their lust and fueling their greed.

"I was there when the armies of Gulam stormed through the mountain passes of Norselandia. I laughed as the Gulamians lanced through the feeble lines of plainsmen pitifully obliged to try and defend their homelands. I led the Gulam cavalry across those places – feeding the fires of their fury, and guiding their blades to the feast.

"And it was I who brought down the great walls of Athenia, and fueled the wild tribesmen of Scythia. Oh what a slaughter that was! The marbled halls of the city are stained red to this day, though they are buried far beneath the sands of time.

"I have led countless slaughters of man. And yet, what of the men whom I served? What were their names? Are they carved in the halls of time beside my own? Did any have a destiny beyond their deaths? No, we both know that they are nothing. You are correct, Executioner, who you are is of little concern. In the end it matters not.

"It is I who is the important one. None can stand before me. My services have been of great demand, and they have always brought great victories to those who enlisted them. I am power, Executioner, pure and proven. None can stop my actions. None can deny my wrath."

"And at what price comes this power?" muttered Kalat.

"The price?" The Djin laughed. "The price is more than you can afford. More than any could afford. Yet all have agreed to the bargain. The price, Executioner, is you. I will own you. You will use the power that I give you to serve me. You will do my will."

Kalat took a sip from the steaming cup. His words were direct, and sharp. "I didn't summon you to become your slave."

The Djin's answer was without treachery, without finesse. "All men are my slaves; slaves to my power, slaves to my destruction; slaves to my will. You are no different. You are weak as are all men. You fear me, not for what I can do, but for what I am. You fear me because I am Afriti!"

The Djin rose to his feet, casting the steaming cup into the desert. The wind swirled around his legs, hiding them in an icy cloud of sand. His voice boomed into the darkness. His mighty frame swelled and doubled in height.

"You had the folly to call me. Do not doubt me, Executioner!" Afriti's words were laced with irony. "I will fulfill the agreement, and I will hold you to your part in it. I will grant you your wish, but your wish has a price. The die has been cast." The Djin loomed above Kalat's squatting position and pointed an accusing finger at Kalat's face. "You are already my slave."

Kalat casually laid aside his cup and dug his frozen hands deep into heavy pockets. He had heard enough. Now, it was time to earn his fees. Kalat's assignments had provided countless opportunities to practice the black arts of his training, and numerous victims on which to hone his skills. He had seen the deadly efficiency of his weapons bring down scores of opponents. His path was dripping with the blood of untold encounters, his blades notched with the deaths they had spawned. His very soul was stained with the blood of his victories. Kalat knew his own strength, and he trusted in the guidance of the Guild. For encounters such as these he had been trained. For challenges such as this he was well prepared.

Yet Kalat paused.

Something about this encounter was different. Kalat's weapons felt puny in his hands, his arms weak, his footing questionable. The threatening force of Afriti loomed over his indecision. An unknown had entered into the equation. For the first time in his many assignments, Kalat knew fear.

Afriti stamped his feet, nearly dousing the fire in a cloud of frozen dust as he drew his scimitar from its scabbard. His voice was like thunder rolling down the icy canyons. "My blade drips with the blood of man" he roared and towered above Kalat. "My belly is bloated with the rotted flesh of your putrid souls. Men are my playthings, and I am eager for sport! Now tell me," the Djin commanded, "what it is that you would have me do? Ask and it will be done! Loose me to your need and I will rampage and destroy. For you, I will kill without pause. I will bring the ruined bodies of the slain to fill your pits. I will toy with those that you would have captured, and at your whim lead them to a slow and tortuous death. This is why I have answered your call. I have come to your summoning for one reason and one reason only – to relish in the fear of your kind."

The Djin swirled his scimitar above his turbaned head. The red blade loosed a spray of blood to fall in a frozen rain of vengeance on the frosted soil. Reflected in those icy drops Kalat could see the faces of doomed men frozen in perpetual fright. In them he could smell the stench of rot. He could hear the sharp screams of death echoed in the drops shattering on the frozen ground.

The Djin, now grown several times in size, stopped his blade in a threatening position above Kalat – drenching him in a stream of dripping blood. "Now tell me, fool, why did you call me?"

Fear, as palatable as the icy sands that swirled around the Djin's legs, clung to Kalat like a frozen cloud. It held his motions and muddied his thoughts. Kalat was afraid to move, afraid to make a mistake that would be his undoing. Fear wrapped him in a death grip that could not be shrugged off. Fear was the opponent, and this enemy was winning.

Kalat's mind swirled with the possibilities. For the first time in his many assignments Kalat doubted his own abilities. Was he to be outdone by this opponent? Was this the assignment that even he could not accomplish? In training, stories had been whispered of agents that had not returned to claim their rewards. The Masters were quick to squelch such tales with the sharp end of the rod, and with drills enforced late into the night. But the seeds of doubt had been planted. Each agent knew his own weaknesses. Each knew that he could be defeated.

Kalat weighted the alternative that Afriti offered. He could succumb to the Djin's wishes. He could use this power against those that had wronged him. Instead of fighting the Djin, Kalat could unleash this horror on the black ships that had appeared at dawn to burn the village of his youth and drag off his sisters to an unknown fate at the hands of slavering barbarians. With a few words, he could reap vengeance to fill the void that all his years of training and assignments had yet to resolve. What did it matter? Wasn't he already a slave to the Guild and the Masters that guided his path? Wouldn't the Djin give him even more power to enact his revenge? Why not point this weapon of destruction to those that he hated?

Kalat wrestled with the outcome, yet he refused to give in to the encompassing fear of Afriti. He looked up to the monster looming over him, struggling to find the answer to the Djin's question. Kalat squinted through the mist of freezing blood and wind, and found his answer in the face of the Djin.

Afriti smiled, and in that smile was his undoing. In his grin was his weakness, revealed like a black cloud in a grey winter sky. Beyond the smirking smile and white teeth of Afriti was darkness, black and empty; void. Hidden by the power and strength of the Djin there was an emptiness; a nothingness. The fear of the Djin was without body; without substance. Afriti was empty. The Djin, fear itself, was nothing!

Kalat's move was well practiced and often used. In each hand he had secreted his incendiaries. The first Kalat dashed to the ground at the Djin's feet, the second he cast directly at Afriti's chest. Each incendiary was laced with shards of quartz and sparked into explosion upon impact, blinding the Djin in the flash of light and flame.

Kalat spun back, out of the reach of the light and into the safety of darkness. Somewhere in his spinning move, he cocked the bows of the short-bolted darter strapped to his wrist. He came out of the spin, crouching in the darkness and loosed three poisoned bolts into Afriti's chest before spinning to a new position further into the black.

This time Kalat retrieved his cuttoe, the razor edged blade preferred by many of the agents. Kalat paused only briefly as Afriti patted at the flames at his chest, and then silently circled to the rear of the Djin. Kalat dashed forward, slashing at the tendons at Afriti's heels and retreating back into the night.

"Here's the answer to your question, you bastard!" Kalat cursed, "I called you to kill you. I summoned you to your death!"

The winds swirled in a maelstrom around Kalat, driving sand and ice into squinted eyes. Afriti struck out blindly with his scimitar in a swirling arc that swept with the force of a hurricane. The blade swung towards Kalat with a heavy arc. But Kalat was not one to be felled by such a blow. He ducked, and then darted into the light once again, his cuttoe biting deep at the Djin's inner thigh. Kalat drew the cuttoe across the wound; widening the gash with the serrated back-blade of his favorite killing tool.

Afriti roared with anger, but he didn't lash out with his scimitar. Instead, he drew his blade closer, as if in defense. He spoke to the darkness that surrounded him. There was a bargaining in his words. "Tell me what you want. You can have whatever you desire! What kingdom would you have me bring down? What empire would you rule?"

But Kalat's blades had already been wetted with fury. His words were echoed by the thud of his throwing knives coming from the darkness to land squarely in the Djin's massive chest. "I will be king of you," he growled. "I will rule over your death!"

"No," Afriti cursed. "I am fear! I am your fear! You make me what I am. With your fear I cannot be defeated. With your service, we cannot be stopped!" There was urgency to Afriti's words, and an understanding of their weakness. "Your fear is my power. You must fear me."

Kalat stepped into the circle of light. His gaze cut through the swirling ice. His cuttoe dripped with the blood of the Djin. "There you are wrong. I don't fear you." Kalat's words were true, his resolve complete. This was his job, his Quest, and his assignment. Let others squirm from the conflict. Let them bask in their ignorance. Let them be slaves to the Djin. Let them fear! Kalat knew his tools, and he knew his abilities. He knew this arena, and he knew that fear was the enemy of the victor. Fear, as palatable as the tea still on his breath, was now Kalat's tool, powering his assault and fueling his resolve.

Already, the poison in Kalat's darts was taking its effect. The Djin's thoughts were blurred, his actions slowed. Each strike of Kalat's weapons had taken its toll. With each new wound, the Djin shrank in stature. Afriti, who moments ago had towered over Kalat, now stood eye to eye with the one who had summoned him.

"We are one and the same, you and I." Afriti's voice was weak and shallow, devoid of the power it had once commanded. "You live for the fear of others. You kill for the power that it gives you. You are skilled at the task, no doubt. But even so, you are no different than me."

"Again, you are wrong," Kalat scoffed. "You feed off the fear of man while I," Kalat's words were little more than a whisper as he turned to step away from the Djin, "kill simply because it is my job."

The dulled senses of the Djin scarcely noticed Kalat's spinning move. Afriti's slow eyes never even saw the razor-edged blade that cut though his mid-section like the plow slices through the field. Far too late, Afriti's hands reflexed to his waist, trying to cup the blood and entrails that would soon ooze from his severed abdomen.

But there was nothing to catch. The Djin fell to his knees as a rush of wind swirled through his fingers. The wind was icy and rank, full of the smells of death – Afriti's death. With his last breath, the Djin strained with a final word, an icy acknowledgement of Kalat's dark occupation.

"Executioner," he whispered.

Kalat squatted and tucked his face to his cloak to ward against the spray of ice and sand that was cast by Afriti's squirming death. In mere moments, only a cloud of swirling sand was left to mark the presence of the Djin. Even this, Kalat knew, would soon be swept clean by the desert winds.

Reaching under the bracer on his left forearm, Kalat retrieved the signal tube and called for the Messenger to return. Kalat knew that the Messenger would hear, and that the raven would soon come. He had only to wait a moment before the dark raven came spiraling down out of the night sky. The Messenger landed easily beside the fire, pecked briefly in the sand and picked up a small insect – a knat, scrambling to flee the circle of light. The raven flapped easily to Kalat's shoulder and waited patiently while he retrieved something from a hidden pocket in his heavy cloak. It was the brass lamp, polished smooth with Kalat's breath. Kalat held the lamp open as the Messenger released the knat into the firebox. He then put the stopper in the neck of the lamp, tied it securely with a barbed cord, and looped it gently over the raven's waiting neck.

Kalat whispered to the Messenger, speaking as if the raven could understand the irony of his words. "Tell the Masters that that third clue was a tricky one. Take the knat. It is nothing really. That should be evidence enough." As if in answer the massive bird bobbed slightly and sprang from Kalat's shoulder. In an instant the Messenger had disappeared into the night sky.

Kalat knew that the Messenger would soon return, and with his return would come another set of instructions. Kalat also understood that the next assignment would draw him through the frozen desert. The Quest was leading consistently north, across the Gobi to the rolling hills and low mountain Steppes that framed the Northern boundary of these desolate lands. He knew that the Quest would not yet lead him back home, that there was more work to be done.

Kalat, agent, spy and executioner, casually brushed the frost from his cloak and gathered up his implements. He allowed himself a brief moment of leisure, fruitlessly trying to warm his hands over the sputtering fire, before stepping away from the light to hide once again, in the dark.

The Adventure of the Second Stain

Arthur Conan Doyle

I HAD INTENDED 'The Adventure of the Abbey Grange' to be the last of those exploits of my friend, Mr. Sherlock Holmes, which I should ever communicate to the public. This resolution of mine was not due to any lack of material, since I have notes of many hundreds of cases to which I have never alluded, nor was it caused by any waning interest on the part of my readers in the singular personality and unique methods of this remarkable man. The real reason lay in the reluctance which Mr. Holmes has shown to the continued publication of his experiences. So long as he was in actual professional practice the records of his successes were of some practical value to him, but since he has definitely retired from London and betaken himself to study and bee-farming on the Sussex Downs, notoriety has become hateful to him, and he has peremptorily requested that his wishes in this matter should be strictly observed. It was only upon my representing to him that I had given a promise that 'The Adventure of the Second Stain' should be published when the times were ripe, and pointing out to him that it is only appropriate that this long series of episodes should culminate in the most important international case which he has ever been called upon to handle, that I at last succeeded in obtaining his consent that a carefully guarded account of the incident should at last be laid before the public. If in telling the story I seem to be somewhat vague in certain details, the public will readily understand that there is an excellent reason for my reticence.

It was, then, in a year, and even in a decade, that shall be nameless, that upon one Tuesday morning in autumn we found two visitors of European fame within the walls of our humble room in Baker Street. The one, austere, high-nosed, eagle-eyed, and dominant, was none other than the illustrious Lord Bellinger, twice Premier of Britain. The other, dark, clear-cut, and elegant, hardly yet of middle age, and endowed with every beauty of body and of mind, was the Right Honourable Trelawney Hope, Secretary for European Affairs, and the most rising statesman in the country. They sat side by side upon our paper-littered settee, and it was easy to see from their worn and anxious faces that it was business of the most pressing importance which had brought them. The Premier's thin, blue-veined hands were clasped tightly over the ivory head of his umbrella, and his gaunt, ascetic face looked gloomily from Holmes to me. The European Secretary pulled nervously at his moustache and fidgeted with the seals of his watch-chain.

"When I discovered my loss, Mr. Holmes, which was at eight o'clock this morning, I at once informed the Prime Minister. It was at his suggestion that we have both come to you."

"Have you informed the police?"

"No, sir," said the Prime Minister, with the quick, decisive manner for which he was famous. "We have not done so, nor is it possible that we should do so. To inform the police must, in the long run, mean to inform the public. This is what we particularly desire to avoid."

"And why, sir?"

"Because the document in question is of such immense importance that its publication might very easily – I might almost say probably – lead to European complications of the utmost moment. It is not too much to say that peace or war may hang upon the issue. Unless its recovery can be attended with the utmost secrecy, then it may as well not be recovered at all, for all that is aimed at by those who have taken it is that its contents should be generally known."

"I understand. Now, Mr. Trelawney Hope, I should be much obliged if you would tell me exactly the circumstances under which this document disappeared."

"That can be done in a very few words, Mr. Holmes. The letter – for it was a letter from a foreign potentate – was received six days ago. It was of such importance that I have never left it in my safe, but have taken it across each evening to my house in Whitehall Terrace, and kept it in my bedroom in a locked despatch-box. It was there last night. Of that I am certain. I actually opened the box while I was dressing for dinner and saw the document inside. This morning it was gone. The despatch-box had stood beside the glass upon my dressing-table all night. I am a light sleeper, and so is my wife. We are both prepared to swear that no one could have entered the room during the night. And yet I repeat that the paper is gone."

"What time did you dine?"

"Half-past seven."

"How long was it before you went to bed?"

"My wife had gone to the theatre. I waited up for her. It was half-past eleven before we went to our room."

"Then for four hours the despatch-box had lain unguarded?"

"No one is ever permitted to enter that room save the house-maid in the morning, and my valet, or my wife's maid, during the rest of the day. They are both trusty servants who have been with us for some time. Besides, neither of them could possibly have known that there was anything more valuable than the ordinary departmental papers in my despatch-box."

"Who did know of the existence of that letter?"

"No one in the house."

"Surely your wife knew?"

"No, sir. I had said nothing to my wife until I missed the paper this morning."

The Premier nodded approvingly.

"I have long known, sir, how high is your sense of public duty," said he. "I am convinced that in the case of a secret of this importance it would rise superior to the most intimate domestic ties."

The European Secretary bowed.

"You do me no more than justice, sir. Until this morning I have never breathed one word to my wife upon this matter."

"Could she have guessed?"

"No, Mr. Holmes, she could not have guessed – nor could anyone have guessed."

"Have you lost any documents before?"

"No, sir."

"Who is there in England who did know of the existence of this letter?"

"Each member of the Cabinet was informed of it yesterday, but the pledge of secrecy which attends every Cabinet meeting was increased by the solemn warning which was given by the Prime Minister. Good heavens, to think that within a few hours I should myself have lost it!" His handsome face was distorted with a spasm of despair, and his hands tore at his hair. For a moment we caught a glimpse of the natural man, impulsive, ardent, keenly sensitive. The next the aristocratic mask was replaced, and the gentle voice had returned. "Besides the members of the Cabinet there are two, or possibly three, departmental officials who know of the letter. No one else in England, Mr. Holmes, I assure you."

"But abroad?"

"I believe that no one abroad has seen it save the man who wrote it. I am well convinced that his Ministers – that the usual official channels have not been employed."

Holmes considered for some little time.

"Now, sir, I must ask you more particularly what this document is, and why its disappearance should have such momentous consequences?"

The two statesmen exchanged a quick glance and the Premier's shaggy eyebrows gathered in a frown.

"Mr. Holmes, the envelope is a long, thin one of pale blue colour. There is a seal of red wax stamped with a crouching lion. It is addressed in large, bold handwriting to —"

"I fear, sir," said Holmes, "that, interesting and indeed essential as these details are, my inquiries must go more to the root of things. What *was* the letter?"

"That is a State secret of the utmost importance, and I fear that I cannot tell you, nor do I see that it is necessary. If by the aid of the powers which you are said to possess you can find such an envelope as I describe with its enclosure, you will have deserved well of your country, and earned any reward which it lies in our power to bestow."

Sherlock Holmes rose with a smile.

"You are two of the most busy men in the country," said he, "and in my own small way I have also a good many calls upon me. I regret exceedingly that I cannot help you in this matter, and any continuation of this interview would be a waste of time."

The Premier sprang to his feet with that quick, fierce gleam of his deep-set eyes before which a Cabinet has cowered. "I am not accustomed, sir," he began, but mastered his anger and resumed his seat. For a minute or more we all sat in silence. Then the old statesman shrugged his shoulders.

"We must accept your terms, Mr. Holmes. No doubt you are right, and it is unreasonable for us to expect you to act unless we give you our entire confidence."

"I agree with you," said the younger statesman.

"Then I will tell you, relying entirely upon your honour and that of your colleague, Dr. Watson. I may appeal to your patriotism also, for I could not imagine a greater misfortune for the country than that this affair should come out."

"You may safely trust us."

"The letter, then, is from a certain foreign potentate who has been ruffled by some recent Colonial developments of this country. It has been written hurriedly and upon his own responsibility entirely. Inquiries have shown that his Ministers know nothing of the matter. At the same time it is couched in so unfortunate a manner, and certain phrases in it are of so provocative a character, that its publication would undoubtedly lead to a most dangerous state of feeling in this country. There would be such a ferment, sir, that I do not hesitate to say that within a week of the publication of that letter this country would be involved in a great war."

Holmes wrote a name upon a slip of paper and handed it to the Premier.

"Exactly. It was he. And it is this letter – this letter which may well mean the expenditure of a thousand millions and the lives of a hundred thousand men – which has become lost in this unaccountable fashion."

"Have you informed the sender?"

"Yes, sir, a cipher telegram has been dispatched."

"Perhaps he desires the publication of the letter."

"No, sir, we have strong reason to believe that he already understands that he has acted in an indiscreet and hot-headed manner. It would be a greater blow to him and to his country than to us if this letter were to come out."

"If this is so, whose interest is it that the letter should come out? Why should anyone desire to steal it or to publish it?"

"There, Mr. Holmes, you take me into regions of high international politics. But if you consider the European situation you will have no difficulty in perceiving the motive. The whole of Europe is an armed camp. There is a double league which makes a fair balance of military power. Great Britain holds the scales. If Britain were driven into war with one confederacy, it would assure the supremacy of the other confederacy, whether they joined in the war or not. Do you follow?"

"Very clearly. It is then the interest of the enemies of this potentate to secure and publish this letter, so as to make a breach between his country and ours?"

"Yes, sir."

"And to whom would this document be sent if it fell into the hands of an enemy?"

"To any of the great Chancelleries of Europe. It is probably speeding on its way thither at the present instant as fast as steam can take it."

Mr. Trelawney Hope dropped his head on his chest and groaned aloud. The Premier placed his hand kindly upon his shoulder.

"It is your misfortune, my dear fellow. No one can blame you. There is no precaution which you have neglected. Now, Mr. Holmes, you are in full possession of the facts. What course do you recommend?"

Holmes shook his head mournfully.

"You think, sir, that unless this document is recovered there will be war?"

"I think it is very probable."

"Then, sir, prepare for war."

"That is a hard saying, Mr. Holmes."

"Consider the facts, sir. It is inconceivable that it was taken after eleven-thirty at night, since I understand that Mr. Hope and his wife were both in the room from that hour until the loss was found out. It was taken, then, yesterday evening between seven-thirty and eleven-thirty, probably near the earlier hour, since whoever took it evidently knew that it was there and would naturally secure it as early as possible. Now, sir, if a document of this importance were taken at that hour, where can it be now? No one has any reason to retain it. It has been passed rapidly on to those who need it. What chance have we now to overtake or even to trace it? It is beyond our reach."

The Prime Minister rose from the settee.

"What you say is perfectly logical, Mr. Holmes. I feel that the matter is indeed out of our hands."

"Let us presume, for argument's sake, that the document was taken by the maid or by the valet —"

"They are both old and tried servants."

"I understand you to say that your room is on the second floor, that there is no entrance from without, and that from within no one could go up unobserved. It must, then, be somebody in the house who has taken it. To whom would the thief take it? To one of several international spies and secret agents, whose names are tolerably familiar to me. There are three who may be said to be the heads of their profession. I will begin my research by going round and finding if each of them is at his post. If one is missing – especially if he has disappeared since last night – we will have some indication as to where the document has gone."

"Why should he be missing?" asked the European Secretary. "He would take the letter to an Embassy in London, as likely as not."

"I fancy not. These agents work independently, and their relations with the Embassies are often strained."

The Prime Minister nodded his acquiescence.

"I believe you are right, Mr. Holmes. He would take so valuable a prize to headquarters with his own hands. I think that your course of action is an excellent one. Meanwhile, Hope, we cannot neglect all our other duties on account of this one misfortune. Should there be any fresh developments during the day we shall communicate with you, and you will no doubt let us know the results of your own inquiries."

The two statesmen bowed and walked gravely from the room.

* * *

When our illustrious visitors had departed Holmes lit his pipe in silence and sat for some time lost in the deepest thought. I had opened the morning paper and was immersed in a sensational crime which had occurred in London the night before, when my friend gave an exclamation, sprang to his feet, and laid his pipe down upon the mantelpiece.

"Yes," said he, "there is no better way of approaching it. The situation is desperate, but not hopeless. Even now, if we could be sure which of them has taken it, it is just possible that it has not yet passed out of his hands. After all, it is a question of money with these fellows, and I have the British treasury behind me. If it's on the market I'll buy it – if it means another penny on the income-tax. It is conceivable that the fellow might hold it back to see what bids come from this side before he tries his luck on the other. There are only those three capable of playing so bold a game – there are Oberstein, La Rothiere, and Eduardo Lucas. I will see each of them."

I glanced at my morning paper.

"Is that Eduardo Lucas of Godolphin Street?"

"Yes."

"You will not see him."

"Why not?"

"He was murdered in his house last night."

My friend has so often astonished me in the course of our adventures that it was with a sense of exultation that I realized how completely I had astonished him. He stared in amazement, and then snatched the paper from my hands. This was the paragraph which I had been engaged in reading when he rose from his chair.

MURDER IN WESTMINSTER

A crime of mysterious character was committed last night at 16 Godolphin Street, one of the old-fashioned and secluded rows of eighteenth century houses which lie between the river and the Abbey, almost in the shadow of the great Tower of the Houses of Parliament. This small but select mansion has been inhabited for some years by Mr. Eduardo Lucas, well known in society circles both on account of his charming personality and because he has the well-deserved reputation of being one of the best amateur tenors in the country. Mr. Lucas is an unmarried man, thirty-four years of age, and his establishment consists of Mrs. Pringle, an elderly housekeeper, and of Mitton, his valet. The former retires early and sleeps at the top of the house. The valet was out for the evening, visiting a friend at Hammersmith. From ten o'clock onward Mr. Lucas had the house to himself. What occurred during that time has not yet transpired, but at a quarter to twelve Police-constable Barrett, passing along Godolphin Street observed that the door of No. 16 was ajar. He knocked, but received no answer. Perceiving a light in the front room, he advanced into the passage and again knocked, but without reply. He then pushed open the door and entered. The room was in a state of wild disorder, the furniture being all swept to one side, and one chair lying on its back in the centre. Beside this chair, and still grasping one of its legs, lay the unfortunate tenant of the house. He had been stabbed to the heart and must have died instantly. The knife with which the crime had been committed was a curved Indian dagger, plucked down from a trophy of Oriental arms which adorned one of the walls. Robbery does not appear to have been the motive of the crime, for there had been no attempt to remove the valuable contents of the room. Mr. Eduardo Lucas was so well known and popular that his violent and mysterious fate will arouse painful interest and intense sympathy in a widespread circle of friends.

"Well, Watson, what do you make of this?" asked Holmes, after a long pause.

"It is an amazing coincidence."

"A coincidence! Here is one of the three men whom we had named as possible actors in this drama, and he meets a violent death during the very hours when we know that that drama was being enacted. The odds are enormous against its being coincidence. No figures could express them. No, my dear Watson, the two events are connected – *must* be connected. It is for us to find the connection."

"But now the official police must know all."

"Not at all. They know all they see at Godolphin Street. They know – and shall know – nothing of Whitehall Terrace. Only *we* know of both events, and can trace the relation between them. There is one obvious point which would, in any case, have turned my suspicions against Lucas. Godolphin Street, Westminster, is only a few minutes' walk from Whitehall Terrace. The other secret agents whom I have named live in the extreme West End. It was easier, therefore, for Lucas than for the others to establish a connection or receive a message from the European Secretary's household – a small thing, and yet where events are compressed into a few hours it may prove essential. Halloa! What have we here?"

Mrs. Hudson had appeared with a lady's card upon her salver. Holmes glanced at it, raised his eyebrows, and handed it over to me.

"Ask Lady Hilda Trelawney Hope if she will be kind enough to step up," said he.

A moment later our modest apartment, already so distinguished that morning, was further honoured by the entrance of the most lovely woman in London. I had often heard of the beauty of the youngest daughter of the Duke of Belminster, but no description of it, and no contemplation of colourless photographs, had prepared me for the subtle, delicate charm and the beautiful colouring of that exquisite head. And yet as we saw it that autumn morning, it was not its beauty which would be the first thing to impress the observer. The cheek was lovely but it was paled with emotion, the eyes were bright but it was the brightness of fever, the sensitive mouth was tight and drawn in an effort after self-command. Terror – not beauty – was what sprang first to the eye as our fair visitor stood framed for an instant in the open door.

"Has my husband been here, Mr. Holmes?"

"Yes, madam, he has been here."

"Mr. Holmes. I implore you not to tell him that I came here." Holmes bowed coldly, and motioned the lady to a chair.

"Your ladyship places me in a very delicate position. I beg that you will sit down and tell me what you desire, but I fear that I cannot make any unconditional promise."

She swept across the room and seated herself with her back to the window. It was a queenly presence – tall, graceful, and intensely womanly. "Mr. Holmes," she said – and her white-gloved hands clasped and unclasped as she spoke – "I will speak frankly to you in the hopes that it may induce you to speak frankly in return. There is complete confidence between my husband and me on all matters save one. That one is politics. On this his lips are sealed. He tells me nothing. Now, I am aware that there was a most deplorable occurrence in our house last night. I know that a paper has disappeared. But because the matter is political my husband refuses to take me into his complete confidence. Now it is essential – essential, I say – that I should thoroughly understand it. You are the only other person, save only these politicians, who knows the true facts. I beg you then, Mr. Holmes, to tell me exactly what has happened and what it will lead to. Tell me all, Mr. Holmes. Let no regard for your client's interests keep you silent, for I assure you that his interests, if he would only see it, would be best served by taking me into his complete confidence. What was this paper which was stolen?"

"Madam, what you ask me is really impossible."

She groaned and sank her face in her hands.

"You must see that this is so, madam. If your husband thinks fit to keep you in the dark over this matter, is it for me, who has only learned the true facts under the pledge of professional secrecy, to tell what he has withheld? It is not fair to ask it. It is him whom you must ask."

"I have asked him. I come to you as a last resource. But without your telling me anything definite, Mr. Holmes, you may do a great service if you would enlighten me on one point."

"What is it, madam?"

"Is my husband's political career likely to suffer through this incident?"

"Well, madam, unless it is set right it may certainly have a very unfortunate effect."

"Ah!" She drew in her breath sharply as one whose doubts are resolved.

"One more question, Mr. Holmes. From an expression which my husband dropped in the first shock of this disaster I understood that terrible public consequences might arise from the loss of this document."

"If he said so, I certainly cannot deny it."

"Of what nature are they?"

"Nay, madam, there again you ask me more than I can possibly answer."

"Then I will take up no more of your time. I cannot blame you, Mr. Holmes, for having refused to speak more freely, and you on your side will not, I am sure, think the worse of me because I desire, even against his will, to share my husband's anxieties. Once more I beg that you will say nothing of my visit."

She looked back at us from the door, and I had a last impression of that beautiful haunted face, the startled eyes, and the drawn mouth. Then she was gone.

"Now, Watson, the fair sex is your department," said Holmes, with a smile, when the dwindling frou-frou of skirts had ended in the slam of the front door. "What was the fair lady's game? What did she really want?"

"Surely her own statement is clear and her anxiety very natural."

"Hum! Think of her appearance, Watson – her manner, her suppressed excitement, her restlessness, her tenacity in asking questions. Remember that she comes of a caste who do not lightly show emotion."

"She was certainly much moved."

"Remember also the curious earnestness with which she assured us that it was best for her husband that she should know all. What did she mean by that? And you must have observed, Watson, how she manoeuvred to have the light at her back. She did not wish us to read her expression."

"Yes, she chose the one chair in the room."

"And yet the motives of women are so inscrutable. You remember the woman at Margate whom I suspected for the same reason. No powder on her nose – that proved to be the correct solution. How can you build on such a quicksand? Their most trivial action may mean volumes, or their most extraordinary conduct may depend upon a hairpin or a curling tongs. Good morning, Watson."

"You are off?"

"Yes, I will while away the morning at Godolphin Street with our friends of the regular establishment. With Eduardo Lucas lies the solution of our problem, though I must admit that I have not an inkling as to what form it may take. It is a capital mistake to theorize in advance of the facts. Do you stay on guard, my good Watson, and receive any fresh visitors. I'll join you at lunch if I am able."

All that day and the next and the next Holmes was in a mood which his friends would call taciturn, and others morose. He ran out and ran in, smoked incessantly, played snatches on his violin, sank into reveries, devoured sandwiches at irregular hours, and hardly answered the casual questions which I put to him. It was evident to me that things were not going well with him or his quest. He would say nothing of the case, and it was from the papers that I learned the particulars of the inquest, and the arrest with the subsequent release of John Mitton, the valet of the deceased. The coroner's jury brought in the obvious Wilful Murder, but the parties remained as unknown as ever. No motive was suggested. The room was full of articles of value, but none had been taken. The dead man's papers had not been tampered with. They were carefully examined, and showed that he was a keen student of international politics, an indefatigable gossip, a remarkable linguist, and an untiring letter writer. He had been on intimate terms with the leading politicians of several countries. But nothing sensational was discovered among the documents which filled his drawers. As to his relations with women, they appeared to have been promiscuous but superficial. He had many acquaintances among them, but few friends, and no one whom he loved. His habits were regular, his conduct inoffensive. His death was an absolute mystery and likely to remain so.

As to the arrest of John Mitton, the valet, it was a council of despair as an alternative to absolute inaction. But no case could be sustained against him. He had visited friends in Hammersmith that night. The *alibi* was complete. It is true that he started home at an hour which should have brought him to Westminster before the time when the crime was discovered, but his own explanation that he had walked part of the way seemed probable enough in view of the fineness of the night. He had actually arrived at twelve o'clock, and appeared to be overwhelmed by the unexpected tragedy. He had always been on good terms with his master. Several of the dead man's possessions – notably a small case of razors – had been found in the valet's boxes, but he explained that they had been presents from the deceased, and the housekeeper was able to corroborate the story. Mitton had been in Lucas's employment for three years. It was noticeable that Lucas did not take Mitton on the Continent with him. Sometimes he visited Paris for three months on end, but Mitton was left in charge of the Godolphin Street house. As to the housekeeper, she had heard nothing on the night of the crime. If her master had a visitor he had himself admitted him.

So for three mornings the mystery remained, so far as I could follow it in the papers. If Holmes knew more, he kept his own counsel, but, as he told me that Inspector Lestrade had taken him into his confidence in the case, I knew that he was in close touch with every development. Upon the fourth day there appeared a long telegram from Paris which seemed to solve the whole question.

A discovery has just been made by the Parisian police [said the Daily Telegraph] which raises the veil which hung round the tragic fate of Mr. Eduardo Lucas, who met his death by violence last Monday night at Godolphin Street, Westminster. Our readers will remember that the deceased gentleman was found stabbed in his room, and that some suspicion attached to his valet, but that the case broke down on an alibi. Yesterday a lady, who has been known as Mme. Henri Fournaye, occupying a small villa in the Rue Austerlitz, was reported to the authorities by her servants as being insane. An examination showed she had indeed developed mania of a dangerous and permanent form. On inquiry, the police have discovered that Mme. Henri Fournaye only returned from a journey to London on Tuesday last, and there is evidence to connect her with the crime at Westminster. A comparison of photographs has proved conclusively that M. Henri Fournaye and Eduardo Lucas were really one and the same person, and that the deceased had for some reason lived a double life in London and Paris. Mme. Fournaye, who is of Creole origin, is of an extremely excitable nature, and has suffered in the past from attacks of jealousy which have amounted to frenzy. It is conjectured that it was in one of these that she committed the terrible crime which has caused such a sensation in London. Her movements upon the Monday night have not yet been traced, but it is undoubted that a woman answering to her description attracted much attention at Charing Cross Station on Tuesday morning by the wildness of her appearance and the violence of her gestures. It is probable, therefore, that the crime was either committed when insane, or that its immediate effect was to drive the unhappy woman out of her mind. At present she is unable to give any coherent account of the past, and the doctors hold out no hopes of the reestablishment of her reason. There is evidence that a woman, who might have been Mme. Fournaye, was seen for some hours upon Monday night watching the house in Godolphin Street.

"What do you think of that, Holmes?" I had read the account aloud to him, while he finished his breakfast.

"My dear Watson," said he, as he rose from the table and paced up and down the room, "You are most long-suffering, but if I have told you nothing in the last three days, it is because there is nothing to tell. Even now this report from Paris does not help us much."

"Surely it is final as regards the man's death."

"The man's death is a mere incident – a trivial episode – in comparison with our real task, which is to trace this document and save a European catastrophe. Only one important thing has happened in the last three days, and that is that nothing has happened. I get reports almost hourly from the government, and it is certain that nowhere in Europe is there any sign of trouble. Now, if this letter were loose – no, it *can't* be loose – but if it isn't loose, where can it be? Who has it? Why is it held back? That's the question that beats in my brain like a hammer. Was it, indeed, a coincidence that Lucas should meet his death on the night when the letter disappeared? Did the letter ever reach him? If so, why is it not among his papers? Did this mad wife of his carry it off with her? If so, is it in her house in Paris? How could I search for it without the French police having their suspicions aroused? It is a case, my dear Watson, where the law is as dangerous to us as the criminals are. Every man's hand is against us, and yet the interests at stake are colossal. Should I bring it to a successful conclusion, it will certainly represent the crowning glory of my career. Ah, here is my latest from the front!" He glanced hurriedly at the note which had been handed in. "Halloa! Lestrade seems to have observed something of interest. Put on your hat, Watson, and we will stroll down together to Westminster."

It was my first visit to the scene of the crime – a high, dingy, narrow-chested house, prim, formal, and solid, like the century which gave it birth. Lestrade's bulldog features gazed out at us from the front window, and he greeted us warmly when a big constable had opened the door and let us in. The room into which we were shown was that in which the crime had been committed, but no trace of it now remained save an ugly, irregular stain upon the carpet. This carpet was a small square drugget in the centre of the room, surrounded by a broad expanse of beautiful, old-fashioned wood-flooring in square blocks, highly polished. Over the fireplace was a magnificent trophy of weapons, one of which had been used on that tragic night. In the window was a sumptuous writing-desk, and every detail of the apartment, the pictures, the rugs, and the hangings, all pointed to a taste which was luxurious to the verge of effeminacy.

"Seen the Paris news?" asked Lestrade.

Holmes nodded.

"Our French friends seem to have touched the spot this time. No doubt it's just as they say. She knocked at the door – surprise visit, I guess, for he kept his life in water-tight compartments – he let her in, couldn't keep her in the street. She told him how she had traced him, reproached him. One thing led to another, and then with that dagger so handy the end soon came. It wasn't all done in an instant, though, for these chairs were all swept over yonder, and he had one in his hand as if he had tried to hold her off with it. We've got it all clear as if we had seen it."

Holmes raised his eyebrows.

"And yet you have sent for me?"

"Ah, yes, that's another matter – a mere trifle, but the sort of thing you take an interest in – queer, you know, and what you might call freakish. It has nothing to do with the main fact – can't have, on the face of it."

"What is it, then?"

"Well, you know, after a crime of this sort we are very careful to keep things in their position. Nothing has been moved. Officer in charge here day and night. This morning, as the man was buried and the investigation over – so far as this room is concerned – we thought we could tidy up a bit. This carpet. You see, it is not fastened down, only just laid there. We had occasion to raise it. We found –"

"Yes? You found –"

Holmes's face grew tense with anxiety.

"Well, I'm sure you would never guess in a hundred years what we did find. You see that stain on the carpet? Well, a great deal must have soaked through, must it not?"

"Undoubtedly it must."

"Well, you will be surprised to hear that there is no stain on the white woodwork to correspond."

"No stain! But there must –"

"Yes, so you would say. But the fact remains that there isn't."

He took the corner of the carpet in his hand and, turning it over, he showed that it was indeed as he said.

"But the under side is as stained as the upper. It must have left a mark."

Lestrade chuckled with delight at having puzzled the famous expert.

"Now, I'll show you the explanation. There *is* a second stain, but it does not correspond with the other. See for yourself." As he spoke he turned over another portion of the carpet, and there, sure enough, was a great crimson spill upon the square white facing of the old-fashioned floor. "What do you make of that, Mr. Holmes?"

"Why, it is simple enough. The two stains did correspond, but the carpet has been turned round. As it was square and unfastened it was easily done."

"The official police don't need you, Mr. Holmes, to tell them that the carpet must have been turned round. That's clear enough, for the stains lie above each other – if you lay it over this way. But what I want to know is, who shifted the carpet, and why?"

I could see from Holmes's rigid face that he was vibrating with inward excitement.

"Look here, Lestrade," said he, "has that constable in the passage been in charge of the place all the time?"

"Yes, he has."

"Well, take my advice. Examine him carefully. Don't do it before us. We'll wait here. You take him into the back room. You'll be more likely to get a confession out of him alone. Ask him how he dared to admit people and leave them alone in this room. Don't ask him if he has done it. Take it for granted. Tell him you *know* someone has been here. Press him. Tell him that a full confession is his only chance of forgiveness. Do exactly what I tell you!"

"By George, if he knows I'll have it out of him!" cried Lestrade. He darted into the hall, and a few moments later his bullying voice sounded from the back room.

"Now, Watson, now!" cried Holmes with frenzied eagerness. All the demoniacal force of the man masked behind that listless manner burst out in a paroxysm of energy. He tore the drugget from the floor, and in an instant was down on his hands and knees clawing at each of the squares of wood beneath it. One turned sideways as he dug his nails into the edge of it. It hinged back like the lid of a box. A small black cavity opened beneath it. Holmes plunged his eager hand into it and drew it out with a bitter snarl of anger and disappointment. It was empty.

"Quick, Watson, quick! Get it back again!" The wooden lid was replaced, and the drugget had only just been drawn straight when Lestrade's voice was heard in the passage. He found Holmes leaning languidly against the mantelpiece, resigned and patient, endeavouring to conceal his irrepressible yawns.

"Sorry to keep you waiting, Mr. Holmes, I can see that you are bored to death with the whole affair. Well, he has confessed, all right. Come in here, MacPherson. Let these gentlemen hear of your most inexcusable conduct."

The big constable, very hot and penitent, sidled into the room.

"I meant no harm, sir, I'm sure. The young woman came to the door last evening – mistook the house, she did. And then we got talking. It's lonesome, when you're on duty here all day."

"Well, what happened then?"

"She wanted to see where the crime was done – had read about it in the papers, she said. She was a very respectable, well-spoken young woman, sir, and I saw no harm in letting her have a peep. When she saw that mark on the carpet, down she dropped on the floor, and lay as if she were dead. I ran to the back and got some water, but I could not bring her to. Then I went round the corner to the Ivy Plant for some brandy, and by the time I had brought it back the young woman had recovered and was off – ashamed of herself, I daresay, and dared not face me."

"How about moving that drugget?"

"Well, sir, it was a bit rumpled, certainly, when I came back. You see, she fell on it and it lies on a polished floor with nothing to keep it in place. I straightened it out afterwards."

"It's a lesson to you that you can't deceive me, Constable MacPherson," said Lestrade, with dignity. "No doubt you thought that your breach of duty could never be discovered, and yet a mere glance at that drugget was enough to convince me that someone had been admitted to the room. It's lucky for you, my man, that nothing is missing, or you would find yourself in Queer Street. I'm sorry to have called you down over such a petty business, Mr. Holmes, but I thought the point of the second stain not corresponding with the first would interest you."

"Certainly, it was most interesting. Has this woman only been here once, constable?"

"Yes, sir, only once."

"Who was she?"

"Don't know the name, sir. Was answering an advertisement about typewriting and came to the wrong number – very pleasant, genteel young woman, sir."

"Tall? Handsome?"

"Yes, sir, she was a well-grown young woman. I suppose you might say she was handsome. Perhaps some would say she was very handsome. 'Oh, officer, do let me have a peep!' says she. She had pretty, coaxing ways, as you might say, and I thought there was no harm in letting her just put her head through the door."

"How was she dressed?"

"Quiet, sir – a long mantle down to her feet."

"What time was it?"

"It was just growing dusk at the time. They were lighting the lamps as I came back with the brandy."

"Very good," said Holmes. "Come, Watson, I think that we have more important work elsewhere."

As we left the house Lestrade remained in the front room, while the repentant constable opened the door to let us out. Holmes turned on the step and held up something in his hand. The constable stared intently.

"Good Lord, sir!" he cried, with amazement on his face. Holmes put his finger on his lips, replaced his hand in his breast pocket, and burst out laughing as we turned down the street. "Excellent!" said he. "Come, friend Watson, the curtain rings up for the last act. You will be relieved to hear that there will be no war, that the Right Honourable Trelawney Hope will suffer no setback in his brilliant career, that the indiscreet Sovereign will receive no punishment for his indiscretion, that the Prime Minister will have no European complication to deal with, and that with a little tact and management upon our part nobody will be a penny the worse for what might have been a very ugly incident."

My mind filled with admiration for this extraordinary man.

"You have solved it!" I cried.

"Hardly that, Watson. There are some points which are as dark as ever. But we have so much that it will be our own fault if we cannot get the rest. We will go straight to Whitehall Terrace and bring the matter to a head."

When we arrived at the residence of the European Secretary it was for Lady Hilda Trelawney Hope that Sherlock Holmes inquired. We were shown into the morning-room.

"Mr. Holmes!" said the lady, and her face was pink with her indignation. "This is surely most unfair and ungenerous upon your part. I desired, as I have explained, to keep my visit to you a secret, lest my husband should think that I was intruding into his affairs. And yet you compromise me by coming here and so showing that there are business relations between us."

"Unfortunately, madam, I had no possible alternative. I have been commissioned to recover this immensely important paper. I must therefore ask you, madam, to be kind enough to place it in my hands."

The lady sprang to her feet, with the colour all dashed in an instant from her beautiful face. Her eyes glazed – she tottered – I thought that she would faint. Then with a grand effort she rallied from the shock, and a supreme astonishment and indignation chased every other expression from her features.

"You – you insult me, Mr. Holmes."

"Come, come, madam, it is useless. Give up the letter."

She darted to the bell.

"The butler shall show you out."

"Do not ring, Lady Hilda. If you do, then all my earnest efforts to avoid a scandal will be frustrated. Give up the letter and all will be set right. If you will work with me I can arrange everything. If you work against me I must expose you."

She stood grandly defiant, a queenly figure, her eyes fixed upon his as if she would read his very soul. Her hand was on the bell, but she had forborne to ring it.

"You are trying to frighten me. It is not a very manly thing, Mr. Holmes, to come here and browbeat a woman. You say that you know something. What is it that you know?"

"Pray sit down, madam. You will hurt yourself there if you fall. I will not speak until you sit down. Thank you."

"I give you five minutes, Mr. Holmes."

"One is enough, Lady Hilda. I know of your visit to Eduardo Lucas, of your giving him this document, of your ingenious return to the room last night, and of the manner in which you took the letter from the hiding-place under the carpet."

She stared at him with an ashen face and gulped twice before she could speak.

"You are mad, Mr. Holmes – you are mad!" she cried, at last.

He drew a small piece of cardboard from his pocket. It was the face of a woman cut out of a portrait.

"I have carried this because I thought it might be useful," said he. "The policeman has recognized it."

She gave a gasp, and her head dropped back in the chair.

"Come, Lady Hilda. You have the letter. The matter may still be adjusted. I have no desire to bring trouble to you. My duty ends when I have returned the lost letter to your husband. Take my advice and be frank with me. It is your only chance."

Her courage was admirable. Even now she would not own defeat.

"I tell you again, Mr. Holmes, that you are under some absurd illusion."

Holmes rose from his chair.

"I am sorry for you, Lady Hilda. I have done my best for you. I can see that it is all in vain."

He rang the bell. The butler entered.

"Is Mr. Trelawney Hope at home?"

"He will be home, sir, at a quarter to one."

Holmes glanced at his watch.

"Still a quarter of an hour," said he. "Very good, I shall wait."

The butler had hardly closed the door behind him when Lady Hilda was down on her knees at Holmes's feet, her hands outstretched, her beautiful face upturned and wet with her tears.

"Oh, spare me, Mr. Holmes! Spare me!" she pleaded, in a frenzy of supplication. "For heaven's sake, don't tell him! I love him so! I would not bring one shadow on his life, and this I know would break his noble heart."

Holmes raised the lady. "I am thankful, madam, that you have come to your senses even at this last moment! There is not an instant to lose. Where is the letter?"

She darted across to a writing-desk, unlocked it, and drew out a long blue envelope.

"Here it is, Mr. Holmes. Would to heaven I had never seen it!"

"How can we return it?" Holmes muttered. "Quick, quick, we must think of some way! Where is the despatch-box?"

"Still in his bedroom."

"What a stroke of luck! Quick, madam, bring it here!" A moment later she had appeared with a red flat box in her hand.

"How did you open it before? You have a duplicate key? Yes, of course you have. Open it!"

From out of her bosom Lady Hilda had drawn a small key. The box flew open. It was stuffed with papers. Holmes thrust the blue envelope deep down into the heart of them, between the leaves of some other document. The box was shut, locked, and returned to the bedroom.

"Now we are ready for him," said Holmes. "We have still ten minutes. I am going far to screen you, Lady Hilda. In return you will spend the time in telling me frankly the real meaning of this extraordinary affair."

"Mr. Holmes, I will tell you everything," cried the lady. "Oh, Mr. Holmes, I would cut off my right hand before I gave him a moment of sorrow! There is no woman in all London who loves her husband as I do, and yet if he knew how I have acted – how I have been compelled to act – he would never forgive me. For his own honour stands so high that he could not forget or pardon a lapse in another. Help me, Mr. Holmes! My happiness, his happiness, our very lives are at stake!"

"Quick, madam, the time grows short!"

"It was a letter of mine, Mr. Holmes, an indiscreet letter written before my marriage – a foolish letter, a letter of an impulsive, loving girl. I meant no harm, and yet he would have thought it criminal. Had he read that letter his confidence would have been forever destroyed. It is years since I wrote it. I had thought that the whole matter was forgotten. Then at last I heard from this man, Lucas, that it had passed into his hands, and that he would lay it before my husband. I implored his mercy. He said that he would return my letter if I would bring him a certain document which he described in my husband's despatch-box. He had some spy in the office who had told him of its existence. He assured me that no harm could come to my husband. Put yourself in my position, Mr. Holmes! What was I to do?"

"Take your husband into your confidence."

"I could not, Mr. Holmes, I could not! On the one side seemed certain ruin, on the other, terrible as it seemed to take my husband's paper, still in a matter of politics I could not understand the consequences, while in a matter of love and trust they were only too clear to me. I did it, Mr. Holmes! I took an impression of his key. This man, Lucas, furnished a duplicate. I opened his despatch-box, took the paper, and conveyed it to Godolphin Street."

"What happened there, madam?"

"I tapped at the door as agreed. Lucas opened it. I followed him into his room, leaving the hall door ajar behind me, for I feared to be alone with the man. I remember that there was a woman outside as I entered. Our business was soon done. He had my letter on his desk, I handed him the document. He gave me the letter. At this instant there was a sound at the door. There were steps in the passage. Lucas quickly turned back the drugget, thrust the document into some hiding-place there, and covered it over.

"What happened after that is like some fearful dream. I have a vision of a dark, frantic face, of a woman's voice, which screamed in French, 'My waiting is not in vain. At last, at last I have found you with her!' There was a savage struggle. I saw him with a chair in his hand, a knife gleamed in hers. I rushed from the horrible scene, ran from the house, and only next morning in the paper did I learn the dreadful result. That night I was happy, for I had my letter, and I had not seen yet what the future would bring.

"It was the next morning that I realized that I had only exchanged one trouble for another. My husband's anguish at the loss of his paper went to my heart. I could hardly prevent myself from there and then kneeling down at his feet and telling him what I had done. But that again would mean a confession of the past. I came to you that morning in order to understand the full enormity of my offence. From the instant that I grasped it my whole mind was turned to the one thought of getting back my husband's paper. It must still be where Lucas had placed it, for it was concealed before this dreadful woman entered the room. If it had not been for her coming, I should not have known where his hiding-place was. How was I to get into the room? For two days I watched the place, but the door was never left open. Last night I made a last attempt. What I did and how I succeeded, you have already learned. I brought the paper back with me, and thought of destroying it, since I could see no way of returning it without confessing my guilt to my husband. Heavens, I hear his step upon the stair!"

The European Secretary burst excitedly into the room. "Any news, Mr. Holmes, any news?" he cried.

"I have some hopes."

"Ah, thank heaven!" His face became radiant. "The Prime Minister is lunching with me. May he share your hopes? He has nerves of steel, and yet I know that he has hardly slept since this terrible event. Jacobs, will you ask the Prime Minister to come up? As to you, dear, I fear that this is a matter of politics. We will join you in a few minutes in the dining-room."

The Prime Minister's manner was subdued, but I could see by the gleam of his eyes and the twitchings of his bony hands that he shared the excitement of his young colleague.

"I understand that you have something to report, Mr. Holmes?"

"Purely negative as yet," my friend answered. "I have inquired at every point where it might be, and I am sure that there is no danger to be apprehended."

"But that is not enough, Mr. Holmes. We cannot live forever on such a volcano. We must have something definite."

"I am in hopes of getting it. That is why I am here. The more I think of the matter the more convinced I am that the letter has never left this house."

"Mr. Holmes!"

"If it had it would certainly have been public by now."

"But why should anyone take it in order to keep it in his house?"

"I am not convinced that anyone did take it."

"Then how could it leave the despatch-box?"

"I am not convinced that it ever did leave the despatch-box."

"Mr. Holmes, this joking is very ill-timed. You have my assurance that it left the box."

"Have you examined the box since Tuesday morning?"

"No. It was not necessary."

"You may conceivably have overlooked it."

"Impossible, I say."

"But I am not convinced of it. I have known such things to happen. I presume there are other papers there. Well, it may have got mixed with them."

"It was on the top."

"Someone may have shaken the box and displaced it."

"No, no, I had everything out."

"Surely it is easily decided, Hope," said the Premier. "Let us have the despatch-box brought in."

The Secretary rang the bell.

"Jacobs, bring down my despatch-box. This is a farcical waste of time, but still, if nothing else will satisfy you, it shall be done. Thank you, Jacobs, put it here. I have always had the key on my watch-chain. Here are the papers, you see. Letter from Lord Merrow, report from Sir Charles Hardy, memorandum from Belgrade, note on the Russo-German grain taxes, letter from Madrid, note from Lord Flowers – Good heavens! What is this? Lord Bellinger! Lord Bellinger!"

The Premier snatched the blue envelope from his hand.

"Yes, it is it – and the letter is intact. Hope, I congratulate you."

"Thank you! Thank you! What a weight from my heart. But this is inconceivable – impossible. Mr. Holmes, you are a wizard, a sorcerer! How did you know it was there?"

"Because I knew it was nowhere else."

"I cannot believe my eyes!" He ran wildly to the door. "Where is my wife? I must tell her that all is well. Hilda! Hilda!" We heard his voice on the stairs.

The Premier looked at Holmes with twinkling eyes.

"Come, sir," said he. "There is more in this than meets the eye. How came the letter back in the box?"

Holmes turned away smiling from the keen scrutiny of those wonderful eyes.

"We also have our diplomatic secrets," said he and, picking up his hat, he turned to the door.

The Moabite Cipher

R. Austin Freeman

A LARGE AND MOTLEY crowd lined the pavements of Oxford Street as Thorndyke and I made our way leisurely eastward. Floral decorations and drooping bunting announced one of those functions inaugurated from time to time by a benevolent Government for the entertainment of fashionable loungers and the relief of distressed pickpockets. For a Russian Grand Duke, who had torn himself away, amidst valedictory explosions, from a loving if too demonstrative people, was to pass anon on his way to the Guildhall; and a British Prince, heroically indiscreet, was expected to occupy a seat in the ducal carriage.

Near Rathbone Place Thorndyke halted and drew my attention to a smart-looking man who stood lounging in a doorway, cigarette in hand.

"Our old friend Inspector Badger," said Thorndyke. "He seems mightily interested in that gentleman in the light overcoat. How d'ye do, Badger?" for at this moment the detective caught his eye and bowed. "Who is your friend?"

"That's what I want to know, sir," replied the inspector. "I've been shadowing him for the last half-hour, but I can't make him out, though I believe I've seen him somewhere. He don't look like a foreigner, but he has got something bulky in his pocket, so I must keep him in sight until the Duke is safely past. I wish," he added gloomily, "these beastly Russians would stop at home. They give us no end of trouble."

"Are you expecting any – occurrences, then?" asked Thorndyke.

"Bless you, sir," exclaimed Badger, "the whole route is lined with plain-clothes men. You see, it is known that several desperate characters followed the Duke to England, and there are a good many exiles living here who would like to have a rap at him. Hallo! What's he up to now?"

The man in the light overcoat had suddenly caught the inspector's too inquiring eye, and forthwith dived into the crowd at the edge of the pavement. In his haste he trod heavily on the foot of a big, rough-looking man, by whom he was in a moment hustled out into the road with such violence that he fell sprawling face downwards. It was an unlucky moment. A mounted constable was just then backing in upon the crowd, and before he could gather the meaning of the shout that arose from the bystanders, his horse had set down one hind-hoof firmly on the prostrate man's back.

The inspector signalled to a constable, who forthwith made a way for us through the crowd; but even as we approached the injured man, he rose stiffly and looked round with a pale, vacant face.

"Are you hurt?" Thorndyke asked gently, with an earnest look into the frightened, wondering eyes.

"No, sir," was the reply; "only I feel queer – sinking – just here."

He laid a trembling hand on his chest, and Thorndyke, still eyeing him anxiously, said in a low voice to the inspector: "Cab or ambulance, as quickly as you can."

A cab was led round from Newman Street, and the injured man put into it. Thorndyke, Badger, and I entered, and we drove off up Rathbone Place. As we proceeded, our patient's face grew more and more ashen, drawn, and anxious; his breathing was shallow and uneven, and his teeth chattered slightly. The cab swung round into Goodge Street, and then – suddenly, in the twinkling of an eye – there came a change. The eyelids and jaw relaxed, the eyes became filmy, and the whole form subsided into the corner in a shrunken heap, with the strange gelatinous limpness of a body that is dead as a whole, while its tissues are still alive.

"God save us! The man's dead!" exclaimed the inspector in a shocked voice – for even policemen have their feelings. He sat staring at the corpse, as it nodded gently with the jolting of the cab, until we drew up inside the courtyard of the Middlesex Hospital, when he got out briskly, with suddenly renewed cheerfulness, to help the porter to place the body on the wheeled couch.

"We shall know who he is now, at any rate," said he, as we followed the couch to the casualty-room. Thorndyke nodded unsympathetically. The medical instinct in him was for the moment stronger than the legal.

The house-surgeon leaned over the couch, and made a rapid examination as he listened to our account of the accident. Then he straightened himself up and looked at Thorndyke.

"Internal haemorrhage, I expect," said he. "At any rate, he's dead, poor beggar! – As dead as Nebuchadnezzar. Ah! Here comes a bobby; it's his affair now."

A sergeant came into the room, breathing quickly, and looked in surprise from the corpse to the inspector. But the latter, without loss of time, proceeded to turn out the dead man's pockets, commencing with the bulky object that had first attracted his attention; which proved to be a brown-paper parcel tied up with red tape.

"Pork-pie, begad!" he exclaimed with a crestfallen air as he cut the tape and opened the package. "You had better go through his other pockets, sergeant."

The small heap of odds and ends that resulted from this process tended, with a single exception, to throw little light on the man's identity; the exception being a letter, sealed, but not stamped, addressed in an exceedingly illiterate hand to Mr. Adolf Schönberg, 213, Greek Street, Soho.

"He was going to leave it by hand, I expect," observed the inspector, with a wistful glance at the sealed envelope. "I think I'll take it round myself, and you had better come with me, sergeant."

He slipped the letter into his pocket, and, leaving the sergeant to take possession of the other effects, made his way out of the building.

"I suppose, Doctor," said he, as we crossed into Berners Street, "you are not coming our way! Don't want to see Mr. Schönberg, h'm?"

Thorndyke reflected for a moment. "Well, it isn't very far, and we may as well see the end of the incident. Yes; let us go together."

No. 213, Greek Street, was one of those houses that irresistibly suggest to the observer the idea of a church organ, either jamb of the doorway being adorned with a row of brass bell-handles corresponding to the stop-knobs.

These the sergeant examined with the air of an expert musician, and having, as it were, gauged the capacity of the instrument, selected the middle knob on the right-hand side and pulled it briskly; whereupon a first-floor window was thrown up and a head protruded. But it afforded us a momentary glimpse only, for, having caught the sergeant's upturned eye, it retired with surprising precipitancy, and before we had time to speculate on the apparition, the street-door was opened and a man emerged. He was about to close the door after him when the inspector interposed.

"Does Mr. Adolf Schönberg live here?"

The new-comer, a very typical Jew of the red-haired type, surveyed us thoughtfully through his gold-rimmed spectacles as he repeated the name.

"Schönberg – Schönberg? Ah, yes! I know. He lives on the third-floor. I saw him go up a short time ago. Third-floor back;" and indicating the open door with a wave of the hand, he raised his hat and passed into the street.

"I suppose we had better go up," said the inspector, with a dubious glance at the row of bell-pulls. He accordingly started up the stairs, and we all followed in his wake.

There were two doors at the back on the third-floor, but as the one was open, displaying an unoccupied bedroom, the inspector rapped smartly on the other. It flew open almost immediately, and a fierce-looking little man confronted us with a hostile stare.

"Well?" said he.

"Mr. Adolf Schönberg?" inquired the inspector.

"Well? What about him?" snapped our new acquaintance.

"I wished to have a few words with him," said Badger.

"Then what the deuce do you come banging at *my* door for?" demanded the other.

"Why, doesn't he live here?"

"No. First-floor front," replied our friend, preparing to close the door.

"Pardon me," said Thorndyke, "but what is Mr. Schönberg like? I mean –"

"Like?" interrupted the resident. "He's like a blooming Sheeny, with a carroty beard and gold gig-lamps!" and, having presented this impressionist sketch, he brought the interview to a definite close by slamming the door and turning the key.

With a wrathful exclamation, the inspector turned towards the stairs, down which the sergeant was already clattering in hot haste, and made his way back to the ground-floor, followed, as before, by Thorndyke and me. On the doorstep we found the sergeant breathlessly interrogating a smartly-dressed youth, whom I had seen alight from a hansom as we entered the house, and who now stood with a notebook tucked under his arm, sharpening a pencil with deliberate care.

"Mr. James saw him come out, sir," said the sergeant. "He turned up towards the Square."

"Did he seem to hurry?" asked the inspector.

"Rather," replied the reporter. "As soon as you were inside, he went off like a lamplighter. You won't catch him now."

"We don't want to catch him," the detective rejoined gruffly; then, backing out of earshot of the eager pressman, he said in a lower tone: "That was Mr. Schönberg, beyond a doubt, and it is clear that he has some reason for making himself scarce; so I shall consider myself justified in opening that note."

He suited the action to the word, and, having cut the envelope open with official neatness, drew out the enclosure.

"My hat!" he exclaimed, as his eye fell upon the contents. "What in creation is this? It isn't shorthand, but what the deuce is it?"

He handed the document to Thorndyke, who, having held it up to the light and felt the paper critically, proceeded to examine it with keen interest. It consisted of a single half-sheet of thin notepaper, both sides of which were covered with strange, crabbed characters, written with a brownish-black ink in continuous lines, without any spaces to indicate the divisions into words; and, but for the modern material which bore the writing, it might have been a portion of some ancient manuscript or forgotten codex.

"What do you make of it, Doctor?" inquired the inspector anxiously, after a pause, during which Thorndyke had scrutinized the strange writing with knitted brows.

"Not a great deal," replied Thorndyke. "The character is the Moabite or Phoenician – primitive Semitic, in fact – and reads from right to left. The language I take to be Hebrew. At any rate, I can find no Greek words, and I see here a group of letters which *may* form one of the few Hebrew words that I know – the word *badim*, 'lies.' But you had better get it deciphered by an expert."

"If it is Hebrew," said Badger, "we can manage it all right. There are plenty of Jews at our disposal."

"You had much better take the paper to the British Museum," said Thorndyke, "and submit it to the keeper of the Phoenician antiquities for decipherment."

Inspector Badger smiled a foxy smile as he deposited the paper in his pocket-book. "We'll see what we can make of it ourselves first," he said; "but many thanks for your advice, all the same, Doctor. No, Mr. James, I can't give you any information just at present; you had better apply at the hospital."

"I suspect," said Thorndyke, as we took our way homewards, "that Mr. James has collected enough material for his purpose already. He must have followed us from the hospital, and I have no doubt that he has his report, with 'full details,' mentally arranged at this moment. And I am not sure that he didn't get a peep at the mysterious paper, in spite of the inspector's precautions."

"By the way," I said, "what do you make of the document?"

"A cipher, most probably," he replied. "It is written in the primitive Semitic alphabet, which, as you know, is practically identical with primitive Greek. It is written from right to left, like the Phoenician, Hebrew, and Moabite, as well as the earliest Greek, inscriptions. The paper is common cream-laid notepaper, and the ink is ordinary indelible Chinese ink, such as is used by draughtsmen. Those are the facts, and without further study of the document itself, they don't carry us very far."

"Why do you think it is a cipher rather than a document in straightforward Hebrew?"

"Because it is obviously a secret message of some kind. Now, every educated Jew knows more or less Hebrew, and, although he is able to read and write only the modern square Hebrew character, it is so easy to transpose one alphabet into another that the mere language would afford no security. Therefore, I expect that, when the experts translate this document, the translation or transliteration will be a mere farrago of unintelligible nonsense. But we shall see, and meanwhile the facts that we have offer several interesting suggestions which are well worth consideration."

"As, for instance – ?"

"Now, my dear Jervis," said Thorndyke, shaking an admonitory forefinger at me, "don't, I pray you, give way to mental indolence. You have these few facts that I have mentioned. Consider them separately and collectively, and in their relation to the circumstances. Don't attempt to suck my brain when you have an excellent brain of your own to suck."

On the following morning the papers fully justified my colleague's opinion of Mr. James. All the events which had occurred, as well as a number that had not, were given in the fullest and most vivid detail, a lengthy reference being made to the paper 'found on the person of the dead anarchist,' and 'written in a private shorthand or cryptogram.'

The report concluded with the gratifying – though untrue – statement that 'in this intricate and important case, the police have wisely secured the assistance of Dr. John Thorndyke, to whose acute intellect and vast experience the portentous cryptogram will doubtless soon deliver up its secret.'

"Very flattering," laughed Thorndyke, to whom I read the extract on his return from the hospital, "but a little awkward if it should induce our friends to deposit a few trifling mementoes in the form of nitro-compounds on our main staircase or in the cellars. By the way, I met Superintendent Miller on London Bridge. The 'cryptogram,' as Mr. James calls it, has set Scotland Yard in a mighty ferment."

"Naturally. What have they done in the matter?"

"They adopted my suggestion, after all, finding that they could make nothing of it themselves, and took it to the British Museum. The Museum people referred them to Professor Poppelbaum, the great palaeographer, to whom they accordingly submitted it."

"Did he express any opinion about it?"

"Yes, provisionally. After a brief examination, he found it to consist of a number of Hebrew words sandwiched between apparently meaningless groups of letters. He furnished the Superintendent off-hand with a translation of the words, and Miller forthwith struck off a number of hectograph copies of it, which he has distributed among the senior officials of his department; so that at present" – here Thorndyke gave vent to a soft chuckle – "Scotland Yard is engaged in a sort of missing word – or, rather, missing sense – competition. Miller invited me to join in the sport, and to that end presented me with one of the hectograph copies on which to exercise my wits, together with a photograph of the document."

"And shall you?" I asked.

"Not I," he replied, laughing. "In the first place, I have not been formally consulted, and consequently am a passive, though interested, spectator. In the second place, I have a theory of my own which I shall test if the occasion arises. But if you would like to take part in the competition, I am authorized to show you the photograph and the translation. I will pass them on to you, and I wish you joy of them."

He handed me the photograph and a sheet of paper that he had just taken from his pocket-book, and watched me with grim amusement as I read out the first few lines.

"Woe, city, lies, robbery, prey, noise, whip, rattling, wheel, horse, chariot, day, darkness, gloominess, clouds, darkness, morning, mountain, people, strong, fire, them, flame."

"It doesn't look very promising at first sight," I remarked. "What is the Professor's theory?"

"His theory – provisionally, of course – is that the words form the message, and the groups of letters represent mere filled-up spaces between the words."

"But surely," I protested, "that would be a very transparent device."

Thorndyke laughed. "There is a childlike simplicity about it," said he, "that is highly attractive – but discouraging. It is much more probable that the words are dummies, and that the letters contain the message. Or, again, the solution may lie in an entirely different direction. But listen! Is that cab coming here?"

It was. It drew up opposite our chambers, and a few moments later a brisk step ascending the stairs heralded a smart rat-tat at our door. Flinging open the latter, I found myself confronted by a well-dressed stranger, who, after a quick glance at me, peered inquisitively over my shoulder into the room.

"I am relieved, Dr. Jervis," said he, "to find you and Dr. Thorndyke at home, as I have come on somewhat urgent professional business. My name," he continued, entering in response to my invitation, "is Barton, but you don't know me, though I know you both by sight. I have come to ask you if one of you – or, better still, both – could come tonight and see my brother."

"That," said Thorndyke, "depends on the circumstances and on the whereabouts of your brother."

"The circumstances," said Mr. Barton, "are, in my opinion, highly suspicious, and I will place them before you – of course, in strict confidence."

Thorndyke nodded and indicated a chair.

"My brother," continued Mr. Barton, taking the proffered seat, "has recently married for the second time. His age is fifty-five, and that of his wife twenty-six, and I may say that the marriage has been – well, by no means a success. Now, within the last fortnight, my brother has been attacked by a mysterious and extremely painful affection of the stomach, to which his doctor seems unable to give a name. It has resisted all treatment hitherto. Day by day the pain and distress increase, and I feel that, unless something decisive is done, the end cannot be far off."

"Is the pain worse after taking food?" inquired Thorndyke.

"That's just it!" exclaimed our visitor. "I see what is in your mind, and it has been in mine, too; so much so that I have tried repeatedly to obtain samples of the food that he is taking. And this morning I succeeded." Here he took from his pocket a wide-mouthed bottle, which, disengaging from its paper wrappings, he laid on the table. "When I called, he was taking his breakfast of arrowroot, which he complained had a gritty taste, supposed by his wife to be due to the sugar. Now I had provided myself with this bottle, and, during the absence of his wife, I managed unobserved to convey a portion of the arrowroot that he had left into it, and I should be greatly obliged if you would examine it and tell me if this arrowroot contains anything that it should not."

He pushed the bottle across to Thorndyke, who carried it to the window, and, extracting a small quantity of the contents with a glass rod, examined the pasty mass with the aid of a lens; then, lifting the bell-glass cover from the microscope, which stood on its table by the window, he smeared a small quantity of the suspected matter on to a glass slip, and placed it on the stage of the instrument.

"I observe a number of crystalline particles in this," he said, after a brief inspection, "which have the appearance of arsenious acid."

"Ah!" ejaculated Mr. Barton, "just what I feared. But are you certain?"

"No," replied Thorndyke; "but the matter is easily tested."

He pressed the button of the bell that communicated with the laboratory, a summons that brought the laboratory assistant from his lair with characteristic promptitude.

"Will you please prepare a Marsh's apparatus, Polton," said Thorndyke.

"I have a couple ready, sir," replied Polton.

"Then pour the acid into one and bring it to me, with a tile."

As his familiar vanished silently, Thorndyke turned to Mr. Barton.

"Supposing we find arsenic in this arrowroot, as we probably shall, what do you want us to do?"

"I want you to come and see my brother," replied our client.

"Why not take a note from me to his doctor?"

"No, no; I want you to come – I should like you both to come – and put a stop at once to this dreadful business. Consider! It's a matter of life and death. You won't refuse! I beg you not to refuse me your help in these terrible circumstances."

"Well," said Thorndyke, as his assistant reappeared, "let us first see what the test has to tell us."

Polton advanced to the table, on which he deposited a small flask, the contents of which were in a state of brisk effervescence, a bottle labelled 'calcium hypochlorite,' and a white porcelain tile. The flask was fitted with a safety-funnel and a glass tube drawn out to a fine jet, to which Polton cautiously applied a lighted match. Instantly there sprang from the jet a tiny, pale violet flame. Thorndyke now took the tile, and held it in the flame for a few seconds, when the appearance of the surface remained unchanged save for a small circle of condensed moisture. His next proceeding was to thin the arrowroot with distilled water until it was quite fluid, and then pour a small quantity into the funnel. It ran slowly down the tube into the flask, with the bubbling contents of which it became speedily mixed. Almost immediately a change began to appear in the character of the flame, which from a pale violet turned gradually to a sickly blue, while above it hung a faint cloud of white smoke. Once more Thorndyke held the tile above the jet, but this time, no sooner had the pallid flame touched the cold surface of the porcelain, than there appeared on the latter a glistening black stain.

"That is pretty conclusive," observed Thorndyke, lifting the stopper out of the reagent bottle, "but we will apply the final test." He dropped a few drops of the hypochlorite solution on to the tile, and immediately the black stain faded away and vanished. "We can now answer your question, Mr. Barton," said he, replacing the stopper as he turned to our client. "The specimen that you brought us certainly contains arsenic, and in very considerable quantities."

"Then," exclaimed Mr. Barton, starting from his chair, "you will come and help me to rescue my brother from this dreadful peril. Don't refuse me, Dr. Thorndyke, for mercy's sake, don't refuse."

Thorndyke reflected for a moment.

"Before we decide," said he, "we must see what engagements we have."

With a quick, significant glance at me, he walked into the office, whither I followed in some bewilderment, for I knew that we had no engagements for the evening.

"Now, Jervis," said Thorndyke, as he closed the office door, "what are we to do?"

"We must go, I suppose," I replied. "It seems a pretty urgent case."

"It does," he agreed. "Of course, the man may be telling the truth, after all."

"You don't think he is, then?"

"No. It is a plausible tale, but there is too much arsenic in that arrowroot. Still, I think I ought to go. It is an ordinary professional risk. But there is no reason why you should put your head into the noose."

"Thank you," said I, somewhat huffily. "I don't see what risk there is, but if any exists I claim the right to share it."

"Very well," he answered with a smile, "we will both go. I think we can take care of ourselves."

He re-entered the sitting-room, and announced his decision to Mr. Barton, whose relief and gratitude were quite pathetic.

"But," said Thorndyke, "you have not yet told us where your brother lives."

"Rexford," was the reply – "Rexford, in Essex. It is an out-of-the-way place, but if we catch the seven-fifteen train from Liverpool Street, we shall be there in an hour and a half."

"And as to the return? You know the trains, I suppose?"

"Oh yes," replied our client; "I will see that you don't miss your train back."

"Then I will be with you in a minute," said Thorndyke; and, taking the still-bubbling flask, he retired to the laboratory, whence he returned in a few minutes carrying his hat and overcoat.

The cab which had brought our client was still waiting, and we were soon rattling through the streets towards the station, where we arrived in time to furnish ourselves with dinner-baskets and select our compartment at leisure.

During the early part of the journey our companion was in excellent spirits. He despatched the cold fowl from the basket and quaffed the rather indifferent claret with as much relish as if he had not had a single relation in the world, and after dinner he became genial to the verge of hilarity. But, as time went on, there crept into his manner a certain anxious restlessness. He became silent and preoccupied, and several times furtively consulted his watch.

"The train is confoundedly late!" he exclaimed irritably. "Seven minutes behind time already!"

"A few minutes more or less are not of much consequence," said Thorndyke.

"No, of course not; but still – Ah, thank Heaven, here we are!"

He thrust his head out of the off-side window, and gazed eagerly down the line; then, leaping to his feet, he bustled out on to the platform while the train was still moving.

Even as we alighted a warning bell rang furiously on the up-platform, and as Mr. Barton hurried us through the empty booking-office to the outside of the station, the rumble of the approaching train could be heard above the noise made by our own train moving off.

"My carriage doesn't seem to have arrived yet," exclaimed Mr. Barton, looking anxiously up the station approach. "If you will wait here a moment, I will go and make inquiries."

He darted back into the booking-office and through it on to the platform, just as the up-train roared into the station. Thorndyke followed him with quick but stealthy steps, and, peering out of the booking-office door, watched his proceedings; then he turned and beckoned to me.

"There he goes," said he, pointing to an iron footbridge that spanned the line; and, as I looked, I saw, clearly defined against the dim night sky, a flying figure racing towards the 'up' side.

It was hardly two-thirds across when the guard's whistle sang out its shrill warning.

"Quick, Jervis," exclaimed Thorndyke; "she's off!"

He leaped down on to the line, whither I followed instantly, and, crossing the rails, we clambered up together on to the foot-board opposite an empty first-class compartment. Thorndyke's magazine knife, containing, among other implements, a railway-key, was already in his hand. The door was speedily unlocked, and, as we entered, Thorndyke ran through and looked out on to the platform.

"Just in time!" he exclaimed. "He is in one of the forward compartments."

He relocked the door, and, seating himself, proceeded to fill his pipe.

"And now," said I, as the train moved out of the station, "perhaps you will explain this little comedy."

"With pleasure," he replied, "if it needs any explanation. But you can hardly have forgotten Mr. James's flattering remarks in his report of the Greek Street incident, clearly giving the impression that the mysterious document was in my possession. When I read that, I knew I must look out for some attempt to recover it, though I hardly expected such promptness. Still, when Mr. Barton called without credentials or appointment, I viewed him with some suspicion. That suspicion deepened when he wanted us both to come. It deepened further when I found an impossible quantity of arsenic in his sample, and it gave place to certainty when, having allowed him to select the trains by which we were to travel, I went up to the laboratory and examined the time-table; for I then found that the last train for London left Rexford ten minutes after we were due to arrive. Obviously this was a plan to get us both safely out of the way while he and some of his friends ransacked our chambers for the missing document."

"I see; and that accounts for his extraordinary anxiety at the lateness of the train. But why did you come, if you knew it was a 'plant'?"

"My dear fellow," said Thorndyke, "I never miss an interesting experience if I can help it. There are possibilities in this, too, don't you see?"

"But supposing his friends have broken into our chambers already?"

"That contingency has been provided for; but I think they will wait for Mr. Barton – and us."

Our train, being the last one up, stopped at every station, and crawled slothfully in the intervals, so that it was past eleven o'clock when we reached Liverpool Street. Here we got out cautiously, and, mingling with the crowd, followed the unconscious Barton up the platform, through the barrier, and out into the street. He seemed in no special hurry, for, after pausing to light a cigar, he set off at an easy pace up New Broad Street.

Thorndyke hailed a hansom, and, motioning me to enter, directed the cabman to drive to Clifford's Inn Passage.

"Sit well back," said he, as we rattled away up New Broad Street. "We shall be passing our gay deceiver presently – in fact, there he is, a living, walking illustration of the folly of underrating the intelligence of one's adversary."

At Clifford's Inn Passage we dismissed the cab, and, retiring into the shadow of the dark, narrow alley, kept an eye on the gate of Inner Temple Lane. In about twenty minutes we observed our friend approaching on the south side of Fleet Street. He halted at the gate, plied the knocker, and after a brief parley with the night-porter vanished through the wicket. We waited yet five minutes more, and then, having given him time to get clear of the entrance, we crossed the road.

The porter looked at us with some surprise.

"There's a gentleman just gone down to your chambers, sir," said he. "He told me you were expecting him."

"Quite right," said Thorndyke, with a dry smile, "I was. Goodnight."

We slunk down the lane, past the church, and through the gloomy cloisters, giving a wide berth to all lamps and lighted entries, until, emerging into Paper Buildings, we crossed at the darkest part to King's Bench Walk, where Thorndyke made straight for the chambers of our friend Anstey, which were two doors above our own.

"Why are we coming here?" I asked, as we ascended the stairs.

But the question needed no answer when we reached the landing, for through the open door of our friend's chambers I could see in the darkened room Anstey himself with two uniformed constables and a couple of plain-clothes men.

"There has been no signal yet, sir," said one of the latter, whom I recognized as a detective-sergeant of our division.

"No," said Thorndyke, "but the M.C. has arrived. He came in five minutes before us."

"Then," exclaimed Anstey, "the ball will open shortly, ladies and gents. The boards are waxed, the fiddlers are tuning up, and –"

"Not quite so loud, if you please, sir," said the sergeant. "I think there is somebody coming up Crown Office Row."

The ball had, in fact, opened. As we peered cautiously out of the open window, keeping well back in the darkened room, a stealthy figure crept out of the shadow, crossed the road, and stole noiselessly into the entry of Thorndyke's chambers. It was quickly followed by a second figure, and then by a third, in which I recognized our elusive client.

"Now listen for the signal," said Thorndyke. "They won't waste time. Confound that clock!"

The soft-voiced bell of the Inner Temple clock, mingling with the harsher tones of St. Dunstan's and the Law Courts, slowly told out the hour of midnight; and as the last reverberations were dying away, some metallic object, apparently a coin, dropped with a sharp clink on to the pavement under our window.

At the sound the watchers simultaneously sprang to their feet.

"You two go first," said the sergeant, addressing the uniformed men, who thereupon stole noiselessly, in their rubber-soled boots, down the stone stairs and along the pavement. The rest of us followed, with less attention to silence, and as we ran up to Thorndyke's chambers, we were aware of quick but stealthy footsteps on the stairs above.

"They've been at work, you see," whispered one of the constables, flashing his lantern on to the iron-bound outer door of our sitting-room, on which the marks of a large jemmy were plainly visible.

The sergeant nodded grimly, and, bidding the constables to remain on the landing, led the way upwards.

As we ascended, faint rustlings continued to be audible from above, and on the second-floor landing we met a man descending briskly, but without hurry, from the third. It was Mr. Barton, and I could not but admire the composure with which he passed the two detectives. But suddenly his glance fell on Thorndyke, and his composure vanished. With a wild stare of incredulous horror, he halted as if petrified; then he broke away and raced furiously down the stairs, and a moment later a muffled shout and the sound of a scuffle told us that he had received a check. On the next flight we met two more men, who, more hurried and less self-possessed, endeavoured to push past; but the sergeant barred the way.

"Why, bless me!" exclaimed the latter, "it's Moakey; and isn't that Tom Harris?"

"It's all right, sergeant," said Moakey plaintively, striving to escape from the officer's grip. "We've come to the wrong house, that's all."

The sergeant smiled indulgently. "I know," he replied. "But you're always coming to the wrong house, Moakey; and now you're just coming along with me to the right house."

He slipped his hand inside his captive's coat, and adroitly fished out a large, folding jemmy; whereupon the discomforted burglar abandoned all further protest.

On our return to the first-floor, we found Mr. Barton sulkily awaiting us, handcuffed to one of the constables, and watched by Polton with pensive disapproval.

"I needn't trouble you tonight, Doctor," said the sergeant, as he marshalled his little troop of captors and captives. "You'll hear from us in the morning. Goodnight, sir."

The melancholy procession moved off down the stairs, and we retired into our chambers with Anstey to smoke a last pipe.

"A capable man, that Barton," observed Thorndyke – "ready, plausible, and ingenious, but spoilt by prolonged contact with fools. I wonder if the police will perceive the significance of this little affair."

"They will be more acute than I am if they do," said I.

"Naturally," interposed Anstey, who loved to 'cheek' his revered senior, "because there isn't any. It's only Thorndyke's bounce. He is really in a deuce of a fog himself."

However this may have been, the police were a good deal puzzled by the incident, for, on the following morning, we received a visit from no less a person than Superintendent Miller, of Scotland Yard.

"This is a queer business," said he, coming to the point at once – "this burglary, I mean. Why should they want to crack your place, right here in the Temple, too? You've got nothing of value here, have you? No 'hard stuff,' as they call it, for instance?"

"Not so much as a silver teaspoon," replied Thorndyke, who had a conscientious objection to plate of all kinds.

"It's odd," said the superintendent, "deuced odd. When we got your note, we thought these anarchist idiots had mixed you up with the case – you saw the papers, I suppose – and wanted to go through your rooms for some reason. We thought we had our hands on the gang, instead of which we find a party of common crooks that we're sick of the sight of. I tell you, sir, it's annoying when you think you've hooked a salmon, to bring up a blooming eel."

"It must be a great disappointment," Thorndyke agreed, suppressing a smile.

"It is," said the detective. "Not but what we're glad enough to get these beggars, especially Halkett, or Barton, as he calls himself – a mighty slippery customer is Halkett, and mischievous, too – but we're not wanting any disappointments just now. There was that big jewel job in Piccadilly, Taplin and Horne's; I don't mind telling you that we've not got the ghost of a clue. Then there's this anarchist affair. We're all in the dark there, too."

"But what about the cipher?" asked Thorndyke.

"Oh, hang the cipher!" exclaimed the detective irritably. "This Professor Poppelbaum may be a very learned man, but he doesn't help *us* much. He says the document is in Hebrew, and he has translated it into Double Dutch. Just listen to this!" He dragged out of his pocket a bundle of papers, and, dabbing down a photograph of the document before Thorndyke, commenced to read the Professor's report. "'The document is written in the characters of the well-known inscription of Mesha, King of Moab' (who the devil's he? Never heard of him. Well known, indeed!) 'The language is Hebrew, and the words are separated by groups of letters, which are meaningless, and obviously introduced to mislead and confuse the reader. The words themselves are not strictly consecutive, but, by the interpellation of certain other words, a series of intelligible sentences is obtained, the meaning of which is not very clear, but is no doubt allegorical. The method of decipherment is shown in the accompanying tables, and the full rendering suggested on the enclosed sheet. It is to be noted that the writer of this document was apparently quite unacquainted with the Hebrew language, as appears from the absence of any grammatical construction.' That's the Professor's report, Doctor, and here are the tables showing how he worked it out. It makes my head spin to look at 'em."

He handed to Thorndyke a bundle of ruled sheets, which my colleague examined attentively for a while, and then passed on to me.

"This is very systematic and thorough," said he. "But now let us see the final result at which he arrives."

"It may be all very systematic," growled the superintendent, sorting out his papers, "but I tell you, sir, it's all BOSH!" The latter word he jerked out viciously, as he slapped down on the table the final product of the Professor's labours. "There," he continued, "that's what he calls the 'full rendering,' and I reckon it'll make your hair curl. It might be a message from Bedlam."

Thorndyke took up the first sheet, and as he compared the constructed renderings with the literal translation, the ghost of a smile stole across his usually immovable countenance.

"The meaning is certainly a little obscure," he observed, "though the reconstruction is highly ingenious; and, moreover, I think the Professor is probably right. That is to say, the words which he has supplied are probably the omitted parts of the passages from which the words of the cryptogram were taken. What do you think, Jervis?"

He handed me the two papers, of which one gave the actual words of the cryptogram, and the other a suggested reconstruction, with omitted words supplied. The first read:

> *Woe city lies robbery prey noise whip rattling wheel horse chariot day darkness gloominess cloud darkness morning mountain people strong fire them flame.*

Turning to the second paper, I read out the suggested rendering:

"'Woe to the bloody city! It is full of lies and robbery; the prey departeth not. The noise of a whip, and the noise of the rattling of the wheels, and of the prancing horses, and of the jumping chariots.

"'A day of darkness and of gloominess, a day of clouds, and of thick darkness, as the morning spread upon the mountains, a great people and a strong.

"'A fire devoureth before them, and behind them a flame burneth.'"

Here the first sheet ended, and, as I laid it down, Thorndyke looked at me inquiringly.

"There is a good deal of reconstruction in proportion to the original matter," I objected. "The Professor has 'supplied' more than three-quarters of the final rendering."

"Exactly," burst in the superintendent; "it's all Professor and no cryptogram."

"Still, I think the reading is correct," said Thorndyke. "As far as it goes, that is."

"Good Lord!" exclaimed the dismayed detective. "Do you mean to tell me, sir, that that balderdash is the real meaning of the thing?"

"I don't say that," replied Thorndyke. "I say it is correct as far as it goes; but I doubt its being the solution of the cryptogram."

"Have you been studying that photograph that I gave you?" demanded Miller, with sudden eagerness.

"I have looked at it," said Thorndyke evasively, "but I should like to examine the original if you have it with you."

"I have," said the detective. "Professor Poppelbaum sent it back with the solution. You can have a look at it, though I can't leave it with you without special authority."

He drew the document from his pocket-book and handed it to Thorndyke, who took it over to the window and scrutinized it closely. From the window he drifted into the adjacent office, closing the door after him; and presently the sound of a faint explosion told me that he had lighted the gas-fire.

"Of course," said Miller, taking up the translation again, "this gibberish is the sort of stuff you might expect from a parcel of crack-brained anarchists; but it doesn't seem to mean anything."

"Not to us," I agreed; "but the phrases may have some pre-arranged significance. And then there are the letters between the words. It is possible that they may really form a cipher."

"I suggested that to the Professor," said Miller, "but he wouldn't hear of it. He is sure they are only dummies."

"I think he is probably mistaken, and so, I fancy, does my colleague. But we shall hear what he has to say presently."

"Oh, I know what he will say," growled Miller. "He will put the thing under the microscope, and tell us who made the paper, and what the ink is composed of, and then we shall be just where we were." The superintendent was evidently deeply depressed.

We sat for some time pondering in silence on the vague sentences of the Professor's translation, until, at length, Thorndyke reappeared, holding the document in his hand. He laid it quietly on the table by the officer, and then inquired:

"Is this an official consultation?"

"Certainly," replied Miller. "I was authorized to consult you respecting the translation, but nothing was said about the original. Still, if you want it for further study, I will get it for you."

"No, thank you," said Thorndyke. "I have finished with it. My theory turned out to be correct."

"Your theory!" exclaimed the superintendent, eagerly. "Do you mean to say – ?"

"And, as you are consulting me officially, I may as well give you this."

He held out a sheet of paper, which the detective took from him and began to read.

"What is this?" he asked, looking up at Thorndyke with a puzzled frown. "Where did it come from?"

"It is the solution of the cryptogram," replied Thorndyke.

The detective re-read the contents of the paper, and, with the frown of perplexity deepening, once more gazed at my colleague.

"This is a joke, sir; you are fooling me," he said sulkily.

"Nothing of the kind," answered Thorndyke. "That is the genuine solution."

"But it's impossible!" exclaimed Miller. "Just look at it, Dr. Jervis."

I took the paper from his hand, and, as I glanced at it, I had no difficulty in understanding his surprise. It bore a short inscription in printed Roman capitals, thus:

THE PICKERDILLEY STUF IS UP THE CHIMBLY 416 WARDOUR ST 2ND FLOUR BACK
IT WAS HID BECOS OF OLD MOAKEYS JOOD MOAKEY IS A BLITER.

"Then that fellow wasn't an anarchist at all?" I exclaimed.

"No," said Miller. "He was one of Moakey's gang. We suspected Moakey of being mixed up with that job, but we couldn't fix it on him. By Jove!" he added, slapping his thigh, "if this is right, and I can lay my hands on the loot! Can you lend me a bag, doctor? I'm off to Wardour Street this very moment."

We furnished him with an empty suit-case, and, from the window, watched him making for Mitre Court at a smart double.

"I wonder if he will find the booty," said Thorndyke. "It just depends on whether the hiding-place was known to more than one of the gang. Well, it has been a quaint case, and instructive, too. I suspect our friend Barton and the evasive Schönberg were the collaborators who produced that curiosity of literature."

"May I ask how you deciphered the thing?" I said. "It didn't appear to take long."

"It didn't. It was merely a matter of testing a hypothesis; and you ought not to have to ask that question," he added, with mock severity, "seeing that you had what turn out to have been all the necessary facts, two days ago. But I will prepare a document and demonstrate to you tomorrow morning."

* * *

"So Miller was successful in his quest," said Thorndyke, as we smoked our morning pipes after breakfast. "The 'entire swag,' as he calls it, was 'up the chimbly,' undisturbed."

He handed me a note which had been left, with the empty suit-case, by a messenger, shortly before, and I was about to read it when an agitated knock was heard at our door. The visitor, whom I admitted, was a rather haggard and dishevelled elderly gentleman, who, as he entered, peered inquisitively through his concave spectacles from one of us to the other.

"Allow me to introduce myself, gentlemen," said he. "I am Professor Poppelbaum."

Thorndyke bowed and offered a chair.

"I called yesterday afternoon," our visitor continued, "at Scotland Yard, where I heard of your remarkable decipherment and of the convincing proof of its correctness. Thereupon I borrowed the cryptogram, and have spent the entire night in studying it, but I cannot connect your solution with any of the characters. I wonder if you would do me the great favour of enlightening me as to your method of decipherment, and so save me further sleepless nights? You may rely on my discretion."

"Have you the document with you?" asked Thorndyke.

The Professor produced it from his pocket-book, and passed it to my colleague.

"You observe, Professor," said the latter, "that this is a laid paper, and has no water-mark?"

"Yes, I noticed that."

"And that the writing is in indelible Chinese ink?"

"Yes, yes," said the savant impatiently; "but it is the inscription that interests me, not the paper and ink."

"Precisely," said Thorndyke. "Now, it was the ink that interested me when I caught a glimpse of the document three days ago. 'Why,' I asked myself, 'should anyone use this troublesome medium' – for this appears to be stick ink – 'when good writing ink is to be had?' What advantages has Chinese ink over writing ink? It has several advantages as a drawing ink, but for writing purposes it has only one: it is quite unaffected by wet. The obvious inference, then, was that this document was, for some reason, likely to be exposed to wet. But this inference instantly suggested another, which I was yesterday able to put to the test – thus."

He filled a tumbler with water, and, rolling up the document, dropped it in. Immediately there began to appear on it a new set of characters of a curious grey colour. In a few seconds Thorndyke lifted out the wet paper, and held it up to the light, and now there was plainly visible an inscription in transparent lettering, like a very distinct water-mark. It was in printed Roman capitals, written across the other writing, and read:

THE PICKERDILLEY STUF IS UP THE CHIMBLY 416 WARDOUR ST 2ND FLOUR BACK IT WAS HID BECOS OF OLD MOAKEYS JOOD MOAKEY IS A BLITER.

The Professor regarded the inscription with profound disfavour.

"How do you suppose this was done?" he asked gloomily.

"I will show you," said Thorndyke. "I have prepared a piece of paper to demonstrate the process to Dr. Jervis. It is exceedingly simple."

He fetched from the office a small plate of glass, and a photographic dish in which a piece of thin notepaper was soaking in water.

"This paper," said Thorndyke, lifting it out and laying it on the glass, "has been soaking all night, and is now quite pulpy."

He spread a dry sheet of paper over the wet one, and on the former wrote heavily with a hard pencil, 'Moakey is a bliter.' On lifting the upper sheet, the writing was seen to be transferred in a deep grey to the wet paper, and when the latter was held up to the light the inscription stood out clear and transparent as if written with oil.

"When this dries," said Thorndyke, "the writing will completely disappear, but it will reappear whenever the paper is again wetted."

The Professor nodded.

"Very ingenious," said he – "a sort of artificial palimpsest, in fact. But I do not understand how that illiterate man could have written in the difficult Moabite script."

"He did not," said Thorndyke. "The 'cryptogram' was probably written by one of the leaders of the gang, who, no doubt, supplied copies to the other members to use instead of blank paper for secret communications. The object of the Moabite writing was evidently to divert attention from the paper itself, in case the communication fell into the wrong hands, and I must say it seems to have answered its purpose very well."

The Professor started, stung by the sudden recollection of his labours.

"Yes," he snorted; "but I am a scholar, sir, not a policeman. Every man to his trade."

He snatched up his hat, and with a curt "Good morning," flung out of the room in dudgeon.

Thorndyke laughed softly.

"Poor Professor!" he murmured. "Our playful friend Barton has much to answer for."

Spooks

Shane Halbach

RACHEL STOOD in the corner of the dirty room that served as a defacto bedroom for the two men who occupied the apartment. She had been in more or less the same spot for almost 48 hours.

Fareed Nadir was talking rapidly in Arabic into a disposable cell phone. Rachel didn't speak Arabic, but she didn't need to. Fareed was planning something. Something big and bad.

Rachel glanced toward the front door for the millionth time. Fareed's brother Hassan would come back eventually. When he did, if she was standing in exactly the right place, she might have a chance to slip out the door before she was noticed.

She began to edge silently toward the door. There were no rugs to muffle her footsteps. The apartment was only inhabited in the technical sense of the word. There was no furniture, not even beds. Only clothes, an old stove and refrigerator, and some dirty blankets for sleeping. It was a temporary location, a staging area, and it could be completely emptied in minutes if need be.

Before Rachel had even crossed the room, Hassan entered through the front door, closing and locking it behind him. Rachel returned to the corner. She'd missed her chance, but there'd be others. She wasn't worried. *(Can I even feel worried anymore? If I've lost that, then what else have I lost?)*

Hassan walked to the bedroom, and his brother acknowledged him with a nod before returning to his conversation. He removed a handgun from the waistband of his khakis and set it carefully on the floor before kicking his loafers into the corner of the room. He turned back around and froze in place.

His handgun rose from the floor seemingly of its own accord and hovered at chest level, pointing at him.

He had time to shout and put his arm up before the gun fired twice into his chest, throwing him backwards into the wall. He slid down to the floor, his eyes wide, leaving a long, dark smear of blood.

Rachel dropped to the floor like a lead weight. Stray bullets had a habit of going where you least expected them. (How is this possible? Am I imagining this? Am I doing this?) She curled up in a ball, trying to make herself as tiny as possible.

The gun turned and fired again, catching Fareed twice in the back before he even had time to turn around.

Rachel opened her mouth, trying to pop her ears. She watched the gun hover at the back of Fareed's head, delivering one final deathblow before moving on and doing the same to Hassan. Finally, the gun dropped to the floor in between the two bodies, as lifeless as they were.

Rachel held her breath, not daring to move a muscle. After a few seconds, the lock on the front door turned and the door opened and shut. Rachel's breath came out in a whoosh as she sat up and leaned back against the wall.

She'd never been happier to be invisible in her entire life.

* * *

It had been almost twenty years since Rachel had last been seen. She was over forty now *(what would my face look like? Would I recognize myself?)*, but she could still remember the cold ceramic on her bare back, the smell of charred flesh, the feeling of power and disorientation as her consciousness leapt from her body like a falcon soaring on the thermals generated by the enormous dynamos buried under C-building. The only thing she could no longer remember about the last day of her life was the sense of purpose she had felt as she climbed in the A-tube. She could only remember remembering it, like a story someone told her about someone else.

She had stood in a room with nineteen other lost souls, wearing street clothes for the last time. *(What did it feel like to wear clothes? Oh God, I can't remember. Why do I even need to remember?)* They had sat through a final presentation that none of them had really paid attention to, and when the lights snapped on she hadn't been the only one to jump.

There had been a graduation ceremony immediately after, even though there was nobody to attend besides the members of Class One. They sat in their folding chairs and Major Spanner gave a speech. Afterwards they had raised their right hands together and said the oath.

"I, Rachel Neelam, do swear to protect these United States and their people from any and all who would do them harm. I freely give my life in this. I protect those who don't know I exist. I am everywhere and nowhere. I am the watcher. I am the Unseen."

There had even been champagne afterward, which Rachel had dutifully sipped in a vain attempt to drown the butterflies in her stomach. The Unseen had been led away one by one, and never seen again by anybody.

* * *

Hanging around waiting for doors to be opened was a skill Rachel had honed to perfection. There were many factors involved: the height and weight of the person opening the door, the speed at which the door closed, even loose fitting clothing or accessories like purses, which must not be bumped. Rachel had been doing it so long that it operated more as a gut feeling than a conscious decision. She could pick her mark with a single glance.

Inside HQ was a row of turnstiles with employees barging through to various offices and cubicles beyond. People put a lot of stock in turnstiles, but if you were invisible and quiet, you could usually just climb over the top or even take a less direct route over a desk or wall. She couldn't pass through walls, but she found she never really needed to.

She rode the elevator up and down twice before a short woman in a pants suit got off on Rachel's floor. Rachel could have pushed the button she needed when she was alone, but elevators often had cameras and you never knew who was watching. She would have done it if she had to, but she was not in a hurry. *(Patience is a virtue. Was I patient before, or was that part of the package? Did I gain patience or lose impatience?)*

Finally she walked down a hall, passing office doors on the left and purposeful looking business-people on the right, until she got to the one labeled, 'Nicholas Denam, Deputy Director, Special Intelligence Unit.' The door was open, so Rachel entered without announcing herself. She looked around his office as a matter of principle, reading the top paper on a neat stack before seating herself in an empty chair.

She waited three minutes until he took a sip of his coffee.

"Good morning, Nick," she said cheerfully, smiling as he almost fumbled his coffee into his lap. *(Oh well, maybe next time.)*

"What is wrong with you people?" he muttered as he stood and closed his door. He looked vaguely in Rachel's direction.

"Who are you? Which one?"

"Rachel."

"What's that?"

She made an effort to strengthen her voice. *"Rachel."*

"You alright, Rachel? You're pretty small and echo-y today. Are you fading out on me?"

She frowned. *(Is it still a frown if no one can see it? A tree in the woods.)*

"I'm here," she said firmly, trying to make it true. "All the way."

"Good. Your country still needs you."

Ah, the old touchstone, worn so smooth by so many retellings that the words had stopped meaning anything to Rachel a long time ago.

"What are you doing here? Did we have an appointment?"

It had probably been ten years since he had asked how she had gotten in unnoticed.

She answered, "One of the Unseen killed two people this morning. I thought you should know."

Nick's face went blank, all at once, like a door slamming shut. Only his eyes seemed alive. She had his attention.

"What are you talking about, Rachel? What did you hear?"

"This isn't a rumor. I saw it with my own eyes."

"Give me the whole story," he said disbelief thick in his voice.

"Not much to tell. I was tailing Fareed Nadir. I was in his apartment. His brother Hassan came home with a tail of his own. Unseen. Two shots in Hassan's chest, with Hassan's own gun. Two in Fareed's back. One more in each of their heads. Very professional."

"Who was it? The rogue agent?"

"How should I know? I was hiding for my life."

"You know all of them. All the ones that are left."

(Precious few of us left. Precious few still managing to hold on. How much longer can I hold on?)

"None of us then."

Nick leaned forward. "Speak up, you're going soft around the edges again."

"None of us would do it, and you know it." She groped for words. "Something's not right. We don't... act. Just watch. It's hard enough to... it takes a certain amount of passion to kill someone. It's too much."

"Rachel, why were you tailing Fareed Nadir?"

"What do you mean? I was told..."

Rachel stopped. Her mind raced. She had gotten a call, like normal. Hadn't the tip come from Nick's office? Who had it come from?"

"I was doing what I was supposed to do," she said instead. "They were terrorists. They were planning something big."

"Well, they're not planning anything anymore, so that's alright at least."

Rachel was incredulous. Her voice was truly in focus for the first time.

"Are you kidding me? Our only leads are dead and we don't know shit! What's their organization, who's involved? Who are their connections? Where is the hardware?"

"If the head is cut off, the body will wither and die."

"The head was cut off before we could even see what the body looked like. Before we even knew it if was the head at all!"

"Look, don't worry about it. I'll handle it. What's done is done. The important thing is to find out who the rogue agent is. You'll just have to find a new terrorist to follow around."

Rachel stood up from her chair, walked to the door and opened it. She wasn't getting any answers, only more questions.

Talking to people was so rarely worth the effort.

* * *

After she opened the door, Rachel remained in Nick's office, standing silently in the corner next to a large picture window with an excellent view of the city. She watched the people and cars below while she waited.

Nick fiddled with things on his desk and pretended to be busy while watching the room out of the corner of his eye. Periodically, he would freeze in place and listen as hard as he could. Sure enough, after less than ten minutes, Nick hurried to his door and closed it before picking up the phone on his desk.

People were always so sure they were alone when they couldn't see anybody. Even Nick, who ought to know better. Rachel had a theory that it was something hardwired in the human brain. *(Out of sight, out of mind; literally)*.

Nick's call connected.

"We have a problem," he said. "One of the Spooks was at Nadir's apartment this morning. Saw the whole thing."

He paused, listening. Rachel couldn't hear what was being said on the other end.

"I have no idea what she was doing there. She said she was following up terrorist leads or something."

...

"Of course not. I've deliberately kept them away from Nadir. But they do get information on their own sometimes too you know."

...

"They're not robots. They're people, and they're good at what they do."

...

Nick banged his fist on the table, his voice getting heated.

"I don't know, damn it! It was just dumb luck. What's done is done. Now the question is, what do we do about it?"

...

"And how am I supposed to do that? I can't even see her for Christ's sake."

...

"Alright, alright! I can handle this. I need a team. Your guys, the new ones. I'll send her a new tip, give her an address. The team will get there first."

Rachel staggered as if punched, barely recovering in time to avoid bumping into the blinds and giving herself away. Was Nick discussing her *death*?

"So what, it doesn't matter. If that happens, she'll run. Trust me on this, I know how they think. She'll go to ground and then it's just a waiting game. She's old, almost gone. I just talked to her, she was barely there. In fact, I'm surprised she's hung on this long, she's Class One."

...

"Give your guys a chance first. It's always better to have a body. Get them together, I'll send you the address in ten minutes."

Nick slammed the phone into its cradle and strode purposefully to the door. Rachel staggered after him on wobbly legs.

* * *

As she followed Nick through the corridors and stairways of HQ, her mind raced.

One of the Unseen had been ordered to kill Fareed, probably by Nick. At least one other person knew about the order, and approved of it. That was bad.

Even worse, Nick had ordered her own death, just as casually. He was obviously willing to keep killing to hush up Fareed's death. No, not Fareed's death, the involvement of the Unseen in his murder.

But why had she received a call telling her to tail Fareed Nadir just before the hit took place? It didn't make sense that Nick or his co-conspirator had called with the information. Could there be some counter-faction who didn't approve of what Nick was up to? Who?

The call itself was pretty routine. The calls didn't usually come from Nick himself and it was not unusual to hear an unfamiliar voice on the other end. In fact, Rachel was pretty certain it had been a familiar voice, one of the few regular anonymous dispatchers who had been around almost as long as she had.

There was also the question of who had actually performed the hit. She was one of only two remaining members of Class One, with four left from Class Two and only three left from Class Three, after which the program has been discontinued. The rest of the graduates had 'moved on' or 'faded away' depending on how religious one was. Losing fifty-one of your sixty graduates was too high of an attribution rate, even for spies.

The Unseen were solitary by nature, but there was a certain bond of shared experience among the only nine living invisible people in the world. Rachel knew them all reasonably well. She couldn't imagine any of them obeying Nick's order to kill Fareed.

It was a question of motivation; what kind of leverage could Nick have applied to overcome the soul-sucking apathy surrounding the Unseen? First off, none of them were killers. They had been selected for certain characteristics, carefully screened to be good at surveillance. Calm, patient, organized; the opposite of hot blooded. Second off, it was hard to bribe or threaten a person who didn't need to eat, didn't get hot or cold, had almost no material possessions, and who had abandoned any connection to what little friends and family they had decades ago. It was no wonder most of the Unseen just decided to... stop. *(What do they have to live for? What do I have to live for?)*

Rachel was so caught up in her thoughts that she almost walked right into Nick's back when he stopped to flash his badge at the card reader positioned to the right of an unmarked door. The door looked identical to the other four doors Rachel could see in the hall.

Nick entered authoritatively, pushing the door wide, so it was no problem for Rachel to slip in after him. She had never been in this particular room before, but she recognized it immediately.

Intelligence hubs were always the same. Analysts sat in cubicles, hunching over computer screen showing grainy images or green waveforms of recorded audio. A low murmur of conversation filled the room, loud enough to be heard, but quiet enough to not disturb any number of phone calls. Against the wall were a series of offices and meeting rooms with maps, banks of phones, and doors that could be closed for private conversations. It was to one of these offices that Nick walked.

Rachel decided to abandon him. She had to get one step ahead of him and stay there. Her life depended on it.

Nick closed the office door behind him, cutting off any second-guessing.

It was possible that the tip to follow Fareed had originated from this room, but Rachel had no idea how to figure out whom it had come from. Stealing a computer password was a piece of cake when you could simply look over someone's shoulder as they logged in. If the system wasn't smart enough to recognize a duplicate logon, and if there was a record of the call, and if she could actually find it on the network... too many ifs.

While she was thinking, she began aimlessly circulating throughout the room.

A woman with tight black curls was arguing quietly and fiercely on the phone with someone who apparently owed her child support. A thin man in a superman t-shirt and thick glasses nervously flipped back and forth between PowerPoint and a furtive game of Solitaire. Two well-dressed older gentlemen argued the relative merits of spell caster classes in a video game.

Rachel absorbed these things without even thinking about it. She had long ago stopped feeling self-conscious about eavesdropping. She allowed the sights and sounds to flow over her, bathing herself in the information stream.

Rachel heard the murmur of another voice floating over the cubical wall and she walked around the end of the row. As she got nearer to the voice, something prickled at her consciousness. The voice was familiar.

Quickly, she followed the sound to a cubicle and peeked in. A man she had never seen before was giving information about a surveillance target over the phone.

He was tall with dark skin; Indian maybe, or Mexican. He was dressed in khakis and a polo shirt. By habit, Rachel registered in quick succession a wedding ring, a picture of a girl of about three, and a coffee mug that said 'Washington Polytechnic' on the side.

Without a doubt, it was the voice that had given her the tip about Fareed.

Rachel was contemplating what to do next when she heard footsteps coming down the aisle. It was Nick. *(Too late, too late! He already knows!)*

She stepped out of the way to let Nick into the cube and then stepped in again as close behind him as she dared. She didn't think Nick would do anything to the man here at the office, but her hand hovered over the coffee mug, just in case.

Nick waited respectfully until the man hung up the phone and turned around.

"Amol, can you send a message for me?"

"Sure boss, what's up?"

Nick held out a post-it note.

"Get a hold of Rachel Neelam. Give her this address and tell her to get over there right away. Oh, and make sure to tell her to be careful."

"Sure Nick, no problem."

A line of ice went down Rachel's spine. She'd known Nick for almost fifteen years. There hadn't even been a hitch in his voice. He was one cold bastard.

Rachel darted out of the way as Nick left, returning to his conference room at the end of the row. She listened numbly as Amol left her a message, unwittingly telling her to report to her own death. Had he known what he was doing when he tipped her off, or was he just passing on a message like he was now? Rachel needed to know, and needed to know now.

This was going to require an approach that was a little more hands on that she was used to.

* * *

Amol walked down the stairs to parking sub-level B. He was almost to the door when he felt a hand on his shoulder. He flinched, and whirled around quickly, but no one was there. His eyes were wide and flicked from corner to corner nervously.

"Hello?" he called in a quivering voice.

"Amol," said Rachel softly. "Please don't panic. I'm Unseen."

If anything, Amol looked more frightened.

"Who are you? What do you want?"

He put his back to the wall and held his hands out in front of himself defensively.

"It's Rachel. You called me, told me to watch Fareed Nadir. I need to know who told you to call me."

Amol's relief was immediate.

"Alhamdulillah! I thought you were… hey, you're pretty clear."

Rachel glanced down at herself, confused.

"Clear?"

"For how old you are. You sound almost normal, like a regular person. I would have sworn you were new."

"Amol, I need to know who gave you the message to trail Fareed. I know it wasn't Nick."

Amol took an excited step forward.

"I knew you were the right person to call! But wait, you should be following Mr. Nadir."

"The Nadirs are dead."

"I knew it! I knew it. Were you too late?"

"Too late for what? What the hell is going on?"

"We can't talk here. It might not be safe."

"Amol, listen. I'm in danger. You might be in danger. I need to know why."

"They restarted the program."

"What? Who did? Why?"

"All the way up. Aaron Davidson, the CIO. They've already graduated a new Class. But Rachel, listen, it's not reconnaissance. It's an ops division."

"But it's a death sentence."

"Listen, we can't talk here. I can explain everything I know when we get somewhere safe."

He turned and opened the door to the parking garage, holding it for her.

"How do you know all this?"

"I'm an analyst. It's my job to see the shape of something based on hints and whispers. Define the outline of something invisible with rumors and innuendos." He looked smug. "You're not the only one who has been working in intelligence for the past twenty years."

He hit the button on his key fob and the lights on a grey sedan blinked in response. There was a car seat in the back.

Amol opened the door and got inside, but Rachel hesitated. It had been a long time since she had ridden in a car. All of her instincts told her not to be confined in such a small space. On top of that, she felt surprisingly self-conscious about affecting the physical world in front of someone. It was like letting Amol see her naked. *(No one can ever see me naked again. Is that good or bad?)*

Finally, she opened the door and got in the car, buckling her seatbelt firmly.

Amol backed out and then drove to the exit. He held his badge up to the card reader and the little arm rose. Amol put his turn signal on.

"Amol, is there any way they could figure out that you were the one who tipped me off?"

"Information is always there, if you're looking in the right place. But I think we're safe. Hypothetically, if someone knew exactly when you were tipped off, they could run a search through all the calls. But they'd need a pretty tight window; otherwise would just be too much data to go through."

"Nick knows when I was tipped off, or at least has a pretty good guess."

Amol sat for a second, letting that sink in before turning out onto the street.

"I think we better not go to my house. Better safe than sorry."

Rachel heard the roar of an engine to her left and turned to look. A black SUV accelerated into the driver's side door of Amol's car.

Rachel hung weightless in that for ever moment before time resumed with a crash. The sound of the impact was tremendous, and even though it must have only taken a second, it seemed to go on and on in Rachel's ears.

The car spun sideways, pressing her against her seat belt. Amol's window shattered, spraying glass into the cabin, and his airbag deployed with a smell like gunfire.

Rachel's head slammed into the doorframe and she lost consciousness.

* * *

The light hurt Rachel's eyes and she put a hand to her head, steadying herself. Amol hung limply by his seatbelt, nestled in the deflated pillow of his airbag. She couldn't see his face, but he wasn't moving.

Rachel undid her seatbelt and leaned over to shake his shoulder. Just as her fingers brushed his shirt, his door was jerked open.

A man Rachel didn't recognize leaned in. He was white, with a strong, clean-shaven jaw and wavy hair brushed to one side. Inexplicably, he wore a pair of black leather gloves. Out of reflex, Rachel flinched away from him and stayed quiet.

The man roughly checked Amol's neck for a pulse. Amol groaned and shifted a little, not quite regaining consciousness. The man in gloves carefully took hold of Amol's chin with his left hand, set his right hand against the top of Amol's head, and twisted violently.

Before she could think, Rachel lunged across the front seat and grabbed at the man. Her invisible nails opened a long gash along one cheek, seemingly by magic. The man jerked away, surprised. He ducked out of the car and out of Rachel's reach.

Snarling in rage, she kicked open her door, but the man was already jumping into the black SUV. It was so damaged from the crash that Rachel wasn't sure if it would be able to drive.

The engine roared to life and Rachel started to run. The tires squealed and Rachel dove for the car, grasping at the door handle. She missed and stumbled, her fingers scrabbling over the side of the car as it pulled away. She was left panting in the street as the SUV squealed around the corner and out of sight.

Only then did she think to go back and check on Amol. His neck was warm under her fingers, but there was no pulse.

Rachel thought of the picture of the little girl on Amol's desk. Forgetting all of her carefully honed instincts collected over years of being invisible, Rachel stood in the center of the road and howled at a cloudless sky.

* * *

Aaron Davidson's house was dark. Rachel had been watching it long enough that the crickets had become accustomed to her presence and once again filled the night with their song.

The Chief Intelligence Officer was apparently doing well for himself. The enormous house stood gleaming and flawless, its manicured lawn an island in the surrounding forest.

It had taken Rachel hours to navigate the network of busses, waiting for passengers to follow on circumspect, less busy routes. Finally, she had walked the last two miles out of town to the secluded mansion.

She crossed into the yard and approached the house. There may have been security cameras, but they would register nothing. The best thing to do would be to wait until morning when somebody left the house, but Rachel wasn't feeling patient for a change. She wanted in tonight.

After a quick circuit of the house, Rachel found what she wanted: the gentle night breeze shifted the curtains on a half-open window. Rachel stood on the back of a stone garden frog and used a jagged stick to punch through the screen. Slowly, she ripped a jagged hole and lifted the window the rest of the way, before landing awkwardly in an enormous bathroom. There was even a helpful night light.

Rachel stepped into the hall and began walking into the house. She passed an alarm system control panel mounted in the hallway, armed, for all the good it was doing. Rachel made a mental note not to open any external doors. She hadn't set off any motion detectors, so they most likely had been disabled by somebody in the house, at least for the ground floor.

Eventually, Rachel found herself in a combination kitchen and dining room, the granite countertops and stainless steel appliances gleaming in the light of the moon streaming in an enormous picture window. Rachel rifled through a stack of papers and checked a few drawers, more out of force of habit than anything else. There was nothing interesting.

She heard the sound of footsteps approaching and retreated quickly behind the table. She had thought everyone would be sleeping by now, so she hadn't been particularly quiet. *(Stupid!)*

Aaron Davidson entered the kitchen. He wore only a white undershirt, a pair of plaid shorts, and black socks pulled up his calf. He looked surprised not to see anybody; maybe he had expected his wife.

As soon as she saw him, Rachel felt her rage kindle to a bonfire. Amol was dead, and his daughter would never see her father again. This man was at least somewhat responsible.

She reached out and snagged a porcelain statue of a cardinal off a curio cabinet in the corner, hurling it with all of her might at the confused expression on Mr. Davidson's face. She missed by two inches and the statue shattered against the dark cherry cabinets.

Davidson flinched away from the sudden explosion of sound and shards of porcelain. He dove behind the counter as she sent a glass vase his way, trailing sunflowers and water behind it.

"Murderer!" she hissed as she stalked toward him.

His head peeked over the top of the counter, but he saw nothing of course. He grabbed a knife out of the block and dived back to safety.

"Traitor," she growled as she rounded the edge of the counter.

He heard her and cried out, slashing the air in front of him to ribbons with his knife. He wasn't anywhere near her.

The room went completely silent; Davidson's heavy breathing was the only noise. He was just cautiously stepping out from behind the counter, his knife probing in front of him, when she came back.

She brought the fire poker from the set in the living room down hard on his outstretched arm and the knife clattered into the corner. Davidson threw himself away from the floating fire poker, landing hard on his butt. He clutched his arm to his chest.

"What do you want?" he moaned. "Who are you?"

She dropped the poker.

"You know who I am."

"Rachel Neelam," he said quietly.

She kicked him in the ribs.

"You don't get to say my name."

He made no move to stand, just sat on the expensive tile and looked at nothing.

"You sent men to kill me. I gave everything for my country. I gave my life! And you sent men to kill me."

"That was a mistake."

"You're damn right it was!" she screamed and punched him in the face. It was only the third time she had voluntarily put her hand on another person in twenty years. It hurt like hell.

Davidson looked like he was going to cry.

"It was a mistake! We should have told you, or at least waited until you were all gone. We knew you wouldn't understand. But don't you see? We couldn't wait, we couldn't sit on the technology. Not when we had the power to save lives!"

"Save lives? How many more people did you condemn to fade away?"

"It's always been a game of numbers. I have to balance the lives of…"

She cut him off. "*We* were saving lives. Within the system."

"It's a bad system, you know that. It's too slow, nobody wants to act. People are more concerned with avoiding blame than actually being successful."

"Do they even know?"

"Every one of them. I swear it. This time they're soldiers, ready to die. That was our mistake with you. It wasn't fair to ask so much from…"

"You fools!" she raged. "You don't know the first thing about it! Soldiers are all wrong. They'll burn out too fast, they'll be lucky to last the year. We could have told you. Why didn't you ask us?"

Davidson gave a wry chuckle. "We were worried how you would react."

Rachel was quiet for a moment. Then she stepped around Davidson and picked up the fallen knife. She crouched behind him and pressed the knife to his throat. She whispered in his ear.

"And what about Amol?"

His body was rigid with fear. She could feel him trembling against her.

"Please. I don't know who that is. Please." He was crying now. "Everything I did, I did for the country. I thought I was doing the right thing."

Rachel pressed the knife until a dark trickle of blood welled out of the dimpled skin. No matter how good his intentions had been, he had ruthlessly order the murder of citizens. A country wasn't worth protecting if it was run by people like him.

With a cry of rage, she threw the knife against the wall. She stood, and Davidson slumped to the floor, weeping.

She had come to a decision.

"I can do worse than kill you. I can haunt you. Every move you make, every order you sign. Every time you go to the bathroom or have sex with your wife, I'll be standing over your shoulder, watching. I am everywhere and nowhere. I am the watcher. I am the Unseen."

She stood, tall and complete. Her voice was strong and unwavering. She was totally, 100%, completely there, filled up with purpose for maybe the first time in her life.

"And God help you if I don't like what I see."

Kim
Chapters I–IV
Rudyard Kipling

Chapter I

O ye who tread the Narrow Way
By Tophet-flare to Judgment Day,
Be gentle when 'the heathen' pray
To Buddha at Kamakura!
Buddha at Kamakura

HE SAT, in defiance of municipal orders, astride the gun Zam Zammah on her brick platform opposite the old Ajaib-Gher – the Wonder House, as the natives call the Lahore Museum. Who hold Zam-Zammah, that 'fire-breathing dragon', hold the Punjab, for the great green-bronze piece is always first of the conqueror's loot.

There was some justification for Kim – he had kicked Lala Dinanath's boy off the trunnions – since the English held the Punjab and Kim was English. Though he was burned black as any native; though he spoke the vernacular by preference, and his mother-tongue in a clipped uncertain sing-song; though he consorted on terms of perfect equality with the small boys of the bazar; Kim was white – a poor white of the very poorest. The half-caste woman who looked after him (she smoked opium, and pretended to keep a second-hand furniture shop by the square where the cheap cabs wait) told the missionaries that she was Kim's mother's sister; but his mother had been nursemaid in a Colonel's family and had married Kimball O'Hara, a young colour-sergeant of the Mavericks, an Irish regiment. He afterwards took a post on the Sind, Punjab, and Delhi Railway, and his Regiment went home without him. The wife died of cholera in Ferozepore, and O'Hara fell to drink and loafing up and down the line with the keen-eyed three-year-old baby. Societies and chaplains, anxious for the child, tried to catch him, but O'Hara drifted away, till he came across the woman who took opium and learned the taste from her, and died as poor whites die in India. His estate at death consisted of three papers – one he called his 'ne varietur' because those words were written below his signature thereon, and another his 'clearance-certificate'. The third was Kim's birth-certificate. Those things, he was used to say, in his glorious opium-hours, would yet make little Kimball a man. On no account was Kim to part with them, for they belonged to a great piece of magic – such magic as men practised over yonder behind the Museum, in the big blue-and-white Jadoo-Gher – the Magic House, as we name the Masonic Lodge. It would, he said, all come right some day, and Kim's horn would be exalted between pillars – monstrous pillars – of beauty and strength.

The Colonel himself, riding on a horse, at the head of the finest Regiment in the world, would attend to Kim – little Kim that should have been better off than his father. Nine hundred first-class devils, whose God was a Red Bull on a green field, would attend to Kim, if they had not forgotten O'Hara – poor O'Hara that was gang-foreman on the Ferozepore line. Then he would weep bitterly in the broken rush chair on the veranda. So it came about after his death that the woman sewed parchment, paper, and birth-certificate into a leather amulet-case which she strung round Kim's neck.

"And some day," she said, confusedly remembering O'Hara's prophecies, "there will come for you a great Red Bull on a green field, and the Colonel riding on his tall horse, yes, and" dropping into English – "nine hundred devils."

"Ah," said Kim, "I shall remember. A Red Bull and a Colonel on a horse will come, but first, my father said, will come the two men making ready the ground for these matters. That is how my father said they always did; and it is always so when men work magic."

If the woman had sent Kim up to the local Jadoo-Gher with those papers, he would, of course, have been taken over by the Provincial Lodge, and sent to the Masonic Orphanage in the Hills; but what she had heard of magic she distrusted. Kim, too, held views of his own. As he reached the years of indiscretion, he learned to avoid missionaries and white men of serious aspect who asked who he was, and what he did. For Kim did nothing with an immense success. True, he knew the wonderful walled city of Lahore from the Delhi Gate to the outer Fort Ditch; was hand in glove with men who led lives stranger than anything Haroun al Raschid dreamed of; and he lived in a life wild as that of the Arabian Nights, but missionaries and secretaries of charitable societies could not see the beauty of it. His nickname through the wards was 'Little Friend of all the World'; and very often, being lithe and inconspicuous, he executed commissions by night on the crowded housetops for sleek and shiny young men of fashion. It was intrigue, – of course he knew that much, as he had known all evil since he could speak, – but what he loved was the game for its own sake – the stealthy prowl through the dark gullies and lanes, the crawl up a waterpipe, the sights and sounds of the women's world on the flat roofs, and the headlong flight from housetop to housetop under cover of the hot dark. Then there were holy men, ash-smeared fakirs by their brick shrines under the trees at the riverside, with whom he was quite familiar – greeting them as they returned from begging-tours, and, when no one was by, eating from the same dish. The woman who looked after him insisted with tears that he should wear European clothes – trousers, a shirt and a battered hat. Kim found it easier to slip into Hindu or Mohammedan garb when engaged on certain businesses. One of the young men of fashion – he who was found dead at the bottom of a well on the night of the earthquake – had once given him a complete suit of Hindu kit, the costume of a lowcaste street boy, and Kim stored it in a secret place under some baulks in Nila Ram's timber-yard, beyond the Punjab High Court, where the fragrant deodar logs lie seasoning after they have driven down the Ravi. When there was business or frolic afoot, Kim would use his properties, returning at dawn to the veranda, all tired out from shouting at the heels of a marriage procession, or yelling at a Hindu festival. Sometimes there was food in the house, more often there was not, and then Kim went out again to eat with his native friends.

As he drummed his heels against Zam-Zammah he turned now and again from his king-of-the-castle game with little Chota Lal and Abdullah the sweetmeat-seller's son, to make a rude remark to the native policeman on guard over rows of shoes at the

Museum door. The big Punjabi grinned tolerantly: he knew Kim of old. So did the water-carrier, sluicing water on the dry road from his goat-skin bag. So did Jawahir Singh, the Museum carpenter, bent over new packing-cases. So did everybody in sight except the peasants from the country, hurrying up to the Wonder House to view the things that men made in their own province and elsewhere. The Museum was given up to Indian arts and manufactures, and anybody who sought wisdom could ask the Curator to explain.

"Off! Off! Let me up!" cried Abdullah, climbing up Zam-Zammah's wheel.

"Thy father was a pastry-cook, Thy mother stole the ghi," sang Kim. "All Mussalmans fell off Zam-Zammah long ago!"

"Let me up!" shrilled little Chota Lal in his gilt-embroidered cap. His father was worth perhaps half a million sterling, but India is the only democratic land in the world.

"The Hindus fell off Zam-Zammah too. The Mussalmans pushed them off. Thy father was a pastry-cook –"

He stopped; for there shuffled round the corner, from the roaring Motee Bazar, such a man as Kim, who thought he knew all castes, had never seen. He was nearly six feet high, dressed in fold upon fold of dingy stuff like horse-blanketing, and not one fold of it could Kim refer to any known trade or profession. At his belt hung a long open-work iron pencase and a wooden rosary such as holy men wear. On his head was a gigantic sort of tam-o'-shanter. His face was yellow and wrinkled, like that of Fook Shing, the Chinese bootmaker in the bazar. His eyes turned up at the corners and looked like little slits of onyx.

"Who is that?" said Kim to his companions.

"Perhaps it is a man," said Abdullah, finger in mouth, staring.

"Without doubt," returned Kim; "but he is no man of India that I have ever seen."

"A priest, perhaps," said Chota Lal, spying the rosary. "See! He goes into the Wonder House!"

"Nay, nay," said the policeman, shaking his head. "I do not understand your talk." The constable spoke Punjabi. "O Friend of all the World, what does he say?"

"Send him hither," said Kim, dropping from Zam-Zammah, flourishing his bare heels. "He is a foreigner, and thou art a buffalo."

The man turned helplessly and drifted towards the boys. He was old, and his woollen gaberdine still reeked of the stinking artemisia of the mountain passes.

"O Children, what is that big house?" he said in very fair Urdu.

"The Ajaib-Gher, the Wonder House!" Kim gave him no title – such as Lala or Mian. He could not divine the man's creed.

"Ah! The Wonder House! Can any enter?"

"It is written above the door – all can enter."

"Without payment?"

"I go in and out. I am no banker," laughed Kim.

"Alas! I am an old man. I did not know." Then, fingering his rosary, he half turned to the Museum.

"What is your caste? Where is your house? Have you come far?" Kim asked.

"I came by Kulu – from beyond the Kailas – but what know you? From the Hills where" – he sighed – "the air and water are fresh and cool."

"Aha! Khitai [a Chinaman]," said Abdullah proudly. Fook Shing had once chased him out of his shop for spitting at the joss above the boots.

"Pahari [a hillman]," said little Chota Lal.

"Aye, child – a hillman from hills thou'lt never see. Didst hear of Bhotiyal [Tibet]? I am no Khitai, but a Bhotiya [Tibetan], since you must know – a lama – or, say, a guru in your tongue."

"A guru from Tibet," said Kim. "I have not seen such a man. They be Hindus in Tibet, then?"

"We be followers of the Middle Way, living in peace in our lamasseries, and I go to see the Four Holy Places before I die. Now do you, who are children, know as much as I do who am old." He smiled benignantly on the boys.

"Hast thou eaten?"

He fumbled in his bosom and drew forth a worn, wooden begging-bowl. The boys nodded. All priests of their acquaintance begged.

"I do not wish to eat yet." He turned his head like an old tortoise in the sunlight. "Is it true that there are many images in the Wonder House of Lahore?" He repeated the last words as one making sure of an address.

"That is true," said Abdullah. "It is full of heathen busts. Thou also art an idolater."

"Never mind him," said. Kim. "That is the Government's house and there is no idolatry in it, but only a Sahib with a white beard. Come with me and I will show."

"Strange priests eat boys," whispered Chota Lal.

"And he is a stranger and a but-parast [idolater]," said Abdullah, the Mohammedan.

Kim laughed. "He is new. Run to your mothers' laps, and be safe. Come!"

Kim clicked round the self-registering turnstile; the old man followed and halted amazed. In the entrance-hall stood the larger figures of the Greco-Buddhist sculptures done, savants know how long since, by forgotten workmen whose hands were feeling, and not unskilfully, for the mysteriously transmitted Grecian touch. There were hundreds of pieces, friezes of figures in relief, fragments of statues and slabs crowded with figures that had encrusted the brick walls of the Buddhist stupas and viharas of the North Country and now, dug up and labelled, made the pride of the Museum. In open-mouthed wonder the lama turned to this and that, and finally checked in rapt attention before a large alto-relief representing a coronation or apotheosis of the Lord Buddha. The Master was represented seated on a lotus the petals of which were so deeply undercut as to show almost detached. Round Him was an adoring hierarchy of kings, elders, and old-time Buddhas. Below were lotus-covered waters with fishes and water-birds. Two butterfly-winged devas held a wreath over His head; above them another pair supported an umbrella surmounted by the jewelled headdress of the Bodhisat.

"The Lord! The Lord! It is Sakya Muni himself," the lama half sobbed; and under his breath began the wonderful Buddhist invocation:

To Him the Way, the Law, apart, Whom Maya held beneath her heart, Ananda's Lord, the Bodhisat.

"And He is here! The Most Excellent Law is here also. My pilgrimage is well begun. And what work! What work!"

"Yonder is the Sahib," said Kim, and dodged sideways among the cases of the arts and manufacturers wing. A white-bearded Englishman was looking at the lama, who gravely turned and saluted him and after some fumbling drew forth a note-book and a scrap of paper.

"Yes, that is my name," smiling at the clumsy, childish print.

"One of us who had made pilgrimage to the Holy Places – he is now Abbot of the Lung-Cho Monastery – gave it me," stammered the lama. "He spoke of these." His lean hand moved tremulously round.

"Welcome, then, O lama from Tibet. Here be the images, and I am here" – he glanced at the lama's face – "to gather knowledge. Come to my office awhile." The old man was trembling with excitement.

The office was but a little wooden cubicle partitioned off from the sculpture-lined gallery. Kim laid himself down, his ear against a crack in the heat-split cedar door, and, following his instinct, stretched out to listen and watch.

Most of the talk was altogether above his head. The lama, haltingly at first, spoke to the Curator of his own lamassery, the Such-zen, opposite the Painted Rocks, four months' march away. The Curator brought out a huge book of photos and showed him that very place, perched on its crag, overlooking the gigantic valley of many-hued strata.

"Ay, ay!" The lama mounted a pair of horn-rimmed spectacles of Chinese work. "Here is the little door through which we bring wood before winter. And thou – the English know of these things? He who is now Abbot of Lung-Cho told me, but I did not believe. The Lord – the Excellent One – He has honour here too? And His life is known?"

"It is all carven upon the stones. Come and see, if thou art rested."

Out shuffled the lama to the main hall, and, the Curator beside him, went through the collection with the reverence of a devotee and the appreciative instinct of a craftsman.

Incident by incident in the beautiful story he identified on the blurred stone, puzzled here and there by the unfamiliar Greek convention, but delighted as a child at each new trove. Where the sequence failed, as in the Annunciation, the Curator supplied it from his mound of books – French and German, with photographs and reproductions.

Here was the devout Asita, the pendant of Simeon in the Christian story, holding the Holy Child on his knee while mother and father listened; and here were incidents in the legend of the cousin Devadatta. Here was the wicked woman who accused the Master of impurity, all confounded; here was the teaching in the Deer-park; the miracle that stunned the fire-worshippers; here was the Bodhisat in royal state as a prince; the miraculous birth; the death at Kusinagara, where the weak disciple fainted; while there were almost countless repetitions of the meditation under the Bodhi tree; and the adoration of the alms-bowl was everywhere. In a few minutes the Curator saw that his guest was no mere bead-telling mendicant, but a scholar of parts. And they went at it all over again, the lama taking snuff, wiping his spectacles, and talking at railway speed in a bewildering mixture of Urdu and Tibetan. He had heard of the travels of the Chinese pilgrims, Fu-Hiouen and Hwen-Tsiang, and was anxious to know if there was any translation of their record. He drew in his breath as he turned helplessly over the pages of Beal and Stanislas Julien. "'Tis all here. A treasure locked." Then he composed himself reverently to listen to fragments hastily rendered into Urdu. For the first time he heard of the labours of European scholars, who by the help of these and a hundred other documents have identified the Holy Places of Buddhism. Then he was shown a mighty map, spotted and traced with yellow. The brown finger followed the Curator's pencil from point to point. Here was Kapilavastu, here the Middle Kingdom, and here Mahabodhi, the Mecca of Buddhism; and here was Kusinagara, sad place of the Holy One's death. The old man bowed his head over the sheets in silence for a while, and the Curator lit another pipe. Kim had fallen asleep. When he waked, the talk, still in spate, was more within his comprehension.

"And thus it was, O Fountain of Wisdom, that I decided to go to the Holy Places which His foot had trod – to the Birthplace, even to Kapila; then to Mahabodhi, which is Buddh Gaya – to the Monastery – to the Deer-park – to the place of His death."

The lama lowered his voice. "And I come here alone. For five – seven – eighteen – forty years it was in my mind that the Old Law was not well followed; being overlaid, as thou knowest, with devildom, charms, and idolatry. Even as the child outside said but now. Ay, even as the child said, with but-parasti."

"So it comes with all faiths."

"Thinkest thou? The books of my lamassery I read, and they were dried pith; and the later ritual with which we of the Reformed Law have cumbered ourselves – that, too, had no worth to these old eyes. Even the followers of the Excellent One are at feud on feud with one another. It is all illusion. Ay, maya, illusion. But I have another desire" – the seamed yellow face drew within three inches of the Curator, and the long forefinger-nail tapped on the table. "Your scholars, by these books, have followed the Blessed Feet in all their wanderings; but there are things which they have not sought out. I know nothing – nothing do I know – but I go to free myself from the Wheel of Things by a broad and open road." He smiled with most simple triumph. "As a pilgrim to the Holy Places I acquire merit. But there is more. Listen to a true thing. When our gracious Lord, being as yet a youth, sought a mate, men said, in His father's Court, that He was too tender for marriage. Thou knowest?"

The Curator nodded, wondering what would come next.

"So they made the triple trial of strength against all comers. And at the test of the Bow, our Lord first breaking that which they gave Him, called for such a bow as none might bend. Thou knowest?"

"It is written. I have read."

"And, overshooting all other marks, the arrow passed far and far beyond sight. At the last it fell; and, where it touched earth, there broke out a stream which presently became a River, whose nature, by our Lord's beneficence, and that merit He acquired ere He freed himself, is that whoso bathes in it washes away all taint and speckle of sin."

"So it is written," said the Curator sadly.

The lama drew a long breath. "Where is that River? Fountain of Wisdom, where fell the arrow?"

"Alas, my brother, I do not know," said the Curator.

"Nay, if it please thee to forget – the one thing only that thou hast not told me. Surely thou must know? See, I am an old man! I ask with my head between thy feet, O Fountain of Wisdom. We know He drew the bow! We know the arrow fell! We know the stream gushed! Where, then, is the River? My dream told me to find it. So I came. I am here. But where is the River?"

"If I knew, think you I would not cry it aloud?"

"By it one attains freedom from the Wheel of Things," the lama went on, unheeding. "The River of the Arrow! Think again! Some little stream, maybe – dried in the heats? But the Holy One would never so cheat an old man."

"I do not know. I do not know."

The lama brought his thousand-wrinkled face once more a handsbreadth from the Englishman's. "I see thou dost not know. Not being of the Law, the matter is hid from thee."

"Ay – hidden – hidden."

"We are both bound, thou and I, my brother. But I" – he rose with a sweep of the soft thick drapery – "I go to cut myself free. Come also!"

"I am bound," said the Curator. "But whither goest thou?"

"First to Kashi [Benares]: where else? There I shall meet one of the pure faith in a Jain temple of that city. He also is a Seeker in secret, and from him haply I may learn. Maybe he will go with me to Buddh Gaya. Thence north and west to Kapilavastu, and there will I seek for the River. Nay, I will seek everywhere as I go – for the place is not known where the arrow fell."

"And how wilt thou go? It is a far cry to Delhi, and farther to Benares."

"By road and the trains. From Pathankot, having left the Hills, I came hither in a te-rain. It goes swiftly. At first I was amazed to see those tall poles by the side of the road snatching up and snatching up their threads," – he illustrated the stoop and whirl of a telegraph-pole flashing past the train. "But later, I was cramped and desired to walk, as I am used."

"And thou art sure of thy road?" said the Curator.

"Oh, for that one but asks a question and pays money, and the appointed persons despatch all to the appointed place. That much I knew in my lamassery from sure report," said the lama proudly.

"And when dost thou go?" The Curator smiled at the mixture of old-world piety and modern progress that is the note of India today.

"As soon as may be. I follow the places of His life till I come to the River of the Arrow. There is, moreover, a written paper of the hours of the trains that go south."

"And for food?" Lamas, as a rule, have good store of money somewhere about them, but the Curator wished to make sure.

"For the journey, I take up the Master's begging-bowl. Yes. Even as He went so go I, forsaking the ease of my monastery. There was with me when I left the hills a chela [disciple] who begged for me as the Rule demands, but halting in Kulu awhile a fever took him and he died. I have now no chela, but I will take the alms-bowl and thus enable the charitable to acquire merit." He nodded his head valiantly. Learned doctors of a lamassery do not beg, but the lama was an enthusiast in this quest.

"Be it so," said the Curator, smiling. "Suffer me now to acquire merit. We be craftsmen together, thou and I. Here is a new book of white English paper: here be sharpened pencils two and three – thick and thin, all good for a scribe. Now lend me thy spectacles."

The Curator looked through them. They were heavily scratched, but the power was almost exactly that of his own pair, which he slid into the lama's hand, saying: "Try these."

"A feather! A very feather upon the face." The old man turned his head delightedly and wrinkled up his nose. "How scarcely do I feel them! How clearly do I see!"

"They be bilaur – crystal – and will never scratch. May they help thee to thy River, for they are thine."

"I will take them and the pencils and the white note-book," said the lama, "as a sign of friendship between priest and priest – and now –" He fumbled at his belt, detached the open-work iron pincers, and laid it on the Curator's table. "That is for a memory between thee and me – my pencase. It is something old – even as I am."

It was a piece of ancient design, Chinese, of an iron that is not smelted these days; and the collector's heart in the Curator's bosom had gone out to it from the first. For no persuasion would the lama resume his gift.

"When I return, having found the River, I will bring thee a written picture of the Padma Samthora such as I used to make on silk at the lamassery. Yes – and of the Wheel of Life," he chuckled, "for we be craftsmen together, thou and I."

The Curator would have detained him: they are few in the world who still have the secret of the conventional brush-pen Buddhist pictures which are, as it were, half written and half drawn. But the lama strode out, head high in air, and pausing an instant before the great statue of a Bodhisat in meditation, brushed through the turnstiles.

Kim followed like a shadow. What he had overheard excited him wildly. This man was entirely new to all his experience, and he meant to investigate further, precisely as he would have investigated a new building or a strange festival in Lahore city. The lama was his trove, and he purposed to take possession. Kim's mother had been Irish, too.

The old man halted by Zam-Zammah and looked round till his eye fell on Kim. The inspiration of his pilgrimage had left him for awhile, and he felt old, forlorn, and very empty.

"Do not sit under that gun," said the policeman loftily.

"Huh! Owl!" was Kim's retort on the lama's behalf. "Sit under that gun if it please thee. When didst thou steal the milkwoman's slippers, Dunnoo?"

That was an utterly unfounded charge sprung on the spur of the moment, but it silenced Dunnoo, who knew that Kim's clear yell could call up legions of bad bazaar boys if need arose.

"And whom didst thou worship within?" said Kim affably, squatting in the shade beside the lama.

"I worshipped none, child. I bowed before the Excellent Law."

Kim accepted this new God without emotion. He knew already a few score.

"And what dost thou do?"

"I beg. I remember now it is long since I have eaten or drunk. What is the custom of charity in this town? In silence, as we do of Tibet, or speaking aloud?"

"Those who beg in silence starve in silence," said Kim, quoting a native proverb. The lama tried to rise, but sank back again, sighing for his disciple, dead in far-away Kulu. Kim watched head to one side, considering and interested.

"Give me the bowl. I know the people of this city – all who are charitable. Give, and I will bring it back filled."

Simply as a child the old man handed him the bowl.

"Rest, thou. I know the people."

He trotted off to the open shop of a kunjri, a low-caste vegetable-seller, which lay opposite the belt-tramway line down the Motee Bazar. She knew Kim of old.

"Oho, hast thou turned yogi with thy begging-bowl?" she cried.

"Nay," said Kim proudly. "There is a new priest in the city – a man such as I have never seen."

"Old priest – young tiger," said the woman angrily. "I am tired of new priests! They settle on our wares like flies. Is the father of my son a well of charity to give to all who ask?"

"No," said Kim. "Thy man is rather yagi [bad-tempered] than yogi [a holy man]. But this priest is new. The Sahib in the Wonder House has talked to him like a brother. O my mother, fill me this bowl. He waits."

"That bowl indeed! That cow-bellied basket! Thou hast as much grace as the holy bull of Shiv. He has taken the best of a basket of onions already, this morn; and forsooth, I must fill thy bowl. He comes here again."

The huge, mouse-coloured Brahmini bull of the ward was shouldering his way through the many-coloured crowd, a stolen plantain hanging out of his mouth. He headed straight for the shop, well knowing his privileges as a sacred beast, lowered his head, and puffed heavily along the line of baskets ere making his choice. Up flew Kim's hard little heel and caught him on his moist blue nose. He snorted indignantly, and walked away across the tram-rails, his hump quivering with rage.

"See! I have saved more than the bowl will cost thrice over. Now, mother, a little rice and some dried fish atop – yes, and some vegetable curry."

A growl came out of the back of the shop, where a man lay.

"He drove away the bull," said the woman in an undertone. "It is good to give to the poor." She took the bowl and returned it full of hot rice.

"But my yogi is not a cow," said Kim gravely, making a hole with his fingers in the top of the mound. "A little curry is good, and a fried cake, and a morsel of conserve would please him, I think."

"It is a hole as big as thy head," said the woman fretfully. But she filled it, none the less, with good, steaming vegetable curry, clapped a fried cake atop, and a morsel of clarified butter on the cake, dabbed a lump of sour tamarind conserve at the side; and Kim looked at the load lovingly.

"That is good. When I am in the bazar the bull shall not come to this house. He is a bold beggar-man."

"And thou?" laughed the woman. "But speak well of bulls. Hast thou not told me that some day a Red Bull will come out of a field to help thee? Now hold all straight and ask for the holy man's blessing upon me. Perhaps, too, he knows a cure for my daughter's sore eyes. Ask him that also, O thou Little Friend of all the World."

But Kim had danced off ere the end of the sentence, dodging pariah dogs and hungry acquaintances.

"Thus do we beg who know the way of it," said he proudly to the lama, who opened his eyes at the contents of the bowl. "Eat now and – I will eat with thee. Ohe, bhisti!" he called to the water-carrier, sluicing the crotons by the Museum. "Give water here. We men are thirsty."

"We men!" said the bhisti, laughing. "Is one skinful enough for such a pair? Drink, then, in the name of the Compassionate."

He loosed a thin stream into Kim's hands, who drank native fashion; but the lama must needs pull out a cup from his inexhaustible upper draperies and drink ceremonially.

"Pardesi [a foreigner]," Kim explained, as the old man delivered in an unknown tongue what was evidently a blessing.

They ate together in great content, clearing the begging bowl. Then the lama took snuff from a portentous wooden snuff-gourd, fingered his rosary awhile, and so dropped into the easy sleep of age, as the shadow of Zam-Zammah grew long.

Kim loafed over to the nearest tobacco-seller, a rather lively young Mohammedan woman, and begged a rank cigar of the brand that they sell to students of the Punjab University who copy English customs. Then he smoked and thought, knees to chin, under the belly of the gun, and the outcome of his thoughts was a sudden and stealthy departure in the direction of Nila Ram's timber-yard.

The lama did not wake till the evening life of the city had begun with lamp-lighting and the return of white-robed clerks and subordinates from the Government offices. He stared dizzily in all directions, but none looked at him save a Hindu urchin in a dirty turban and Isabella-coloured clothes. Suddenly he bowed his head on his knees and wailed.

"What is this?" said the boy, standing before him. "Hast thou been robbed?"

"It is my new chela [disciple] that is gone away from me, and I know not where he is."

"And what like of man was thy disciple?"

"It was a boy who came to me in place of him who died, on account of the merit which I had gained when I bowed before the Law within there." He pointed towards the Museum. "He came upon me to show me a road which I had lost. He led me into the Wonder House, and by his talk emboldened me to speak to the Keeper of the Images, so that I was cheered and made strong. And when I was faint with hunger he begged for me, as would a chela for his teacher. Suddenly was he sent. Suddenly has he gone away. It was in my mind to have taught him the Law upon the road to Benares."

Kim stood amazed at this, because he had overheard the talk in the Museum, and knew that the old man was speaking the truth, which is a thing a native on the road seldom presents to a stranger.

"But I see now that he was but sent for a purpose. By this I know that I shall find a certain River for which I seek."

"The River of the Arrow?" said Kim, with a superior smile.

"Is this yet another Sending?" cried the lama. "To none have I spoken of my search, save to the Priest of the Images. Who art thou?"

"Thy chela," said Kim simply, sitting on his heels. "I have never seen anyone like to thee in all this my life. I go with thee to Benares. And, too, I think that so old a man as thou, speaking the truth to chance-met people at dusk, is in great need of a disciple."

"But the River – the River of the Arrow?"

"Oh, that I heard when thou wast speaking to the Englishman. I lay against the door."

The lama sighed. "I thought thou hadst been a guide permitted. Such things fall sometimes – but I am not worthy. Thou dost not, then, know the River?"

"Not I," Kim laughed uneasily. "I go to look for – for a bull – a Red Bull on a green field who shall help me." Boylike, if an acquaintance had a scheme, Kim was quite ready with one of his own; and, boylike, he had really thought for as much as twenty minutes at a time of his father's prophecy.

"To what, child?" said the lama.

"God knows, but so my father told me. I heard thy talk in the Wonder House of all those new strange places in the Hills, and if one so old and so little – so used to truth-telling – may go out for the small matter of a river, it seemed to me that I too must go a-travelling. If it is our fate to find those things we shall find them – thou, thy River; and I, my Bull, and the Strong Pillars and some other matters that I forget."

"It is not pillars but a Wheel from which I would be free," said the lama.

"That is all one. Perhaps they will make me a king," said Kim, serenely prepared for anything.

"I will teach thee other and better desires upon the road," the lama replied in the voice of authority. "Let us go to Benares."

"Not by night. Thieves are abroad. Wait till the day."

"But there is no place to sleep." The old man was used to the order of his monastery, and though he slept on the ground, as the Rule decrees, preferred a decency in these things.

"We shall get good lodging at the Kashmir Serai," said Kim, laughing at his perplexity. "I have a friend there. Come!"

The hot and crowded bazars blazed with light as they made their way through the press of all the races in Upper India, and the lama mooned through it like a man in a dream. It was his first experience of a large manufacturing city, and the crowded tram-car with its continually squealing brakes frightened him. Half pushed, half towed, he arrived at the high gate of the Kashmir Serai: that huge open square over against the railway station, surrounded with arched cloisters, where the camel and horse caravans put up on their return from Central Asia. Here were all manner of Northern folk, tending tethered ponies and kneeling camels; loading and unloading bales and bundles; drawing water for the evening meal at the creaking well-windlasses; piling grass before the shrieking, wild-eyed stallions; cuffing the surly caravan dogs; paying off camel-drivers; taking on new grooms; swearing, shouting, arguing, and chaffering in the packed square. The cloisters, reached by three or four masonry steps, made a haven of refuge around this turbulent sea. Most of them were rented to traders, as we rent the arches of a viaduct; the space between pillar and pillar being bricked or boarded off into rooms, which were guarded by heavy wooden doors and cumbrous native padlocks. Locked doors showed that the owner was away, and a few rude – sometimes very rude – chalk or paint scratches told where he had gone. Thus: 'Lutuf Ullah is gone to Kurdistan.' Below, in coarse verse: 'O Allah, who sufferest lice to live on the coat of a Kabuli, why hast thou allowed this louse Lutuf to live so long?'

Kim, fending the lama between excited men and excited beasts, sidled along the cloisters to the far end, nearest the railway station, where Mahbub Ali, the horse-trader, lived when he came in from that mysterious land beyond the Passes of the North.

Kim had had many dealings with Mahbub in his little life, especially between his tenth and his thirteenth year – and the big burly Afghan, his beard dyed scarlet with lime (for he was elderly and did not wish his grey hairs to show), knew the boy's value as a gossip. Sometimes he would tell Kim to watch a man who had nothing whatever to do with horses: to follow him for one whole day and report every soul with whom he talked. Kim would deliver himself of his tale at evening, and Mahbub would listen without a word or gesture. It was intrigue of some kind, Kim knew; but its worth lay in saying nothing whatever to anyone except Mahbub, who gave him beautiful meals all hot from the cookshop at the head of the serai, and once as much as eight annas in money.

"He is here," said Kim, hitting a bad-tempered camel on the nose. "Ohe. Mahbub Ali!" He halted at a dark arch and slipped behind the bewildered lama.

The horse-trader, his deep, embroidered Bokhariot belt unloosed, was lying on a pair of silk carpet saddle-bags, pulling lazily at an immense silver hookah. He turned his head very slightly at the cry; and seeing only the tall silent figure, chuckled in his deep chest.

"Allah! A lama! A Red Lama! It is far from Lahore to the Passes. What dost thou do here?"

The lama held out the begging-bowl mechanically.

"God's curse on all unbelievers!" said Mahbub. "I do not give to a lousy Tibetan; but ask my Baltis over yonder behind the camels. They may value your blessings. Oh, horseboys, here is a countryman of yours. See if he be hungry."

A shaven, crouching Balti, who had come down with the horses, and who was nominally some sort of degraded Buddhist, fawned upon the priest, and in thick gutturals besought the Holy One to sit at the horseboys' fire.

"Go!" said Kim, pushing him lightly, and the lama strode away, leaving Kim at the edge of the cloister.

"Go!" said Mahbub Ali, returning to his hookah. "Little Hindu, run away. God's curse on all unbelievers! Beg from those of my tail who are of thy faith."

"Maharaj," whined Kim, using the Hindu form of address, and thoroughly enjoying the situation; "my father is dead – my mother is dead – my stomach is empty."

"Beg from my men among the horses, I say. There must be some Hindus in my tail."

"Oh, Mahbub Ali, but am I a Hindu?" said Kim in English.

The trader gave no sign of astonishment, but looked under shaggy eyebrows.

"Little Friend of all the World," said he, "what is this?"

"Nothing. I am now that holy man's disciple; and we go a pilgrimage together – to Benares, he says. He is quite mad, and I am tired of Lahore city. I wish new air and water."

"But for whom dost thou work? Why come to me?" The voice was harsh with suspicion.

"To whom else should I come? I have no money. It is not good to go about without money. Thou wilt sell many horses to the officers. They are very fine horses, these new ones: I have seen them. Give me a rupee, Mahbub Ali, and when I come to my wealth I will give thee a bond and pay."

"Um!" said Mahbub Ali, thinking swiftly. "Thou hast never before lied to me. Call that lama – stand back in the dark."

"Oh, our tales will agree," said Kim, laughing.

"We go to Benares," said the lama, as soon as he understood the drift of Mahbub Ali's questions. "The boy and I, I go to seek for a certain River."

"Maybe – but the boy?"

"He is my disciple. He was sent, I think, to guide me to that River. Sitting under a gun was I when he came suddenly. Such things have befallen the fortunate to whom guidance was allowed. But I remember now, he said he was of this world – a Hindu."

"And his name?"

"That I did not ask. Is he not my disciple?"

"His country – his race – his village? Mussalman – Sikh Hindu – Jain – low caste or high?"

"Why should I ask? There is neither high nor low in the Middle Way. If he is my chela – does – will – can anyone take him from me? For, look you, without him I shall not find my River." He wagged his head solemnly.

"None shall take him from thee. Go, sit among my Baltis," said Mahbub Ali, and the lama drifted off, soothed by the promise.

"Is he not quite mad?" said Kim, coming forward to the light again. "Why should I lie to thee, Hajji?"

Mahbub puffed his hookah in silence. Then he began, almost whispering: "Umballa is on the road to Benares – if indeed ye two go there."

"Tck! Tck! I tell thee he does not know how to lie – as we two know."

"And if thou wilt carry a message for me as far as Umballa, I will give thee money. It concerns a horse – a white stallion which I have sold to an officer upon the last time I returned from the Passes. But then – stand nearer and hold up hands as begging – the pedigree of the white stallion was not fully established, and that officer, who is now at Umballa, bade me make it clear." (Mahbub here described the horse and the appearance of the officer.) "So the message to that officer will be: 'The pedigree of the white stallion is fully established.' By this will he know that thou comest from me. He will then say 'What proof hast thou?' and thou wilt answer: 'Mahbub Ali has given me the proof.'"

"And all for the sake of a white stallion," said Kim, with a giggle, his eyes aflame.

"That pedigree I will give thee now – in my own fashion and some hard words as well." A shadow passed behind Kim, and a feeding camel. Mahbub Ali raised his voice.

"Allah! Art thou the only beggar in the city? Thy mother is dead. Thy father is dead. So is it with all of them. Well, well –"

He turned as feeling on the floor beside him and tossed a flap of soft, greasy Mussalman bread to the boy. "Go and lie down among my horseboys for tonight – thou and the lama. Tomorrow I may give thee service."

Kim slunk away, his teeth in the bread, and, as he expected, he found a small wad of folded tissue-paper wrapped in oilskin, with three silver rupees – enormous largesse. He smiled and thrust money and paper into his leather amulet-case. The lama, sumptuously fed by Mahbub's Baltis, was already asleep in a corner of one of the stalls. Kim lay down beside him and laughed. He knew he had rendered a service to Mahbub Ali, and not for one little minute did he believe the tale of the stallion's pedigree.

But Kim did not suspect that Mahbub Ali, known as one of the best horse-dealers in the Punjab, a wealthy and enterprising trader, whose caravans penetrated far and far into the Back of Beyond, was registered in one of the locked books of the Indian Survey Department as C25 IB. Twice or thrice yearly C25 would send in a little story, baldly told but most interesting, and generally – it was checked by the statements of R17 and M4 – quite true. It concerned all manner of out-of-the-way mountain principalities, explorers of nationalities other than English, and the guntrade – was, in brief, a small portion of that vast mass of 'information received' on which the Indian Government acts. But, recently, five confederated Kings, who had no business to confederate, had been informed by a kindly Northern Power that there was a leakage of news from their territories into British India. So those Kings' Prime Ministers were seriously annoyed and took steps, after the Oriental fashion. They suspected, among many others, the bullying, red-bearded horsedealer whose caravans ploughed through their fastnesses belly-deep in snow. At least, his caravan that season had been ambushed and shot at twice on the way down, when Mahbub's men accounted for three strange ruffians who might, or might not, have been hired for the job. Therefore Mahbub had avoided halting at the insalubrious city of Peshawur, and had come through without stop to Lahore, where, knowing his country-people, he anticipated curious developments.

And there was that on Mahbub Ali which he did not wish to keep an hour longer than was necessary – a wad of closely folded tissue-paper, wrapped in oilskin – an impersonal, unaddressed statement, with five microscopic pin-holes in one corner, that most scandalously betrayed the five confederated Kings, the sympathetic Northern Power, a Hindu banker in Peshawur, a firm of gun-makers in Belgium, and an important, semi-independent Mohammedan ruler to the south. This last was R17's work, which Mahbub had picked up beyond the Dora Pass and was carrying in for R17, who, owing to circumstances over which he had no control, could not leave his post of observation. Dynamite was milky and innocuous beside that report of C25; and even an Oriental, with an Oriental's views of the value of time, could see that the sooner it was in the proper hands the better. Mahbub had no particular desire to die by violence, because two or three family blood-feuds across the Border hung unfinished on his hands, and when these scores were cleared he intended to settle down as a more or less virtuous citizen. He had never passed the serai gate since his arrival two days ago, but had been ostentatious in sending telegrams to Bombay, where he banked some of his money; to Delhi, where a sub-partner of his own clan was selling horses to the agent of a Rajputana state; and to Umballa, where an Englishman was excitedly demanding the pedigree of a white stallion. The public letter-writer, who knew English, composed excellent telegrams, such as: 'Creighton, Laurel Bank, Umballa. Horse is Arabian as already advised. Sorrowful delayed pedigree which am translating.' And later to the same address: 'Much sorrowful delay. Will forward pedigree.' To his sub-partner at Delhi he wired: 'Lutuf Ullah. Have wired two thousand rupees your credit Luchman Narain's bank –' This was entirely in the way of trade, but every one of those telegrams was discussed and rediscussed, by parties who conceived themselves to be interested, before they went over to the railway station in charge of a foolish Balti, who allowed all sorts of people to read them on the road.

When, in Mahbub's own picturesque language, he had muddied the wells of inquiry with the stick of precaution, Kim had dropped on him, sent from Heaven; and, being as prompt as he was unscrupulous, Mahbub Ali used to taking all sorts of gusty chances, pressed him into service on the spot.

A wandering lama with a low-caste boy-servant might attract a moment's interest as they wandered about India, the land of pilgrims; but no one would suspect them or, what was more to the point, rob.

He called for a new light-ball to his hookah, and considered the case. If the worst came to the worst, and the boy came to harm, the paper would incriminate nobody. And he would go up to Umballa leisurely and – at a certain risk of exciting fresh suspicion – repeat his tale by word of mouth to the people concerned.

But R17's report was the kernel of the whole affair, and it would be distinctly inconvenient if that failed to come to hand. However, God was great, and Mahbub Ali felt he had done all he could for the time being. Kim was the one soul in the world who had never told him a lie. That would have been a fatal blot on Kim's character if Mahbub had not known that to others, for his own ends or Mahbub's business, Kim could lie like an Oriental.

Then Mahbub Ali rolled across the serai to the Gate of the Harpies who paint their eyes and trap the stranger, and was at some pains to call on the one girl who, he had reason to believe, was a particular friend of a smooth-faced Kashmiri pundit who had waylaid his simple Balti in the matter of the telegrams. It was an utterly foolish thing to do; because they fell to drinking perfumed brandy against the Law of the Prophet, and Mahbub grew wonderfully drunk, and the gates of his mouth were loosened, and he pursued the Flower of Delight with the feet of intoxication till he fell flat among the cushions, where the Flower of Delight, aided by a smooth-faced Kashmiri pundit, searched him from head to foot most thoroughly.

About the same hour Kim heard soft feet in Mahbub's deserted stall. The horse-trader, curiously enough, had left his door unlocked, and his men were busy celebrating their return to India with a whole sheep of Mahbub's bounty. A sleek young gentleman from Delhi, armed with a bunch of keys which the Flower had unshackled from the senseless one's belt, went through every single box, bundle, mat, and saddle-bag in Mahbub's possession even more systematically than the Flower and the pundit were searching the owner.

"And I think," said the Flower scornfully an hour later, one rounded elbow on the snoring carcass, "that he is no more than a pig of an Afghan horse-dealer, with no thought except women and horses. Moreover, he may have sent it away by now – if ever there were such a thing."

"Nay – in a matter touching Five Kings it would be next his black heart," said the pundit. "Was there nothing?"

The Delhi man laughed and resettled his turban as he entered. "I searched between the soles of his slippers as the Flower searched his clothes. This is not the man but another. I leave little unseen."

"They did not say he was the very man," said the pundit thoughtfully. "They said, 'Look if he be the man, since our counsels are troubled.'"

"That North country is full of horse-dealers as an old coat of lice. There is Sikandar Khan, Nur Ali Beg, and Farrukh Shah all heads of kafilas [caravans] – who deal there," said the Flower.

"They have not yet come in," said the pundit. "Thou must ensnare them later."

"Phew!" said the Flower with deep disgust, rolling Mahbub's head from her lap. "I earn my money. Farrukh Shah is a bear, Ali Beg a swashbuckler, and old Sikandar Khan – yaie! Go! I sleep now. This swine will not stir till dawn."

When Mahbub woke, the Flower talked to him severely on the sin of drunkenness. Asiatics do not wink when they have outmanoeuvred an enemy, but as Mahbub Ali cleared his throat, tightened his belt, and staggered forth under the early morning stars, he came very near to it.

"What a colt's trick!" said he to himself. "As if every girl in Peshawur did not use it! But 'twas prettily done. Now God He knows how many more there be upon the Road who have orders to test me – perhaps with the knife. So it stands that the boy must go to Umballa – and by rail – for the writing is something urgent. I abide here, following the Flower and drinking wine as an Afghan coper should."

He halted at the stall next but one to his own. His men lay there heavy with sleep. There was no sign of Kim or the lama.

"Up!" He stirred a sleeper. "Whither went those who lay here last even – the lama and the boy? Is aught missing?"

"Nay," grunted the man, "the old madman rose at second cockcrow saying he would go to Benares, and the young one led him away."

"The curse of Allah on all unbelievers!" said Mahbub heartily, and climbed into his own stall, growling in his beard.

But it was Kim who had wakened the lama – Kim with one eye laid against a knot-hole in the planking, who had seen the Delhi man's search through the boxes. This was no common thief that turned over letters, bills, and saddles – no mere burglar who ran a little knife sideways into the soles of Mahbub's slippers, or picked the seams of the saddle-bags so deftly. At first Kim had been minded to give the alarm – the long-drawn choor – choor! [thief! thief!] that sets the serai ablaze of nights; but he looked more carefully, and, hand on amulet, drew his own conclusions.

"It must be the pedigree of that made-up horse-lie," said he, "the thing that I carry to Umballa. Better that we go now. Those who search bags with knives may presently search bellies with knives. Surely there is a woman behind this. Hai! Hai!" In a whisper to the light-sleeping old man, "Come. It is time – time to go to Benares."

The lama rose obediently, and they passed out of the serai like shadows.

Chapter II

And whoso will, from Pride released;
Contemning neither creed nor priest,
May feel the Soul of all the East.
About him at Kamakura.
Buddha at Kamakura

THEY ENTERED the fort-like railway station, black in the end of night; the electrics sizzling over the goods-yard where they handle the heavy Northern grain-traffic.

"This is the work of devils!" said the lama, recoiling from the hollow echoing darkness, the glimmer of rails between the masonry platforms, and the maze of girders above. He stood in a gigantic stone hall paved, it seemed, with the sheeted dead third-class passengers who had taken their tickets overnight and were sleeping in the waiting-rooms. All hours of the twenty-four are alike to Orientals, and their passenger traffic is regulated accordingly.

"This is where the fire-carriages come. One stands behind that hole" – Kim pointed to the ticket-office – "who will give thee a paper to take thee to Umballa."

"But we go to Benares," he replied petulantly.

"All one. Benares then. Quick: she comes!"

"Take thou the purse."

The lama, not so well used to trains as he had pretended, started as the 3.25 a.m. south-bound roared in. The sleepers sprang to life, and the station filled with clamour and shoutings, cries of water and sweetmeat vendors, shouts of native policemen, and shrill yells of women gathering up their baskets, their families, and their husbands.

"It is the train – only the te-rain. It will not come here. Wait!" Amazed at the lama's immense simplicity (he had handed him a small bag full of rupees), Kim asked and paid for a ticket to Umballa. A sleepy clerk grunted and flung out a ticket to the next station, just six miles distant.

"Nay," said Kim, scanning it with a grin. "This may serve for farmers, but I live in the city of Lahore. It was cleverly done, Babu. Now give the ticket to Umballa."

The Babu scowled and dealt the proper ticket.

"Now another to Amritzar," said Kim, who had no notion of spending Mahbub Ali's money on anything so crude as a paid ride to Umballa. "The price is so much. The small money in return is just so much. I know the ways of the te-rain.... Never did yogi need chela as thou dost," he went on merrily to the bewildered lama. "They would have flung thee out at Mian Mir but for me. This way! Come!" He returned the money, keeping only one anna in each rupee of the price of the Umballa ticket as his commission – the immemorial commission of Asia.

The lama jibbed at the open door of a crowded third-class carriage. "Were it not better to walk?" said he weakly.

A burly Sikh artisan thrust forth his bearded head. "Is he afraid? Do not be afraid. I remember the time when I was afraid of the te-rain. Enter! This thing is the work of the Government."

"I do not fear," said the lama. "Have ye room within for two?"

"There is no room even for a mouse," shrilled the wife of a well-to-do cultivator – a Hindu Jat from the rich Jullundur, district. Our night trains are not as well looked after as the day ones, where the sexes are very strictly kept to separate carriages.

"Oh, mother of my son, we can make space," said the blueturbaned husband. "Pick up the child. It is a holy man, see'st thou?"

"And my lap full of seventy times seven bundles! Why not bid him sit on my knee, Shameless? But men are ever thus!" She looked round for approval. An Amritzar courtesan near the window sniffed behind her head drapery.

"Enter! Enter!" cried a fat Hindu money-lender, his folded account-book in a cloth under his arm. With an oily smirk: "It is well to be kind to the poor."

"Ay, at seven per cent a month with a mortgage on the unborn calf," said a young Dogra soldier going south on leave; and they all laughed.

"Will it travel to Benares?" said the lama.

"Assuredly. Else why should we come? Enter, or we are left," cried Kim.

"See!" shrilled the Amritzar girl. "He has never entered a train. Oh, see!"

"Nay, help," said the cultivator, putting out a large brown hand and hauling him in. "Thus is it done, father."

"But – but – I sit on the floor. It is against the Rule to sit on a bench," said the lama. "Moreover, it cramps me."

"I say," began the money-lender, pursing his lips, "that there is not one rule of right living which these te-rains do not cause us to break. We sit, for example, side by side with all castes and peoples."

"Yea, and with most outrageously shameless ones," said the wife, scowling at the Amritzar girl making eyes at the young sepoy.

"I said we might have gone by cart along the road," said the husband, "and thus have saved some money."

"Yes – and spent twice over what we saved on food by the way. That was talked out ten thousand times."

"Ay, by ten thousand tongues," grunted he.

"The Gods help us poor women if we may not speak. Oho! He is of that sort which may not look at or reply to a woman." For the lama, constrained by his Rule, took not the faintest notice of her. "And his disciple is like him?"

"Nay, mother," said Kim most promptly. "Not when the woman is well-looking and above all charitable to the hungry."

"A beggar's answer," said the Sikh, laughing. "Thou hast brought it on thyself, sister!" Kim's hands were crooked in supplication.

"And whither goest thou?" said the woman, handing him the half of a cake from a greasy package.

"Even to Benares."

"Jugglers belike?" the young soldier suggested. "Have ye any tricks to pass the time? Why does not that yellow man answer?"

"Because," said Kim stoutly, "he is holy, and thinks upon matters hidden from thee."

"That may be well. We of the Ludhiana Sikhs" – he rolled it out sonorously – "do not trouble our heads with doctrine. We fight."

"My sister's brother's son is naik [corporal] in that regiment," said the Sikh craftsman quietly. "There are also some Dogra companies there." The soldier glared, for a Dogra is of other caste than a Sikh, and the banker tittered.

"They are all one to me," said the Amritzar girl.

"That we believe," snorted the cultivator's wife malignantly.

"Nay, but all who serve the Sirkar with weapons in their hands are, as it were, one brotherhood. There is one brotherhood of the caste, but beyond that again" – she looked round timidly – "the bond of the Pulton – the Regiment – eh?"

"My brother is in a Jat regiment," said the cultivator. "Dogras be good men."

"Thy Sikhs at least were of that opinion," said the soldier, with a scowl at the placid old man in the corner. "Thy Sikhs thought so when our two companies came to help them at the Pirzai Kotal in the face of eight Afridi standards on the ridge not three months gone."

He told the story of a Border action in which the Dogra companies of the Ludhiana Sikhs had acquitted themselves well. The Amritzar girl smiled; for she knew the talk was to win her approval.

"Alas!" said the cultivator's wife at the end. "So their villages were burnt and their little children made homeless?"

"They had marked our dead. They paid a great payment after we of the Sikhs had schooled them. So it was. Is this Amritzar?"

"Ay, and here they cut our tickets," said the banker, fumbling at his belt.

The lamps were paling in the dawn when the half-caste guard came round. Ticket-collecting is a slow business in the East, where people secrete their tickets in all sorts of curious places. Kim produced his and was told to get out.

"But I go to Umballa," he protested. "I go with this holy man."

"Thou canst go to Jehannum for aught I care. This ticket is only –"

Kim burst into a flood of tears, protesting that the lama was his father and his mother, that he was the prop of the lama's declining years, and that the lama would die without his care. All the carriage bade the guard be merciful – the banker was specially eloquent here – but the guard hauled Kim on to the platform. The lama blinked – he could not overtake the situation and Kim lifted up his voice and wept outside the carriage window.

"I am very poor. My father is dead – my mother is dead. O charitable ones, if I am left here, who shall tend that old man?"

"What – what is this?" the lama repeated. "He must go to Benares. He must come with me. He is my chela. If there is money to be paid –"

"Oh, be silent," whispered Kim; "are we Rajahs to throw away good silver when the world is so charitable?"

The Amritzar girl stepped out with her bundles, and it was on her that Kim kept his watchful eye. Ladies of that persuasion, he knew, were generous.

"A ticket – a little tikkut to Umballa – O Breaker of Hearts!" She laughed. "Hast thou no charity?"

"Does the holy man come from the North?"

"From far and far in the North he comes," cried Kim. "From among the hills."

"There is snow among the pine-trees in the North – in the hills there is snow. My mother was from Kulu. Get thee a ticket. Ask him for a blessing."

"Ten thousand blessings," shrilled Kim. "O Holy One, a woman has given us in charity so that I can come with thee – a woman with a golden heart. I run for the tikkut."

The girl looked up at the lama, who had mechanically followed Kim to the platform. He bowed his head that he might not see her, and muttered in Tibetan as she passed on with the crowd.

"Light come – light go," said the cultivator's wife viciously.

"She has acquired merit," returned the lama. "Beyond doubt it was a nun."

"There be ten thousand such nuns in Amritzar alone. Return, old man, or the te-rain may depart without thee," cried the banker.

"Not only was it sufficient for the ticket, but for a little food also," said Kim, leaping to his place. "Now eat, Holy One. Look. Day comes!"

Golden, rose, saffron, and pink, the morning mists smoked away across the flat green levels. All the rich Punjab lay out in the splendour of the keen sun. The lama flinched a little as the telegraph-posts swung by.

"Great is the speed of the te-rain," said the banker, with a patronizing grin. "We have gone farther since Lahore than thou couldst walk in two days: at even, we shall enter Umballa."

"And that is still far from Benares," said the lama wearily, mumbling over the cakes that Kim offered. They all unloosed their bundles and made their morning meal. Then the banker, the cultivator, and the soldier prepared their pipes and wrapped the compartment in choking, acrid smoke, spitting and coughing and enjoying themselves. The Sikh and the cultivator's wife chewed pan; the lama took snuff and told his beads, while Kim, cross-legged, smiled over the comfort of a full stomach.

"What rivers have ye by Benares?" said the lama of a sudden to the carriage at large.

"We have Gunga," returned the banker, when the little titter had subsided.

"What others?"

"What other than Gunga?"

"Nay, but in my mind was the thought of a certain River of healing."

"That is Gunga. Who bathes in her is made clean and goes to the Gods. Thrice have I made pilgrimage to Gunga." He looked round proudly.

"There was need," said the young sepoy drily, and the travellers' laugh turned against the banker.

"Clean – to return again to the Gods," the lama muttered. "And to go forth on the round of lives anew – still tied to the Wheel." He shook his head testily. "But maybe there is a mistake. Who, then, made Gunga in the beginning?"

"The Gods. Of what known faith art thou?" the banker said, appalled.

"I follow the Law – the Most Excellent Law. So it was the Gods that made Gunga. What like of Gods were they?"

The carriage looked at him in amazement. It was inconceivable that anyone should be ignorant of Gunga.

"What – what is thy God?" said the money-lender at last.

"Hear!" said the lama, shifting the rosary to his hand. "Hear: for I speak of Him now! O people of Hind, listen!"

He began in Urdu the tale of the Lord Buddha, but, borne by his own thoughts, slid into Tibetan and long-droned texts from a Chinese book of the Buddha's life. The gentle, tolerant folk looked on reverently. All India is full of holy men stammering gospels in strange tongues; shaken and consumed in the fires of their own zeal; dreamers, babblers, and visionaries: as it has been from the beginning and will continue to the end.

"Um!" said the soldier of the Ludhiana Sikhs. "There was a Mohammedan regiment lay next to us at the Pirzai Kotal, and a priest of theirs – he was, as I remember, a naik – when the fit was on him, spake prophecies. But the mad all are in God's keeping. His officers overlooked much in that man."

The lama fell back on Urdu, remembering that he was in a strange land. "Hear the tale of the Arrow which our Lord loosed from the bow," he said.

This was much more to their taste, and they listened curiously while he told it. "Now, O people of Hind, I go to seek that River. Know ye aught that may guide me, for we be all men and women in evil case."

"There is Gunga – and Gunga alone – who washes away sin," ran the murmur round the carriage.

"Though past question we have good Gods Jullundur-way," said the cultivator's wife, looking out of the window. "See how they have blessed the crops."

"To search every river in the Punjab is no small matter," said her husband. "For me, a stream that leaves good silt on my land suffices, and I thank Bhumia, the God of the Home-stead." He shrugged one knotted, bronzed shoulder.

"Think you our Lord came so far North?" said the lama, turning to Kim.

"It may be," Kim replied soothingly, as he spat red pan-juice on the floor.

"The last of the Great Ones," said the Sikh with authority, "was Sikander Julkarn [Alexander the Great]. He paved the streets of Jullundur and built a great tank near Umballa. That pavement holds to this day; and the tank is there also. I never heard of thy God."

"Let thy hair grow long and talk Punjabi," said the young soldier jestingly to Kim, quoting a Northern proverb. "That is all that makes a Sikh." But he did not say this very loud.

The lama sighed and shrank into himself, a dingy, shapeless mass. In the pauses of their talk they could hear the low droning "Om mane pudme hum! Om mane pudme hum!" – and the thick click of the wooden rosary beads.

"It irks me," he said at last. "The speed and the clatter irk me. Moreover, my chela, I think that maybe we have over-passed that River."

"Peace, peace," said Kim. "Was not the River near Benares? We are yet far from the place."

"But – if our Lord came North, it may be any one of these little ones that we have run across."

"I do not know."

"But thou wast sent to me – wast thou sent to me? – For the merit I had acquired over yonder at Such-zen. From beside the cannon didst thou come – bearing two faces – and two garbs."

"Peace. One must not speak of these things here," whispered Kim. "There was but one of me. Think again and thou wilt remember. A boy – a Hindu boy – by the great green cannon."

"But was there not also an Englishman with a white beard holy among images – who himself made more sure my assurance of the River of the Arrow?"

"He – we – went to the Ajaib-Gher in Lahore to pray before the Gods there," Kim explained to the openly listening company. "And the Sahib of the Wonder House talked to him – yes, this is truth as a brother. He is a very holy man, from far beyond the Hills. Rest, thou. In time we come to Umballa."

"But my River – the River of my healing?"

"And then, if it please thee, we will go hunting for that River on foot. So that we miss nothing – not even a little rivulet in a field-side."

"But thou hast a Search of thine own?" The lama – very pleased that he remembered so well – sat bolt upright.

"Ay," said Kim, humouring him. The boy was entirely happy to be out chewing pan and seeing new people in the great good-tempered world.

"It was a bull – a Red Bull that shall come and help thee and carry thee – whither? I have forgotten. A Red Bull on a green field, was it not?"

"Nay, it will carry me nowhere," said Kim. "It is but a tale I told thee."

"What is this?" The cultivator's wife leaned forward, her bracelets clinking on her arm. "Do ye both dream dreams? A Red Bull on a green field, that shall carry thee to the heavens or what? Was it a vision? Did one make a prophecy? We have a Red Bull in our village behind Jullundur city, and he grazes by choice in the very greenest of our fields!"

"Give a woman an old wife's tale and a weaver-bird a leaf and a thread, they will weave wonderful things," said the Sikh. "All holy men dream dreams, and by following holy men their disciples attain that power."

"A Red Bull on a green field, was it?" the lama repeated. "In a former life it may be thou hast acquired merit, and the Bull will come to reward thee."

"Nay – nay – it was but a tale one told to me – for a jest belike. But I will seek the Bull about Umballa, and thou canst look for thy River and rest from the clatter of the train."

"It may be that the Bull knows – that he is sent to guide us both," said the lama, hopefully as a child. Then to the company, indicating Kim: "This one was sent to me but yesterday. He is not, I think, of this world."

"Beggars aplenty have I met, and holy men to boot, but never such a yogi nor such a disciple," said the woman.

Her husband touched his forehead lightly with one finger and smiled. But the next time the lama would eat they took care to give him of their best.

And at last – tired, sleepy, and dusty – they reached Umballa City Station.

"We abide here upon a law-suit," said the cultivator's wife to Kim. "We lodge with my man's cousin's younger brother. There is room also in the courtyard for thy yogi and for thee. Will – will he give me a blessing?"

"O holy man! A woman with a heart of gold gives us lodging for the night. It is a kindly land, this land of the South. See how we have been helped since the dawn!"

The lama bowed his head in benediction.

"To fill my cousin's younger brother's house with wastrels –" the husband began, as he shouldered his heavy bamboo staff.

"Thy cousin's younger brother owes my father's cousin something yet on his daughter's marriage-feast," said the woman crisply. "Let him put their food to that account. The yogi will beg, I doubt not."

"Ay, I beg for him," said Kim, anxious only to get the lama under shelter for the night, that he might seek Mahbub Ali's Englishman and deliver himself of the white stallion's pedigree.

"Now," said he, when the lama had come to an anchor in the inner courtyard of a decent Hindu house behind the cantonments, "I go away for a while – to – to buy us victual in the bazar. Do not stray abroad till I return."

"Thou wilt return? Thou wilt surely return?" The old man caught at his wrist. "And thou wilt return in this very same shape? Is it too late to look tonight for the River?"

"Too late and too dark. Be comforted. Think how far thou art on the road – an hundred miles from Lahore already."

"Yea – and farther from my monastery. Alas! It is a great and terrible world."

Kim stole out and away, as unremarkable a figure as ever carried his own and a few score thousand other folk's fate slung round his neck. Mahbub Ali's directions left him little doubt of the house in which his Englishman lived; and a groom, bringing a dog-cart home from the Club, made him quite sure. It remained only to identify his man, and Kim slipped through the garden hedge and hid in a clump of plumed grass close to the veranda. The house blazed with lights, and servants moved about tables dressed with flowers, glass, and silver. Presently forth came an Englishman, dressed in black and white, humming a tune. It was too dark to see his face, so Kim, beggar-wise, tried an old experiment.

"Protector of the Poor!"

The man backed towards the voice.

"Mahbub Ali says –"

"Hah! What says Mahbub Ali?" He made no attempt to look for the speaker, and that showed Kim that he knew.

"The pedigree of the white stallion is fully established."

"What proof is there?" The Englishman switched at the rose-hedge in the side of the drive.

"Mahbub Ali has given me this proof." Kim flipped the wad of folded paper into the air, and it fell in the path beside the man, who put his foot on it as a gardener came round the corner. When the servant passed he picked it up, dropped a rupee – Kim could hear the clink – and strode into the house, never turning round. Swiftly Kim took up the money; but for all his training, he was Irish enough by birth to reckon silver the least part of any game. What he desired was the visible effect of action; so, instead of slinking away, he lay close in the grass and wormed nearer to the house.

He saw – Indian bungalows are open through and through – the Englishman return to a small dressing-room, in a comer of the veranda, that was half office, littered with papers and despatch-boxes, and sit down to study Mahbub Ali's message. His face, by the full ray of the kerosene lamp, changed and darkened, and Kim, used as every beggar must be to watching countenances, took good note.

"Will! Will, dear!" called a woman's voice. "You ought to be in the drawing-room. They'll be here in a minute."

The man still read intently.

"Will!" said the voice, five minutes later. "He's come. I can hear the troopers in the drive."

The man dashed out bareheaded as a big landau with four native troopers behind it halted at the veranda, and a tall, black haired man, erect as an arrow, swung out, preceded by a young officer who laughed pleasantly.

Flat on his belly lay Kim, almost touching the high wheels. His man and the black stranger exchanged two sentences.

"Certainly, sir," said the young officer promptly. "Everything waits while a horse is concerned."

"We shan't be more than twenty minutes," said Kim's man. "You can do the honours – keep 'em amused, and all that."

"Tell one of the troopers to wait," said the tall man, and they both passed into the dressing-room together as the landau rolled away. Kim saw their heads bent over Mahbub Ali's message, and heard the voices – one low and deferential, the other sharp and decisive.

"It isn't a question of weeks. It is a question of days – hours almost," said the elder. "I'd been expecting it for some time, but this" – he tapped Mahbub Ali's paper – "clinches it. Grogan's dining here tonight, isn't he?"

"Yes, sir, and Macklin too."

"Very good. I'll speak to them myself. The matter will be referred to the Council, of course, but this is a case where one is justified in assuming that we take action at once. Warn the Pined and Peshawar brigades. It will disorganize all the summer reliefs, but we can't help that. This comes of not smashing them thoroughly the first time. Eight thousand should be enough."

"What about artillery, sir?"

"I must consult Macklin."

"Then it means war?"

"No. Punishment. When a man is bound by the action of his predecessor –"

"But C25 may have lied."

"He bears out the other's information. Practically, they showed their hand six months back. But Devenish would have it there was a chance of peace. Of course they used it to make themselves stronger. Send off those telegrams at once – the new code, not the old – mine and Wharton's. I don't think we need keep the ladies waiting any longer. We can settle the rest over the cigars. I thought it was coming. It's punishment – not war."

As the trooper cantered off, Kim crawled round to the back of the house, where, going on his Lahore experiences, he judged there would be food – and information. The kitchen was crowded with excited scullions, one of whom kicked him.

"Aie," said Kim, feigning tears. "I came only to wash dishes in return for a bellyful."

"All Umballa is on the same errand. Get hence. They go in now with the soup. Think you that we who serve Creighton Sahib need strange scullions to help us through a big dinner?"

"It is a very big dinner," said Kim, looking at the plates.

"Small wonder. The guest of honour is none other than the Jang-i-Lat Sahib [the Commander-in-Chief]."

"Ho!" said Kim, with the correct guttural note of wonder. He had learned what he wanted, and when the scullion turned he was gone.

"And all that trouble," said he to himself, thinking as usual in Hindustani, "for a horse's pedigree! Mahbub Ali should have come to me to learn a little lying. Every time before that I have borne a message it concerned a woman. Now it is men. Better. The tall man said that they will loose a great army to punish someone – somewhere – the news goes to Pindi and Peshawur. There are also guns. Would I had crept nearer. It is big news!"

He returned to find the cultivator's cousin's younger brother discussing the family law-suit in all its bearings with the cultivator and his wife and a few friends, while the lama dozed. After the evening meal some one passed him a water-pipe; and Kim felt very much of a man as he pulled at the smooth coconut-shell, his legs spread abroad in the moonlight, his tongue clicking in remarks from time to time. His hosts were most polite; for the cultivator's wife had told them of his vision of the Red Bull, and of his probable descent from another world. Moreover, the lama was a great and venerable curiosity.

* * *

The family priest, an old, tolerant Sarsut Brahmin, dropped in later, and naturally started a theological argument to impress the family. By creed, of course, they were all on their priest's side, but the lama was the guest and the novelty. His gentle kindliness, and his impressive Chinese quotations, that sounded like spells, delighted them hugely; and in this sympathetic, simple air, he expanded like the Bodhisat's own lotus, speaking of his life in the great hills of Such-zen, before, as he said, "I rose up to seek enlightenment."

Then it came out that in those worldly days he had been a master-hand at casting horoscopes and nativities; and the family priest led him on to describe his methods; each giving the planets names that the other could not understand, and pointing upwards as the big stars sailed across the dark. The children of the house tugged unrebuked at his rosary; and he clean forgot the Rule which forbids looking at women as he talked of enduring snows, landslips, blocked passes, the remote cliffs where men find sapphires and turquoise, and that wonderful upland road that leads at last into Great China itself.

"How thinkest thou of this one?" said the cultivator aside to the priest.

"A holy man – a holy man indeed. His Gods are not the Gods, but his feet are upon the Way," was the answer. "And his methods of nativities, though that is beyond thee, are wise and sure."

"Tell me," said Kim lazily, "whether I find my Red Bull on a green field, as was promised me."

"What knowledge hast thou of thy birth-hour?" the priest asked, swelling with importance.

"Between first and second cockcrow of the first night in May."

"Of what year?"

"I do not know; but upon the hour that I cried first fell the great earthquake in Srinagar which is in Kashmir." This Kim had from the woman who took care of him, and she again from Kimball O'Hara. The earthquake had been felt in India, and for long stood a leading date in the Punjab.

"Ai!" said a woman excitedly. This seemed to make Kim's supernatural origin more certain. "Was not such an one's daughter born then –"

"And her mother bore her husband four sons in four years all likely boys," cried the cultivator's wife, sitting outside the circle in the shadow.

"None reared in the knowledge," said the family priest, "forget how the planets stood in their Houses upon that night." He began to draw in the dust of the courtyard. "At least thou hast good claim to a half of the House of the Bull. How runs thy prophecy?"

"Upon a day," said Kim, delighted at the sensation he was creating, "I shall be made great by means of a Red Bull on a green field, but first there will enter two men making all things ready."

"Yes: thus ever at the opening of a vision. A thick darkness that clears slowly; anon one enters with a broom making ready the place. Then begins the Sight. Two men – thou sayest? Ay, ay. The Sun, leaving the House of the Bull, enters that of the Twins. Hence the two men of the prophecy. Let us now consider. Fetch me a twig, little one."

He knitted his brows, scratched, smoothed out, and scratched again in the dust mysterious signs – to the wonder of all save the lama, who, with fine instinct, forbore to interfere.

At the end of half an hour, he tossed the twig from him with a grunt.

"Hm! Thus say the stars. Within three days come the two men to make all things ready. After them follows the Bull; but the sign over against him is the sign of War and armed men."

"There was indeed a man of the Ludhiana Sikhs in the carriage from Lahore," said the cultivator's wife hopefully.

"Tck! Armed men – many hundreds. What concern hast thou with war?" said the priest to Kim. "Thine is a red and an angry sign of War to be loosed very soon."

"None – none," said the lama earnestly. "We seek only peace and our River."

Kim smiled, remembering what he had overheard in the dressing-room. Decidedly he was a favourite of the stars.

The priest brushed his foot over the rude horoscope. "More than this I cannot see. In three days comes the Bull to thee, boy."

"And my River, my River," pleaded the lama. "I had hoped his Bull would lead us both to the River."

"Alas, for that wondrous River, my brother," the priest replied. "Such things are not common."

Next morning, though they were pressed to stay, the lama insisted on departure. They gave Kim a large bundle of good food and nearly three annas in copper money for the needs of the road, and with many blessings watched the two go southward in the dawn.

"Pity it is that these and such as these could not be freed from –"

"Nay, then would only evil people be left on the earth, and who would give us meat and shelter?" quoth Kim, stepping merrily under his burden.

"Yonder is a small stream. Let us look," said the lama, and he led from the white road across the fields; walking into a very hornets' nest of pariah dogs.

Chapter III

Yea, voice of every Soul that clung
To life that strove from rung to rung
When Devadatta's rule was young,
The warm wind brings Kamakura.
Buddha at Kamakura

BEHIND THEM an angry farmer brandished a bamboo pole. He was a market-gardener, Arain by caste, growing vegetables and flowers for Umballa city, and well Kim knew the breed.

"Such an one," said the lama, disregarding the dogs, "is impolite to strangers, intemperate of speech and uncharitable. Be warned by his demeanour, my disciple."

"Ho, shameless beggars!" shouted the farmer. "Begone! Get hence!"

"We go," the lama returned, with quiet dignity. "We go from these unblessed fields."

"Ah," said Kim, sucking in his breath. "If the next crops fail, thou canst only blame thine own tongue."

The man shuffled uneasily in his slippers. "The land is full of beggars," he began, half apologetically.

"And by what sign didst thou know that we would beg from thee, O Mali?" said Kim tartly, using the name that a market-gardener least likes. "All we sought was to look at that river beyond the field there."

"River, forsooth!" the man snorted. "What city do ye hail from not to know a canal-cut? It runs as straight as an arrow, and I pay for the water as though it were molten silver. There is a branch of a river beyond. But if ye need water I can give that – and milk."

"Nay, we will go to the river," said the lama, striding out.

"Milk and a meal," the man stammered, as he looked at the strange tall figure. "I – I would not draw evil upon myself – or my crops. But beggars are so many in these hard days."

"Take notice." The lama turned to Kim. "He was led to speak harshly by the Red Mist of anger. That clearing from his eyes, he becomes courteous and of an affable heart. May his fields be blessed! Beware not to judge men too hastily, O farmer."

"I have met holy ones who would have cursed thee from hearthstone to byre," said Kim to the abashed man. "Is he not wise and holy? I am his disciple."

He cocked his nose in the air loftily and stepped across the narrow field-borders with great dignity.

"There is no pride," said the lama, after a pause, "there is no pride among such as follow the Middle Way."

"But thou hast said he was low-caste and discourteous."

"Low-caste I did not say, for how can that be which is not? Afterwards he amended his discourtesy, and I forgot the offence. Moreover, he is as we are, bound upon the Wheel of Things; but he does not tread the way of deliverance." He halted at a little runlet among the fields, and considered the hoof-pitted bank.

"Now, how wilt thou know thy River?" said Kim, squatting in the shade of some tall sugar-cane.

"When I find it, an enlightenment will surely be given. This, I feel, is not the place. O littlest among the waters, if only thou couldst tell me where runs my River! But be thou blessed to make the fields bear!"

"Look! Look!" Kim sprang to his side and dragged him back. A yellow-and-brown streak glided from the purple rustling stems to the bank, stretched its neck to the water, drank, and lay still – a big cobra with fixed, lidless eyes.

"I have no stick – I have no stick," said Kim. "I will get me one and break his back."

"Why? He is upon the Wheel as we are – a life ascending or descending – very far from deliverance. Great evil must the soul have done that is cast into this shape."

"I hate all snakes," said Kim. No native training can quench the white man's horror of the Serpent.

"Let him live out his life." The coiled thing hissed and half opened its hood. "May thy release come soon, brother!" the lama continued placidly. "Hast thou knowledge, by chance, of my River?"

"Never have I seen such a man as thou art," Kim whispered, overwhelmed. "Do the very snakes understand thy talk?"

"Who knows?" He passed within a foot of the cobra's poised head. It flattened itself among the dusty coils.

"Come, thou!" he called over his shoulder.

"Not I," said Kim. "I go round."

"Come. He does no hurt."

Kim hesitated for a moment. The lama backed his order by some droned Chinese quotation which Kim took for a charm. He obeyed and bounded across the rivulet, and the snake, indeed, made no sign.

"Never have I seen such a man." Kim wiped the sweat from his forehead. "And now, whither go we?"

"That is for thee to say. I am old, and a stranger – far from my own place. But that the rail-carriage fills my head with noises of devil-drums I would go in it to Benares now.... Yet by so going we may miss the River. Let us find another river."

Where the hard-worked soil gives three and even four crops a year through patches of sugar-cane, tobacco, long white radishes, and nol-kol, all that day they strolled on, turning aside to every glimpse of water; rousing village dogs and sleeping villages at noonday; the lama replying to the volleyed questions with an unswerving simplicity. They sought a River: a River of miraculous healing. Had any one knowledge of such a stream?

Sometimes men laughed, but more often heard the story out to the end and offered them a place in the shade, a drink of milk, and a meal. The women were always kind, and the little children as children are the world over, alternately shy and venturesome.

Evening found them at rest under the village tree of a mud-walled, mud-roofed hamlet, talking to the headman as the cattle came in from the grazing-grounds and the women prepared the day's last meal. They had passed beyond the belt of market-gardens round hungry Umballa, and were among the mile-wide green of the staple crops.

He was a white-bearded and affable elder, used to entertaining strangers. He dragged out a string bedstead for the lama, set warm cooked food before him, prepared him a pipe, and, the evening ceremonies being finished in the village temple, sent for the village priest.

Kim told the older children tales of the size and beauty of Lahore, of railway travel, and such-like city things, while the men talked, slowly as their cattle chew the cud.

"I cannot fathom it," said the headman at last to the priest. "How readest thou this talk?" The lama, his tale told, was silently telling his beads.

"He is a Seeker," the priest answered. "The land is full of such. Remember him who came only last, month – the fakir with the tortoise?"

"Ay, but that man had right and reason, for Krishna Himself appeared in a vision promising him Paradise without the burning-pyre if he journeyed to Prayag. This man seeks no God who is within my knowledge."

"Peace, he is old: he comes from far off, and he is mad," the smooth-shaven priest replied. "Hear me." He turned to the lama. "Three koss [six miles] to the westward runs the great road to Calcutta."

"But I would go to Benares – to Benares."

"And to Benares also. It crosses all streams on this side of Hind. Now my word to thee, Holy One, is rest here till tomorrow. Then take the road" (it was the Grand Trunk Road he meant) "and test each stream that it overpasses; for, as I understand, the virtue of thy River lies neither in one pool nor place, but throughout its length. Then, if thy Gods will, be assured that thou wilt come upon thy freedom."

"That is well said." The lama was much impressed by the plan. "We will begin tomorrow, and a blessing on thee for showing old feet such a near road." A deep, sing-song Chinese half-chant closed the sentence. Even the priest was impressed, and the headman feared an evil spell: but none could look at the lama's simple, eager face and doubt him long.

"Seest thou my chela?" he said, diving into his snuff-gourd with an important sniff. It was his duty to repay courtesy with courtesy.

"I see – and hear." The headman rolled his eye where Kim was chatting to a girl in blue as she laid crackling thorns on a fire.

"He also has a Search of his own. No river, but a Bull. Yea, a Red Bull on a green field will some day raise him to honour. He is, I think, not altogether of this world. He was sent of a sudden to aid me in this search, and his name is Friend of all the World."

The priest smiled. "Ho, there, Friend of all the World," he cried across the sharp-smelling smoke, "what art thou?"

"This Holy One's disciple," said Kim.

"He says thou are a but [a spirit]."

"Can buts eat?" said Kim, with a twinkle. "For I am hungry."

"It is no jest," cried the lama. "A certain astrologer of that city whose name I have forgotten –"

"That is no more than the city of Umballa where we slept last night," Kim whispered to the priest.

"Ay, Umballa was it? He cast a horoscope and declared that my chela should find his desire within two days. But what said he of the meaning of the stars, Friend of all the World?"

Kim cleared his throat and looked around at the village greybeards.

"The meaning of my Star is War," he replied pompously.

Somebody laughed at the little tattered figure strutting on the brickwork plinth under the great tree. Where a native would have lain down, Kim's white blood set him upon his feet.

"Ay, War," he answered.

"That is a sure prophecy," rumbled a deep voice. "For there is always war along the Border – as I know."

It was an old, withered man, who had served the Government in the days of the Mutiny as a native officer in a newly raised cavalry regiment. The Government had given him a good holding in the village, and though the demands of his sons, now grey-bearded officers on their own account, had impoverished him, he was still a person of consequence. English officials – Deputy Commissioners even – turned aside from the main road to visit him, and on those occasions he dressed himself in the uniform of ancient days, and stood up like a ramrod.

"But this shall be a great war – a war of eight thousand." Kim's voice shrilled across the quick-gathering crowd, astonishing himself.

"Redcoats or our own regiments?" the old man snapped, as though he were asking an equal. His tone made men respect Kim.

"Redcoats," said Kim at a venture. "Redcoats and guns."

"But – but the astrologer said no word of this," cried the lama, snuffing prodigiously in his excitement.

"But I know. The word has come to me, who am this Holy One's disciple. There will rise a war – a war of eight thousand redcoats. From Pindi and Peshawur they will be drawn. This is sure."

"The boy has heard bazar-talk," said the priest.

"But he was always by my side," said the lama. "How should he know? I did not know."

"He will make a clever juggler when the old man is dead," muttered the priest to the headman. "What new trick is this?"

"A sign. Give me a sign," thundered the old soldier suddenly. "If there were war my sons would have told me."

"When all is ready, thy sons, doubt not, will be told. But it is a long road from thy sons to the man in whose hands these things lie." Kim warmed to the game, for it reminded him of experiences in the letter-carrying line, when, for the sake of a few pice, he pretended to know more than he knew. But now he was playing for larger things – the sheer excitement and the sense of power. He drew a new breath and went on.

"Old man, give me a sign. Do underlings order the goings of eight thousand redcoats – with guns?"

"No." Still the old man answered as though Kim were an equal.

"Dost thou know who He is, then, that gives the order?"

"I have seen Him."

"To know again?"

"I have known Him since he was a lieutenant in the topkhana (the Artillery)."

"A tall man. A tall man with black hair, walking thus?" Kim took a few paces in a stiff, wooden style.

"Ay. But that anyone may have seen." The crowd were breathless – still through all this talk.

"That is true," said Kim. "But I will say more. Look now. First the great man walks thus. Then He thinks thus." (Kim drew a forefinger over his forehead and downwards till it came to rest by the angle of the jaw.) "Anon He twitches his fingers thus. Anon He thrusts his hat under his left armpit." Kim illustrated the motion and stood like a stork.

The old man groaned, inarticulate with amazement; and the crowd shivered.

"So – so – so. But what does He when He is about to give an order?"

"He rubs the skin at the back of his neck – thus. Then falls one finger on the table and He makes a small sniffing noise through his nose. Then He speaks, saying: 'Loose such and such a regiment. Call out such guns.'"

The old man rose stiffly and saluted.

"'For'" – Kim translated into the vernacular the clinching sentences he had heard in the dressing-room at Umballa – "'For,' says He, 'we should have done this long ago. It is not war – it is a chastisement. Snff!'"

"Enough. I believe. I have seen Him thus in the smoke of battles. Seen and heard. It is He!"

"I saw no smoke" – Kim's voice shifted to the rapt sing-song of the wayside fortune-teller. "I saw this in darkness. First came a man to make things clear. Then came horsemen. Then came He standing in a ring of light. The rest followed as I have said. Old man, have I spoken truth?"

"It is He. Past all doubt it is He."

The crowd drew a long, quavering breath, staring alternately at the old man, still at attention, and ragged Kim against the purple twilight.

"Said I not – said I not he was from the other world?" cried the lama proudly. "He is the Friend of all the World. He is the Friend of the Stars!"

"At least it does not concern us," a man cried. "O thou young soothsayer, if the gift abides with thee at all seasons, I have a red-spotted cow. She may be sister to thy Bull for aught I know –"

"Or I care," said Kim. "My Stars do not concern themselves with thy cattle."

"Nay, but she is very sick," a woman struck in. "My man is a buffalo, or he would have chosen his words better. Tell me if she recover?"

Had Kim been at all an ordinary boy, he would have carried on the play; but one does not know Lahore city, and least of all the fakirs by the Taksali Gate, for thirteen years without also knowing human nature.

The priest looked at him sideways, something bitterly – a dry and blighting smile.

"Is there no priest, then, in the village? I thought I had seen a great one even now," cried Kim.

"Ay – but –" the woman began.

"But thou and thy husband hoped to get the cow cured for a handful of thanks." The shot told: they were notoriously the closest-fisted couple in the village. "It is not well to cheat the temples. Give a young calf to thine own priest, and, unless thy Gods are angry past recall, she will give milk within a month."

"A master-beggar art thou," purred the priest approvingly. "Not the cunning of forty years could have done better. Surely thou hast made the old man rich?"

"A little flour, a little butter and a mouthful of cardamoms," Kim retorted, flushed with the praise, but still cautious – "Does one grow rich on that? And, as thou canst see, he is mad. But it serves me while I learn the road at least."

He knew what the fakirs of the Taksali Gate were like when they talked among themselves, and copied the very inflection of their lewd disciples.

"Is his Search, then, truth or a cloak to other ends? It may be treasure."

"He is mad – many times mad. There is nothing else."

Here the old soldier bobbled up and asked if Kim would accept his hospitality for the night. The priest recommended him to do so, but insisted that the honour of entertaining the lama belonged to the temple – at which the lama smiled guilelessly. Kim glanced from one face to the other, and drew his own conclusions.

"Where is the money?" he whispered, beckoning the old man off into the darkness.

"In my bosom. Where else?"

"Give it me. Quietly and swiftly give it me."

"But why? Here is no ticket to buy."

"Am I thy chela, or am I not? Do I not safeguard thy old feet about the ways? Give me the money and at dawn I will return it." He slipped his hand above the lama's girdle and brought away the purse.

"Be it so – be it so." The old man nodded his head. "This is a great and terrible world. I never knew there were so many men alive in it."

Next morning the priest was in a very bad temper, but the lama was quite happy; and Kim had enjoyed a most interesting evening with the old man, who brought out his cavalry sabre and, balancing it on his dry knees, told tales of the Mutiny and young captains thirty years in their graves, till Kim dropped off to sleep.

"Certainly the air of this country is good," said the lama. "I sleep lightly, as do all old men; but last night I slept unwaking till broad day. Even now I am heavy."

"Drink a draught of hot milk," said Kim, who had carried not a few such remedies to opium-smokers of his acquaintance. "It is time to take the Road again."

"The long Road that overpasses all the rivers of Hind," said the lama gaily. "Let us go. But how thinkest thou, chela, to recompense these people, and especially the priest, for their great kindness? Truly they are but parast, but in other lives, maybe, they will receive enlightenment. A rupee to the temple? The thing within is no more than stone and red paint, but the heart of man we must acknowledge when and where it is good."

"Holy One, hast thou ever taken the Road alone?" Kim looked up sharply, like the Indian crows so busy about the fields.

"Surely, child: from Kulu to Pathankot – from Kulu, where my first chela died. When men were kind to us we made offerings, and all men were well-disposed throughout all the Hills."

"It is otherwise in Hind," said Kim drily. "Their Gods are many-armed and malignant. Let them alone."

"I would set thee on thy road for a little, Friend of all the World, thou and thy yellow man." The old soldier ambled up the village street, all shadowy in the dawn, on a punt, scissor-hocked pony. "Last night broke up the fountains of remembrance in my so-dried heart, and it was as a blessing to me. Truly there is war abroad in the air. I smell it. See! I have brought my sword."

He sat long-legged on the little beast, with the big sword at his side – hand dropped on the pommel – staring fiercely over the flat lands towards the North. "Tell me again how He showed in thy vision. Come up and sit behind me. The beast will carry two."

"I am this Holy One's disciple," said Kim, as they cleared the village-gate. The villagers seemed almost sorry to be rid of them, but the priest's farewell was cold and distant. He had wasted some opium on a man who carried no money.

"That is well spoken. I am not much used to holy men, but respect is always good. There is no respect in these days – not even when a Commissioner Sahib comes to see me. But why should one whose Star leads him to war follow a holy man?"

"But he is a holy man," said Kim earnestly. "In truth, and in talk and in act, holy. He is not like the others. I have never seen such an one. We be not fortune-tellers, or jugglers, or beggars."

"Thou art not. That I can see. But I do not know that other. He marches well, though."

The first freshness of the day carried the lama forward with long, easy, camel-like strides. He was deep in meditation, mechanically clicking his rosary.

They followed the rutted and worn country road that wound across the flat between the great dark-green mango-groves, the line of the snowcapped Himalayas faint to the eastward. All India was at work in the fields, to the creaking of well-wheels, the shouting of ploughmen behind their cattle, and the clamour of the crows. Even the pony felt the good influence and almost broke into a trot as Kim laid a hand on the stirrup-leather.

"It repents me that I did not give a rupee to the shrine," said the lama on the last bead of his eighty-one.

The old soldier growled in his beard, so that the lama for the first time was aware of him.

"Seekest thou the River also?" said he, turning.

"The day is new," was the reply. "What need of a river save to water at before sundown? I come to show thee a short lane to the Big Road."

"That is a courtesy to be remembered, O man of good will. But why the sword?"

The old soldier looked as abashed as a child interrupted in his game of make-believe.

"The sword," he said, fumbling it. "Oh, that was a fancy of mine an old man's fancy. Truly the police orders are that no man must bear weapons throughout Hind, but" – he cheered up and slapped the hilt – "all the constabeels hereabout know me."

"It is not a good fancy," said the lama. "What profit to kill men?"

"Very little – as I know; but if evil men were not now and then slain it would not be a good world for weaponless dreamers. I do not speak without knowledge who have seen the land from Delhi south awash with blood."

"What madness was that, then?"

"The Gods, who sent it for a plague, alone know. A madness ate into all the Army, and they turned against their officers. That was the first evil, but not past remedy if they had then held their hands. But they chose to kill the Sahibs' wives and children. Then came the Sahibs from over the sea and called them to most strict account."

"Some such rumour, I believe, reached me once long ago. They called it the Black Year, as I remember."

"What manner of life hast thou led, not to know The Year? A rumour indeed! All earth knew, and trembled!"

"Our earth never shook but once – upon the day that the Excellent One received Enlightenment."

"Umph! I saw Delhi shake at least – and Delhi is the navel of the world."

"So they turned against women and children? That was a bad deed, for which the punishment cannot be avoided."

"Many strove to do so, but with very small profit. I was then in a regiment of cavalry. It broke. Of six hundred and eighty sabres stood fast to their salt – how many, think you? Three. Of whom I was one."

"The greater merit."

"Merit! We did not consider it merit in those days. My people, my friends, my brothers fell from me. They said: 'The time of the English is accomplished. Let each strike out a little holding for himself.' But I had talked with the men of Sobraon, of Chilianwallah, of Moodkee and Ferozeshah. I said: 'Abide a little and the wind turns. There is no blessing in this work.' In those days I rode seventy miles with an English Memsahib and her babe on my saddle-bow. (Wow! That was a horse fit for a man!) I placed them in safety, and back came I to my officer – the one that was not killed of our five. 'Give me work,' said I, 'for I am an outcast among my own kind, and my cousin's blood is wet on my sabre.' 'Be content,' said he. 'There is great work forward. When this madness is over there is a recompense.'"

"Ay, there is a recompense when the madness is over, surely?" the lama muttered half to himself.

"They did not hang medals in those days on all who by accident had heard a gun fired. No! In nineteen pitched battles was I; in six-and-forty skirmishes of horse; and in small affairs without number. Nine wounds I bear; a medal and four clasps and the medal of an Order, for my captains, who are now generals, remembered me when the Kaisar-i-Hind had accomplished fifty years of her reign, and all the land rejoiced. They said: 'Give him the Order of Berittish India.' I carry it upon my neck now. I have also my jaghir [holding] from the hands of the State – a free gift to me and mine. The men of the old days – they are now Commissioners – come riding to me through the crops – high upon horses so that all the village sees – and we talk out the old skirmishes, one dead man's name leading to another."

"And after?" said the lama.

"Oh, afterwards they go away, but not before my village has seen."

"And at the last what wilt thou do?"

"At the last I shall die."

"And after?"

"Let the Gods order it. I have never pestered Them with prayers. I do not think They will pester me. Look you, I have noticed in my long life that those who eternally break in upon Those Above with complaints and reports and bellowings and weepings are presently sent for in haste, as our Colonel used to send for slack-jawed down-country men who talked too much. No, I have never wearied the Gods. They will remember this, and give me a quiet place where I can drive my lance in the shade, and wait to welcome my sons: I have no less than three Rissaldar – majors all – in the regiments."

"And they likewise, bound upon the Wheel, go forth from life to life – from despair to despair," said the lama below his breath, "hot, uneasy, snatching."

"Ay," the old soldier chuckled. "Three Rissaldar – majors in three regiments. Gamblers a little, but so am I. They must be well mounted; and one cannot take the horses as in the old days one took women. Well, well, my holding can pay for all. How thinkest thou? It is a well-watered strip, but my men cheat me. I do not know how to ask save at the lance's point. Ugh! I grow angry and I curse them, and they feign penitence, but behind my back I know they call me a toothless old ape."

"Hast thou never desired any other thing?"

"Yes – yes – a thousand times! A straight back and a close-clinging knee once more; a quick wrist and a keen eye; and the marrow that makes a man. Oh, the old days – the good days of my strength!"

"That strength is weakness."

"It has turned so; but fifty years since I could have proved it otherwise," the old soldier retorted, driving his stirrup-edge into the pony's lean flank.

"But I know a River of great healing."

"I have drank Gunga-water to the edge of dropsy. All she gave me was a flux, and no sort of strength."

"It is not Gunga. The River that I know washes from all taint of sin. Ascending the far bank one is assured of Freedom. I do not know thy life, but thy face is the face of the honourable and courteous. Thou hast clung to thy Way, rendering fidelity when it was hard to give, in that Black Year of which I now remember other tales. Enter now upon the Middle Way which is the path to Freedom. Hear the Most Excellent Law, and do not follow dreams."

"Speak, then, old man," the soldier smiled, half saluting. "We be all babblers at our age."

The lama squatted under the shade of a mango, whose shadow played checkerwise over his face; the soldier sat stiffly on the pony; and Kim, making sure that there were no snakes, lay down in the crotch of the twisted roots.

There was a drowsy buzz of small life in hot sunshine, a cooing of doves, and a sleepy drone of well-wheels across the fields. Slowly and impressively the lama began. At the end of ten minutes the old soldier slid from his pony, to hear better as he said, and sat with the reins round his wrist. The lama's voice faltered, the periods lengthened. Kim was busy watching a grey squirrel. When the little scolding bunch of fur, close pressed to the branch, disappeared, preacher and audience were fast asleep, the old officer's strong-cut head pillowed on his arm, the lama's thrown back against the tree-bole, where it showed like yellow ivory. A naked child toddled up, stared, and, moved by some quick impulse of reverence, made a solemn little obeisance before the lama – only the child was so short and fat that it toppled over sideways, and Kim laughed at the sprawling, chubby legs. The child, scared and indignant, yelled aloud.

"Hai! Hai!" said the soldier, leaping to his feet. "What is it? What orders? … It is… a child! I dreamed it was an alarm. Little one – little one – do not cry. Have I slept? That was discourteous indeed!"

"I fear! I am afraid!" roared the child.

"What is it to fear? Two old men and a boy? How wilt thou ever make a soldier, Princeling?"

The lama had waked too, but, taking no direct notice of the child, clicked his rosary.

"What is that?" said the child, stopping a yell midway. "I have never seen such things. Give them me."

"Aha," said the lama, smiling, and trailing a loop of it on the grass:

> *"This is a handful of cardamoms,*
> *This is a lump of ghi:*
> *This is millet and chillies and rice,*
> *A supper for thee and me!"*

The child shrieked with joy, and snatched at the dark, glancing beads.

"Oho!" said the old soldier. "Whence hadst thou that song, despiser of this world?"

"I learned it in Pathankot – sitting on a doorstep," said the lama shyly. "It is good to be kind to babes."

"As I remember, before the sleep came on us, thou hadst told me that marriage and bearing were darkeners of the true light, stumbling-blocks upon the Way. Do children drop from Heaven in thy country? Is it the Way to sing them songs?"

"No man is all perfect," said the lama gravely, recoiling the rosary. "Run now to thy mother, little one."

"Hear him!" said the soldier to Kim. "He is ashamed for that he has made a child happy. There was a very good householder lost in thee, my brother. Hai, child!" He threw it a pice. "Sweetmeats are always sweet." And as the little figure capered away into the sunshine: "They grow up and become men. Holy One, I grieve that I slept in the midst of thy preaching. Forgive me."

"We be two old men," said the lama. "The fault is mine. I listened to thy talk of the world and its madness, and one fault led to the next."

"Hear him! What harm do thy Gods suffer from play with a babe? And that song was very well sung. Let us go on and I will sing thee the song of Nikal Seyn before Delhi – the old song."

And they fared out from the gloom of the mango tope, the old man's high, shrill voice ringing across the field, as wail by long-drawn wail he unfolded the story of Nikal

Seyn [Nicholson] – the song that men sing in the Punjab to this day. Kim was delighted, and the lama listened with deep interest.

"Ahi! Nikal Seyn is dead – he died before Delhi! Lances of the North, take vengeance for Nikal Seyn." He quavered it out to the end, marking the trills with the flat of his sword on the pony's rump.

"And now we come to the Big Road," said he, after receiving the compliments of Kim; for the lama was markedly silent. "It is long since I have ridden this way, but thy boy's talk stirred me. See, Holy One – the Great Road which is the backbone of all Hind. For the most part it is shaded, as here, with four lines of trees; the middle road – all hard – takes the quick traffic. In the days before rail-carriages the Sahibs travelled up and down here in hundreds. Now there are only country-carts and such like. Left and right is the rougher road for the heavy carts – grain and cotton and timber, fodder, lime and hides. A man goes in safety here for at every few koss is a police-station. The police are thieves and extortioners (I myself would patrol it with cavalry – young recruits under a strong captain), but at least they do not suffer any rivals. All castes and kinds of men move here.

"Look! Brahmins and chumars, bankers and tinkers, barbers and bunnias, pilgrims and potters – all the world going and coming. It is to me as a river from which I am withdrawn like a log after a flood."

And truly the Grand Trunk Road is a wonderful spectacle. It runs straight, bearing without crowding India's traffic for fifteen hundred miles – such a river of life as nowhere else exists in the world. They looked at the green-arched, shade-flecked length of it, the white breadth speckled with slow-pacing folk; and the two-roomed police-station opposite.

"Who bears arms against the law?" a constable called out laughingly, as he caught sight of the soldier's sword. "Are not the police enough to destroy evil-doers?"

"It was because of the police I bought it," was the answer. "Does all go well in Hind?"

"Rissaldar Sahib, all goes well."

"I am like an old tortoise, look you, who puts his head out from the bank and draws it in again. Ay, this is the Road of Hindustan. All men come by this way..."

"Son of a swine, is the soft part of the road meant for thee to scratch thy back upon? Father of all the daughters of shame and husband of ten thousand virtueless ones, thy mother was devoted to a devil, being led thereto by her mother. Thy aunts have never had a nose for seven generations! Thy sister – What Owl's folly told thee to draw thy carts across the road? A broken wheel? Then take a broken head and put the two together at leisure!"

The voice and a venomous whip-cracking came out of a pillar of dust fifty yards away, where a cart had broken down. A thin, high Kathiawar mare, with eyes and nostrils aflame, rocketed out of the jam, snorting and wincing as her rider bent her across the road in chase of a shouting man. He was tall and grey-bearded, sitting the almost mad beast as a piece of her, and scientifically lashing his victim between plunges.

The old man's face lit with pride. "My child!" said he briefly, and strove to rein the pony's neck to a fitting arch.

"Am I to be beaten before the police?" cried the carter. "Justice! I will have Justice –"

"Am I to be blocked by a shouting ape who upsets ten thousand sacks under a young horse's nose? That is the way to ruin a mare."

"He speaks truth. He speaks truth. But she follows her man close," said the old man. The carter ran under the wheels of his cart and thence threatened all sorts of vengeance.

"They are strong men, thy sons," said the policeman serenely, picking his teeth.

The horseman delivered one last vicious cut with his whip and came on at a canter.

"My father!" He reigned back ten yards and dismounted.

The old man was off his pony in an instant, and they embraced as do father and son in the East.

Chapter IV

Good Luck, she is never a lady,
But the cursedest quean alive,
Tricksy, wincing, and jady –
Kittle to lead or drive.
Greet her – she's hailing a stranger!
Meet her – she's busking to leave!
Let her alone for a shrew to the bone
And the hussy comes plucking your sleeve!
Largesse! Largesse, O Fortune!
Give or hold at your will.
If I've no care for Fortune,
Fortune must follow me still!
The Wishing-Caps

THEN, lowering their voices, they spoke together. Kim came to rest under a tree, but the lama tugged impatiently at his elbow.

"Let us go on. The River is not here."

"Hai mai! Have we not walked enough for a little? Our River will not run away. Patience, and he will give us a dole."

"This," said the old soldier suddenly, "is the Friend of the Stars. He brought me the news yesterday. Having seen the very man Himself, in a vision, giving orders for the war."

"Hm!" said his son, all deep in his broad chest. "He came by a bazar-rumour and made profit of it."

His father laughed. "At least he did not ride to me begging for a new charger, and the Gods know how many rupees. Are thy brothers' regiments also under orders?"

"I do not know. I took leave and came swiftly to thee in case –"

"In case they ran before thee to beg. O gamblers and spendthrifts all! But thou hast never yet ridden in a charge. A good horse is needed there, truly. A good follower and a good pony also for the marching. Let us see – let us see." He thrummed on the pommel.

"This is no place to cast accounts in, my father. Let us go to thy house."

"At least pay the boy, then: I have no pice with me, and he brought auspicious news. Ho! Friend of all the World, a war is toward as thou hast said."

"Nay, as I know, the war," returned Kim composedly.

"Eh?" said the lama, fingering his beads, all eager for the road.

"My master does not trouble the Stars for hire. We brought the news bear witness, we brought the news, and now we go." Kim half-crooked his hand at his side.

The son tossed a silver coin through the sunlight, grumbling something about beggars and jugglers. It was a four-anna piece, and would feed them well for days. The lama, seeing the flash of the metal, droned a blessing.

"Go thy way, Friend of all the World," piped the old soldier, wheeling his scrawny mount. "For once in all my days I have met a true prophet – who was not in the Army."

Father and son swung round together: the old man sitting as erect as the younger.

A Punjabi constable in yellow linen trousers slouched across the road. He had seen the money pass.

"Halt!" he cried in impressive English. "Know ye not that there is a takkus of two annas a head, which is four annas, on those who enter the Road from this side-road? It is the order of the Sirkar, and the money is spent for the planting of trees and the beautification of the ways."

"And the bellies of the police," said Kim, slipping out of arm's reach. "Consider for a while, man with a mud head. Think you we came from the nearest pond like the frog, thy father-in-law? Hast thou ever heard the name of thy brother?"

"And who was he? Leave the boy alone," cried a senior constable, immensely delighted, as he squatted down to smoke his pipe in the veranda.

"He took a label from a bottle of belaitee-pani [soda-water], and, affixing it to a bridge, collected taxes for a month from those who passed, saying that it was the Sirkar's order. Then came an Englishman and broke his head. Ah, brother, I am a town-crow, not a village-crow!"

The policeman drew back abashed, and Kim hooted at him all down the road.

"Was there ever such a disciple as I?" he cried merrily to the lama. "All earth would have picked thy bones within ten mile of Lahore city if I had not guarded thee."

"I consider in my own mind whether thou art a spirit, sometimes, or sometimes an evil imp," said the lama, smiling slowly.

"I am thy chela." Kim dropped into step at his side – that indescribable gait of the long-distance tramp all the world over.

"Now let us walk," muttered the lama, and to the click of his rosary they walked in silence mile upon mile. The lama as usual, was deep in meditation, but Kim's bright eyes were open wide. This broad, smiling river of life, he considered, was a vast improvement on the cramped and crowded Lahore streets. There were new people and new sights at every stride – castes he knew and castes that were altogether out of his experience.

They met a troop of long-haired, strong-scented Sansis with baskets of lizards and other unclean food on their backs, their lean dogs sniffing at their heels. These people kept their own side of the road', moving at a quick, furtive jog-trot, and all other castes gave them ample room; for the Sansi is deep pollution. Behind them, walking wide and stiffly across the strong shadows, the memory of his leg-irons still on him, strode one newly released from the jail; his full stomach and shiny skin to prove that the Government fed its prisoners better than most honest men could feed themselves. Kim knew that walk well, and made broad jest of it as they passed. Then an Akali, a wild-eyed, wild-haired Sikh devotee in the blue-checked clothes of his faith, with polished-steel quoits glistening on the cone of his tall blue turban, stalked past, returning from a visit to one of the independent Sikh States, where he had been singing the ancient glories of the Khalsa to College-trained princelings in top-boots and white-cord breeches. Kim was careful not to irritate that man; for the Akali's temper is short and his arm quick. Here and there they met or were overtaken by the gaily dressed crowds of whole villages turning out to some local fair; the women, with their babes on their hips, walking behind the men, the older boys prancing on sticks of sugar-cane, dragging rude brass models of locomotives such as they sell for a halfpenny, or flashing the sun into the eyes of their betters from cheap toy mirrors. One could see at a glance what each had bought; and if there were any doubt it needed only to watch the wives comparing, brown arm against brown arm, the newly purchased dull glass bracelets that come from the North-West. These merry-makers stepped slowly, calling one to the other and stopping to haggle with sweetmeat-sellers, or to make a prayer before one of the wayside shrines – sometimes Hindu, sometimes Mussalman – which the low-caste of both creeds share with beautiful impartiality. A solid line of blue, rising and falling like the back of a caterpillar in haste, would swing up through the quivering dust and trot past to a chorus of quick cackling. That was a gang of changars – the women who have taken all the embankments of all the Northern railways under their charge – a flat-footed, big-bosomed, strong-limbed, blue-petticoated clan of earth-carriers, hurrying north on news of a job, and wasting no time by the road. They belong to the caste whose men do not count, and they walked with squared elbows, swinging hips, and heads on high, as suits women who carry heavy weights. A little later a marriage procession would strike into the Grand Trunk with music and shoutings, and a smell of marigold and jasmine stronger even than the reek of the dust. One could see the bride's litter, a blur of red and tinsel, staggering through the haze, while the bridegroom's bewreathed pony turned aside to snatch a mouthful from a passing fodder-cart. Then Kim would join the Kentish-fire of good wishes and bad jokes, wishing the couple a hundred sons and no daughters, as the saying is. Still more interesting and more to be shouted over it was when a strolling juggler with some half-trained monkeys, or a panting, feeble bear, or a woman who tied goats' horns to her feet, and with these danced on a slack-rope, set the horses to shying and the women to shrill, long-drawn quavers of amazement.

The lama never raised his eyes. He did not note the money-lender on his goose-rumped pony, hastening along to collect the cruel interest; or the long-shouting, deep-voiced little mob – still in military formation – of native soldiers on leave, rejoicing to be rid of their breeches and puttees, and saying the most outrageous things to the most respectable women in sight. Even the seller of Ganges-water he did not see, and Kim expected that he would at least buy a bottle of that precious stuff. He looked steadily at the ground, and strode as steadily hour after hour, his soul busied elsewhere. But Kim was in the seventh heaven of joy. The Grand Trunk at this point was built on an embankment to guard against winter floods from the foothills, so that one walked, as it were, a little above the country, along a stately corridor, seeing all India spread out to left and right. It was beautiful to behold the many-yoked grain and cotton wagons crawling over the country roads: one could hear their axles, complaining a mile away, coming nearer, till with shouts and yells and bad words they climbed up the steep incline and plunged on to the hard main road, carter reviling carter. It was equally beautiful to watch the people, little clumps of red and blue and pink and white and saffron, turning aside to go to their own villages, dispersing and growing small by twos and threes across the level plain. Kim felt these things, though he could not give tongue to his feelings, and so contented himself with buying peeled sugar-cane and spitting the pith generously about his path. From time to time the lama took snuff, and at last Kim could endure the silence no longer.

"This is a good land – the land of the South!" said he. "The air is good; the water is good. Eh?"

"And they are all bound upon the Wheel," said the lama. "Bound from life after life. To none of these has the Way been shown." He shook himself back to this world.

"And now we have walked a weary way," said Kim. "Surely we shall soon come to a parao [a resting-place]. Shall we stay there? Look, the sun is sloping."

"Who will receive us this evening?"

"That is all one. This country is full of good folk. Besides," he sunk his voice beneath a whisper – "we have money."

The crowd thickened as they neared the resting-place which marked the end of their day's journey. A line of stalls selling very simple food and tobacco, a stack of firewood, a police-station, a well, a horse-trough, a few trees, and, under them, some trampled ground dotted with the black ashes of old fires, are all that mark a parao on the Grand Trunk; if you except the beggars and the crows – both hungry.

By this time the sun was driving broad golden spokes through the lower branches of the mango-trees; the parakeets and doves were coming home in their hundreds; the chattering, grey-backed Seven Sisters, talking over the day's adventures, walked back and forth in twos and threes almost under the feet of the travellers; and shufflings and scufflings in the branches showed that the bats were ready to go out on the night-picket. Swiftly the light gathered itself together, painted for an instant the faces and the cartwheels and the bullocks' horns as red as blood. Then the night fell, changing the touch of the air, drawing a low, even haze, like a gossamer veil of blue, across the face of the country, and bringing out, keen and distinct, the smell of wood-smoke and cattle and the good scent of wheaten cakes cooked on ashes. The evening patrol hurried out of the police-station with important coughings and reiterated orders; and a live charcoal ball in the cup of a wayside carter's hookah glowed red while Kim's eye mechanically watched the last flicker of the sun on the brass tweezers.

The life of the parao was very like that of the Kashmir Serai on a small scale. Kim dived into the happy Asiatic disorder which, if you only allow time, will bring you everything that a simple man needs.

His wants were few, because, since the lama had no caste scruples, cooked food from the nearest stall would serve; but, for luxury's sake, Kim bought a handful of dung-cakes to build a fire. All about, coming and going round the little flames, men cried for oil, or grain, or sweetmeats, or tobacco, jostling one another while they waited their turn at the well; and under the men's voices you heard from halted, shuttered carts the high squeals and giggles of women whose faces should not be seen in public.

Nowadays, well-educated natives are of opinion that when their womenfolk travel – and they visit a good deal – it is better to take them quickly by rail in a properly screened compartment; and that custom is spreading. But there are always those of the old rock who hold by the use of their forefathers; and, above all, there are always the old women – more conservative than the men – who toward the end of their days go on a pilgrimage. They, being withered and undesirable, do not, under certain circumstances, object to unveiling. After their long seclusion, during which they have always been in business touch with a thousand outside interests, they love the bustle and stir of the open road, the gatherings at the shrines, and the infinite possibilities of gossip with like-minded dowagers. Very often it suits a longsuffering family that a strong-tongued, iron-willed old lady should disport herself about India in this fashion; for certainly pilgrimage is grateful to the Gods. So all about India, in the most remote places, as in the most public, you find some knot of grizzled servitors in nominal charge of an old lady who is more or less curtained and hid away in a bullock-cart. Such men are staid and discreet, and when a European or a high-caste native is near will net their charge with most elaborate precautions; but in the ordinary haphazard chances of pilgrimage the precautions are not taken. The old lady is, after all, intensely human, and lives to look upon life.

Kim marked down a gaily ornamented ruth or family bullock-cart, with a broidered canopy of two domes, like a double-humped camel, which had just been drawn into the par. Eight men made its retinue, and two of the eight were armed with rusty sabres – sure signs that they followed a person of distinction, for the common folk do not bear arms. An increasing cackle of complaints, orders, and jests, and what to a European would have been bad language, came from behind the curtains. Here was evidently a woman used to command.

Kim looked over the retinue critically. Half of them were thin-legged, grey-bearded Ooryas from down country. The other half were duffle-clad, felt-hatted hillmen of the North; and that mixture told its own tale, even if he had not overheard the incessant sparring between the two divisions. The old lady was going south on a visit – probably to a rich relative, most probably to a son-in-law, who had sent up an escort as a mark of respect. The hillmen would be of her own people – Kulu or Kangra folk. It was quite clear that she was not taking her daughter down to be wedded, or the curtains would have been laced home and the guard would have allowed no one near the car. A merry and a high-spirited dame, thought Kim, balancing the dung-cake in one hand, the cooked food in the other, and piloting the lama with a nudging shoulder. Something might be made out of the meeting. The lama would give him no help, but, as a conscientious chela, Kim was delighted to beg for two.

He built his fire as close to the cart as he dared, waiting for one of the escort to order him away. The lama dropped wearily to the ground, much as a heavy fruit-eating bat cowers, and returned to his rosary.

"Stand farther off, beggar!" The order was shouted in broken Hindustani by one of the hillmen.

"Huh! It is only a pahari [a hillman]," said Kim over his shoulder. "Since when have the hill-asses owned all Hindustan?"

The retort was a swift and brilliant sketch of Kim's pedigree for three generations.

"Ah!" Kim's voice was sweeter than ever, as he broke the dung-cake into fit pieces. "In my country we call that the beginning of love-talk."

A harsh, thin cackle behind the curtains put the hillman on his mettle for a second shot.

"Not so bad – not so bad," said Kim with calm. "But have a care, my brother, lest we – we, I say – be minded to give a curse or so in return. And our curses have the knack of biting home."

The Ooryas laughed; the hillman sprang forward threateningly. The lama suddenly raised his head, bringing his huge tam-o'-shanter hat into the full light of Kim's new-started fire.

"What is it?" said he.

The man halted as though struck to stone. "I – I – am saved from a great sin," he stammered.

"The foreigner has found him a priest at last," whispered one of the Ooryas.

"Hai! Why is that beggar-brat not well beaten?" the old woman cried.

The hillman drew back to the cart and whispered something to the curtain. There was dead silence, then a muttering.

"This goes well," thought Kim, pretending neither to see nor hear.

"When – when – he has eaten" – the hillman fawned on Kim – "it – it is requested that the Holy One will do the honour to talk to one who would speak to him."

"After he has eaten he will sleep," Kim returned loftily. He could not quite see what new turn the game had taken, but stood resolute to profit by it. "Now I will get him his food." The last sentence, spoken loudly, ended with a sigh as of faintness.

"I – I myself and the others of my people will look to that – if it is permitted."

"It is permitted," said Kim, more loftily than ever. "Holy One, these people will bring us food."

"The land is good. All the country of the South is good – a great and a terrible world," mumbled the lama drowsily.

"Let him sleep," said Kim, "but look to it that we are well fed when he wakes. He is a very holy man."

Again one of the Ooryas said something contemptuously.

"He is not a fakir. He is not a down-country beggar," Kim went on severely, addressing the stars. "He is the most holy of holy men. He is above all castes. I am his chela."

"Come here!" said the flat thin voice behind the curtain; and Kim came, conscious that eyes he could not see were staring at him. One skinny brown finger heavy with rings lay on the edge of the cart, and the talk went this way:

"Who is that one?"

"An exceedingly holy one. He comes from far off. He comes from Tibet."

"Where in Tibet?"

"From behind the snows – from a very far place. He knows the stars; he makes horoscopes; he reads nativities. But he does not do this for money. He does it for kindness and great charity. I am his disciple. I am called also the Friend of the Stars."

"Thou art no hillman."

"Ask him. He will tell thee I was sent to him from the Stars to show him an end to his pilgrimage."

"Humph! Consider, brat, that I am an old woman and not altogether a fool. Lamas I know, and to these I give reverence, but thou art no more a lawful chela than this my finger is the pole of this wagon. Thou art a casteless Hindu – a bold and unblushing beggar, attached, belike, to the Holy One for the sake of gain."

"Do we not all work for gain?" Kim changed his tone promptly to match that altered voice. "I have heard" – this was a bow drawn at a venture – "I have heard –"

"What hast thou heard?" she snapped, rapping with the finger.

"Nothing that I well remember, but some talk in the bazars, which is doubtless a lie, that even Rajahs – small Hill Rajahs –"

"But none the less of good Rajput blood."

"Assuredly of good blood. That these even sell the more comely of their womenfolk for gain. Down south they sell them – to zemindars and such – all of Oudh."

If there be one thing in the world that the small Hill Rajahs deny it is just this charge; but it happens to be one thing that the bazars believe, when they discuss the mysterious slave-traffics of India. The old lady explained to Kim, in a tense, indignant whisper, precisely what manner and fashion of malignant liar he was. Had Kim hinted this when she was a girl, he would have been pommelled to death that same evening by an elephant. This was perfectly true.

"Ahai! I am only a beggar's brat, as the Eye of Beauty has said," he wailed in extravagant terror.

"Eye of Beauty, forsooth! Who am I that thou shouldst fling beggar-endearments at me?" And yet she laughed at the long-forgotten word. "Forty years ago that might have been said, and not without truth. Ay. Thirty years ago. But it is the fault of this gadding up and down Hind that a king's widow must jostle all the scum of the land, and be made a mock by beggars."

"Great Queen," said Kim promptly, for he heard her shaking with indignation, "I am even what the Great Queen says I am; but none the less is my master holy. He has not yet heard the Great Queen's order that –"

"Order? I order a Holy One – a Teacher of the Law – to come and speak to a woman? Never!"

"Pity my stupidity. I thought it was given as an order –"

"It was not. It was a petition. Does this make all clear?"

A silver coin clicked on the edge of the cart. Kim took it and salaamed profoundly. The old lady recognized that, as the eyes and the ears of the lama, he was to be propitiated.

"I am but the Holy One's disciple. When he has eaten perhaps he will come."

"Oh, villain and shameless rogue!" The jewelled forefinger shook itself at him reprovingly; but he could hear the old lady's chuckle.

"Nay, what is it?" he said, dropping into his most caressing and confidential tone – the one, he well knew, that few could resist. "Is – is there any need of a son in thy family? Speak freely, for we priests –" That last was a direct plagiarism from a fakir by the Taksali Gate.

"We priests! Thou art not yet old enough to –" She checked the joke with another laugh. "Believe me, now and again, we women, O priest, think of other matters than sons. Moreover, my daughter has borne her man-child."

"Two arrows in the quiver are better than one; and three are better still." Kim quoted the proverb with a meditative cough, looking discreetly earthward.

"True – oh, true. But perhaps that will come. Certainly those down-country Brahmins are utterly useless. I sent gifts and monies and gifts again to them, and they prophesied."

"Ah," drawled Kim, with infinite contempt, "they prophesied!" A professional could have done no better.

"And it was not till I remembered my own Gods that my prayers were heard. I chose an auspicious hour, and – perhaps thy Holy One has heard of the Abbot of the Lung-Cho lamassery. It was to him I put the matter, and behold in the due time all came about as I desired. The Brahmin in the house of the father of my daughter's son has since said that it was through his prayers – which is a little error that I will explain to him when we reach our journey's end. And so afterwards I go to Buddh Gaya, to make shraddha for the father of my children."

"Thither go we."

"Doubly auspicious," chirruped the old lady. "A second son at least!"

"O Friend of all the World!" The lama had waked, and, simply as a child bewildered in a strange bed, called for Kim.

"I come! I come, Holy One!" He dashed to the fire, where he found the lama already surrounded by dishes of food, the hillmen visibly adoring him and the Southerners looking sourly.

"Go back! Withdraw!" Kim cried. "Do we eat publicly like dogs?" They finished the meal in silence, each turned a little from the other, and Kim topped it with a native-made cigarette.

"Have I not said an hundred times that the South is a good land? Here is a virtuous and high-born widow of a Hill Rajah on pilgrimage, she says, to Buddha Gay. She it is sends us those dishes; and when thou art well rested she would speak to thee."

"Is this also thy work?" The lama dipped deep into his snuff-gourd.

"Who else watched over thee since our wonderful journey began?" Kim's eyes danced in his head as he blew the rank smoke through his nostrils and stretched him on the dusty ground. "Have I failed to oversee thy comforts, Holy One?"

"A blessing on thee." The lama inclined his solemn head. "I have known many men in my so long life, and disciples not a few. But to none among men, if so be thou art woman-born, has my heart gone out as it has to thee – thoughtful, wise, and courteous; but something of a small imp."

"And I have never seen such a priest as thou." Kim considered the benevolent yellow face wrinkle by wrinkle. "It is less than three days since we took the road together, and it is as though it were a hundred years."

"Perhaps in a former life it was permitted that I should have rendered thee some service. Maybe" – he smiled – "I freed thee from a trap; or, having caught thee on a hook in the days when I was not enlightened, cast thee back into the river."

"Maybe," said Kim quietly. He had heard this sort of speculation again and again, from the mouths of many whom the English would not consider imaginative. "Now, as regards that woman in the bullock-cart. I think she needs a second son for her daughter."

"That is no part of the Way," sighed the lama. "But at least she is from the Hills. Ah, the Hills, and the snow of the Hills!"

He rose and stalked to the cart. Kim would have given his ears to come too, but the lama did not invite him; and the few words he caught were in an unknown tongue, for they spoke some common speech of the mountains. The woman seemed to ask questions which the lama turned over in his mind before answering. Now and again he heard the singsong cadence of a Chinese quotation. It was a strange picture that Kim watched between drooped eyelids. The lama, very straight and erect, the deep folds of his yellow clothing slashed with black in the light of the parao fires precisely as a knotted tree-trunk is slashed with the shadows of the low sun, addressed a tinsel and lacquered ruth which burned like a many-coloured jewel in the same uncertain light. The patterns on the gold-worked curtains ran up and down, melting and reforming as the folds shook and quivered to the night wind; and when the talk grew more earnest the jewelled forefinger snapped out little sparks of light between the embroideries. Behind the cart was a wall of uncertain darkness speckled with little flames and alive with half-caught forms and faces and shadows. The voices of early evening had settled down to one soothing hum whose deepest note was the steady chumping of the bullocks above their chopped straw, and whose highest was the tinkle of a Bengali dancing-girl's sitar. Most men had eaten and pulled deep at their gurgling, grunting hookahs, which in full blast sound like bull-frogs.

At last the lama returned. A hillman walked behind him with a wadded cotton-quilt and spread it carefully by the fire.

"She deserves ten thousand grandchildren," thought Kim. "None the less, but for me, those gifts would not have come."

"A virtuous woman – and a wise one." The lama slackened off, joint by joint, like a slow camel. "The world is full of charity to those who follow the Way." He flung a fair half of the quilt over Kim.

"And what said she?" Kim rolled up in his share of it.

"She asked me many questions and propounded many problems – the most of which were idle tales which she had heard from devil-serving priests who pretend to follow the Way. Some I answered, and some I said were foolish. Many wear the Robe, but few keep the Way."

"True. That is true." Kim used the thoughtful, conciliatory tone of those who wish to draw confidences.

"But by her lights she is most right-minded. She desires greatly that we should go with her to Buddh Gaya; her road being ours, as I understand, for many days' journey to the southward."

"And?"

"Patience a little. To this I said that my Search came before all things. She had heard many foolish legends, but this great truth of my River she had never heard. Such are the priests of the lower hills! She knew the Abbot of Lung-Cho, but she did not know of my River – nor the tale of the Arrow."

"And?"

"I spoke therefore of the Search, and of the Way, and of matters that were profitable; she desiring only that I should accompany her and make prayer for a second son."

"Aha! 'We women' do not think of anything save children," said Kim sleepily.

"Now, since our roads run together for a while, I do not see that we in any way depart from our Search if so be we accompany her – at least as far as – I have forgotten the name of the city."

"Ohe!" said Kim, turning and speaking in a sharp whisper to one of the Ooryas a few yards away. "Where is your master's house?"

"A little behind Saharunpore, among the fruit gardens." He named the village.

"That was the place," said the lama. "So far, at least, we can go with her."

"Flies go to carrion," said the Oorya, in an abstracted voice.

"For the sick cow a crow; for the sick man a Brahmin." Kim breathed the proverb impersonally to the shadow-tops of the trees overhead.

The Oorya grunted and held his peace.

"So then we go with her, Holy One?"

"Is there any reason against? I can still step aside and try all the rivers that the road overpasses. She desires that I should come. She very greatly desires it."

Kim stifled a laugh in the quilt. When once that imperious old lady had recovered from her natural awe of a lama he thought it probable that she would be worth listening to.

He was nearly asleep when the lama suddenly quoted a proverb: "The husbands of the talkative have a great reward hereafter." Then Kim heard him snuff thrice, and dozed off, still laughing.

The diamond-bright dawn woke men and crows and bullocks together. Kim sat up and yawned, shook himself, and thrilled with delight. This was seeing the world in real truth; this was life as he would have it – bustling and shouting, the buckling of belts, and beating of bullocks and creaking of wheels, lighting of fires and cooking of food, and new sights at every turn of the approving eye. The morning mist swept off in a whorl of silver, the parrots shot away to some distant river in shrieking green hosts: all the well-wheels within ear-shot went to work. India was awake, and Kim was in the middle of it, more awake and more excited than anyone, chewing on a twig that he would presently use as a toothbrush; for he borrowed right- and left-handedly from all the customs of the country he knew and loved. There was no need to worry about food – no need to spend a cowrie at the crowded stalls. He was the disciple of a holy man annexed by a strong-willed old lady. All things would be prepared for them, and when they were respectfully invited so to do they would sit and eat. For the rest – Kim giggled here as he cleaned his teeth – his hostess would rather heighten the enjoyment of the road. He inspected her bullocks critically, as they came up grunting and blowing under the yokes. If they went too fast – it was not likely – there would be a pleasant seat for himself along the pole; the lama would sit beside the driver. The escort, of course, would walk. The old lady, equally of course, would talk a great deal, and by what he had heard that conversation would not lack salt. She was already ordering, haranguing, rebuking, and, it must be said, cursing her servants for delays.

"Get her her pipe. In the name of the Gods, get her her pipe and stop her ill-omened mouth," cried an Oorya, tying up his shapeless bundles of bedding. "She and the parrots are alike. They screech in the dawn."

"The lead-bullocks! Hai! Look to the lead-bullocks!" They were backing and wheeling as a grain-cart's axle caught them by the horns. "Son of an owl, where dost thou go?" This to the grinning carter.

"Ai! Yai! Yai! That within there is the Queen of Delhi going to pray for a son," the man called back over his high load. "Room for the Queen of Delhi and her Prime Minister the grey monkey climbing up his own sword!" Another cart loaded with bark for a down-country tannery followed close behind, and its driver added a few compliments as the ruth-bullocks backed and backed again.

From behind the shaking curtains came one volley of invective. It did not last long, but in kind and quality, in blistering, biting appropriateness, it was beyond anything that even Kim had heard. He could see the carter's bare chest collapse with amazement, as the man salaamed reverently to the voice, leaped from the pole, and helped the escort haul their volcano on to the main road. Here the voice told him truthfully what sort of wife he had wedded, and what she was doing in his absence.

"Oh, shabash!" murmured Kim, unable to contain himself, as the man slunk away.

"Well done, indeed? It is a shame and a scandal that a poor woman may not go to make prayer to her Gods except she be jostled and insulted by all the refuse of Hindustan – that she must eat gali [abuse] as men eat ghi. But I have yet a wag left to my tongue – a word or two well spoken that serves the occasion. And still am I without my tobacco! Who is the one-eyed and luckless son of shame that has not yet prepared my pipe?"

It was hastily thrust in by a hillman, and a trickle of thick smoke from each corner of the curtains showed that peace was restored.

If Kim had walked proudly the day before, disciple of a holy man, today he paced with tenfold pride in the train of a semi-royal procession, with a recognized place under the patronage of an old lady of charming manners and infinite resource. The escort, their heads tied up native-fashion, fell in on either side the cart, shuffling enormous clouds of dust.

The lama and Kim walked a little to one side; Kim chewing his stick of sugarcane, and making way for no one under the status of a priest. They could hear the old lady's tongue clack as steadily as a rice-husker. She bade the escort tell her what was going on on the road; and so soon as they were clear of the parao she flung back the curtains and peered out, her veil a third across her face. Her men did not eye her directly when she addressed them, and thus the proprieties were more or less observed.

A dark, sallowish District Superintendent of Police, faultlessly uniformed, an Englishman, trotted by on a tired horse, and, seeing from her retinue what manner of person she was, chaffed her.

"O mother," he cried, "do they do this in the zenanas? Suppose an Englishman came by and saw that thou hast no nose?"

"What?" she shrilled back. "Thine own mother has no nose? Why say so, then, on the open road?"

It was a fair counter. The Englishman threw up his hand with the gesture of a man hit at sword-play. She laughed and nodded.

"Is this a face to tempt virtue aside?" She withdrew all her veil and stared at him.

It was by no means lovely, but as the man gathered up his reins he called it a Moon of Paradise, a Disturber of Integrity, and a few other fantastic epithets which doubled her up with mirth.

"That is a nut-cut [rogue]," she said. "All police-constables are nut-cuts; but the police-wallahs are the worst. Hai, my son, thou hast never learned all that since thou camest from Belait [Europe]. Who suckled thee?"

"A pahareen – a hillwoman of Dalhousie, my mother. Keep thy beauty under a shade – O Dispenser of Delights," and he was gone.

"These be the sort" – she took a fine judicial tone, and stuffed her mouth with pan – "These be the sort to oversee justice. They know the land and the customs of the land. The others, all new from Europe, suckled by white women and learning our tongues from books, are worse than the pestilence. They do harm to Kings." Then she told a long, long tale to the world at large, of an ignorant young policeman who had disturbed some small Hill Rajah, a ninth cousin of her own, in the matter of a trivial land-case, winding up with a quotation from a work by no means devotional.

Then her mood changed, and she bade one of the escort ask whether the lama would walk alongside and discuss matters of religion. So Kim dropped back into the dust and returned to his sugar-cane. For an hour or more the lama's tam-o'shanter showed like a moon through the haze; and, from all he heard, Kim gathered that the old woman wept. One of the Ooryas half apologized for his rudeness overnight, saying that he had never known his mistress of so bland a temper, and he ascribed it to the presence of the strange priest. Personally, he believed in Brahmins, though, like all natives, he was acutely aware of their cunning and their greed. Still, when Brahmins but irritated with begging demands the mother of his master's wife, and when she sent them away so angry that they cursed the whole retinue (which was the real reason of the second off-side bullock going lame, and of the pole breaking the night before), he was prepared to accept any priest of any other denomination in or out of India. To this Kim assented with wise nods, and bade the Oorya observe that the lama took no money, and that the cost of his and Kim's food would be repaid a hundred times in the good luck that would attend the caravan henceforward. He also told stories of Lahore city, and sang a song or two which made the escort laugh. As a town-mouse well acquainted with the latest songs by the most fashionable composers – they are women for the most part – Kim had a distinct advantage over men from a little fruit-village behind Saharunpore, but he let that advantage be inferred.

At noon they turned aside to eat, and the meal was good, plentiful, and well-served on plates of clean leaves, in decency, out of drift of the dust. They gave the scraps to certain beggars, that all requirements might be fulfilled, and sat down to a long, luxurious smoke. The old lady had retreated behind her curtains, but mixed most freely in the talk, her servants arguing with and contradicting her as servants do throughout the East. She compared the cool and the pines of the Kangra and Kulu hills with the dust and the mangoes of the South; she told a tale of some old local Gods at the edge of her husband's territory; she roundly abused the tobacco which she was then smoking, reviled all Brahmins, and speculated without reserve on the coming of many grandsons.

The complete and unabridged text is available online, from *flametreepublishing.com/extras*

Under the Shield

Stephen Kotowych

THE CLAUSTROPHOBIC sound of breathing filled Peter Trevelyan's gas mask as he surveyed the subway platform. Bodies lay everywhere, even on the stairs and hanging over the platform's edge, shrouded in a yellow-green fog of chlorine gas.

What a horrible way to die, thought Trevelyan as he stepped carefully so as to not disturb the corpses. He'd investigated more anarchist attacks in the four years since Tunguska than he cared to remember, including gassings. These people had died in agony, their lungs bleeding and destroyed.

Tsar Nicolas' agents in New York were growing bold in attacking a subway station. The creeping mist had been delivered through the ventilation system, descending on a platform packed with rush-hour commuters.

Fulton Street Station was in the Financial District, so most of the dead were businessmen, but there was also an old woman who lay in a bloody heap by the stairs, trampled to death in the pandemonium. And a mother who'd thrown herself over her two sons, vainly trying to shelter them from the gas. The younger boy still clutched one of those new stuffed bears; the one's named for President Roosevelt.

Something odd caught Trevelyan's eye: at the far end of the station a single body, a woman, sat upright on a bench. He made his way to her.

She was dark-haired, no more than twenty. He tugged at the long hose and canister of his gas hood, pulling the canvas taut to get a better view through the hood's round, glass eyes.

Wearing a flower-print dress under a beige overcoat, she'd been pretty. Her body sat facing the downtown tracks, her head tilted down and to the side, looking peaceful. Trevelyan might have thought she were asleep if he didn't know better.

All the other bodies were on the ground. Why hadn't she joined the stampede? Who sits calmly on a bench through an agonizing death?

Trevelyan waved his arms to get the attention of the photographer and motioned for a picture of the dead girl. As the flash bulb fired, Trevelyan wondered who the freelancer was this time. City cops usually contracted crime-scene photography to whoever slipped them a twenty first. It was even-money whether the photo would be in the morning papers before it was on his desk at the Bureau.

He checked the dead girl's pockets for identification, finding none. One did yield a small, crumpled paper bag with a smeared purple stamp. Peering inside by flashlight, Trevelyan made out a few pinches of grit. Birdseed? No purse accompanied the body – her ID may have been in there, wherever it had ended up.

Pulling at the long gold chain around her neck revealed a golden crucifix hidden within her dress. He fingered the three crossbeams of the Orthodox cross for a moment and then placed it carefully back within the woman's dress.

* * *

Once he was at street level, Trevelyan tore off the gas mask, glad to be free of its close, damp heat. The pepper-and-pineapple tang of the gas hung vaguely in the air. Only two years earlier the anarchists had still been throwing homemade bombs at police wagons and trying to gun down politicians from the backs of speeding Model Ts.

But an unknown number of tsarist secret police, the Okhrana, had been smuggled into the United States since then to agitate amongst Russian immigrants, as well as those opposed to the war and Tesla's peace-beam. The Okhrana trained agents to fight the only kind of war Tesla shields couldn't defend against: sabotage and terror.

Flash-bulbs popped amongst the crowd at the barricades as stretcher-bearers carried the shrouded bodies up from the subway and laid them on the cobble. Newsmen were never far behind one of the Russian attacks.

Vultures, thought Trevelyan.

The Okhrana had been effective. Trevelyan had never seen a more lethal attack: twenty-six dead from gas, by his count, and probably the same again in the hospital who would succumb to the effects of the chlorine after several agonizing days. Ten or twelve more had been trampled to death.

One of the stretcher men approached and removed his gas mask. "That's the last, sir. Shall I have them start the hoses?"

"Yes, constable," said Trevelyan. "And thank you," he added, not used to such deference from the NYPD. City cops usually resented Bureau agents assuming command.

At the constable's signal the assembled firemen started their pumps and trained hoses down the station stairs. Water would neutralize the vapors, washing them harmlessly into the sewers.

A distant siren sounded, followed momentarily by a chorus of others. The all-clear.

Reflexively, everyone in the street – from Trevelyan, to the cordon of police riflemen, to the crowd of onlookers behind the barricades – craned their heads skyward.

Above the building tops, the Tesla shield dome of electromagnetic energy flickered out in spasms of forked lightning and crashes of thunder as the generating stations on Roosevelt Island powered down. Trevelyan felt again the drizzle of rain that the shield had temporarily blocked.

Every tsarist bomb was treated as a possible prelude to invasion, so up went the shield. Impervious to external attack, New York had only to worry about the rot within.

Trevelyan found the stretcher with the girl in the flower-print dress and motioned to one of the coroner's assistants. "No ID," he said. "Tell the coroner I want her examined first. Let me know what the autopsy says."

* * *

At 3 a.m., after hours of interviewing witnesses and survivors, Trevelyan finally reached home. He locked his apartment door and pulled down the blinds, then unlocked a small cabinet that stood in the eastern corner of his bedroom. Its plain exterior belied the glints of gold and silver revealed within as Peter struck a match. The wooden doors were divided into ornate arches painted with images of saints, martyrs, the Madonna and Child – a private *iconostasis* for Peter. The contents were all manner of icons, holy medals, and crucifixes, some passed down for generations.

Peter lit a candle before icons of the Theotokos of Kazan and of Saint Mark of the Caves that had belonged to his grandmother – his *paternal* grandmother – and stood quietly for a moment watching the flame dance off deeply-burnished gold-leaf halos and ornate silver frames.

He prayed for the dead girl, who wore a Byzantine cross even though signs of her Orthodox faith risked recrimination.

And though he lived alone and the door was locked, because Peter prayed all this in Russian, he whispered.

* * *

Trevelyan arrived at the Bureau of Investigation's New York field office on three hours of sleep. The bright, clear day stood not only as an unwelcome reminder of how little sleep he'd managed, but also in stark contrast to the headlines he passed at the newsstands.

The *Times* ran 'SUBWAY TERROR-ANARCHISTS GAS COMMUTERS-DOZENS DEAD' while the reliably sensational *New York Herald* trumpeted 'UNDERGROUND DEATH!' above a photo of the subway platform littered with bodies.

A thick yellow envelope waited on Peter's desk. As the BOI Russian Affairs Liaison with the NYPD, he was provided with crime scene photos and notes of the interviews made with all survivors of anarchist attacks.

The shuffling sound of heavy feet let Trevelyan know Assistant Director Swan approached. He turned as Swan struck a match, lighting a cigar and puffing until a veil of thick smoke hung around his head. He always looked to Trevelyan like a man who had wallowed all day, fully dressed, on an unmade bed.

Swan tossed a missing persons report on Trevelyan's desk. The small glossy photo paperclipped to the pages – some kind of official ID photo – showed the dark-haired girl from the night before.

"She's one of yours."

"Sir?" Trevelyan managed, though his heart was momentarily in his throat. Swan would know about the name change if he'd read Trevelyan's permanent file, but he'd never brought up Peter's Russian heritage.

"The girl. She was killed last night in the attack," said Swan. "The coroner matched the photo with the body this morning. He needs to see you – there's been a development."

Trevelyan scanned the missing persons report. His victim had a name, at last. Alice Bester. It wasn't Russian. An alias?

"This report was filed today," Trevelyan said, flipping through the pages. "She's been missing... less than eighteen hours? How did this get acted on so quickly?"

"She's one of Tesla's." Swan puffed his cigar.

"Wardenclyffe?"

The assistant director nodded and Trevelyan's jaw tensed. Wardenclyffe was the last thing he wanted to get involved with Tesla, too. Not again.

"What the hell was one of Tesla's people doing in Manhattan?" Trevelyan asked aloud. Wardenclyffe was in Shoreham, on Long Island. "I'll need an automobile."

"A car and driver are waiting downstairs," said Swan, and he picked a bit of tobacco off his tongue. Trevelyan grabbed his coat and followed Swan into the elevator.

Ever since Wardenclyffe had been militarized, Trevelyan's understanding was that staff lived on the base, and, given the secrecy of their work, their movements were closely monitored. The missing persons report said Alice Bester had been ordered to the city on official business – she was one of Tesla's secretaries – and failed to return to base.

"Peter," Swan said as they stepped out on to street, "this is going to be a very sensitive case." They stopped at the curb where a grey-haired constable in need of a shave leaned against a Model T. "Makes me uneasy, having one of Tesla's people involved. Very powerful people will want to know why she was on that platform last night. Solve this – fast."

Trevelyan thought a moment before he spoke. "Am I working the subway gassing or Alice Bester?" He'd been involved in politically sensitive cases before and this was starting to feel uncomfortably like another one.

Swan merely smiled. "The automobile is yours for the duration of the case. Hargrave here will be your driver. Good hunting," he said, and disappeared back inside the BOI offices in a cloud of cigar smoke.

Hargrave appraised Trevelyan coolly. He didn't offer his hand.

"The Bureau's taken jurisdiction in this case, constable," said Trevelyan, sensing a city cop's territoriality in the man.

"Yes, *sir*," said Hargrave, in a tone just short of insubordination. "Always happy to drive around you fellas from the Bureau."

Trevelyan climbed in the passenger side as the auto rocked side-to-side several times, Hargrave giving the starter crank two or three quarter turns at full choke. The engine turned over and sputtered to a start as Hargrave gave one final good spin of the crank. He rushed to the driver's side, hopped in, and advanced the spark coil. The auto lurched forward into the street.

"Must be a big case if the Department's letting us take out the flivver, eh?" Hargrave said. When Trevelyan said nothing Hargrave added: "I mean this is a lot of fuss for one dead girl, ain't it?"

"It's Hargrave, right?" Trevelyan said without looking up from the report he was reading. "Truth be told, Hargrave, I've only been in one of these damned 'flivver' things once before. I'm not looking forward to another trip."

Hargrave scoffed under his breath but said nothing else. Trevelyan often found a little well-placed rudeness had wonderful results. He had too much on his mind to make chitchat with some flatfoot.

Very powerful people would want answers, Swan had said. Hoover was probably watching this case himself.

They came to a stop at the corner, where a patrolman directed traffic as a work crew replaced the traffic signal with one using the new Tesla glow globes. Caricature portraits of the Entente heads of state were painted on the side of a nearby building: Tsar Nicolas (looking fey and gaunt); George V (his moustache exaggerated to make him look like a walrus); and Poincaré, President of France (fat-cheeked, with a nose red from too much wine).

'KNOW YOUR ENEMY!' read the painted banner above the three portraits.

"To the morgue, Hargrave." Tongues of lightning arced across the clear sky and a sharp staccato of thunderclaps echoed through the canyon of buildings around them as the sirens began their piercing whine. The Tesla shield flickered to life.

* * *

"Strangulation?" said Trevelyan, reading aloud from the coroner's report. He exhaled a lungful of cigarette smoke into the dimness. Trevelyan didn't smoke often, but it masked the smell of antiseptic and death that permeated the morgue. Hargrave, who'd produced a sandwich from somewhere, stood by the swinging doors chewing wetly.

"You can see the bruising here, and here," said the coroner – a Dr. Northey – lifting the sheet covering the girl and indicated the bruising on both sides of her neck.

"This girl was dead *before* the gas started," Northey continued, lighting himself a cigarette. He was a short, bespectacled man who might have been mistaken for a barber but for the grim stains on his apron.

"Small mercy, if you ask me," he said. "Chlorine gas…" He shook his head.

If Ms. Bester was dead before the gas attack, Trevelyan realized, it explained her positioning on the bench – she'd been staged by whoever killed her. Passersby would have thought the young woman had simply dozed off waiting for a train.

Northey tipped his glasses to the end of his nose and began filling out paperwork. "What I can't figure is why the killer would leave a body on a subway platform where it could be discovered."

Trevelyan thought a moment. "Unless the killer knew of the attack in advance." Who would notice one more body when it was all over?

* * *

How different Wardenclyffe is, Trevelyan thought, as the Model T trundled to a halt at a guard booth. There had been no guards on his last visit, and they were still several miles from where he remembered the old main gates being. A decorative gate with no lock had been replaced by a high fence topped with razor wire, guard towers, riflemen, and cavalry patrolling the perimeter…. Land in every direction had been annexed by the military and the whole area was designated the Wardenclyffe National Research Laboratory.

Hargrave presented their badges and explained their investigation. The MP on duty looked them over and picked up a telephone.

"Straight ahead. Park on the left," he said after receiving instructions. "You'll be met by Colonel Hilroy's adjutant."

The giant Tesla tower – the first, Trevelyan realized, of hundreds that now protected cities all over the United States – was visible above the trees for more than a mile before they reached the main base. And where once there had been only the main laboratory and the great transmission tower, the Wardenclyffe grounds were now covered in all manner of low buildings, and stretches of apartment blocks.

The great mushroom-domed Tesla tower – transmitter for both shield and death ray – rushed heavenward like a steel geyser. Stepping from the Model T, Hargrave gawked upward and Trevelyan found himself doing the same, sunlight reflecting blindingly off the tower's metal sheathing. The clouds rushing past made the tower appear to be falling toward them, and Trevelyan looked away, dizzy.

It was the Tunguska Event that changed everything.

Though it happened in June of nineteen hundred and eight, the world didn't learn of the explosion in the Tunguska river valley of Siberia until November of that year, when the Russians produced the first photographic evidence.

It looked like the vengeful fist of God Himself had smashed into the Russian frontier.

The blast, equivalent to millions of tons of TNT, had a radius of nearly 900 miles. Estimates counted 80 million trees destroyed, splintered and tossed over the hillsides like matchsticks.

Eyewitnesses spoke of a flash and explosion like an artillery barrage. The shockwave threw people to the ground and shattered windows seven hundred miles away. Seismic stations in Great Britain registered the blast as an earthquake.

Then came Mr. Tesla's remarkable announcement.

He had, claimed the inventor himself, been working on a weapon to end war for all time: a focused energy beam, an application of teleforce which he called his 'peace beam,' but which all the papers heralded as Tesla's 'death ray,' a terror weapon sprung to life seemingly from the pages of an H.G. Wells tale.

His beam had rendered war obsolete for all time, he said, and ushered in an age of eternal peace. He urged the military powers of Europe and the Orient to abandon their arms races and entangling alliances.

And then he took questions from the press.

* * *

Waiting at the motor pool was a tall lieutenant who identified himself as Carlson, the colonel's adjutant. They followed him to a smartly appointed office on the second floor of the main building, where a bristle-haired Army colonel waited.

"The Bureau telephoned this morning to let me know we should expect you," said Colonel Hilroy as he and Trevelyan shook hands. "We were very sorry to hear about Miss Bester. My people will do anything they can to assist you in your investigation."

"Thank you, Colonel," Trevelyan said, sitting and pulling out a notepad. "I understand Miss Bester was a secretary?"

"Doctor Tesla's social secretary, that's right," said Hilroy. "I was told Miss Bester died in the subway gas attack last night. Can I ask what the Bureau's interest is in this case?"

"We're keeping it from the press, colonel, but Miss Bester was murdered before the gas attack and left in the subway so it would appear she'd died with everyone else."

"I see," Hilroy said, his eyebrows raised.

"Can you think of any reason why someone might have wanted to harm Miss Bester?"

"I didn't know much about her, personally. I can arrange for you to talk with Mrs. Wilson, if you'd like. She's the head of the secretaries and the typing pool."

"Would Miss Bester have had access to classified materials, anything worth killing for?"

"No, no. Doctor Tesla's for ever being requested as a guest at charity dinners, ribbon cuttings, that sort of thing. The most sensitive information she might have known was his itinerary."

"Do you have any idea why Miss Bester was off-base last night?"

"As I say, she is – was Doctor Tesla's social secretary. My understanding is that she went to Manhattan yesterday afternoon on an errand related to her position."

* * *

The colonel's adjutant showed Trevelyan and Hargrave to the dead girl's small house on base, which was guarded by two MPs on the colonel's orders. Like all housing at Wardenclyffe it had been built since Tunguska and so included the latest amenities, like running hot water and wireless Tesla lamps. He and Hargrave spent an hour scouring the small space, finding nothing. A few books, some unremarkable paperwork related to her job as Tesla's social secretary, and almost nothing personal.

There were no photographs of herself or her family, nothing to hint at a sweetheart. Her bed was unmade, her dressing table cluttered with make-up and perfume. The closet was full of dozens of dresses, some almost unworn, in a very staid palette of browns, dark blues, and blacks. The flower-print dress she died in appeared to be the most colorful item in her wardrobe.

But what disturbed Trevelyan most was the lack of any sign of her faith. She was devout enough to wear the Byzantine cross daily, yet had no candles or icons in her home? No prayer book or bible?

They'd looked behind every painting for a safe, behind every piece of furniture…

Trevelyan grabbed the small coffee table. "Help me with this rug, Hargrave," he said, pulling up the corner of a large Persian that covered much of the living room floor. Rolling it back toward the sofa revealed two small planks cut from the floorboards. Hargrave pried up the boards, reached into the small compartment below, and pulled up a dusty hatbox.

"Bingo!" he said, lifting the lid and getting a glimpse inside. "I can't make out the name, but that's your girl, right?" Hargrave handed Trevelyan a small stack of documents.

An ID card and passport, both in Russian and bearing the name and image of an Alisa Bestemianova. A baptismal certificate in that name was also in the stack.

"Yeah, that's her," said Trevelyan. Alice Bester, indeed.

"And there's these –" Hargrave produced a bundle of newspapers tied with string. "Russian," he said. "Or looks like it to me. There's more of them down here."

Trevelyan recognized them instantly, and read the blocky Cyrillic headline of the top issue to himself: 'TSAR AND HIS DUMA BETRAY WORKERS IN NAME OF WAR WITH AMERICA.'

Why the hell would someone at Wardenclyffe have his brother's propaganda rag?

Alisa Bestemianova had immigrated as a child, apparently. Her passport was valid, though, so she was still a subject of the tsar, at least technically. She'd returned from a trip to St. Petersburg just prior to the Tunguska Event and the closing of the borders.

How does a Russian citizen get a job at the most highly-secure military research facility in the United States during a war with Russia, Trevelyan wondered as he flipped through her ID documents.

"Living under an assumed identity? Doesn't surprise me," said Hargrave, pulling books from the shelves in the parlor. He flipped through each one quickly before discarding it to the floor. "This whole place is run by a damned Russian. It's probably crawling with them."

"Tesla's Serbian, not Russian," said Trevelyan.

Hargrave gave Trevelyan a long, incredulous look. "What's the difference?" he said as another book thudded to the floor. "You know, *sir*, I got a friend who used to be with the Bureau. Left for the Pinkertons, though. Said he didn't like how the Bureau was running things." Hargrave shook a book by its cover and dropped it when nothing fell out.

"My buddy says there used to be this Russian guy at the Bureau. And after the Russians declared war, the Bureau just let him change his name and carry on like nothing had happened. Funny, huh? But I'm pretty sure I can tell the difference between a real American and someone pretending to be one. So maybe you would know the difference between a Serbian and a Russian, after all."

"See to the car, constable," Trevelyan said icily. "I'll meet you there when I'm finished."

* * *

"Impossible," said Colonel Hilroy in a tightly controlled voice. He'd met Trevelyan in the foyer of the main building, a grand, ornate space lit by the soft glow of Tesla globes.

"I'm afraid not, colonel," said Trevelyan, producing one of the Russian-language papers and the passport for his inspection.

"You've had a serious breach of security. I suggest you do a thorough double-check on all staff, even the civilians."

"Find Jones," Hilroy snapped to Carlson. "Have him in my office *now*."

Heavy doors swung open behind Hilroy, and from a laboratory beyond them the *buzz-crackle* sounds of electrical discharge flooded into the hall.

Nikola Tesla strode briskly across the foyer amidst a gaggle of assistants. He wore a white lab coat over black tie and tails, and his shoes were soled with thick cork that exaggerated his already towering height.

"The resistance across the terminals is at an unacceptable level," Tesla was saying to a lab coat-wearing aid that frantically scribbled down on a flip pad everything the inventor said.

"Special Agent Tretyak! What a pleasant surprise," said Tesla as he noticed Peter.

Trevelyan cleared his throat, feeling the colonel's eyes on him. "Actually it's *Trevelyan*, sir."

Tesla paused a moment and then smiled. "Yes. Of course. Please pardon my mistake. It has been a long time."

"Yes, it has," Trevelyan said, clearing his throat again.

"Colonel, Mr. Trevelyan saved my life once. I insist that we treat him as an honored guest!"

"Special Agent Trevelyan is here on official business, Doctor Tesla," said Hilroy. "Miss Bester has been killed."

Tesla gasped and his shoulders slumped. "How did this happen?"

Carlson appeared in a doorway at the far end of the foyer and nodded to Hilroy.

"Carlson will see to anything else you need, Agent Trevelyan. Doctor Tesla..." the colonel said, excusing himself and marching down the hallway.

"They call me doctor even though I have no degree," said Tesla, smiling wistfully. "Tell me," he said, shooing away his assistants, "what became of Miss Bester?"

"She died in the subway last night," said Trevelyan, following Tesla as the inventor wandered outside, "during the gas attack. How well did you know her?"

"She was –" Tesla paused as if looking for the right words. "My social secretary. For almost two years now. The best I've ever had. She'd just arranged the details for my trip to Cambridge. Massachusetts," Tesla added. "I'm to receive an honorary degree next month."

"Did she ever mention being in any kind of trouble? Can you think of any reason that someone might want to hurt her?"

"No," said Tesla, sounding dazed. "No."

Trevelyan let the man walk for a few moments, examining him in silence. He was shaken by his secretary's death, yes, but there was something more...

Tesla led them to a small wooden bench in the middle of a great lawn between the main laboratory and the tower.

"Had you ever had any difficulties with Miss Bester?" he asked, trying to gauge Tesla's reaction. "Any reason to be unhappy with her or her work?"

"None," said Tesla. "She was a very capable staff member, helping me with my great work." No sooner had the inventor sat down than a flock of pigeons arrived at his feet, seemingly from thin air, cooing and flapping. Tesla pulled a small bag of birdseed from his lab coat and absently began to feed them.

"Forgive me, Agent Trevelyan," he said after a few moments silence. "I should like to be alone with my birds."

* * *

"You seem to have a good rapport with Tesla, sir," said Hargrave as he opened the Model T's passenger door. Trevelyan had seen him watching from the motor pool and there was accusation in the man's voice.

"I brought him into protective custody once."

Trevelyan meant to be curt and left it there. He'd been mulling over his first encounter with Tesla, though, from the moment he'd learned Alice Bester worked at Wardenclyffe.

No sooner had Tesla's press conference about Tunguska finished and the headline 'ELECTRICAL PIONEER INVENTS DEATH RAY!' gone out across the telegraph than Trevelyan was ordered to Wardenclyffe.

He had arrived by Model T near midnight, not long after two assassins dispatched by the tsar's spymaster. Brilliant blue-white light flashed from the windows of the laboratory building, illuminating the night like insane Morse code.

Inside, the high-power electrical generators rained storms of lightning across their terminals. The stench of burnt hair and cooked flesh filled the space. Trevelyan found Tesla huddled in a corner of his laboratory.

The inventor had been too wily for the tsar's assassins.

After that President Roosevelt had no choice. The United States had not been responsible for the attack, but there could be no acquiescing to Russian demands for Tesla's extradition, no handing over of a man capable of building such devices.

The rest followed quickly: the declaration of war by the Russian Empire and its Entente allies, Great Britain and France; the destruction of the Great White Fleet in Manila harbor by an Anglo-Russian naval assault; Hawaii occupied; the militarization of the border with Canada and construction of a fence along the frontier.

* * *

Hargrave drove in silence, which allowed Trevelyan to review his notes. He had interviewed all the girls in the steno pool, but none had been close to Alice and none were able to offer much insight. She'd started two years earlier and kept mainly to herself, not even partaking in the usual gossip about suitors. Mrs. Wilson, the head of the steno pool, wasn't aware of Alice ever mentioning any family, and the next of kin box on her personnel record had been left blank.

The only oddity was in something Mrs. Wilson said.

Tesla had a number of idiosyncrasies she claimed were well-known to the staff and the laboratory personnel: he experienced great agitation if he came in contact with human hair; he hated fat people; he detested the sight of women in floral dresses, or wearing pearls. They were largely accepted as the eccentricities of genius by the staff, said Mrs. Wilson.

And yet Alice had been found dead in a flower-print dress.

"Oh yes," said Mrs. Wilson when Trevelyan asked. "Mr. Tesla was forever ordering her out of his sight when she'd wear such things. He'd send her to the city to buy a new dress before allowing her to return to work. Seems like it happened every other week."

"And you put up with this?" he'd asked.

"I spoke to her about it *repeatedly*," she had said, taking offense at Trevelyan's implication. "She'd swear not to wear such dresses in future, but in a few weeks... Claimed she kept forgetting." Mrs. Wilson had shaken her head.

"Why not fire her?"

"Oh, I tried," said Mrs. Wilson. "Several times. But Mr. Tesla wouldn't allow it. Said she was simply the only social secretary he could work with. And when Mr. Tesla makes up his mind about such things, well, there's nothing for it. He's very loyal and generous to people in his employ. Another one of his quirks, I suppose. A good one, generally speaking."

"When was the last time Mr. Tesla sent Miss Bester to Manhattan for a new dress?"

"Why, only yesterday," Mrs. Wilson had said.

Trevelyan closed his notebook and pulled an evidence envelope from the pocket of his great coat. Inside was the small paper bag with the purple stamp that he'd taken from Alice Bester's body.

"Hargrave, I've got something here I need you to run down for me."

* * *

Trevelyan watched the coffee shop and its clientele for nearly an hour before entering.

The shop was on the ground floor of a brick building that was all fire escapes up the front, and its customers were either angry-looking young men who hung about the front window for a time before slipping in, or somewhat older men who looked generally not in funds.

Doubtless many fancied themselves would-be anarchists and freedom fighters. In truth, Trevelyan knew, most had no job and nowhere else to go.

The bell over the door clattered as he entered.

The shop was dark wood with a low tin ceiling, a haze of pipe smoke hanging sweet in the air. The ne'er-do-wells he'd watched enter now sat at a hodgepodge of unmatched tables, sipping coffee and conversing in low tones.

"Pyotr!" the woman behind the counter exclaimed. Her voice, so out of place – loud and feminine – drew everyone's attention to Trevelyan.

"Katya," he said just as surprised. It had been four years since he'd seen his brother Mikhail, longer still Katya.

With hands plunged deep in their coat pockets, every man in the shop filed out, dodging past Trevelyan sideways, shoulder first, as if they might have to ram him.

Katya stood silently behind the coffee bar, trembling visibly, her face pale. Her hair was different, worn now in the Grecian style popular since the outbreak of the war. She looked older, too: crow's-feet starting at the edges of her eyes, her mouth newly downcast. Where had the fire in her eyes gone, the fire he'd known all through their youth?

It took Trevelyan a moment to remember why he had come. "Is –" he tried, and cleared his throat. "Is he here?"

"Are you here to arrest him?"

Trevelyan shook his head. Wordlessly, Katya lifted up the flap at the end of the counter to let him pass and held back the curtain that covered the door behind the bar.

She led him through the back parlor, which was full of furniture that was littered with stacked books and scattered papers. The *biss-clang-swoosh* of printing presses was audible in the basement below.

Katya showed him to a steep flight of stairs at the end of a long hallway. The caustic odor of printer's ink and oiled machines wafted through the open door.

For a moment Katya looked about to say something, but instead turned and left the way they had come.

Trevelyan could feel the narrow, rubber-treaded wooden stairs creak as he descended, but their groaning was drowned out by the mechanical clatter of the printing press. Under the light of a bare Edison bulb a lone man in a leather smock stood by the press, checking the printing on the broadsheets that were being run off.

He looked up from his work and, seeing Trevelyan, paused a long while before hitting a button that wound the press down to a standstill.

"Special Agent Trevelyan."

"Hello Michael."

"Who? *You* changed your name, brother, not me."

"Can we not do this? I'm here for –"

"I thought I told you never to come here. It's bad for business. My customers are Russians. They can spot the secret police when they see them."

Still trying to goad, to rile. All these years and nothing has changed, Trevelyan thought. "Mich – Mikhail!" he said. "I didn't come here to fight with you. I need you to answer some questions."

"Oh, you don't mean to arrest, then?" said Mikhail, speaking in rapid Russian.

"I'm not here to arrest you," Trevelyan answered in English. "I need some information. About a girl you might know."

Mikhail made a puzzled face and spoke again in Russian. *"I'm afraid I don't understand,"* he said. *"If only you spoke Russian."*

The muscles in Trevelyan's jaw flexed.

"Zhopa," he cursed. *"Do you know Alice Bester?"*

"So you do remember how to speak your language? I don't know any girl. Who is she?"

"Who *was* she," said Trevelyan. "She's dead."

He watched his brother try to hide his shock: a noticeable pause, and then he busied himself with the ink for the presses.

"Mischa," said Trevelyan softly. "Who was she?"

After a moment Mikhail, just as softly, said: "She would come in to the coffee shop. How did she die?"

"The gas attack in the subway. Was she a subscriber to your paper?"

Mikhail made an effort to deny it, but Trevelyan tossed across the press a sheaf of the roughly printed propaganda sheets he'd collected from Alice Bester's apartment.

"So? They are my papers. It's not a crime to subscribe to them. Not yet. Or is the BOI finally going to shut me down? I wondered how long freedom of speech would last in this country for Russians."

"You were born in Brooklyn! You're an American."

"That's not what Americans think."

Trevelyan took a deep breath. "Did you know she was Alisa Bestemianova, a Russian living under an assumed name?"

"Many of us change our names these days."

"Mischa, this girl worked at Wardenclyffe," Trevelyan said, moving around the press and close to his brother. "She lied on her application. Your propaganda was found in her house. They'll trace the papers to you and come asking questions. They won't be as *forgiving* as me."

"I don't need your forgiveness."

"As *understanding*, then. I know you have contacts among the anarchists. Are you caught up in something? If you tell me what you know, I can protect you. Katya, too."

"You turned your back on us," said Mikhail, darkly. "Collaborating against your own people."

"Collaborating? You publish propaganda supporting anarchists who gas civilians in subways. Who blow up buses and fire-bomb police stations!"

"You work for a government that protects that Serb and his death ray. You hold the whole world hostage! That's what they do at Wardenclyffe – plan when and where they'll strike next with their terror ray, while the world holds its breath. And you, running away just when we needed you. Like Father."

"*Poshyol ty*," Trevelyan said, his voice a low rumble.

"Father was a pig," Mikhail spit. "Like you. Poor little Sonja, lying there in the parlor stiff and cold, mother wailing. What kind of man leaves his family at a moment like that? Tell me!"

"It wasn't like –"

"He's in the ground, Pyotr, stop making excuses for him. He left because mother was a Jew. He knew she was a Jew when he married her. And when she sat shiva for Sonja – the *one time* she acted as a Jew after marrying him – he left. That's why he's a pig."

Peter remembered during that time their mother, Sarra, insisted he take Mikhail to church on Sundays. "Look for your father there," she said to them. But as soon as the boys rounded the block, Mikhail would run away.

Peter would hide in the back of the dark church, praying his father wouldn't discover him.

"Father came back," said Trevelyan, the ache of an old wound in his voice. He had returned after some months, and no one – except Mikhail – spoke again of that time.

"Alexei never came back," said Mikhail. "Not for me. He was there, in the apartment, but he never came back. I never understood how you could side with him, with his church. How you could forgive his cruelty. Maybe that's why you can side with Teddy, and Hoover, and Tesla. You need cruel masters."

Mikhail hit a button and the presses whirred back to life, drowning out anything Peter had to say.

* * *

Trevelyan crept to his door with pistol in hand. The pounding came again. He'd been tending his icons, saying evening prayers, and was not expecting visitors.

"Pyotr!" called a voice he immediately recognized as Katya's. *"Open the door!"*

A quick peek though the peephole to ensure she was alone and Trevelyan unlocked the deadbolts and chains. Pulling Katya inside by the arm elicited a squeak of surprise from her and he smelled the acrid reek of old booze as she whirled past him. He glanced down the hall in both directions and thought he saw a door closing.

At least one nosy neighbor. Dammit.

"What the hell are you doing here?" he demanded. It was obvious Katya had been crying. "I don't need some drunk woman at my door at midnight screaming in Russian."

"Pyotr, Pyotr," she sobbed. "You can get him released. Tell them Mischa didn't do it."

"Tell who? What happened?"

"Mischa went to the police and told them he killed that girl. The one you were asking about."

"What?"

"Then the *politsiya* –" She flopped down on the sofa. "They came to the shop," she said, sniffling and trying to get her composure back. "Ransacked it. Smashed up the printing press. They won't let me see him – you have to help!"

In a flash, Trevelyan ran everything that he knew of the case through his mind. Mikhail killing Alice? It made no sense. What was the motive?

"He was screwing that *blyadischa*," Katya said, venomously. "How could he do that to me?"

Trevelyan felt like he might throw up. In a cascade the facts fell together in his mind, proofs colliding on their way to inescapable conclusion.

"You killed her," said Trevelyan. It was not a question.

Katya, tears rolling down her cheeks, sat down at the small kitchen table. Trevelyan joined her.

"Tell me what happened."

"I found out they were meeting, in secret. She wasn't one of *us*," Katya said.

Wasn't Russian, she meant. He couldn't tell her.

"I knew there was going to be an attack. So I set up a meeting at the subway station. I wanted her to get caught in the attack, to suffer. But when I saw her.... It was rage, pure rage. Before I knew it, it was over. I left her there, on the bench. I was so angry, Pyotr."

Trevelyan could say nothing for a time except "Katya, Katya."

"After your visit Mikhail realized what I'd done. He turned himself in to protect me. So noble," she scoffed. "Oh God, why do I still love him?" She began sobbing again.

"I didn't know you and Mikhail were – Not until I walked into the shop."

She nodded her head. "We only had each other after you left. Please, Pyotr, you have to get him out of there."

"I can't get him released unless I can give them someone else. The real killer." He stood, pushing the chair away.

She reached in her coat for a packet of cigarettes and lit one with shaking hands.

"Maybe we can work out a deal with the district attorney," he said. "You've got contacts among the anarchists. Turn state's evidence."

"Betray our cause? Mischa was right about you!"

Peter stalked to his desk and from a drawer he pulled the photos from the subway attack, tossing them on the coffee table. Katya looked away.

"That's what your politics cost, Katya! Innocent people, on their way home from work. Dead. Think of their last moments. Think of their agony as the gas choked them. As they were crushed to death. Tell me they don't deserve justice."

"That's not why you want me to turn them in, Petya. You know it."

"If you love him, you won't leave him in there for what you did." Trevelyan took a cigarette from her pack and lit it with shaking hands.

* * *

"They so rarely allow me to leave Wardenclyffe, and then never to a park to feed the pigeons."

Tesla sat on the same bench where Trevelyan had left him two days before. At the inventor's feet were dozens of pigeons cooing and pecking the ground as he hunched over and delicately spread seed for them. "I used to spend wonderful hours in Bryant Park feeding my pigeons."

"In the south-west corner," said Trevelyan.

Tesla turned, a look of delighted surprise on his face.

"It's the same corner you sent Alice Bester to, once a month, to feed your birds." Trevelyan held up the small ID photo from the missing persons report. "Several of the vendors remember seeing this girl there with some frequency over the last two years."

Tesla's smile faded and he turned back to the birds. "I understand Miss Bester's killer has turned herself in. A matter of simple jealousy, I'm told."

"Jealousy, yes," said Trevelyan taking a seat on the bench. "But simple? There are a few things that don't add up. You and Alice were close. You both loved birds. She would bring you birdseed from Capar's Dry Goods on Houston."

"I am impressed, Mr. Trevelyan."

"There was a bag of seed in her pocket when we found her. I noticed the same purple stamp on your bag when I was here last. I understand from the proprietor that a young woman placed an order every other week for a very special blend of birdseed. He mixes it only for her, and she pays a premium for the service. Quite a bill on a secretary's salary."

Tesla smiled weakly. "I gave her the ratios for the mix myself, and arranged payment through Miss Bester. It is what my birds like best, you understand."

"But you ordered Alice to the city at least twice a month, according to Mrs. Wilson. Witnesses only put Alice in Bryant Park once a month. Why the second trip? Was the flower-print dress her signal that her contact wanted to meet?"

"I've no idea what you mean. It's well known –"

"That you hate flower-print dresses, yes. Strange, though, that a social secretary you claimed was the best you'd ever worked with and whom you forbade Mrs. Wilson to fire seemed incapable of remembering such a simple thing. She had dozens of dresses, yet she wore her only flower-print dress twice a month? Tell me, Mr. Tesla, did she also routinely wear pearls, or brush her hair in your face?"

Tesla cringed visibly at the thought.

"I didn't think so," said Trevelyan, leaning close. "How long did it take you to deduce that Miss Bester was Miss Bestemianova and take her into your confidence?"

Tesla paused his feeding, considering the last handful of seed carefully. "You seem to have figured out a great deal, Mr. Trevelyan," said Tesla. "Very well," he said before sprinkling the feed delicately before the cooing, flapping mass of birds. "Let us speak frankly with one another. I knew almost immediately that she was Russian. Her accent. She had been here since she was a child and to anyone born here I'm sure her English was flawless. But I have an ear for such things. A certain lilt when she vocalized certain sounds, and the way she pronounced 'Tesla.'"

"You were in love with her."

"Dear me, no!" Tesla laughed. "I love only my work and my birds. Anything else is a distraction I cannot afford. No, Miss Bester was assisting me in my great work."

"Providing the Russians with plans for your peace beam."

Tesla glowered at Trevelyan. "No doubt you believe the tsar is paying me vast sums for this knowledge? Do you think me so coldly mercenary as that?" Tesla stood and stalked away.

"The thought had occurred to me," said Trevelyan, following.

Tesla rounded on him. "You should call it my death ray, Special Agent. Everyone else does, and they are right. I was terribly naive to think my beam could stop war. It can only make it more terrible, and more random.

"The incident in Siberia was an accident, and not intended whatsoever. I had aimed my teleforce beam for the skies above the Arctic, to a spot I had calculated was west of the Peary expedition. He was then making his second attempt to reach the North Pole and I had asked him to report back to me anything unusual that he might witness on the open tundra.

"When I first energized my tower –" Tesla turned to stare up at the giant mushroom-like transmitter, "it was hard to tell whether it was even working. Then an owl tried to perch on the tower and was disintegrated instantaneously. We powered down at once. That was the extent of the test. Forty seconds, perhaps a minute. But the destruction it caused…

"The beam did not behave as my calculations suggested it would. Instead of discharging into the sky the energy traveled through the crust of the earth itself, erupting in the Tunguska valley. I have still been unable to deduce how or why this happened.

"My death ray is not like an arrow or artillery shell. It follows no predictable path or parabola. It is as random and capricious as lightning. It might strike halfway around the world, or ten feet from you. It is useless as a weapon and a hazard to any nation that would deploy it."

Trevelyan was for a moment too stunned to speak. The whole world thrown into chaos for a weapon no one could use safely?

"Then why give the ray to the Russians?"

Tesla's brow furrowed and he straightened to his full height. "I would destroy the death ray, if I could," he said, voice quavering. "I am thankful beyond measure that the explosion at Tunguska killed no one. But lesser souls will pervert the device for destructive ends. I was a fool not to see this before. I understand now something of what poor Nobel must have felt. I gave the world alternating current, harnessed the power of Niagara Falls, but all I shall be remembered for is my death ray. No, I would never share that technology. It's too terrible to contemplate.

"What I gave Miss Bester were plans and schematics for my defensive shield. The act with the flower-print dress was, as you surmise, to get her to the city when necessary. She said only that she had contacts in the Russian community that could pass the information to the tsar's agents."

Trevelyan staggered back and sat hard on the bench. "Mikhail was her contact?" *Katya, what have you done? They weren't lovers.*

"I wish she did not have to become involved. But Miss Bester was considered such a low security risk that she was allowed off base with greater ease and frequency than would be other members of the staff. And since she was leaving at my eccentric request..."

Trevelyan understood. No one would suspect Tesla of collaborating with the Entente that had tried to kill him.

"Getting the shield to the Russians is the only way to ensure, nay, *enforce* global peace," said Tesla. "If the Entente can shield their cities as we can, it renders not only conventional warfare obsolete, but also my death ray.

"There are elements, within our military and our government who wish to use the death ray even knowing its flaws. Edison – that fool! – has convinced them that the accuracy of the weapon can be refined and a targeting system devised."

Trevelyan lifted his head from his hands. "Is this possible?"

"Possible," said Tesla slowly. "But only at terrible cost. Edison's plan for calibration might take as many as several hundred firings of the weapon. Several hundred Tunguskas.

"This is what Miss Bester – let us call her by her proper name at last, Miss Bestemianova – was working to prevent. But with her dead the Russians will never build the shield towers, now. They are still missing key components of the plans. Everything I have worked for – that *she* worked for – has come to naught. I have unleashed a *terror* upon the world."

Tesla staggered to the bench and began to weep.

* * *

Trevelyan had spent a long night in prayer before his icon of St. Mark of the Caves, asking help and guidance from a saint known for his gift of discernment. And as he descended the creaking stairs to Mikhail's basement it struck him how cave-like the space was. Carved from the bedrock of Manhattan, the walls were dark and slick with moisture.

Given the contents of the briefcase Trevelyan carried he thought it appropriate, too, that St. Mark was also known as the Gravedigger.

In the harsh light of the single Edison bulb, Trevelyan saw that the basement and the printing press had been worked over. Paper was everywhere, both printed issues and sheaves of blank stock: shredded, wrinkled, stepped on and torn. The presses were battered and bent, like someone – or several someones – had taken a sledgehammer to them.

In the damp chill, Mikhail stood with his back to the stairs, leaning over his smashed press and trying to repair the dented rollers with nothing more than a wrench.

Mikhail mumbled something that Trevelyan couldn't make out, and as his brother turned toward him Trevelyan got his first look at Mikhail's battered face. Deep purple bruises, a split through the left eyebrow, a swollen lip.

"*Bozhe moy...*" whispered Trevelyan.

"This is what they think of us," Mikhail mumbled. Only then did Trevelyan realize his brother's jaw was wired shut.

"I'm so sorry, Mischa."

Mikhail sucked back spittle leaking through the wiring. "Save your pity for Katya. I wasn't sleeping with Alice. I never told Katya what we were doing so I could *protect* her if it went bad. Instead... this. She told me you wanted her to make a deal, turn in her contacts. She won't do it. She'd never betray the movement. Just like I didn't tell the police your precious secret. You have no radical brother to embarrass you."

"Mischa, if I could have protected her –"

"Don't," he said, turning back to his ruined press. After a moment: "I was only ever worried that Katya loved *you*. I had no idea that she would –" He began to silently shake.

After a long pause Trevelyan said: "Alice was getting the plans directly from Tesla." At that, Mikhail turned around. "Told me so himself. We both misjudged him. He wants his death ray stopped as badly as anyone." Trevelyan held up the briefcase. "These are the last blueprints they need to build shield generators of their own."

"Is this a trick? A trap?"

Trevelyan shook his head. Mikhail managed a "Why?" after a moment of stunned silence.

"I know you have contacts with the tsarists," Trevelyan said. "I know you've been passing Tesla's plans to them. I need you to finish the job."

"There's no money in this. No glory," said Mikhail, defensive. "We are doing only what needs doing."

"I never thought you were being paid, Mischa," said Trevelyan, handing him the briefcase.

Mikhail quickly examined the papers inside before closing the case. "They will shoot us for this, you know," he said. "If we are caught. This is treason."

Peter never imagined doing anything like this. Everything was upside down. He simply nodded and said, "Then let us hope it's a noble treason."

Induction

Colt Leasure

EWEN RUMELL sat in his office. The room had oak paneled walls and a smooth mahogany desk placed near a large window overlooking a grassy lot. He had enough filled bookshelves to open up his own second hand literary store, if the public were more interested in buying works on esoteric subjects. Texts on occultism, astrology, the I-ching and Solomon's magic rituals were placed next to hardcover tomes on meditation. Lining the topmost shelf were amulets, crystals, and hand crafted talismans he had collected during his travels through the Sahara.

Rumell was a hypnotist by profession. Describing his occupation made interesting small talk at parties, but it usually aroused heavy judgment in whomever he was speaking to. Skeptics loved to roll their eyes at him. When being honest about what he did for a living, the cynical would ask him if he was a parlor magician, a carnival stage performer, or a children's birthday party entertainer.

This used to offend him, but he had grown a thick skin. He would end the talk by handing over a business card and telling them to come and see him if they ever needed help changing their problematic thought processes. He preferred to think of himself as an entrepreneur who convinced the stubborn and nourished the open minded, as opposed to someone who the vast public had disregarded as a simple snake oil salesman who indulged in street tricks.

Rumell was about to close up early on that day. Only two patients had come in, and the sessions were short. The first one needed help to quit wasting time playing crossword puzzles, and the second was spending too much money on lottery tickets, and they asked him to help cure them of their habits.

There were no other people scheduled to visit him, so he was only a few seconds away from retrieving the keys to his office and locking the place up for the rest of the evening before there was a loud knock on his door.

He stood from his chair, walked over to the main entrance and peered through the peephole. There was a woman wearing a burgundy sweatshirt standing on the other side. She was in her mid twenties, and had pale skin and black hair.

Rumell opened the door.

"Hello," she said, extending a hand. "Are you Dr. Rumell?"

"Yes," he said, taking her hand in his and shaking it.

"Can I come in?"

"Sure," he said, opening the door further and then pointing to the crimson leather inclined stretcher chair in front of his desk.

When she was seated and he was behind his computer, he put on his glasses and checked his list, asking her what her name was.

"Tiffany McAllister," she said.

"You're not on my scheduled appointments. I like to set my sessions up ahead of time."

"I'm sorry," she said. "I didn't feel comfortable doing that. I've been monitoring your office for a few days now. Not many people came in or out. I thought you wouldn't be busy enough to justify turning me away."

Rumell laughed, assuring her that no offense was taken, although he did feel a bit strange about her admitting to having stalked his premises.

"You're right," he said. "So tell me, what is it you'd like to do? Keep in mind that I will have you sign a waiver before we get started. Are you curious about the pricing?"

"Not a problem, and no. I have one question. Is everything I say in this office confidential? I'm afraid that I may have done some bad things that I can't recall, things that may not be… legal. I just want assurance from you that you're not going to get me in trouble."

Rumell thought of all the people at the low end of society that he had treated, such as rapists who wanted to keep their worst temptations for power at bay, drug addicts who needed to be reprogrammed in order to stop stealing to feed their habits, and amnesiacs whose neurological conditions stemmed from incidents of driving while drunk. As much as he wanted to call the authorities on some of the legitimately sick and depraved men he had dealt with over the years, he had taken an oath to fix, to cure, to treat, and not to play as an informant or perceive their reaching out for help from a place of judgment.

"I guarantee the full sealing of any and all information," he said. "This room is not recorded. Any notes I take are for the sake of managing, tracking and modifying progress for statistical purposes, nothing else, and all of those notes are barricaded away in my files and destroyed when I deem them to be irrelevant once you are cured of whatever ailment you have."

"What if a law enforcement agency has a warrant for your notes?"

"That never happens," he said. "I am a hypnotist. Authorities don't think of me a licensed source of information, not in the same way a shrink or even priest may be. I am, first and foremost, someone you can trust and be open with. I need you to be that way with me, if you want any real help. So tell me – what are you here for?"

"I can't recall anything from before two weeks ago," she said. "I don't remember where I was born or where I went to school, but I found out that I can play the piano fluently, having somehow burned to memory every note of Rachmaninoff from a past that I cannot distinguish. I could not describe the voices or physical appearances of my parents, friends, or significant other, but I can recite every Blake poem and give a visual synopsis of every classic portraiture. I am a chef when it comes to certain cuisines, and one of my other talents is hitting the bull's eye on a dartboard every time without fail whenever I enter a bar. I can throw a knife at a tree branch from any distance and have the blade connect. I can sprint and jump high hurdles. In other words, I need you to tell me who I am, doctor."

He sat back in his chair and contemplated her words. "So your life, until two weeks ago, is a blur?"

"No," she said. "It's a black out. I have tried to retrace the steps I can't remember taking. I hit a wall every time. That's why I've come to you. I've heard that you specialize in summoning scenes from people's past lives. I need that for the life I'm in."

"Tell me what happened two weeks ago, when you woke up without any memory."

Tiffany readjusted herself on the couch, and pointed to a black water pitcher on his desk, asking Rumell if she could have a glass. He retrieved a decanter from his drawer, filled it to the brim with the water, and then handed it to her. She drank it before starting her story.

"I woke up at dusk," she said. "Looking around, I saw that I was in a decrepit and windowless building. Every gap in the walls gave me a view of a surrounding of trees, and they were rotted and swaying with the wind. From the signs describing different wings where various medical practices had happened at some point. I was in an abandoned hospital. It was clear that looters, squatters, homeless and junkies had taken over the place, with explicit graffiti all over the walls. Then I found the bodies.

"There were three men sprawled out near me who were butchered. They were covered in blood, and as I inched closer to them, they were not breathing. They had been dead a while based on the dryness of the red on their clothes. They had been murdered with something sharp. I do not know what compelled me to be curious instead of scared, but I did a quick search of the perimeter with the hopes of finding the weapon, and I did. I saw an ice pick drenched in blood on one of the lower hanging roofs minutes later. What's strange is, it took me even longer to find out that I myself was covered in blood.

"I was not in any pain, and there were no scrapes on me, so that meant it all came from someone else. Did I murder those men? I don't know. The next thing I did was search for scrubs or any kind of clothing that had not been eaten by moths or stolen by vagrants, and I found some eventually, along with a sink that actually had running water. I headed to the woods to try to find my way back to town. I walked for seven miles, not finding anything besides nature. It was another hour of wandering before I began to get the feeling that I was being followed.

"After another fifteen minutes of contemplating how maybe it was a bear or a deer, I finally saw the silhouette of a figure trailing behind me – one in the shape of a man. When he saw that I had spotted him, he charged at me. He was wearing a black bag over his head and was holding a knife. I don't know how or where I learned to do this, but I fought him, disarmed him, and killed him in self-defense. I blocked his right hand which held the blade, used my left to steal it, swept his foot out from under him, and when he was on his knees I slashed his carotid artery. I ran for twenty minutes straight, until finally coming across a freeway. I managed to get picked up by a trucker, who brought me to a nearby motel and paid for my room. In the following weeks, having no money to my name, I found a storage shed that was not checked on frequently by the landlords of the unit, so I lived in there. I take showers at a nearby recreation center, and maintain a low profile. I have this constant feeling that more people are out to kill me."

"Did you call the police?" Rumell asked. "Did you go to a real hospital to get checked out? A doctor of neurology might be able to help you to determine if the reason for your amnesia could be a result of some kind of an impact."

"I was too scared," she said, lowering her head and taking another sip of water. "I thought I might be guilty, and although I had no recollection of what had transpired, I knew that telling a judge 'I don't remember anything' wouldn't be a good defense. I must be a victim of something. There are indicators that they tried to kill me not once, but at least four times, judging by the body count. How could I prove it, though, when I woke up in a room full of the dead? None of this makes me look good. Again, this is why I've come to you. I want you to help me determine what my next step should be. Help me remember."

"Alright," Rumell said. He stood up, dimmed the lights, and pulled out a flat screen situated on a rolling table from his closet, positioning it in front of her. He told her to sit back as he went near the bookshelves and turned on a stereo. Vibrant nature sounds filled the room.

"Close your eyes and relax," he said. "Picture each part of your body turning off – all of the tenseness and uptightness is floating away."

Hypnotizing someone, Rumell knew, was never that difficult. It was not something that required years of research or study. All it took was practice, an approach similar to that of a method actor's, and a little bit of tenacity. Using a mixture of guided visualization, meditation, and convincing her through brief physical contact that there was an 'energy transmission,' he was able to put her in a state of what magicians liked to call gnosis.

"What was your name before you adopted the one of Tiffany McAllister?"

A brief pause. "La… Larisa."

"Larisa what?"

"Larisa Snezhana."

"Where are you from originally?"

"Lake Baikal. Siberia."

"When and why did you come to the states?" "An assignment."

"To do what?"

"Escape."

"From who? From what?"

"My agency. They are going to kill me…"

Over the course of the next fifteen minutes, he found out everything. How she was actually what the media would call a 'honey trapper,' a female Russian spy who used seductiveness to gain the confidence and eventual secrecy of major politicians or people of influence. However, she had broken the ties with her agency by revealing sensitive information. This was an act of treason with only one outcome of punishment, and that was death.

When he snapped his fingers, she woke up again. Her eyes not only opened, but they were now bulging.

It then dawned on Rumell that in addition to her finally knowing everything she wanted, he, too, was the one who knew way too much. This was beyond simple murder. In that second, based on the animalistic nature of her eyes, he knew that he would be lucky to leave that room alive with the true stories that he had just brought out of her.

Larisa stood up quickly and dove at Rumell. He was on the ground now, her on top of him, her hands clasped around his throat, strangling him. He reached up and tried to strike her in the face, his first two punches being relatively weak, the third one finally hitting her hard enough to make her bleed. Rumell then struck her a fourth time, and when her body shifted to the right with the blunt force, he kicked her off of him.

He ran over to the book shelf, grabbing a sharp crystal that he had collected during his trips overseas. He turned around to find that she was running at him. With one full swing, he jabbed the piece at her, which in turn slashed her face open. She was now spraying blood everywhere, on his desk, his books, the reclining chair, screaming hysterically while still trying to claw at him. He then drove the amulet into her forehead, recklessly pushing forward until she collapsed.

Rumell went over to his landline phone and dialed 911. While doing so, he felt a tingling on the back of his neck. Turning around, he looked out at the grassy lot that his office faced, and saw two men in the distance. Both were stocky, wearing sunglasses and suits. When they saw him staring at them, they took a few steps back, turned around and got into a black Mercedes, driving away out of the hypnotist's sight.

The Mysterious Railway Passenger

Maurice Leblanc

THE EVENING before, I had sent my automobile to Rouen by the highway. I was to travel to Rouen by rail, on my way to visit some friends that live on the banks of the Seine.

At Paris, a few minutes before the train started, seven gentlemen entered my compartment; five of them were smoking. No matter that the journey was a short one, the thought of traveling with such a company was not agreeable to me, especially as the car was built on the old model, without a corridor. I picked up my overcoat, my newspapers and my time-table, and sought refuge in a neighboring compartment.

It was occupied by a lady, who, at sight of me, made a gesture of annoyance that did not escape my notice, and she leaned toward a gentleman who was standing on the step and was, no doubt, her husband. The gentleman scrutinized me closely, and, apparently, my appearance did not displease him, for he smiled as he spoke to his wife with the air of one who reassures a frightened child. She smiled also, and gave me a friendly glance as if she now understood that I was one of those gallant men with whom a woman can remain shut up for two hours in a little box, six feet square, and have nothing to fear.

Her husband said to her:

"I have an important appointment, my dear, and cannot wait any longer. Adieu."

He kissed her affectionately and went away. His wife threw him a few kisses and waved her handkerchief. The whistle sounded, and the train started.

At that precise moment, and despite the protests of the guards, the door was opened, and a man rushed into our compartment. My companion, who was standing and arranging her luggage, uttered a cry of terror and fell upon the seat. I am not a coward – far from it – but I confess that such intrusions at the last minute are always disconcerting. They have a suspicious, unnatural aspect.

However, the appearance of the new arrival greatly modified the unfavorable impression produced by his precipitant action. He was correctly and elegantly dressed, wore a tasteful cravat, correct gloves, and his face was refined and intelligent. But, where the devil had I seen that face before? Because, beyond all possible doubt, I had seen it. And yet the memory of it was so vague and indistinct that I felt it would be useless to try to recall it at that time.

Then, directing my attention to the lady, I was amazed at the pallor and anxiety I saw in her face. She was looking at her neighbor – they occupied seats on the same side of the compartment – with an expression of intense alarm, and I perceived that one of her trembling hands was slowly gliding toward a little traveling bag that was lying on the seat about twenty inches from her. She finished by seizing it and nervously drawing it to her. Our eyes met, and I read in hers so much anxiety and fear that I could not refrain from speaking to her:

"Are you ill, madame? Shall I open the window?"

Her only reply was a gesture indicating that she was afraid of our companion. I smiled, as her husband had done, shrugged my shoulders, and explained to her, in pantomime, that she had nothing to fear, that I was there, and, besides, the gentleman appeared to be a very harmless individual. At that moment, he turned toward us, scrutinized both of us from head to foot, then settled down in his corner and paid us no more attention.

After a short silence, the lady, as if she had mustered all her energy to perform a desperate act, said to me, in an almost inaudible voice:

"Do you know who is on our train?"

"Who?"

"He… he… I assure you…"

"Who is he?"

"Arsene Lupin!"

She had not taken her eyes off our companion, and it was to him rather than to me that she uttered the syllables of that disquieting name. He drew his hat over his face. Was that to conceal his agitation or, simply, to arrange himself for sleep? Then I said to her:

"Yesterday, through contumacy, Arsene Lupin was sentenced to twenty years' imprisonment at hard labor. Therefore it is improbable that he would be so imprudent, today, as to show himself in public. Moreover, the newspapers have announced his appearance in Turkey since his escape from the Sante."

"But he is on this train at the present moment," the lady proclaimed, with the obvious intention of being heard by our companion; "my husband is one of the directors in the penitentiary service, and it was the stationmaster himself who told us that a search was being made for Arsene Lupin."

"They may have been mistaken –"

"No; he was seen in the waiting-room. He bought a first-class ticket for Rouen."

"He has disappeared. The guard at the waiting-room door did not see him pass, and it is supposed that he had got into the express that leaves ten minutes after us."

"In that case, they will be sure to catch him."

"Unless, at the last moment, he leaped from that train to come here, into our train… which is quite probable… which is almost certain."

"If so, he will be arrested just the same; for the employees and guards would no doubt observe his passage from one train to the other, and, when we arrive at Rouen, they will arrest him there."

"Him – never! He will find some means of escape."

"In that case, I wish him 'bon voyage.'"

"But, in the meantime, think what he may do!"

"What?"

"I don't know. He may do anything."

She was greatly agitated, and, truly, the situation justified, to some extent, her nervous excitement. I was impelled to say to her:

"Of course, there are many strange coincidences, but you need have no fear. Admitting that Arsene Lupin is on this train, he will not commit any indiscretion; he will be only too happy to escape the peril that already threatens him."

My words did not reassure her, but she remained silent for a time. I unfolded my newspapers and read reports of Arsene Lupin's trial, but, as they contained nothing that was new to me, I was not greatly interested. Moreover, I was tired and sleepy. I felt my eyelids close and my head drop.

"But, monsieur, you are not going to sleep!"

She seized my newspaper, and looked at me with indignation.

"Certainly not," I said.

"That would be very imprudent."

"Of course," I assented.

I struggled to keep awake. I looked through the window at the landscape and the fleeting clouds, but in a short time all that became confused and indistinct; the image of the nervous lady and the drowsy gentleman were effaced from my memory, and I was buried in the soothing depths of a profound sleep. The tranquility of my response was soon disturbed by disquieting dreams, wherein a creature that had played the part and bore the name of Arsene Lupin held an important place. He appeared to me with his black laden with articles of value; he leaped over walls, and plundered castles. But the outlines of that creature, who was no longer Arsene Lupin, assumed a more definite form. He came toward me, growing larger and larger, leaped into the compartment with incredible agility, and landed squarely on my chest. With a cry of fright and pain, I awoke. The man, the traveller, our companion, with his knee on my breast, held me by the throat.

My sight was very indistinct, for my eyes were suffused with blood. I could see the lady, in a corner of the compartment, convulsed with fright. I tried even not to resist. Besides, I did not have the strength. My temples throbbed; I was almost strangled. One minute more, and I would have breathed my last. The man must have realized it, for he relaxed his grip, but did not remove his had. Then he took a cord, in which he had prepared a slip-knot, and tied my wrists together. In an instant, I was bound, gagged, and helpless.

Certainly, he accomplished the trick with an ease and skill that revealed the hand of a master; he was, no doubt, a professional thief. Not a word, not a nervous movement; only coolness and audacity. And I was there, lying on the bench, bound like a mummy, I – Arsene Lupin!

It was anything but a laughing matter, and yet, despite the gravity of the situation, I keenly appreciated the humor and irony that it involved. Arsene Lupin seized and bound like a novice! Robbed as if I were an unsophisticated rustic – for, you must understand, the scoundrel had deprived me of my purse and wallet! Arsene Lupin, a victim, duped, vanquished…. What an adventure!

The lady did not move. He did not even notice her. He contented himself with picking up her traveling-bag that had fallen to the floor and taking from it the jewels, purse, and gold and silver trinkets that it contained. The lady opened her eyes, trembled with fear, drew the rings from her fingers and handed them to the man as if she wished to spare him unnecessary trouble. He took the rings and looked at her. She swooned.

Then, quite unruffled, he resumed his seat, lighted a cigarette, and proceeded to examine the treasure that he had acquired. The examination appeared to give him perfect satisfaction.

But I was not so well satisfied. I do not speak of the twelve thousand francs of which I had been unduly deprived: that was only a temporary loss, because I was certain that I would recover possession of that money after a very brief delay, together with the important papers contained in my wallet: plans, specifications, addresses, lists of correspondents, and compromising letters. But, for the moment, a more immediate and more serious question troubled me: How would this affair end? What would be the outcome of this adventure?

As you can imagine, the disturbance created by my passage through the Saint-Lazare station has not escaped my notice. Going to visit friends who knew me under the name of Guillaume Berlat, and amongst whom my resemblance to Arsene Lupin was a subject of many innocent jests, I could not assume a disguise, and my presence had been remarked. So, beyond question, the commissary of police at Rouen, notified by telegraph, and assisted by numerous agents, would be awaiting the train, would question all suspicious passengers, and proceed to search the cars.

Of course, I had foreseen all that, but it had not disturbed me, as I was certain that the police of Rouen would not be any shrewder than the police of Paris and that I could escape recognition; would it not be sufficient for me to carelessly display my card as 'depute,' thanks to which I had inspired complete confidence in the gate-keeper at Saint-Lazare? – But the situation was greatly changed. I was no longer free. It was impossible to attempt one of my usual tricks. In one of the compartments, the commissary of police would find Mon. Arsene Lupin, bound hand and foot, as docile as a lamb, packed up, all ready to be dumped into a prison-van. He would have simply to accept delivery of the parcel, the same as if it were so much merchandise or a basket of fruit and vegetables. Yet, to avoid that shameful denouement, what could I do? – bound and gagged, as I was? And the train was rushing on toward Rouen, the next and only station.

Another problem was presented, in which I was less interested, but the solution of which aroused my professional curiosity. What were the intentions of my rascally companion? Of course, if I had been alone, he could, on our arrival at Rouen, leave the car slowly and fearlessly. But the lady? As soon as the door of the compartment should be opened, the lady, now so quiet and humble, would scream and call for help. That was the dilemma that perplexed me! Why had he not reduced her to a helpless condition similar to mine? That would have given him ample time to disappear before his double crime was discovered.

He was still smoking, with his eyes fixed upon the window that was now being streaked with drops of rain. Once he turned, picked up my time-table, and consulted it.

The lady had to feign a continued lack of consciousness in order to deceive the enemy. But fits of coughing, provoked by the smoke, exposed her true condition. As to me, I was very uncomfortable, and very tired. And I meditated; I plotted.

The train was rushing on, joyously, intoxicated with its own speed.

Saint Etienne! ... At that moment, the man arose and took two steps toward us, which caused the lady to utter a cry of alarm and fall into a genuine swoon. What was the man about to do? He lowered the window on our side. A heavy rain was now falling, and, by a gesture, the man expressed his annoyance at his not having an umbrella or an overcoat. He glanced at the rack. The lady's umbrella was there. He took it. He also took my overcoat and put it on.

We were now crossing the Seine. He turned up the bottoms of his trousers, then leaned over and raised the exterior latch of the door. Was he going to throw himself upon the track? At that speed, it would have been instant death. We now entered a tunnel. The man opened the door half-way and stood on the upper step. What folly! The darkness, the smoke, the noise, all gave a fantastic appearance to his actions. But suddenly, the train diminished its speed. A moment later it increased its speed, then slowed up again. Probably, some repairs were being made in that part of the tunnel which obliged the trains to diminish their speed, and the man was aware of the fact. He immediately stepped down to the lower step, closed the door behind him, and leaped to the ground. He was gone.

The lady immediately recovered her wits, and her first act was to lament the loss of her jewels. I gave her an imploring look. She understood, and quickly removed the gag that stifled me. She wished to untie the cords that bound me, but I prevented her.

"No, no, the police must see everything exactly as it stands. I want them to see what the rascal did to us."

"Suppose I pull the alarm-bell?"

"Too late. You should have done that when he made the attack on me."

"But he would have killed me. Ah! Monsieur, didn't I tell you that he was on this train. I recognized him from his portrait. And now he has gone off with my jewels."

"Don't worry. The police will catch him."

"Catch Arsene Lupin! Never."

"That depends on you, madame. Listen. When we arrive at Rouen, be at the door and call. Make a noise. The police and the railway employees will come. Tell what you have seen: the assault made on me and the flight of Arsene Lupin. Give a description of him – soft hat, umbrella – yours – gray overcoat..."

"Yours," said she.

"What! Mine? Not at all. It was his. I didn't have any."

"It seems to me he didn't have one when he came in."

"Yes, yes... unless the coat was one that some one had forgotten and left in the rack. At all events, he had it when he went away, and that is the essential point. A gray overcoat – remember! ... Ah! I forgot. You must tell your name, first thing you do. Your husband's official position will stimulate the zeal of the police."

We arrived at the station. I gave her some further instructions in a rather imperious tone:

"Tell them my name – Guillaume Berlat. If necessary, say that you know me. That will save time. We must expedite the preliminary investigation. The important thing is the pursuit of Arsene Lupin. Your jewels, remember! Let there be no mistake. Guillaume Berlat, a friend of your husband."

"I understand... Guillaume Berlat."

She was already calling and gesticulating. As soon as the train stopped, several men entered the compartment. The critical moment had come.

Panting for breath, the lady exclaimed:

"Arsene Lupin... he attacked us... he stole my jewels... I am Madame Renaud... my husband is a director of the penitentiary service... Ah! Here is my brother, Georges Ardelle, director of the Credit Rouennais... you must know..."

She embraced a young man who had just joined us, and whom the commissary saluted. Then she continued, weeping:

"Yes, Arsene Lupin... while monsieur was sleeping, he seized him by the throat... Mon. Berlat, a friend of my husband."

The commissary asked:

"But where is Arsene Lupin?"

"He leaped from the train, when passing through the tunnel."

"Are you sure that it was he?"

"Am I sure! I recognized him perfectly. Besides, he was seen at the Saint-Lazare station. He wore a soft hat –"

"No, a hard felt, like that," said the commissary, pointing to my hat.

"He had a soft hat, I am sure," repeated Madame Renaud, "and a gray overcoat."

"Yes, that is right," replied the commissary, "the telegram says he wore a gray overcoat with a black velvet collar."

"Exactly, a black velvet collar," exclaimed Madame Renaud, triumphantly.

I breathed freely. Ah! The excellent friend I had in that little woman.

The police agents had now released me. I bit my lips until they ran blood. Stooping over, with my handkerchief over my mouth, an attitude quite natural in a person who has remained for a long time in an uncomfortable position, and whose mouth shows the bloody marks of the gag, I addressed the commissary, in a weak voice:

"Monsieur, it was Arsene Lupin. There is no doubt about that. If we make haste, he can be caught yet. I think I may be of some service to you."

The railway car, in which the crime occurred, was detached from the train to serve as a mute witness at the official investigation. The train continued on its way to Havre. We were then conducted to the station-master's office through a crowd of curious spectators.

Then, I had a sudden access of doubt and discretion. Under some pretext or other, I must gain my automobile, and escape. To remain there was dangerous. Something might happen; for instance, a telegram from Paris, and I would be lost.

Yes, but what about my thief? Abandoned to my own resources, in an unfamiliar country, I could not hope to catch him.

"Bah! I must make the attempt," I said to myself. "It may be a difficult game, but an amusing one, and the stake is well worth the trouble."

And when the commissary asked us to repeat the story of the robbery, I exclaimed:

"Monsieur, really, Arsene Lupin is getting the start of us. My automobile is waiting in the courtyard. If you will be so kind as to use it, we can try..."

The commissary smiled, and replied:

"The idea is a good one; so good, indeed, that it is already being carried out. Two of my men have set out on bicycles. They have been gone for some time."

"Where did they go?"

"To the entrance of the tunnel. There, they will gather evidence, secure witnesses, and follow on the track of Arsene Lupin."

I could not refrain from shrugging my shoulders, as I replied:

"Your men will not secure any evidence or any witnesses."

"Really!"

"Arsene Lupin will not allow anyone to see him emerge from the tunnel. He will take the first road –"

"To Rouen, where we will arrest him."

"He will not go to Rouen."

"Then he will remain in the vicinity, where his capture will be even more certain."

"He will not remain in the vicinity."

"Oh! Oh! And where will he hide?"

I looked at my watch, and said:

"At the present moment, Arsene Lupin is prowling around the station at Darnetal. At ten fifty, that is, in twenty-two minutes from now, he will take the train that goes from Rouen to Amiens."

"Do you think so? How do you know it?"

"Oh! It is quite simple. While we were in the car, Arsene Lupin consulted my railway guide. Why did he do it? Was there, not far from the spot where he disappeared, another line of railway, a station upon that line, and a train stopping at that station? On consulting my railway guide, I found such to be the case."

"Really, monsieur," said the commissary, "that is a marvelous deduction. I congratulate you on your skill."

I was now convinced that I had made a mistake in displaying so much cleverness. The commissary regarded me with astonishment, and I though a slight suspicion entered his official mind... Oh! Scarcely that, for the photographs distributed broadcast by the police department were too imperfect; they presented an Arsene Lupin so different from the one he had before him, that he could not possibly recognize me by it. But, all the same, he was troubled, confused and ill-at-ease.

"Mon Dieu! nothing stimulates the comprehension so much as the loss of a pocketbook and the desire to recover it. And it seems to me that if you will give me two of your men, we may be able..."

"Oh! I beg of you, monsieur le commissaire," cried Madame Renaud, "listen to Mon. Berlat."

The intervention of my excellent friend was decisive. Pronounced by her, the wife of an influential official, the name of Berlat became really my own, and gave me an identity that no mere suspicion could affect. The commissary arose, and said:

"Believe me, Monsieur Berlat, I shall be delighted to see you succeed. I am as much interested as you are in the arrest of Arsene Lupin."

He accompanied me to the automobile, and introduced two of his men, Honore Massol and Gaston Delivet, who were assigned to assist me. My chauffer cranked up the car and I took my place at the wheel. A few seconds later, we left the station. I was saved.

Ah! I must confess that in rolling over the boulevards that surrounded the old Norman city, in my swift thirty-five horse-power Moreau-Lepton, I experienced a deep feeling of pride, and the motor responded, sympathetically to my desires. At right and left, the trees flew past us with startling rapidity, and I, free, out of danger, had simply to arrange my little personal affairs with the two honest representatives of the Rouen police who were sitting behind me. Arsene Lupin was going in search of Arsene Lupin!

Modest guardians of social order – Gaston Delivet and Honore Massol – how valuable was your assistance! What would I have done without you? Without you, many times, at the cross-roads, I might have taken the wrong route! Without you, Arsene Lupin would have made a mistake, and the other would have escaped!

But the end was not yet. Far from it. I had yet to capture the thief and recover the stolen papers. Under no circumstances must my two acolytes be permitted to see those papers, much less to seize them. That was a point that might give me some difficulty.

We arrived at Darnetal three minutes after the departure of the train. True, I had the consolation of learning that a man wearing a gray overcoat with a black velvet collar had taken the train at the station. He had bought a second-class ticket for Amiens. Certainly, my debut as detective was a promising one.

Delivet said to me:

"The train is express, and the next stop is Monterolier-Buchy in nineteen minutes. If we do not reach there before Arsene Lupin, he can proceed to Amiens, or change for the train going to Cleres, and, from that point, reach Dieppe or Paris."

"How far to Monterolier?"

"Twenty-three kilometres."

"Twenty-three kilometres in nineteen minutes... We will be there ahead of him."

We were off again! Never had my faithful Moreau-Repton responded to my impatience with such ardor and regularity. It participated in my anxiety. It indorsed my determination. It comprehended my animosity against that rascally Arsene Lupin. The knave! The traitor!

"Turn to the right," cried Delivet, "then to the left."

We fairly flew, scarcely touching the ground. The mile-stones looked like little timid beasts that vanished at our approach. Suddenly, at a turn of the road, we saw a vortex of smoke. It was the Northern Express. For a kilometre, it was a struggle, side by side, but an unequal struggle in which the issue was certain. We won the race by twenty lengths.

In three seconds we were on the platform standing before the second-class carriages. The doors were opened, and some passengers alighted, but not my thief. We made a search through the compartments. No sign of Arsene Lupin.

"Sapristi!" I cried, "he must have recognized me in the automobile as we were racing, side by side, and he leaped from the train."

"Ah! There he is now! Crossing the track."

I started in pursuit of the man, followed by my two acolytes, or rather followed by one of them, for the other, Massol, proved himself to be a runner of exceptional speed and endurance. In a few moments, he had made an appreciable gain upon the fugitive. The man noticed it, leaped over a hedge, scampered across a meadow, and entered a thick grove. When we reached this grove, Massol was waiting for us. He went no farther, for fear of losing us.

"Quite right, my dear friend," I said. "After such a run, our victim must be out of wind. We will catch him now."

I examined the surroundings with the idea of proceeding alone in the arrest of the fugitive, in order to recover my papers, concerning which the authorities would doubtless ask many disagreeable questions. Then I returned to my companions, and said:

"It is all quite easy. You, Massol, take your place at the left; you, Delivet, at the right. From there, you can observe the entire posterior line of the bush, and he cannot escape without you seeing him, except by that ravine, and I shall watch it. If he does not come out voluntarily, I will enter and drive him out toward one or the other of you. You have simply to wait. Ah! I forgot: in case I need you, a pistol shot."

Massol and Delivet walked away to their respective posts. As soon as they had disappeared, I entered the grove with the greatest precaution so as to be neither seen nor heard. I encountered dense thickets, trough which narrow paths had been cut, but the overhanging boughs compelled me to adopt a stooping posture. One of these paths led to a clearing in which I found footsteps upon the wet grass. I followed them; they led me to the foot of a mound which was surmounted by a deserted, dilapidated hovel.

"He must be there," I said to myself. "It is a well-chosen retreat."

I crept cautiously to the side of the building. A slight noise informed me that he was there; and, then, through an opening, I saw him. His back was turned toward me. In two bounds, I was upon him. He tried to fire a revolver that he held in his hand. But he had no time. I threw him to the ground, in such a manner that his arms were beneath him, twisted and helpless, whilst I held him down with my knee on his breast.

"Listen, my boy," I whispered in his ear. "I am Arsene Lupin. You are to deliver over to me, immediately and gracefully, my pocketbook and the lady's jewels, and, in return therefore, I will save you from the police and enroll you amongst my friends. One word: yes or no?"

"Yes," he murmured.

"Very good. Your escape, this morning, was well planned. I congratulate you."

I arose. He fumbled in his pocket, drew out a large knife and tried to strike me with it.

"Imbecile!" I exclaimed.

With one hand, I parried the attack; with the other, I gave him a sharp blow on the carotid artery. He fell – stunned!

In my pocketbook, I recovered my papers and bank-notes. Out of curiosity, I took his. Upon an envelope, addressed to him, I read his name: Pierre Onfrey. It startled me. Pierre Onfrey, the assassin of the rue Lafontaine at Auteuil! Pierre Onfrey, he who had cut the throats of Madame Delbois and her two daughters. I leaned over him. Yes, those were the features which, in the compartment, had evoked in me the memory of a face I could not then recall.

But time was passing. I placed in an envelope two bank-notes of one hundred francs each, with a card bearing these words: "Arsene Lupin to his worthy colleagues Honore Massol and Gaston Delivet, as a slight token of his gratitude." I placed it in a prominent spot in the room, where they would be sure to find it. Beside it, I placed Madame Renaud's handbag. Why could I not return it to the lady who had befriended me? I must confess that I had taken from it everything that possessed any interest or value, leaving there only a shell comb, a stick of rouge Dorin for the lips, and an empty purse. But, you know, business is business. And then, really, her husband is engaged in such a dishonorable vocation!

The man was becoming conscious. What was I to do? I was unable to save him or condemn him. So I took his revolver and fired a shot in the air.

"My two acolytes will come and attend to his case," I said to myself, as I hastened away by the road through the ravine. Twenty minutes later, I was seated in my automobile.

At four o'clock, I telegraphed to my friends at Rouen that an unexpected event would prevent me from making my promised visit. Between ourselves, considering what my friends must now know, my visit is postponed indefinitely. A cruel disillusion for them!

At six o'clock I was in Paris. The evening newspapers informed me that Pierre Onfrey had been captured at last.

Next day, – let us not despise the advantages of judicious advertising, – the *Echo de France* published this sensational item:

"Yesterday, near Buchy, after numerous exciting incidents, Arsene Lupin effected the arrest of Pierre Onfrey. The assassin of the rue Lafontaine had robbed Madame Renaud, wife of the director in the penitentiary service, in a railway carriage on the Paris-Havre line. Arsene Lupin restored to Madame Renaud the hand-bag that contained her jewels, and gave a generous recompense to the two detectives who had assisted him in making that dramatic arrest."

To Catch A Mole

Jonathan MacGregor

IT'S BEEN fifteen minutes since Safehouse 5 detonated in downtown Manhattan. Four operatives sit opposite me in the confines of Safehouse 6; the representative of the Syrian Opposition paces without pause in the adjacent chamber. My Sig Sauer P229 – the only weapon in the room – rests on the arm of my chair. At least one of the agents before me is a mole. None of us are leaving until I discover the truth.

"Tell me what happened," I say, straightening the cuff of my shirt.

"Special Agent Sanborne..." One of the women, an African-American agent with short, cropped hair speaks up. "We had no idea –"

"That's the problem, Agent Lewis," I say, running a hand through my hair. "The CIA is an intelligence agency. How does one of our safehouses become wired with explosives without our knowledge?"

A pale, lanky officer leans forward; his eyes are dull, and his nose seems slightly too large for his face. "Sir, it could've been a terrorist att—"

"Bullshit." I practically spit the word. "Are you really that naive, Agent Kent? One of you, maybe more, placed those explosives. Only the four of you had unhindered access to Safehouse 5 over the past week."

A brawny Indian man raises a veiny hand. "You think one of us –"

"I *know* one of you placed those charges, Agent Reddy. The Agency has intercepted messages to the Russians. It's no secret that their government would benefit from the representative's death."

"But that doesn't mean –" Lewis starts.

"The Agency has suspected that the Russians have at least one double-agent in the Agency." My pause is deliberate. "At the very least, one of you. We intercepted a message originating from the laptop in the safehouse that contained the order to detonate the bombs. Two of you logged in to the laptop's guest account during the twenty minutes immediately preceding the bombs' detonation." I pause. "There's no guarantee that those who logged in were moles, or if the moles even know who each other are." I tighten my grip on my weapon. "But they will be dealt with."

The silence that follows is uneasy. Each of the agents seem to view each other with new eyes, processing their comrades through the filter of paranoia.

I adjust my tie. "Knowledge of the bombs' placement was limited to the person – or people – who planted them. So tell me, which of your colleagues was itching to leave the safehouse today?"

Each of the agents jumps in, rushing to tell their side of the story, save for one. I hold up my hand, and the cacophony ceases. I consider the agent who has chosen to remain silent. Her prominent cheekbones offer her face an elegant, sculpted appearance that – while not unattractive – is decidedly too harsh for conventional beauty.

"Agent Preston," I say, "please recount for me everything that happened today in Safehouse 5. Spare no detail."

The operative brushes a strand of blonde hair from her eye. "When we found the bomb –"

"Everything," I repeat. "From the start."

Agent Preston

I LEVEL a stern gaze at Preston as I produce a notepad and uncap my pen. "Please start with the layout of Safehouse 5. I don't visit Manhattan often."

"The apartment is like this one," she says, "except for its location in the hallway." She bites her lip and squints. "The apartment door is at the corner of a hallway. Exiting straight from the door takes you down the north corridor, and turning right takes you down the east corridor."

I jot down a crude drawing on my pad. "Give me details on the rooms too; I don't want to assume anything." I return my pen to the page, ready to add to my sketch.

"There's a main room with two closets and a bathroom on the left as you walk in. A door to the kitchen on the right. The kitchen has a door to the representative's bedroom, and the bedroom has its own bath. I was posted guard at the door when Reddy arrived."

Reddy cuts in. "I was out –"

I raise my hand. "I will be the only one to interrupt Preston." I give her a nod. "Continue."

Preston glances at Reddy. "Reddy ran to the corner store to buy antacid for the rep."

"Did this strike you as strange?" I ask.

She shakes her head. "He's been complaining about his stomach ever since his plane landed."

"What happened next?"

"When Reddy entered the apartment, he delivered the antacid to the rep."

"Did you see him do this?" I ask, propping my head with my hand.

She shakes her head.

"Please tell me what you observed. Nothing more."

She sighs. "Lewis followed Reddy as he walked through the room."

"And where was she standing?"

"By the window in the main room, near the laptop."

I produce a notepad and scribble as she talks. "The laptop that the detonation command was sent from?"

"I… um, that's not something I observed."

"But you were alone with the laptop that gave the command?"

"Actually, I followed Lewis and Reddy into the kitchen. They both entered the rep's room – per our orders never to be alone with him. I asked Kent to cover my post at the door so I could make myself a snack."

Kent shifts uneasily in his chair.

"So Kent was alone with the laptop?"

Preston nods.

"For how long?"

She shrugs. "It took me maybe four minutes to make myself a sandwich."

"It takes less time than that to send an email," I remark, jotting down more notes on my pad. "What then?"

She scratches her chin. "I think Reddy had to use the restroom then."

Reddy's face flusters at this comment.

"So he left the rep's room?"

She shakes her head. "The toilet in the bathroom just off the living room is out of order. The only functional bathroom was the one in the rep's room, so Reddy called Kent into the rep's quarters so he could use the rep's bathroom. When Kent left the living room, I resumed my post."

"Alone?"

She nods.

"With the laptop."

She nods, albeit slower this time.

"What then?"

"After a few minutes –"

"How long, Preston? This is important."

She sighs, massaging her temples. "Seven minutes, or close to that. After seven minutes, I hear Lewis, Kent, and Reddy enter the kitchen. Lewis and Kent stay in the kitchen, and Reddy enters the living room and begins searching the walk-in closet for surveillance gear."

"Why?"

"Lewis and Reddy spotted a suspicious-looking vehicle across the street. They wanted a pair of binoculars to get a closer look at the license plate."

"Did you see this vehicle?"

She nods. "Lewis called me into the kitchen and pointed out a white van across the street. I didn't think anything of it, but she said that she saw the same van when we picked up the rep from the airport. Said it was worth checking out."

"Did you run the plates?"

"Reddy never came back with the binoculars. Lewis went into the living room, leaving Kent and I to monitor the van from the window. About five minutes later, we're all back in the kitchen debating what to do about the van. We start arguing over who would be the one to investigate."

"Who wanted to leave the apartment first?"

"Lewis. She's the newest recruit; she wanted to investigate."

Lewis opens her mouth, as if to object, but one stern look from me closes it.

"Did anyone object?"

Preston stares at the floor. "We all did. Kent made a bid for investigating, and Reddy claimed that we should change safehouses, because this one was compromised."

"Did *you* want to leave?"

"I'd been cooped inside on guard duty for the past seven hours. Of course I did."

I jot another note. "I must admit that it strikes me as odd that you all expressed a strong desire to leave the apartment just minutes before at least one of you knew that the place would blow." I nod. "Continue."

"We were all in a fairly heated argument when I hear glass shatter on the floor. Kent went to clean it up and discovered the bomb when he knelt beside the refrigerator."

"The bomb was in the refrigerator?"

"Under it. I still don't know how Kent saw it. He called out 'Bomb' and we scrambled to grab the rep and rush him off to safety."

"Who was the first to leave the apartment?"

"I don't remember. Kent and I flanked the rep on our way out. It was either Lewis or Reddy."

"How much time passed between the bomb's discovery and detonation?"

"I honestly have no idea."

Agent Lewis

AFTER PENNING my notes on Preston's account, I turn to Lewis. "I'd like to hear your account next. Nothing omitted."

Lewis nods. "Like Preston said, when Reddy comes in with his bag from the 7-11, I'm standing at the living room window. He walks in to deliver his bag to the rep, so I follow him in, because Kent is neck-deep in the fridge looking for the last beer.

"So I follow Reddy into the rep's room, and Reddy gives him his antacid. He makes a big show of telling the guy that he had to visit three stores to get the brand that the rep asked for. Asked the guy if he needed anything else, and the guy said something about football scores. Then Reddy and the rep talk for a few minutes about soccer before Reddy asks to use the private bathroom because the other one has low water pressure."

"What was his reaction?"

"After Reddy found his antacid, he seemed pretty agreeable. Anyway, I poke my head out to call for Kent, because we're not allowed to be alone with the rep. I'm pretty surprised to see Preston making a sandwich in the kitchen instead of Kent getting his drink on, but we call Kent in from the living room while Reddy does his thing in the private bathroom."

"Did he take anything inside with him?"

"Kent brought a glass of water."

"I meant Reddy."

"No."

"Did his bathroom break seem suspicious to you?"

She shrugs. "Reddy was the one hopping to three different 7-11's. Seems like he could've fit a bathroom break in there somewhere."

"What then?"

"Kent and I felt pretty awkward after being forced to wait for Reddy to do his business, so when he gets out of the bathroom, the three of us immediately leave for the kitchen. Maybe a minute or two later, I spot the van outside."

"You'd seen it before?"

She nods. "At the airport. I tell Reddy to grab some binoculars to get a look at the plate. He goes in the other room, and Preston comes in to see what's happening."

"She mentioned that you called her in."

Lewis pauses. "I could've. I don't remember who said what. Anyway, I walk back into the living room to see if I can get a better look at the plate."

"Did you see Reddy?"

"He was looking for binoculars in the closet."

"Could Preston and Kent see you?" I ask.

"They were looking at the van."

"So you were alone with the laptop."

Lewis' lips tighten. "For a few minutes, before Reddy gives up looking for the binoculars and goes to the kitchen. I follow him in, asking where the binoculars were. He says he couldn't find them. Then Preston jumps in, saying that she should be the one to go down and check it out. I tell her no way."

"Why? She's the most experienced agent."

"Because she's always pulling rank like this. How am I supposed to get more experience if she's always swooping in when something unexpected happens?" She pauses. "Anyway, the two of us argue. She tries throwing her weight around. Reddy says something, but I can't hear what. Then Kent cracks a joke about him going instead of us, because he's the only one who didn't want to go.

"After three more minutes of listening to Preston air her grievances, Kent breaks a glass. When he and Reddy go to clean it up, they find the bomb. We waste no time getting the rep the hell out of there."

"Who was the first to leave?"

"Reddy left first, then Kent and Preston with the rep. I followed them."

"How did you exit the building?"

"East corridor. Don't ask me why. Like I said, Reddy led us out."

Agent Reddy

I SIGH as I turn to the third agent. "Okay, Agent Reddy, your turn. Perhaps you should tell us why you went to the store."

The athletic man's large frame is hunched over in his chair. He's fidgeting with his hands. "The rep needed some antacid, but the corner store didn't carry the brand he wanted, so I began searching the nearby 7-11's. Lucky I did, too. Manchester vs. Arsenal was on, and I got to see the winning goal as I paid for the rep's antacid." He pauses. "So I came back –"

"Which way?"

Reddy looks up, searching the ceiling. "North corridor."

"Why?"

"It's the shortest route."

I make note of this on my pad. "Did you see a white van on your way up?" My pen hovers over the page.

Reddy moistens his lips. "Like I said, I came back through the north corridor. That's the opposite direction from where we saw the van parked later." He pauses. "When I returned to the safehouse, I greeted Preston at the door, then grabbed Lewis so I could deliver the antacid to the rep. We entered his room, I gave him the bag, and we started talking about soccer. I shared about the game-winning goal I'd seen; he mentioned that he saw several Al-Jaish matches in Damascus. Then I asked to use his bathroom, so we called in Kent to accompany Lewis with the rep."

"Did you notice anything out of place in the bathroom?"

He pauses. "No."

I jot a few lines on my pad. "A second bomb was found in that bathroom."

Reddy's eyes widen. "I didn't take anything in with me."

I continue writing on my pad. "No one's accusing you."

Reddy takes a moment to compose himself before resuming his story. "When I'm done in the bathroom, Kent, Lewis, and I go into the kitchen, and we see the van across the street. While Lewis and Kent chatter about whether they'd seen it before, I run into the other room to grab some binoculars from the walk-in closet."

"How long did that take you?"

"I couldn't find them. I searched for –"

"Did you know that Preston left the living room?"

"I called out to her at one point, asking her where she left the binoculars; I guess that's why she didn't answer."

"Could you have slipped into the living room without anyone else noticing?"

Reddy fidgets in his chair. "I suppose."

"And accessed the laptop?"

He nods reluctantly. "But that's not what I did. After a few more minutes of searching, I joined everyone else at the window. Preston and Lewis were arguing over who was going to investigate the van, so Kent and I mostly stayed out of it. While the ladies were going at it, Kent found the bomb, then we evacuated the rep."

"You left first?"

He nods.

"Which way did you exit the building?"

"East corridor."

"Didn't you say that the north corridor was the shortest route?"

"I made a snap decision and followed my gut."

Agent Kent

I FLIP to a blank page of my rapidly-filling notepad. "Alright, Kent. Let's hear your story."

"I'm looking for a beer when Reddy comes in. He and Lewis go into the rep's room, delivering their bag. Then Preston comes in asking me to cover her post while she makes a sandwich. I'm still dying of thirst, so I take a glass with me from the kitchen when I cover Preston's post."

"And how long were you alone with the laptop?"

Kent squirms in his chair. "Like I said, I was thirsty by this point, so I go into the main bathroom and fill the glass with water from the tap. But the water pressure's low, so I'm working with just a trickle to fill my glass. By the time it's halfway full, Lewis calls me in to watch the rep while Reddy takes a piss."

"Did you notice anything unusual?"

Kent considers the question for a moment before shaking his head. "Not then, but right after we left, Reddy spotted the van outside."

My pen halts its path across the page. "Agent Reddy saw the van first?"

Kent nods. "He points it out to Lewis, who says she remembers seeing it at the airport." He waits until I'm done writing my note to continue. "Reddy goes to the other room to grab some binoculars to read the plate, leaving Lewis and me discussing what should be done. We call in Preston, who has the most experience, and I give her the details while Lewis goes back into the living room for a better look.

"A few minutes later, Lewis and Reddy return to the kitchen, and Lewis and Preston get in this big tiff about who was going downstairs to scope out the van. Reddy and I try to diffuse the situation, but it gets more heated. Reddy backs into me, and knocks the glass from my hand. It breaks on the floor by the fridge."

"Reddy knocked the glass from your hand? Was it an accident?"

Kent rubs his neck. "Didn't have much time to think about it. Some of the broken glass slipped under the fridge, and when I reached for it to clean it up, I found the bomb. Preston and I ran into the other room, grabbed the rep, and left."

"Who left the safehouse first?"

Kent scratches his chin. "Reddy was out the door first, then Preston and me with the rep, then Lewis."

Special Agent Sanborne

I FLIP THROUGH my notebook, reviewing the case as the agents' eyes bore into my skull. All the agents were alone with the laptop at some point in the window during which the message was sent. Two of them logged in, but none of them admit to it. A smile creeps across my face. "Agent Reddy?"

Reddy practically jumps from his chair. "Yes, sir?"

"Kent says that you were the first one to point out the white van. Is this true?"

He nods.

"The double-agent knew that he or she would need an excuse to leave the apartment for a few minutes, and they needed a cover story for doing so. Your white van was the perfect excuse."

"Sir, I saw it at the airport, what do you want me to –"

"When you heard that there was a bomb, not only were you the first one out the door, but you also exited the building via the east corridor: the more inconvenient route."

"With all due respect, sir, that hardly –"

"What if a bomb had been placed in one of the closets? Or the bathroom that's hardly used? An escape route through the north corridor is the most efficient escape. The eastern corridor would double back over the potential blast radius... unless, of course, you knew where the bombs were planted... and it should be noted that none were found in any of the rooms I just mentioned. Only the mole would view this as the safest escape route."

Reddy jumps to his feet; I ready my gun.

"I'm not the mole," he says. "It's one of –"

He takes an unexpected step toward Lewis. I fire. My suppressor reduces the noise to the same level as a dull clap. Reddy's lifeless form falls to the floor. The agents look at me in shock.

"A necessary evil," I say. I appeal to Lewis. "I couldn't afford to let him make a move on a fellow agent" – I motion to the next room – "or our asset." I rest my gun on the arm of my chair. "We're done here."

The agents are slow to rise – understandably so – but Preston and Kent stand on shaky feet and visit the kitchen. I rise, turning to leave, but Lewis stops me.

"Special Agent Sanborne, didn't you say that there were *two* logins to the laptop this afternoon?"

I nod. The weight of my Sig feels uncomfortable in my hand as it hangs against my side. "Reddy could've logged in twice."

She shakes her head. "I think that when Reddy logged on, he discovered that the detonation command had been sent, and according to Preston's testimony, he tried evacuating the apartment by inventing the van story to convince us that the safehouse had been compromised."

I nod. "An interesting theory."

"When that didn't work, he 'accidentally' broke Kent's glass near one of the bombs planted in the apartment so that someone else could discover them."

"Who logged on first then?"

She leans in closer. "Preston. If Reddy found the message when he logged on, it had to be sent by either Preston or Kent. Preston's the only one who knew that she would have enough uninterrupted time to send the message while Reddy was in the bathroom. And since Kent found the bomb, he's in the clear. A mole wouldn't undermine his own mission."

I offer her a polite smile. "But if Reddy knew the bomb was there the whole time, why not say something instead of resorting to tricks?"

Lewis looks over my shoulder before answering. "I think that Reddy was working for both teams. He was pretending to be a mole for the Russians to get snippets of their intel, but he always remained loyal to the US. He couldn't directly tell us any of that without blowing his cover." She stares at Reddy's body. "I think he was one of us."

I chuckle. "But he wasn't one of *us*."

Firing my Sig at this close range gives me a guaranteed kill shot. Lewis' body hits the floor as Kent and Preston run in. It takes me two shots to finish Kent.

I stare at Preston. "Get me the rep."

Preston retrieves the representative, and I finish the job that she'd attempted to start. She marches over the bodies, surveying the scene. "We're going to need one hell of a cover story to come back from this one."

I point my Sig into my left forearm and pull the trigger. Pain erupts from my hand to my shoulder, but I shake it off.

Preston stares at me agape. "Why the *hell* did you do that?"

"To make my story more believable when I tell the Agency how I disarmed the mole."

I fire at Preston. I'm now alone in Safehouse 6, wondering if this lie will earn me a medal from the CIA.

The Empathy Bomb

Jo Miles

GUESTS WHO didn't know when to leave were always an annoyance. Doubly so when that over-persistent guest stood between you and your target, while you crouched outside the window with a fifty-foot drop beside you and the wind numbed your extremities.

Dahl had been waiting on the narrow parapet for an hour, and not only was his time running out, but his leg was beginning to cramp.

Venta would laugh to see me seizing up like a raw recruit. She'd probably chuck pebbles at me like in training, make me scramble to catch them before the sound gives me away...

Or maybe she wouldn't laugh, considering what he aimed to do.

Gentian summers were marginally less unpleasant than Gentian winters, but only just: chill and damp instead of frigid and icy. The thin sun warmed the coal-black stones of the castle at his back, but up here, the wind outbalanced it.

He thumbed open his pocket watch. Ten minutes. He'd give Lord Allisan ten minutes to rid himself of his guest, then Dahl would have to take a risk. If Allisan left for the Circle of Lords' meeting before Dahl got him with the substance, well... it might not be ruinous. He'd already secured the rest of his targets. But as a professional, Dahl disliked loose ends; they tended to muck things up.

And Allisan was the muckiest of the bunch.

Dahl braced his shoulder against the wall, freeing his hands to reach over and press the stethoscopic cup to the window glass. A thin tube connected it to an earpiece. It should have been impossible to eavesdrop on the Circle, but the Black Veils always left themselves a chink or two in the palace's security to exploit at need.

"But, m'lord! Conditions in those factories are most unsavory for children..."

"Yes, what a *shame* the urchins aren't having fun. But fun is a luxury of the past. Who will keep the gears of our economy grinding, if not the children? Our dead? In such times as these, we survivors all must sacrifice for the sake of the realm –"

Dahl drew back, a sour smile on his face. Oh, yes. Sometimes he did enjoy his work.

There, now. The susurrus of voices grew louder, cadences changing as they bid each other farewell. A door closed, and when Dahl peeked, Lord Allisan sat at his desk, frosty head bent as he composed a letter.

With practiced efficiency, Dahl set to work.

First, to pierce the window. He pulled out a metal tube and removed from it a vial of liquid. He poured the vial into the tube, stoppered it, and shook it to speed the chemical reaction. At the key moment, he set the end of the tube (now glowing white-hot) to the glass, and a soft pop announced its successful penetration.

He withdrew at once, held his breath, waited. No movement within. If Allisan heard the sound, he probably attributed it to the ancient building's usual creaks and groans.

The darts were almost too small for his chilled fingers to manipulate. He picked one up with his fingernails from his folio and loaded it into the spring-gun. It was unworthy of the name 'gun,' little more than a metal tube with a trigger attached – but deadly accurate over short distances, and silent.

The riskiest part of the business: he lifted his veil and leaned out, far enough to sight Allisan through the little hole in the glass. He aimed, held his breath, and pulled the trigger.

The dart sailed true. So tiny, it was invisible to the eye, but Allisan slapped his neck where it struck him as if brushing away a redwing fly. That was all he'd think of it: an insect bite, and the 'insect' would fall to the carpet, blending among the patterned fibers. If anyone ever noticed it, it even looked like a fly until scrutinized.

Satisfied, Dahl gathered his gear. The substance wouldn't take effect for a few minutes, and he had another appointment. He leaped up, grabbed the gilded edging of the roof above, and worked his way onto it. From there, he could see the whole of the city falling away, and beyond it, the dung-brown hills and muddy fields that were Gentia's dubious pride.

Escape was easy across the sloping rooftops, but something made him pause. A familiar feeling, impossible to tie to the senses' evidence, but the Black Veils trained you to heed your gut. He kept moving to cover his suspicion, but he scanned the usual surveillance points on the palace itself and the surrounding buildings. He saw no one, just an expanse of black stone and black tile punctuated with striking gold accents.

Still, he felt watched.

Not until he reached the street did Dahl feel secure again. He jogged along the alley and hid himself just back from its mouth, watching for his next appointment.

A woman rounded the corner, surveying the alley dubiously. Pretty brown curls framed a face that was all business; she wore what must be her very best dress, well worn, with a thinning fur coat drawn loosely over it. From her handbag she pulled out a chymical bolt gun, meant to stun an assailant and put him to sleep. Not a bad idea for a woman in her profession, especially one who agreed to meetings with strangers in shadowy alleys.

"Is anyone there?"

Afraid, but trying not to sound it. Dahl liked her. He stepped forward. "Miss Venetta."

"Are you…" Her eyes widened as she took in his black steel-cloth body suit, his distinctive veil. The question would be foolish: who would dare wear that veil, except one of that order? She breathed deep of the brackish air. "You requested to meet with me."

"I have advice for you. For this afternoon."

"Then tell me. If you know where I'm going, you know I haven't got much time to spare."

He smiled, though she couldn't see it. "Don't worry, I won't make you late. My advice is this: ignore all the *other* advice you've gotten about how to make your request of the Circle. You'll do best to tell them about the children. About the administrator's treatment of them. About how you would improve upon his methods. Play on the lords' empathy."

"The Lords of the Circle are reputed to have no empathy. If I do as you say, they'll give me nothing but sneers." She blanched, remembering who she was talking to. "I mean no…"

"Any other day, you'd be right. But today, you'll find them disposed to listen. Act boldly, Miss Venetta. Seize this opportunity."

She stared at him. "Why should the Black Veils take an interest in my affairs?"

"Is it so surprising? The Veils work for the good of the realm."

Miss Venetta bit down on her startled objection to that claim. Even her bold tongue had limits.

"Remember what I said, Miss Venetta. Play upon their empathy. Make them listen."

He melted into the shadows. She stared after him, then hastened back onto the busy street.

From the rooftop high above, a flash of movement. A bird, or...? Impossible to tell with the sun angled into his eyes.

Dahl considered, then headed back toward the palace. A risky indulgence, maybe, but he liked to see the outcome of his work for himself. And maybe he could draw out his pursuers.

* * *

Spying on the Circle of Lords as they held council was an ancient tradition, so common as to be a rite of passage for newly-minted Veils. For Dahl, it was child's play. Still, he took care as he approached the rooftop cupola that decorated the Lords' Hall, in case he wasn't the only one listening today.

When he squeezed through the shoulder-wide well (easier than last time, with the weight he'd lost) and dropped from extended arms into the darkness, he found only that: darkness. Unoccupied. He'd have felt better with a lookout; he and Venta always took turns, listening and watching, but as things stood, he'd have to trust to luck.

He relied on luck far too much these days. Luck was a beast when it turned on you.

His hidey-hole was in the ceiling above where the lords gathered, an access point for artists when they made repairs to the mural on the domed ceiling. The acoustics of the hall were marvelous; Dahl could hear every word. He hunkered down to listen.

The subject of the day was the orphanages. Mister Palt, the state-appointed overseer of the system (and thus the appointed guardian of every registered orphan in the city) reviewed the budget while the seven ruling lords of Gentia listened. Coin spent on food, coal, bedding, and clothes. Income from alms-collection and factory work – mostly from factory work.

"These totals are not what you promised us, Mister Palt."

"Regretfully no, m'lord, but they're improving. The new waifs are learning what's expected of them, so they'll soon be earning better. We can't cut back more on food, but we can save on coal by..."

"What about the staff? Do you really need two nurses at each facility? If we..."

The questions went on, delving into budgetary minutiae. Caught between boredom and aggravation, Dahl flipped open a knife and scratched at the floor, invisible carvings mimicking the ones he'd like to make on Palt's shiny scalp.

"My lords? If you'll permit the interruption..." Miss Venetta's voice. She paused, waiting for permission. "Yes, well, there are certain figures missing from Mister Palt's report. You haven't asked about the deaths."

"Oh?"

"We've lost ninety-seven boys and girls since Mister Palt took charge."

Dahl's eyes squeezed shut. *Alia.*

"Ninety-seven? Palt, how do you explain this?"

Palt cleared his throat, trying and failing to sound imperious. "That figure is accurate, but Miss Venetta is exaggerating the implications. This is not an unusual number for a system of this size. Most of the losses are due to sickness."

"Not to the plague!"

"Oh, no." This latest and most virulent wave of plague spared the very young; that was the only hope Gentia clung to. Of those adults over thirty who caught the sickness, nine would die for every one who recovered. Dahl himself was young enough to escape its worst, but his parents, his aunts and uncles… gone. That was how the Circle came to its present power: when the Gentian czar fell ill, the lords stepped in. To help, of course.

And as parents died, the orphanages swelled.

"No, children remain immune to the plague as ever, but the sicknesses of childhood have no respect for our situation. Ordinary colds turned bad, the welting fever, all these little things take their toll."

"Certainly so, if you give them too little food and not enough blankets and no medicine to speak of, my lords. They come home from the factories wheezing, coughing up soot, and there's no rest for them. They get paler and paler, thinner and thinner. And Mister Palt gives no child special treatment, no matter what their nurses say. Only last week, I saw Mister Palt order a six-year-old girl out of bed and to work when she was too weak to walk! Lila had to lean on a pair of her friends just to make it out the door, and she was dead by day's end. Indeed, my lords, let's do away with the nurses, because as things stand, they have no power to help these children."

Dahl smiled in the darkness. He'd judged well. Venetta had guts of iron, to speak so in front of the Circle. The lords murmured together, an undertone of astonishment as Venetta talked on, gathering momentum, naming child after child and how Palt sent them, directly or indirectly, to their graves. And this was only at the single orphanage she ran under Palt's supervision. No other orphanage director had dared to speak out.

And until today, it wouldn't have mattered if they did. The lords would only have cared about the expense. But today…

"It is true," one lord began, and then paused for an astonishingly robust nose-blowing. It was old Allisan. "Excuse me. These stories are new to me, and most unfortunate." He sniffed, loudly, and searched for the safest political couching for what his heart wanted to say. "It is true that our children are our greatest asset… our greatest *economic* asset and as such, we cannot waste them like twigs on the fire. We cannot afford it. We must take better care of our young charges. So that, ah, they can grow into productive members of our new society of young people."

Allisan couldn't bring himself to express his feelings outright, but he couldn't bear to ignore them, either. Nor could the others, not with the substance flowing through their veins. Every one of the lords, every crotchety old man, spoke in agreement. Dahl wished he could see Venetta's face, almost as much as he wished to see Palt's as the man scrambled to defend his methods, baffled to find himself under attack. Today (as it happened) the lords saw more clearly than usual, and the debate ended with Palt's removal from his office, and Venetta appointed in his place. Dahl's smile grew to a tear-streaked grin.

For you, Alia.

A good day. This victory would make all the difference for some of the orphans. Yet it was a small victory, a single rock braced against the avalanche. They needed so much more than these patchwork solutions. He'd best keep his eye on his greater aim.

When Dahl felt collected enough to venture back into the open, he gripped the sill of the cuppola above him, hoisted himself up – and dropped down again as a dagger whistled past his head.

A thrown dagger, not a stab. He vaulted up and out the narrow opening in one smooth motion, rolling to an upright stop on the roof. His assailant moved to intercept him, closing fast. All in black, with a black veil.

Slim build, long legs. Could be Stala? No, Stala wouldn't have missed.

Dahl dropped as a second dagger flew past. His attacker gave a coded warning cry, three sharp hoots: there were more Veils about, and scanning the rooftops, he found them: one straight ahead, another to his left. He dodged right, leaping over peaked roofs, sliding down slopes with a clatter.

A fourth attacker flew from behind a low gable and slammed into him, forcing him to his knees.

"Easy there, Brocke, you don't need to break my kneecaps." Brocke's red hair always was a handicap to his anonymity.

"Sure I don't." Brocke's elbow locked around Dahl's throat, pinning him. "Then you'll come peaceably?"

In answer, Dahl drove an elbow back into Brocke's gut. He broke free, but Brocke lunged for him again, and the two men grappled.

"Damn you, Dahl, you know how this has to end." A chymical bolt blasted the tiles beside them. Dahl rolled to the right, using the bigger man as a shield. "Give it up, and no one has to break anything."

As Brocke threw his weight the other way, Dahl rolled with him, and they tumbled together off the roof.

They hit the next level some fifteen feet down. Dahl's onetime colleague broke his fall and took a blow to the head, stunning him enough to let Dahl scramble away. Now he was trapped on an isolated corner of the roof. Street below thick with guards. No escape by jumping down, even if the height wouldn't break him. But Dahl still had a few tricks they might not anticipate.

He ran straight for the balustrade at the roof's edge. He leapt onto it, landed in a crouch, and just before his momentum would have carried him over, he tapped the activators on his boots.

And he flew.

Not true flight, but his spring-loaded boots turned his flying leap into a thirty-foot soar across the gap and onto the roof of the building beyond. He rolled the landing and came up with a grin.

Try to follow me now, friends.

They didn't try. Dahl glanced over his shoulder long enough to see that the Veils had halted. Their captain was shouting orders, pointing at him. But Dahl recognized the posture of defeat. By the time they caught up to him, he'd be long gone.

* * *

With a safe distance between him and the palace, Dahl dropped down into an alley. He landed in something fetid and damp. Probably the better to blend in, he told himself. He completed the blending by tucking his veil into a pocket and donning an ill-fitting pair of canvas trousers and a mismatched fur coat over his blacks.

Stepping onto the street, he was the same as any poor sot in this city.

Here, in the city center, people had drawn together in the plague's wake. Windows were broken on the ground floors of row-homes, but the homes were occupied. A cluster of children played tug-the-rope with an old rag, fierce and unlaughing in their struggle. Wild children, those who avoided the orphanages and hid from the slave-runners, living in abandoned buildings. Things might not improve immediately under Miss Venetta's care, but perhaps in time these urchins would find their way under her protection.

Adults passed him, too. The adults were the ones who frightened him, with their empty, starving eyes. Children were resilient, and if they survived, they'd get used to the new way of things. The adults never would. They'd lost their entire generation.

"Spare a coin, sir?"

The urchin stared up – not at him, but another passing man – and held out a grubby hand.

The man spat in it.

"For shame, girl. We all got enough troubles."

The little girl revealed no shame as she wiped her hand on her skirt. Dahl's spring-gun found his hand before he knew his intention; he launched the dart before he questioned it. It was wrong to use the substance frivolously – he needed every drop – but the dart was already away. The false-fly found its mark on the back of the man's neck, and he swatted at it, already too late. A single prick of the substance would do its work.

When the curmudgeon encountered the next beggar-girl, he'd be in a more giving mood.

Too slow. Dispensing the substance person by person, need by need, it was too slow. A drip, when their crisis demanded a torrent. Disease had torn Gentia apart, but greed and self-interest would unravel what was left, unless someone took counter-measures.

All he needed was a little more time to finish his work. A few days, maybe a week, without the Veils catching up to him.

"Coin, sir?"

The orphan girl was watching him now. She didn't look a thing like Alia, her hair limp and matte-brown instead of curly black, but she was about the same age, and his heart twisted. He dropped a coin into her hand.

A few streets over, he stopped at the grocer's stall, an open-air shop under the suspicious eye of the thirty-odd-year-old Helmin, who'd recently inherited his father's business and already had a talent for driving off beggars with his glares. Today, he watched Dahl and a rare grey-haired lady, who in turn covetously watched a pile of persimmons that looked too mealy to evoke such hunger.

"I'll have a loaf of bread, a soft sheep's cheese, four turnips… and a persimmon," Dahl said. That would keep him for a week if he was careful. That ought to be long enough.

"That's eight coppers."

He reached into his coin-purse, though he already knew what was in it. The last of his coins, and no more would come, not with his line of work. And some he needed for his supplies.

"I haven't got it. I could pay you back next week."

"Then you get your bread and turnips next week. I'm no moneylender."

Dahl sighed. If he had to…

"It's all right, man, I understand. You've got a family to feed, and I'll starve only myself." He slapped Helmin on the shoulder. The grocer showed no sign that he felt the sting of the palmed dart.

Dahl circled the stall again, examining produce, muttering calculations under his breath, trying to look wretched with hunger. Not looking at Helmin, but counting the moments until he'd soften.

And sure enough: "Fine. You're my regular customer, so this once, I'll give you the bread, the fruit, and two turnips. You owe me five coppers next week, or I'll beat it out of you."

"Good sir, your generosity in these dire times is an example to us all," Dahl told him, gathering up his haul. With a flourish, he handed his persimmon to the old woman. "One good turn deserves another, don't you think?"

Her face brightened as she clutched the orange jewel in blue-white hands. "You, sir, you are a kind spirit."

"I do what I can."

* * *

Dahl listened at the door to his nest before he slipped inside. Dagger in hand, he made a circuit of the little room, checking behind barrels and workbenches, scanning the bare rafters and the hand-sized holes where shingles were missing from the roof. An over-cautious check; there weren't so many places to hide.

Satisfied, he relieved himself of his burdens: first the food, set on the table; then his outer layer of clothing and the tools of his trade, tucked back in their places; finally, the vial of the substance, no bigger than his little finger. This he poured with utmost care into the jar on his workbench, then sealed it tight.

Nearly full. One more raid on the Veils' laboratory ought to yield the remainder of what he needed, along with the iridun fuses. The rest of his supplies, he could buy. And then Gentia's problems would have their solution.

The substance was always meant to be that. Some of his comrades sneered, too literal-minded to see the point of an elixir that infected with empathy, as if only poisons and sleeping draughts and memory-erasers had any value to operatives. But Dahl and Venta understood at once: kindness could be a lever as effective as any blackmail, and better, because it left the victim believing he'd done a good deed. They learned to apply it with precision.

Venta was satisfied with that. Dahl never was.

Abruptly weary, he wished for a cup of hot, smoky tea to warm his fingers and his insides, but he had no tea nor fuel to boil water. Instead he stretched his arms over his head with a groan, working his shoulders, moving into a familiar series of limbering exercises. The constant missions he assigned himself took their toll in bruises and exhaustion, but he had to keep pushing. This afternoon made that more clear than ever: his plan *would* work, if he could keep the Veils off him long enough to complete the bomb.

The empathy bomb. That was an unpleasant term for his project, but it had a certain poetry, and thus was how he'd come to think of the device during its painstaking construction. The plans he followed were derived from those of deadly explosives, and in his darker moods, it was satisfying to think that his bomb would wreak only kindness. The Veils used the substance cynically, for power and manipulation, but he would unleash it upon the city at large, shunning no one.

Once the substance took effect, every person in Gentia would be full of empathy and good will for their fellows. Everyone, from the crustiest old lord to the most street-hardened urchin. Give Gentia a single day of free-flowing empathy, and they could help each other out of the pit they'd fallen in. They could force the Veils to make the substance available to all, for ever… and with it, the people of Gentia would rise anew.

A floorboard creaked, and not under his foot. He swung about into a fighter's stance, estimating whether he could reach his dagger on the table before the blow fell.

But there was no blow. Only a black-veiled figure, waiting just beyond arm's reach.

"There's no need for that, is there?" said Venta.

"That depends on you. Why are you here?"

"You know why."

"To bring me in." He swallowed, and held his stance. "Why am I still standing, then? My back was to you."

"Because I want to talk to my old partner first. Can I have that?" She lifted her hands, slowly, palms outward to prove she was weaponless, and drew back her veil.

But empty hands meant nothing in a Black Veil. Dahl looked past her, into the shadows of his shabby room.

"I'm alone. You proved this afternoon that numbers are no good against you."

"They would have been, if you were there."

"Well, they preferred to get you without using me, if they could." A slight stress in her voice, a hitch on the word *using*. Dahl let himself look into her face: rust-brown hair, broad cheekbones standing out against a new thinness in her face, a mouth quick to laugh or sneer or grin. Eyes grey as a gathering storm. He'd seen the terror of her victims a thousand times as they quailed before those eyes, but never thought to be one of them.

He gestured to a chair – the room's only chair – and she took it. He drew up a crate for himself, putting the makeshift table between them. His hand brushed his leg, the secret pocket there, before coming to rest on the rough-hewn boards.

"Are you well, Dahl?" she asked after too long a pause.

He had to laugh. "How unwell must things be, if you and I are resorting to small talk?"

Her lips curled in the smile he knew so well. Idle talk was a dangerous habit in their trade. Good partners learned to work in silence. And Venta, she'd been a good partner.

"True. Well." The smile faded, and he followed her gaze to the painting on the wall, which stood out like a gash in the otherwise raw, unadorned attic. A family portrait, from a time when there were families and painters and leisure to sit for them. Mother, father, son… daughter.

"I'm sorry about Alia. I never got a chance to tell you that."

"It… wasn't your fault."

Weeks later, and it still caught in his throat, any mention of his little sister. Even after losing both parents, five-year-old Alia was a matchstick-flame of joy in his life, lively and tiny and bright and determined. And despite all that, snuffed out.

Dahl took in Alia after their parents' deaths, but the Veils had lost too many of their own, they were stretched too thin. Missions became ordeals. Shifts lasted days. Keeping the barest grip on order took everything they had.

Amid all that, one time he stayed away too long. He'd never know if Alia thought him dead, or if she grew too hungry, or merely too lonely, but she went to an orphanage. Three days later, that strong, healthy girl was dead and no one could tell him why. *It's sad, but these things happen*, the orphanage director said to him, and *that* he found unacceptable.

"When I found out, when I learned what Alia had done and that the Veils didn't let me go to her... I thought: *we should have used the substance on ourselves first*. You can imagine how our superiors took that." Venta blinked once in acknowledgment. "I knew what we had to do, then. I tried to tell them, tried and tried, but they refused to listen. They told you?"

"Yes."

"And what do you think of my plan? You think I'm mad?"

"Worse. An idealist." With the barest edge of irony, she shook her head. "How did they ever let you into our ranks?"

"I'm serious! You must see..."

"We don't get to choose our targets. That's the first thing they teach us: they assign missions, we complete them. The head makes its decisions without bias, and the hands execute them without guilt. You, Dahl, are the definition of bias."

"Maybe the head could use a little bias." He hesitated. "And the rest? My empathy bomb?"

"Is that what you're calling it?" She pursed her lips. "No, I don't believe spreading the substance to everyone will save us. It's not effective, not sane, not right. I know you think that once they taste it, they'll want to stay on it, to stay that pure and caring. But people don't work that way, Dahl. Having empathy doesn't mean they make good choices."

"But they'd have to make better ones –"

"Empathy *hurts*, Dahl. All the pain this city is suffering, you want to make every person feel *that*? They'd never want that, and if they had it... we can predict what one person will do under the substance's influence, but not what ten thousand people will do. The substance has to stay a secret, in our hands, where we can use it appropriately."

Dahl bowed his head. Callousness was killing Gentia as surely as the plague, and the substance was the only solution. But even Venta, who'd seen everything he had, didn't believe.

He tightened and relaxed his fingers, shifting the tiny object in his palm. She lay her hands on the table, near his but not touching.

"What will you do with me now?"

"I'll bring you in, and they can help you. They're willing to forgive, to let you work your way back up. You're damn good, Dahl. Who else ever evaded the Veils for so long? They've invested a lot in you, and they – we – don't want to lose you."

"They want me to submit to conditioning."

"Well... yes."

They both shuddered. They'd seen people subjected to conditioning. They'd put people through it.

"Dahl," she said, as gentle as he'd ever heard her, and as cold. "You're my assignment. My highest order target."

Highest order. For a Black Veil, that meant failure was inadmissible. She couldn't return to headquarters without her quarry in tow. Loyalty to the institution went far beyond loyalty to a partner. One way or another, she would bring him in.

Dahl could run. He could fight. Though Venta was as good as he was, there was a fair chance he'd get away. But he couldn't bring himself to kill her, and because she was that good, she'd find him again. And again. And again. And someday he'd get careless. Someday she'd win.

Or...

His fingers tightened again on the dart's narrow shaft. Venta's hands lay flat on the table, easily within reach, hands rich with veins to carry the substance to her brain. He could prick her with the dart and then she'd have to let him go. Wouldn't she? With her new-found empathy for him, for his plight if not his ideals, for all he'd lost and all he would suffer if she brought him in, she'd have to let him go. Since she couldn't return empty-handed, maybe she'd come with him. His supply of the substance could keep her empathy-high for a long time, more than long enough to finish his work.

Unless... unless her loyalty was stronger even than the substance. And that, he thought, was possible. In that case, the substance would heighten her guilt, hone the edge on her torment as she led him away. Agony, for having to put her partner and friend through agony. But she would follow her orders nevertheless.

He looked into her storm-grey eyes, and that was a mistake: she stared back unflinching, as if the choices he weighed were transparent to her. His chest tightened.

How to escape this? Could he even escape, with his conscience intact?

Oh. Of course.

There was an easy way to discover the right choice. Or at least the choice that felt most right. Knowing and dreading what it would tell him, Dahl closed his hand tight.

The dart-tip penetrated his skin.

The substance felt like nothing. There was no rush, no boozy wooziness. He waited for it, but it never came. None of his targets ever realized they'd been drugged, either. All he felt was a slow, warm-molasses feeling in his chest, and a countervailing queasiness wrenching his gut. Two feelings, growing and waning in opposition to each other as he contemplated his options, like a compass pointing him toward righteousness.

Yet not true righteousness, as he realized for the first time. Merely a narrow angle of it, like the view through an arrow-loop in the palace walls: true, but incomplete. He knew, he *knew* that completing the bomb would be better for the masses of Gentia, that thousands of people would live better for it if he succeeded. The arithmetic of morality was on his side. Therefore, logically, he should fight her to the end.

But he couldn't see Gentia's masses. He saw *her*, Venta, those cool, familiar eyes that had watched him through her veil during so many missions. He saw pain in those eyes, frustration so intense that every muscle of her body should have been rigid with it. Not Venta, though. She was too well-trained for that. Bringing him in was hard for her; hunting him would be torment. If he escaped, she would track him down, again and again, miserable through every minute of it, and only her eyes would reveal her suffering.

Venta was the closest thing to family he had left. With the substance slipping silent through his veins, he could not put her through that.

Holding her gaze, Dahl opened his fingers and let the dart fall to the table like a swatted fly.

"You'd better do your job."

"Thank you." In her eyes, gratitude mingled with regret enough for both of them. The substance would have done nothing to her, he realized. He already had all the empathy she could give.

As he rose to his feet, she touched him on the shoulder. "I'll ask them to go easy on you, partner."

Then her grip tightened, and she led him away.

The Defenestration of Prague

Josh Pachter

PILOTING HIS rented Mercedes down endless bleak thoroughfares and side streets, McKenna grows hot with frustration despite the November chill. He has approached the hotel three times now – from the north, from the east, from the west. On his third attempt, he gets close enough to glimpse the dull green of the oxidized copper cupolas that crown the once-majestic old five-story building and the words 'Hotel Continental' spelled out in weathered three-foot letters between them. But each time Prague's tangled maze of one-way streets fools him and carries him blithely past his destination.

On his fourth try, from the south, he reaches a point where he needs to turn left, but six intersections in a row all deny him that option. When he spots construction blocking off the road before him, and the only cross-street between where he is and the barricade is marked with a right-turn-only arrow, he grips the padded steering wheel tightly and begins to swear as his knuckles bleach white with the pressure.

Ten minutes later, after circling around past the National Theater and paralleling the course of the Vltava River for half a kilometer, he finally reaches the Continental.

The woman at the Čedok tourist office has promised him that he will find ample parking in front of the hotel. 'Ample parking' turns out to mean four narrow spaces labeled 'Reserved for Guests' in both German and what McKenna assumes must be Czech. Or Slovak. Or whatever the hell they speak in this godforsaken city.

All four spaces are filled, of course, and with a final expletive he leaves the Mercedes on the sidewalk across from the four stone steps leading up to the plate-glass doors. He doesn't give a damn if they ticket him; the car has German plates, he rented it at the airport in Munich, where he flew in yesterday afternoon for a briefing by the bureau chief there before driving across the border into Czechoslovakia early this morning.

The doorman is a stocky type, with close-cropped brown hair, wearing a black tuxedo. As McKenna brushes past him, the man offers to change his dollars or D-Marks into crowns at double the official exchange rate. McKenna ignores him. A parking ticket is one thing, but black marketeering is another matter entirely.

The receptionist tries to tell him that Stebbins is not registered at the hotel. She must have been an attractive woman, McKenna thinks, thirty pounds and a dozen years ago. Her complexion is still creamy smooth, and this surprises him. He expects Czech women to be rough-skinned, raw-boned, dulled by a repressive system and a harsh life. But this receptionist is still soft and gentle, though time and too many carbohydrates have added blowse to her body. She has considerable English, and she explains patiently that there is no Stebbins staying at the Hotel Continental.

"Check your records," McKenna says. "Please."

He parts with this last word grudgingly, given the jetlag and the five-hour drive from Munich, the one-way streets and the parking and the general dreariness of the day. But this once-attractive woman in her severe white blouse and royal blue blazer draws it out of him, and he is surprised again when the single syllable produces the desired result.

With a sigh, she looks down the columns of the oversized ledger before her, and her index finger stops at the name Stebbins and taps it thoughtfully

"Ah, yes," she says, without apology. "Mr. Stebbins. Room 511."

McKenna finds the elevator, a cranky piece of machinery that whines in protest as it carries him upward toward the fifth floor. The ride is slow, and the voice at the back of his head uses the time to tell him the story of his mission once more before his meeting with Stebbins.

A distinguished Czech biologist working on the cutting edge of genetic experimentation has decided to turn over the invaluable results of his recent research to the West. McKenna does not know the scientist's name or how to locate him, not yet. That's where Stebbins comes into the picture. The biologist, fearful for the safety of his family, refuses to defect. He is, however, determined to pass on his knowledge to the free world in spite of his government's opposition. He has sent out certain cautious feelers within the American community and has been put in touch with Stebbins, a low-level embassy staffer who doubles as the Agency's point man in Prague. The scientist insists he will only deliver his information to someone qualified to understand it, and it is for this reason that McKenna, a skilled biogeneticist in his own right but little known outside the small circle of his field, has been contacted by the Agency and, eventually, sent to Munich for a detailed briefing and then on to Prague. A meet with Stebbins has been set up for this day, in this hotel, at this time, and from here Stebbins will take him to wherever it is that the Czech is waiting.

Stebbins is, of course, not Stebbins' real name, any more than McKenna is McKenna's.

Games, the man who is traveling as McKenna thinks, as the crotchety old elevator wheezes to a stop, *games for grown-up children.* But he recognizes the potential importance of the data this anonymous Czech scientist has to offer, and this is why he is here, why he has agreed to take time away from his own research to play this game of espionage, where both the prizes and the risks, he knows, are very, very real.

He steps out of the elevator and walks down the corridor to his left. The first room he passes is number 519 and the next is 521, so he about-faces and returns the way he has come, past the elevator, which is already rumbling back down to the lobby, past rooms 517 and 515 and 513 to an off-white door marked 511. He knocks softly on the door, but there is no response from within. He knocks again, more loudly, but still there is no reply.

He checks his watch and sees that he is almost half an hour late. "Dammit," he says aloud, and his irritation echoes down the corridor. He had thought to be early, but Prague's one-way streets have tricked him into failure on that score. Has Stebbins given up and left already, he asks himself – and, if so, what is he supposed to do next? Call up the embassy and ask to speak with their resident spy?

He tries the door handle and finds that it responds to his touch. The door swings outward, toward him, revealing a second door set six inches behind it. This double door setup is a way for the hotel staff to collect and deliver dry cleaning to guests without disturbing them, McKenna assumes, but then he notices there is no hook for hanging laundry on either door. Nothing could be less important under the circumstances, yet the scientist in him toys unsuccessfully with the puzzle for several moments before letting go of it and returning to the more important question at hand.

The inner door swings inward, and McKenna finds himself in an enormous high-ceilinged bedroom, the largest hotel room he has ever seen. There are two single beds side-by-side on a raised platform jutting out from the wall to his right. There are two wooden wardrobes, two dressers, a sofa, a plush armchair, and a writing desk with a straight-backed wooden chair set neatly in place before it. None of this furniture is decorative in the least; it is simple, drab and severely functional. There is worn carpeting on the floor, tired wallpaper running only three quarters of the way up three of the room's walls. The fourth wall, to his left, is hidden behind dingy green drapery, an arrangement that makes no sense to McKenna. One of the far wall's three tall windows is open, and the weather outside flutters its gauzy white curtains. On a small table by the door is a television set with pushbuttons for eight channels. A two-tiered wall shelf holds an old-fashioned telephone below, a bulky box radio above.

The room is empty. The beds have not been slept in. McKenna wonders if they *can* be slept in: instead of mattresses, they have a series of thin cushions placed end to end, with a sheet and blanket laid out on top of them but folded so the cushions are visible beneath. The pillows are feather, and not many birds can have given up their plumage to fill them.

There is no clothing anywhere. There are no personal effects of any kind. Stebbins is not only not among those present, there is no indication that he has ever been in this room at all.

McKenna checks the wardrobes and finds them bare. There are not even any hangers. The dresser drawers and the desk prove equally empty. He pulls aside the floor-to-ceiling drapes along the left-hand wall, revealing a bathroom only four feet deep but stretching the entire length of the immense bedroom. In all that space, there is no toilet. There is a sink, with a mirror above it and an empty wastepaper basket beneath it, and an assortment of mismatched towels on a rack by its side. There is a large white freestanding bathtub on lion's paws. Laid out in the tub is the body of a small, thin black man, impeccably dressed in a pinstriped three-piece suit. The suit is gray, over a white shirt and a subdued blue tie; the man's face and hands are the color of strong coffee, and his shoes are a highly polished black with bright gold buckles at the sides. But the color McKenna stares at in horrified fascination is crimson: Stebbins' throat has been cut, and his blood has drenched his clothing and pooled beneath his body on the floor of the tub.

McKenna turns blindly away from the dead man and staggers to the sink to vomit. Quite some time passes before he can raise his head. He hardly recognizes the terrified features that peer back at him from the mirror. The phrase *children's games* comes into his mind, and he bends forward and retches again and again, beyond the point where there is nothing left in his stomach to lose. His legs are weak, his head is filled with cotton, and the sourness in his mouth has been there forever and will never go away again as long as he lives.

As long as I live, he thinks. And for the first time in his forty-eight years it becomes horribly real to him that his life is not an ongoing process, but a discrete event with a beginning and a middle and an end.

He risks turning away from the sink and looking back down into the bathtub, and his body twitches with renewed revulsion as if the puppet master has jerked on his strings without concern for the normal niceties of fluid human motion, of grace. He closes his eyes and wills his pulse to slow, his hoarse breathing to calm, the taste of bile in his throat to melt, the frantic acrobatics of his stomach to settle. When he has brought himself under control at last, he opens his eyes. The body is still there. He forces himself to go through its pockets, but there is nothing to find. Wallet, keys, handkerchief, loose change, cigarettes, lighter, comb, pen, notebook, passport – all personal items have been taken away. If Stebbins had been fool enough to have carried any clue to the Czech scientist's identity or whereabouts on his person, that clue has been carried off by his killer.

McKenna washes the feel of the dead man's clothes from his hands and goes out of the bathroom, pulling its heavy green drapery shut behind him to screen Stebbins' body from sight.

He is cold, almost to the point of shivering, and he cannot decide if he feels that way because of the corpse in the bathtub or the open window admitting November into the bedroom.

Right, he thinks. *Stebbins is dead,* he thinks. *So* now *what?*

His briefings at Langley and in Munich have not prepared him for this contingency. No one has told him what to do if he finds Stebbins lying in a bathtub with his throat slit.

McKenna is not used to dealing with murder victims. He is not used to dead bodies, period. He has seen a total of one dead human being in his life, and that was his father at the funeral home; the old man had died of a coronary, and the mortician had made it look as if he was only sleeping. Even *that* had turned McKenna's stomach, and he was no fun at all at the wake. His mother has still not forgiven him for that.

His mind is wandering, he realizes with a start. His father has been dead for fifteen years. Stebbins is dead *now.* Murdered. *Here.*

Get the police, he tells himself. He moves woodenly to the telephone on the wall shelf by the door and stretches out a hand to the receiver. There are ten numbered finger holes on the dial, he notices, but instead of three letters for each number there is only one: A, B, C, F, H, I, K, L, M, R.

Strange, he thinks, and wonders why Ma Bell has made it that way. Then he remembers that he is in Czechoslovakia, in the Soviet sphere of influence, and he snatches his hand back from the phone as if he is afraid it will bite him.

Right, sure, get the police. That's all he needs, to spend the next twenty years in some Commie jail cell if they should get it into their heads that he was the wacko with the razor blade.

No, thank you, he frowns. *No police.*

Well, what then?

He turns on the radio to help himself think, but what comes out of the speaker is an angry tirade in some damn Slavic language. He goes to change the station, but there is only one knob on the bulky old box, the one he used to switch the thing on in the first place. He turns it further and the sound gets louder. There is no way to tune in any other frequency than the one to which the radio has been pre-set.

Curious, McKenna crosses to the television and turns *it* on. There is snow at first, and then the screen fills with black-and-white images of a massive parade. There are thousands of soldiers marching in perfect formation. There are missiles rolling by on flatbed trucks. There are huge banners of Marx and Lenin and other faces he does not recognize. He pushes one of the channel-selector buttons, but the program does not change. He tries all eight buttons, and all eight of them have been set to receive the same channel. There is no way he can find to tamper with the settings.

Welcome to Czechoslovakia, he thinks, and it strikes him that he really knows very little about this foreign place he has allowed an assortment of bureaucrats to convince him it is his patriotic duty to visit. He knows that Franz Kafka was born here, and lived and wrote here. He remembers the Prague Spring of 1968, when even American television screens had been filled with grim, grainy footage of troops and tanks. For a moment, he can almost see old Prof. Stasheff standing at his lectern, a map of Europe on the wall behind him, droning on about the causes of the Thirty Years' War. History 334, McKenna's junior year at Columbia. With a sardonic chuckle and expressive gestures, Stasheff told them about the governors being tossed out the windows of the fortress on the hill, across the river in the Hradcany section of the city. McKenna can no longer recall the year in which it happened, but it was around the beginning of the seventeenth century, he is sure of that. "The Defenestration of Prague," Prof. Stasheff called the incident. The *second* Defenestration of Prague, no less.

McKenna's teeth are beginning to chatter, and he crosses to the open window and shuts and latches it.

He stands there with his hand on the latch, and a question furrows his forehead. *What the hell's the window doing open in the first place? It's* cold *outside!*

The second Defenestration of Prague, he thinks. *Well, if there was a second, then why not a third?*

He reopens the window and looks out. He can see his car five stories below, and a corner of his mind notes with relief that there is no flimsy pink rectangle tucked beneath the blade of the windshield wiper. Not yet, anyway. There is a line of traffic moving slowly past the hotel entrance, there are gray pedestrians crowding to and fro.

But, thinks McKenna, *so what?*

He shifts the focus of his eyes from far to near and sees a greenish rain gutter clamped to the stone exterior of the hotel, just below the bottom shelf of the window. There is a crumpled ball of paper in the gutter, and McKenna fishes it out and closes the window and spreads the paper out on the writing desk, smoothing it as best he can with his palms.

It is a long thin paper bag, with a maroon cross printed at the top and then three lines of text in each of five different languages. English comes fourth, below Czech and Russian and German but ahead of French. 'Hygienic bag for sanitary towels. After use, please leave in the basket of the lavatory. Do not throw anything into the WC.' On the flip side of the bag someone has scrawled the word BALKAM in capital letters.

Balkan, McKenna figures, *only they spelled it wrong, so they threw it away.*

Why not in the basket of the lavatory, though? Why defenestrate the thing instead? The answer to that one seems obvious. You toss something out the window instead of in the wastepaper basket because you know if you toss it in the basket someone will find it and you don't *want* them to.

All right, then, fine. Only, if you toss it out the window, it winds up in the street, not the rain gutter, right? Right, unless maybe the wind catches it and blows it back. Except wadded up like it was, it would've been too heavy for the wind to play with.

No, the only way for it to have gotten into the gutter would've been for someone to have leaned out the window and *put* it there. But why do that, if you don't want it found?

You do that, McKenna realizes, *if you do want it found, but only by someone who takes the time to really look for it.*

My God, he thinks. *It's a message from Stebbins!*

He was sitting here waiting for me when he heard someone fumbling at the door. He knew it wasn't me, I'd just walk up and knock. So, who, then? The maid, maybe. But the room was already clean. What if it was someone who wanted to keep him from leading me to Dr. Whatever-His-Name-Is? Stebbins was a little guy. He had no reason to be carrying any kind of a weapon. He only had a matter of seconds before whoever was at the door would manage to pick the lock. So he grabbed the nearest bit of paper and scribbled a message to me and dropped it into the gutter, hoping that, when I got here, I'd be smart enough to search the room and find it.

Or maybe not, McKenna frowns. *Maybe the damn bag's been sitting out there for days.*

But maybe. And it's all he has to go on.

BALKAM. Could Dr. Whatever-his-name-is be Dr. Balkam? He goes back to the telephone shelf, looking for a phone book. But there is no phone book there, just the box radio and the phone itself.

The phone itself.

McKenna grabs up the receiver but bangs it down again. *Probably bugged*, he guesses. He pulls a handkerchief from his pocket and starts wiping his fingerprints from the phone, but then realizes the receptionist will remember him being there and asking for Stebbins, so the hell with it.

He folds the hygienic bag as neatly as its crumpled condition will allow and puts it away in his pocket. He considers looking in on Stebbins one more time, to say thank you for what he hopes is a clue that will help him complete his mission after all, to say how sorry he is that the man has died for his country, to promise to do his damnedest to apprehend his killer, but he shakes off all these thoughts as idiotic and gives the curtained bathroom a wide berth on his way out of the room.

Stebbins has not died for his country, McKenna tells himself bitterly as he waits for the elevator. He has not died *for* anything. He has died because the madmen on one side of the Iron Curtain are apparently incapable of dealing rationally and intelligently with the madmen on the other side. That is why Stebbins has died.

And he, McKenna, is as mad as the worst of them.

He will not apprehend Stebbins' killer, of course. He is not crazy enough to even *think* about trying to avenge his countryman's death. This is real life, after all, and not some intricate novel by Len Deighton or Ken Follett or John le Carré. He will be very grateful to get out of this country and back to his nice, safe laboratory with his *own* skin intact, and the hell with the faceless Socialist goon who cut Stebbins' throat. No, no, McKenna is not quite *that* mad.

But he is mad enough, he knows, as the elevator door slides open before him and, seeing that the cage is empty of secret police, he expels the breath he has not noticed himself holding. He is mad enough to take the next step in this lunatic game of espionage, now that Stebbins has told him – or, at least, so he believes – what that next step must be.

In the hotel lobby, he forces a smile for the once-pretty receptionist and turns down a repeated offer from the doorman, who shrugs wryly and holds the glass door open for him with a look that says, *Well, I tried.*

McKenna crosses the street and gets into his car, pulls off the sidewalk and into the thinning traffic. This time, he lets Prague's network of one-way streets take him where it will, careful only to keep increasing the distance between himself and the Hotel Continental. He checks his rear-view mirror frequently, and, as far as he can tell, he is not being followed.

Twenty minutes later, in an industrial sector on the eastern fringe of the city, he finds a phone booth on a quiet side street.

He lifts the receiver, drops change into the coin slot until he hears the buzz of a dial tone. The number he dials is 218719, but he does not think of it in terms of numbers.

B-A-L, he thinks as he dials, not needing to refer to the scrawled capital letters on the back of the paper bag in his pocket, K-A-M.

Let this work, he thinks, just beginning to develop an awareness of how important the game has become to him.

And then there is the muted sound of ringing, and an abrupt click, and a low-pitched male voice speaks a cautious syllable in a language McKenna does not understand.

"Hello," he replies in English, the only language in which he feels comfortable. "My name is McKenna. I got your number from Mr. Stebbins."

And what if the man at the other end of the line cannot understand him? What if the name Stebbins is meaningless to him, if he knows the dead man only by his *real* name, or by some other name entirely? What if the man at the other end of the line is not his anonymous biogeneticist at all, if BALKAM is merely a name, as it appears, and not a telephone number, if it is only coincidence that the wadded-up paper bag happened to be in the rain gutter outside the window of room 511?

These thoughts flicker swiftly through McKenna's mind, and then are thrust aside when he hears a sharp intake of breath and the low-pitched voice whispers, in lightly accented English, "Where have you been? I have been terribly frightened. Why are *you* calling me, and not Mr. Stebbins?"

McKenna allows himself a tight smile before he responds. He has found his scientist, after all.

But one man has already died on the way to this moment. Will there be more deaths before he can return home with the information he has come for?

And, if there are, will the man who is traveling as McKenna finish the game as one of the survivors – or as one of the victims?

We Who Steal Faces

Tony Pi

January 4, 1588

MAFEO PREMARIN, my eyes and ears in the shadows of Venice, was dying of poison.

I knelt by Mafeo's bedside and took his trembling hand. His flesh felt cold, patches of red mottled his skin. He tried to speak but fell into a fit of coughs instead. I looked for blood in the sputum on his beard. None yet, a small relief.

The assassin had left a trail of bodies: intelligencers in Amsterdam, Paris, and Lisbon. They were good men, all, loyal to England. Whoever killed them was blinding us to the intrigues abroad. In these times when Spain sought to overthrow Elizabeth's reign, we needed the vigilance of every spy. I refused to let the killer take any more of my operatives, least of all my top man. "Who did this to you, old friend?"

The point of a stiletto grazed the side of my throat.

"The poison's robbed him of his voice," Luca said in his father's stead. "If you are Flea, you know how to earn my trust. Show me his face."

His caution was wise. In these times of looming war, spies like us had to take every precaution to know friend from foe.

"I'll need that mirror in the Restello frame."

Luca allowed me to stand. I took the mirror and slid open a secret compartment along its top. Inside lay the handkerchief Mafeo had hidden there when I first taught him how to thieve. I felt the prickle of Lightning magic dancing within the silk threads. Mafeo, last to touch the kerchief decades ago, had left an impression of his younger self trapped in the silk like a fly in a spider's web.

I willed the Lightning to enter my flesh, letting the magic shape my body into the exact image of my apprentice as he had been in his prime. My brawny physique thinned and shortened, and my skin darkened to a sun-bronze.

Pain blossomed in my left hand. Teeth marks from a mastiff's bite, still scabbing over, reminded me of our first burglary together as master and pupil.

Luca gasped at my transformation, but Mafeo managed a faint smile.

"Proof enough?" I asked with Mafeo's voice as it had been.

Luca sheathed his stiletto. "Forgive me, Master Flea. I had to be sure. Father prepared me for this moment with many tales of your magic, but I never believed him till now!"

"Tell me what happened."

"Two days ago, at the height of Carnivale, Father met with a Spaniard who claimed to know Álvaro de Bazán's plans for the Armada. I waited for him in a gondola, watching the costumed revelers go by. On his way back, a man in a white Volto mask pushed past him. In the space of a few steps Father had stumbled to the ground in a seizure.

The masked man was long gone by the time Father's fits had calmed." He pulled up his father's sleeve and showed me a sickly red scratch.

I had seen poisonings like this before, administered by a needle hidden in a ring. "What of the Spaniard?"

Luca sighed. "I don't know how to find him. He would only meet with Father."

Mafeo wheezed, his breath stinking of rotten eggs.

"Rest, Mafeo. Your only task is to live." I held a cup of water to his lips. "I will find the antidote."

Mafeo closed his eyes.

"Come, let my sister tend to him," Luca whispered.

I hooded myself and donned my Harlequin mask as we left. Luca called to his sister and whispered instructions in her ear. Thereafter, we descended the stairs to the water door. I still wore Mafeo's face, and would for the remainder of the evening.

"Is there an antidote?" Luca asked.

"Your father's been given a concoction of many poisons tailored for a slow, agonizing death. One antidote is not enough."

"How do you know?"

I told him of the others who died in the same way. "I tried cure after cure, but unless all the poisons are countered, death comes within a day when the victim first coughs blood."

Luca paled. "What do we do?"

"The killer might carry the right antidotes or know the recipe for the poisons, but he will be hard to catch." I opened the water door and stepped into the moored gondola beyond. "But there is another way. The mithridate."

"What is it?" asked Luca, his voice regaining hope.

"Legend has it that King Mithridates the Sixth of Pontus so feared that he might be poisoned by his enemies, that he took small doses of many poisons to harden himself against them. He even made a special antidote that would protect him against all poisons, which came to bear his name."

Luca untied the rope and took hold of the oar. "But it's only a legend, isn't it?"

"They say the same of me. What has your father told you about me?"

"That you're a shapeshifter, centuries old. That you were once the outlaw Little John of the English ballads. That you now serve England's spymaster."

"Then believe me when I say that there are others far older than me, one of whom dwells in Venice and may keep the secret of the mithridate. Do you know *Ca' Clessidra*?"

"House Sandglass on Murano." Luca frowned. "Father said never to enter or steal from that place."

"An excellent and inviolable rule I taught him myself. Take me there."

* * *

As Luca ferried me across Laguna Veneta towards the isle of Murano, his silhouette against the setting sun reminded me much of his father. A gondolier by trade, Mafeo had given me my first tour of the city by canal thirty years ago. I had grown fond of the young Venetian during our explorations, even more so after he tried to cut the strings of my purse at the end of the day. Having centuries more experience at pick pocketing than he, he did not succeed, but I was so impressed by his audacity and potential that I took him as my apprentice. And now, the son followed in his father's footsteps.

By the light of dusk, I could see the palatial *Ca' Clessidra* on the approaching shore.

We were not the only ones heading there. The sound of music drew masked revelers through its doors like sand streaming into the bottom half of an hourglass.

"Wait here," I said.

"You might need me," Luca insisted. "Father's taught me everything he knows."

"He may be the best thief and spy in Venice, but even he would find great danger in this house."

"What makes it so dangerous?"

"Antlion," I replied, and said no more. "Besides, I may need a quick escape should things turn sour."

Luca nodded, but beneath his cloak he drummed his fingers on the hilt of his stiletto. I left him to brood while I hopped out of the gondola and followed a group of tittering masqueraders into House Sandglass, my Harlequin costume easily fitting in with the Columbines and Bautas.

Antlion, the master of *Ca' Clessidra*, was a legend whose genius shone through his names of old. Daedalus. Archimedes. Leonardo da Vinci. His mind conceived incredible things while his hands gave them shape, like the infamous Labyrinth at Knossos and fantastic machines of war. Indeed, his reputation had earned him much trust among our kind. Since ancient times, many of the Elect vested Antlion with the stewardship of their most prized possessions, trusting his traps and mazes to keep their treasures safe.

It was my hope that the mithridate was among those things.

Inside, masked guests mingled in the opulent hall. The décor illuminated Antlion's wealth, and the masterful paintings doubtlessly came from his own hand. Women behind feathered masks called to me to share wine with them, and had I not come to see Antlion on a singular mission, I might have sought their company.

The old shapeshifter proved easy to find. When a portly man with a handheld golden mask came into the grand hall, the musicians silenced their instruments and the dancers ceased their dance. Two guards accompanied him, one in a Sun mask and the other the Moon, each bearing a lit oil lamp resembling the symbols they wore. Antlion's own mask played upon his secret name, a gold-leafed lion with rows of ants in amber set into the mane.

A servant quickly brought Antlion a goblet of wine. He lowered his mask, revealing the face of a charismatic bearded man in his forties. He tasted the wine and smiled. "I approve. To a perfect night!"

The cheer echoed throughout House Sandglass, returning the celebration to its liveliness. Men flocked to Antlion's side to curry favour, while women gazed longingly at him. To them, he was Vincenzo Scamozzi, an architect of much renown in the Veneto region. But Antlion also ruled Venice from the shadows. Little happened in the city that he did not know or approve of. Even we Elect gave Antlion due respect, for he who ruled Venice also controlled the amber and silk trades in Europe. Since we depended on those commodities for our immortality, only the brave or the foolish dared risk Antlion's wrath.

I approached. "Signor Scamozzi, might I have a private word?"

Antlion's eyes met mine. "And you are?"

I bowed. "Filippo Gamba." I had used that alias in Florence in 1506 when I studied with him during his time as Leonardo da Vinci.

"Flea?" His mood darkened. "What have you come to steal this time?"

"Still haven't forgiven me for stealing that codex of yours, I see. I must say, those notes on shape-shifting were quite illuminating." The tricks of healing and organ-shifting in the book had saved my life on more than a few occasions.

Antlion scowled. "Then you also know how many ways I could kill you before your powers could save you."

"Listen to my plea, first. I suppose you know why I've come?"

"I've heard whispers of trouble for your network of spies."

"Someone's been poisoning them, letting them die slow deaths. I need your help to save them."

"Why should I help you, thief?"

"In exchange for the return of the Proteus Codex, I hope."

He stared at me. "You dare bargain with something that is rightfully mine?"

Despite his icy tone, I caught the faintest curl of a smile. He was tempted.

"That, and my incomparable skills for a theft of your choosing."

Antlion raised an eyebrow. "Anything, anytime?"

I nodded.

"Where is my notebook?"

"Safe and near. You have my word you'll get it back."

He gave it some thought. "Then let us continue this conversation in the *Sala di Enea*." He bade his admirers to enjoy the party and led me to the stairs, his protectors flanking me as I followed.

We entered a room with pale green walls and glass doors opening onto a portico. The Room of Aeneas must have been named for the magnificent tapestry that covered the north wall, showing a scene from the myth of the Trojan War.

"Take watch, men," Antlion said. The Sun-masked guard took his place in the hallway outside the room while the Moon stepped out onto the portico. Antlion said to me, "Your assassin kills for Bee."

I frowned. Bee claimed among her early shapes Medea, Delilah, Cleopatra, and Empress Messalina: poisoners and betrayers, all. A century ago she abandoned the guise of Lucrezia Borgia to become Catherine de Médicis, Queen Mother to Henry III of France.

"Why does she want my spies dead? Why aid Spain against England?"

"My sources tell me that she's turning her sights on the New World. She tires of her present form and eyes the throne of Spain. There are reports of untapped reserves of amber in New Spain, and the Spanish Conquest of the Yucatan has brought additional reports of different species of bees and honey. For her, it is a means to new powers and conquests."

We who steal faces were few, relying on two sources of Lightning to transform our bodies: amber for permanent changes, silk for fleeting disguises. Honey also held Lightning, but Bee alone knew how to free the magic from that sweetness, and had known that secret since her time as Medea.

"And England stands in her way."

Antlion nodded.

I now understood. To win the New World, Bee would have to blind England to Spain's strategies, and that meant killing my best spies. "Who's Drone this time?" She always named her favourite minion that.

"His face changes, of course, but his voice betrays him as a Frenchman."

"I must have the mithridate, Antlion," I said. "You boasted once that Bee entrusted its secret to you."

"I have guarded treasures and secrets for thousands of years, Flea, for pharaohs, kings, and Doges. What I keep in my Labyrinth vault stays protected until the owner demands it back. No man has ever bested the traps in my maze or breached the vault at its centre or ever will," he said.

"No maze is unsolvable. Where does your Labyrinth lie?"

He laughed. "If I tell you, you will certainly die mangled in one of my traps. A pleasant thought, that, but how would I get my Proteus Codex back?"

"Either you have your revenge on me or I make amends once I have the mithridate. You win either way."

"True. All the same, tell me now what tragic tale you wish told of your many lives, so I may engrave it upon your tombstone."

I shrugged. "I am only fit for an unmarked grave."

"So be it." With a flourish, Antlion gestured at the tapestry depicting the Trojan War. "Let *Il Dono di Ulisse*, the Gift of Ulysses, lead you to your doom."

So, Antlion had hidden the path to his new Labyrinth in the imagery. He could never resist flaunting his brilliance, even when it could spell his own downfall. That was how King Minos lured him out when he was Daedalus in hiding: with a puzzle only he could solve.

Antlion called to his guards. "Sun, come with me. Moon, stay with our guest." He paused at the doorway but did not look back. "Make certain he steals nothing."

With that, he was gone.

Moon watched as I set aside my harlequin mask to better study the tapestry, a marvel of weaving with exquisite detail. I was familiar enough with Antlion's work to know he had a hand in its creation. The silk portrayed in painstaking detail the procession of the Trojan Horse. The wooden horse loomed tall over the dozen soldiers pulling it through the gates of Troy. Tricks of light and shadow suggested more Trojans were pushing the great beast on wheels from behind.

In the foreground, a wild-haired Cassandra in a crimson flowing robe beat at the soldiers with a branch. According to myth, she possessed the gift of prophecy, and foresaw how the horse would bring about the fall of the city. But the god Apollo had cursed her so that no one would ever believe her. A severed tongue upon the dirt at her feet symbolized her words falling on deaf ears.

But how did these things point to the whereabouts of Antlion's new Labyrinth? I memorized as many details as I could, from the architecture of the stone gate, to the stance of the Wooden Horse, to the petals of mulberry flowers upon the branch she held.

So enthralled in the puzzle, I almost did not notice the light in the room change. When my shadow suddenly grew large and shifted on the tapestry, I ducked Moon's swing towards my head with his oil lamp staff. The lamp missed my head but broke against the tapestry, spilling burning oil onto the silk and setting it afire.

My assailant dropped the staff and drew a knife. I threw my full weight into a low tackle, sending him reeling backward, but he managed a cut at my throat. The sharp edge sliced into my jugular.

The wound would have been grievous had I not still been wearing Mafeo's image. Instead, the form I borrowed from the silk unraveled, shielding me from the otherwise devastating cut. As I regained my previous shape, the wound to my throat vanished. I kicked Moon in the stomach, knocking him stumbling backward.

Moon steadied himself and threw the knife. I turned just in time, avoiding the steel sinking into my chest but taking its bite on my left upper arm. I gritted my teeth and grabbed his abandoned staff, but the fire behind me was spreading fast, the smoke stinging my eyes.

He drew another knife, but suddenly he startled as his own stolen form unraveled. Bee's Drone. He had infiltrated Antlion's home and meant to kill me as well as my spies. A stiletto clattered to the floor behind him.

My tearing eyes caught a glimpse of Luca on the portico.

Caught between Luca and me, Moon sped through the interior door and into House Sandglass. I hastened after him, but the only trace of him was the mask of the Moon abandoned on the floor of the corridor.

"Should we go after him?" Luca asked.

I shook my head. The fire would soon grow deadly if I didn't alert Antlion and his masquerade guests. I raised my voice and shouted *Fire*.

Frantic shouts and footfalls rose from below.

"I thought I told you to stay in the gondola."

"Father's first rule: protect you even if I must disobey your orders," Luca confessed.

I smiled. Mafeo would say that. "Remind me later that I owe Antlion a book."

Once we were safely back on water, I tended to the wound on my arm. I retrieved a hidden piece of amber and held it in my left hand. It was too dark to see if it was the one with the midge or the gnat trapped inside, but either way, the amber held bottled Lightning. I drew the jewel's Lightning up my arm and imagined my arm whole. Shaped by my thoughts, the magic closed the cut.

"What a night of marvels," Luca said. "Is this how you stave off death?"

"We can still die. Thank you for saving my life."

Drone must have overheard everything, which meant he knew I was going after the mithridate. "You know Venice better than I, Luca." I relayed what I discovered to him. "What do the clues in the tapestry mean?"

Luca asked for more details, and after a while gave his opinion. "There's a walled town on the mainland, like Troy, west of here called Padua. They say that its legendary founder was Antenor, a Trojan."

"What else?" I asked, unsure if that alone pointed to the Labyrinth.

"The tongue. The town's Basilica is named after their patron saint, Saint Anthony of Padua," Luca said. "Legend has it that Saint Anthony's body inside the Basilica had turned to dust, all except his tongue, which is still fresh and untouched."

Saint Anthony of Padua, the patron saint of lost things. Antlion *would* find perverse delight in that.

"Padua it is."

* * *

Hours later, Luca and I stood in a circle of lamplight, gazing up at the great wooden horse on the grounds of the Palazzo Capodilista in Padua.

The majestic wooden horse before us had been built for a fairground joust in 1466 by the order of Annibale Capodilista. Though the horse had not been designed by Donatello, it bore many similarities to the bronze equestrian statue of Gattamelata in the Piazza del Santo in Venice. I would not be surprised if Antlion had a hand in its construction or even claimed Donatello as a past identity. The tapestry might not have led us directly to the Labyrinth, but I gambled that the next clue lay with the great beast.

"Where do we start?" Luca asked.

I considered the possibilities. The horse, easily the height of three men, stood upon a wooden base that made it taller still. The base and the horse itself had been designed for men to enter and hide for the purpose of the joust. Its head and tail had not withstood the passing of the years well, appearing damaged.

I thought back to Cassandra's tongue in the painting, a deviation from classical myth. "Let's try the mouth. Give me a hand."

I climbed onto Luca's shoulders and pulled myself onto the horse's back. I could not easily reach the horse's mouth unless I hung one-handed from the horse's neck, but I had built this body strong and acrobatic: perfect for such a challenge. Gripping its wooden mane, I swung myself towards its mouth and grabbed onto its jaw. Searching inside with my fingers, I found a piece of hardwood that came loose.

I let go of the horse's neck and dropped to the ground. Inscribed upon the hardwood plaque was a phrase in *Venesiàn*. *'To find the paths in darkness, raise your eyes to the stars.'* I smiled. "If you were an astronomer at the University of Padua, Luca, where would you look to the stars?"

"Someplace high?"

"Exactly, the tallest tower in Padua. Come, let's find these paths in darkness."

The highest tower in Padua stood in the southern outskirts of town, once part of the old Castle. Situated near where two of Padua's canals met, it had served as a prison in the past. Luca and I found our way into the tower cellar where I found a loose stone high on one wall. When I pressed the stone, a hidden door shuddered open.

Taking the lamp from Luca, I peered inside. A small antechamber, with a single earth passage leading into the depths. Luca tried to follow me into the antechamber, but I stopped him.

"Too dangerous. If I do not return by dawn, assume I am dead and go back to Venice."

"You know I'd just come after you again," Luca said. "Besides, if the killer followed us, I'll be safer with you."

I lit a torch with flame from his lamp. "Then do exactly as I say: step where I step, touch nothing without leave, and –"

"– and keep you in sight. You taught Father that too."

I grinned. "Then you know I mean it."

Paved earthen tunnels lay beyond the antechamber. To trace our path, I held a piece of amber to the torchlight and gazed at the gnat caught within. I borrowed a lick of its power to mark my path in a carmine tattoo on the back of my right hand, tracing our route as we ventured deeper.

Luca followed my instructions precisely. "It seems safe thus far."

"Only because we've stepped around three pitfalls." I pointed out the edges of the one we just passed. "There will be deadlier traps."

Together, we stalked the winding corridors beneath Padua. Deeper into the maze, hewn stone lined the passages. By my reckoning, we had traveled so far underground that we stood somewhere beneath Padua's university. It would not surprise me in the least to learn that Antlion had laid the foundations for the Paduan Labyrinth ages ago when the university was founded. He and his minions had centuries to perfect the maze.

A tunnel led us to a stone door carved with the symbol of the Winged Lion of Venice. I studied the door from three paces back. Was it another mock portal, or a trapped gateway leading deeper into the maze?

"Another dead end?" Luca asked.

"You tell me."

I took the lamp from Luca. He knelt to examine the door without touching it, then the tiles in the floor. "Since Antlion would need to visit his vault, the true path would show signs of his passage. By the way the door's constructed, it should pull towards us, but I see no scratch marks on the floor. This is a dead end."

"Your reasoning is excellent, Luca. But what of the trap?"

Luca frowned and examined the door again. "Faint stains on the door, darker ones in the groove of the symbol. Blood." He looked up. "A twin stain on the ceiling. I see. A catch holds the hinged marble slab above in place, and when a thief tries the door, the swinging slab crushes him between the stones."

"Let's try a different passage." I touched amber and inked this branch of the maze as impassable with a blue tattoo.

We returned the way we came to a corridor we had passed earlier. The tunnel, covered in spider-webs, gave an impression of disuse, but could Antlion have somehow woven the webs? It would be an effective way to mislead a would-be thief. After all, our power to change shapes came from bugs and the like, leeching magic from amber and silk. Given Antlion's genius, he might know a way to command a legion of spiders.

I burned away the webs with my torch and entered the passage, inking the new path on my skin with another spark of Lightning. Luca followed. More webs concealed a bend in the passageway. I touched my torch to the webs again, but as they burned, I caught gleams of objects falling from crevices in the ceiling. Glass!

I dropped the torch and stumbled to my knees, grabbing for the falling vials. But they were too far apart. My free hand snatched one of the delicate vials, but the other –

Luca caught the second vial inches above the ground.

We caught our breaths and exchanged glances.

A colourless liquid rippled within the sealed vials. The pretty containers, most certainly made from Murano glass, had threads of white silk tied around their necks. Clever of Antlion to hide the threads among the webs, knowing the touch of flame or a rough tug might make the vials fall and break.

Luca took up the torch. "What's in them?"

"Antlion loves alchemy. Had the glass shattered, no doubt the concoction's fumes would have overcome or killed us." I took the vial from Luca and put both against a wall, out of the path of a stray foot.

The tunnel snaked for twenty paces before ending at a flight of stairs leading down to another stone door. Did the door below conceal another trap?

"Wait at the top," I said, taking the torch back.

I descended the stairs with caution. No loose stones or hidden threads on the way down, eleven steps in all. I studied the new stone door from the last step, not yet ready to set foot on the lower landing.

The jambs and lintel framing the plain door bore stone roundels carved with heraldic beasts. They numbered eleven, three above and four on either side.

The roundels on the left jamb, from lowest to highest: Eagle. Winged Lion. Horse. Goat. Continuing on the lintel, from left to right: Dog. Panther. Serpent. Finally, to the right, from top to bottom: Double-headed Eagle. Dragon. Minotaur. Unicorn.

"What did you find?" Luca called from the top of the stairs.

"Symbols. They may be the key to opening the door." The roundels had been designed to be turned, not pressed. Surely one would unlock the door, while the others delivered death.

I searched the surroundings again. If I knew the manner of the trap, I might better understand the puzzle of the heraldic beasts.

The ceiling did not seem to hide a swinging slab as before. The floor looked solid and unlikely to give way. I took a tentative step onto the landing, ready to leap back onto the stairs.

Nothing.

I knelt and examined the stairs. Each step had borne my full weight, but it took a careful eye to notice that the rise of the steps were not natural stone. Linen canvas painted to resemble bare rock concealed the true stone. A convincing illusion. I used my dagger to cut away a swath of cloth from the fourth step from the bottom to see what hid beneath.

The step had a line of seven round holes cut into it, oddly spaced, each the width of a large thumb. I could not see what lay on the other side, but had an inkling as to their true purpose. I had once admired Antlion's designs for giant crossbows, but those same arbalests could mean my death here. Antlion likely set such weapons under the stairs, rigged to impale someone who twisted the wrong symbol.

I told Luca my suspicions. Together, we tore the canvas away. Eleven steps, seven holes each, made for a terrifying storm of arrows.

"Ten roundels might lead to death, and one to the treasures beyond. Luca, do these symbols mean anything to you?"

Luca considered the symbols in turn. "A few. This is the heraldic device of Lombardia. This Eagle here's for Friuli. And the Winged Lion of Venice of course."

"The Winged Lion's too obvious." Antlion could be counting on the thief to choose the symbol of Saint Mark. "The Minotaur, beast of Crete, once the guardian of the ancient Labyrinth. Again, an obvious choice. But the Panther – myths tell that the traitor Antenor helped Odysseus open the gates of Troy. To reward his betrayal, Antenor's house, marked by a panther skin hung above the door, had been spared in the sack of Troy. That must mean Padua."

Luca frowned. "It seems too simple. Why not pick a random image?"

I reconsidered the roundel with the heraldic Panther, venting fire from its ears and mouth. Did I overlook something? Would Antlion really hide the key to the stone door in an obvious symbol?

I decided to trust what I knew of Antlion. "When Antlion delights in riddles and hidden meanings. Given that he kept true to the clues in *Il Dono di Ulisse* and the Capodilista Horse, these symbols likely hold secret meaning as well. Look where he chose to put the Panther: directly over the threshold, alluding to the myth of Antenor."

"You can't be sure the bolts won't fire even if you turn the right symbol," Luca said. "These things turn. They don't work by push, so you can't prod them with a staff from a safe distance. You'd have to know where and how to stand."

I saw his point. Even if I changed back to my first shape, with the reach of seven-foot tall Little John, I could not turn a symbol from a position safe from the array of crossbows. I had to place myself in the maw of the trap.

I looked up. The walls at the landing stood five feet apart, and the ceiling six feet high. I handed the torch to Luca. "Go back to the top." Though it was a tight squeeze, I braced my hands and feet against opposite walls and climbed up, my body flat and facing down. I climbed until my back hit the ceiling.

Luca held the torch low to give me light.

I twisted the Panther roundel.

Three bolts flew out of the stairs. One hit where my head would have been, had I been standing in front of the door, breaking against the stone. The second struck the left wall. The third arrow, angled upward from the rise of the second step, buried its sharp head in my thigh. I held in a cry of pain and kept myself from falling.

Damned Antlion had anticipated that a thief might try exactly what I did. Had I been turned the other way, the bolt might have pierced my heart.

There came a shout of surprise and sounds of a struggle, and then the torch rolled down the stairs. I dropped down to the ground and looked up. Luca was struggling with a man at the top of the stairs, desperately keeping a dagger from being plunged into his chest.

Drone!

I hobbled up the stairs, every other step sending a jolt of pain through my injured leg. I forced Drone's knife hand away from Luca. Drone kicked my thigh and broke the arrow, driving the arrowhead deeper into my flesh and unbalancing me. I cried out and fell backward, but dragged him with me, tumbling together down to the lower landing. I twisted him so that he was the one who fell on the flaming torch and he screamed. But he wrestled me with all his strength and rolled us further towards the portal, smashing my head against the floor.

I couldn't keep my mind clear. All I saw was a gleam coming towards my right eye.

I grabbed his wrist just in time, and with all my strength turned his hand and broke his wrist.

He howled and dropped the dagger, but grabbed for the amber set in its pommel with his good hand. I grabbed his throat and reached for the amber as well, but he touched it first and drained its Lightning. He began to grow. I couldn't let him gain an advantage in size. I grabbed Drone and pressed him against the steps with my full weight while I still could. "Luca! Trigger the arrows!"

Luca leapt over our heads and used my back as a step, forcing the air from my lungs, but it helped me keep Drone down even as he grew larger.

The arbalests fired, a single bolt flying past my ear. The other two bolts buried themselves in Drone's back. He coughed blood on my bare chest, shuddered, and was still.

I tried to ask Luca how he was, but my voice would not come. Then I saw a scratch across my left palm. I had been poisoned.

Luca saw it too. "Maybe he has the antidote," he said, searching through Drone's clothes.

I reached for the other amber in my pocket, but it had been crushed beyond usefulness in my fall.

"Nothing!" Luca said.

I could barely hold on to consciousness. The mithridate that could save me was on the other side of the puzzle door. With a trembling hand, I indicated the roundels.

"But which?" Luca said, despair in his voice.

Darkness took me then.

* * *

I awakened in a round, vaulted chamber lit by tall brass candle stands with beeswax candles standing at the base of eight Doric columns. Dark alcoves set into the walls held chests of gold and silver that glimmered in the fading torchlight.

Luca breathed a sigh of relief. "The antidote worked."

"How...?"

"I figured out how to open the door," he said. "Well, not straight away; I made a couple of mistakes before figuring it out. Luckily, Drone's corpse took some arrows that might have killed me." He knelt. "But then I thought about you and Antlion. You're both proud of who you once were, and who you are now. If the Panther of Padua is the key to Antlion's current Labyrinth, then maybe the Minotaur is the key to his past. I tried both roundels at the same time and it worked." He pressed a piece of amber into my hand. "There are lots of these here."

I willed the spark of Lightning in the amber to heal me, forcing out the arrowhead and closing the wounds in my flesh.

Whole again, I stood with Luca's help. "Thank you."

"No, Master Flea, it is I who must thank you. There are more vials of mithridate, enough to save Father."

I walked the perimeter of the chamber, marveling at the heart of Antlion's Labyrinth. A passage curving behind the entrance likely led to Antlion's ballistae trap. Eight alcoves in the walls bore their own carved emblem at the top of each arch. Mantis. Locust. Cicada. Dragonfly. Butterfly. Spider. Scorpion. Bee. Ancient shape-shifters, all, elders among the Elect.

Luca showed me Bee's alcove. An open chest there bore a latch with the same bee emblem. Atop a bed of gleaming gold dinar, silver drachm coins, jewels and gems, lay two slender vials filled with honey-gold liquid, and a slab of basalt inscribed with Greek words. The mithridate and its recipe. Bee would never poison another of my men again.

I gave the vials to Luca. "We must return to Venice at once. Take as well what treasure you can from Bee, so long as it does not weigh us down."

* * *

Under the magic of the mithridate, Mafeo began to regain his strength.

True to his nature, his first utterance to me was his report of his meeting with the Spaniard. At the end of it, he clasped my hands. "Master Flea, once again I owe you my life."

"Ah, but if you hadn't taught your son to defy me, Mafeo, I might well be dead myself." I regarded Luca with heartfelt thanks. "And what you have learned of the Armada may save all of England."

The Black Hand

Arthur B. Reeve

KENNEDY AND I had been dining rather late one evening at Luigi's, a little Italian restaurant on the lower West Side. We had known the place well in our student days, and had made a point of visiting it once a month since, in order to keep in practice in the fine art of gracefully handling long shreds of spaghetti. Therefore we did not think it strange when the proprietor himself stopped a moment at our table to greet us. Glancing furtively around at the other diners, mostly Italians, he suddenly leaned over and whispered to Kennedy: "I have heard of your wonderful detective work, Professor. Could you give a little advice in the case of a friend of mine?"

"Surely, Luigi. What is the case?" asked Craig, leaning back in his chair.

Luigi glanced around again apprehensively and lowered his voice. "Not so loud, sir. When you pay your check, go out, walk around Washington Square, and come in at the private entrance. I'll be waiting in the hall. My friend is dining privately upstairs."

We lingered a while over our Chianti, then quietly paid the check and departed.

True to his word, Luigi was waiting for us in the dark hall. With a motion that indicated silence, he led us up the stairs to the second floor, and quickly opened a door into what seemed to be a fair-sized private dining room. A man was pacing the floor nervously. On a table was some food, untouched. As the door opened I thought he started as if in fear, and I am sure his dark face blanched, if only for an instant. Imagine our surprise at seeing Gennaro, the great tenor, with whom merely to have a speaking acquaintance was to argue oneself famous.

"Oh, it is you, Luigi," he exclaimed in perfect English, rich and mellow. "And who are these gentlemen?"

Luigi merely replied, "Friends," in English also, and then dropped off into a voluble, low-toned explanation in Italian.

I could see, as we waited, that the same idea had flashed over Kennedy's mind as over my own. It was now three or four days since the papers had reported the strange kidnapping of Gennaro's five-year-old daughter Adelina, his only child, and the sending of a demand for ten thousand dollars ransom, signed, as usual, with the mystic Black Hand – a name to conjure with in blackmail and extortion.

As Signor Gennaro advanced toward us, after his short talk with Luigi, almost before the introductions were over, Kennedy anticipated him by saying: "I understand, Signor, before you ask me. I have read all about it in the papers. You want someone to help you catch the criminals who are holding your little girl."

"No, no!" exclaimed Gennaro excitedly. "Not that. I want to get my daughter first. After that, catch them if you can – yes, I should like to have someone do it. But read this first and tell me what you think of it. How should I act to get my little Adelina back without harming a hair of her head?" The famous singer drew from a capacious pocketbook a dirty, crumpled letter, scrawled on cheap paper.

Kennedy translated it quickly. It read:

> *Honourable sir: Your daughter is in safe hands. But, by the saints, if you give this letter to the police as you did the other, not only she but your family also, someone near to you, will suffer. We will not fail as we did Wednesday. If you want your daughter back, go yourself, alone and without telling a soul, to Enrico Albano's Saturday night at the twelfth hour. You must provide yourself with $10,000 in bills hidden in Saturday's Il Progresso Italiano. In the back room you will see a man sitting alone at a table. He will have a red flower on his coat. You are to say, "A fine opera is 'I Pagliacci.'" If he answers, "Not without Gennaro," lay the newspaper down on the table. He will pick it up, leaving his own, the Bolletino. On the third page you will find written the place where your daughter has been left waiting for you. Go immediately and get her. But, by the God, if you have so much as the shadow of the police near Enrico's your daughter will be sent to you in a box that night. Do not fear to come. We pledge our word to deal fairly if you deal fairly. This is a last warning. Lest you shall forget we will show one other sign of our power tomorrow.*
>
> *La Mano Nera.*

The end of this letter was decorated with a skull and crossbones, a rough drawing of a dagger thrust through a bleeding heart, a coffin, and, under all, a huge black hand. There was no doubt about the type of letter. It was such as have of late years become increasingly common in all our large cities.

"You have not showed this to the police, I presume?" asked Kennedy.

"Naturally not."

"Are you going Saturday night?"

"I am afraid to go and afraid to stay away," was the reply, and the voice of the fifty-thousand-dollars-a-season tenor was as human as that of a five-dollar-a-week father, for at bottom all men, high or low, are one.

"'We will not fail as we did Wednesday,'" reread Craig. "What does that mean?"

Gennaro fumbled in his pocketbook again, and at last drew forth a typewritten letter bearing the letterhead of the Leslie Laboratories, Incorporated.

"After I received the first threat," explained Gennaro, "my wife and I went from our apartments at the hotel to her father's, the banker Cesare, you know, who lives on Fifth Avenue. I gave the letter to the Italian Squad of the police. The next morning my father-in-law's butler noticed something peculiar about the milk. He barely touched some of it to his tongue, and he has been violently ill ever since. I at once sent the milk to the laboratory of my friend Doctor Leslie to have it analyzed. This letter shows what the household escaped."

"My dear Gennaro," read Kennedy. "The milk submitted to us for examination on the 10th inst. has been carefully analyzed, and I beg to hand you herewith the result:

"*Specific gravity 1.036 at 15 degrees Cent.*

Water	84.60	per cent
Casein	3.49	per cent
Albumin	.56	per cent

Globulin	*1.32*	*per cent*
Lactose	*5.08*	*per cent*
Ash	*.72*	*per cent*
Fat	*3.42*	*per cent*
Ricinus	*1.19*	*per cent*

"Ricinus is a new and little-known poison derived from the shell of the castor-oil bean. Professor Ehrlich states that one gram of the pure poison will kill 1,500,000 guinea pigs. Ricinus was lately isolated by Professor Robert, of Rostock, but is seldom found except in an impure state, though still very deadly. It surpasses strychnine, prussic acid, and other commonly known drugs. I congratulate you and yours on escaping and shall of course respect your wishes absolutely regarding keeping secret this attempt on your life. Believe me,

"Very sincerely yours,

"C.W. Leslie."

As Kennedy handed the letter back, he remarked significantly: "I can see very readily why you don't care to have the police figure in your case. It has got quite beyond ordinary police methods."

"And tomorrow, too, they are going to give another sign of their power," groaned Gennaro, sinking into the chair before his untasted food.

"You say you have left your hotel?" inquired Kennedy.

"Yes. My wife insisted that we would be more safely guarded at the residence of her father, the banker. But we are afraid even there since the poison attempt. So I have come here secretly to Luigi, my old friend Luigi, who is preparing food for us, and in a few minutes one of Cesare's automobiles will be here, and I will take the food up to her – sparing no expense or trouble. She is heartbroken. It will kill her, Professor Kennedy, if anything happens to our little Adelina.

"Ah, sir, I am not poor myself. A month's salary at the opera-house, that is what they ask of me. Gladly would I give it, ten thousand dollars – all, if they asked it, of my contract with Signor Cassinelli, the director. But the police – bah! – They are all for catching the villains. What good will it do me if they catch them and my little Adelina is returned to me dead? It is all very well for the Anglo-Saxon to talk of justice and the law, but I am – what you call it? – an emotional Latin. I want my little daughter – and at any cost. Catch the villains afterward – yes. I will pay double then to catch them so that they cannot blackmail me again. Only first I want my daughter back."

"And your father-in-law?"

"My father-in-law, he has been among you long enough to be one of you. He has fought them. He has put up a sign in his banking-house, 'No money paid on threats.' But I say it is foolish. I do not know America as well as he, but I know this: the police never succeed – the ransom is paid without their knowledge, and they very often take the credit. I say, pay first, then I will swear a righteous vendetta – I will bring the dogs to justice with the money yet on them. Only show me how, show me how."

"First of all," replied Kennedy, "I want you to answer one question, truthfully, without reservation, as to a friend. I am your friend, believe me. Is there any person, a relative or acquaintance of yourself or your wife or your father-in-law, whom you even have reason to suspect of being capable of extorting money from you in this way? I needn't say that is the experience of the district attorney's office in the large majority of cases of this so-called Black Hand."

"No," replied the tenor without hesitation. "I know that, and I have thought about it. No, I can think of no one. I know you Americans often speak of the Black Hand as a myth coined originally by a newspaper writer. Perhaps it has no organization. But, Professor Kennedy, to me it is no myth. What if the real Black Hand is any gang of criminals who choose to use that convenient name to extort money? Is it the less real? My daughter is gone!"

"Exactly," agreed Kennedy. "It is not a theory that confronts you. It is a hard, cold fact. I understand that perfectly. What is the address of this Albano's?"

Luigi mentioned a number on Mulberry Street, and Kennedy made a note of it.

"It is a gambling saloon," explained Luigi. "Albano is a Neapolitan, a Camorrista, one of my countrymen of whom I am thoroughly ashamed, Professor Kennedy."

"Do you think this Albano had anything to do with the letter?"

Luigi shrugged his shoulders.

Just then a big limousine was heard outside. Luigi picked up a huge hamper that was placed in a corner of the room and, followed closely by Signor Gennaro, hurried down to it. As the tenor left us he grasped our hands in each of his.

"I have an idea in my mind," said Craig simply. "I will try to think it out in detail tonight. Where can I find you tomorrow?"

"Come to me at the opera-house in the afternoon, or if you want me sooner at Mr. Cesare's residence. Goodnight, and a thousand thanks to you, Professor Kennedy, and to you, also, Mr. Jameson. I trust you absolutely because Luigi trusts you."

We sat in the little dining room until we heard the door of the limousine bang shut and the car shoot off with the rattle of the changing gears.

"One more question, Luigi," said Craig as the door opened again. "I have never been on that block in Mulberry Street where this Albano's is. Do you happen to know any of the shopkeepers on it or near it?"

"I have a cousin who has a drug store on the corner below Albano's, on the same side of the street."

"Good! Do you think he would let me use his store for a few minutes Saturday night – of course without any risk to himself?"

"I think I could arrange it."

"Very well. Then tomorrow, say at nine in the morning, I will stop here, and we will all go over to see him. Goodnight, Luigi, and many thanks for thinking of me in connection with this case. I've enjoyed Signor Gennaro's singing often enough at the opera to want to render him this service, and I'm only too glad to be able to be of service to all honest Italians; that is, if I succeed in carrying out a plan I have in mind."

A little before nine the following day Kennedy and I dropped into Luigi's again. Kennedy was carrying a suitcase which he had taken over from his laboratory to our rooms the night before. Luigi was waiting for us, and without losing a minute we sallied forth.

By means of the tortuous twists of streets in old Greenwich village we came out at last on Bleecker Street and began walking east amid the hurly-burly of races of lower New York. We had not quite reached Mulberry Street when our attention was attracted by a large crowd on one of the busy corners, held back by a cordon of police who were endeavouring to keep the people moving with that burly good nature which the six-foot Irish policeman displays toward the five-foot burden-bearers of southern and eastern Europe who throng New York.

Apparently, we saw, as we edged up into the front of the crowd, here was a building whose whole front had literally been torn off and wrecked. The thick plate-glass of the windows was smashed to a mass of greenish splinters on the sidewalk, while the windows of the upper floors and for several houses down the block in either street were likewise broken. Some thick iron bars which had formerly protected the windows were now bent and twisted. A huge hole yawned in the floor inside the doorway, and peering in we could see the desk and chairs a tangled mass of kindling.

"What's the matter?" I inquired of an officer near me, displaying my reporter's fire-line badge, more for its moral effect than in the hope of getting any real information in these days of enforced silence toward the press.

"Black Hand bomb," was the laconic reply.

"Whew!" I whistled. "Anyone hurt?"

"They don't usually kill anyone, do they?" asked the officer by way of reply to test my acquaintance with such things.

"No," I admitted. "They destroy more property than lives. But did they get anyone this time? This must have been a thoroughly overloaded bomb, I should judge by the looks of things."

"Came pretty close to it. The bank hadn't any more than opened when, bang! went this gas-pipe-and-dynamite thing. Crowd collected before the smoke had fairly cleared. Man who owns the bank was hurt, but not badly. Now come, beat it down to headquarters if you want to find out any more. You'll find it printed on the pink slips – the 'squeal book' – by this tune. 'Gainst the rules for me to talk," he added with a good-natured grin, then to the crowd: "Gwan, now. You're blockin' traffic. Keep movin'."

I turned to Craig and Luigi. Their eyes were riveted on the big gilt sign, half broken, and all askew overhead. It read:

CIRO DI CESARE & CO. BANKERS
NEW YORK, GENOA, NAPLES, ROME, PALERMO

"This is the reminder so that Gennaro and his father-in-law will not forget," I gasped.

"Yes," added Craig, pulling us away, "and Cesare himself is wounded, too. Perhaps that was for putting up the notice refusing to pay. Perhaps not. It's a queer case – they usually set the bombs off at night when no one is around. There must be more back of this than merely to scare Gennaro. It looks to me as if they were after Cesare, too, first by poison, then by dynamite."

We shouldered our way out through the crowd, and went on until we came to Mulberry Street, pulsing with life. Down we went past the little shops, dodging the children, and making way for women with huge bundles of sweat-shop clothing accurately balanced on their heads or hugged up under their capacious capes. Here was just one little colony of the hundreds of thousands of Italians – a population larger than the Italian population of Rome – of whose life the rest of New York knew and cared nothing.

At last we came to Albano's little wine-shop, a dark, evil, malodorous place on the street level of a five-story, alleged 'new-law' tenement. Without hesitation Kennedy entered, and we followed, acting the part of a slumming party. There were a few customers at this early hour, men out of employment and an inoffensive-looking lot, though of course they eyed us sharply. Albano himself proved to be a greasy, low-browed fellow who had a sort of cunning look. I could well imagine such a fellow spreading terror in the hearts of simple folk by merely pressing both temples with his thumbs and drawing his long bony forefinger under his throat – the so-called Black Hand sign that has shut up many a witness in the middle of his testimony even in open court.

We pushed through to the low-ceilinged back room, which was empty, and sat down at a table. Over a bottle of Albano's famous California 'red ink' we sat silently. Kennedy was making a mental note of the place. In the middle of the ceiling was a single gas-burner with a big reflector over it. In the back wall of the room was a horizontal oblong window, barred, and with a sash that opened like a transom. The tables were dirty and the chairs rickety. The walls were bare and unfinished, with beams innocent of decoration. Altogether it was as unprepossessing a place as I had ever seen.

Apparently satisfied with his scrutiny, Kennedy got up to go, complimenting the proprietor on his wine. I could see that Kennedy had made up his mind as to his course of action.

"How sordid crime really is," he remarked as we walked on down the street. "Look at that place of Albano's. I defy even the police news reporter on the *Star* to find any glamour in that."

Our next stop was at the corner at the little store kept by the cousin of Luigi, who conducted us back of the partition where prescriptions were compounded, and found us chairs.

A hurried explanation from Luigi brought a cloud to the open face of the druggist, as if he hesitated to lay himself and his little fortune open to the blackmailers. Kennedy saw it and interrupted.

"All that I wish to do," he said, "is to put in a little instrument here and use it tonight for a few minutes. Indeed, there will be no risk to you, Vincenzo. Secrecy is what I desire, and no one will ever know about it."

Vincenzo was at length convinced, and Craig opened his suitcase. There was little in it except several coils of insulated wire, some tools, a couple of packages wrapped up, and a couple of pairs of overalls. In a moment Kennedy had donned overalls and was smearing dirt and grease over his face and hands. Under his direction I did the same.

Taking the bag of tools, the wire, and one of the small packages, we went out on the street and then up through the dark and ill-ventilated hall of the tenement. Halfway up a woman stopped us suspiciously.

"Telephone company," said Craig curtly. "Here's permission from the owner of the house to string wires across the roof."

He pulled an old letter out of his pocket, but as it was too dark to read even if the woman had cared to do so, we went on up as he had expected, unmolested. At last we came to the roof, where there were some children at play a couple of houses down from us.

Kennedy began by dropping two strands of wire down to the ground in the back yard behind Vincenzo's shop. Then he proceeded to lay two wires along the edge of the roof.

We had worked only a little while when the children began to collect. However, Kennedy kept right on until we reached the tenement next to that in which Albano's shop was.

"Walter," he whispered, "just get the children away for a minute now."

"Look here, you kids," I yelled, "some of you will fall off if you get so close to the edge of the roof. Keep back."

It had no effect. Apparently they looked not a bit frightened at the dizzy mass of clothes-lines below us.

"Say, is there a candy store on this block?" I asked in desperation.

"Yes, sir," came the chorus.

"Who'll go down and get me a bottle of ginger ale?" I asked.

A chorus of voices and glittering eyes was the answer. They all would. I took a half-dollar from my pocket and gave it to the oldest.

"All right now, hustle along, and divide the change."

With the scamper of many feet they were gone, and we were alone. Kennedy had now reached Albano's, and as soon as the last head had disappeared below the scuttle of the roof he dropped two long strands down into the back yard, as he had done at Vincenzo's.

I started to go back, but he stopped me. "Oh, that will never do," he said. "The kids will see that the wires end here. I must carry them on several houses farther as a blind and trust to luck that they don't see the wires leading down below."

We were several houses down, still putting up wires when the crowd came shouting back, sticky with cheap trust-made candy and black with East Side chocolate. We opened the ginger ale and forced ourselves to drink it so as to excite no suspicion, then a few minutes later descended the stairs of the tenement, coming out just above Albano's.

I was wondering how Kennedy was going to get into Albano's again without exciting suspicion. He solved it neatly.

"Now, Walter, do you think you could stand another dip into that red ink of Albano's?"

I said I might in the interests of science and justice – not otherwise.

"Well, your face is sufficiently dirty," he commented, "so that with the overalls you don't look very much as you did the first time you went in. I don't think they will recognize you. Do I look pretty good?"

"You look like a coal-heaver on the job," I said. "I can scarcely restrain my admiration."

"All right. Then take this little glass bottle. Go into the back room and order something cheap, in keeping with your looks. Then when you are all alone break the bottle. It is full of gas drippings. Your nose will dictate what to do next. Just tell the proprietor you saw the gas company's wagon on the next block and come up here and tell me."

I entered. There was a sinister-looking man, with a sort of unscrupulous intelligence, writing at a table. As he wrote and puffed at his cigar, I noticed a scar on his face, a deep furrow running from the lobe of his ear to his mouth. That, I knew, was a brand set upon him by the Camorra. I sat and smoked and sipped slowly for several minutes, cursing him inwardly more for his presence than for his evident look of the '*mala vita.*' At last he went out to ask the barkeeper for a stamp.

Quickly I tiptoed over to another corner of the room and ground the little bottle under my heel. Then I resumed my seat. The odor that pervaded the room was sickening.

The sinister-looking man with the scar came in again and sniffed. I sniffed. Then the proprietor came in and sniffed.

"Say," I said in the toughest voice I could assume, "you got a leak. Wait. I seen the gas company wagon on the next block when I came in. I'll get the man."

I dashed out and hurried up the street to the place where Kennedy was waiting impatiently. Rattling his tools, he followed me with apparent reluctance.

As he entered the wine-shop he snorted, after the manner of gasmen, "Where's de leak?"

"You find-a da leak," grunted Albano. "What-a you get-a you pay for? You want-a me do your work?"

"Well, half a dozen o' you wops get out o' here, that's all. D'youse all wanter be blown ter pieces wid dem pipes and cigarettes? Clear out," growled Kennedy.

They retreated precipitately, and Craig hastily opened his bag of tools.

"Quick, Walter, shut the door and hold it," exclaimed Craig, working rapidly. He unwrapped a little package and took out a round, flat disk-like thing of black vulcanized rubber. Jumping up on a table, he fixed it to the top of the reflector over the gas-jet.

"Can you see that from the floor, Walter?" he asked, under his breath.

"No," I replied, "not even when I know it is there."

Then he attached a couple of wires to it and led them across the ceiling toward the window, concealing them carefully by sticking them in the shadow of a beam. At the window he quickly attached the wires to the two that were dangling down from the roof and shoved them around out of sight.

"We'll have to trust that no one sees them," he said. "That's the best I can do at such short notice. I never saw a room so bare as this, anyway. There isn't another place I could put that thing without its being seen."

We gathered up the broken glass of the gas-drippings bottle, and I opened the door.

"It's all right now," said Craig, sauntering out before the bar. "Only de next time you has anyt'ing de matter call de company up. I ain't supposed to do dis wit'out orders, see?"

A moment later I followed, glad to get out of the oppressive atmosphere, and joined him in the back of Vincenzo's drug store, where he was again at work. As there was no back window there, it was quite a job to lead the wires around the outside from the back yard and in at a side window. It was at last done, however, without exciting suspicion, and Kennedy attached them to an oblong box of weathered oak and a pair of specially constructed dry batteries.

"Now," said Craig, as we washed off the stains of work and stowed the overalls back in the suitcase, "that is done to my satisfaction. I can tell Gennaro to go ahead safely now and meet the Black Handers."

From Vincenzo's we walked over toward Center Street, where Kennedy and I left Luigi to return to his restaurant, with instructions to be at Vincenzo's at half-past eleven that night.

We turned into the new police headquarters and went down the long corridor to the Italian Bureau. Kennedy sent in his card to Lieutenant Giuseppe in charge, and we were quickly admitted. The lieutenant was a short, full-faced fleshy Italian, with lightish hair and eyes that were apparently dull, until you suddenly discovered that that was merely a cover to their really restless way of taking in every thing and fixing it on his mind, as if on a sensitive plate.

"I want to talk about the Gennaro case," began Craig. "I may add that I have been rather closely associated with Inspector O'Connor of the Central Office on a number of cases, so that I think we can trust each other. Would you mind telling me what you know about it if I promise you that I, too, have something to reveal?"

The lieutenant leaned back and watched Kennedy closely without seeming to do so. "When I was in Italy last year," he replied at length, "I did a good deal of work in tracing up some Camorra suspects. I had a tip about some of them to look up their records – I needn't say where it came from, but it was a good one. Much of the evidence against some of those fellows who are being tried at Viterbo was gathered by the Carabinieri as a result of hints that I was able to give them – clues that were furnished to me here in America from the source I speak of. I suppose there is really no need to conceal it, though. The original tip came from a certain banker here in New York."

"I can guess who it was," nodded Craig.

"Then, as you know, this banker is a fighter. He is the man who organized the White Hand – an organization which is trying to rid the Italian population of the Black Hand. His society had a lot of evidence regarding former members of both the Camorra in Naples and the Mafia in Sicily, as well as the Black Hand gangs in New York, Chicago, and other cities. Well, Cesare, as you know, is Gennaro's father-in-law.

"While I was in Naples looking up the record of a certain criminal I heard of a peculiar murder committed some years ago. There was an honest old music master who apparently lived the quietest and most harmless of lives. But it became known that he was supported by Cesare and had received handsome presents of money from him. The old man was, as you may have guessed, the first music teacher of Gennaro, the man who discovered him. One might have been at a loss to see how he could have an enemy, but there was one who coveted his small fortune. One day he was stabbed and robbed. His murderer ran out into the street, crying out that the poor man had been killed. Naturally a crowd rushed up in a moment, for it was in the middle of the day. Before the injured man could make it understood who had struck him the assassin was down the street and lost in the maze of old Naples where he well knew the houses of his friends who would hide him. The man who is known to have committed that crime – Francesco Paoli – escaped to New York. We are looking for him today. He is a clever man, far above the average – son of a doctor in a town a few miles from Naples, went to the university, was expelled for some mad prank – in short, he was the black sheep of the family. Of course over here he is too high-born to work with his hands on a railroad or in a trench, and not educated enough to work at anything else. So he has been preying on his more industrious countrymen – a typical case of a man living by his wits with no visible means of support.

"Now I don't mind telling you in strict confidence," continued the lieutenant, "that it's my theory that old Cesare had seen Paoli here, knew he was wanted for that murder of the old music master, and gave me the tip to look up his record. At any rate, Paoli disappeared right after I returned from Italy, and we haven't been able to locate him since. He must have found out in some way that the tip to look him up had been given by the White Hand. He had been a Camorrista, in Italy, and had many ways of getting information here in America."

He paused, and balanced a piece of cardboard in his hand.

"It is my theory of this case that if we could locate this Paoli we could solve the kidnapping of little Adelina Gennaro very quickly. That's his picture."

Kennedy and I bent over to look at it, and I started in surprise. It was my evil-looking friend with the scar on his cheek.

"Well," said Craig, quietly handing back the card, "whether or not he is the man, I know where we can catch the kidnappers tonight, Lieutenant."

It was Giuseppe's turn to show surprise now.

"With your assistance I'll get this man and the whole gang tonight," explained Craig, rapidly sketching over his plan and concealing just enough to make sure that no matter how anxious the lieutenant was to get the credit he could not spoil the affair by premature interference.

The final arrangement was that four of the best men of the squad were to hide in a vacant store across from Vincenzo's early in the evening, long before anyone was watching. The signal for them to appear was to be the extinguishing of the lights behind the coloured bottles in the druggist's window. A taxicab was to be kept waiting at headquarters at the same time with three other good men ready to start for a given address the moment the alarm was given over the telephone.

We found Gennaro awaiting us with the greatest anxiety at the opera house. The bomb at Cesare's had been the last straw. Gennaro had already drawn from his bank ten crisp one-thousand-dollar bills, and already he had a copy of *Il Progresso* in which he had hidden the money between the sheets.

"Mr. Kennedy," he said, "I am going to meet them tonight. They may kill me. See, I have provided myself with a pistol – I shall fight, too, if necessary for my little Adelina. But if it is only money they want, they shall have it."

"One thing I want to say," began Kennedy.

"No, no, no!" cried the tenor. "I will go – you shall not stop me."

"I don't wish to stop you," Craig reassured him. "But one thing – do exactly as I tell you, and I swear not a hair of the child's head will be injured and we will get the blackmailers, too."

"How?" eagerly asked Gennaro. "What do you want me to do?"

"All I want you to do is to go to Albano's at the appointed time. Sit down in the back room. Get into conversation with them, and, above all, Signor, as soon as you get the copy of the *Bolletino* turn to the third page, pretend not to be able to read the address. Ask the man to read it. Then repeat it after him. Pretend to be overjoyed. Offer to set up wine for the whole crowd. Just a few minutes, that is all I ask, and I will guarantee that you will be the happiest man in New York tomorrow."

Gennaro's eyes filled with tears as he grasped Kennedy's hand. "That is better than having the whole police force back of me," he said. "I shall never forget, never forget."

As we went out Kennedy remarked: "You can't blame them for keeping their troubles to themselves. Here we send a police officer over to Italy to look up the records of some of the worst suspects. He loses his life. Another takes his place. Then after he gets back he is set to work on the mere clerical routine of translating them. One of his associates is reduced in rank. And so what does it all come to? Hundreds of records have become useless because the three years within which the criminals could be deported have elapsed with nothing done. Intelligent, isn't it? I believe it has been established that all but about fifty of seven hundred known Italian suspects are still at large, mostly in this city. And the rest of the Italian population is guarded from them by a squad of police in number scarcely one-thirtieth of the number of known criminals. No, it's our fault if the Black Hand thrives."

We had been standing on the corner of Broadway, waiting for a car.

"Now, Walter, don't forget. Meet me at the Bleecker Street station of the subway at eleven thirty. I'm off to the university. I have some very important experiments with phosphorescent salts that I want to finish today."

"What has that to do with the case?" I asked mystified.

"Nothing," replied Craig. "I didn't say it had. At eleven thirty, don't forget. By George, though, that Paoli must be a clever one – think of his knowing about ricinus. I only heard of it myself recently. Well, here's my car. Goodbye."

Craig swung aboard an Amsterdam Avenue car, leaving me to kill eight nervous hours of my weekly day of rest from the *Star*.

They passed at length, and at precisely the appointed time Kennedy and I met. With suppressed excitement, at least on my part, we walked over to Vincenzo's. At night this section of the city was indeed a black enigma. The lights in the shops where olive oil, fruit, and other things were sold, were winking out one by one; here and there strains of music floated out of wine-shops, and little groups lingered on corners conversing in animated sentences. We passed Albano's on the other side of the street, being careful not to look at it too closely, for several men were hanging idly about – pickets, apparently, with some secret code that would instantly have spread far and wide the news of any alarming action.

At the corner we crossed and looked in Vincenzo's window a moment, casting a furtive glance across the street at the dark empty store where the police must be hiding. Then we went in and casually sauntered back of the partition. Luigi was there already. There were several customers still in the store, however, and therefore we had to sit in silence while Vincenzo quickly finished a prescription and waited on the last one.

At last the doors were locked and the lights lowered, all except those in the windows which were to serve as signals.

"Ten minutes to twelve," said Kennedy, placing the oblong box on the table. "Gennaro will be going in soon. Let us try this machine now and see if it works. If the wires have been cut since we put them up this morning Gennaro will have to take his chances alone."

Kennedy reached over and with a light movement of his forefinger touched a switch.

Instantly a babel of voices filled the store, all talking at once, rapidly and loudly. Here and there we could distinguish a snatch of conversation, a word, a phrase, now and then even a whole sentence above the rest. There was the clink of glasses. I could hear the rattle of dice on a bare table, and an oath. A cork popped. Somebody scratched a match.

We sat bewildered, looking at Kennedy.

"Imagine that you are sitting at a table in Albano's back room," was all he said. "This is what you would be hearing. This is my 'electric ear' – in other words the dictagraph, used, I am told, by the Secret Service of the United States. Wait, in a moment you will hear Gennaro come in. Luigi and Vincenzo, translate what you hear. My knowledge of Italian is pretty rusty."

"Can they hear us?" whispered Luigi in an awestruck whisper.

Craig laughed. "No, not yet. But I have only to touch this other switch, and I could produce an effect in that room that would rival the famous writing on Belshazzar's wall – only it would be a voice from the wall instead of writing."

"They seem to be waiting for someone," said Vincenzo. "I heard somebody say: 'He will be here in a few minutes. Now get out.'"

The babel of voices seemed to calm down as men withdrew from the room. Only one or two were left.

"One of them says the child is all right. She has been left in the back yard," translated Luigi.

"What yard? Did he say?" asked Kennedy.

"No, they just speak of it as the 'yard.'"

"Jameson, go outside in the store to the telephone booth and call up headquarters. Ask them if the automobile is ready, with the men in it."

I rang up, and after a moment the police central answered that everything was right.

"Then tell central to hold the line clear – we mustn't lose a moment. Jameson, you stay in the booth. Vincenzo, you pretend to be working around your window, but not in such a way as to attract attention, for they have men watching the street very carefully. What is it, Luigi?"

"Gennaro is coming. I just heard one of them say, 'Here he comes.'"

Even from the booth I could hear the dictagraph repeating the conversation in the dingy little back room of Albano's, down the street.

"He's ordering a bottle of red wine," murmured Luigi, dancing up and down with excitement.

Vincenzo was so nervous that he knocked a bottle down in the window, and I believe that my heartbeats were almost audible over the telephone which I was holding, for the police operator called me down for asking so many times if all was ready.

"There it is – the signal," cried Craig. "'A fine opera is "I Pagliacci."' Now listen for the answer."

A moment elapsed, then, "Not without Gennaro," came a gruff voice in Italian from the dictagraph.

A silence ensued. It was tense.

"Wait, wait," said a voice which I recognized instantly as Gennaro's. "I cannot read this. What is this, 23½ Prince Street?"

"No, 33½. She has been left in the back yard."

"Jameson," called Craig, "tell them to drive straight to 33½, Prince Street. They will find the girl in the back yard – quick, before the Black-Handers have a chance to go back on their word."

I fairly shouted my orders to the police headquarters. "They're off," came back the answer, and I hung up the receiver.

"What was that?" Craig was asking of Luigi. "I didn't catch it. What did they say?"

"That other voice said to Gennaro, 'Sit down while I count this.'"

"Sh! He's talking again."

"If it is a penny less than ten thousand or I find a mark on the bills I'll call to Enrico, and your daughter will be spirited away again," translated Luigi.

"Now, Gennaro is talking," said Craig. "Good – he is gaining time. He is a trump. I can distinguish that all right. He's asking the gruff-voiced fellow if he will have another bottle of wine. He says he will. Good. They must be at Prince Street now – we'll give them a few minutes more, not too much, for word will be back to Albano's like wildfire, and they will get Gennaro after all. Ah, they are drinking again. What was that, Luigi? The money is all right, he says? Now, Vincenzo, out with the lights!"

A door banged open across the street, and four huge dark figures darted out in the direction of Albano's.

With his finger Kennedy pulled down the other switch and shouted: "Gennaro, this is Kennedy! To the street! *Polizia! Polizia!*"

A scuffle and a cry of surprise followed. A second voice, apparently from the bar, shouted, "Out with the lights, out with the lights!"

Bang! went a pistol, and another.

The dictagraph, which had been all sound a moment before, was as mute as a cigar-box.

"What's the matter?" I asked Kennedy, as he rushed past me.

"They have shot out the lights. My receiving instrument is destroyed. Come on, Jameson; Vincenzo, stay back if you don't want to appear in this."

A short figure rushed by me, faster even than I could go. It was the faithful Luigi.

In front of Albano's an exciting fight was going on. Shots were being fired wildly in the darkness, and heads were popping out of tenement windows on all sides. As Kennedy and I flung ourselves into the crowd we caught a glimpse of Gennaro, with blood streaming from a cut on his shoulder, struggling with a policeman while Luigi vainly was trying to interpose himself between them. A man, held by another policeman, was urging the first officer on. "That's the man," he was crying. "That's the kidnapper. I caught him."

In a moment Kennedy was behind him. "Paoli, you lie. You are the kidnapper. Seize him – he has the money on him. That other is Gennaro himself."

The policeman released the tenor, and both of them seized Paoli. The others were beating at the door, which was being frantically barricaded inside.

Just then a taxicab came swinging up the street. Three men jumped out and added their strength to those who were battering down Albano's barricade.

Gennaro, with a cry, leaped into the taxicab. Over his shoulder I could see a tangled mass of dark brown curls, and a childish voice lisped: "Why didn't you come for me, papa? The bad man told me if I waited in the yard you would come for me. But if I cried he said he would shoot me. And I waited, and waited –"

"There, there, 'Lina, papa's going to take you straight home to mother."

A crash followed as the door yielded, and the famous Paoli gang was in the hands of the law.

The Creaking Door

Sapper

Chapter I

RONALD STANDISH lay back in his chair with a worried look on his usually cheerful face. In his hand he held a letter, which he read over for the second time before tossing it across to me.

"The devil and all, Bob," he said, shaking his head. "From what I saw in the papers a clearer case never existed."

I glanced at the note.

> *Dear Mr. Standish (it ran), I do hope you will forgive a complete stranger writing to you, but I am in desperate trouble. You will probably remember a very great friend of mine – Isabel Blount, whom you helped some months ago. Well, it was she who advised me to come to you. Would it be possible for you to see me tomorrow after noon at three o'clock? I shall come, anyway, on the chance of finding you disengaged.*
> *Yours sincerely,*
> *Katherine Moody*

"Which means today, in a quarter of an hour," he said, as I laid down the note.

"And I fear it's pretty hopeless."

"You know who she is, then?" I remarked.

He nodded gravely and crossed to a corner of the room where a pile of newspapers was lying on a chair. And as I watched him I wondered, not for the first time what had made him take up the profession he had. A born player of games, wealthy, and distinctly good-looking, he seemed the last person in the world to become a detective. And yet that was what he was when one boiled down to hard facts. True, he picked and chose his cases, and sometimes for months on end he never handled one at all. But sooner or later some crime would interest him, and then he would drop everything until he had either solved it or was beaten. With the official police he was on excellent terms, which was not to be wondered at in view of the fact that on many occasions he had put them on the right track. At times some new man was tempted to smile contemptuously at the presumption of an amateur pitting himself against the official force, but the smile generally faded before long. For there was no denying that he had a most uncanny flair for picking out the points that mattered from a mass of irrelevant detail.

"It's bad to prejudge a case," he remarked, coming back with two papers, "but this looks pretty damaging on the face of it."

He pointed to a paragraph, and I ran my eye down it.

SHOCKING TRAGEDY IN LEICESTERSHIRE BRUTAL MURDER OF YOUNG ARTIST

A crime of unparalleled ferocity was committed yesterday in the grounds of Mexbury Hall, the home of Mr. John Playfair, who has lived there for some years with his ward, Miss Katherine Moody, and her companion. Standing amongst the trees, some way from the Hall and out of sight of it, there is a summer-house which commands a magnificent view over the surrounding country. And it was in this summer-house that the tragedy occurred.

It appears that for some weeks past Mr. Playfair has allowed a young artist named Bernard Power to use it as a studio. Yesterday, on returning in the afternoon from a motor trip, Mr. Playfair, while taking a stroll in the grounds, happened to pass by the summer-house, where he was horrified to see a red stream dripping sluggishly down the wooden steps that led to the door. He rushed in, to find the unfortunate young man lying dead on the floor with his head literally crushed in like a broken egg-shell.

Touching nothing, he rushed back to the house, where he telephoned for the police and a doctor, who arrived post-haste.

The doctor stated, after examining the body, that Mr. Power had been dead about five hours, which placed the time of the crime at ten o'clock that morning. Then, with the help of Inspector Savage, who has charge of the case, the body was moved, and instantly the weapon with which the deed was done was discovered. A huge stone weighing over fourteen pounds was lying on the floor, and adhering to it were blood and several hairs that obviously had belonged to the dead man. Mr. Playfair explained that the stone had originally come from an old heap which had been left over when the foundations of the summer-house had been laid. This particular one, he went on to say, had been used as a weight on the floor to prevent the door from banging when the artist wanted it open: he had suggested it to him some weeks previously.

It is clear that a particularly brutal murder has been committed, as any possibility of accident or suicide can be ruled out. The murderer must have approached from behind while the unfortunate young man was at work on his picture, and bashed in his head with one blow.

The police are in possession of several clues, and sensational developments are expected.

I looked at the date. It was yesterday's paper. Then I looked at the other paragraph he was indicating.

"These are the sensational developments," said Ronald, "which are doubtless responsible for Miss Moody's letter."

The police have lost no time in following up the clues they obtained in the shocking tragedy that occurred the day before yesterday at Mexbury Hall. It will be recalled that the body of a young artist named Bernard Power was found in the summer house with the head battered in in a fashion which proved conclusively that a singularly brutal murder had been committed.

Yesterday Inspector Savage arrested a neighbouring landowner, Mr. Hubert Daynton, on the charge of being the murderer. It is understood that a stick belonging to the accused was found in the summer and the butt end of a cigarette of a brand he habitually smokes was discovered lying on the floor.

The accused protests his complete ignorance of the affair, a further developments are awaited hourly. Needless to say, Mr. Playfair, in whose grounds the tragedy occurred, is much upset, as the dead man was a protégé of his.

I put down the paper and glanced at my companion.

"It certainly seems pretty bad for Mr. Hubert Daynton," I said. "He seems to have gone out of his way to leave the evidence lying about."

"Exactly," Standish remarked. "Which may be a point in his favour. However, there goes the bell. We'll hear what Miss Moody has to say."

The door opened, and his man ushered in a delightfully pretty girl of about twenty-one or two, who looked from one to the other of us with a worried expression on her face.

"Sit down, Miss Moody," said Ronald. "And let me introduce a great pal of mine, Bob Miller. You can say anything you like in front of him."

"I suppose you know what I've come about, Mr. Standish," cried the girl. "I know what has appeared in the papers," said Ronald, "which summarises into the fact that Hubert Daynton has been arrested for the murder of an artist called Bernard Power in the summer-house of your guardian's place."

"But he never did it, Mr. Standish," she cried, clasping her hands together.

"So, I gather, he states. At the same time, the police seem to think otherwise. Now will you be good enough to fill in all the gaps, as far as you can, which have been left by the papers? And one thing I beg of you – don't keep anything back. It is absolutely imperative that I should have all the facts, even if they appear to you to be damaging."

"I will conceal nothing," she said. "You know from the papers that I live at Mexbury Hall with my guardian, and Hubert Daynton has the neighbouring house, Gadsby Tower. He was often over with us, and we did the same thing at his place –"

"Was?" put in Ronald. "Do you imply anything by using the past tense?"

"During recent months matters have become a little strained," she said, a slightly heightened colour coming into her cheeks. "To be brief, he wanted to marry me, and my guardian didn't like the idea."

"Why not?" said Ronald bluntly. "Was there any particular reason, or just general disapproval?"

"I don't know," she answered, "Uncle John – he's not really any relation, of course – is very old-fashioned in some ways, and has the most absurd ideas about what girls ought to be told. But one thing is certain: the moment Hubert made it clear that he wanted to marry me, Uncle John's manner towards him changed completely."

"One further point, Miss Moody," said Ronald, with a faint smile. "What were your feelings on the subject?"

"Well," she answered frankly, "I didn't say I would and I didn't say I wouldn't. He's rather a dear, and I like him immensely, but I can't say I'm in love with him. In addition, I'm terribly fond of Uncle John who has been a sort of mother and father to me, and the fact that he disapproved did influence me. There was an idea at the back of my mind, I think, that in time I might get him to change his mind about Hubert, which would have made a difference."

"I understand perfectly," said Ronald. "And that was the condition of affairs between you and Hubert Daynton at the time of his arrest?"

"I'm afraid it wasn't," she answered slowly. "Two months ago Bernard Power came to stay at the village inn. He was an artist, as you know, and in some way or other he got to know Uncle John. Now, my guardian is a photographic maniac – it is the one absorbing hobby of his life – and as Bernard went in for landscape work they seemed to find something in common. He was continually asking Bernard to dinner; and fitted him up, as you read in the papers, in the summer-house as a studio."

She paused for a moment, and glanced from Ronald to me.

"The poor man is dead now," she went on, "and if it wasn't for Hubert's sake, I'd say nothing. But there's no getting away from the fact that Bernard Power was a nasty bit of work. You both of you look thoroughly uman, and you'll know what I mean when I say he was always pawing one, touching one's arm or something like that – a thing I loathe. But matters came to a head three days ago. I happened to be passing the summer-house when he called out to me to come and have a look at his picture.

"Without thinking, I went in. To do him justice, he was a very clever painter. And before I knew where I was, he'd seized me in his arms and was trying to kiss me. I was perfectly furious. I'd never given him the slightest encouragement. However, after I'd smacked his face as hard as I could, he let me go. And then I told him a few home truths and left."

Again she paused, and bit her lip.

"I left, Mr. Standish, and, as evil fortune would have it, I ran into Hubert paying one of his very infrequent visits, He had come over to see me about a spaniel I wanted. If only it had been an hour later it wouldn't have mattered; I should have recovered. As it was he saw, of course, that I was angry, and realising I'd come from the direction of the summer-house, he jumped at once to the correct conclusion.

"'Has that damned painter been up to his monkey tricks again?' he cried.

"And very foolishly I told him what had happened. He was furious, and there's no denying that Hubert has a very nasty temper when roused. I regretted having said anything the moment the words were out of my mouth, but then it was too late. And it was only with the greatest difficulty that I prevented him going on then and there to put it across Bernard Power. I told him that I was quite capable of looking after myself, and that the matter was over and done with.

"In the middle of our conversation Uncle John joined us. He saw at once that something was up and asked what had happened. Hubert told him and he didn't mince his words, which got Uncle John's back up. And finally the two of them very nearly had a row.

"Uncle John's point of view was that he was the proper person for me to go to, and that it was no business of Hubert's. Hubert on the contrary said it was any decent man's business if some swab of a painter kissed a girl against her will. And then he made the damning statement that he personally proposed to interview Mr. Bernard Power the following morning."

"Did anyone else hear that remark besides you and your guardian?" asked Ronald.

"No one," she said. "Of that I'm positive."

"Why did he specify the following morning? Why didn't he go right away?"

"He had people coming to lunch, and it was getting late."

"And the following morning was the morning of the murder," said Ronald thoughtfully. "Now let's hear exactly what Daynton says took place."

"He says that he started from Gadsby Tower at half-past nine and walked over to the summer-house. He found Bernard Power had no yet arrived, so he lit a cigarette and waited for him – a cigarette which he admits he threw on the floor and put out with his shoe.

"Then Bernard Power came in, and apparently Hubert went for him like a pickpocket. He called him a leprous mess, and a few more things of that sort, and they had a fearful quarrel, in the course of which Hubert put his stick up against the wall, because he was afraid he might hit the other with it, and he was a much smaller man than Hubert. Then he left, and went back to his own house, which he reached at twenty past ten."

Ronald Standish nodded thoughtfully.

"Forgetting all about his stick," he remarked. "A very important point, that."

"He was so excited, Mr. Standish," said the girl. "I know the police think as you do, but surely it's understandable"

"My dear Miss Moody," he said with a smile, "you quite mistake my meaning. Now that I've heard your full story I think it tells enormously in his favour. It is certain that he must have discovered he had left his stick in the summer-house on his way back to Gadsby Tower. There is nothing that a man notices quicker. If, then, he had murdered Power he would at all costs have had to go back to get it. To leave such a damning piece of evidence lying about was tantamount to putting a noose round his neck. But what was more natural than that he, rather than renew the quarrel, should decide to leave it there, and get it some other time?"

"Then you don't think he did it?" she cried eagerly.

"What I may think," said Ronald guardedly, "is one thing. What we've got to prove is another. If he didn't do it – who did? The crime, according to the doctor's evidence, must have been committed very shortly after Daynton left the summer-house. It is, therefore, I think, a justifiable assumption that the murderer was near by during the interview, heard the quarrel, and seized the opportunity of throwing suspicion on somebody else. So that at any rate one line of exploration must be to find out if this man Power had an enemy who was so bitter against him that he wouldn't stick at murder. And from what you tell me of his manners with you, it would not be surprising if he has gone even further with some other girl. In which case there may be a man who was not as forbearing as Daynton."

"Then you'll help Hubert?" she cried.

"Certainly, Miss Moody," he said. "Now that I've heard the details my opinion is quite different. Bob and I will come down with you this afternoon. But before we start there are just one or two points I'd like cleared up. First – what were your movements on the day of the murder?"

"I stayed in the house till lunch; and in the afternoon I played tennis at a house five miles away."

"You had no communication with Daynton of any sort – over the telephone, for instance?"

"None."

"And Mr. Playfair – what did he do?"

"He went out on one of his photography expeditions. He started in the car about half-past eight in the morning, and was not back till after lunch."

"One last point. You have already said that no one could have overheard the conversation between the three of you on the drive. But did you by any chance mention it to anybody afterwards?"

"No," she said. "I said nothing about it. And I'm sure Uncle John didn't either, as he was in the whole afternoon fiddling about with his latest camera."

"Then it must either have been an unfortunate coincidence for Bernard Power or –" He broke off and stared out of the window thoughtfully.

"Come along," he said, rousing himself at length. "Let's go down and look at this summer-house. I hope your nerves are good, Miss Moody. Bob generally drives, and never at less than sixty miles an hour."

Chapter II

THE GROUNDS of Mexbury Hall were extensive, and the summer-house was a good quarter of a mile from the Hall itself. Trees surrounded it on three sides, affording admirable cover for anyone who wished to hide. The fourth was open, and gave a magnificent view over the country to the south. It was simply built of wood, with a sunblind that could be let down over the big window.

A policeman was on guard as we approached, and he looked doubtful when Ronald explained his business.

"Inspector's orders, sir, were that no one was to be allowed in. Still, I suppose you're different."

"Come in yourself, officer, and you'll see that I'm not going to touch anything. I take it nothing has been moved except the body?"

"Nothing, sir."

"Were you here yourself when the body was found?"

"I came with the Inspector, sir."

Ronald knelt down by the wooden steps leading to the door, and carefully examined the ominous red stain. Then, with a shake of his head, he got up.

"Too late," he said, "Nothing to be got out of that now."

He pushed open the door and stepped inside. Then, according to his invariable custom, he stood absolutely motionless, with only his eyes moving from side to side as he absorbed every detail. On the easel stood the half-finished picture spattered with the dead man's blood. The overturned chair still lay where it had fallen as the artist had crashed to the floor.

"Not much doubt about what happened, sir," remarked the constable. "Never seen a clearer case in all ray service. Fair battered to pieces, he was, poor gentleman."

"What's the meaning of this, Roberts?" said a gruff voice from outside.

"I ordered you to admit no one."

Ronald Standish swung round. A choleric looking man in uniform was standing in the doorway.

"Inspector Savage, I take it?" Standish said genially. "I have been commissioned by Miss Moody to make a few inquiries on behalf of Mr. Daynton."

He held out his card, and the Inspector grunted.

"I've heard of you, Mr. Standish," he remarked. "And if I was you I'd wash my hands of it. You'll get no credit out of this case."

"Perhaps not," agreed Ronald. "Still, when a lady asks one to do something for her it is hard to refuse."

"Kinder in the long run," said the other. "There's no good in raising false hopes in her mind. You've seen in the newspapers what we've discovered. What you may not know is that Daynton admits to having had a furious quarrel with the murdered man at the very time the deed was done."

"It was that fact, amongst others, my dear Inspector, that caused me to take up the case. Surely no one out of a lunatic asylum would go out of his way to damn himself so completely if he had done the murder. His stick, I admit, he couldn't get over, since he was imbecile enough to leave it here; the cigarette stump is awkward. But why he should then add a quarrel which no one had heard is really more than one can swallow."

He was swinging the door backwards and forwards as he spoke, and I saw by the glint in his eye that he was hot on something.

"Very clever, Mr. Standish," laughed the Inspector, "but not quite clever enough. Both Miss Moody and Mr. Playfair knew of his intention. So how could he deny it? I say, sir, must you go on making that squeaking noise with the door?"

"Both ways, you notice," said Ronald. "It creaks when it opens and it creaks when it shuts. Moreover, it shuts of its own accord. Very interesting."

We stared at him in amazement, but he took no notice, and at last the Inspector turned to go, with a significant glance at me.

"By the way, Inspector," said Ronald suddenly, "had the dead man got a brush in his hand?"

"No; but one was lying on the floor beside him."

"Was there any paint on it?"

For a moment the Inspector looked nonplussed.

"I really couldn't tell you at the moment," he said, and Ronald shook his head.

"My dear fellow," he remarked, "you surprise me. Get hold of it and examine it. And if there's paint on it, sit down and think things over, bearing in mind the fact that the door creaks."

"And if there isn't paint on it?" said the other with ponderous sarcasm.

"There will be," answered Ronald quietly.

"Anything else you can suggest?"

"Yes; but I don't think you're likely to do it."

"What's that?"

"Release that unfortunate chap, Daynton."

"Release Daynton?" gasped the other.

"Why not? For I can assure you that he had no more to do with the murder of Bernard Power than you or I had."

"Then who did do it?"

"I promise you shall know at the first possible moment," said Ronald.

"Well, until I do," grinned the other, "Mr. Daynton remains under lock and key."

Ronald was silent as we strolled back to the house, and I knew him too well to interrupt his reverie.

"By the way, Bob," he said suddenly, as we neared the door, "say nothing – even to Miss Moody – about our thinking Daynton innocent. It might get round to the servants."

She met us on the drive, and with her was a man of about forty-five, who we correctly surmised was her guardian, Mr. Playfair.

"Well," she cried, after introducing us, "what luck?"

Ronald shook his head. "Early days yet, Miss Moody," he said gravely. "I've seen the Inspector, and I'm bound to confess it doesn't look too good."

"I blame myself very much," said her guardian, "but never in my wildest imagination did I dream of such a tragedy occurring."

"In what way do you blame yourself, Mr. Playfair?" asked Ronald.

"In going out so early that morning. I ought to have waited here and been present at the interview. Hubert is such a hot headed chap."

"But, Uncle John, he didn't do it!" cried the girl.

"My dear," said the other sadly, "I wish I could think so. And let us hope that Mr. Standish succeeds in proving it. Candidly," he went on as she left us, "I wish she hadn't been to you. You understand how I mean it. The case is so painfully clear that I fear even you can do no good. And the sooner she realises it the better."

"Perhaps so," agreed Ronald. "As you say, it's a pity you went out as early as you did."

"Well, I wanted to get to Comber Ness by noon, and it's very nearly a four hours' run. I don't know whether my ward has told you," he went on, with a faint smile, "but I'm a most enthusiastic photographer. And I have just acquired a new toy. Are you by any chance interested?"

"Very," said Ronald. "I do a bit that way myself."

"Then come and have a drink, and I will show it to you." He led the way into the house and we followed him. "It is a stereoscopic camera," he explained, as he took it off a table in the hall. "And doubtless you know the principle on which it works. The two lenses are the same distance apart as one's eyes, and two negatives are taken at each exposure. Then by making positives and holding them in one of those machines that you probably remember from your early youth, the whole thing stands out as in real life."

"And you went over to Comber Ness to get a photograph," said Ronald.

"Exactly," said the other, and then gave a rueful laugh. "And didn't get it – at least, not what I wanted. I've only just got the machine. In fact, it was my first load of plates. Now, if you examine it, you will see a little number at one end of the plate-carrier. Every time you change a plate after taking a photo the number goes up one, so that you always know how many plates are left. The numbers range from one to twelve, and the night before Wilkinson, my butler, who is almost as keen as I am on it, happened to mention to me that number twelve was showing, which meant that there was only one more plate left. And I forgot all about it till I arrived at Comber Ness."

"But one exposure was surely enough?" said Ronald.

"Quite – if I hadn't wanted to take two different views. It is, as you know, one of the most celebrated beauty spots of England, and I had promised an American friend of mine two photographs taken from totally separate points. And I had only one plate. So there was nothing for it but to use the camera as an ordinary one by covering one lens with a cap and taking one view on half the plate, and then covering the other lens and taking the second view on the other half. But, of course, it spoiled things from a stereoscopic point altogether. However, I'm glad to say they both came out well. I left them to be developed that day, and they were sent up this afternoon with the other eleven."

He was examining some of the results as he was speaking, and at moment his ward came into the hall.

"Good Heavens! Uncle John," she cried, "this is hardly the time for photographs."

"Sorry, dear," he said contritely. "The matter came up in the course of conversation with Mr. Standish. You see, this was the camera I was using that day at Comber Ness."

She seemed sorry at having spoken so sharply, and laid her hand on his shoulder.

"It's all right, old 'un," she said "So that's the new toy, is it? Can we see the pretty pictures?"

"I've got to make the positives first," he answered. "These are the negatives."

"Well, it's all beyond me. And I thought they were going to be much bigger. Each of them seems just the same size as that other camera takes – the little one."

"Quite right. This camera takes two identical pictures on every plate, each of which is the same size as the little one."

"And when were these very good views of the grounds here taken?" said Ronald.

"Let me see. I think I took those the day before I went to Comber Ness."

"A very fine machine," cried Ronald. "They are so clear cut. And these two separate ones of Comber Ness. Beautiful! Beautiful! I should very much like prints of those myself, if you would be good enough."

"Certainly," said our host. "Delighted. And now I expect you'd like to see your rooms."

He led the way upstairs and, having told us the time of dinner, left us. And shortly after Ronald came sauntering into my room and sat on the bed.

"What do you make of it, Bob?" he said.

"Nothing at all," I answered. "And though you may be perfectly clear in your own mind, old lad, that this man Daynton didn't do it, I don't see that you've got much forrader as to who did."

He made no reply, and was staring out of the window as the butler knocked to find out if there was anything we wanted.

"I hear you're very keen on photography, Wilkinson," said Ronald pleasantly.

"In a small way I dabble in it, sir."

"Mr. Playfair was telling me it was a great hobby of yours. What do you think of that new camera of his?"

"I've only seen it once, sir. He asked me to tell him the number showing at the end. Twelve it was, I remember. That was the night before the tragedy, sir. I do hope that you may be able to do something for poor Mr. Daynton. Such a nice gentleman, sir."

"I hope so, too, Wilkinson. By the way, Mr. Playfair does most of his developing himself, doesn't he?"

"Invariably, sir," said the butler, looking faintly surprised.

"But he had this last lot developed for him?" persisted Ronald.

"Yes, sir. He apparently lunched at Barminster on the day of the murder, and left them with a chemist there."

"Thank you, Wilkinson. No – nothing to drink."

The butler left the room, and I stared at him.

"You seem very interested in our host's photography," I said.

"Bob;" he remarked, "if you had just bought a new stereoscopic camera and had motored over a hundred miles for a view, would you suddenly be so overcome by a promise given to an American friend that you wouldn't use your new acquisition as such?"

"What in the name of fortune are you driving at?" I cried. "Anyway, whatever I might or might not do, we have seen what our host did. There's the proof in the negative. Why, good Lord, man, you can't suspect him."

"I didn't say I did. I merely asked a question. You see, Bob, one thing is perfectly clear. A man who was at Comber Ness in the morning and arrived at Barminster for lunch could not possibly have left here as late as ten o'clock."

"Very well, then?"

"A perfect alibi. But it would have been an equally good alibi if he had carried out the same time-table and taken a stereoscopic picture there instead of two separate views. So again I ask – why those two different views?"

"It must be the American," I cried.

"Must it? Or is it because he couldn't take a stereoscopic picture?"

"Then he couldn't have taken the other two?"

"Sound logic," he grinned. "Well, time to change, I suppose."

"Look here, Ronald," I almost shouted, "what do you mean?"

The grin departed, and he looked at me gravely. "It means," he said, "that we are dealing with a particularly dangerous and unprincipled man, whose only slip up to date is that he did not expend a pennyworth of oil on the hinges of the summer-house door."

And with that he left the room.

All through the evening his words kept recurring to me, and the more I thought of them the more amazing did they become. It seemed to me he must be wrong, and yet Ronald Standish was not in the habit of making a definite statement without good reason. And when, next morning, he suddenly announced his intention of returning to London, I was even more dumbfounded.

The girl was terribly disappointed, and it struck me that his attempts at consolation were very half-hearted. He seemed to have lost interest in the case, though he gave her a few perfunctory words of hope.

"I'll be back this evening, Miss Moody," he said, "and perhaps by then I may have something to report."

But I heard him expressing a different opinion to our host when she was out of hearing. For some reason he did not want me to go with him, and so I spent most of the day with her trying to cheer her up. It was a little difficult, since I manifestly could not allude to the amazing hints he had dropped the preceding evening. In fact, the more I thought of them the more fantastic did they seem. If Ronald had a fault it was that he sometimes seemed to go out of his way to find a complicated solution to a thing when a simple one fitted the facts. And for the life of me I could not see wherein lay the difficulty over our host's explanation of the two different photos on the one plate.

He returned about six, looking weary and dispirited, and my heart sank.

"Waste of time, I fear," he said, as we all met him in the hall. "I'm afraid it's a case of going back to London for good."

"And throwing up the case?" cried the girl.

"I fear I was to blame, Miss Moody, in speaking too hopefully in my rooms," he said. "So if you could give orders for our things to be packed, we'll be getting along. By the way, Mr. Playfair, don't forget those two photographs you promised me."

"I did them for you today," said our host. "I'll see if they are dry."

He left the hall, and for a moment we were alone.

"Got him, Bob," he said, and his eyes were blazing with excitement, "by an amazing piece of luck."

But he was his apathetic self when Playfair returned with the prints.

"Astoundingly good," he remarked, as he examined them. "How did you manage to do it, Mr. Playfair?"

"Do what?" cried the other, staring at him.

"Avoid taking the steam-roller which has been standing idle in the centre of this particular view for the last ten days."

For a moment there was dead silence, and I saw that every atom of colour had left our host's face.

"I did not go to London today," went on Ronald. "I went to Comber Ness, where I took this photograph. Not fixed yet – but look at it."

He flung it on the table; it was the same as the other. But in the centre was a steam-roller with a tarpaulin over it.

"You devil!" screamed Playfair, and made a dash for the passage leading to the back of the house.

"Hold him, Bob!" roared Ronald, and I collared him. He struggled like a maniac, but I kept him till Ronald came running back with the plate in his hand.

"He was going to destroy that," he cried. "Well, Mr. Playfair, have you any explanation as to why that steam-roller is missing from your photo?" And then with a sudden shout – "Stop him, Bob!"

But it was too late. I felt his body relax in my arms, almost immediately after his hand came away from his mouth. Then he slithered to the floor – dead.

Chapter III

"I'M BLOWED if I see how you did it, Mr. Standish."

It was three hours later, and Inspector Savage was gazing at Ronald in undisguised admiration.

"By starting with a theory diametrically opposed to yours," said Ronald.

"You were convinced Hubert Daynton had done it; I was convinced he hadn't. Then who had? My first idea was that the murderer was some man Power had wronged – probably over some woman. He had been hiding near by, and had taken advantage of the quarrel he heard to do the deed and throw the suspicion on someone else. Then I suddenly realised the enormous significance of the fact that the door creaked, and shut of its own accord.

"Now, Power was sitting at his easel some four yards from the door. Suppose the door was shut when the murderer entered; it would creak as he opened it. Suppose it was being kept open by the stone with which the deed was done; it would creak as it shut, after the stone was picked up. In either event it would creak.

"Now, what does anybody do who hears a door creak behind him – especially if there has just been a quarrel and the creak may mean that the other person has returned? He looks over his shoulder to see who it is. And if he sees some enemy of his, someone he has wronged, he does not continue his job with his back to the newcomer. But Power went on with his painting. There fore the person he saw he did not regard as an enemy, but looked on as a friend. So much of a friend, in fact, that he did not object to this new arrival walking about behind his back – always an uncomfortable sensation unless your mind is completely at rest. And at once a very different complexion was put on the matter.

"Then came my interview with Mr. John Playfair, and the question of the two separate pictures of different views of Comber Ness on the one plate – the point that puzzled you so much, Bob. You remember that when I said it might be because he couldn't take a stereoscopic picture, you countered by saying that in that case he equally could not have taken the two separate views. Which was right, up to a point. He couldn't have taken either, but that doesn't prevent a negative appearing on a plate.

"The man was a skilled photographer, and he was faced with the necessity of proving to the world that he had been to Comber Ness. If he could do so he was safe. But since he had ho intention of going anywhere near Comber Ness, what was he to do? He knew that if you take a negative and make a positive from it, you can produce a second negative in a dark room on exactly the same principle as you produce a print. But he had no stereoscopic picture of Comber Ness; he'd only just bought the machine. What he had got were two separate views taken with his smaller camera!

"So he makes two positives – you remember Miss Moody told us he was fiddling about in the dark room all the afternoon before the murder – and then he takes out his last stereoscopic plate. You see the importance of its being the last one; that accounted for his having to put them both on one plate. And that was why he took three unnecessary photos of his own grounds. On to that last plate he clips the two positives, side by side, exposes it in his dark room, and returns the plate to the camera. There is his alibi. He need never go near Comber Ness, and, in fact, he never did.

"He had Wilkinson's evidence that twelve was the number showing – you noticed there, Bob, the slight discrepancy between Playfair's statement and the butler's. He had the chemist's evidence that the plates were handed over to him to be developed; he had the hotel evidence that he lunched at Barminster.

"Exactly what he did we shall never know. He drove away at eight-thirty, and presumably concealed his car in some lane. Then he returned and hid near the summer-house. He was taking no risk up to date; if he was found there was no reason why he shouldn't be in his own grounds. And everything came off. He murdered Power, and drove quietly over to Barminster, where he lunched."

"But why. This cold-blooded murder of a man he apparently liked?" I asked.

"The usual reason," he answered. "Once or twice after dinner last night I caught the look in his eyes as they rested on the girl. He was in love with her himself, which can account for many things. Why he took up Power at all I can't tell you – possibly at the beginning he had some idea of choking off Daynton by making him jealous. Then he may have feared that instead of doing that the artist's attentions to the girl might have the opposite result and bring Daynton and the girl closer together. Or perhaps he may have become jealous of Power himself. Anyway, he saw his opportunity of getting rid of both of them. And but for the astounding piece of luck of my finding that steam-roller where it was, he'd have gone darned near doing it. Being a clever man, he realised at once that his whole alibi had become worse than useless – it had become a rope round his neck. For what possible reason could there be, save the true one, for his saying he'd been to Comber Ness when he hadn't? That was why I was so off-hand today. At the first hint of suspicion he would have destroyed the plate and never given me the prints, trusting to the chemist's evidence that it had been a view of Comber Ness."

"Well, I'm sure I'm much obliged to you, Mr. Standish," said the Inspector. "Mr. Daynton has already been released."

"And doubtless will provide the necessary consolation for Miss Moody," said Ronald, with a smile. "For I don't think we need waste one second's pity on that singularly cold-blooded murderer."

And it wasn't until we were driving into London that he turned to me thoughtfully.

"I think the lie was justified, Bob, don't you?"

"What lie?" I said.

"That steam-roller only arrived at Comber Ness early this morning."

Spies and Taboos

S.L. Scott

TYRUS KNEW he had gone too far when he enjoyed being called by a Margas name. They chose one close to his own so it would be easy for him to adjust. Tomas. It had taken weeks to remember to respond to it, and even after two years living in the Margas capitol, weeks away from any dhan'ya, the name had always felt like a costume, a masquerade where he danced with his enemies. It had never been who he was – until now.

"Tomas," Gamel's voice called from the stable door. "I'm heading out, prepare Riversong."

"As you wish, m'lord." Tyrus bowed his head, his smile hidden beneath his hair fallen free of his braid, and waited to hear the man turn away before he looked up again.

Gamel walked only few feet away. The thick riding cloak hid a body trained for a battle he had yet to enter, and the calm expression on his face held a naiveté Tyrus had not expected in anyone on either side of this eighty-year war. Gamel kept a stilted gaze on the main house, but Tyrus could feel the anticipation to turn to the stables itching at the back of his consciousness. The feeling only fed Tyrus's own contentment as he went through the motions of preparing the horse.

All dhan'ya received a gift from the Spirits. Tyrus was destined to feel the emotions of those around him. It was that gift that had brought the head of the dhan'ya army to his family's *des* – a house of lashi mael, the flesh traders – to recruit him to serve the realm. Dhan'ya were not suited to being spies, who hid their gifts, but Tyrus's allowed him to manipulate people with ease and could not be revealed in a physical way. His training as a lashi mael made him all the more useful.

When Tyrus was first hired as a stable hand, he'd intended to seduce one of the lady's maids for information. Gamel's father, Ranulf, was lord of the house, but he rarely met the stable hand except to deliver his horse upon his return. It was a surprise when the person he sensed the most attraction from was the young lord of the house.

Of course his restraint outweighed any desire. Margas taboos against men being with men made no sense to the dhan'ya – Tyrus served more men than women in his *des* – but it controlled Gamel's every move and passing glance. Tyrus spent months simply encouraging him to face the yearning within himself. Looks that lasted too long. A hand on Gamel's thigh while he adjusted the saddle. Half-hidden smiles whenever he approached, quickly covered should another come by. Breaking through Margas taboos was an arduously tedious task, especially for those who had a great deal to lose, but over the years Tyrus had learned how to offer himself without being as obvious as a dhan'ya who didn't fear his desire.

Tyrus remembered the first time he reciprocated. Gamel asked to brush down his horse after his ride, something none of the family had ever done before. Gamel was so nervous, Tyrus ended up trembling as well when Gamel slid his hand over Tyrus's hidden in the horse's mane. It made his act all the more believable, but Tyrus spent hours afterwards regaining control of his gift. The emotions burned like fire under his skin. Their first kiss was maddened and desperate, but the euphoric release of finally yielding to his passion was spoiled by the terror they'd be caught.

These days Gamel displayed a serious interest in the care of his horse. He came for it himself and waited outside the stable, eager for a glimpse of Tyrus that wouldn't be noticed by the other servants. The almost paralyzing fear he'd been conditioned to feel had faded to a lingering worry, long since overwhelmed by pleasure and joy and love.

Tyrus guided the brindle mare from her stall and paused a moment before closing the stall to gaze back at Gamel. A content grin was all that revealed the searing desire within as he watched Tyrus work. Love from a human. Perhaps that was what made him seem so innocent compared to the world around him. All the people Tyrus had been with since coming to this backwards kingdom used him to satisfy their lust in a way their world couldn't, and on some level they knew he was using them for something as well. But Gamel fell in love with him. There was never suspicion or deceit behind his actions, and part of Tyrus ached with shame each time he inquired about the condition of the war.

"Riversong's ready, m'lord," Tyrus said, bringing the mare around for inspection.

Gamel ran a hand through her brown mane as he searched the saddle and harness for any inconsistencies. Slightly over-cautious for a rider, but not unheard of. He tugged on the clasp of the saddle and his eyes settled on Tyrus. "Tomas, I think you forgot something."

Tyrus stroked the saddle, his hand caressing Gamel's in the process. Nothing was missing. There never was. "Forgive me, I'll fetch it immediately."

"I had best make sure you do."

Gamel tied Riversong to the stable door and followed Tyrus back to her stall. He always remained a step behind in case someone should come upon them, but once they entered the small sanctuary of the mare's stall, Gamel yanked Tyrus close and kissed him with the fury only repression produced.

"I'm glad we found that, m'lord."

Gamel laughed, stroking Tyrus's face in search of all the connection he could get in so short a time. "I'm going to miss the freedom of this once my father returns. We'll have to be far more discreet then."

"That's not for weeks. Let's enjoy this."

Gamel shook his head. "A messenger arrived today. He'll be back the day after tomorrow."

"Did something happen in the war?" Tyrus asked, hiding the eagerness and guilt that welled up at the sudden change in the husky voice of his lust.

"No, something happened at Montegard. The king's called all the marchen lords to the palace."

Tyrus inhaled long and deep to keep his body from exposing the sudden rush of adrenaline that made his head spin. Over two years he'd been hiding amongst these people, his enemies, waiting for news of the king. So little was known outside the palace, and few – even those noble men and women he seduced – knew what happened behind the castle walls. Was he finally going to learn what he needed to return home? Would he finally get to be dhan'ya again?

Spinning Gamel around, Tyrus pinned him against the wall to conceal the thundering of his heart or the heat burning his face. "Is the king well? Rumors in the streets say he's been ill for years."

Any suspicion Gamel might have had at Tyrus's hasty tone was drowned beneath a wave of carnality barely kept in check. He kissed Tyrus, hands tugging at his waist but not delving further. "I don't know, but it must be important to call on all the lords."

Tyrus shoved their excitement back and focused on Gamel. "Will you come tonight, then? Let's make the most of what time we have left."

Gamel ran his hands up Tyrus's torso, his fingers dipping into each ripple of muscle beneath his shirt. "Come to my room tonight."

"Are you certain?"

Gamel never allowed their trysts inside the main house where they could be caught by the servants. The stables were dangerous enough, but there at least Tyrus had control.

"You always tell me you can get there without the servants seeing. Who knows how long Father will remain here. I want to have you like a real lover just once."

Tyrus smiled and rested his forehead against Gamel's. "You talk as if it's the last time I'll ever be with you."

"It'll have to be until Father leaves. If he ever found out, he'd kill you, and I don't know what he'd do to me. We can't let that happen."

Tyrus struggled to resist the love flowing from Gamel. Strong as his heart beat, it was a steady ebb and flow that slowly broke down his defenses. Tyrus kissed him again, forgetting everything except the desire so wholly theirs that one's emotion couldn't be separated from the other's.

"I'll be there tonight."

"I'll wait." Gamel kissed Tyrus one last time and playfully tugged at the black braid swaying between Tyrus's shoulder blades. "I should go before someone notices Riversong."

Tyrus followed Gamel back to his horse, staying a step behind for propriety's sake. Once mounted, there was a regal air to the young lord. He held his body straight and strong. Given a few years on the battlefield and that raw power would be honed into a warrior. If only Gamel wasn't his enemy; Tyrus would have been pleased to wait for his return – more experienced and stalwart.

When Gamel spurred the horse forward, Tyrus rested against the stable door and closed his eyes. He always indulged in the love lingering around Gamel, fading away the further from the house he fled. It was one of the few times Tyrus allowed himself to simply enjoy his gift instead of sullying it by manipulating others. He missed the unadulterated act of being dhan'ya without fear. Being with his family and feeling their love, their security.

Human families weren't the same, not the ones in power at least. The common family relied on each other for survival, but the warriors and marchen lords turned his gift into a cancer. Many lacked any kind of familial bond. Resentment, fear, hate – Tyrus couldn't imagine growing up surrounded by that. His mother and father, sisters and brothers, aunts and uncles, he loved them all. They gave him strength when his gift threatened to overwhelm him as a child and welcomed him home once he'd gained control. They were the reason he came to this foul kingdom, and his memory of them kept the distorted emotions of the Margas from taking hold in his heart.

Perhaps that's what made Gamel's love seem so much purer than those he'd sensed it from before. Despite knowing how much revulsion his family would condemn him with if they learned the truth, Gamel still allowed himself to love so strongly that it had barely diminished in Tyrus despite the distance. It was almost dhan'ya, and that made Tyrus miss home so much more. Sometimes, when they lay together in the safety of an empty stall, Tyrus imagined what it would have been if Gamel had been born in the Dhan'ya Realm. He would never have hidden his preferences. He could have offered that love freely or come to a lashi mael like Tyrus without any condemnation. Plenty of men would have found his firm physique as appealing as Tyrus did, and Gamel would have experienced happiness – acceptance.

Tyrus opened his eyes, a smile still on his face, and searched the road leading away from the estate. The love Tyrus felt was too strong for Gamel to have gotten far, and many times before he double backed with some foolish excuse simply to say goodbye again. But the road was empty. The only sign of Gamel's departure was a settling trail of dust. Tyrus ran to the nearby tree line that blocked his view of the bend, but all he found in the distance was dirt and broken sunlight.

Gamel was gone, but the love remained.

No one's but his own.

* * *

Tyrus almost didn't go to Gamel that night. It took three false starts before he forced himself to leave the stables, and as he snuck through the empty halls, he wasn't sure if it was duty or his own feelings urging him forward. He focused on the moonlit halls to try and smother the confusion. The outside edifice of Margas homes may have been different, but halls and doors all looked the same.

To Tyrus, the stone was nothing but cold. Dhan'ya used masonry as well, but in the exterior for support or protection and always mixed with earth and lumbar so that the Spirits could enter and protect the home. And such color decorated Tyrus's home. Golds and paints of bright reds, blues, and greens covered every surface inside and out. They walked on mosaics of colored ceramic, and shaped glass made the sunlight dance through the windows. The Spirits lived in those halls, from the winds that entered through the arched doors, to the forests and flowers that surrounded their home, to the heat and waters of the nearby springs. But it was more than fixtures and gardens that he longed for.

In his *des*, Tyrus knew who he was and why he was there. He was a lashi mael, apprenticed and mastered into the craft of physical pleasure. He enjoyed his work, and his sister, Tal'Resh'Resh, kept him from crossing a line that his gift kept hidden from his sight, a fact she was never quiet about. If only he'd heeded to her warnings.

He could still hear the fear in her voice upon their final meeting before he left for Margas lands. Tal'Resh rounded the edge of Tyrus's cushioned bed and yanked the satchel he was packing to the floor. "It's too dangerous."

"So you've told me many times. It hasn't changed my mind yet."

"This is my last chance, since I may never see you again."

Tyrus picked up his satchel and packed small vials of oils into a hidden sleeve inside. They would serve him well, but so many together could reveal him as lashi mael, and thus dhan'ya. "I'll come home, Tal. I promise."

"When? How many months will I have to worry that you've been discovered and those monsters have killed you?"

It was difficult for him to keep his spirits up about his coming journey under the oppression of her long-fed fear. Half a year of training to become Margas, an ordinary human, and several more months to learn the basics of trades that could provide him with work in the right places, had turned what started as a simmering dislike into blazing terror searing his sister's heart. He wanted his farewell to be on better terms, especially with his dearest sister.

"When I learn that either the rumors are false and their king is well or the rumors are true and the king will soon be replaced. If we don't know who is ruling our enemy, we won't be prepared to fight them."

"Why must it be you that goes? Rishi can read minds, you can only sense feelings. Rishi is a better choice." Tal'Resh's stubbornness dug in despite knowing every reply he'd give to her arguments.

"Rishi is the Huntmaster," Tyrus answered, as he always did. "Remove him from command of the army and you may as well hand the realm over to the Margas. My gift will keep me ahead of them without revealing me, and I can hold my own in battle."

Reaching out, Tal'Resh took his hand and urged him to sit next to her. She was only four years older than him, yet Tal'Resh had mastered the ability to be both his elder commanding and sister asking at the same time. "Tyrus," she started, her voice much quieter in her seriousness, "you aren't ready to deal with deception like this. You still allow yourself to feel what others feel far too much. You'll become too close and be hurt."

Tyrus was silent for a moment, taking in an implication she had never insinuated before. "Do you think I'll betray the realm – you – for a Margas?"

"I think it will be difficult for you to not sympathize when your enemy is no longer faceless but a warm body flooding you with lust. You've always struggled with separating yourself from the client, and this time I won't be there to bring you back." She caressed his cheek, a tender affection that filled him with her fears and proved the weakness in his gift. "You're not ready to be Margas when you can't entirely control your dhan'ya gift."

Tyrus fought to do just that, pushing away her fears as best he could with her still touching him. Touch made the emotions strong and vital. Tal'Resh knew too well how to focus his gift on her, especially when she was determined to make him feel what she did. Normally that was a relief amid an excess of emotions driving him mad, but now it was an unwelcome reminder of his deficits.

He'd been with many Margas since Tal'Resh warned him of his weakness, and none had been more than tools for him to use. Their own depravities kept him from connecting too deeply with his enemy. But now, standing in front of the heavy wood door that separated him from the young man within, he'd lost himself. What was his and what was Gamel's intertwined too closely, like roots reaching out until two plants became one. To uproot one was to take the other with it.

Tyrus rested his head against the cold wood. So close to Gamel, the excitement, the anticipation, but mostly the love overwhelmed him. Tal'Resh was right, it was too dangerous, and Tyrus knew it, but if he didn't enter, he'd never be able to fulfill his mission. If he did though, he may never escape it. Tyrus wasn't sure he wanted to anymore.

The door slowly gave way without even a creak to mark an affair neither side should have allowed. Gamel stood near his window as Tyrus sealed the door, locking them together with their fate.

"I was beginning to worry you wouldn't come," Gamel said, his voice shaking a little with relief.

He was dressed only in his breeches with a single tie at his waist to keep them on as he waited. Gamel's skin seemed pale, like moonlight at dawn. He wasn't as dark in complexion as Tyrus, but the mild tan that normally bronzed his face and arms was subdued in the glow of the fading candles.

Tyrus didn't say anything in reply. It was too late for words. Love and lust fogged his mind as his hands pulled Gamel's breeches loose enough to fall to the floor, and Gamel yanked his shirt free. Enemy or lover, spy or stable hand, his two worlds were now one that he never wanted to separate again.

* * *

The lull after sex had never been so comforting to Tyrus. The musty smell of their sweat-dripped bodies. The soft rise and fall of Gamel's chest. His hands urging Gamel closer for a connection beyond the carnality. A content smile remained ever present on his lover's face as they lay in the near darkness of the bed.

"I wish we could be like this always," Gamel whispered like a secret given voice.

Tyrus kissed Gamel's shoulder, enjoying the gritty tang that remained on his lips. He didn't know if the love he felt was born from his own heart or stolen from Gamel's, but since allowing it in Tyrus would have given Gamel anything he asked. He wanted to bask in Gamel's happiness for ever.

"If the stories are true, we could be if we were dhan'ya. They say many like us live freely over there."

"I've heard many deviants exist within the dhan'ya," Gamel said, and for a moment shame slipped into his mind. Tyrus hadn't felt it from him as much in the last month, but whenever Tyrus made their love seem normal, Gamel often cowered again.

"Gamel," Tyrus drawled, pulling him closer beneath the cover. "Imagine for a moment, will you? If we were over there, we could live together with everyone knowing and no one would care. I could kiss you on our doorstep and no one would consider us deviants or depraved because we love each other. Our friends would ask how we are, if we planned to stay together, if we were going to start a family."

Gamel scoffed, a thick sound deep in his throat. "And how would we start a family?"

"We could take a child in," Tyrus said quickly to cover his slip. There was only so much of the dhan'ya he should know as a Margas, and the obscure dealings of lashi mael bearing children for those who couldn't wasn't among them. Though even as he said it, the image of his sister bearing Gamel's child for them brought a smile to his lips.

The answer seemed to mollify Gamel's skepticism. "I suppose there are orphans on both sides of the war. So, would we have a family?"

"Oh yes, many children."

"And who's going to tend to these children without a woman in the house?"

Tyrus bit back the reply that dhan'ya families raised children together. Family was important to the dhan'ya. "We'll hire help, of course."

"So we're rich over there?"

"I don't know about you, but I was born into a very good family," Tyrus joked, knowing he was walking a fine line hanging the truth before his Margas lover.

"If you're from a good family, then I must be as well."

"Everything you could want." Tyrus ran his fingers through Gamel's sweat-streaked hair, turning his head so their eyes met. Love. All he felt was love. "Let's go."

"Go? Go where?"

"To the border. We can run away tomorrow night before your father arrives. Gather enough to make it to the border and let's start a new life together." The words tumbled from Tyrus before his judgment or sense of duty could stop them. He wanted Gamel, wanted to feel that endless, unconditional love that left him in a heady rush of bliss. "There are Margas villages controlled by the dhan'ya. We could go there and we wouldn't have to hide anymore. We can be together."

Gamel shoved Tyrus away and sat up, his face twisted with an indignation that seemed to choke the joy from Tyrus. "Among monsters? You want to live with the demons trying to kill us."

"I want to live with you, Gamel. I want to be able to hold you without being afraid, and if that means living with my enemy, is that really so much of a sacrifice?"

"How can you say that?" Gamel demanded so loudly he paused to make sure no one was nearby to hear. Once it was safe, he continued in a cold whisper. "They're the *enemy*. Nothing is worth being near them."

Tyrus had felt positive and negative emotions together before because of his gift, but none compared to the grief, shame, and guilt that swelled in the center of his soul, creeping out like a lizard climbing from a bog until his entire body numbed where his heart could not. He was no longer within himself; he was beyond, trapped in Gamel's condemnation and his own love.

Swallowing, Tyrus forced his mouth to move before he gave himself away. When he spoke, even his own words felt distant. "You couldn't tolerate a single dhan'ya for me, for us?"

Gamel crawled over to him and cradled Tyrus's face in his hands. Several times Gamel kissed him, a worthless apology for a wound he didn't understand. "Tomas. You know I love you, but living with the dhan'ya… it's a fantasy. What you imagine could never be real. They're monsters that need to be killed. Our enjoyment isn't worth suffering them, Tomas. We may have to hide when Father's here, but not terrible, not like them."

Tomas. That morning Tyrus had loved hearing that name. He waited for it – the anticipation making the sound actualized so much more pleasurable. Now that name was a curse, burning him with his own lies. The only possible relief was a truth that would never come to pass. "I just want to be with you."

Gamel smiled and let his hands trace down Tyrus's neck and chest, slipping along the line of muscle on his stomach to reach lower with a touch far less novice than their first encounter. "Then let's make the most of tonight, Tomas. When my father leaves for the front again, we'll be free to enjoy each other."

It seemed Tyrus would never get the smile to form on his face. He thought of his family and a muscle moved. He remembered the sound of Tal'Resh's voice chastising him and another twitched. He breathed in the sweet scents of spice and flowers that never left his home and a grin finally showed for Gamel. He had been a fool to think his enemy would ever understand him. Or love him as he was.

He was a spy, and he'd forgotten that. There was only one thing left to do.

"Then let us hope the king is well, and your father goes swiftly." Tyrus forced his thoughts to his family – his duty – and kissed Gamel as a lashi mael should. "Please, tell me what happens, so I know when I can be with you again."

The Hula-Hoop Heart

Dan Stout

Sammie's Stand was a cobbled together lean-to with faded paint that sat at the far end of the grounds shared by the Fillmore Middle School and Junior High. The stand straddled the property line between the school playground and the adjacent city park. That put it in a legal gray zone – both the teachers and park officials figured it was the others' problem. All that confusion made it a nice place to go if you didn't want an adult breathing down your neck.

I bellied up to the stand and rapped my knuckles twice on the wood countertop, just like I did every weekday about that time.

"The usual," I said. A moment later Sammie appeared with a Dixie cup full of lemonade and a single lemon wedge.

I reached into my pocket, pretending to hunt for a quarter. Sammie waved it off.

"On the house, Sera," he said, and gave me a grin.

"You're aces, Sammie." Sammie was a sixth grader; a year older than me, but he let me drink for free in exchange for me not coming down on his operation.

I threw back the lemonade in a single sugary shot, and then sucked on the wedge. The sour chasing the sweet made my jaw ache, especially where I'd recently lost a baby tooth. I shook my head, sending my pigtails whipping back and forth.

I stepped away from the lemonade stand and adjusted my neon-yellow vest. I wanted another round but I was still on the clock. It was almost the end of the school day, and pretty soon there'd be kids who had to cross the street. I was about to head for the crosswalk when a voice stopped me cold.

"Well, well. Whatta we got here?"

I knew that whiny, just beginning to crack voice. I turned around slowly, hoping I'd be wrong. But there he was: Kevin Breyers, accompanied by his oversized flunkie, Matt Stahl. They both wore dopey smiles and the orange sashes that marked them as Hall Monitors.

I hate Hall Monitors.

I squared my shoulders and hitched my belt.

"You're outta your jurisdiction," I said. "Shouldn't you be inside busting kids for no hall pass, instead of wandering around on my turf?"

Behind me I could hear kids surreptitiously walking away from illicit card games, leaving forgotten Pokémon cards to languish in the dirt. No one wanted to cross the Monitors. They were nothing but a bunch of thugs with detention pads, but they could make life hard for a kid.

"Special assignment," said Breyers. Stahl said nothing.

Breyers and me go way back. Back in kindergarten we were even what you'd call pals, until he developed a sweet tooth and started making candy grabs from the class jar when the teacher wasn't looking. I caught him in the act, my first bust. I got a gold star out of the deal while Breyers did a stint in timeout. He cleaned up his act afterwards and we'd both ended up in the services: me a crossing guard, him a monitor. But there was bad blood between us ever since. The bruiser with him – Stahl – I didn't know anything about, other than he was twice the size of a normal sixth grader and had been following Breyers around like a puppy for the last month or so.

I asked Breyers. "What kind of special assignment?"

He looked smug. "Someone's been swiping gym equipment."

"I heard." I wasn't sure about the going price for hot football flags and orange cones, but I guessed someone was making a pretty profit from them. Anyway, it wasn't my problem.

Breyers nodded. "You hear that whoever it was left a broken Hula-Hoop in the shed?"

"I got ears, don't I?"

"Well we turned up a matching hoop. Bent up to fit in a locker."

"Oh?" Ears or no, I hadn't heard any of this.

"The perp's turning himself in today."

That was unexpected. Why would they turn themselves in? And why out here? Breyers crossed his arms and gave me a self-satisfied grin.

"Stick around," he said. "You'll see how a real bust goes down when I take this twerp in."

"You will..." I shrugged. "Or you won't. It's all the same to me." My lack of admiration pushed his buttons.

"Oh, it'll matter to you," he said. "I know all about your little empire out here, Vasquez. Shaking down Sammie for free drinks, turning a blind eye to kids running with suckers. Pretty soon you're gonna take a tumble, and I'm gonna be here to watch you fall."

I didn't say anything. There wasn't any 'empire,' just kids being kids. And as long as things stayed civil, that was fine with me. I figured a crossing guard should be judicious about her use of authority.

"Besides," he said, "there's another angle on the gym heist."

I kept my mouth shut, knowing he'd talk. He didn't disappoint.

"Those Hula-Hoops? They were on loan from the Junior High."

My blood ran cold at that. It meant that whoever had swiped the hoops had crossed the Big Kids. Dangerous and unpredictable, they were more like adults than kids. I pitied whoever was going to be taking the fall for this one.

There was movement in the grove of trees along the park.

"Here he comes now." Breyers elbowed Stahl nervously. The bigger monitor shot an irritated glance at Breyers, but let it pass.

Then I saw who stepped from the trees. It was the last person I'd have expected to see caught up in something like this: maybe the only good soul in all of Fillmore Middle School. My sweet Markus.

Markus, the library assistant. He of the argyle sweaters and soft brown eyes. Jay-Z in coke-bottle glasses. He had perfect attendance and a gentle smile, and we'd once held hands on a field trip to the art museum. He had librarian's hands, soft and finely boned. The kind of hands that would never know the burden that came with carrying a crossing flag.

Right now those same hands were holding a broken Hula-Hoop. It was bent in the top, the arc bisected and coming together. The bottom side pinched in and pointed down. Markus held it in front of him and it looked all the world like an oversized, blue-and-white-striped valentine. My own heart melted a little to see him.

Markus looked at Breyers and stammered out, "I am here to turn myself in."

Breyers widened his eyes. "Is that so? I am shocked to see you here, Markus."

My librarian took a deep breath. "I am overcome with remorse."

I'd heard less-rehearsed dialogue at Christmas pageants. I didn't know what was going on, but someone had forced Markus into this.

"Stop talking," I said.

"Shaddup." It was big Stahl, the first thing he'd said since he and Breyers had shown their mugs on my playground. I glared back at him.

"Don't you have something else to say, librarian?" Breyers stared at Markus and nodded his head, as if prompting him somehow.

Markus nodded back. "Yes –" I caught his eye, wordlessly pleading with him to stop this madness. I knew he could barely hold twenty Hula-Hoops, let alone run off with them. He sighed and looked back to Breyers.

"Just that I did this alone, is all."

Breyers's face went red. He opened his mouth to say something but I spoke first.

"So is this why you came out here, Breyers? So you could write him a detention slip in front of me?"

Markus swayed on his feet at the word 'detention.' I reached out to steady him. "It'll be okay," I whispered. "You'll do your time and get out. I'll be waiting for you."

Breyers shot forward and pushed himself between us, bumping my shoulder and knocking the crossing guard badge from my vest. It struck Sammie's bar, spinning a lazy dance across the plywood before falling to the ground. Breyers and I were almost nose to nose.

"Detention?" Up close Breyers's breath was a foul blend of Twizzlers and lemonade. "Nah, I don't think so, Vasquez. There's folks want to talk to this kid." He jerked his chin to the north, across the parking lot towards Fillmore Junior High. Big Kids. My hand instinctively tightened on the crossing flag. I turned back to Markus, in a last desperate bid to talk sense into him.

"Markus, you didn't do anything! Why are you caving in like this?"

My librarian couldn't even look me in the eye, just stared past me to Sammie's stand, as if he longed for one last Dixie cup-sized swig of sugar before he was hauled off to meet his fate.

"I acted alone –"

Stahl's deeper voice rumbled over all of ours. "Save it. You're coming with us."

He and Breyers sidled up to either side of my sweet librarian.

Markus gave them a weak smile. "Hey fellas. How about you do me a solid and let me say goodbye to Seraphina, huh?"

Breyers sneered. "Say goodbye while you're walking, bookworm." He pushed Markus forward, and all three of them started towards the junior high. From what sounded like a million miles away, I heard the end-of-day bell ringing its shrill declaration of release.

My brain and heart both screamed for me to do something.

No, no, no. This was all wrong, such a heavy-handed setup, and I was useless. If I couldn't save Markus, then I couldn't save anyone. What was the whole point of being a crossing guard, anyway?

I looked down at the grimy badge by my feet. There was still some shine to it, even laying there in the dirt. I picked it up and cradled it in my hand, like an orphaned bunny. The shield had meant so much to me back when I first started guarding. Maybe it was time to make it mean something again.

"Sammie!" I barked. "Gimmie one for the road."

My eyes were on the three figures walking away from me, but I heard the Dixie cup slam down next to me, and from the pour I could tell Sammie's hand was shaking.

"You're not about to do something stupid, Sera?"

I threw back the shot of lemonade and bit down on the lemon slice, but I didn't spit it out. The yellow rind ringed my teeth, and acted like a makeshift mouthpiece.

"We don't use that word," I said, though I suppose the lemon probably muffled it. I sprinted forward, dodging in and out among the stream of kids exiting school doors, waving my flag to clear them, running through the playground like I owned it. My heart was pumping. The movement felt good, felt right. The world may still have been a cold and callous place, but for the first time in forever, I was doing something about it.

I caught up to the monitors and Markus halfway across the playground. Breyers was still whispering into Markus' ear, and my librarian wobbled slightly on his feet as they walked. Probably telling him stories of wedgies and swirlies, and all the other enhanced detention techniques the Big Kids used.

I ran in front of them and dropped my crossing flag in their path. They halted immediately.

"Thith thetup thtinks."

I got back only stares.

Breyers shaded his eyes. "What?"

I spit the lemon rind out of my mouth and tried again. "Something stinks about this, Breyers, and not just your breath. This is a frame job."

"You know," said Breyers, "I think you're right. In fact, Markus here was just telling us that he'd maybe rather not deal with the Big Kids. He'd maybe like to tell us who he's working for." He smacked Markus on the back. "Isn't that right, kid?"

Markus was quiet for a long breath. Never looking up from his feet, in a small voice he said, "Seraphina made me do it. She's the mastermind."

Breyers beamed.

My throat constricted, and I hunched over. I looked up at Markus and willed myself not to show how hurt I was.

"Why?" I said.

"All of you shaddup." It was Stahl again, pushing us around like a typical monitor.

Well I was sick of getting pushed around. I was sick of good kids being ground up like yesterday's meatloaf. And most of all I was sick to my stomach of Breyers's sense of triumph, of his leering grin and foul breath, that unholy combination of Twizzlers and –

It hit me like a dodge ball across the face.

"Lemonade," I said.

They all looked at me when I spoke. Everyone except Markus. His guilty eyes were still boring holes into the ground. I couldn't believe I hadn't seen it before. If someone wanted to move stolen gym goods, they'd need someone to act as a fence. Someone who operated in a gray zone at the border of the school's authority. I turned slowly. Sammie wasn't at his stand. In fact, he was nowhere to be seen.

I pretend-spit on the ground. "That little booger-eater..."

Stahl rumbled, "Language, Vasquez."

Breyers forced a nervous laugh. "What are you talking about? Stahl, do you know what she's talking about?" His eyes danced back and forth. "I don't know what she's –"

"Shaddup," Stahl cut him off. The brute was looking at me. "Breyers hasn't talked to the perp in weeks, if that's what you're thinking. But he did tell Markus what'll happen if he doesn't come clean." He turned to Markus. "I'd like to remind you that the Big Kids and I will look very unfavorably on any mistruths. You better come clean."

"Markus," I said, "I know who put you up to this. And I'll bust him. So anything he has on you will come out in the open sooner or later."

Finally breaking, Markus screamed, "Sammie made me!"

I pulled Markus away from the monitors, holding his shoulders and doing my best not to shake sense into him. "But why? Why were you taking a dive for Sammie?"

Markus covered his face with his hands, as if he could hide from what he'd done. "He was putting the squeeze on me, Sera. He knew about my library fines. If he went public with that, I'd be ruined. Ruined! All I had to do was turn you in."

"He needed me out of the way before I got wise to his fence operation."

"He said if I blamed you, I'd walk and he'd keep quiet about my – my overdues." He dropped his hands then and looked at me. "But I couldn't do it. When I saw you there, I couldn't go through with it. I didn't know what I was doing, I just –"

Stahl broke in. "So it was you and Sammie."

I turned to him, ready to chew him a new one for still thinking either I or Markus was involved. But Stahl wasn't looking at us. Instead, he had hold of Breyers's shirt in one of his over-sized fists. "I knew you had a stooge, I just wasn't sure who it was."

Then I got it: all the times Stahl had spoken that day – the broken, barely intelligible commands of 'Shaddup' – he hadn't been telling me to stop talking, he'd been trying to get Markus to stop incriminating himself.

I pointed at Stahl. "So you're…"

"Internal Affairs," he said. The hulking Monitor was still up in Breyers's face. "I've been on you for a month now," he thunked Breyers in the chest with an over-sized finger. "I wanted to pop you for so many small things, but this… this is too good."

Breyers was pale, shaking and – for once in his life – quiet. I wish I could say I didn't enjoy seeing him twist, but it did my heart glad to be there to watch him fall.

Stahl spun Breyers around, facing the Junior High, then looked my way. "That was pretty fast thinking. And acting." He paused, and I could practically hear the gears turning. "You ever think about joining the Monitors?"

I hacked out a laugh and swung an arm, a gesture that encompassed the playground and parking lot. "What, and give all this up?"

Stahl grunted.

"You're alright, Vasquez." He shoved Breyers forward with one of his over-sized mitts. "But keep your nose clean or I'll be back for you." Then he and Breyers headed off towards the Big Kids' school.

"Seraphina…." It was Markus. He held out one of his gentle librarian's hands.

My voice was so cold it even surprised me. "That's Officer Vasquez to you."

His hand dropped to his side.

"I'm sorry," he said. "I didn't know what to do. Sammie said…" Those big brown eyes started to water up behind his glasses. When I spoke my voice was softer.

"You're not cut out for this life. Get outta here."

He started to say something else, but I cut him off.

"Go on, kid. There's a Dewey Decimal System that needs tending to."

Markus looked away and waited a heartbeat, just long enough for me to hope that he'd refuse. Then he turned and began the long walk back to the library.

I watched him go, then looked back at the Big Kids school. Stahl and Breyers had reached the big glass doors of the Junior High. Justice was about to be served. I tugged my Hello Kitty shirt and turned my back to them, standing a little straighter in my neon-yellow vest.

It ain't easy out here. There's candy wrappers in the bushes and gum on the sidewalk. Two times a day there's kids that need to cross the street.

And me? I'm Seraphina Vasquez.

I'm the crossing guard.

No Regrets on Fourth Street

Lauren C. Teffeau

I WEAR the skin the job requires.

It's supposed to be enough. This is my mantra, unassailable even now, my only tether in the darkness that fills my head, blunting all thought as I drift. Long enough to know something's wrong, but not enough to care. Behind me, a metal door screeches open. I'm no longer alone.

Water slaps me in the face, forcing open my eyes. I rear back at the rush of cold, and an ache in my right temple kindles to life. Plastic zip ties halt my wrists, anchoring me to a straight-backed chair. My mind stutters. I was headed for a rave in the factory district, took a shortcut, but…

A naked bulb glares down, my eyes watering as I try to figure out where I am. Nowhere I've been before –I'd remember the meat locker vibe and the overwhelming stench of ammonia.

The water dribbles down my neck, collecting in the collar of my shirt. The restraints abrade my new tattoos. All I can do is shiver in the cramped little room and blink back the fierce light shining down.

"Where's your handler?"

The owner of the voice remains backlit, but I make out enough of his form – maybe a foot taller than me with linebacker shoulders. That's right. He's the thug who jumped me in the alley on my way to the drop. I was supposed to be at the rave by now, making sure to refill my glass at exactly 1:43 a.m. to alert the client to my presence. The skin would do the rest.

"Don't know what you're talking about," I say through a mouth of sandpaper. Coarse grit. I wobble the chair back and forth. "Seriously, what the hell is all this?"

"Took us a while to pin you down. But we've been watching, Callie."

My name sound like a curse on his lips, and a shudder tears through me, knocking my spine against the chair back. "You're crazy. Let me go."

My skin is perfect down to the last detail: blue-green tattoos wreathing my light brown forearms, metal cuffs studded with LEDs fitted across my shins and thighs, exposed by my floor-length skirt's transparent panels. If I squint I can make out the faint glow of the bioluminescent protein grafted to the soft skin under my eyes. Jellyfish, I think. Everything Marco specified. Only he and the client that was supposed to approach me during the rave should know the combination of mods for this particular job.

But somehow this guy knows who – no, *what* – I am.

I've been compromised. That's never happened before, and the novelty of it wars with the dead feeling in my stomach. Pushing past my headache, I try to access my implant. Offline. Hazy sensory impressions rise to the top. I remember a brief scuffle, a blow to the head and a sharp prick on my neck before the darkness came. The man must have taken care of my implant then. Marco probably doesn't know what happened yet.

The man chuckles and steps closer. The light falls on the Taser in his tanned hand. Blue electricity arcs between the contact points. He holds it up to my neck, where my silenced implant sits under my skin. "Cut the act. We know you know, sweetheart."

Scalp prickling, I can only stare up at him. Bullet shaped head, a fake scar running below his right eye – too calculated to be real. Lots of thugs sign up for that particular mod to look tough without having to earn it. Hired help. But for whom?

Marco always said skins are an information courier's best weapon. Constantly changing, they allow us to stump the cameras and operate safely in plain sight. He said it would be enough.

The Taser starts to hum.

He was wrong.

* * *

"Well?" the parlor tech asked as he held the mirror in front of me. "What do you think?"

Long graphene rectangles had been grafted to both of my cheeks, along my collarbones, down my arms, the long line of my shins. My fingers tripped along the seam between skin and the digital plaques. Amazing. And mine.

The tech laughed at my silence. "First time, huh?"

I sheepishly nodded. It had taken me a long time to decide on this particular parlor. Reviews said they were welcoming of first-timers, and the warm wood-paneled interior had set me at ease as soon as I walked in.

"Well, you'll be able to use your implant to program them to display... anything really, so have fun."

I finally pulled my gaze away from my altered reflection and gave the tech a smile. "Thank you."

When I got home, I dressed myself with care, selecting clothes that would keep the plaques uncovered as they shuddered through different colors according to my mood. Then I went back out.

Some people blithely drifted by, their implant's proximity sensor helping them navigate the crowd as they synched. But others saw. They had to peer beyond the information clogging their view, but when they saw me, that little pause, the slight widening of the eyes, I knew I existed outside of myself.

It gave me a heady feeling, despite the confusion, the disgust even, that cycled across their faces. But at least I didn't get lost in the competing noise.

Across the street, a man watched me. Not a disbelieving stare or a furtive glance like the ones who'd come before – he didn't look away when my gaze connected with his. For a moment, I thought he'd walk on. But no, his steps slowed, then he decisively turned and took the crosswalk to my side of the world.

He looked so comfortable in his skin. His dark arms were bare, alive with electric ink. The tattoos writhed, changing too quickly for the eye to settle on any one design. They held me rapt as he came to stand in front of me.

"Well? Is it working?" he asked.

"What do you mean?"

His gaze traveled from the plaques on my cheeks down my body with languid ease. "Performance art? Social experiment?"

Those terms were inadequate, but the truth seemed weak by comparison. "I just wanted to be seen."

Something kindled to life in his liquid dark eyes. "Well, *I* see you." A tattoo, not quite as chaotic as the rest of them, peeked out above the collar of his shirt. A small, ink-black tree, branches constantly fluttering as if stirred by an invisible breeze. Remarkable.

"Are you…. Do you…" *feel the same*, but I couldn't bring myself to ask.

He shifted closer, allowing me to touch the warm skin of his arm. My fingers followed the lines of ink as they jumped over lean muscle, then got lost at the edges of his shirt. The tattoos were beautiful and bizarre, and I wanted.

"Where did you get this done?" I asked.

A grin lifted the corner of his mouth. "It's a secret. What about yours?"

"No Regrets on Fourth Street."

He nodded, a finger hovering out between us, before ever so gently sliding across the plaque mounted to my right cheek. My skin had fully healed, but it was still tender at his touch. "They do good work. I could get lost in your colors." His voice was throaty with the hint of an accent.

Using my implant, I tried to see who he was, but his signal was cloaked. Smiling kindly at my disappointment, he handed me a card to a club – the Plastic Factory. He gestured to the people swerving to avoid us. "When this is no longer enough, come find me."

Then he walked on, leaving my digital plaques in kaleidoscopic chaos.

* * *

My body convulses awake, the memory of static discharge still sharp in my mind. Must have passed out. I bite down on my tongue, willing the sensations away. The metallic taste in my mouth grounds me slightly.

I'm almost myself again except I don't remember how I got from the chair to an exam table. An IV port interrupts the vines of blue-green ink wrapped around my left arm.

I lift my aching head. A high ceiling studded with skylights, walls of thin metal sheeting… some sort of warehouse? Air leaks out of my lungs when I see another exam table – a woman strapped there. Then another. And another. Dozens of them. All unconscious, but each with the same height and build as me.

A shudder rolls through me. Skins are convincing, but they can't alter the frame underneath. They've been *hunting* for me.

My heart monitor squeals, and I jump.

I thought maybe I slipped up, or they got lucky. Not such a large-scale operation. Marco said a lot was riding on this job, but who –

A door slams open. The man from before looms over my table with his scar in all its fake glory. "Ready to talk?"

I try to look helpless. It's not hard in my current state. "I don't know what you mean." If he's still asking questions, then I have to believe they haven't found the data. Yet. Maybe there's still a way out of this.

The man sneers, his scar stretching across his cheekbone. "Marco. The jobs you do for him." His gaze turns predatory. "We already know about the rest."

Marco deals in information; the kind that can't be securely transmitted through the networks. Which is all of it these days. Anything sent online can be tracked, cached, or reconstructed. Confidential data, classified intel, trade secrets, crooked books, communiqués between clandestine lovers... Marco doesn't discriminate. Couriers never know what we're carrying. We just get outfitted with our new skins, play pretend at being someone else for a few hours, make the exchange, and do it all over again.

I shake my head, if only so his gaze slides away.

He fiddles with my IV. "No matter. If you won't talk, *he* will."

A strange warmth washes through my body, the darkness calling me once more. "He won't come. He wouldn't be so foolish," I say in a burred voice.

"We'll see," is the last thing I hear.

* * *

"Oh my god." My roommate Aimee lurched off the couch as I entered our apartment and dropped my purse on the kitchen counter. "You look fantastic."

I stood patiently as she circled around me. Horn plates trailed down my neck like vestigial gills. I ran a nervous hand through my new pixie cut. "What about the hair? Too much?"

"No, it's perfect. Shows it off." She touched one of the plates with the tip of her finger. "Feel that?"

"It's muted, but yeah, I can."

"That is *so* cool." She flashed me a grin. "We should go out tonight. Celebrate your new look. There's a place I heard about that'll be perfect." Aimee dashed into her room.

I followed after her, leaning against the doorframe as she dug through her closet. "What's it called?"

"The Plastic Factory."

I was suddenly very glad she was too busy deciding what to wear to see my reaction. It had been months since that day on the sidewalk. Still had the business card. It smelled of leather and springtime – evidence that the man was flesh and blood and waiting for me. Or not. Maybe it had all been an elaborate come-on.

But he'd been right about one thing. As time passed, I needed more elaborate mods to hold onto that feeling of liberation the simple digital plaques had given me.

Aimee glanced up from a daring tank top. "Well, go get ready. It'll be fun. This is supposed to be your thing, right?"

I wasn't so sure. Still wasn't by the time we crossed town and passed through the doors of the Plastic Factory.

The place was full of people with increasingly outlandish body mods – mine tame by comparison. One woman had fiber optic hairs erupting out of her scalp, her braids winking as she shouldered her way to the bathrooms. Another man had stainless steel horns riveted to his forehead that could retract and expand with a blink. One area was cordoned off for the 'Highly Evolved' – people with three or more different kinds of mods. Everyone was so covered in ink, piercings, and grafts, they stopped being individuals and became one with the phantasmagorical horde.

My skin itched at all the possibilities I'd been too cowardly to try.

I lost Aimee in the crush on the dance floor and consoled myself with a whisky from the bar. Here I was, yet I still didn't feel like I belonged. Sure, I'd had some work done, but seeing everyone else's absolute commitment to the mods was humbling.

When I reached the bottom of my glass, the man on the neighboring stool bought a refill. I turned to him in thanks, and then froze at the dark ridges that covered the right side of his face like a mask.

I was already reaching out to touch when I stopped. "May I?"

He nodded, and my hand ranged over the surprisingly warm ridges that got lost in his curly dark hair. His fingers trailed down my neck along the smooth horn plates.

He leaned in, his breath ticklish against my ear. "When anything is possible, it is important to understand the power of restraint," he said in a voice my body recognized over the music. He gestured toward the wild throng on the dance floor. "I find it refreshing compared to the alternative."

His words were a balm on my bruised pride. He focused on my face for a long moment, a slight wrinkle in his brow. "Do I know you?"

Instead of answering, I held out my hand and counted the seconds until he took it. I towed him to the dark hall leading to the bathrooms, and when I let him back me up against the wall and kiss me, I was certain.

I inhaled one last lungful of springtime and eased back. "I *see* you."

Breathing heavily, he blinked down at me, his dark brown eyes now even darker.

I tugged down the neck of my shirt, revealing the digital plaque along my collarbone shifting through colors in time with my erratic heartbeat.

"It *is* you." He bucked his hips against me and pressed a kiss to the hollow of my throat. "We should celebrate properly."

He moved away, and I slid back down to the floor. My body didn't want to stop – I didn't want to stop. "We don't have to…. We could…" I grabbed his belt.

He crowded me up against the wall again. "Yes. But not here."

I ditched Aimee. In that moment, it wasn't even a question. He lived in one of the lofts above the club. We rode the elevator to his floor. The throbbing bass had faded, leaving only the thumping blood in my veins. When we passed through the door to his apartment, he finally uncloaked himself. Marco Addams, my implant told me. Twenty-six, only two years older than me.

The rest could wait as I kissed my way down his altered face.

* * *

Hot needle pain radiates though my arm. I struggle to lift my bruised eyelids. A med tech comes into focus as he futzes with the port on my arm. How did I get here? The rave? No, before that, in the alley. Then the man with the fake scar…. The tech eases the IV out, and I hiss.

"Shh…" he says to me.

I blink back tears and really look at him. Warm, dark eyes. Wide shoulders. He holds a finger to his lips through a facemask.

"Who sent you?" Do I look as pathetic as I sound?

The med tech doesn't answer as he helps me sit up. Gunfire explodes from the next room. I can only cling to him as he carries me out of there and into the adjoining alley. I peer over the tech's shoulder. Vision blurs as men with guns try to follow us, but other men with guns stop them. At least that's what I think is happening. The concussive gunfire turns everything to a dull roar.

My eyes are slow to find the ink just visible under the med tech's scrubs. A tree. There's something off about it, but my head's pounding and it's safe and warm in the tech's arms.

I've felt this way with only one other person. Even if everything smells like antiseptic. "Marco…"

"I'm here." His voice rumbles through me.

"You shouldn't have come," I say in a raw voice. "They'll –"

"They can't hurt us anymore."

* * *

Late morning sun gilded the loft's concrete walls. Marco left the windows uncovered, the view of the river breathtaking. He stretched, and I watched the play of ink across his chest. His closely cropped hair, his large frame, and the tree tattoo were the only things this Marco had in common with the man I had met on the sidewalk months ago.

I slowly sat up under the thin bed sheet, my body twinging with delicious tenderness. "Why the change?" I gestured to his face.

He trailed his fingers down the plates along my neck, his hand drifting lower. I nearly purred. "I could ask you the same."

"You were right. The mods... they aren't enough. But the people at the club? That's not who I am either."

"If I may ask, what were you trying to prove with those plaques in the first place?"

I blinked. "I wanted to defy expectations." It sounded pathetic out loud but Marco just gave me a thoughtful nod. "Everything I was working toward, college, a career.... It felt like a trap. At least with these," I fingered the smooth horn, "people couldn't ignore me." The only way I could compete with the world around me, the only way I still felt real. By being that one disharmonious note in a sea of homogeneity.

I placed my fingers over his tree tattoo, dancing in time with his pulse. "Is that how it works for you?"

"Yes. It started out that way."

"And now?"

He smiled. "Now I use the different mods to do my job."

"What job?"

His fingers drifted across the plaque along my collarbone, so long I wondered if he was going to answer. "I facilitate offline data transfers, and to do that, my couriers adopt different skins."

"Skins?"

"Mods working together for a specific purpose." He gestured to the ridges eclipsing half of his face. "What do you see when you look at me?"

"If I didn't know you... defensiveness, self-hatred maybe, since your face is partially covered."

He nodded. "Or perhaps it could signify overconfidence, aggression even, depending on what costume I wear, where you encounter me – say the alley behind your apartment instead of a club – changing your interpretation."

"Context is everything."

He leaned down and kissed the corner of my mouth. "Yes, but equally important is being able to match the mods to an environment in the first place so my couriers can operate in plain sight. It requires subtlety and..."

"Restraint?" I asked, thinking back to his words last night.

He nodded. "You see? I was right about you. Normally, this would be the point where I'd ask you if you wanted a job."

"Why don't you?"

"Because." He rolled me onto my back. "I like this a lot better."

"Why can't we do both?"

He stilled. Later, I learned Marco recruited his couriers from the Plastic Factory since many of the club's customers were already into pretty invasive mods. They were less likely to balk at the need to constantly adopt different skins to evade biometrics and other surveillance measures that could tie couriers to Marco, the clients, or both. But out of his recruits, I was the first he'd taken to bed.

After a moment's deliberation, he leaned down and whispered, "If you could use skins to make a living – a good one – would you do it?"

* * *

I wake in Marco's bed. The loft's natural light surrounds me. It's been too long. I snuggle into the covers, seeking out his scent. But all I can smell is laundry soap.

"How are you feeling?" Marco's basso voice filters into my ears from far away.

"All right." I sit up. "I missed this place."

Once I started working as an information courier, my visits here had been few and far between – Marco said it was safer that way. If we were spotted together, it could ruin my ability to do the job. So we had to get creative for our debriefings, each of us adopting skins to meet up at various places across the city. It was fun, at first.

"What did you miss about it?"

I walk to the window. "This view. With the sun rising over the river, it makes the noise almost worth it when the club empties out in the early mornings."

He cocks his head. "What club?"

"The Plastic Factory, silly." I step toward him and give him a saucy smile as I run my hand along his chest, testing him to see how long he can stand my touch. "Remember when you nearly ravished me in the back?"

I still when my eyes find his tree tattoo. Static. Unmoving. A mere facsimile.

I stare up at not-Marco. He gives me a grin. "You've been *so* helpful, Callie." The way he says my name...

Gooseflesh breaks out all over my body. "No..." They tricked me. They must have.... The edges of the room bleed together, colors desaturating, and Marco's face – the one he was wearing when I first met him – melts into darkness.

* * *

Cellophane and the faint scent of burnt hair was the first thing I noticed when the parlor technician moved my bed into a sitting position.

Marco stood by, a dark goatee, gold studs rimming both ears, and a sleeveless shirt revealing overly muscled arms that had to be mods. He looked like a gothic gangbanger. He gave the parlor tech a sharp nod of dismissal. "Callie, listen carefully."

"You should wear a gold cross necklace. Looks more convincing that way."

His mouth pursed as he thought that over, then nodded. "So I should. But enough about that. We have only so much time before the rendezvous."

He helped me to my feet. I giggled as I fell into him, his arms coming around me automatically. His sigh ruffled my new stick straight ebony hair.

"I won't be here after every procedure. You understand why?"

I nodded. "Because you're a big important information broker, and I'm just a lowly courier." I giggled again.

Marco rolled his eyes. "Close enough. I'll tell the technician to dial back the anesthesia next time. You're a lightweight." He held out the knee-length dress, blue with tiny white polka dots. "Now tell me what you'll do."

I pulled the dress over my head and shimmied it into place. "I'm to go to the botanical gardens for the festival and sit under the cherry blossoms. I'm supposed to read..."

Marco handed me a chemistry textbook. "...this."

It was the combination of mods, working in concert with costume and environment, that gave skins power. People saw what they wanted to – even more so with implants distracting them from the everyday.

"Then someone will approach me before the festival ends."

He nodded. "They'll scan a part of your body, and that'll be the end of it. Come right back here. I'll be waiting for you."

I ran a hand through my new hair in front of the mirror. My cheeks were fuller, my forehead wider, my eyelids stretched. The structure of my face changed just enough to fool the cameras.

Marco smoothed the edge of my dress over my digital plaque. He insisted we keep one part of me consistent for identification purposes.

"There's just one thing I don't understand."

He gave me a patient smile in the mirror.

"Why don't I just carry the information on a datakey? Why does it have to be embedded inside me?"

"It's a security feature. Anything can go wrong – lost or damaged datakeys, theft, detainment by the authorities, you name it. What you don't know will keep you safe. That way my clients can be assured of their information's security."

I peered at myself in the mirror. The thought of some chip festering somewhere in my body... "Give me a hint. I don't want to be molested in the middle of the park."

He chuckled. "Don't worry – the locations are randomized, but they're almost always accessible, with minimum discomfort to you."

This was it – my first job. A rush of adrenaline burned off the last of the painkillers, leaving my new body prickly and very much awake.

I turned around. "And you'll be waiting?" I asked in a small voice.

"Always." Marco pressed a kiss to my forehead. "Now show me what you've learned."

* * *

"Wake her," a new voice demands. The side of my neck with my implant stings. Tears lodge in my throat as I try to banish the image of not-Marco from my mind. Ice trickles through my veins moments later, turning into a sharp burn that cracks open my eyes.

"Ah, there she is." A middle-aged Hispanic man leans over me, eyes glinting in the dull light. The thug from before guards the door.

I tremble. Did they find the data with whatever tricks they played with my implant? Worse, did they find Marco? I force myself to smile despite my chapped lips, despite everything. "Finally. I nearly despaired of only having Scarface for company."

He chuckles. "Believe me, Callie, I'm happy to oblige." Then with a flip of a switch, whatever friendliness he has in his face disappears. "Where's the data you were carrying for Marco?"

"What data?" I try to say it lightly but my voice cracks from disuse.

"The data you had on you three nights ago."

The man's eyes crinkle at the corners when I have nothing to say to that. At least not right away. Three nights? Have I been here that long?

I lift a shoulder. "If you didn't find it, I must have lost it in the scuffle with your boy there."

I'm rewarded when the men exchange a glance, and Scarface shakes his head vehemently. Interesting. They know about me and Marco, but not the fundamentals of our operation.

"Datakeys do have a pesky way of getting lost," I add for good measure.

I contract my leg muscles, wiggle my toes. Whatever they've been pumping me full of must pack a punch since they haven't bothered with restraints this time. My body tenses as I run through my options. Jump out of bed, bash Bossman on the head with my IV stand before squaring off with Scarface. A tray table is to the side, gleaming with metal instruments. It might do some damage if properly applied.

The man chuckles and gestures to his lackey. "Look at her, trying to figure out a way out of here."

Scarface grins. "Like a rat in a maze."

Bossman looks at me again with a slight sniff. "We heard you were Marco's best, but I'm disappointed so far. To think one smart-mouthed *puta* is all that stands between me and this city's info market."

Everything clicks into place. "You must be Basilio." A low-level competitor. Marco's never been too concerned about them since their data transfer techniques lack sophistication. After all, they still use datakeys. I snort. "And what, you thought nabbing me would get you in the big leagues?"

Something dangerous flashes in his eyes. "Guess we're going to have to do things the hard way. I thought Marco would come for you – I was wrong. I see that now. You are disposable," he whispers in my ear.

Skins *are* disposable. But not me. Not to Marco. I have to believe –

Basilio taps my neck and the implant there. "We have all the time in the world to take you apart and discover your secrets."

They can't know, can they? Fear clamps down, overriding my lethargy. If I'm going to make a play, it has to be now. Basilio glances at Scarface.

That's when I launch off the bed. My feet hit cool concrete, and my legs nearly buckle. Am I so weak? Basilio doesn't move, just watches me with cold assessment as he waves Scarface forward.

No, no, no. I back up, the IV pole lurching with me on its casters. I reach back for the tray of tools, hoping for something sharp, pointy.... My hip catches the tray's edge and it falls, dashing any hope of making a stand.

I don't fight Scarface as he bundles me back onto the hospital bed, Basilio watching on impassively.

"Your resistance is quite... admirable. Especially when Marco's closed up shop. His loft was already cleaned out by the time we got there. I'm not sure I'd be so loyal if I were the one left holding the bag."

"Closed up shop?" No. He would have told me. I'm supposed to...

Scarface draws straps tight against my chest, binding me to the bed. Then he adjusts my IV fluids. *No.* Not again. I spit in his face.

His fist strikes out, and I find darkness once more.

* * *

Callie, get out of there. Marco's voice filtered into my head via my implant. That he broke radio silence on a job a rarity.

But I'm supposed to stay in position for another ten minutes.

Some jobs didn't require data transfers. Sometimes the combination of mods was information enough. A red blouse instead of green. Blonde hair instead of black. The minute changes imbued with meaning for whoever was paying attention and paying Marco to make it happen.

Today, I wore a maroon pea coat I got second-hand over a pair of faded jeans. The mod parlor had made tweaks to my facial structure, and my newly-installed hair reached the small of my back in near-perfect ringlets. The bulk of it was bundled into a large updo secured with a bright yellow scarf – that was the key. I had commandeered a stretch of wall in front of the art museum where I pretended to sketch, occasionally pitching breadcrumbs to the pigeons.

I was supposed to hold my position for two hours, time enough for whoever to get the message my skin signified.

Now. Cops received a tip and will be on the scene soon.

I didn't ask how he knew that or what could happen if I was found there. I simply gathered up my belongings and tossed out the rest of the breadcrumbs for the pigeons to fight over.

Good. The Carleton, in a half-hour. Then he cut the connection.

There was enough legalese in courier-client agreements to absolve me and by extension Marco of any wrongdoing. Eventually. But that didn't mean law enforcement couldn't make trouble for us. Or our clients once they found out the deal went sideways.

The subway dumped me out a few blocks from the hotel. When I arrived, the concierge gave me a smile. "You are in Room 1644, miss. Have a nice stay."

Marco bounded off the bed when I entered the hotel suite. Without preamble, he wrenched down the neck of my shirt, and grunted at the sight of my digital plaque, quiescent whenever I was on a job.

His shoulders relaxed, his frame screamed Marco, but the color of his eyes and the blond highlights in his hair seemed all wrong. But there was enough of *him* in his mannerisms as he began to pace.

I took off my coat and set my bag on the dresser.

He whirled toward me. "When I give you an order, you do it, no questions asked."

"Ten minutes, Marco. I had everything under control. Besides, I didn't pass one cop on my way to the train." I was still riding the high of another job pulled off under the noses of virtually everyone, and he was all about the buzzkill.

He ran a hand through his hair, drawing my eye to the unnatural highlights. "And the next time? What happens if you guess wrong, Callie?" He stepped toward me and put his hands on my shoulders. "I can't lose you."

I laughed bitterly. "You just don't want to lose your best courier."

Shrugging him off me, I pulled back the curtains to stare out across the city. He stood behind me. Close enough I could feel the heat of his body even though we weren't touching.

"Callie, these are the rules we agreed to when all this started."

I cocked my head, neither agreeing with or refuting his statement. "I'm tired of the rules, Marco. All this sneaking around... it feels like I'm your dirty little secret."

"How can you say that? You know what could happen if we –"

I ducked my head. "I know, I know." Things between us had happened so quickly, we skipped over so many steps, and I hated how insecure that made me. "I'm just tired of hiding what I feel."

One of his hands came up to rest on my hip, the other smoothed away the collar of my shirt so he could place a kiss on the back of my neck. "You don't have to hide it now, not with me," his voice rasped in my ear.

"What if that's not enough?"

He tensed. I felt it from the back of my thighs to my shoulder blades. "You love this as much as I do." He pulled the scarf from my hair, and it fell down in heavy waves. "No matter what skin you wear, that I wear, this... connection between us remains. Recognizable despite everything."

He kissed the hollow below my ear, then my cheek, turning me around to face him. He knew what he was doing to me, the way my bones seemed to melt at his touch. And yet a small voice protested.

"I can't do it. This with you now, the jobs." I thought we could do both, but I was wrong. I wouldn't make him choose between me and his first love – the skins that had brought us together. "After tonight, I'm a courier only."

He hissed. "Callie..."

"I mean it, Marco."

His gaze shuttered at that. Then he kissed me, hard, possessively. I pulled him closer. He stopped too soon, leaving me aching, my lungs starved for air.

He stepped away from me a stranger. "If that's what you want."

* * *

I can barely move. I'm still in the warehouse. Gunfire just like before filters into my ears. But this time smoke and metal fills my nose. It's another dream, they're trying to extract more information from me. I have to be strong. I have to –

Basilio slams into the room, looking a lot less confident than before. Scarface follows, firing into the hallway behind him. Then he goes down, blood leaking out of his chest in gouts.

Swearing, Basilio gets the door shut and barricades it with a chair. Advancing to my bed, he rips away my restraints and pulls out my IV and the electrodes keeping me tethered to the machines.

Pain burns down my arm. "Leave me alone."

"Not gonna to happen. You're the only one who can tell us where the data is." He yanks me to my feet.

I clutch the IV pole with trembling hands to keep from falling over. "I told you already. I don't know."

Gunfire draws his gaze to the door. Somehow, I haul the pole up and around, ramming Basilio in the back of the head. I stumble back, scanning the room for anything to defend myself with. My gaze lands on Scarface, and the gun still held in his blood-slicked hands.

I reach for it at the same time Basilio pulls himself off the floor. He hollers something, then slams into me. I fall back against the concrete floor, the gun twisting between us. Everything narrows into this one moment. I squeeze the trigger, the discharge rattling through me. Basilio goes still, his lifeblood seeping over my body.

Somehow, I'm still breathing.

I push him off me and gain my feet, the gun still clutched in my hand. Dimly, I hear someone banging against the door. The plastic and metal chair gives way, and the door groans open. Another man with a gun.

I crouch behind the hospital bed as he moves through the room ripping the smocks off the left shoulder of each woman. I keep the gun trained on him as he – Marco – approaches my side of the room. This version is even more convincing, his eyes, the hard line of his jaw.... He hasn't bothered with a disguise.

When he sees me, a bright flash of relief passes over his face. "Callie, thank god." Then he sees the gun and goes still a few feet away. "It's me."

Even his voice sounds right. "Prove it."

Slowly he pulls down the collar of his shirt. My eyes focus on the tree, dancing and jerking across his skin. Let it be real this time.

He steps closer. "Now you."

The gun wavers as I slide the smock off my shoulder. I close my eyes as he reaches out, his hand passing over the digital plaque along my collarbone almost reverently.

"It's going to be okay."

Another man bangs into the room. "You found her? Hurry! Basilio's men are regrouping."

"We're coming," Marco says. He looks at me, tentative, as with a wounded animal. "Right?"

The gun's still pointed at his chest. With shaking hands, I finally lower it. He pulls me into his arms, tucking my head against his neck. I breathe Marco in. Springtime and leather. The fidelity is even better this time.

I shed the rest of my doubts. "Did they get it?"

"No, the data's safe. You're safe. Well, once we get out of here."

Marco helps me into an idling car in a nearby alley. No sooner than the door closes, gunfire pelts the exterior. A man I don't know in the passenger seat yells, "Go, go, go." Then, "God, what did they do to her?" as the car lurches forward.

I reach for my face, but Marco takes my hand and squeezes. "Callie, don't. We'll fix it. We'll fix everything."

* * *

I took up position underneath the one tree in the park, an old elm heavy with leaves, and settled in for a long wait. A couple of hours past sunset, but people still lingered, sitting on benches and staring off into space or walking the same circuit around and around again as they synched with friends or did whatever they did with their implants. Marco could have been any one of the men in the park. That he was there without me knowing sent an illicit little thrill through me even if I wouldn't act on it.

What skin would he come to me in this time? Slightly crossing my eyes, I tracked the visitors. That way I didn't get caught up on individual details and could just focus on the overall shape of the person. I narrowed down the candidates, but none of them would dare touch the steel points that traveled my spine and flanked my shoulders. The heat of Marco's fingers transmitted directly to my nerves, and I shivered despite the humid summer air. Fooled again.

"I confess, I've developed a fascination for these studs," Marco said in a heavy voice.

I faced him. His hair was slicked back and he was clean-shaven. He wore a suit that belonged on a used car lot. I arched a brow. "And the rest?"

His eyes drifted over the facial piercings, the bleached butch-cut hair, the contacts that made my eyes all pupil. Then he tugged at my neckline, checking for the digital plaque grafted to my left collarbone.

Merely a formality at this point. But I leaned in and pressed my face to his neck. I found the tattoo of the tree, winking with electronic ink. I also breathed him in. This was the closest I allowed myself to get to him these days.

He pulled back and shrugged, an elegant lift of his shoulders at odds with the sleaze radiating off his skin. "I think the eyes are the worst part."

"But I got into the biker rally."

A genuine smile graced his lips before he pushed it away. "So you did." I could still make him proud.

He stood next to me, our shoulders brushing, then he pressed closer, a folded piece of paper slipping into my pocket. "Your parlor assignment." By now I knew each one in the city. "They'll know which mods you'll need to pass."

He was all work tonight. "What is it this time?"

"Now, now. You know the rules."

"You're no fun anymore, Marco." I meant to be flip, but it cut too closely.

His eyes flashed, then reverted back to practiced indifference. "You're the only one who can change that." His hand slid back down along the studs, and I hissed. "After this," he said, "we should talk."

"I haven't changed my mind. Whatever you have to say, you can say now."

My voice pitched higher than normal. If he noticed, he didn't press his advantage. Instead he merely inclined his head. "Fine. You should know this is the last job."

"What? You're firing me?" That was low, even for him.

"No. And keep your voice down." He ran a hand through his hair and grimaced at the product that clung to his fingers. "I'm getting out. For good. I can't give you all the details yet, but you get this one right, and we walk away clean."

His gaze returned to my back. A gusty sigh escaped him. When he faced me again, the rawness I saw in his eyes hollowed me out. Our break was hurting both of us. He took my hand. Not a touch to cajole or capitulate. Just pure contact. My breath hitched when he squeezed.

"Come to the loft when it's finished. Please?"

I turned to go. Any longer, and I wouldn't be able to behave myself.

"And Callie, be careful on this one."

Something in his voice made me stop. "I'm always careful." I gave him a quick smile over my shoulder, then strode out of the park.

* * *

The plasticky smell of new mods fills my lungs. *No.* Not again. My body tenses, expecting restraints, but I can move – slowly but under my own power.

I claw the gauze off my face. Not the warehouse. Instead, the warm wood paneling of 'No Regrets' greets my eyes. My body relaxes before my brain catches up.

Marco stirs in the chair next to my bed. How fitting he brought me here. This must really be it. The end of an era. He looks exhausted but more like himself than ever before – what remains when his former skins are stripped away.

My hands go to my face – *my* face – free of mods. "They snatched me on the way to the meet. They wanted you. They were after…" I shake my head. "Your apartment. I told them… I didn't mean to. I –"

"Callie, it's okay. They tampered with your implant to extract information. It's not your fault."

The burning pain along my neck, the fact that they couldn't recreate Marco's tattoos or his scent. They could access my memories, but they needed *me* to put them into context, translating them into concrete information they could use to track him down.

I gasp, my hands checking over my arms and legs, the common places the information disks were embedded. "And the data?"

"Safe." Marco takes my hand. "A few weeks ago, the authorities approached me after investigating one of my long-term clients. Said if I turned over what info I had, they'd be able to protect us. When the competition found out I was trying to close shop, they started sniffing around for my records that weren't supposed to exist for the last three years. If not for you –"

Some of that hardness from before comes back into his eyes.

He squeezes my hand. "I almost didn't take the deal with the feds, but it was an easy way out. No more danger of being discovered, no more hiding. And I thought…"

"What?" I hold my breath as he struggles for words.

Finally his eyes meet mine. "That we could start over. Do things properly this time." There would be no more sneaking around, no more hiding what we felt. "But I'm not sure what'll happen when we get bored of being invisible."

Tugging him close, I trail my hand down his neck, along the tattooed tree branches dancing under my fingers. I breathe him in, chest tight with possibilities. "I don't know, but I'm sure we'll figure something out."

For right now, at least, we're exactly who we need to be.

The Ebony Box

Ellen Wood

Chapter I

IN ONE OR TWO of the papers already written for you, I have spoken of 'Lawyer Cockermuth,' as he was usually styled by his fellow-townspeople at Worcester. I am now going to tell of something that happened in his family; that actually did happen, and is no invention of mine.

Lawyer Cockermuth's house stood in the Foregate Street. He had practised in it for a good many years; he had never married, and his sister lived with him. She had been christened Betty; it was a more common name in those days than it is in these. There was a younger brother named Charles. They were tall, wiry men with long arms and legs. John, the lawyer, had a smiling, homely face; Charles was handsome, but given to be choleric.

Charles had served in the militia once, and had been ever since called Captain Cockermuth. When only twenty-one he married a young lady with a good bit of money; he had also a small income of his own; so he abandoned the law, to which he had been bred, and lived as a gentleman in a pretty little house on the outskirts of Worcester. His wife died in the course of a few years, leaving him with one child, a son, named Philip. The interest of Mrs. Charles Cockermuth's money would be enjoyed by her husband until his death, and then would go to Philip.

When Philip left school he was articled to his uncle, Lawyer Cockermuth, and took up his abode with him. Captain Cockermuth (who was of a restless disposition, and fond of roving), gave up his house then and went travelling about. Philip Cockermuth was a very nice steady young fellow, and his father was liberal to him in the way of pocket-money, allowing him a guinea a-week. Every Monday morning Lawyer Cockermuth handed (for his brother) to Philip a guinea in gold; the coin being in use then. Philip spent most of this in books, but he saved some of it; and by the time he was of age he had sixty golden guineas put aside in a small round black box of carved ebony. "What are you going to do with it, Philip?" asked Miss Cockermuth, as he brought it down from his room to show her. "I don't know what yet, Aunt Betty," said Philip, laughing. "I call it my nest-egg."

He carried the little black box (the sixty guineas quite filled it), back to his chamber and put it back into one of the pigeon-holes of the old-fashioned bureau which stood in the room, where he always kept it, and left it there, the bureau locked as usual. After that time, Philip put his spare money, now increased by a salary, into the Old Bank; and it chanced that he did not again look at the ebony box of gold, never supposing but that it was safe in its hiding-place. On the occasion of his marriage some years later, he laughingly remarked to Aunt Betty that he must now take his box of guineas into use; and he went up to fetch it. The box was not there.

Consternation ensued. The family flocked upstairs; the lawyer, Miss Betty, and the captain – who had come to Worcester for the wedding, and was staying in the house – one and all put their hands into the deep, dark pigeon-holes, but failed to find the box. The captain, a hot-tempered man, flew into a passion and swore over it; Miss Betty shed tears; Lawyer Cockermuth, always cool and genial, shrugged his shoulders and absolutely joked. None of them could form the slightest notion as to how the box had gone or who was likely to have taken it, and it had to be given up as a bad job.

Philip was married the next day, and left his uncle's house for good, having taken one out Barbourne way. Captain Cockermuth felt very sore about the loss of the box, he strode about Worcester talking of it, and swearing that he would send the thief to Botany Bay if he could find him.

A few years more yet, and poor Philip became ill. Ill of the disorder which had carried off his mother – decline. When Captain Cockermuth heard that his son was lying sick, he being (as usual) on his travels, he hastened to Worcester and took up his abode at his brother's – always his home on these visits. The disease was making very quick progress indeed; it was what is called 'rapid decline.' The captain called in all the famed doctors of the town – if they had not been called before: but there was no hope.

The day before Philip died, his father spoke to him about the box of guineas. It had always seemed to the captain that Philip must have, or ought to have, *some* notion of how it went. And he put the question to him again, solemnly, for the last time.

"Father," said the dying man – who retained all his faculties and his speech to the very end – "I declare to you that I have none. I have never been able to set up any idea at all upon the loss, or attach suspicion to a soul, living or dead. The two maids were honest; they would not have touched it; the clerks had no opportunity of going upstairs. I had always kept the key safely, and you know that we found the lock of the bureau had not been tampered with."

Poor Philip died. His widow and four children went to live at a pretty cottage on Malvern Link – upon a hundred pounds a-year, supplied to her by her father-in-law. Mr. Cockermuth added the best part of another hundred. These matters settled, Captain Cockermuth set off on his rovings again, considering himself hardly used by Fate at having his limited income docked of nearly half its value. And yet some more years passed on.

This much has been by way of introduction to what has to come. It was best to give it.

Mr. and Mrs. Jacobson, our neighbours at Dyke Manor, had a whole colony of nephews, what with brothers' sons and sisters' sons; of nieces also; batches of them would come over in relays to stay at Elm Farm, which had no children of its own. Samson Dene was the favourite nephew of all; his mother was sister to Mr. Jacobson, his father was dead. Samson Reginald Dene he was christened, but most people called him 'Sam.' He had been articled to the gentleman who took to his father's practice; a lawyer in a village in Oxfordshire. Later, he had gone to a firm in London for a year, had passed, and then came down to his uncle at Elm Farm, asking what he was to do next. For, upon his brother-in-law's death, Mr. Jacobson had taken upon himself the expenses of Sam, the eldest son.

"Want to know what you are to do now, eh?" cried old Jacobson, who was smoking his evening pipe by the wide fire of the dark-wainscoted, handsome dining-parlour, one evening in February. He was a tall, portly man with a fresh-coloured, healthy face; and not, I dare say, far off sixty years old. "What would you like to do? – What is your own opinion upon it, Sam?"

"I should like to set up in practice for myself, uncle."

"Oh, indeed! In what quarter of the globe, pray?"

"In Worcester. I have always wished to practise at Worcester. It is the assize town: I don't care for pettifogging places: one can't get on in them."

"You'd like to emerge all at once into a full-blown lawyer there? That's your notion, is it, Sam?"

Sam made no answer. He knew by the tone his notion was being laughed at.

"No, my lad. When you have been in some good office for another year or two maybe, then you might think about setting-up. The office can be in Worcester if you like."

"I am hard upon twenty-three, Uncle Jacobson. I have as much knowledge of law as I need."

"And as much steadiness also, perhaps?" said old Jacobson.

Sam turned as red as the table-cover. He was a frank-looking, slender young fellow of middle height, with fine wavy hair almost a gold colour and worn of a decent length. The present fashion – to be cropped as if you were a prison-bird and to pretend to like it so – was not favoured by gentlemen in those days.

"You may have been acquiring a knowledge of law in London, Sam; I hope you have; but you've been kicking up your heels over it. What about those sums of money you've more than once got out of your mother?"

Sam's face was a deeper red than the cloth now. "Did she tell you of it, uncle?" he gasped.

"No, she didn't; she cares too much for her graceless son to betray him. I chanced to hear of it, though."

"One has to spend so much in London," murmured Sam, in lame apology.

"I dare say! In my past days, sir, a young man had to cut his coat according to his cloth. We didn't rush into all kinds of random games and then go to our fathers or mothers to help us out of them. Which is what you've been doing, my gentleman."

"Does aunt know?" burst out Sam in a fright, as a step was heard on the stairs.

"I've not told her," said Mr. Jacobson, listening – "she is gone on into the kitchen. How much is it that you've left owing in London, Sam?"

Sam nearly choked. He did not perceive this was just a random shot: he was wondering whether magic had been at work.

"Left owing in London?" stammered he.

"That's what I asked. How much? And I mean to know. 'Twon't be of any use your fencing about the bush. Come! Tell it in a lump."

"Fifty pounds would cover it all, sir," said Sam, driven by desperation into the avowal.

"I want the truth, Sam."

"That is the truth, uncle, I put it all down in a list before leaving London; it comes to just under fifty pounds."

"How could you be so wicked as to contract it?"

"There has not been much wickedness about it," said Sam, miserably, "indeed there hasn't. One gets drawn into expenses unconsciously in the most extraordinary manner up in London. Uncle Jacobson, you may believe me or not, when I say that until I added it up, I did not think it amounted to twenty pounds in all."

"And then you found it to be fifty! How do you propose to pay this?"

"I intend to send it up by installments, as I can."

"Instead of doing which, you'll get into deeper debt at Worcester. If it's Worcester you go to."

"I hope not, uncle. I shall do my best to keep out of debt. I mean to be steady."

Mr. Jacobson filled a fresh pipe, and lighted it with a spill from the mantelpiece. He did not doubt the young fellow's intentions; he only doubted his resolution.

"You shall go into some lawyer's office in Worcester for two years, Sam, when we shall see how things turn out," said he presently. "And, look here, I'll pay these debts of yours myself, provided you promise me not to get into trouble again. There, no more" – interrupting Sam's grateful looks – "your aunt's coming in."

Sam opened the door for Mrs. Jacobson. A little pleasant-faced woman in a white net cap, with small flat silver curls under it. She carried a small basket lined with blue silk, in which lay her knitting.

"I've been looking to your room, my dear, to see that all's comfortable for you," she said to Sam, as she sat down by the table and the candles. "That new housemaid of ours is not altogether to be trusted. I suppose you've been telling your uncle all about the wonders of London?"

"And something else, too," put in old Jacobson gruffly. "He wanted to set up in practice for himself at Worcester: off-hand, red-hot!"

"Oh dear!" said Mrs. Jacobson.

"That's what the boy wanted, nothing less. No. Another year or two's work in some good house, to acquire stability and experience, and then he may talk about setting up. It will be all for the best, Sam; trust me."

"Well, uncle, perhaps it will." It was of no use for him to say perhaps it won't: he could not help himself. But it was a disappointment.

Mr. Jacobson walked over to Dyke Manor the next day, to consult the Squire as to the best lawyer to place Sam with, himself suggesting their old friend Cockermuth. He described all Sam's wild ways (it was how he put it) in that dreadful place, London, and the money he had got out of amidst its snares. The Squire took up the matter with his usual hearty sympathy, and quite agreed that no practitioner in the law could be so good for Sam as John Cockermuth.

John Cockermuth proved to be agreeable. He was getting to be an elderly man then, but was active as ever, saving when a fit of the gout took him. He received young Dene in his usual cheery manner, upon the day appointed for his entrance, and assigned him his place in the office next to Mr. Parslet. Parslet had been there more than twenty years; he was, so to say, at the top and tail of all the work that went on in it, but he was not a qualified solicitor. Samson Dene was qualified, and could therefore represent Mr. Cockermuth before the magistrates and what not: of which the old lawyer expected to find the benefit.

"Where are you going to live?" he questioned of Sam that first morning.

"I don't know yet, sir. Mr. and Mrs. Jacobson are about the town now, I believe, looking for lodgings for me. Of course they couldn't let *me* look; they'd think I should be taken in," added Sam.

"Taken in and done for," laughed the lawyer. "I should not wonder but Mr. Parslet could accommodate you. Can you, Parslet?"

Mr. Parslet looked up from his desk, his thin cheeks flushing. He was small and slight, with weak brown hair, and had a patient, sad sort of look in his face and in his meek, dark eyes.

James Parslet was one of those men who are said to spoil their own lives. Left alone early, he was looked after by a bachelor uncle, a minor canon of the cathedral, who perhaps tried to do his duty by him in a mild sort of manner. But young Parslet liked to go his own ways, and they were not very good ways. He did not stay at any calling he was put to, trying first one and then another; either the people got tired of him, or he of them. Money (when he got any) burnt a hole in his pocket, and his coats grew shabby and his boots dirty. "Poor Jamie Parslet! How he has spoilt his life," cried the town, shaking its pitying head at him: and thus things went on till he grew to be nearly thirty years of age. Then, to the public astonishment, Jamie pulled up. He got taken on by Lawyer Cockermuth as copying clerk at twenty shillings a-week, married, and became as steady as Old Time. He had been nothing but steady from that day to this, had forty shillings a-week now, instead of twenty, and was ever a meek, subdued man, as if he carried about with him a perpetual repentance for the past, regret for the life that might have been. He lived in Edgar Street, which is close to the cathedral, as every one knows, Edgar Tower being at the top of it. An old gentleman attached to the cathedral had now lodged in his house for ten years, occupying the drawing room floor; he had recently died, and hence Lawyer Cockermuth's suggestion.

Mr. Parslet looked up. "I should be happy to, sir," he said; "if our rooms suited Mr. Dene. Perhaps he would like to look at them?"

"I will," said Sam. "If my uncle and aunt do not fix on any for me."

Is there any subtle mesmeric power, I wonder, that influences things unconsciously? Curious to say, at this very moment Mr. and Mrs. Jacobson were looking at these identical rooms. They had driven into Worcester with Sam very early indeed, so as to have a long day before them, and when breakfast was over at the inn, took the opportunity, which they very rarely got, of slipping into the cathedral to hear the beautiful ten-o'clock service. Coming out the cloister way when it was over, and so down Edgar Street, Mrs. Jacobson espied a card in a window with 'Lodgings' on it. "I wonder if they would suit Sam?" she cried to her husband. "Edgar Street is a nice, wide, open street, and quiet. Suppose we look at them?"

A young servant-maid, called by her mistress 'Sally,' answered the knock. Mrs. Parslet, a capable, bustling woman of ready speech and good manners, came out of the parlour, and took the visitors to the floor above. They liked the rooms and they liked Mrs. Parslet; they also liked the moderate rent asked, for respectable country people in those days did not live by shaving one another; and when it came out that the house's master had been clerk to Lawyer Cockermuth for twenty years, they settled the matter off-hand, without the ceremony of consulting Sam. Mrs. Jacobson looked upon Sam as a boy still. Mr. Jacobson might have done the same but for the debts made in London.

And all this, you will say, has been yet more explanation; but I could not help it. The real thing begins now, with Sam Dene's sojourn in Mr. Cockermuth's office, and his residence in Edgar Street.

The first Sunday of his stay there, Sam went out to attend the morning service in the cathedral, congratulating himself that that grand edifice stood so conveniently near, and looking, it must be confessed, a bit of a dandy, for he had put a little bunch of spring violets into his coat, and 'button-holes' were quite out of the common way then. The service began with the Litany, the earlier service of prayers being held at eight o'clock. Sam Dene has not yet forgotten that day, for it is no imaginary person I am telling you of, and never will forget it. The Reverend Allen Wheeler chanted, and the prebendary in residence (Somers Cocks) preached. While wondering when the sermon (a very good one) would be over, and thinking it rather prosy, after the custom of young men, Sam's roving gaze was drawn to a young lady sitting in the long seat opposite to him on the other side of the choir, whose whole attention appeared to be given to the preacher, to whom her head was turned. It is a nice face, thought Sam; such a sweet expression in it. It really was a nice face, rather pretty, gentle and thoughtful, a patient look in the dark brown eyes. She had on a well-worn dark silk, and a straw bonnet; all very quiet and plain; but she looked very much of a lady. 'Wonder if she sits there always?' thought Sam.

Service over, he went home, and was about to turn the handle of the door to enter (looking another way) when he found it turned for him by some one who was behind and had stretched out a hand to do it. Turning quickly, he saw the same young lady.

"Oh, I beg your pardon," said Sam, all at sea; "did you wish to come in here?"

"If you please," she answered – and her voice was sweet and her manner modest.

"Oh," repeated Sam, rather taken aback at the answer. "You did not want me, did you?"

"Thank you, it is my home," she said.

"Your home?" stammered Sam, for he had not seen the ghost of any one in the house yet, saving his landlord and landlady and Sally. "Here?"

"Yes. I am Maria Parslet."

He stood back to let her enter; a slender, gentle girl of middle height; she looked about eighteen, Sam thought (she was that and two years on to it), and he wondered where she had been hidden. He had to go out again, for he was invited to dine at Lawyer Cockermuth's, so he saw no more of the young lady that day; but she kept dancing about in his memory. And somehow she so fixed herself in it, and as the time went on so grew in it, and at last so filled it, that Sam may well hold that day as a marked day – the one that introduced him to Maria Parslet. But that is anticipating.

On the Monday morning all his ears and eyes were alert, listening and looking for Maria. He did not see her; he did not hear a sound of her. By degrees he got to learn that the young lady was resident teacher in a lady's school hard by; and that she was often allowed to spend the whole day at home on Sundays. One Sunday evening he ingeniously got himself invited to take tea in Mrs. Parslet's parlour, and thus became acquainted with Maria; but his opportunities for meeting her were rare.

There's not much to tell of the first twelvemonth. It passed in due course. Sam Dene was fairly steady. He made a few debts, as some young men, left to themselves, can't help making – at least, they'd tell you they can't. Sundry friends of Sam's in Worcester knew of this, and somehow it reached Mr. Cockermuth's ears, who gave Sam a word of advice privately.

This was just as the first year expired. According to agreement, Sam had another year to stay. He entered upon it with inward gloom. On adding up his scores, which he deemed it as well to do after his master's lecture, he again found that they amounted to far more than he had thought for, and how he should contrive to pay them out of his own resources he knew no more than the man in the moon. In short, he could not do it; he was in a fix; and lived in perpetual dread of its coming to the ears of his uncle Jacobson.

* * *

The spring assize, taking place early in March, was just over; the judges had left the town for Stafford, and Worcester was settling down again to quietness. Miss Cockermuth gave herself and her two handmaidens a week's rest – assize time being always a busy and bustling period at the lawyer's, no end of chance company looking in – and then the house began its spring cleaning, a grand institution with our good grandmothers, often lasting a couple of weeks. This time, at the lawyer's house, it was to be a double bustle; for visitors were being prepared for.

It had pleased Captain Cockermuth to write word that he should be at home for Easter; upon which, the lawyer and his sister decided to invite Philip's widow and her children also to spend it with them; they knew Charles would be pleased. Easter Day was very early indeed that year, falling at the end of March.

To make clearer what's coming, the house had better have a word or two of description. You entered from the street into a wide passage; no steps. On the left was the parlour and general sitting room, in which all meals were usually taken. It was a long, low room, its two rather narrow windows looking upon the street, the back of the room being a little dark. Opposite the door was the fireplace. On the other side the passage, facing the parlour-door, was the door that opened to the two rooms (one front, one back) used as the lawyer's offices. The kitchens and staircase were at the back of the passage, a garden lying beyond; and there was a handsome drawing room on the first floor, not much used.

The house, I say, was in a commotion with the spring cleaning, and the other preparations. To accommodate so many visitors required contrivance: a bedroom for the captain, a bedroom for his daughter-in-law, two bedrooms for the children. Mistress and maids held momentous consultations together.

"We have decided to put the three little girls in Philip's old room, John," said Miss Betty to her brother, as they sat in the parlour after dinner on the Monday evening of the week preceding Passion Week; "and little Philip can have the small room off mine. We shall have to get in a child's bed, though; I can't put the three little girls in one bed; they might get fighting. John, I do wish you'd sell that old bureau for what it will fetch."

"Sell the old bureau!" exclaimed Mr. Cockermuth.

"I'm sure I should. What good does it do? Unless that bureau goes out of the room, we can't put the extra bed in. I've been in there half the day with Susan and Ann, planning and contriving, and we find it can't be done any way. Do let Ward take it away, John; there's no place for it in the other chambers. He'd give you a fair price for it, I dare say."

Miss Betty had never cared for this piece of furniture, thinking it more awkward than useful: she looked eagerly at her brother, awaiting his decision. She was the elder of the two; tall, like him; but whilst he maintained his thin, wiry form, just the shape of an upright gas-post with arms, she had grown stout with no shape at all. Miss Betty had dark, thick eyebrows and an amiable red face. She wore a 'front' of brown curls with a high and dressy cap perched above it. This evening her gown was of soft twilled shot-green silk, a white net kerchief was crossed under its body, and she had on a white muslin apron.

"I don't mind," assented the lawyer, as easy in disposition as Miss Betty was; "it's of no use keeping it that I know of. Send for Ward and ask him, if you like, Betty."

Ward, a carpenter and cabinet-maker, who had a shop in the town and sometimes bought second-hand things, was sent for by Miss Betty on the following morning; and he agreed, after some chaffering, to buy the old bureau. It was the bureau from which Philip's box of gold had disappeared – but I dare say you have understood that. In the midst of all this stir and clatter, just as Ward betook himself away after concluding the negotiation, and the maids were hard at work above stairs with mops and pails and scrubbing-brushes, the first advance-guard of the visitors unexpectedly walked in: Captain Cockermuth.

Miss Betty sat down in an access of consternation. She could do nothing but stare. He had not been expected for a week yet; there was nothing ready and nowhere to put him.

"I wish you'd take to behaving like a rational being, Charles!" she exclaimed. "We are all in a mess; the rooms upside down, and the bedside carpets hanging out at the windows."

Captain Cockermuth said he did not care for bedside carpets, he could sleep anywhere – on the brewhouse-bench, if she liked. He quite approved of selling the old bureau, when told it was going to be done.

Ward had appointed five o'clock that evening to fetch it away. They were about to sit down to dinner when he came, five o'clock being the hour for late dinners then in ordinary life. Ward had brought a man with him and they went upstairs.

Miss Betty, as carver, sat at the top of the dining-table, her back to the windows, the lawyer in his place at the foot, Charles between them, facing the fire. Miss Betty was cutting off the first joint of a loin of veal when the bureau was heard coming down the staircase, with much bumping and noise.

Mr. Cockermuth stepped out of the dining room to look on. The captain followed: being a sociable man with his fellow-townspeople, he went to ask Ward how he did.

The bureau came down safely, and was lodged at the foot of the stairs; the man wiped his hot face, while Ward spoke with Captain Cockermuth. It seemed quite a commotion in the usual quiet dwelling. Susan, a jug of ale in her hand, which she had been to the cellar to draw, stood looking on from the passage; Mr. Dene and a younger clerk, coming out of the office just then to leave for the evening, turned to look on also.

"I suppose there's nothing in here, sir?" cried Ward, returning to business and the bureau.

"Nothing, I believe," replied Mr. Cockermuth.

"Nothing at all," called out Miss Betty through the open parlour-door. "I emptied the drawers this morning."

Ward, a cautious man and honest, drew back the lid and put his hand in succession into the pigeon-holes; which had not been used since Philip's time. There were twelve of them; three above, and three below on each side, and a little drawer that locked in the middle. "Halloa!" cried Ward, when his hand was in the depth of one of them: "here's something."

And he drew forth the lost box. The little ebony box with all the gold in it.

Well now, that was a strange thing. Worcester thinks so, those people who are still living to remember it, to this day. How it was that the box had appeared to be lost and was searched for in vain over and over again, by poor Philip and others; and how it was that it was now recovered in this easy and natural manner, was never explained or accounted for. Ward's opinion was that the box must have been put in, side upwards, that it had in some way stuck to the back of the deep, narrow pigeon-hole, which just about held the box in width, that those who had searched took the box for the back of the hole when their fingers touched it and that the bumping of the bureau now in coming downstairs had dislodged the box and brought it forward. As a maker of bureaus, Ward's opinion was listened to with deference. Any way, it was a sort of theory, serving passably well in the absence of any other. But who knew? All that was certain about it was the fact; the loss and the recovery after many years. It happened just as here described, as I have already said.

Sam Dene had never heard of the loss. Captain Cockermuth, perfectly beside himself with glee, explained it to him. Sam laughed as he touched with his forefinger the closely packed golden guineas, lying there so snug and safe, offered his congratulations, and walked home to tea.

It chanced that on that especial Tuesday evening, matters were at sixes and sevens in the Parslets' house. Sally had misbehaved herself and was discharged in consequence; and the servant engaged in her place, who was to have entered that afternoon, had not made her appearance. When Sam entered, Maria came out of the parlour, a pretty blush upon her face. And to Sam the unexpected sight of her, it was not often he got a chance of it, and the blush and the sweet eyes came like a gleam of Eden, for he had grown to love her dearly. Not that he had owned it to himself yet.

Maria explained. Her school had broken up for the Easter holidays earlier than it ought, one of the girls showing symptoms of measles; and her mother had gone out to see what had become of the new servant, leaving a request that Mr. Dene would take his tea with them in the parlour that evening, as there was no one to wait on him.

Nothing loth, you may be sure, Mr. Dene accepted the invitation, running up to wash his hands, and give a look at his hair, and running down in a trice. The tea-tray stood in readiness on the parlour table, Maria sitting behind it. Perhaps she had given a look at *her* hair, for it was quite more lovely, Sam thought, more soft and silken than any hair he had ever seen. The little copper kettle sang away on the hob by the fire.

"Will papa be long, do you know?" began Maria demurely, feeling shy and conscious at being thus thrown alone into Sam's company. "I had better not make the tea until he comes in."

"I don't know at all," answered Sam. "He went out on some business for Mr. Cockermuth at half-past four, and was not back when I left. Such a curious thing has just happened up there, Miss Parslet!"

"Indeed! What is it?"

Sam entered on the narrative. Maria, who knew all about the strange loss of the box, grew quite excited as she listened. "Found!" she exclaimed. "Found in the same bureau! And all the golden guineas in it!"

"Every one," said Sam: "as I take it. They were packed right up to the top!"

"Oh, what a happy thing!" repeated Maria, in a fervent tone that rather struck Sam, and she clasped her fingers into one another, as one sometimes does in pleasure or in pain.

"Why do you say that, Miss Parslet?"

"Because papa – but I do not think I ought to tell you," added Maria, breaking off abruptly.

"Oh yes, you may. I am quite safe, even if it's a secret. Please do."

"Well," cried the easily persuaded girl, "papa has always had an uncomfortable feeling upon him ever since the loss. He feared that some people, knowing he was not well off, might think perhaps it was he who had stolen upstairs and taken it."

Sam laughed at that.

"He has never *said* so, but somehow we have seen it, my mother and I. It was altogether so mysterious a loss, you see, affording no clue as to *when* it occurred, that people were ready to suspect anything, however improbable. Oh, I am thankful it is found!"

The kettle went on singing, the minutes went on flitting, and still nobody came. Six o'clock struck out from the cathedral as Mr. Parslet entered. Had the two been asked the time, they might have said it was about a quarter-past five. Golden hours fly quickly; fly on angels' wings.

Now it chanced that whilst they were at tea, a creditor of Sam's came to the door, one Jonas Badger. Sam went to him: and the colloquy that ensued might be heard in the parlour. Mr. Badger said (in quite a fatherly way) that he really could not be put off any longer with promises; if his money was not repaid to him before Easter he should be obliged to take steps about it, should write to Mr. Jacobson, of Elm Farm, to begin with. Sam returned to the tea-table with a wry face.

Soon after that, Mrs. Parslet came in, the delinquent servant in her rear. Next, a friend of Sam's called, Austin Chance, whose father was a solicitor in good practice in the town. The two young men, who were very intimate and often together, went up to Sam's room above.

"I say, my good young friend," began Chance, in a tone that might be taken for jest or earnest, "don't you go and get into any entanglement in that quarter."

"What d'you mean now?" demanded Sam, turning the colour of the rising sun.

"I mean Maria Parslet," said Austin Chance, laughing. "She's a deuced nice girl; I know that; just the one a fellow might fall in love with unawares. But it wouldn't do, Dene."

"Why wouldn't it do?"

"Oh, come now, Sam, you know it wouldn't. Parslet is only a working clerk at Cockermuth's."

"I should like to know what has put the thought in your head?" contended Sam. "You had better put it out again. I've never told you I was falling in love with her; or told herself, either. Mrs. Parslet would be about me, I expect, if I did. She looks after her as one looks after gold."

"Well, I found you in their room, having tea with them, and –"

"It was quite an accident; an exceptional thing," interrupted Sam.

"Well," repeated Austin, "you need not put your back up, old fellow; a friendly warning does no harm. Talking of gold, Dene, I've done my best to get up the twenty pounds you wanted to borrow of me, and I can't do it. I'd let you have it with all my heart if I could; but I find I am harder up than I thought for."

Which was all true. Chance was as good-natured a young man as ever lived, but at this early stage of his life he made more debts than he could pay.

"Badger has just been here, whining and covertly threatening," said Sam. "I am to pay up in a week, or he'll make me pay – and tell my uncle, he says, to begin with."

"Hypocritical old skinflint!" ejaculated Chance, himself sometimes in the hands of Mr. Badger – a worthy gentleman who did a little benevolent usury in a small and quiet way, and took his delight in accommodating safe young men. A story was whispered that young M., desperately hard-up, borrowed two pounds from him one Saturday night, undertaking to repay it, with two pounds added on for interest, that day month; and when the day came and M. had not got the money, or was at all likely to get it, he carried off a lot of his mother's plate under his coat to the pawnbroker's.

"And there's more besides Badger's that is pressing," went on Dene. "I must get money from somewhere, or it will play the very deuce with me. I wonder whether Charley Hill could lend me any?"

"Don't much think so. You might ask him. Money seems scarce with Hill always. Has a good many ways for it, I fancy."

"Talking of money, Chance, a lot has been found at Cockermuth's today. A boxful of guineas that has been lost for years."

Austin Chance stared. "You don't mean that box of guineas that mysteriously disappeared in Philip's time?"

"Well, they say so. It is a small, round box of carved ebony, and it is stuffed to the brim with old guineas. Sixty of them, I hear."

"I can't believe it's true; that *that's* found."

"Not believe it's true, Chance! Why, I saw it. Saw the box found, and touched the guineas with my fingers. It has been hidden in an old bureau all the time," added Sam, and he related the particulars of the discovery.

"What an extraordinary thing!" exclaimed young Chance: "the queerest start I ever heard of." And he fell to musing.

But the 'queer start,' as Mr. Austin Chance was pleased to designate the resuscitation of the box, did not prove to be a lucky one.

Chapter II

THE SUN SHONE brightly on Foregate Street, but did not yet touch the front-windows on Lawyer Cockermuth's side of it. Miss Betty Cockermuth sat near one of them in the parlour, spectacles on nose, and hard at work unpicking the braid off some very old woollen curtains, green once, but now faded to a sort of dingy brown. It was Wednesday morning, the day following the wonderful event of finding the box, lost so long, full of its golden guineas. In truth nobody thought of it as anything less than marvellous.

The house-cleaning, in preparation for Easter and Easter's visitors, was in full flow today, and would be for more than a week to come; the two maids were hard at it above. Ward, who did not disdain to labour with his own hands, was at the house, busy at some mysterious business in the brewhouse, coat off, shirt-sleeves stripped up to elbow, plunging at that moment something or other into the boiling water of the furnace.

"How I could have let them remain up so long in this state, I can't think," said Miss Betty to herself, arresting her employment, scissors in hand, to regard the dreary curtains. She had drawn the table towards her from the middle of the room, and the heavy work was upon it. Susan came in to impart some domestic news.

"Ward says there's a rare talk in the town about the finding of that box, missis," cried she, when she had concluded it. "My! How bad them curtains look, now they're down!"

Servants were on more familiar terms with their mistresses in those days without meaning, or showing, any disrespect; identifying themselves, as it were, with the family and its interests. Susan, a plump, red-cheeked young woman turned thirty, had been housemaid in her present place for seven years. She had promised a baker's head man to marry him, but never could be got to fix the day. In winter she'd say to him, "Wait till summer;" and when summer came, she'd say, "Wait till winter." Miss Betty commended her prudence.

"Yes," said she now, in answer to the girl, "I've been wondering how we could have kept them up so long; they are not fit for much, I'm afraid, save the ragbag. Chintz will make the room look much nicer."

As Susan left the parlour, Captain Cockermuth entered it, a farmer with him who had come in from Hallow to the Wednesday's market. The captain's delighted excitement at the finding of the box had not at all subsided; he had dreamt of it, he talked of it, he pinned every acquaintance he could pick up this morning and brought him in to see the box of gold. Independently of its being a very great satisfaction to have had the old mysterious loss cleared up, the sixty guineas would be a huge boon to the captain's pocket.

"But how was it that none of you ever found it, if it remained all this while in the pigeon-hole?" cried the wondering farmer, bending over the little round box of guineas, which the captain placed upon the table open, the lid by its side.

"Well, we didn't find it, that's all I know; or poor Philip, either," said Captain Cockermuth.

The farmer took his departure. As the captain was showing him to the front-door, another gentleman came hustling in. It was Thomas Chance the lawyer, father of the young man who had been the previous night with Samson Dene. He and Lawyer Cockermuth were engaged together just then in some complicated, private, and very disagreeable business, each acting for a separate client, who were the defendants against a great wrong – or what they thought was one.

"Come in, Chance, and take a look at my box of guineas, resuscitated from the grave," cried the captain, joyously. "You can go into the office to John afterwards."

"Well, I've hardly time this morning," answered Mr. Chance, turning, though, into the parlour and shaking hands with Miss Betty. "Austin told me it was found."

Now it happened that Lawyer Cockermuth came then into the parlour himself, to get something from his private desk-table which stood there. When the box had been discussed, Mr. Chance took a letter from his pocket and placed it in his brother practitioner's hands.

"What do you think of that?" he asked. "I got it by post this morning."

"Think! Why, that it is of vital importance," said Mr. Cockermuth when he had read it.

"Yes; no doubt of that. But what is to be our next move in answer to it?" asked the other.

Seeing they were plunging into business, the captain strolled away to the front-door, which stood open all day, for the convenience of those coming to the office, and remained there whistling, his hands in his pockets, on the look out for somebody else to bring in. He had put the lid on the box of guineas, and left the box on the table.

"I should like to take a copy of this letter," said Mr. Cockermuth to the other lawyer.

"Well, you can take it," answered Chance. "Mind who does it, though – Parslet, or somebody else that's confidential. Don't let it go into the office."

"You are wanted, sir," said Mr. Dene, from the door.

"Who is it?" asked his master.

"Mr. Chamberlain. He says he is in a hurry."

"I'm coming. Here, Dene!" he called out as the latter was turning away: and young Dene came back again.

"Sit down here, now, and take a copy of this letter," cried the lawyer, rapidly drawing out and opening the little writing-desk table that stood against the wall at the back of the room. "Here's pen, ink and paper, all ready: the letter is confidential, you perceive."

He went out of the room as he spoke, Mr. Chance with him; and Sam Dene sat down to commence his task, after exchanging a few words with Miss Betty, with whom he was on good terms.

"Charles makes as much fuss over this little box as if it were filled with diamonds from Golconda, instead of guineas," remarked she, pointing with her scissors to the box, which stood near her on the table, to direct the young man's attention to it. "I don't know how many folks he has not brought in already to have a look at it."

"Well, it was a capital find, Miss Betty; one to be proud of," answered Sam, settling to his work.

For some little time nothing was heard but the scratching of Mr. Dene's pen and the clicking of Miss Betty's scissors. Her task was nearing completion. A few minutes more, and the last click was given, the last bit of the braid was off. "And I'm glad of it," cried she aloud, flinging the end of the curtain on the top of the rest.

"This braid will do again for something or other," considered Miss Betty, as she began to wind it upon an old book. "It was put on fresh only three or four years ago. Well brushed, it will look almost like new."

Again Susan opened the door. "Miss Betty, here's the man come with the chintz: five or six rolls of it for you to choose from," cried she. "Shall he come in here?"

Miss Betty was about to say "Yes," but stopped and said "No," instead. The commotion of holding up the chintzes to the light, to judge of their different merits, might disturb Mr. Dene; and she knew better than to interrupt business.

"Let him take them to the room where they are to hang, Susan; we can judge best there."

Tossing the braid to Susan, who stood waiting at the door, Miss Betty hastily took up her curtains, and Susan held the door open for her mistress to pass through.

Choosing chintz for window-curtains takes some time; as everybody knows whose fancy is erratic. And how long Miss Betty and Susan and the young man from the chintz-mart had been doubting and deciding and doubting again, did not quite appear, when Captain Cockermuth's voice was heard ascending from below.

"Betty! Are you upstairs, Betty?"

"Yes, I'm here," she called back, crossing to the door to speak. "Do you want me, Charles?"

"Where have you put the box?"

"What box?"

"The box of guineas."

"It is on the table."

"It is not on the table. I can't see it anywhere."

"It was on the table when I left the parlour. I did not touch it. Ask Mr. Dene where it is: I left him there."

"Mr. Dene's not here. I wish you'd come down."

"Very well; I'll come in a minute or two," concluded Miss Betty, going back to the chintzes.

"Why, I saw that box on the table as I shut the door after you had come out, ma'am," observed Susan, who had listened to the colloquy.

"So did I," said Miss Betty; "it was the very last thing my eyes fell on. If young Mr. Dene finished what he was about and left the parlour, I dare say he put the box up somewhere for safety. I think, Susan, we must fix upon this light pea-green with the rosebuds running up it. It matches the paper: and the light coming through it takes quite a nice shade."

A little more indecision yet; and yet a little more, as to whether the curtains should be lined, or not, and then Miss Cockermuth went downstairs. The captain was pacing the passage to and fro impatiently.

"Now then, Betty, where's my box?"

"But how am I to know where the box is, Charles, if it's not on the table?" she remonstrated, turning into the parlour, where two friends of the captain's waited to be regaled with the sight of the recovered treasure. "I had to go upstairs with the young man who brought the chintzes; and I left the box here" – indicating the exact spot on the table. "It was where you left it yourself. I did not touch it at all."

She shook hands with the visitors. Captain Cockermuth looked gloomy – as if he were at sea and had lost his reckoning.

"If you had to leave the room, why didn't you put the box up?" asked he. "A boxful of guineas shouldn't be left alone in an empty room."

"But Mr. Dene was in the room; he sat at the desk there, copying a letter for John. As to why didn't I put the box up, it was not my place to do so that I know of. You were about yourself, Charles – only at the front-door, I suppose."

Captain Cockermuth was aware that he had not been entirely at the front-door. Two or three times he had crossed over to hold a chat with acquaintances on the other side the way; had strolled with one of them nearly up to Salt Lane and back. Upon catching hold of these two gentlemen, now brought in, he had found the parlour empty of occupants and the box not to be seen.

"Well, this is a nice thing – that a man can't put his hand upon his own property when he wants to, or hear where it is!" grumbled he. "And what business on earth had Dene to meddle with the box?"

"To put it in safety – if he did meddle with it, and a sensible thing to do," retorted Miss Betty, who did not like to be scolded unjustly. "Just like you, Charles, making a fuss over nothing! Why don't you go and ask young Dene where it is?"

"Young Dene is not in. And John's not in. Nobody is in but Parslet; and he does not know anything about it. I must say, Betty, you manage the house nicely!" concluded the captain ironically, giving way to his temper.

This was, perhaps the reader may think, commotion enough 'over nothing,' as Miss Betty put it. But it was not much as compared with the commotion which set in later. When Mr. Cockermuth came in, he denied all knowledge of it, and Sam Dene was impatiently waited for.

It was past two o'clock when he returned, for he had been home to dinner. The good-looking young fellow turned in at the front-door with a fleet step, and encountered Captain Cockermuth, who attacked him hotly, demanding what he had done with the box.

"Ah," said Sam, lightly and coolly, "Parslet said you were looking for it." Mr. Parslet had in fact mentioned it at home over his dinner.

"Well, where is it?" said the captain. "Where did you put it?"

"I?" cried young Dene. "Not anywhere. Should I be likely to touch the box, sir? I saw the box on that table while I was copying a letter for Mr. Cockermuth; that's all I know of it."

The captain turned red, and pale, and red again. "Do you mean to tell me to my face, Mr. Dene, that the box is *gone*?"

"I'm sure I don't know," said Sam in the easiest of all easy tones. "It seems to be gone."

The box was gone. Gone once more with all its golden guineas. It could not be found anywhere; in the house or out of the house, upstairs or down. The captain searched frantically, the others helped him, but no trace of it could be found.

At first it was impossible to believe it. That this self-same box should mysteriously have vanished a second time, seemed to be too marvellous for fact. But it was true.

Nobody would admit a share in the responsibility. The captain left the box safe amidst (as he put it) a roomful of people: Miss Betty considered that she left it equally safe, with Mr. Dene seated at the writing-table, and the captain dodging (as *she* put it) in and out. Mr. Cockermuth had not entered the parlour since he left it, when called to Mr. Chamberlain, with whom he had gone out. Sam Dene reiterated that he had not meddled with the box; no, nor thought about it.

Sam's account, briefly given, was this. After finishing copying the letter, he closed the little table-desk and pushed it back to its place against the wall, and had carried the letter and the copy into the office. Finding Mr. Cockermuth was not there, he locked them up in his own desk, having to go to the Guildhall upon some business. The business there took up some time, in fact until past one o'clock, and he then went home to dinner.

"And did you consider it right, Sam Dene, to leave a valuable box like that on the table, unguarded?" demanded Captain Cockermuth, as they all stood together in the parlour, after questioning Sam; and the captain had been looking so fierce and speaking so sharply that it might be thought he was taking Sam for the thief, off-hand.

"To tell the truth, captain, I never thought of the box," answered Sam. "I might not have noticed that the box was in the room at all but for Miss Betty's drawing my attention to it. After that, I grew so much interested in the letter I was copying (for I know all about the cause, as Mr. Cockermuth is aware, and it was curious news) that I forgot everything else."

Lawyer Cockermuth nodded to confirm this. The captain went on.

"Betty drew your attention to it, did she? Why did she draw it? In what way?"

"Well, she remarked that you made as much fuss over that box as if it were filled with diamonds," replied the young man, glad to pay out the captain for his angry and dictatorial tone. But the captain was in truth beginning to entertain a very ominous suspicion.

"Do you wish to deny, Samson Dene, that my sister Betty left that box on the table when she quitted the room?"

"Why, who does?" cried Sam. "When Miss Betty says she left the box on the table, of course she did leave it. She must know. Susan, it seems, also saw that it was left there."

"And you could see that box of guineas standing stark staring on the table, and come out of the room and leave it to its fate!" foamed the captain. "Instead of giving me a call to say nobody was on guard here!"

"I didn't see it," returned Sam. "There's no doubt it was there, but I did not see it. I never looked towards the table as I came out, that I know of. The table, as I dare say you remember, was not in its usual place; it was up there by the window. The box had gone clean out of my thoughts."

"Well, Mr. Dene, my impression is that *you have got the box*," cried the angry captain.

"Oh, is it!" returned Sam, with supreme good humour, and just the least suspicion of a laugh. "A box like that would be uncommonly useful to me."

"I expect, young man, the guineas would!"

"Right you are, captain."

But Captain Cockermuth regarded this mocking pleasantry as particularly ill-timed. *He believed the young man was putting it on to divert suspicion from himself.*

"Who did take the box?" questioned he. "Tell me that."

"I wish I could, sir."

"How could the box vanish off the table unless it was taken, I ask you?"

"That's a puzzling question," coolly rejoined Sam. "It was too heavy for the rats, I expect."

"Oh dear, but we have no rats in the house," cried Miss Betty. "I wish we had, I'm sure – and could find the box in their holes." She was feeling tolerably uncomfortable. Placid and easy in a general way, serious worry always upset her considerably.

Captain Cockermuth's suspicions were becoming certainties. The previous night, when his brother had been telling him various items of news of the old town, as they sat confidentially over the fire after Miss Betty had gone up to bed, Mr. Cockermuth chanced to mention the fact that young Dene had been making a few debts. Not speaking in any ill-natured spirit, quite the contrary, for he liked the young man amazingly. Only a few, he continued; thoughtless young men would do so; and he had given him a lecture. And then he laughingly added the information that Mr. Jacobson had imparted to him twelve months ago, in their mutual friendship – of the debts Sam had made in London.

No sensible person can be surprised that Charles Cockermuth recalled this now. It rankled in his mind. Had Sam Dene taken the box of guineas to satisfy these debts contracted during the past year at Worcester? It looked like it. And the longer the captain dwelt on it, the more and more likely it grew to look.

All the afternoon the search was kept up by the captain. Not an individual article in the parlour but was turned inside out; he wanted to have the carpet up. His brother and Sam Dene had returned to their work in the office as usual. The captain was getting to feel like a raging bear; three times Miss Betty had to stop him in a dreadful fit of swearing; and when dinner-time came he could not eat. It was a beautiful slice of Severn salmon, which had its price, I can tell you, in Worcester then, and minced veal, and a jam tart, all of which dishes Charles Cockermuth especially favoured. But the loss of the sixty guineas did away with his appetite. Mr. Cockermuth, who took the loss very coolly, laughed at him.

The laughing did not mend the captain's temper: neither did the hearing that Sam Dene had departed for home as usual at five o'clock. Had Sam been innocent, he would at least have come to the parlour and inquired whether the box was found, instead of sneaking off home to tea.

Fretting and fuming, raging and stamping, disturbing the parlour's peace and his own, strode Charles Cockermuth. His good-humoured brother John bore it for an hour or two, and then told him he might as well go outside and stamp on the pavement for a bit.

"I will," said Charles. Catching up his hat, saying nothing to anybody, he strode off to see the sergeant of police – Dutton – and laid the case concisely before him: The box of guineas was on the table where his sister sat at work; her work being at one end, the box at the other. Sam Dene was also in the room, copying a letter at the writing-table. Miss Betty was called upstairs; she went, leaving the box on the table. It was the last thing she saw as she left the room; the servant, who had come to call her, also saw it standing there. Presently young Dene also left the room and the house; and from that moment the box was never seen.

"What do you make of that, Mr. Dutton?" summed up Captain Cockermuth.

"Am I to understand that no other person entered the room after Mr. Dene quitted it?" inquired the sergeant.

"Not a soul. I can testify to that myself."

"Then it looks as though Mr. Dene must have taken the box."

"Just so," assented the complainant, triumphantly. "And I shall give him into custody for stealing it."

Mr. Dutton considered. His judgment was cool; the captain's hot. He thought there might be ins and outs in this affair that had not yet come to the surface. Besides that, he knew young Dene, and did not much fancy him the sort of individual likely to do a thing of this kind.

"Captain Cockermuth," said he, "I think it might be best for me to come up to the house and see a bit into the matter personally, before proceeding to extreme measures. We experienced officers have a way of turning up scraps of evidence that other people would never look at. Perhaps, after all, the box is only mislaid."

"But I tell you it's *lost*," said the captain. "Clean gone. Can't be found high or low."

"Well, if that same black box is lost again, I can only say it is the oddest case I ever heard of. One would think the box had a demon inside it."

"No, sergeant, you are wrong there. The demon's inside him that took it. Listen while I whisper something in your ear – that young Dene is over head and ears in debt: he has debts here, debts there, debts everywhere. For some little time now, as I chance to know, he has been at his very wits' end to think where or how he could pick up some money to satisfy the most pressing; fit to die of fear, lest they should travel to the knowledge of his uncle at Elm Farm."

"*Is* it so?" exclaimed Mr. Dutton, severely. And his face changed, and his opinion also. "Are you sure of this, sir?"

"Well, my informant was my brother; so you may judge whether it is likely to be correct or not," said the captain. "But, if you think it best to make some inquiries at the house, come with me now and do so."

They walked to Foregate together. The sergeant looked a little at the features of the parlour, where the loss had taken place, and heard what Miss Betty had to say, and questioned Susan. This did not help the suspicion thrown on Sam Dene, saving in one point – their joint testimony that he and the box were left alone in the room together.

Mr. Cockermuth had gone out, so the sergeant did not see him: but, as he was not within doors when the loss occurred, he could not have aided the investigation in any way.

"Well, Dutton, what do you think now?" asked Captain Cockermuth, strolling down the street with the sergeant when he departed.

"I confess my visit has not helped me much," said Dutton, a slow-speaking man, given to be cautious. "If nobody entered the room between the time when Miss Cockermuth left it and you entered it, why then, sir, there's only young Dene to fall back upon."

"I tell you nobody did enter it," cried the choleric captain; "or *could*, without my seeing them. I stood at the front-door. Ward was busy at the house that morning, dodging perpetually across the top of the passage, between the kitchen and brewhouse: he, too, is sure no stranger could have come in without being seen by him."

"Did you see young Dene leave the room, sir?"

"I did. Hearing somebody come out of the parlour, I looked round and saw it was young Dene with some papers in his hand. He went into the office for a minute or two, and then passed me, remarking, with all the impudence in life, that he was going to the town hall. He must have had my box in his pocket then."

"A pity but you had gone into the parlour at once, captain," remarked the sergeant. "If only to put the box in safety – provided it was there."

"But I thought it was safe. I thought my sister was there. I did go in almost directly."

"And you never stirred from the door – from first to last?"

"I don't say that. When I first stood there I strolled about a little, talking with one person and another. *But I did not stir from the door after I saw Sam Dene leave the parlour.* And I do not think five minutes elapsed before I went in. Not more than five, I am quite certain. What are you thinking about, Dutton? – You don't seem to take me."

"I take you well enough, sir, and all you say. But what is puzzling me in the matter is this; strikes me as strange, in fact: that Mr. Dene should do the thing (allowing that he has done it) in so open and barefaced a manner, laying himself open to immediate suspicion. Left alone in the room with the box by Miss Betty, he must know that if, when he left it, the box vanished with him, only one inference would be drawn. Most thieves exercise some caution."

"Not when they are as hard up as Dene is. Impudence with them is the order of the day, and often carries luck with it. Nothing risk, nothing win, they cry, and they *do* risk – and win. Dene has got my box, sergeant."

"Well, sir, it looks dark against him; almost *too* dark; and if you decide to give him into custody, of course we have only to – Good evening, Badger!"

They had strolled as far as the Cross, and were standing on the wide pavement in front of St. Nicholas' Church, about to part, when that respectable gentleman, Jonas Badger, passed by. A thought struck the captain. He knew the man was a money-lender in a private way.

"Here, Badger, stop a minute," he hastily cried. "I want to ask you a question about young Dene – my brother's clerk, you know. Does he owe you money? – Much?"

Mr. Badger, wary by nature and by habit, glanced first at the questioner and then at the police-sergeant, and did not answer. Whereupon Captain Cockermuth, as an excuse for his curiosity, plunged into the history of what had occurred: the finding of the box of guineas yesterday and the losing it again today, and the doubt of Sam.

Mr. Badger listened with interest; for the news of that marvellous find had not yet reached his ears. He had been shut up in his office all the morning, very busy over his account-books; and in the afternoon had walked over to Kempsey, where he had a client or two, getting back only in time for tea.

"That long-lost box of guineas come to light at last!" he exclaimed. "What an extraordinary thing! And Mr. Dene is suspected of – Why, good gracious!" he broke off in fresh astonishment, "I have just seen him with a guinea in his pocket!"

"Seen a guinea in Sam Dene's pocket!" cried Captain Cockermuth, turning yellow as the gas-flame under which they were standing.

"Why yes, I have. It was –"

But there Mr. Badger came to a full stop. It had suddenly struck him that he might be doing harm to Sam Dene; and the rule of his life was not to harm any one, or to make an enemy, if his own interest allowed him to avoid it.

"I won't say any more, Captain Cockermuth. It is no business of mine."

But here Mr. Sergeant Dutton came to the fore. "You must, Badger. You must say all you know that bears upon the affair; the law demands it of you. What about the guinea?"

"Well, if you force me to do so – putting it in that way," returned the man, driven into a corner.

Mr. Badger had just been down to Edgar Street to pay another visit to Sam. Not to torment him; he did not do that more than he could help; but simply to say he would accept smaller instalments for the liquidation of his debt – which of course meant giving to Sam a longer time to pay the whole in. This evening he was admitted to Sam's sitting room. During their short conversation, Sam, searching impatiently for a pencil in his waistcoat-pocket, drew out with it a few coins in silver money, and one coin in gold. Mr. Badger's hungry eyes saw that it was an old guinea. These particulars he now imparted.

"What did he *say* about the guinea?" cried Captain Cockermuth, his own eyes glaring.

"Not a word," said Badger; "neither did I. He slipped it back into his pocket."

"I hope you think there's some proof to go upon *now*," were Charles Cockermuth's last words to the police-officer as he wished him goodnight.

On the following morning, Sam Dene was apprehended, and taken before the magistrates. Beyond being formally charged, very little was done; Miss Betty was in bed with a sick headache, brought on by the worry, and could not appear to give evidence; so he was remanded on bail until Saturday.

Chapter III

I'M SURE you might have thought all his rick-yards were on fire by the way old Jacobson came bursting in. It was Saturday morning, and we were at breakfast at Dyke Manor. He had run every step of the way from Elm Farm, two miles nearly, not having patience to wait for his gig, and came in all excitement, the *Worcester Herald* in his hand. The Squire started from his chair; Mrs. Todhetley, then in the act of pouring out a cup of coffee, let it flow over on to the tablecloth.

"What on earth's amiss, Jacobson?" cried the Squire.

"Ay, what's amiss," stuttered Jacobson in answer; "*this* is amiss," holding out the newspaper. "I'll prosecute the editor as sure as I'm a living man. It is a conspiracy got up to sell it; a concocted lie. It can't be anything else, you know, Todhetley. And I want you to go off with me to Worcester. The gig's following me."

When we had somewhat collected our senses, and could look at the newspaper, there was the account as large as life. Samson Reginald Dene had been had up before the magistrates on Thursday morning on a charge of stealing a small box of carved ebony, containing sixty guineas in gold, from the dwelling house of Lawyer Cockermuth; and he was to be brought up again that day, Saturday, for examination.

"A pretty thing this is to see, when a man opens his weekly newspaper at his breakfast-table!" gasped Jacobson, flicking the report with his angry finger. "I'll have the law of them – accusing *my* nephew of such a thing as that! You'll go with me, Squire!"

"Go! Of course I'll go!" returned the Squire, in his hot partisanship. "We were going to Worcester, any way; I've things to do there. Poor Sam! Hanging would be too good for the printers of that newspaper, Jacobson."

Mr. Jacobson's gig was heard driving up to the gate at railroad speed; and soon our own carriage was ready. Old Jacobson sat with the Squire, I behind with Giles;

the other groom, Blossom, drove Tod in the gig; and away we went in the blustering March wind. Many people, farmers and others, were on the road, riding or driving to Worcester market.

Well, we found it was true. And not the mistake of the newspapers: they had but reported what passed before the magistrates at the town hall.

The first person we saw was Miss Cockermuth. She was in a fine way, not knowing what to think or believe, and sat in the parlour in that soft green gown of twilled silk (that might have been a relic of the silk made in the time of the Queen of Sheba), her cap and front all awry. Rumour said old Jacobson had been a sweetheart of hers in their young days; but I'm sure I don't know. Any way they were very friendly with one another, and she sometimes called him 'Frederick.' He sat down by her on the horse-hair sofa, and we took chairs.

She recounted the circumstances (ramblingly) from beginning to end. Not that the end had come yet by a long way. And – there it was, she wound up, when the narrative was over: the box had disappeared, just for all the world as mysteriously as it disappeared in the days gone by.

Mr. Jacobson had listened patiently. He was a fine, upright man, with a healthy colour and bright dark eyes. He wore a blue frock-coat today with metal buttons, and top-boots. As yet he did not see how they had got up grounds for accusing Sam, and he said so.

"To be sure," cried the Squire. "How's that, Miss Betty?"

"Why, it's this way," said Miss Betty – "that nobody was here in the parlour but Sam when the box vanished. It is my brother Charles who has done it all; he is so passionate, you know. John has properly quarrelled with him for it."

"It is not possible, you know, Miss Betty, that Sam Dene could have done it," struck in Tod, who was boiling over with rage at the whole thing. "Some thief must have stolen in at the street-door when Sam had left the room."

"Well, no, that could hardly have been, seeing that Charles never left the street-door after that," returned Miss Betty, mildly. "It appears to be a certain fact that not a soul entered the room after the young man left it. And there lies the puzzle of it."

Putting it to be as Miss Betty put it – and I may as well say here that nothing turned up, then or later, to change the opinion – it looked rather suspicious for Sam Dene. I think the Squire saw it.

"I suppose you are sure the box was on the table when you left the room, Miss Betty?" said he.

"Why, of course I am sure, Squire," she answered. "It was the last thing my eyes fell on; for, as I went through the door, I glanced back to see that I had left the table tidy. Susan can bear witness to that. Dutton, the police-sergeant, thinks some demon of mischief must be in that box – meaning the deuce, you know. Upon my word it looks like it."

Susan came in with some glasses and ale as Miss Betty spoke, and confirmed the testimony – which did not need confirmation. As she closed the parlour-door, she said, after her mistress had passed out, she noticed the box standing on the table.

"Is Sam here today – in the office?" asked Mr. Jacobson.

"Oh, my goodness, no," cried Miss Betty in a fluster. "Why, Frederick, he has not been here since Thursday, when they had him up at the Guildhall. He couldn't well come while the charge is hanging over him."

"Then I think we had better go out to find Sam, and hear what he has to say," observed Mr. Jacobson, drinking up his glass of ale.

"Yes, do," said Miss Betty. "Tell poor Sam I'm as sorry as I can be – pestered almost out of my mind over it. And as to their having found one of the guineas in his pocket, please just mention to him that I say it might have slipped in accidentally."

"One of the guineas found in Sam's pocket!" exclaimed Mr. Jacobson, taken aback.

"Well, I hear so," responded Miss Betty. "The police searched him, you see."

As the Squire and Mr. Jacobson went out, Mr. Cockermuth was coming in. They all turned into the office together, while we made a rush to Sam Dene's lodgings in Edgar Street: as much of a rush, at least, as the Saturday's streets would let us make. Sam was out, the young servant said when we got there, and while parleying with her Mrs. Parslet opened her sitting room door.

"I do not suppose Mr. Dene will be long," she said. "He has to appear at the town hall this morning, and I think it likely he will come home first. Will you walk in and wait?"

She handed us into her parlour, where she had been busy, marking sheets and pillow-cases and towels with 'prepared' ink; the table was covered with them. Tod began telling her that Mr. Jacobson was at Worcester, and went on to say what a shame it was that Sam Dene should be accused of this thing.

"We consider it so," said Mrs. Parslet; who was a capable, pleasant-speaking woman, tall and slender. "My husband says it has upset Mr. Cockermuth more than anything that has occurred for years past. He tells his brother that he should have had it investigated privately, not have given Mr. Dene into custody."

"Then why did he let him do it, Mrs. Parslet?"

She looked at Tod, as if surprised at the question. "Mr. Cockermuth knew nothing of it; you may be sure of that. Captain Cockermuth had the young man at the Guildhall and was preferring the charge, before Mr. Cockermuth heard a word of what was agate. Certainly that is a most mysterious box! It seems fated to give trouble."

At this moment the door opened, and a young lady came into the parlour. It was Maria. What a nice face she had! – What sweet thoughtful eyes! – What gentle manners! Sam's friends in the town were accusing him of being in love with her – and small blame to him.

But Sam did not appear to be coming home, and time was getting on. Tod decided not to wait longer, and said good-morning.

Flying back along High Street, we caught sight of the tray of Dublin buns, just put fresh on the counter in Rousse's shop, and made as good a feast as time allowed. Some people called them Doubling buns (from their shape, I take it), and I don't know to this day which was right.

Away with fleet foot again, past the bustle round the town hall, and market house, till we came to the next confectioner's and saw the apple-tarts. Perhaps somebody remembers yet how delicious those apple-tarts were. Bounding in, we began upon them.

While the feast was in progress, Sam Dene went by, walking very fast. We dashed out to catch him. Good Mrs. Mountford chanced to be in the shop and knew us, or they might have thought we were decamping without payment.

Sam Dene, in answer to Tod's hasty questions, went into a passion; swearing at the world in general, and Captain Cockermuth in particular, as freely as though the justices, then taking their places in the Guildhall, were not as good as within earshot.

"It is a fearful shame, Todhetley! – to bring such a charge against me, and to lug me up to the criminal bar like a felon. Worse than all, to let it go forth to the town and county in today's glaring newspapers that I, Sam Dene, am a common thief!"

"Of course it is a fearful shame, Sam – it's infamous, and all your friends know it is," cried Tod, with eager sympathy. "My father wishes he could hang the printers. I say, what do you think has become of the box?"

"Become of it! – Why, that blundering Charles Cockermuth has got it. He was off his head with excitement at its being found. He must have come into the room and put it somewhere and forgotten it: or else he put it into his pocket and got robbed of it in the street. That's what I think. Quite off his head, I give you my word."

"And what fable is it the wretches have got up about finding one of the guineas in your pocket, Sam?"

"Oh, bother that! It was my own guinea. I swear it – there! I can't stay now," went on Sam, striding off down High Street. "I am due at the town hall this minute; only out on bail. You'll come with me."

"You go in and pay for the tarts, Johnny," called back Tod, as he put his arm within Sam Dene's. I looked in, pitched a shilling on the counter, said I didn't know how many we had eaten; perhaps ten; and that I couldn't wait for change.

Crushing my way amidst the market women and their baskets in the Guildhall yard, I came upon Austin Chance. His father held some post connected with the law, as administered there, and Austin said he would get me in.

"Can it be true that the police found one of the guineas about him?" I asked.

Chance pulled a long face. "It's true they found one when they searched him –"

"What right had they to search him?"

"Well, I don't know," said Austin, laughing a little; "they did it. To see perhaps whether all the guineas were about him. And I am afraid, Johnny Ludlow, that the finding of that guinea will make it rather hard for Sam. It is said that Maria Parslet can prove the guinea was Sam's own, and that my father has had a summons served on her to appear here today. He has taken Sam's case in hand; but he is closer than wax, and tells me nothing."

"You don't think he can have stolen the box, Chance?"

"I don't. I shouldn't think him capable of anything so mean; let alone the danger of it. Not but that there are circumstances in the case that tell uncommonly strong against him. And where the deuce the box can have got to, otherwise, is more than mortal man can guess at. Come along."

Chapter IV

NOT FOR A LONG while had Worcester been stirred as it was over this affair of Samson Dene's. What with the curious discovery of the box of guineas after its mysterious disappearance of years, and then its second no less mysterious loss, with the suspicion that Sam Dene stole it, the Faithful City was so excited as hardly to know whether it stood on its head or its heels.

When the police searched the prisoner on Thursday morning, after taking him into custody, and found the guinea upon him (having been told that he had one about him), his guilt was thought to be as good as proved. Sam said the guinea was his own, an heirloom, and stood to this so indignantly resolute that the police let him have it back. But now, what did Sam go and do? When released upon bail by the magistrates – to come up again on the Saturday – he went straight off to a silversmith's, had a hole stamped in the guinea and hung it to his watch-chain across his waistcoat, that the public might feast their eyes upon it. It was in this spirit of defiance – or, as the town called it, bravado – that he met the charge. His lodgings had been searched for the rest of the guineas, but they were not found.

The hour for the Saturday's examination – twelve o'clock – was striking, as I struggled my way with Austin Chance through the crush round the Guildhall. But that Austin's father was a man of consequence with the door-keepers, we should not have got in at all.

The accused, arraigned by his full name, Samson Reginald Dene, stood in the place allotted to prisoners, cold defiance on his handsome face. As near to him as might be permitted, stood Tod, just as defiant as he. Captain Charles Cockermuth, a third in defiance, stood opposite to prosecute; while Lawyer Cockermuth, who came in with Sam's uncle, Mr. Jacobson, openly wished his brother at Hanover. Squire Todhetley, being a county magistrate, sat on the bench with the City magnates, but not to interfere.

The proceedings began. Captain Cockermuth related how the little box, his property, containing sixty golden guineas, was left on the table in a sitting room in his brother's house, the accused being the only person in the room at the time, and that the box disappeared. He, himself (standing at the front-door), saw the accused quit the room; he went into it almost immediately, but the box was gone. He swore that no person entered the room after the prisoner left it.

Miss Betty Cockermuth, flustered and red, appeared next. She testified that she was in the room nearly all the morning, the little box being upon the table; when she left the room, Mr. Dene remained in it alone, copying a letter for her brother; the box was still on the table. Susan Edwards, housemaid at Lawyer Cockermuth's, spoke to the same fact. It was she who had fetched her mistress out, and she saw the box standing upon the table.

The accused was asked by one of the magistrates what he had to say to this. He answered, speaking freely, that he had nothing to say in contradiction, except that he did not know what became of the box.

"Did you see the box on the table?" asked the lawyer on the opposite side, Mr. Standup.

"I saw it there when I first went into the room. Miss Betty made a remark about the box, which drew my attention to it. I was sitting at the far end of the room, at Mr. Cockermuth's little desk-table. I did not notice the box afterwards."

"Did you not see it there after Miss Cockermuth left the room?"

"No, I did not; not that I remember," answered Sam. "Truth to say, I never thought about it. My attention was confined to the letter I was copying, to the exclusion of everything else."

"Did any one come into the room after Miss Cockermuth left it?"

"No one came into it. Somebody opened the door and looked in."

This was fresh news. The town hall pricked up its ears.

"I do not know who it was," added Sam. "My head was bent over my writing, when the door opened quickly, and as quickly shut again. I supposed somebody had looked in to see if Mr. or Miss Cockermuth was there, and had retreated on finding they were not."

"Could that person, whomsoever it might be, have advanced to the table and taken the box?" asked the chief of the magistrates.

"No, sir. For certain, no!" – and Sam's tone here, he best knew why, was aggravatingly defiant. "The person might have put his head in – and no doubt did – but he did not set a foot inside the room."

Captain Cockermuth was asked about this: whether he observed any one go to the parlour and look in. He protested till he was nearly blue with rage (for he regarded it as Sam's invention), that such a thing never took place, that no one whatever went near the parlour-door.

Next came up the question of the guinea, which was hanging from his watch-guard, shining and bold as if it had been brass. Sam had been questioned about this by the justices on Thursday, and his statement in answer to them was just as bold as the coin.

The guinea had been given him by his late father's uncle, old Thomas Dene, who had jokingly enjoined him never to change it, always to keep it by him, and then he would never be without money. Sam had kept it; kept it from that time to this. He kept it in the pocket of an old-fashioned leather case, which contained some letters from his father, and two or three other things he valued. No, he was not in the habit of getting the guinea out to look at, he had retorted to a little badgering; had not looked at it (or at the case either, which lay in the bottom of his trunk) for months and months – yes, it might be years, for all he recollected. But on the Tuesday evening, when talking with Miss Parslet about guineas, he fetched it to show to her; and slipped it into his pocket afterwards, where, the police found it on the Thursday. This was the substance of his first answer, and he repeated it now.

"Do you know who is said to be the father of lies, young man?" asked Justice Whitewicker in a solemn tone, suspecting that the prisoner was telling an out-and-out fable.

"I have heard," answered Sam. "Have never seen him myself. Perhaps you have, sir." At which a titter went round the court, and it put his worship's back up. Sam went on to say that he had often thought of taking his guinea into wear, and had now done it. And he gave the guinea a flick in the face of us all.

Evidently little good could come of a hardened criminal like this; and Justice Whitewicker, who thought nothing on earth so grand as the sound of his own voice from the bench, gave Sam a piece of his mind. In the midst of this a stir arose at the appearance of Maria Parslet. Mr. Chance led her in; her father, sad and shrinking as usual, walked behind them. Lawyer Cockermuth – and I liked him for it – made a place for his clerk next to himself. Maria looked modest, gentle and pretty. She wore black silk, being in slight mourning, and a dainty white bonnet.

Mr. Dene was asked to take tea with them in the parlour on the Tuesday evening, as a matter of convenience, Maria's evidence ran, in answer to questions, and she briefly alluded to the reason why. Whilst waiting together, he and she, for her father to come in, Mr. Dene told her of the finding of the ebony box of guineas at Mr. Cockermuth's. She laughingly remarked that a guinea was an out-of-date coin now, and she was not sure that she had ever seen one. In reply to that, Mr. Dene said he had one by him, given him by an old uncle some years before; and he went upstairs and brought it down to show to her. There could be no mistake, Maria added to Mr. Whitewicker, who wanted to insinuate a word of doubt, and her sweet brown eyes were honest and true as she said it; she had touched the guinea and held it in her hand for some moments.

"Held it and touched it, did you, Miss Parslet?" retorted Lawyer Standup. "Pray what appearance had it?"

"It was a thin, worn coin, sir," replied Maria; "thinner, I think, than a sovereign, but somewhat larger; it seemed to be worn thin at the edge."

"Whose image was on it? – What king's?"

"George the Third's. I noticed that."

"Now don't you think, young lady, that the accused took this marvellous coin from his pocket, instead of from some receptacle above stairs?" went on Mr. Standup.

"I am quite sure he did not take it from his pocket when before me," answered Maria. "He ran upstairs quickly, saying he would fetch the guinea: he had nothing in his hands then."

Upon this Lawyer Chance inquired of his learned brother why he need waste time in useless questions; begging to remind him that it was not until Wednesday morning the box disappeared, so the prisoner could not well have had any of its contents about him on Tuesday.

"Just let my questions alone, will you," retorted Mr. Standup, with a nod. "I know what I am about. Now, Miss Parslet, please attend to me. Was the guinea you profess to have seen a perfect coin, or was there a hole in it?"

"It was a perfect coin, sir."

"And what became of it?"

"I think Mr. Dene put it in his waistcoat-pocket: I did not particularly notice. Quite close upon that, my father came home, and we sat down to tea. No, sir, nothing was said to my father about the guinea; if it was, I did not hear it. But he and Mr. Dene talked of the box of guineas that had been found."

"Who was it that called while you were at tea?"

"Young Mr. Chance called. We had finished tea then, and Mr. Dene took him upstairs to his own sitting room."

"I am not asking you about young Mr. Chance; we shall come to him presently," was the rough-toned, but not ill-natured retort. "Somebody else called: who was it?"

Maria, blushing and paling ever since she stood up to the ordeal, grew white now. Mr. Badger had called at the door, she answered, and Mr. Dene went out to speak to him. Worried by Lawyer Standup as to whether he did not come to ask for money, she said she believed so, but she did not hear all they said.

Quiet Mr. Parslet was the next witness. He had to acknowledge that he did hear it. Mr. Badger appeared to be pressing for some money owing to him; could not tell the amount, knew nothing about that. When questioned whether the accused owed him money, Parslet said not a shilling; Mr. Dene had never sought to borrow of him, and had paid his monthly accounts regularly.

Upon that, Mr. Badger was produced; a thin man with a neck as stiff as a poker; who gave his reluctant testimony in a sweet tone of benevolence. Mr. Dene had been borrowing money from him for some time; somewhere about twenty pounds, he thought, was owing now, including interest. He had repeatedly asked for its repayment, but only got put off with (as he believed) lame excuses. Had certainly gone to ask for it on the Tuesday evening; was neither loud nor angry, oh dear, no; but did tell the accused he thought he could give him some if he would, and did say that he must have a portion of it within a week, or he should apply to Mr. Jacobson, of Elm Farm. Did not really mean to apply to Mr. Jacobson, had no wish to do any one an injury, but felt vexed at the young man's off-handedness, which looked like indifference. Knew besides that Mr. Dene had other debts.

Now I'll leave you to judge how this evidence struck on the ears of old Jacobson. He leaped to the conclusion that Sam had been going all sorts of ways, as he supposed he went when in London, and might be owing, the mischief only knew how much money; and he shook his fist at Sam across the justice-room.

Mr. Standup next called young Chance, quite to young Chance's surprise; perhaps also to his father's. He was questioned upon no end of things – whether he did not know that the accused was owing a great deal of money, and whether the accused had shown any guinea to him when he was in Edgar Street on the Tuesday night. Austin answered that he believed Mr. Dene owed a little money, not a great deal, so far as he knew; and that he had not seen the guinea or heard of it. And in saying all this, Austin's tone was just as resentfully insolent to Mr. Standup as he dared to make it.

Well, it is of no use to go on categorically with the day's proceedings. When they came to an end, the magistrates conferred pretty hotly in a low tone amongst themselves, some apparently taking up one opinion, as to Sam's guilt, or innocence, and some the other. At length they announced their decision, and it was as follows.

"Although the case undoubtedly presents grave grounds of suspicion against the accused, Samson Reginald Dene – 'Very grave indeed,' interjected Mr. Whitewicker, solemnly – we do not consider them to be sufficient to commit him for trial upon; therefore, we give him the benefit of the doubt, and discharge him. Should any further evidence transpire, he can be brought up again."

"It was Maria Parslet's testimony about the guinea that cleared him," whispered the crowd, as they filed out.

And I think it must have been. It was just impossible to doubt her truth, or the earnestness with which she gave it.

Mr. Jacobson 'interviewed' Sam, as the Americans say, and the interview was not a loving one. Being in the mood, he said anything that came uppermost. He forbade Sam to appear at Elm Farm ever again, as 'long as oak and ash grew;' and he added that as Sam was bent on going to the deuce head foremost, he might do it upon his own means, but that he'd never get any more help from him.

The way the Squire lashed up Bob and Blister when driving home – for, liking Sam hitherto, he was just as much put out as old Jacobson – and the duet they kept together in abuse of his misdeeds, was edifying to hear. Tod laughed; I did not. The gig was given over this return journey to the two grooms.

"I do not believe Sam took the box, sir," I said to old Jacobson, interrupting a fiery oration.

He turned round to stare at me. "What do you say, Johnny Ludlow? *You do not believe he took the box?*"

"Well, to me it seems quite plain that he did not take it. I've hardly ever felt more sure of anything."

"Plain!" struck in the Squire. "How is it plain, Johnny? What grounds do you go upon?"

"I judge by his looks and his tones, sir, when denying it. They are to be trusted."

They did not know whether to laugh or scoff at me. It was Johnny's way, said the Squire; always fancying he could read the riddles in a man's face and voice. But they'd have thrown up their two best market-going hats with glee to be able to think it true.

Chapter V

SAMSON REGINALD DENE was relieved of the charge, as it was declared 'not proven;' all the same, Samson Reginald Dene was ruined. Worcester said so. During the following week, which was Passion Week, its citizens talked more of him than of their prayers.

Granted that Maria Parslet's testimony had been honestly genuine, a theory cropped up to counteract it. Lawyer Standup had been bold enough to start it at the Saturday's examination: a hundred tongues were repeating it now. Sam Dene, as may be remembered, was present at the finding of the box on Tuesday; he had come up the passage and touched the golden guineas in it with the tips of his fingers; those fingers might have deftly extracted one of the coins. No wonder he could show it to Maria when he went home to tea! Captain Cockermuth admitted that in counting the guineas subsequently he had thought he counted sixty; but, as he knew there were (or ought to be) that number in the box, probably the assumption misled him, causing him to reckon them as sixty when in fact there were only fifty-nine. Which was a bit of logic.

Still, popular opinion was divided. If part of the town judged Sam to be guilty, part believed him to be innocent. A good deal might be said on both sides. To a young man who does not know how to pay his debts from lack of means, and debts that he is afraid of, too, sixty golden guineas may be a great temptation; and people did not shut their eyes to that. It transpired also that Mr. Jacobson, his own uncle, his best friend, had altogether cast Sam off and told him he might now go to the dogs his own way.

Sam resented it all bitterly, and defied the world. Far from giving in or showing any sense of shame, he walked about with an air, his head up, and that brazen guinea dangling in front of him. He actually had the face to appear at college on Good Friday (the congregation looking askance at him), and sat out the cold service of the day: no singing, no organ, and the little chorister-boys in black surplices instead of white ones.

But the crowning act of boldness was to come. Before Easter week had lapsed into the past, Sam Dene had taken two rooms in a conspicuous part of the town and set-up in practice. A big brass plate on the outer door displayed his name: 'Mr. Dene, Attorney-at-law.' Sam's friends extolled his courage; Sam's enemies were amazed at his impudence. Captain Cockermuth prophesied that the ceiling of that office would come tumbling down on its crafty occupant's head: it was *his* gold that was paying for it.

The Cockermuths, like the town, were divided in opinion. Mr. Cockermuth could not believe Sam guilty, although the mystery as to where the box could be puzzled him as few things had ever puzzled him in this life. He would fain have taken Sam back again, had it been a right thing to do. What the captain thought need not be enlarged upon. While Miss Betty felt uncertain; veering now to this belief, now to that, and much distressed either way.

There is one friend in this world that hardly ever deserts us – and that is a mother. Mrs. Dene, a pretty little woman yet, had come flying to Worcester, ready to fight everybody in it on her son's behalf. Sam of course made his own tale good to her;

whether it was a true one or not he alone knew, but not an angel from heaven could have stirred her faith in it. She declared that, to her positive knowledge, the old uncle had given Sam the guinea.

It was understood to be Mrs. Dene who advanced the money to Sam to set up with; it was certainly Mrs. Dene who bought a shutting-up bed (at old Ward's), and a gridiron, and a tea-pot, and a three-legged table, and a chair or two, all for the back-room of the little office, that Sam might go into housekeeping on his own account, and live upon sixpence a-day, so to say, until business came in. To look at Sam's hopeful face, he meant to do it, and to live down the scandal.

Looking at the thing impartially, one might perhaps see that Sam was not swayed by impudence in setting-up, so much as by obligation. For what else lay No firm would engage him as clerk with that doubt sticking to his coat-tails. He paid some of his debts, and undertook to pay the rest before the year was out. A whisper arose that it was Mrs. Dene who managed this. Sam's adversaries knew better; the funds came out of the ebony box: that, as Charles Cockermuth demonstrated, was as sure as heaven.

But now there occurred one thing that I, Johnny Ludlow, could not understand, and never shall: why Worcester should have turned its back, like an angry drake, upon Maria Parslet. The school, where she was resident teacher, wrote her a cool, polite note, to say she need not trouble herself to return after the Easter recess. That example was followed. Pious individuals looked upon her as a possible story-teller, in danger of going to the bad in Sam's defence, nearly as much as Sam had gone.

It was just a craze. Even Charles Cockermuth said there was no sense in blaming Maria: of course Sam had deceived her (when pretending to show the guinea as his own), just as he deceived other people. Next the town called her 'bold' for standing up in the face and eyes of the Guildhall to give her evidence. But how could Maria help that? It was not her own choice: she'd rather have locked herself up in the cellar. Lawyer Chance had burst in upon her that Saturday morning (not ten minutes after we left the house), giving nobody warning, and carried her off imperatively, never saying 'Will you, or Won't you.' It was not his way.

Placid Miss Betty was indignant when the injustice came to her ears. What did people mean by it? She wanted to know. She sent for Maria to spend the next Sunday in Foregate Street, and marched with her arm-in-arm to church (St. Nicholas'), morning and evening.

As the days and the weeks passed, commotion gave place to a calm; Sam and his delinquencies were let alone. One cannot be on the grumble for ever. Sam's lines were pretty hard; practice held itself aloof from him; and if he did not live upon the sixpence a-day, he looked at every halfpenny that he had to spend beyond it. His face grew thin, his blue eyes wistful, but he smiled hopefully.

* * *

"You keep up young Dene's acquaintance, I perceive," remarked Lawyer Chance to his son one evening as they were finishing dinner, for he had met the two young men together that day.

"Yes: why shouldn't I?" returned Austin.

"Think that charge was a mistaken one, I suppose?"

"Well I do, father. He has affirmed it to me in terms so unmistakable that I can but believe him. Besides, I don't think Dene, as I have always said, is the sort of fellow to turn rogue: I don't, indeed."

"Does he get any practice?"

"Very little, I'm afraid."

Mr. Chance was a man with a conscience. On the whole, he felt inclined to think Sam had not helped himself to the guineas, but he was by no means sure of it: like Miss Betty Cockermuth, his opinion veered, now on this side, now on that, like a haunted weathercock. If Sam was not guilty, why, then, Fate had dealt hardly with the young fellow – and what would the end be? These thoughts were running through the lawyer's mind as he talked to his son and sat playing with his bunch of seals, which hung down by a short, thick gold chain, in the old-fashioned manner.

"I should like to say a word to him if he'd come to me," he suddenly cried. "You might go and bring him, Austin."

"What – this evening?" exclaimed Austin.

"Ay; why not? One time's as good as another."

Austin Chance started off promptly for the new office, and found his friend presiding over his own tea-tray in the little back-room; the loaf and butter on the table, and a red herring on the gridiron.

"Hadn't time to get any dinner today; too busy," was Sam's apology, given briefly with a flush of the face. "Mr. Chance wants me? Well, I'll come. What is it for?"

"Don't know," replied Austin. And away they went.

The lawyer was standing at the window, his hands in the pockets of his pepper-and-salt trousers, tinkling the shillings and sixpences there. Austin supposed he was not wanted, and shut them in.

"I have been thinking of your case a good bit lately, Sam Dene," began Mr. Chance, giving Sam a seat and sitting down himself; "and I should like to feel, if I can, more at a certainty about it, one way or the other."

"Yes, sir," replied Sam. And you must please to note that manners in those days had not degenerated to what they are in these. Young men, whether gentle or simple, addressed their elders with respect; young women also. "Yes, sir," replied Sam. "But what do you mean about wishing to feel more at a certainty?"

"When I defended you before the magistrates, I did my best to convince them that you were not guilty: you had assured me you were not: and they discharged you. I believe my arguments and my pleadings went some way with them."

"I have no doubt of it, sir, and I thanked you at the time with all my heart," said Sam warmly. "Some of my enemies were bitter enough against me."

"But you should not speak in that way – calling people your enemies!" reproved the lawyer. "People were only at enmity with you on the score of the offence. Look here, Sam Dene – did you commit it, or did you not?"

Sam stared. Mr. Chance had dropped his voice to a solemn key, his head was pushed forward, gravity sat on his face.

"No, sir. No."

The short answer did not satisfy the lawyer. "Did you filch that box of guineas out of Cockermuth's room; or were you, and are you, as you assert, wholly innocent?" he resumed. "Tell me the truth as before Heaven. Whatever it be, I will shield you still."

Sam rose. "On my sacred word, sir, and before Heaven, I have told nothing but the truth. I did not take or touch the box of guineas. I do not know what became of it."

Mr. Chance regarded Sam in silence. He had known young men, when under a cloud, prevaricate in a most extraordinary and unblushing manner: to look at them and listen to them, one might have said they were fit to be canonized. But he thought truth lay with Sam now.

"Sit down, sit down, Dene," he said. "I am glad to believe you. Where the deuce could the box have got to? It could not take flight through the ceiling up to the clouds, or down to the earth through the floor. *Whose hands took it?*"

"The box went in one of two ways," returned Sam. "If the captain did not fetch it out unconsciously, and lose it in the street, why, somebody must have entered the parlour after I left it and carried off the box. Perhaps the individual who looked into the room when I was sitting there."

"A pity but you had noticed who that was."

"Yes, it is. Look here, Mr. Chance; a thought has more than once struck me – if that person did not come back and take the box, why has he not come forward openly and honestly to avow it was himself who looked in?"

The lawyer gave his head a dissenting shake. "It is a ticklish thing to be mixed up in, he may think, one that he had best keep out of – though he may be innocent as the day. How are you getting on?" he asked, passing abruptly from the subject.

"Oh, middling," replied Sam. "As well, perhaps, as I could expect to get on at first, with all the prejudice abroad against me."

"Earning bread-and-cheese?"

"Not quite – yet."

"Well, see here, Dene – and this is what I chiefly sent for you to say, if you could assure me on your conscience you deserved it – I may be able to put some little business in your hands. Petty matters are brought to us that we hardly care to waste time upon: I'll send them to you in future. I dare say you'll be able to rub on by dint of patience. Rome was not built in a day, you know."

"Thank you, sir; I thank you very truly," breathed Sam. "Mr. Cockermuth sent me a small matter the other day. If I can make a bare living of it at present, that's all I ask. Fame and fortune are not rained down upon black sheep."

Which was so true a remark as to need no contradiction.

May was nearing its close then, and the summer evenings were long and lovely. As Sam went forth from the interview, he thought he would take a walk by the river, instead of turning in to his solitary rooms. Since entering upon them he had been as steady as old Time: the accusation and its attendant shame seemed to have converted him from a heedless, youthful man into a wise old sage of age and care. Passing down Broad Street towards the bridge, he turned to the left and sauntered along beside the Severn. The water glittered in the light of the setting sun; barges, some of them bearing men and women and children, passed smoothly up and down on it; the opposite fields, towards St. John's, were green as an emerald: all things seemed to wear an aspect of brightness.

All on a sudden things grew brighter – and Sam's pulses gave a leap. He had passed the grand old red-stoned wall that enclosed the Bishop's palace, and was close upon the gates leading up to the Green, when a young lady turned out of them and came towards him with a light, quick step. It was Maria Parslet, in a pretty summer muslin, a straw hat shading her blushing face. For it did blush furiously at sight of Sam.

"Mr. Dene!"

"Maria!"

She began to say, hurriedly, that her mother had sent her with a message to the dressmaker on the Parade, and she had taken that way, as being the shortest – as if in apology for having met Sam.

He turned with her, and they paced slowly along side by side, the colour on Maria's cheeks coming and going with every word he spoke and every look he gave her – which seemed altogether senseless and unreasonable. Sam told her of his conversation with Austin Chance's father, and his promise to put a few things in his way.

"Once let me be making two hundred a-year, Maria, and then –"

"Then what?" questioned Maria innocently.

"Then I should ask you to come to me, and we'd risk it together."

"Risk what?" stammered Maria, turning her head right round to watch a barge that was being towed by.

"Risk our luck. Two hundred a-year is not so bad to begin upon. I should take the floor above as well as the ground-floor I rent now, and we should get along. Any way, I hope to try it."

"Oh, Mr. Dene!"

"Now don't 'Mr. Dene' me, young lady, if you please. Why, Maria, what else can we do? A mean, malicious set of dogs and cats have turned their backs upon us both; the least we should do is to see if we can't do without them. I know you'd rather come to me than stay in Edgar Street."

Maria held her tongue, as to whether she would or not. "Mamma is negotiating to get me a situation at Cheltenham," she said.

"You will not go to Cheltenham, or anywhere else, if I get any luck," he replied dictatorially. "Life would look very blue to me now without you, Maria. And many a man and wife, rolling in riches at the end, have rubbed on with less than two hundred a-year at the beginning. I wouldn't say, mind, but we might risk it on a hundred and fifty. My rent is low, you see."

"Ye–es," stammered Maria "But – I wish that mystery of the guineas could be cleared up!"

Sam stood still, turned, and faced her. "Why do you say *that*? You are not suspecting that I took them?"

"Oh dear, *NO!*" returned Maria, losing her breath. "I *know* you did not take them: could not. I was only thinking of your practice: so much more would come in."

"Cockermuth has sent me a small matter or two. I think I shall get on," repeated Sam.

They were at their journey's end by that time, at the dressmaker's door. "Good evening," said Maria, timidly holding out her hand.

Sam Dene took it and clasped it. "Goodbye, my darling. I am going home to my bread-and-cheese supper, and I wish you were there to eat it with me!"

Maria sighed. She wondered whether that wonderful state of things would ever come to pass. Perhaps no; perhaps yes. Meanwhile no living soul knew aught of these treasonable aspirations; they were a secret between her and Sam. Mr. and Mrs. Parslet suspected nothing.

Time went on. Lawyer Chance was as good as his word, and put a few small matters of business into the hands of Sam Dene. Mr. Cockermuth did the same. The town came down upon him for it; though it let Chance alone, who was not the sort of man to be dictated to. "Well," said Cockermuth in answer, "I don't believe the lad is guilty; never have believed it. Had he been of a dishonest turn, he could have helped himself before, for a good deal of my cash passed at times through his hands. And, given that he was innocent, he has been hardly dealt by."

Sam Dene was grateful for these stray windfalls, and returned his best thanks to the lawyers for them. But they did not amount to much in the aggregate; and a gloomy vision began to present itself to his apprehension of being forced to give up the struggle, and wandering out in the world to seek a better fortune. The summer assizes drew near. Sam had no grand cause to come on at them, or small one either; but it was impossible not to give a thought now and again to what his fate might have been, had he stood committed to take his trial at them. The popular voice said that was only what he merited.

Chapter VI

THE ASSIZES were held, and passed. One hot day, when July was nearing its meridian, word was brought to Miss Cockermuth – who was charitable – that a poor sick woman whom she befriended, was worse than usual, so she put on her bonnet and cloak to pay her a visit. The bonnet was a huge Leghorn, which shaded her face well from the sun, its trimming of straw colour; and the cloak was of thin black "taffeta," edged with narrow lace. It was a long walk on a hot afternoon, for the sick woman lived but just on this side Henwick. Miss Betty had got as far as the bridge, and was about to cross it when Sam Dene, coming over it at a strapping pace, ran against her.

"Miss Betty!" he cried. "I beg your pardon."

Miss Betty brought her bonnet from under the shade of her large grass-green parasol. "Dear me, is it you, Sam Dene?" she said. "Were you walking for a wager?"

Sam laughed a little. "I was hastening back to my office, Miss Betty. I have no clerk, you know, and a client *might* come in."

Miss Betty gave her head a twist, something between a nod and a shake; she noticed the doubtful tone in the 'might.' "Very hot, isn't it?" said she. "I'm going up to see that poor Hester Knowles; she's uncommon bad, I hear."

"You'll have a warm walk."

"Ay. Are you pretty well, Sam? You look thin."

"Do I? Oh, that's nothing but the heat of the weather. I am quite well, thank you. Good-afternoon, Miss Betty."

She shook his hand heartily. One of Sam's worst enemies, who might have run in a curricle with Charles Cockermuth, as to an out-and-out belief in his guilt, was passing at the moment, and saw it.

Miss Betty crossed the bridge, turned off into Turkey, for it was through those classical regions that her nearest and coolest way lay, and so onwards to the sick woman's room. There she found the blazing July sun streaming in at the wide window, which had no blind, no shelter whatever from it. Miss Betty had had enough of the sun out-of-doors, without having it in. Done up with the walk and the heat, she sat down on the first chair, and felt ready to swoon right off.

"Dear me, Hester, this is bad for you!" she gasped.

"Did you mean the sun, ma'am?" asked the sick woman, who was sitting full in it, wrapped in a blanket or two. "It is a little hot just now, but I don't grumble at it; I'm so cold mostly. As soon as the sun goes off the window, I shall begin to shiver."

"Well-a-day!" responded Miss Betty, wishing she could be cool enough to shiver. "But if you feel it cold now, Hester, what will you do when the autumn winds come on?"

"Ah, ma'am, please do not talk of it! I just can't tell what I shall do. That window don't fit tight, and the way the wind pours in through it upon me as I sit here at evening, or lie in my little bed there, passes belief. I'm coughing always then."

"You should have some good thick curtains put up," said Miss Betty, gazing at the bare window, which had a pot of musk on its sill. "Woollen ones."

The sick woman smiled sadly. She was very poor now, though it had not always been so; she might as well have hoped to buy the sun itself as woollen curtains – or cotton curtains either. Miss Betty knew that.

"I'll think about it, Hester, and see if I've any old ones that I could let you have. I'm not sure; but I'll look," repeated she – and began to empty her capacious dimity pockets of a few items of good things she had brought.

By-and-by, when she was a little cooler, and had talked with Hester, Miss Betty set off home again, her mind running upon the half-promised curtains. "They are properly shabby," thought she, as she went along, "but they'll serve to keep the sun and the wind off her."

She was thinking of those warm green curtains that she had picked the braid from that past disastrous morning – as the reader heard of, and all the town as well. Nothing had been done with them since.

Getting home, Miss Betty turned into the parlour. Susan – who had not yet found leisure to fix any time for her wedding – found her mistress fanning her hot face, her bonnet untied and tilted back.

"I've been to see that poor Hester Knowles, Susan," began Miss Betty.

"Law, ma'am!" interposed Susan. "What a walk for you this scorching afternoon! All up that wide New Road!"

"You may well say that, girl: but I went Turkey away. She's very ill, poor thing; and that's a frightfully staring window of hers, the sun on it like a blazing fire, and not as much as a rag for a blind; and the window don't fit, she says, and in cold weather the biting wind comes in and shivers her up. I think I might give her those shabby old curtains, Susan – that were up in Mr. Philip's room, you know, before we got the new chintz ones in."

"So you might, ma'am," said Susan, who was not a bad-hearted girl, excepting to the baker's man. "They can't go up at any of our windows as they be; and if you had 'em dyed, I don't know as they'd answer much, being so shabby."

"I put them – let me see – into the spare ottoman, didn't I? Yes, that was it. And there I suppose they must be lying still."

"Sure enough, Miss Betty," said Susan. "I've not touched 'em."

"Nor I," said Miss Betty. "With all the trouble that got into our house at that time, I couldn't give my mind to seeing after the old things, and I've not thought about them since. Come upstairs with me now, Susan; we'll see what sort of a state they are in."

They went up; and Miss Betty took off her bonnet and cloak and put her cap on. The spare ottoman, soft, and red, and ancient, used as a receptacle for odds and ends that were not wanted, stood in a spacious linen-closet on the first-floor landing. It was built out over the back-door, and had a skylight above. Susan threw back the lid of the ottoman, and Miss Betty stood by. The faded old brown curtains, green once, lay in a heap at one end, just as Miss Betty had hastily flung them in that past day in March, when on her way to look at the chintzes.

"They're in a fine rabble, seemingly," observed Susan, pausing to regard the curtains.

"Dear me!" cried Miss Betty, conscience-stricken, for she was a careful housewife, "I let them drop in any way, I remember. I did mean to have them well shaken out-of-doors and properly folded, but that bother drove it all out of my head. Take them out, girl."

Susan put her strong arms underneath the heap and lifted it out with a fling. Something heavy flew out of the curtains, and dropped on the boarded floor with a crash. Letting fall the curtains, Susan gave a wild shriek of terror and Miss Betty gave a wilder, for the floor was suddenly covered with shining gold coins. Mr. Cockermuth, passing across the passage below at the moment, heard the cries, wondered whether the house was on fire, and came hastening up.

"Oh," said he coolly, taking in the aspect of affairs. "So the thief was you, Betty, after all!"

He picked up the ebony box, and bent his head to look at the guineas. Miss Betty sank down on a three-legged stool – brought in for Philip's children – and grew as white as death.

Yes, it was the missing box of guineas, come to light in the same extraordinary and unexpected manner that it had come before, without having been (as may be said) truly lost. When Miss Betty gathered her curtains off the dining room table that March morning, a cumbersome and weighty heap, she had unwittingly gathered up the box with them. No wonder Sam Dene had not seen the box on the table after Miss Betty's departure! It was a grievous misfortune, though, that he failed to take notice it was not there.

She had no idea she was not speaking truth in saying she saw the box on the table as she left the room. Having seen the box there all the morning she thought it was there still, and that she saw it, being quite unconscious that it was in her arms. Susan, too, had noticed the box on the table when she opened the door to call her mistress, and believed she was correct in saying she saw it there to the last: the real fact being that she had not observed it was gone. So there the box with its golden freight had lain undisturbed, hidden in the folds of the curtains. But for Hester Knowles's defective window, it might have stayed there still, who can say how long?

Susan, no less scared than her mistress, stood back against the closet wall for safety, out of reach of those diabolical coins; Miss Betty, groaning and half-fainting on the three-legged stool, sat pushing back her cap and her front. The lawyer picked up the guineas and counted them as he laid them flat in the box. Sixty of them: not one missing. So Sam's guinea *was* his own! He had not, as Worcester whispered, trumped up the story with Maria Parslet.

"John," gasped poor Miss Betty, beside herself with remorse and terror, "John, what will become of me now? Will anything be done?"

"How 'done'?" asked he.

"Will they bring me to trial – or anything of that – in poor Sam's place?"

"Well, I don't know," answered her brother grimly; "perhaps not this time. But I'd have you take more care in future, Betty, than to hide away gold in old curtains."

Locking the box securely within his iron safe, Mr. Cockermuth put on his hat and went down to the town hall, where the magistrates, after dispensing their wisdom, were about to disperse for the day. He told them of the wonderful recovery of the box of guineas, of how it had been lost, and that Sam Dene was wholly innocent. Their worships were of course charmed to hear it, Mr. Whitewicker observing that they had only judged Sam by appearances, and that appearances had been sufficient (in theory) to hang him.

From the town hall, Mr. Cockermuth turned off to Sam's office. Sam was making a great show of business, surrounded by a tableful of imposing parchments, but with never a client to the fore. His old master grasped his hand.

"Well, Sam, my boy," he said, "the tables have turned for you. That box of guineas is found."

Sam never spoke an answering word. His lips parted with expectation: his breath seemed to be a little short.

"Betty had got it all the time. She managed somehow to pick it up off the table with those wretched old curtains she had there, all unconsciously, of course, and it has lain hidden with the curtains upstairs in a lumber-box ever since. Betty will never forgive herself. She'll have a fit of the jaundice over this."

Sam drew a long breath. "You will let the public know, sir?"

"Ay, Sam, without loss of an hour. I've begun with the magistrates – and a fine sensation the news made amidst 'em, I can tell you; and now I'm going round to the newspapers; and I shall go over to Elm Farm the first thing tomorrow. The town took up the cause against you, Sam: take care it does not eat you now in its repentance. Look here, you'll have to come round to Betty, or she'll moan her heart out: you won't bear malice, Sam?"

"No, that I won't," said Sam warmly. "Miss Betty did not bear it to me. She has been as kind as can be all along."

The town did want to eat Sam. It is the custom of the true Briton to go to extremes. Being unable to shake Sam's hands quite off, the city would fain have chaired him round the streets with honours, as it used to chair its newly returned members.

Captain Cockermuth, sent for post haste, came to Worcester all contrition, beseeching Sam to forgive him fifty times a-day, and wanting to press the box of guineas upon him as a peace-offering. Sam would not take it: he laughingly told the captain that the box did not seem to carry luck with it.

And then Sam's troubles were over. And no objection was made by his people (as it otherwise might have been) to his marrying Maria Parslet, by way of recompense. "God never fails to bring good out of evil, my dear," said old Mrs. Jacobson to Maria, the first time they had her on a visit at Elm Farm. As to Sam, he had short time for Elm Farm, or anything else in the shape of recreation. Practice was flowing in quickly: litigants arguing, one with another, that a young man, lying for months under an imputation of theft, and then coming out of it with flying colours, must needs be a clever lawyer.

"But, Johnny," Sam said to me, when talking of the past, "there's one thing I would alter if I made the laws. No person, so long as he is only suspected of crime, should have his name proclaimed publicly. I am not speaking of murder, you understand, or charges of that grave nature; but of such a case as mine. My name appeared in full, in all the local newspapers, Samson Reginald Dene, coupled with theft, and of course it got a mark upon it. It is an awful blight upon a man when he is innocent, one that he may never quite live down. Suspicions must arise, I know that, of the innocent as well as the guilty, and they must undergo preliminary examinations in public and submit to legal inquiries: but time enough to proclaim who the man is when evidence strengthens against him, and he is committed for trial; until then let his name be suppressed. At least that is my opinion."

And it is mine as well as Sam's.

Biographies & Sources

Sara Dobie Bauer
The Youngest Brother
(Originally Published in *Solarcide Magazine*, 2015)
Sara Dobie Bauer is an Amazon bestselling author, model, and mental health advocate with a creative writing degree from Ohio University. Her short story 'Don't Ball the Boss' was nominated for the Pushcart Prize. She lives in Northeast Ohio, although she'd really like to live in a Tim Burton film. She is author of the paranormal rom-com *Bite Somebody*, among other ridiculously entertaining things, and her biggest literary influences are Christopher Moore and Rainbow Rowell. Learn more at SaraDobieBauer.com.

Arnold Bennett
Murder!
(Originally Published in *The Night Visitor and Other Stories,* 1931)
Arnold Bennett (1867–1931) worked in theatre, journalism and film but is mainly remembered for his work as a novelist. Bennett was born in Hanley, Staffordshire – one of the towns that joined to form Stoke-on-Trent. Bennett refers to these towns in many of his novels as the 'Five Towns' such as in *Anna of the Five Towns* and *Clayhanger*. Bennett spent some time as editor of *Woman* magazine before moving to Paris in 1903 and dedicating his time to writing. He had a great love for mystery fiction and was particularly well known for *The Grand Babylon Hotel*, a novel about the disappearance of a German prince. In 1931 he published *The Night Visitor and Other Stories*, inspired by real-life experiences in a big hotel.

Ernest Bramah
The Tilling Shaw Mystery
(Originally Published in *Max Carrados,* 1914)
English writer Ernest Bramah (1868–1942) was born in Manchester and began writing after failing to pursue a career in farming. His first creation was the Chinese storyteller Kai Lung, who tells short stories featuring fantasy aspects, such as dragons. Bramah is also known for Max Carrados, a blind detective who uses his other senses to solve crimes. One of the Carrados books begins with an essay defending the creation of the first blind detective and listing other blind people who have achieved great things. Little is known about Bramah's private life, leading to rumours that his name was a pseudonym and a famous writer was in fact the author of his work.

John Buchan
The Thirty-Nine Steps
(Originally Published by William Blackwood and Sons, 1915)
John Buchan (1875–1940) was born in Scotland and throughout his life worked as a novelist, journalist, historian, politician and soldier. After graduating from Oxford he spent much of his time writing, while exploring a career as a barrister and then as private secretary to the High Commissioner for South Africa. Buchan carried out the

role of war correspondent for *The Times* during the First World War until he joined the army. His most famous novel *The Thirty-Nine Steps* was published in 1915 and follows Richard Hannay who protects Britain from German spies whilst following the notes of a murdered secret agent. The novel is still hugely successful and has been made into various film adaptations. Buchan continued writing a number of adventure and thriller novels, producing over 100 works throughout his life, making him popular in the UK and Scotland in particular, as well as internationally.

G.K. Chesterton

The Man Who Was Thursday (chapters I–VIII)
(Originally Published by J.W. Arrowsmith, 1908)
The Invisible Man
(Originally Published in The Saturday Evening Post, 1911)
Gilbert Keith Chesterton (1874–1936) is best known for his creation of the worldly priest detective Father Brown. The Edwardian writer's literary output was immense: around 200 short stories, nearly 100 novels and about 4000 essays, as well as weekly columns for multiple newspapers. Chesterton was a valued literary critic, and his own authoritative works included biographies of Charles Dickens and Thomas Aquinas, and the theological book *The Everlasting Man*. Chesterton also debated with such notable figures as George Bernard Shaw and Bertrand Russell. His detective stories were essentially moral; Father Brown is an empathetic force for good, battling crime while defending the vulnerable.

Joseph Conrad

The Secret Agent (chapters I–V)
(Originally Published by Methuen & Co., 1907)
Joseph Conrad (1857–1924) was a Polish-British author born in Ukraine and influenced by his years at sea. Travelling first on French ships and spending 16 years as a British merchant marine enabled him to gain experiences in various countries including Australia, Africa and Singapore. His writings show clear roots from his seafaring career, as many are exotic tales and display themes of imperialism and colonialism. One of his most famous novels *Lord Jim* follows the story of a sailor dealing with his past. But he is perhaps best known for his novella *Heart of Darkness*, inspired by his time as captain of a steamer on the Congo River in Africa. *The Secret Agent* deals with themes of anarchism, espionage and terrorism, and is often cited. His works have influenced a number of authors, such as F. Scott Fitzgerald (1896–1940), George Orwell (1903–50) and Salman Rushdie.

Joseph Cusumano

The Vigil
(First Publication)
Joseph Cusumano is a physician living in St. Louis. His major hobby, other than writing, is the design and construction of radio controlled airplanes. His piloting skills need a lot of work. His writing has been accepted by *Crimson Streets*, *Pseudopod*, *Mystery Weekly*, *Disturbed Digest*, *Flash Fiction Press*, *Heater*, and *Litmag* (University of Missouri). His writing tastes are eclectic, including crime, horror, science fiction and literary pieces.

David R. Downing

Afriti

(Originally Published in *New Realm Magazine* Vol. 04 No. 10, 2016)

David R. Downing lives a dual life; mild-mannered informatics consultant by day and fanatical writer at night. You may come across David frantically typing on his laptop in some lonely hotel lobby, airport waiting area, or cramped airplane seat. David travels frequently for his day job, and it is often while he is on the road that his better efforts come to life. David has had over a dozen short stories see the light of day with publications in various magazines. His first novel *The Executioner*, featuring Kalat from a series of his short stories, is due out soon.

Arthur Conan Doyle

The Adventure of the Second Stain

(Originally Published in *The Return of Sherlock Holmes*, 1903)

Arthur Conan Doyle (1859–1930) was born in Edinburgh, Scotland. As a medical student he was so impressed by his professor's powers of deduction that he was inspired to create the illustrious and much-loved figure Sherlock Holmes. Holmes is known for his keen power of observation and logical reasoning, which often astounds his companion Dr. Watson. However, Doyle became increasingly interested in spiritualism, leaving him keen to explore more fantastical elements in his stories. Whatever the subject, Doyle's vibrant and remarkable characters have breathed life into all of his stories, engaging readers throughout the decades. *The Adventure of the Second Stain* made it into Doyle's top twelve Sherlock Holmes Stories. It is rated as being just ahead of *The Devil's Foot* and *The Priory School*.

Martin Edwards

Foreword: Agents & Spies Short Stories

Martin Edwards is the author of 18 novels, including the Lake District Mysteries, and the Harry Devlin series. His groundbreaking genre study *The Golden Age of Murder* has won the Edgar, Agatha, and H.R.F. Keating awards. He has edited 28 crime anthologies, has won the CWA Short Story Dagger and the CWA Margery Allingham Prize, and is series consultant for the British Library's Crime Classics. In 2015, he was elected eighth President of the Detection Club, an office previously held by G.K. Chesterton, Agatha Christie, and Dorothy L. Sayers.

R. Austin Freeman

The Moabite Cipher

(Originally Published in *Pearson's Magazine*, 1909)

Richard Austin Freeman (1862–1943) studied at Middlesex Hospital and pursued a career in medicine. His work influenced his writing as he created Dr. Thorndyke, a forensic investigator who features in a number of his detective novels. Freeman would make sure to be extremely thorough in his writing, often using his job as a way to test that everything he wrote was plausible. Dr. Thorndyke and Freeman had many similarities as they both strove for accuracy and had a love for science. Freeman was the first to write the 'inverted detective story' – he would begin by revealing the criminal, leaving the suspense to come from how Thorndyke would be able to catch the perpetrator and solve the crime.

Shane Halbach

Spooks

(First Publication)

Shane Halbach is a writer, blogger, and international man of mystery living in Chcago with his wife and three kids, where he writes software by day and avoids writing stories by night. He has been accused of being obsessed with pirates, bacon, zombies and his kids (not necessarily in that order). His fiction has appeared in *Analog, Orson Scott Card's Intergalactic Medicine Show*, and *The Year's Best YA Speculative Fiction*, among others. Find him on his blog shanehalbach.com, or on Twitter @shanehalbach.

Rudyard Kipling

Kim (chapters I–IV)

(Originally Published by Macmillan & Co. Ltd, 1901)

English writer and poet Rudyard Kipling (1865–1936) was born in Bombay, India. He was educated in England but returned to India in his youth, which would inspire many of his later writings. He was awarded the Nobel Prize for Literature in 1907, which made him the first English-language writer to receive the accolade. His narrative style is inventive and engaging, making it no surprise that his works have become classics.

Stephen Kotowych

Under the Shield

(Originally Published in *Orson Scott Card's Intergalactic Medicine Show #24*, 2011)

Stephen Kotowych is a winner of the Writers of the Future Grand Prize; Spain's Ictineu Award; and a two-time finalist for Canada's Aurora Award. His stories have appeared in *Interzone, Orson Scott Card's Intergalactic Medicine Show*, numerous anthologies, and been translated into a dozen languages. His first collection of short stories, *Seven Against Tomorrow*, is available now. He lives in Toronto with his family. He enjoys guitar, tropical fish, and writing about himself in the third person. For more information about Stephen and his writing visit his website: www.kotowych.com.

Colt Leasure

Induction

(Originally Published on the webzine *Aphelion*, 2017)

Colt Randy Leasure is a writer and bouncer from South Lake Tahoe, California. His work has been featured in publications such as *Lovecraftiana, Blood Moon Rising, Aphelion, Yellow Mama*, and *Schlock*. He was raised on a diet of crime films, horror paperbacks, and heavy metal albums. In the horror genre he admires Poe, Lovecraft, King, Ketchum, Pizzolatto, Joseph Pulver, Cormac McCarthy, Laird Barron and countless others. In regards to spy fiction, he bows down to John Le Carre, Jason Matthews, Daniel Silva and many more. You can find him on Twitter @ColtLeasure.

Maurice Leblanc

The Mysterious Railway Passenger

(Originally Published in *The Extraordinary Adventures of Arsene Lupin, Gentleman Burglar*, 1910)

French novelist and playwright Maurice Leblanc (1864–1941) was the creator of detective Arsène Lupin. Leblanc dropped out of law school in his early life and moved to Paris where he began writing crime novels and short stories. Leblanc gained little fame until the publishing of his first Arsène Lupin story in 1905: *The Arrest of Arsène Lupin*. The Arsène Lupin stories would often parody the crime genre, with some featuring the British detective 'Herlock Sholmes'. They were widely considered to be the French version of Sherlock Holmes, however the stories have a different feel. Leblanc continued to write 21 novels featuring the famous detective Lupin, which were greatly received.

Jonathan MacGregor

To Catch a Mole
(First Publication)
Jonathan MacGregor is a freelance writer who lives in Commack, New York. He wrote 'To Catch a Mole' specifically for Flame Tree Publishing, and this short story is his first publication. He grew up reading Agatha Christie novels and locked-room mysteries, and he is enthused that his first story in print pays homage to the mystery genre. Readers interested in his work should investigate his other work at jdmacgregor.wixsite.com/index or visit his facebook page at fb.com/JonathanDMacGregor.

Jo Miles

The Empathy Bomb
(First Publication)
Jo Miles is a science fiction and fantasy writer. She's a 2016 graduate of the Viable Paradise writers' workshop, and she has upcoming publications in Diabolical Plots and the *Mad Scientists Journal*. She also runs FutureShift, a project working to broaden the intersection between speculative fiction and social change work. She lives in Maryland, where she is owned by two cats. When she's not writing, you'll likely find her hiking up a mountain or riding her bike.

Josh Pachter

The Defenestration of Prague
(Copyright © 1986, 2017 by Josh Pachter. Originally published in *Espionage*. Reprinted by permission of the author.)
Josh Pachter is the author of more than 80 short stories, which have appeared in *Ellery Queen's Mystery Magazine*, *Alfred Hitchcock's Mystery Magazine*, and many other periodicals and anthologies. *The Tree of Life*, a collection of his Mahboob Chaudri stories, was published in 2015. He has edited numerous anthologies, including three coming up in 2018: *Amsterdam Noir* (Akashic Press), *The Misadventures of Ellery Queen* (Perfect Crime Books), and *The Man Who Read Mr. Strang* (Crippen & Landru). He lives in Virginia, where he teaches communication studies and film at Northern Virginia Community College.

Tony Pi

We Who Steal Faces
(Originally Published in *Orson Scott Card's Intergalactic Medicine Show*, 2011)
Tony Pi lives in Toronto, Canada, and has published widely in magazines such as *Beneath Ceaseless Skies*, *Clarkesworld Magazine*, *Orson Scott Card's InterGalactic Medicine Show*, and *On Spec*, as well as anthologies like *Clockwork Canada*, *Ages of Wonder*, the *Tesseracts* series, and many others. His short fiction has previously been

nominated for the Aurora Awards and the Parsec Awards, and he was once a finalist for the John W. Campbell Award for Best New Writer. Visit his website at www.tonypi.com.

Arthur B. Reeve
The Black Hand
(Originally Published in *The Poised Pen: The Further Adventures of Craig Kennedy*, 1911)
Arthur Benjamin Reeve (1880–1936) was born in New York, graduating from Princeton and going on to study law. However he ended up working as an editor and journalist, writing about several famous crime cases, before gaining wide popularity for his stories about fictional detective Professor Craig Kennedy, the first of which were published in *Cosmopolitan* magazine. Kennedy shares many similarities with both Conan Doyle's Holmes and Freeman's Dr. Thorndyke, as he solves crimes with science, logic and a knowledge of technology, as well as having a companion in several stories who chronicles his work, very similarly to Watson.

Sapper (H.C. McNeile)
The Creaking Door
(Originally Published in *Ronald Standish*, 1933)
Soldier and author Herman Cyril McNeile (1888–1937) was born in Cornwall and travelled to France as part of the British Expeditionary Force in 1914. During the war he wrote stories for the *Daily Mail* and adopted the pseudonym 'Sapper', a name for Royal Engineers as officers in the British Army were unable to publish under their own name. In 1920 *Bull-dog Drummond* was published and became McNeile's most famous publication. The character was based on himself, his friend and English gentleman and featured in a number of thrillers. Another famous character created by McNeile was Ronald Standish, a private detective. Much of his work centered on the war, displaying how his career had impacted him.

S.L. Scott
Spies and Taboos
(First Publication)
S.L. Scott lives in St. Louis, Missouri, and has a Master's degree in Professional Writing and Publishing. She has been published in *Bewildering Stories* magazine, *Wild Musette* magazine, *Eyes that Pour Forth and Other Stories* anthology, and *The Rogue's Gallery* anthology. She's also received an Honorable Mention in both the 2012 Tuscany Prize and the Writers of the Future 2014 First Quarter. Currently, she writes about the craft of world-building in her blog: 'Woman in the Red Room'.

Dan Stout
The Hula-Hoop Heart
(Originally Published in *The Saturday Evening Post*, July 2016)
Dan Stout lives in Columbus, Ohio, where he writes about fever dreams and half-glimpsed shapes in the shadows. His prize-winning fiction draws on his travels throughout Europe, Asia, and the Pacific Rim, as well as an employment history spanning everything from subpoena server to assistant well driller. Dan's stories have appeared in publications such as *The Saturday Evening Post*, *Nature*, and *Mad Scientist Journal*. Follow him on Facebook or visit him on the web at www.DanStout.com.

Lauren C. Teffeau
No Regrets on Fourth Street
(Originally Published in *Perihelion Science Fiction*, 2017)
Lauren C. Teffeau is an American writer from New Mexico. Whether it's James Bond or Jason Bourne, Ethan Hunt or Evelyn Salt, Agent Smith or Sterling Archer, she's always had a soft spot for all things espionage. She may not be a spy in real life, but she does enjoy hiding in plain sight and listening in on other people's conversations – to aid her writing, of course. Her short fiction can be found in a wide variety of speculative fiction magazines and anthologies. To learn more, please visit laurencteffeau.com.

Ellen Wood (Mrs. Henry Wood)
The Ebony Box
(Originally Published in *Johnny Ludlow, Fifth Series*, 1890)
Ellen Price (1814–87) was born in Worcester and upon marrying Henry Wood in 1836, spent 20 years in the South of France before returning to England. On her return to England Mrs. Henry Wood began writing a number of novels and short stories. Her most famous novel was the 1861 *East Lynne,* which was followed by many other successful novels including *Danesbury House* and *Oswald Cray.* In 1867 Wood bought the English magazine *Argosy* where she published many of her short stories. She was known for writing mystery and supernatural fiction. Her works were translated into multiple languages and many of her books became international bestsellers.

FLAME TREE PUBLISHING
Short Story Series
New & Classic Writing

Flame Tree's Gothic Fantasy books offer a carefully curated series of new titles, each with combinations of original and classic writing:

Chilling Horror Short Stories
Chilling Ghost Short Stories
Science Fiction Short Stories
Murder Mayhem Short Stories
Crime & Mystery Short Stories
Swords & Steam Short Stories
Dystopia Utopia Short Stories
Supernatural Horror Short Stories
Lost Worlds Short Stories
Time Travel Short Stories
Heroic Fantasy Short Stories
Pirates & Ghosts Short Stories

as well as new companion titles which offer rich collections of classic fiction from masters of the gothic fantasy genres:

H.G. Wells Short Stories
Lovecraft Short Stories
Sherlock Holmes Short Stories
Edgar Allan Poe Short Stories

Available from all good bookstores, worldwide, and online at
flametreepublishing.com

GOTHIC FANTASY

For our books, calendars, blog
and latest special offers please see:
flametreepublishing.com